Praise F

AN

'Engaging characters…shivering suspense and
captivating romance. Want it all?
Read Ann Major.'
—Nora Roberts, *New York Times* bestselling author

REBECCA YORK

'Rebecca York's writing is fast-paced, suspenseful
and loaded with tension.'
—Jayne Ann Krentz, *New York Times* bestselling author

LINDSAY McKENNA

'Page after page of non-stop excitement,
breathtaking adventure and hot passion…'
—*Romantic Times*

ABOUT THE AUTHORS

The author of more than thirty novels, **Ann Major** is a firm reader favourite and her books have appeared repeatedly on international bestseller lists. She is the proud mother of three children and lists hiking in the Colorado mountains with her husband, enjoying her cats and playing the piano among her hobbies.

Rebecca York has always loved making up stories of adventure, romance and suspense. The creator of the highly successful **43 Light Street** series in Silhouette Intrigue®, this author has been honoured with a Career Achievement Award by *Romantic Times* magazine.

Lindsay McKenna is a practising homeopath and emergency medical technician on the Navajo Reservation in Arizona. She comes from an Eastern Cherokee medicine family and is a member of the Wolf Clan. Dividing her energies between alternative medicine and writing, she lives with her husband, David, near Sedona.

Dangerous
L I A I S O N S

ANN MAJOR
REBECCA YORK
LINDSAY McKENNA

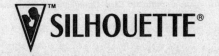

*Silhouette and Colophon are registered trademarks of
Harlequin Books S.A., used under licence.*

*First published in Great Britain 1999
Silhouette Books, Eton House, 18-24 Paradise Road,
Richmond, Surrey TW9 1SR*

DANGEROUS LIAISONS © Harlequin Books S.A. 1999

The publisher acknowledges the copyright holders
of the individual works as follows:

SECRET CHILD © Ann Major 1998
FACE TO FACE © Ruth Glick and Eileen Buckholtz 1996
HEART OF THE JAGUAR © Eileen Nauman 1999
Heart of the Jaguar was originally published as
Morgan's Mercenaries: Heart of the Jaguar in the USA.

ISBN 0 373 59688 X
81-9907

*Printed and bound in Great Britain
by Caledonian International Book Manufacturing Ltd, Glasgow*

CONTENTS

Secret Child

ANN MAJOR

DEDICATION

I am grateful to my editor, Tara Gavin, and to her colleagues and staff for their hard work and encouragement; to my late agent, Anita Diamant, for her years of encouragement and friendship; I am grateful to my new agent, Robin Rue; to my late colleague, Sondra Stanford, and to Mary Lynn Baxter, as well.

Many other people helped me. Kay Telle invited me to Vail, where inspiration for this novel struck. Morgan Thaxton, Chili Robinson, Elizabeth Stowe, and Ann and Dick Jones gave generous interviews and advice. Robert Lund, Tad Cleaves, David Cleaves, Kim Cleaves and Jason Nichols helped correct several drafts. I am also grateful to my talented secretary, Patricia Patterson, and to my housekeeper, Ella Mae Lescuer.

Last but not least, I thank Ted.

Prologue

Bronte felt a raindrop hit her cheek. Involuntarily her fingers tightened on the metal clasp of her purse.

A second drop splashed her prim, white collar.

The urge to run was almost overwhelming.

But it was nine long blocks back to her hotel.

Bronte Devlin hated big cities.

But this one should have been different.

She preferred wide-open spaces and big blue skies. She preferred men who wore jeans and Stetsons and lived outside to stuffy, pale-skinned businessmen in suits and ties.

She had been standing on Fifty-fourth Street for thirty minutes, trying without success to hail a cab during the evening rush hour.

It was October, but it felt like July.

The sky was so black she thought it could start raining any second. She felt lost and forlorn, almost fainting in the thick, humid heat.

Not that New York City wasn't bustling with an endless stream of cabs. Buses, too. Not that the air wasn't dense with their exhaust fumes. But the cabs were full. Just as the sidewalks were jammed. People of all races, ages, classes, shapes and sizes jostled past her, hurrying toward jobs, restaurants, hotels and homes.

Thunder reverberated through the air. Suddenly, she was a thousand times more anxious as she imagined these strangers having what she didn't—purposeful lives, marriages. And children.

They had somewhere to go. And someone who loved them.

They still believed in something.

She had to get out of this city that had once been home—and fast.

As soon as she got back to her hotel, she would throw her clothes into her suitcase and leave. She had no idea where she'd go, certainly not back to Wimberley, Texas, where she had stood in her principal's prison-green office and torn up her teaching contract. She'd sold her clothes in a garage sale, given away her cat, Pogo, to a friend. She had no home now.

Kindergarten would be starting soon, but she had known she couldn't face teaching the children another year. She couldn't bear the way she saw Jimmy's face every time another long-lashed, little boy with copper-colored curls looked up shyly from his coloring book or raised his hand to ask a question. A kindergarten teacher needed illusions. She had lost hers.

Her Jimmy was dead.

With his pale skin, fiery hair and constant grin, he had been the joy of her life. Light boned and hyperactive, Jimmy had loved his dog, his cat, his horse, his skateboard, his chocolate-chip cookies with ice-cold milk and his three best friends. She had loved the hectic job of raising him, and entertaining the children who were always dashing in and out of their house. She hadn't even minded if they used their outdoor voices indoors or slammed the screen door a hundred times a day. And then suddenly one rainy afternoon, with no warning, he was gone.

When they had buried Jimmy in his boots and cowboy hat, Bronte had died, too. So had her marriage to her cowboy husband and her dreams of other children—although more gradually. So had her belief in life.

Bronte had tried to go on as Bryan—dear placid, staid, unimaginative Bryan, who had never seemed to be as deeply touched by life as she—had so wisely pontificated she should. She had tried to live with the rage and then the hollow pain of their loss. Even after Bryan had walked out, she had kept teaching kindergarten, struggling to go on, hoping that something would happen to renew her faith. Then suddenly, a month ago, she had torn up her contract and fled back to New York, her childhood home. She had even taken her maiden name back.

Running away was as hard as teaching. The overwhelming emptiness inside her seemed to be expanding. Sometimes she just wanted to give up and die.

But she hadn't.

Not yet, anyway.

Who had said, "Everywhere I go, there I am"?

She didn't know anyone in Manhattan anymore. Still, she had gone to West 69th Street, where she'd lived as a child. Where her beautiful mother had practiced arias in between screaming matches with her equally famous father.

But the street had felt every bit as strange and alien

as it had when Bronte had been a child. Only it was alien in a different way.

Her mother's handsome brownstone mansion was divided into a dozen fashionable apartments. Strangers raised canaries on the second floor, where her mother had lavishly entertained movie stars and dictators. The fourth-floor balcony where their cook had kept pots of red geraniums, where their black cat had sunned and where Bronte had hidden from her mother's rages, was now jammed with bicycles.

A young career woman in black, chewing gum, had rushed out of the front door. When she saw Bronte staring up at the building, the girl had demanded to know whether she was looking for somebody or just lost.

"I think I am...a little of both," Bronte had admitted. Then she added shyly, "Did...did you know that this used to be Madame Devlin's house?"

"The diva who ran off with the Brazilian shipping tycoon? Wasn't there some tragedy?" The girl paused. "Her picture is in the foyer. She was very beautiful."

"Back then they said she was the most beautiful woman in the world. There was this huge cult surrounding her. She...she was my mother."

"Really? Well, you don't look much like her," the girl said. "Too bad." Then someone shouted to her and she waved and dashed off down the street with her friend.

Yes. Bronte had been the ugly duckling and her mother, the swan, had been so ashamed of her.

All that had once been a problem. Until Bronte had rebelled against the beauty god. And the success god. Until she'd realized the world was filled with ordinary people. Until she had become a teacher and had mar-

ried easy-going Bryan, who had said she was pretty;
Bryan who hadn't gone to college, who hardly knew
there was such a thing as opera. They'd had Jimmy,
and Bronte had made a whole new life for herself—
a laid-back, ordinary life her attention-seeking
mother, who had been driven by inner demons to ex-
cel and cause scandal, would never have approved of
nor understood.

Bronte had failed at that life, too.

She had wanted to come back to her mother's
house. To remember how her life had been. To try to
see where she had gone wrong.

She remembered herself as a child parading up and
down the staircase in long, glittering robes, and her
mother's rage later when she'd found the costume
torn. Bronte remembered all the other rages, too.
Rages over dirty fingernails, over clumsy curtsies
when Bronte was introduced to somebody her mother
had wanted to impress at one of her soirees.

Bronte had been so…so ordinary. Unable to sing
even the simplest melody. And so plain.

Suddenly, she didn't want to remember that first
life, which had been such an immense burden to her
once. She still wanted to keep that time far away and
unreal.

Too late Bronte realized that this was not a city to
offer comfort to one with profound grief and loss and
guilt. So here she was, all alone on busy Fifty-fourth
Street. Hadn't her mother pitied her and told her she
was nothing special, that she would fail at whatever
she tried?

Despite her striking red hair, slim figure and her
almost-pretty, sweet face, which had an appeal all its
own, Bronte might as well have been invisible on that
crowded street corner. Nobody noticed her.

Suddenly two large men sprang from a shop door and charged after a teenager like a pair of stampeding bulls.

"Thief!" a bull bellowed as rain pelted the sidewalk.

"Get him!"

Bronte barely got a glimpse of the boy. She'd been looking up, panicked by the dark sky with its keening wind and huge raindrops.

The biggest man lunged, ripping the bundle of money out of the boy's arm.

The brown paper sack burst.

Fifty-dollar bills exploded everywhere. A gust from the storm caught the money and sent green bills drifting over the crowd. Everybody started pushing and grabbing and jumping to catch them.

The tough-faced store owner slugged the boy hard in the stomach and then in the jaw, sending him reeling backward into Bronte, whose leather-soled flats slid on the slick sidewalk. She careened backward off the curb just as the light turned yellow and the downpour really began. Just as a speeding taxi driver stomped on his accelerator to make the light.

While money and rain flooded the street, Bronte held up her hands helplessly—in a vain attempt to signal the taxi to stop.

A woman saw her and screamed.

"Get out of the street, girlie!" a bystander yelled.

Terror froze Bronte's raised hands as the taxi driver braked too late, and the blur of yellow and chrome kept hurtling toward her.

Funny how she hardly felt the blow, how there was only an odd, numbing warmth as she was lifted into the air. Then she was falling. Still, she felt nothing as black asphalt rushed up to meet her face.

While she lay on the street, a vast dome seemed to close over the skyscrapers and encase her lifeless body like a huge jar. Only there weren't any holes punched in the lid, and she had to fight for every breath. The ferment of people and taxis and buses were all on the other side of the glass. Even the rain couldn't touch her.

The cabdriver got out and screamed at her in some foreign language she didn't understand. Others were screaming as well, but their babble seemed to come from a long way away.

High above her, against a liver-colored skyscraper, a huge matinee sign with the bold image of her favorite movie star, Garth Brown, floated. He had dark skin, dark hair and an incredibly fierce demeanor. How many nights had she stayed up late watching his old movies, and fantasizing after Bryan had walked out that she'd fall in love again and start over? But it hadn't happened. Now it never would.

Someone knelt and touched her face with fingertips she couldn't feel. A white-haired lady called 911.

In the absolute silence and aloneness inside her jar, Bronte felt the beating of her heart. She tasted blood. She watched fluttering green bills sift slowly down on top of her.

Shadows began to darken.

Garth's face dissolved.

Was she dying?

Her fierce moan of denial was so loud it startled her.

Jimmy was dead.

Bryan had needed more attention than she could give him and had left her for a younger, more cheerful woman who adored him, a woman who was not haunted by ghosts.

Bronte had lost everything.

But suddenly, miraculously, she knew that she wanted to live.

When she heard sirens, the pain in her chest began. First it was only pressure, deep and constricting, holding her down.

As she gasped for every breath, the wall of brown buildings seemed to move together. The sky darkened. Then everything dissolved in a rush of black.

Jimmy. Jimmy. Jimmy.

Bronte felt her little boy's rowdy presence as she'd dreamed so many times of feeling it.

Happiness filled her.

He was all right. He was all around her.

The doctors had lied to her. Bryan had lied to her. She hadn't failed.

Jimmy wasn't dead.

He wasn't.

She'd been right all along. God couldn't be that cruel.

She tried to open her eyes and see her son.

But her eyelids were as heavy as lead.

She didn't have the strength to move even the tiniest muscle.

Still, his presence instilled a wonderful peace as well as a belief that she had to live....

When Bronte regained consciousness, she was lying on a gurney in a crowded emergency room. Someone was squeezing her hand.

She could barely feel the firm, blunt fingers of the stranger who probed expertly for her pulse. All she could feel was the searing pain every time she tried to breathe.

''God Almighty!'' a young nurse behind him said. ''What happened to her face?''

''She was hit by a cab,'' a sterner, older voice said.

''Hey—shut up!'' the doctor said. ''I'm getting a pulse!''

''Poor thing. Who'd want to live looking like that?''

''Bronte Devlin?'' Webster's heart was racing as he thumbed through the young woman's chart.

He had noticed her red hair when he'd seen her staring at her mother's home.

He hadn't been sure who she was, but he had followed her. But before he'd had a chance to speak, she'd been hit by that cab.

Coincidence?

Synchronicity was the current buzzword. Webster Quinn was used to blessings from the gods.

Any other plastic surgeon might have blanched at the sight of the young woman in the blood-smeared, white dress, but the notorious, silver-haired Dr. Webster Quinn, famed for his bizarre genius and immense ego, thrived as both a rebel and an outcast. At fifty, he had three passions—work, the opera and a mysterious woman.

Professionally, nothing turned him on more than achieving the unachievable. His successes had dazzled the world. Secretive by nature, he rarely shared his innovative methods and aggressive procedures with colleagues. Naturally, he did not advertise his failures.

Awestruck, Webster knelt low, fingering a matted lock of the girl's hair with a trembling hand.

Even in his blue scrubs, he looked more like a television actor playing a doctor than a real doctor. His keen blue eyes, which were usually so cold, blazed with an almost fanatical light.

Incredible.

He couldn't believe his good fortune.

Madame Devlin's daughter.

Her hair, as bright as spun flame, was a perfect match.

When he probed the young girl's eyelids, she made a small, whimpering sound. But it wasn't compassion for her obvious discomfort as she struggled for every breath that made his heart stop. It was the vivid green hue of one swollen eye.

Her eye color was an exact match, too.

She was slim and tall.

Like the *other*.

And the bone structure...

She was the *original*'s daughter. Closer to the genuine article than the *other*.

His palms grew sweaty. His heart raced faster.

He felt like Michelangelo stumbling upon a perfect piece of Carrara marble.

Finally, Webster studied the mangled face of Bronte Devlin.

Instead of pity or revulsion, he felt an excitement he imagined to be like that of the elation of a gifted sculptor who saw what other fools could not see.

This poor, broken creature would be the raw material for his second masterpiece.

The damage wasn't nearly as extensive as it might appear to those less talented and less sure.

As soon as the other doctors patched her ribs and saved her life, he would spirit her away to his clinic in Costa Rica. Although it was perfectly legal for any simpleminded goose with a medical degree to perform the most complex sort of plastic surgery in the

United States, Webster preferred to do his highly innovative procedures out of the country, as far as possible from the prying eyes of his critical colleagues. Not that he couldn't make a few basic repairs here while she was healing from her other, life-threatening injuries.

Webster, who had left California and moved east under a cloud of scandal ten years ago, was the most controversial plastic surgeon in the state of New York. Yet his credentials were impeccable. He had a wall full of diplomas. He had graduated first in his class from UCLA Medical School. He had operated on some of the most famous movie stars in Hollywood. One of cinema's oldest and most glamorous stars, who was over sixty but looked twenty on the screen, had made Quinn a household name by proclaiming on national television that he had magic fingers.

Everybody agreed that he was a creative genius who routinely worked miracles. But since Webster played by his own rules, his creativity and genius were considered his most dangerous liabilities. His few admirers in New York cited that he had donated as much of his time and expertise to charity cases as he had to the rich.

But neither his admirers nor his enemies would have suspected his motivations as he studied the injured young woman on the gurney.

For a moment Webster remembered another tall, slim redhead who had slipped inside his office after hours five years ago.

He had given her a new face, which had been her key to wealth and fame. She had become his lover. And his obsession.

He had shown her into a suite of offices called the

Magic Rooms. The walls had been painted black, and his magic paraphernalia and memorabilia had been on display in lighted, glass cases.

"You have to change my face," she had said in a desperate whisper. "It's a matter of life and death." She had picked up a pair of dice and rolled them.

A pair of sixes lay on his desk.

"Whose?"

If only he had not stared straight into her green eyes.

"Terrible people…you cannot imagine how terrible have forced me to do this, or I would never… You must make me beautiful. Very beautiful. The most beautiful woman in the world."

"Plastic surgeons are not magicians. The idea that I am a sculptor of the flesh who can transform an ordinary woman into a magnificent goddess is fantasy."

She stroked a case that contained a top hat and a black velvet cloak lined with red satin. "You underestimate us both. I am no ordinary woman. You are no ordinary surgeon."

He had started to argue, but she had exerted such an incredible power over him that he was dumbstruck. He had noticed that her perfume smelled of gardenias.

A framed portrait of Madame Devlin, the diva, whose voice and beauty had electrified him for as long as he could remember, had graced the wall behind the mysterious woman in his office.

He had felt a sudden shocking rush of inspiration as he had compared Madame's slender face to the real woman's pale, triangular features. A stillness had descended upon him as he began to wonder if he could perform such a miracle.

She would believe it to be *her* miracle.

But it would be *his*.

"Can you do it?"

"It will be risky and expensive."

"I'm not afraid. Money is no object. Neither is…this…." She loosened his tie and jerked his top two shirt buttons apart.

Pushing her hands away, he gasped, "I live with someone."

"Not any longer."

She had undressed him before he could protest. She had begun to touch him, and the moment he'd felt her talented fingertips stroking his bare skin, an electric stillness had descended upon him.

Then his flesh had started to burn, and a meteoric burst of lust had overpowered his will. Forgetting his rigid code of medical ethics that forbade sex with a patient, he had torn off her black dress and pushed her down on the floor, falling on top of her like a heavy animal. All that had mattered was to shove himself savagely inside her again and again, to plunge deeply, to know the fierce ecstasy of her long limbs writhing under his. Their bodies had been fluid and electric, like two snakes on a dark forest floor, as graceful as eels in a dark undersea world.

When it was over, there had been red marks on his back and purple bruises on her breasts. He had never hit a woman before, and he had felt cheap and dirty. He had sworn to himself that the new perversions she had introduced him to would lose their appeal, and her hold on him would soon be over.

He hadn't known then that the well-ordered pattern of his life had shifted into something obscene, that even then she was already a dangerous obsession.

He thought of his secret mistress constantly, of the things she did to him when they were alone. Of the things she did with other men when she was away. It had been a mistake to give her the face of a goddess. Sometimes he fancied she was the devil and that she'd stolen his soul.

She was a cruel master.

She had used him and abused him. Not that she didn't rationalize everything she did.

Sometimes he hated her.

Sometimes he wanted to escape.

Sometimes he wanted revenge.

Most of the time he did as she ordered.

He had waited for this moment.

He had a plan.

He would make another one.

The wretched young woman on the stretcher, whom he'd believed to be unconscious, moaned. Startled, he came back to the present and to the gravity of the matter at hand.

He felt shaken by a twinge of conscience. What would this young woman think and feel when she found out what he had done? It didn't matter.

He leaned down and whispered very gently, very soothingly in his much-practiced, movie-star doctor's voice against her ear.

She opened her eyes, and he noted with relief that the peculiar frightening aspect in the *other*'s eyes was absent. This woman could never hold him in thrall. She would be easy to manage.

"Go away!" the girl said as she grew aware of his presence.

"Do you want to live or die?" he whispered kindly.

"Without my face?" She turned away from him with a thready sob. "My son is dead. Everybody's dead. I'm all alone. I have failed at everything. I thought I wanted to die before this happened…''

''Your parents?''

''Dead.''

He felt a wave of unwanted pity for her. "I'm a plastic surgeon. I can leave you as you are…or I can make you into the most beautiful woman in the world. I can give you paradise on earth. You will be the envy of every woman, and every man will desire you.''

Every man but me.

He told himself this rather too forcefully. He would have other uses for her.

''Your injuries are not as terrible as you believe them to be. But I must get started at once if we are to have even a chance at success. Do you want to live or die?'' he repeated.

His deep, melodious voice was soothingly hypnotic. His cool blue eyes were tender.

Of the evil in his soul there was no trace.

I

Chapter 1

The siren was shrill, cutting the eerie silence like a knife.

Jack West awoke with a start, his black gaze as alert as a cat's as he glanced fiercely about his cheap, San Antonio motel room. He half expected to find himself back in cell block C, a knife-tip against his throat, a murderer's legs straddling his waist.

He was alone.

Safe.

Even so, his heart pounded a few seconds longer, his senses having been honed by the constant danger.

He felt the familiar loneliness close over him. It was deep and dark, but he surrendered to it.

The name Jack West once had meant something in south Texas. He'd been rich and famous.

No more.

Jack West. Crisp, prison-cropped black hair. Indian dark eyes with long bristly lashes, brooding eyes that could flame with hate as hot as tar-tipped torches or go as cold as black ice and stare straight through his enemy.

Before prison he'd been tough.

His carved face and tall, muscular body were harder and leaner than ever. Scars crisscrossed his broad back from the night he'd gotten drunk on smuggled gin with a black inmate named Brickhouse.

When Jack had sobered up he'd been in lockdown. He'd been badly beaten and slashed. The bulging muscle of his left forearm had throbbed almost as much as the deeper cuts on his hands and shoulders. He'd had vague memories of being held down while Brickhouse used a ballpoint pen and a sewing needle to tattoo matching hunting knives onto their forearms. There had been even cloudier memories of the fight when they'd been jumped by six inmates with knives.

Jack's once healthy, dark skin was sallow, and the scars on his back were nothing compared to the ones on his soul. He couldn't forget that even before his conviction, Theodora had thrown him off the ranch, seized his daughter and cut him off from his old life forever. Once he had almost believed his life might count for something, after all.

No more.

Jack West wasn't much different than a dead man.

He was even worse off now than when he'd started as a beggar and a thief in Matamoros, Mexico. His mama had been a cheap Mexican whore, his father an Anglo ranch foreman who'd paid for his five minutes with her. He'd known his father's name only because his mother had stolen his wallet.

Jack had spent his earliest years in a small shack in a dusty Mexican barrio, where he'd had to steal or starve. He'd lived on the fringes even there. He'd lived the second half of his life like a cowboy prince in the big, white, stucco house on El Atascadero, one of the grandest of the great, legendary ranches in south Texas. But he'd existed on the fringes there, too. Because nobody forgot where he'd come from and what his mother had been, least of all him.

Jack owed his Anglo looks and height and his ranching talent to his father, but on the inside he was more Mexican than Anglo. He knew that because when they'd locked him up, his soul had left him. He'd watched it go.

His mother would have said he had the *susto*.

Whatever. His soul hadn't come back yet—even though they'd let him out. He didn't want it back, either.

What he wanted was a drink.

But he hadn't let himself touch the stuff.

He'd decided to stay sober for at least one full night.

Outside in the sweltering dark, an ambulance raced north on San Antonio's Loop 410, its scream dying as if suffocated by the Texas heat.

Jack blinked, forcing himself to relax when he didn't hear the sound of boots racing toward his cell. Instead of blue uniforms and fists bulging with brass knuckles or spoons sharpened into clumsy knives, he saw the rosy rectangle of light behind thin drapes and heard the muted roar of traffic. The lumpy pillow he'd used to cover the phone because he'd taken it off the hook when the reporters kept calling still lay across the telephone on the nightstand.

There were drapes on the windows. Instead of bars.

The soft mattress and clean sheets were real, too.

The five-year nightmare in an eight-by-six cell was over.

He was free.

Whatever that meant.

Bastard from a barrio. Ex-con. Starting over at the bottom again.

When he laughed harshly, his neck began to ache, so he pulled the pillow off the telephone and bunched it under his head. Gently he replaced the receiver on the hook.

He couldn't sleep; he hadn't slept through a night in years. Still, he lay back and closed his eyes, dreading the dawn.

Yesterday he'd been in solitary, his ankles shackled, his hands cuffed to his waist. His toilet had been overflowing, permeating his narrow cell with a foul stench. When he'd asked for something to clean up the mess with, the fat guard had laughed and told him to wallow in the rot like the pig he was.

Then this morning the same guard had yelled at him to grab his bedroll; he was moving.

Jack had been stunned when they'd handcuffed him and driven him to San Antonio and then set him free.

Nobody, not even his lawyer, had bothered to inform him about the serial killer who'd made headlines all over Texas when he'd confessed to one of the murders Jack had been locked up for.

Jack hadn't been prepared to deal with reporters demanding to know how freedom felt when he'd been shoved out the gate into blinding sunshine and sweltering heat.

Since he had nowhere to go and there was no one to care, freedom had only changed the nature of his fears. He'd blinked and rubbed his wrists, stalling, keeping his eyes on his cheap, prison-issue running shoes, not knowing what to say. Not wanting to say anything. Five years ago the press had crucified him. So when reporters had pestered him with calls after he'd checked into the motel, he'd taken the phone off the hook.

To survive the violence, he'd shut off his emotions. He'd learned to keep his thoughts to himself, to trust no one. He'd learned regimentation. He'd obeyed his jailers with curt grunts and nods.

He was little better than an animal. Guards and inmates alike had beaten him and taught him how to cower like a dog and to hate deeply.

He was free...but he was embittered and unfit company for most decent folk. Maybe that wouldn't have mattered if he'd had a family who'd stood by him.

But Theodora had made her feelings clear right from the first. Never once had she written or come to see him. After his conviction, he'd lost custody of his daughter, Carla.

All his letters to Carla and to Theodora had come back. *Return to sender.* The guards had chanted that line aloud when they'd thrown his letters through the bars of his cell.

To hell with Theodora. To hell with the whole damn world. He'd started alone; he might as well end alone. Never again would he let anybody get close to him. He'd take some low job and drink till he found oblivion.

If Jack hated thinking about Carla and Theodora, he hated thinking about Chantal, his wife, even more.

For she had betrayed him in every way that a wife could betray a husband. He had put up with her abuse and then her absences and infidelities for years. Then one day, she had pushed him too far.

When had the deeply rooted hatred between them gotten its start? Had the seeds of it been between them even on that first day Theodora had brought him home to El Atascadero?

As a small boy growing up in Mexico, Jack had dreamed of *el norte,* the United States.

But the reality hadn't been like his dream.

He had dreamed of a mother who could feed him. Of a world where children had homes and clothes. Of a father who'd claim him.

Instead Chantal had been swinging on the ranch gates, waiting with a seething heart for Theodora's limousine to rush up the palm-lined drive with the ten-year-old boy from Mexico.

Theodora had rolled down the car window and let in the blistering heat. Not that he'd felt it. He was used to heat. Besides, he'd been too pop-eyed from his first glimpse of the big house.

Then the girl had snickered, and he'd seen her. Oh, but she'd been a marvel to behold. She had charmed a whip snake. Dozing, its monstrous head dangling, its thick body had been coiled around her arm. The girl and the snake had been so still they'd seemed like enchanted creatures. Then he had looked into Chantal's eyes—strange green eyes that looked out at him but did not allow him to look inside her. Snake's eyes in the pale, unusually pretty face of a redheaded little girl.

Even then she had been blaming him for her problems and waiting there with that snake of hers to attack him.

She had known his mother had just died—his father, too. But she hadn't minced her words. "Go home, you son of a Mexican *puta*. If your father had wanted you here he would have come for you himself."

Chantal had smiled, and her white teeth had been pretty. But her icy eyes had despised him as if he were something less than human, less than nothing.

Still, his voice had been as tight and cold as hers. "You may be a *puta*, too, someday. You're meaner than one right now."

"You two are going to live like brother and sister," Theodora had said. "Say you're sorry and be polite." When he'd only stared sullenly at the girl, Theodora had scolded him.

Chantal had been a skinny thing then in her jeans and cowboy hat. She'd jumped off the gate with her dangling snake and spat at the ground in front of his feet. "I'm not sorry! Catch this, *basura*." Before Theodora could stop her, Chantal had uncoiled the snake, shaken it and thrown it straight at his face. Trying to ward off fangs, flicking tongue and writhing coils, he'd lunged for Chantal, who had leaped on her pony. Flying hooves spewed dirt and rocks into his face as she raced away.

The snake had wrapped around his shoulders, and as he'd screamed, it had coiled tighter.

"Shut up, boy. It's just a whip snake."

Finally, Theodora had untangled the snake and tossed it gently into the high brown grasses, where it slithered away.

"It's not poisonous. It can't hurt you."

Maybe the snake was harmless. But the girl wasn't.

Chantal had made him feel dirty and low and cowardly, too, but he'd been right about her. When she'd grown up, she'd been the sexiest, hottest girl anybody in three counties had ever seen.

Everybody had had her. Lots of times. Including him.

But he'd been the only one fool enough to marry her.

He hadn't wanted to marry anybody so young.

But she'd tricked him. And he'd felt sorry for her. Sorry for the kid, too.

He still wasn't sure the fair-skinned, delicate-looking Carla was his.

Jack's jaw clenched.

Chantal was dead.

He'd best forget her.

There was no way now ever to even that score.

He wanted to lock his memories of her deep inside him and throw away the key.

But memories like he had weren't so easily bottled.

Not till he knew she was dead for sure.

Her body had never been found.

Her lover's killer, Nick Busby, the gas-station attendant with the thin face and the scrawny goatee, had become an instant celebrity that night two weeks ago when he'd confessed to a dozen murders all over Texas, that night when he'd told a bunch of Houston cops that he'd met Chantal and her young lover in a bar and followed the two of them back to El Atascadero. Busby had bragged that he'd watched them have sex and had then shot the boy for kicks.

But he hadn't confessed to killing *her*.

What Jack wanted to know was where the hell she had gone that night.

How could a woman just vanish without a trace? If she were alive, why would she have stayed away?

For five damn years? Without a thought that her husband was rotting in prison for her murder? Without a thought for her daughter, whom she loved, even in her own bizarre and highly destructive way? Without a thought to the immense inheritance that was her birthright?

Not that Chantal, who wasn't normal, had ever given a damn about him once she'd tricked him to the altar and given birth to Carla seven months later. With lightning speed, she'd moved to Houston and into the bed of her less-than-discriminating brother-in-law, Martin Lord.

Jack's lawyer, Bobby Doyle, kept telling him to forget about her, that she had to be dead. To make a fresh start of it.

But it wasn't that easy.

Jack lay in the dark awhile longer, wishing he could turn off his mind and go back to sleep.

Half an hour later his mind was still festering with uneasy memories about Chantal when the phone rang.

He let it ring.

Six. Eight times.

Persistent devil.

Who the hell could be calling that he'd want to talk to?

Nobody. Curiosity would be the sinking of him yet, he decided as he grabbed the phone, expecting a stranger.

A familiar, raspy, bourbon-slurred tone made his chest knot with a poignant rush of rage, regret and bitter anguish.

Theodora.

When his eyes filled with quick, hot tears, he savagely brushed his fingers across his lashes. He was so upset, he almost slammed the phone down.

"I've been trying and trying to call you, boy," she snapped, as full of venom and vigor as always, never for a second thinking he might not know her, nor caring that he might not want to hear from her. "I've been up half the night dialing this damned phone, trying to get you. As if I don't have a ranch to run come dawn. Like always, you don't mind a bit putting me to trouble."

"You've been drinking while you dialed, I reckon." His voice was deceptively soft and very cold.

"Maybe. A little."

"More than a little. I'd say half a bottle."

"Maybe so. You'd know. Well, it's been a long night, Jack."

"A long five years," he muttered.

She laughed huskily. "You haven't changed."

"I have. You haven't." It cost him to make his tone so low and hard.

"I've been watching your half brother's old movies tonight. Got me thinking…about you."

People said Jack could double for his world-famous half brother, who'd made it big in Hollywood playing cowboys and tough guys. Raised by different mothers, the siblings had never even met. Some cowboy. But Jack had damn sure had Garth thrown up to him all his life. The actor had never set foot on the ranch. Jack didn't think much of his brother's shallow movies. He didn't much like the attention he'd received because of their resemblance, either. Guys in prison had gotten ticked off about his pretty face. They'd called him Hollywood and had wanted to beat him up because of it. Still, he'd always envied his brother because everybody loved him.

"What the hell do you want, Theodora?"

"I've been thinking about things. About what you've been through. About the ranch. I want you to come home, boy."

"Home?" He hated how the word made his voice shake. "You never once wrote me or came to visit. Only Mario and Caroline did."

And Cheyenne. At least she'd written.

Every time Mario had come, he'd glanced around the prison mournfully and complained that Caesar, his oldest son, had fallen in with a wild crowd and was going bad.

Caroline, Theodora's beautiful, classy sister-in-law from the East Coast, had visited him once. She'd sat across from him as cool and pale as ivory. Always a perfectionist in dress and decorum, she'd sat straight backed and frozen in a beige silk, designer suit, too upset by the violent prison setting to ask more than if he was getting enough to eat. He had been too ashamed to tell her starvation was the least of his worries. Still, he'd been touched that she'd come. He'd always envied Maverick having such a sweet, pure woman as a mother. Caroline had been good to Jack, too. If it hadn't been for Caroline Jack might not have known that such a woman could exist.

Why the hell had he brought up Theodora's not coming? He didn't give a damn about her or anybody now.

"I expect I had my reasons for not visiting you."

"I didn't kill her."

"I wasn't the only one to think you did. A jury convicted you."

"I didn't kill anybody. I couldn't—not ever, no matter how much—" Damn. How could he care what she thought.

"I believe you—now."

"No. You believe some lying, psychopathic, serial killer! You believe that damn perverted stranger bragging to a bunch of federal marshals up in Houston so he could show them how stupid they all were for not catching him sooner."

"No. I believe what he showed me. They brought the skinny bastard down here, you know. He killed somebody down in Val Verde. They were taking him there for questioning, you see. The ranch was on their way, so they stopped off here, marched him all around the place. In jangling leg shackles that made him trip over every cactus. But he knew stuff he couldn't have known if he hadn't been here that night. They let me talk to him private like. He told me he heard all those things you accused Chantal of doing. The same things I heard. He quoted you word for word. He's got a scar from a bullet in his shoulder. He says Chantal shot him."

"I told you five years ago—I'm innocent." Jack had been drunk that night. Too drunk to remember much or know for sure what he'd done or hadn't done. Without an alibi, without even his own memory, he'd found nobody had believed him.

Theodora made no apology. As far as Jack knew, she had never said she was sorry to a single soul in her whole damned life. She was into controlling people and land; she was like a steamroller. Heaven help you if you got in her way. So he wasn't surprised when nothing more came from her but a deep and brooding silence.

Her silence wrapped around Jack.

He lay in the dark, his heavy, unwanted emotions suffocating him.

He wanted to feel nothing.

He should hang up.

"You think you can just dial me up, and I'll come running back to you like I did when I was a half-starved kid and you were the grand queen of El Atascadero? Maybe I was once your number-one charity case," he muttered bitterly, "but not anymore, old woman. You don't have anything I want."

"So, what will you do? El Atascadero is the only home you've ever known. You spent every dime you had on lawyers. I'm the closest thing you've got to family."

"I used to think so. I took a lot from Chantal—because of you. But you turned on me." That had hurt way more than anything Chantal had ever done.

Silence.

"As if you have so many better offers," she said at last. "At minimum wage, you won't be much better off than you were in Mexico."

"I guess I can survive on the bottom. What the hell do you want, anyway?"

"I want you to find my daughter and bring her home."

Jack's heart sank.

So—Theodora wanted Chantal.

Not him.

Like always.

Not that he gave a damn. Not that he gave a damn about a living soul now.

"Hasn't she caused you enough grief, old woman?"

"She's my daughter. Then there's…Carla."

"I don't want to hear about Carla!"

Again there was silence.

"You called the wrong man, Theodora. I don't want to find Chantal. I want to forget her. To be free of her. I lost five years and everything I ever cared about. Hell, six guys beat me so bad one night, I damn near died because of her. As for Carla, my daughter's better off without an ex-con for a father."

He lowered the phone, intending to hang up.

But Theodora wasn't about to let him off that easy.

She knew all of his buttons.

Which ones to punch. Which ones not to.

She zeroed in on the right ones and rammed her gnarled and blue-veined fist on them fast and hard.

"Oh, you're a fine one to say Carla's better off with no daddy. A fine one. You with that boulder-size chip on your shoulder ever since you were a boy because your daddy never claimed you, and I did. You were always wishing I'd go easier on you and treat you with kid gloves like Caroline treated Maverick. You never have forgiven me for taking you in, and you can't forgive the world. Poor Jack. Or do you want to be Mocho now? You gonna feel sorry for yourself the rest of your life—Mocho?"

He was surprised that she brought up his birth name. Mocho.

"No. I'm not going to feel a damn thing. I'm going to hang up on you and get as roaring drunk as you. And I'm going to stay that way—till I die."

Chapter 2

"Go ahead. Drink yourself to an early grave. Nobody cares about you. Nobody ever tried to give you a chance. Who's going to care if your little girl needs her daddy when her own daddy doesn't care?" Theodora persisted in a soft slur.

"I don't want to hear about her." His voice sounded oddly choked.

"Damn right, you don't. What father in his right mind would want a kid that won't go to school half the time? She runs away, too. Her friends ain't much to write home about, either. Sometimes she retreats into deep, scary silences—just like Chantal did. She draws terrible pictures. She's so lonely, Jack. The kids at school…she has the same kinds of problems there you used to. When the other kids won't play with her she acts so proud, closes herself off…."

"Aren't you done yet, old woman?"

"Hell no…!" she drawled, Texas-style. "I'm just

getting started. Next there's Maverick's running the ranch into the ground the same way he's done Caroline's. I think maybe…maybe I was wrong to set my hopes on him. Caroline and he like to live too high. And that takes money. Plenty of it.'' She paused. ''Oh, well, I was damn sure wrong to set any hopes on you. If you came back, you'd just hit the booze. There's a better chance of seeing an ice storm in hell than for you to straighten yourself out and me to ever change my mind and let you run this place.''

Damn, she knew how to get under a man's hide. First his kid. Now she was throwing Maverick in his face.

Maverick was Chantal's first cousin, a favorite lover, too. He had been raised by his mother, the elegant Caroline Henley, Theodora's sister-in-law from the next ranch. Maverick had been sent East to prep school and college. He'd always looked down his snoot at Jack. Once he'd even called him border trash.

''Maverick's no rancher,'' Jack said, riled about being drawn in despite his best intentions.

''Well, he's blood kin. You're a con. Not that some cons can't change. I'll bet there's some that don't wallow in the gutter feeling sorry for themselves. Some men might say, 'I'm free now. I know the people and the land. I understand cattle and horses. I could help that old woman…that raised me, that set her hopes on me, that shared her dreams with me…if I took a mind to. She's too old to be facing all that she's facing.'''

Damn her. He didn't want to feel anything. She'd always been a controlling witch. What he needed was a drink. He didn't want to feel anything.

With cynical, self-deprecating humor he laughed.

She was easy to figure out. But then, so was he.

He was glad she couldn't see the neon-orange carrot flashing in his mind's eye. Glad she couldn't know he felt as hungry for a nibble of that carrot as any half-starved jackrabbit in a drought-stricken pasture.

"Yeah. Sure you'll let me run the ranch. You've used that line before, old woman, when you talked me into marrying Chantal and claiming Carla."

"I talked you into doing what was right. I'm trying to talk you into doing what's right now."

"Right for you, you mean."

"Right for the ranch."

They say that childhood forms us, that we are never free of it or of our boyhood dreams.

Maybe because his dark memories of going hungry in Mexico had haunted him, Jack had loved being a boy and growing into manhood on the ranch. Had loved the wide-open spaces and freedom he'd found in those endless pastures with their waving grasses so tall he could polish his boots by riding through them. Grass meant cows. Cows meant food.

Jack had loved the pastures even with their thistles and thorns, salt cedar and mesquite trees. He'd loved climbing windmills and staring out at the vast kingdom of prairie that seemed to stretch forever, loved imagining that he was king of it. Huge dreams for a poor Mexican boy who'd once starved and fought street gangs. Huge dreams for a bastard with no right to the land. Later he'd developed the same keen eye for cattle and horses his father had had, as well as a talent and dedication for land and livestock management.

Ranching was in his blood. Ranchers turned grass into meat. With the world's population exploding, meat was vital. The dream of being king had taken hold of Jack in his teens. And Theodora had always known it. Dreams of the ranch had kept him sane these past five years.

His memories of the endless range made the four walls of the motel room feel like a prison cell. Did Carla really need him?

He couldn't bear to think about the child he hadn't seen for five years. Then Jack's future loomed before him, meaningless and empty without the little girl. If he didn't go back to the ranch, would he ever feel whole again?

He thought of Mexico and other countries like it that were full of starving kids.

A good rancher helped feed starving kids.

Feelings. He didn't want them.

But he couldn't stop them.

As he lifted the receiver back to his ear, his fingers were clenched.

Theodora had raised him up from nothing. She'd taught him to dream her dreams. He would have been dead long ago but for her. Maybe he did owe her.

He hated owing anybody. Just as he hated looking back.

But he couldn't stop himself.

Good memories flooded his mind right along with bad ones. If he'd dreamed of being king, Theodora West had been born queen in her little corner of the world. When she'd gone down to Mexico and brought back a poor Mexican boy to raise, she had gone against the normal prejudices of her race and class, as well as against the desires of her husband and daughter. After Shanghai Dawes's death she'd found a letter from Jack's mother in Shanghai's cabin. Im-

elda had written pleadingly that she was bad sick and
would die soon and that their boy would desperately
need a home.

Theodora couldn't have known what Shanghai
would have done if he'd lived. But she'd gone down
to Mexico, snooped around in the barrio asking prying questions till she found the boy. His mother had
just died. Even after Theodora had been told Jack was
a very bad boy who stole liquor and food, she had
arranged his mother's funeral mass and burial.

Jack's fingers tightened on the phone. He didn't
believe in giving anybody a second chance, but he
owed Theodora more than he owed anyone.

She had been a big-time rancher of the Old West.
He had been the bastard son of the foreman who had
gotten himself trampled during July roundup after a
rattler had spooked Theodora's horse. She'd been
thrown, her leg crushed, helpless when a bull had
charged her. Shanghai had jumped under the bull.

Maybe she'd figured she owed Shanghai.

Plucking his bastard son out of that barrio had been
her way of repaying him. Not that Jack believed
Shanghai had ever given a damn one way or the other
about him.

Jack remembered the first time he'd seen Theodora.
Only his name hadn't been Jack West then. It had
been Mocho Salinas.

His mother had lain in a cheap pine coffin in an
impoverished Mexican church. The hot, Matamoros
sun had streamed through the broken, stained-glass
window in that tiny, airless chapel with its dirty,
stucco walls, causing dust motes to sparkle as they
sifted and came to rest on top the coffin.

There had been only two mourners at Imelda Salinas's funeral mass—the Mexican boy and the older, Anglo woman who'd been asking everybody about him. They'd sat as far from one another as possible, each nursing a festering terror and a resentment for the other.

Jack's thin, dark body had been as tight as a clenched fist in his ill-fitting, threadbare suit, a garment he'd stolen off a clothesline. He had never been inside a chapel before and wasn't sure how to act, so he sat glued to the front bench, too scared to fidget, sweating profusely and yet oblivious to the heavy, stifling heat.

But not oblivious to the woman behind him, the woman who was paying to bury his mother, even though he stubbornly refused to acknowledge her presence.

Instead of staring back at her through grief-ravaged eyes, he'd concentrated on his mother's coffin, as if by sheer force of will he could drag her back to life.

Even though he'd found no comfort from the crosses, the frosted chromolithographs, the flickering candles, the priest or from all the other religious images, he'd bowed his head and fervently whispered a solemn prayer. "*Por favor, Dios.* Please, God, I'll do anything. Just make her wake up so I can tell her I'm sorry."

He'd remembered his mother laughing, his mother whoring. He'd stared expectantly at her worn, young face, which had remained gray and frozen, her lifeless eyes closed.

Never had he felt so utterly alone and guilt stricken. Despair had opened inside him like a chasm. How many times had he prayed to the angels for some escape from his hateful childhood.

But he had not meant for his mother to die, to change into this pale, waxen creature.

If she couldn't live, maybe he could die, too, he'd thought.

He'd drawn a deep breath and clamped his lips shut, holding the air in his lungs till his cheeks and neck ached and his chest felt about to explode.

He had tried to imagine what it would be like to be dead. For his heart to stop and his blood to congeal. For his eyes to pop open and not be able to see.

When he conjured an image of a bloated dog he'd seen in the barrio, Mocho had exhaled in terror. It was no use. He'd gulped in a mouthful of air. Dying was too hard. Besides that…he'd stared down at his hand and imagined his own flesh rotting away like the dog's had. And death had seemed a mighty fearsome prospect.

Finally, he'd turned and dared a look at the other mourner.

On the last bench, her beak of a nose perched loftily, her thin lips pursed as if in distaste, Theodora West—not that Mocho had known her name then— had sat with the unhappy resignation of one forced to perform an unpleasant charitable duty.

He resented her for being the only one to come and for having the money to bury his mother. Who did she think she was, this woman with her nose in the air whose hair was steel gray, whose tanned face was lined from the sun? He hadn't noticed how small she was, for he'd been too awed by the terrifying power that had radiated from her like that of a fierce bull in a ring. He hadn't known then that she was still badly injured and in pain from the fall that had cost Shanghai his life, that she hated churches, that she longed

for a drink from the flask she always carried but had
left in her limousine.

If he wanted her gone, he wanted it no more than
she.

But when he stared at her with cold dislike, she
stared back at him unblinkingly. Then her bench
creaked, her ivory cane tapping ominously as she
rose.

Terrified, Mocho ducked. His muscles tightened
when he heard the brisk clicks of her cane and the
stiff rustling of her dress. With all his heart he wished
he could turn himself into a wild creature, a wolf or
an ocelot maybe. Then he would run away from this
woman who dragged a leg, and would howl all night
in the woods.

Abruptly the tapping stopped, too near him.

In the awful silence, Mocho's heart gave a leap of
pure terror. Then he hunkered so low his unruly black
mop shrank entirely from view.

Theodora stiffened. In cold flawless Spanish, without a trace of enthusiasm, she said, "Come, boy.
Don't be afraid. I promised your father I would take
care of you."

She had done no such thing. But he hadn't known
that then. He'd learned it later. All he knew was that
he couldn't allow himself to believe she could possibly want him. He was dirt. A whore's son. Nobody
had ever wanted him.

"I don't have a father."

She didn't smile. He didn't know that she was
touched by his proud grief. "Yes, you do."

Mocho's lips curled into an insolent sneer. "I don't
like you. Go away and leave me alone."

"Nobody but me wants you, boy."

The coldness inside him expanded when her cane tapped his bench sharply, and she took another dragging step toward him. He shook his head and dived under the bench and then crawled up to his mother's coffin.

Theodora rapped her cane sharply on the coffin.

When he didn't come out, Theodora turned. As if on command, the doors at the back of the chapel swung open and a monstrous giant filled the narrow doorway.

"Boy, this is Ramón. If you don't come willingly, he'll carry you to my car."

When the tall, dark man lumbered up the aisle, Mocho bolted out from under the coffin, straight into the man's big belly. Mocho began biting and clawing and kicking, and the chauffeur bellowed. Maddened, he grabbed Mocho by the ear and cuffed him. Wrapping Mocho's wrists and crushing bone and flesh in his big fist, Ramón shoved Mocho to the wall and whispered in a voice too low for Theodora to hear, "Maybe you're Shanghai Dawes's son. Maybe you ain't. I liked Shanghai, though, same as *la Señora* liked him, so I'll give you the benefit of the doubt. If you're Shanghai's brat, I figure to like you, too. Stop kicking me, damn it, or I'll bite your ear off and break both your arms."

Immediately Mocho stopped fighting.

"Boy, Theodora don't mean you no harm—you do what she says."

Mocho, who by then had been beaten, shrank lower when Theodora frowned and began limping toward him. With great difficulty she knelt, so that she was on eye level with him.

Mocho stared at her sullenly. Then he saw his reflection in a windowpane.

His lip was cut and bleeding. The right side of his
face was growing purple, the eye swelling shut.

He looked like a wild boy. But again Theodora
seemed more impressed with his spirit and fierce determination than depressed by his appearance.

"For a small boy who has lost his mother, you
have much courage," she said, pulling out a handkerchief and wiping the blood from his mouth. "They
told me in the barrio that you are very bad, that you
steal. But they told me, too, that you give the smaller
children the food. A boy who thinks of others can't
be all bad. Your father was like that. You've learned
bad habits, boy, but you've got good blood in you. If
you're half the man your father was, the ranch needs
you."

Mocho drew back, startled by her kind touch and
words. Startled to think of himself as having good
blood, as being of value…to anyone. Before she'd
said that, he'd seen himself only as an unwanted bastard and a thief. As nothing.

"If you obey me, I won't ever let anybody hurt
you again," she said.

He didn't believe her because it was too scary
somehow.

"If I go away, you'll just be another beggar. And
Mexico has enough beggars."

Mocho glowered at the floor, not wanting to want
what she offered.

"If Ramón lets your arms go, will you promise not
to run?"

When Mocho fixed his bruised, coal black eye on
her, she paled. Fearlessly, she persisted. "If you don't

promise, Ramón will keep holding you. If you come with me, I'll send you to school.''

Her Spanish was that of an educated woman.

She spoke his own language better than he.

He had never been to school.

He couldn't read or write. Once he had found a broken pencil in the dirt, and he had tried to draw the letters he'd seen on a license plate. But his efforts had been clumsy, and the bullies who'd gone to school had laughed at him. He'd felt stupid. The world belonged to those with knowledge.

Bitterness flashed in his heart at the unfairness of life—that some are born with so much and most with so little—but he was too tired to fight her.

The instant his forceful energy had abated, hers did, too. For a moment she looked so exhausted he almost pitied her.

She had known his father. He felt a dim glimmer of curiosity about the man he had never known.

''Why didn't my father come?''

''He died saving my life. I owe him. Maybe you do, too, a little.'' When an entire minute had gone by, she said, ''It's a long drive to El Atascadero. We need to leave.''

''I won't go till my mother's buried,'' Mocho said defiantly.

Her gaze ran over his high cheekbones, his aquiline nose, and lingered on the stubborn set of his strong jaw. Later he would watch her cull cattle with that same sure eye for bone-deep quality.

Maybe she sensed how desperate he felt to show her he was somebody, too. ''I see more of Shanghai in you than your mother,'' she said at last. ''If you didn't glower so, in the right clothes, with your hair cut, you know…you just might be an appealing boy.''

"I won't go unless I see her—"

To his surprise Theodora suddenly relented. "All right." When he stared at her uncomprehendingly, she snapped, "Well, don't just stand there. Let's see her in the ground."

Stunned, he stared at her despite his swollen, black eye. He wasn't used to anybody ever considering his feelings.

This time when she looked down at him, she caught her breath at his smile. The sudden warmth in her gaze caused him to have a peculiar urge to touch her.

He forgot their racial differences, her wealth and his poverty. Even for a second, he forgot his pride. Briefly, he let his rough knuckles brush her wrist, but then, like a shy puppy making a new acquaintance, he pulled his hand away quickly.

Still, his simple gesture seemed to affect her. Just for a moment or two, her strong, sun-tanned fingers settled on top of his impossible hair.

They stared at each other in surprise, each wondering if somehow they had reached an uneasy truce. If so, it would be the first of many in what was to be for both of them a difficult relationship. For always, always she strove to control him and everybody and everything.

He hadn't known then how lonely she was. That with her plain face and bossy personality she had troubles with relationships; that she needed him as much as he needed her.

When Mocho had placed the last of his wilted wildflowers on top of the fresh dirt clods in the graveyard and Ramón had started the limousine, Theodora took the boy's hand and told him it was time to go.

He yanked free of her and flung himself across the withering flowers and howled like a trapped animal, his fingers digging into the dry earth. Finally, he stood up and walked to the car. When he got in, he pressed his thin face against the rear window glass and howled again. Even when she told him she had packed a picnic basket full of food, he kept his nose glued to the glass. Only when they'd driven out of the cemetery did his hoarse cries decrease.

He smelled meat, and his empty stomach grumbled, but when he opened the basket and unwrapped a sandwich, beggars raced up to the car. He shut his eyes, sinking his teeth into soft white bread and delicious ham. But he couldn't forget their desperate, dirty faces and the rancid garbage that would be their meal that day. He choked on the soft, sweet meat when he tried to swallow.

Through sobs, he said, "Stop the car...."

After he'd set the basket out, he began weeping again—this time over the loss of the ham.

"Tears don't ever change anything, boy. I wanted to be pretty when I was a girl...." Theodora stopped. It was not her manner to reveal herself.

Mocho squeezed his eyes shut.

"I lost my mother younger than you. I've hated funerals ever since," Theodora said, unscrewing the cap of a silver flask. "I don't like the sight of hungry children much, either. Life's hard—even for rich, old women."

He doubted that this willful woman who had a bully for a chauffeur and a big car and a full belly had a hard life.

"I keep this for just such depressing emergencies." When she thought he wasn't watching, she hastily sneaked three long swigs.

He watched her reflection in the window as she belted her liquor like a man, and wondered if she would get drunk and beat him.

After a while she said, "I have a daughter. Not an easy daughter, either. Chantal doesn't care about the ranch the way a boy would." Theodora drew a deep breath. "Maybe you and I will surprise ourselves. Shanghai and I saw eye to eye about most things."

She didn't tell him then of her loveless marriage to Ben West. Nor of Ben's long-term affair with a younger, fascinating beauty, Ivory Rose, who some said had bewitched him. Nor of Ben's other daughter, Cheyenne, who of late was so much sweeter and more appealing than Theodora's own daughter. Nor of Theodora's heavy ranching responsibilities.

Mocho's sobs died by fits and starts.

"Boy…" In sudden inspiration she offered him her flask. "Normally I wouldn't suggest this, but you're no ordinary child. Take a sip!" she ordered. "You'll feel better. All cowboys drink. Your father did."

She smiled. Mocho didn't know she was remembering the long nights she'd spent drinking with Shanghai while Ben stayed with his other woman.

Mocho wrinkled his nose. Just the smell of the liquor brought back the beatings he had endured in the barrio from his mother's drunken boyfriends. He had stolen liquor to sell it. "I'm no cowboy."

"Your father was the best that ever lived."

Mocho grew sullen as he thought of his father, who had never come for him.

Theodora pressed the flask to his lips, and Mocho

tipped his head back. She hadn't left much for him, but he swallowed, choking on what there was.

She patted his back, while he sputtered and smeared the back of his suit sleeve across his mouth. The stuff quit burning his throat after a minute or two. Then he found that she was right about it making him feel better.

A strange, relaxing warmth was soon spreading through him. His hunger lessened. Her brown face looked softer, blurrier—almost friendly now.

He began to feel very sleepy, so sleepy that the scary images of his mother's coffin and the bloated dog began to recede. When he rubbed his eyes and yawned, Theodora drew his black head down onto her lap as if he were her boy. As if it didn't matter that she was a rich Anglo and he a poor barrio brat.

"It was my fault that Mama died," he confessed guiltily, fixing her with his one good eye again. "I prayed that I wouldn't have to live in the barrio anymore. I wanted to go to *el norte*. I wanted to live like an Anglo. Now she is dead, and I'm with you."

"That's not your fault," Theodora stated in a tone that brooked no nonsense. "You know, since you're going to live in Texas, we're going to have to think up an English name for you."

He flinched, feeling sullen again.

"You must have a name that goes better with—"

"I won't take my father's name!"

"Then you can take mine." Her voice rang with even more authority. "West."

"Jack," he muttered swiftly, feeling defeated at the thought of giving up his own name even if she was willing to share hers. Jack was the name of an older kid he'd met at the river who'd once helped him fight a bully.

"Jack," she repeated, regarding him as she tested the name.

Jack. The name echoed inside his brain, an alien, hollow sound. It wasn't him. It never would be.

But he was too tired to worry about it.

Mocho wearily gulped in two ragged breaths and fell asleep.

He didn't wake up till Theodora ruffled his springy hair and said they were home.

"Here we are, Jack."

Jack? Who was she talking to? But he got up on wobbly legs and peered out the window.

Palm fronds that lined the drive roared in the Gulf breeze. The driveway made a graceful loop in front of a majestic main entrance, where the tall white walls of a red-roofed mansion loomed above gnarled mesquite and oak.

He muttered a Spanish curse word and shrank violently against Theodora. His new home felt even stranger and more alien than his new name.

Fresh panic surged through him as she opened the window and he saw the skinny little redheaded girl holding a fat, dozing snake. The girl's cold green eyes fastened on his face with fierce dislike. Then she smiled and hissed bad things about his mother and father.

Jack regarded the girl narrowly, knowing she'd probably always think she was better than he was. When he muttered the worst insult that he could think of, the girl laughed.

Theodora told them to stop fighting. "Get out of the car, boy. You behave, too, Chantal."

The second he jumped out, Chantal spat at him and then uncoiled the snake from her arm and threw it. When the thing had wrapped itself around his neck, he screamed like a girl.

Disgusted, Theodora pulled the snake off him. Later she'd said, "Don't worry about Chantal. She's been the ranch princess—till you came. Just give her time." But there was a strange hardness in her voice every time she spoke of her daughter.

Chantal was just a girl, he'd told himself. One stuck-up white girl who knew how to make snakes go to sleep. In the barrio he'd been outnumbered by dozens of thugs.

But this girl was rich and mean. So mean even her mother was uneasy around her.

He knew the girl would get meaner when she caught him alone.

Maybe his new house was a mansion.

Maybe he had a new Anglo name. Maybe he wouldn't have to beg or steal.

But nothing had changed. He was still dirt. He was still alone—with no friends. He was going to have to fight very hard for his place here. If Chantal made her mother hate him, Theodora would throw him out, and he'd be poor and alone in some garbage-strewn alley again.

Funny how he almost felt poorer and lonelier in this rich, Anglo world. At least in the barrio he had known the rules.

Later he found out that there were plenty of people besides Chantal on El Atascadero. Many despised him for his birth, but a few accepted him because he was Shanghai's son. Mario, the *caporal* of cow camp one, took him under his wing right along with his own son, Caesar, and taught him everything he knew, which made Caesar jealous.

Jack had had to work very hard to prove himself, and nobody had been more amazed than he at how fast he caught on to everything—school as well as cowboying. Theodora told him that he could be whatever he wanted. Not that he believed her. Not that he ever relaxed or stopped trying to better himself. But the higher he'd climbed, Chantal had always been there to bring him down and to tempt the dark side of him to wildness. And no matter how high he'd risen, he'd never felt sure. One false move and he'd be at the bottom again.

He'd been right, too.

Because of Chantal, a man had died in their barn, and Jack had served time for two murders.

Another ambulance rushed past Jack's motel on the San Antonio freeway. But Theodora's voice cut his bitter thoughts short.

"Come home, Jack. Maverick needs a wake-up call. We're in the middle of the worst drought of this century. We're burning the needles off prickly pears to feed our cattle. I've sold half the herd and leased land in east Texas to feed the rest."

"You threw me out. Why should I give a damn about your problems?"

"In four months, if she's still alive, Chantal will be thirty-five. I have been holding her shares of El Atascadero in trust while you were gone. On her birthday her shares revert to me if she's dead or if she doesn't claim them. I can give them to anybody. If you stay sober and prove you're better at running things than Maverick, I could will them to Carla and give you control till she comes of age. It'd look better if Chantal's alive, by your side. She's your wife. The shares would then legally belong to the two of you.'' Theodora paused. ''I need you. The ranch needs you. Carla needs—''

''Leave Carla out of this!''

Carla. He remembered the last time he'd seen her, the afternoon he'd tried to tell her goodbye.

He'd been drunk, not so it showed, but she'd run away from him and climbed *her* tree. He had watched the branches bend with her weight as she'd scampered to the top. Then she'd sat on a skinny branch high above him and rocked back and forth, staring down at him as white-faced as she'd been that night in the barn. He'd stood there, under her, scared out of his wits she'd fall. But he'd just stayed where he was, watching that limb rock, thinking about how he'd once climbed windmills, thinking about how he might never see her again. The very next day they'd found him guilty and sentenced him to life.

Carla.

Little girls change a lot in five years.

Jack felt as if all the air in the room had been sucked out. ''You're not promising me anything really—''

''Life's always a gamble.''

Pain tightened his lungs.

He wasn't used to choices. He didn't want them.

''This is as close as you'll get, Jack, to having a chance to get back everything you lost—your daughter, the ranch, your good name.''

''My good name? That's a laugh if ever there was one. You don't care about me. All you care about is controlling your ranch.''

"I need you...for that. Mario and the others—they want you back, too."

Mario. Jack had too many tender memories of the tough old man who had been so kind to him, who was disappointed in his own son.

Carla, the ranch...

Jack wanted to yell, to bang his head against the wall.

He didn't want feelings. He didn't want this hollowness in the pit of his stomach, either.

"What about Chantal? What if she's alive and I find her? What makes you think she's changed? What if she starts lavishing Carla with expensive gifts instead of her attention again? Aren't you scared of what the two of us might do to each other the next time?"

"Hell, yes. But not nearly as scared as you are."

The hollow feeling was expanding inside him. "I'm not scared."

"Jack, maybe it's January, but, hell, you know how the weather is down here. Most days it's as warm as May. A few wildflowers are already in bloom—bluebonnets, pink primroses. A few hummers stayed instead of migrating south. They feed outside my window. You know how pretty it can be here when it's warm, and all the scissortails and Mexican eagles are flying about. I expect you'd feel mighty free if you got back in the saddle and just rode off as far as you pleased toward the horizon. You could take your guitar, and sometime, maybe... I got a mighty big hankering to hear you sing again, Jack. Remember how we used to sit out on the verandah and you'd strum your guitar? All you ever wanted to do was grow grass and cows and help feed the poor. Remember how it was to go hungry…?''

Damn.

Her voice died away. It was a habit of hers, letting her words trail into nothing like smoke in the wind.

His freedom hadn't meant much till she said all that. He could camp out. He could build a fire. He could watch the stars, roam the endless prairies. He hadn't sung in years. His life would have a purpose.

He was a rancher. That was all he knew. All he wanted to know. The work meant something to him. He had a daughter.

His throat constricted. When he couldn't speak, she didn't bother, either. He imagined her sitting back, taking a swig or two, giving her hooks time to settle deep inside his hide. She had him, and she knew it.

"Why don't you come home," she persisted. "Stay awhile. And then decide."

"Okay," he rasped. "You win." His voice grew more hoarse and shaky. "I lose. Like always."

When she broke the connection without saying goodbye, unwanted pain flashed through him.

Why the hell was he opening himself up to her again? He'd sworn he'd never…

He squeezed his eyes shut and opened them. Then he threw back the covers. His bare feet made contact with the threadbare carpet.

Slowly, step by step, he padded to the window. Pulling the curtain to one side, he looked out, his eyes straining, his dark face hard as he studied the freeway.

Chantal could be anywhere.

Whether she was dead or alive, he'd find her.

But if he brought her back to the ranch, it would be on his terms.

Not Chantal's.
Not Theodora's, either.
He had a score to settle.

Chapter 3

Jimmy was running down the driveway with his skateboard and shouting excitedly to his friend, Ronnie. The sun was shining through the trees, backlighting leaves and branches with shimmering golden light. Backlighting Jimmy's hair so that it looked like it was on fire.

Bronte called after him.

He never looked back.

Then it started raining, and he was lying there. And she was holding him and weeping, not knowing what to do.

Jimmy's bright head began to dissolve.

Tires whirred softly outside on the gravel drive of Webster's Connecticut farmhouse. The diesel engine of a big Mercedes pinged and went silent.

She called to Jimmy, but he vanished into a red, misty haze of raindrops and sunlight.

Bronte's new reality was the hollow feeling in her

soul and a charming bedroom with a slanting ceiling papered with tiny yellow flowers, and dormer windows that looked out onto rolling dark hills and shadowy trees.

The screen of her television set was flickering from across the room as she awakened slowly, feeling strange and lost. She had no idea that Webster's car had awakened her, but she guessed that she'd overslept by nearly an hour.

For one thing, the thick aroma of the chicken browning in thyme and sherry now filled Webster's farmhouse. Thank heavens the bird didn't smell like it was charred to a crisp this time. For another thing, moonlight and starlight were glimmering off the windows of the loft in the barn where Webster's mysterious study was.

As her gaze wandered to the distant trees, a bolt of lightning forked. Then thunder echoed, sounding faraway.

The front door beneath her bedroom was cautiously opened and shut.

Webster was late, much later than usual.

"A-a-a-a-choo! A-a-a-a-choo!" His hard, masculine sneezes erupted as soon as he stepped inside. Next came his curse. "Damn it!"

Bronte sprang up guiltily, knocking her gardening book and botanical catalogue from the bed. Two Garth Brown movie videos fell, too.

Oh, dear. Why had she brought the lilacs inside? And why did a man of such invincible ego and ferocious will have to be allergic to every flower in Connecticut? Why was she beginning to dread his dark moods the way she had once dreaded her mother's?

Not that he had discouraged her from her passion for planting, which had been her chief pastime during the spring while she had convalesced. No. Thank goodness. So long as she followed his medical advice, he was arrogantly indifferent about her other interests.

Webster sneezed and cursed again. He put on the highlights of *Madama Butterfly*. Then he yelled Bronte's name, and she raced out to the landing— only to linger there like a naughty child, reluctant to go down because he made her so nervous. Maybe it was the soaring opera lyrics, but Bronte felt like she was a little girl in her mother's house again. Webster had rules for everything just as her mother had had, and Bronte could never remember them all.

It was April. Which meant the pastures and the woods and the rolling hills and the stone cliffs and ledges were green and beautiful, especially with the lilacs in bloom.

It had been almost six months since Bronte's accident, and other than that one occasion after her second operation, when she'd looked at herself and then been terrified by how ugly she was with the swelling and bruises, she still had almost no idea what she looked like. She didn't care much, either. A lot of things had ceased to matter to her. A couple of times when she'd been mildly curious, Webster had intimidated her by hinting that any interference from her might jinx the outcome. She had decided maintaining his enthusiasm was more important than satisfying her curiosity.

Bronte had tried to tell herself that the main thing, after all, was that she was so much better. Maybe she was all alone in the world. Maybe she didn't understand Webster as well as she would have liked to.

Maybe Jimmy was dead, but her grief had abated when she'd felt his presence in the emergency room.

Perhaps he had really been there. Or perhaps coming so close to death had taught her that her life might be precious to her again. She still didn't feel much, but these months had been a time of healing and waiting. Gone were the hateful respirator, the casts, the crutches. Dental implants had replaced the three teeth that had been knocked out. He had cleaned out the dead tissue, put bones back together, and done trauma repair.

Still, Webster, ever the perfectionist, wasn't quite satisfied despite all he'd done.

Bronte felt guilty that she couldn't feel closer to Webster. He had saved her life and her face. In the beginning, he had even stayed at her bedside day and night.

Now Webster held himself aloof. He asked only one thing of her—that she live with him and not look at her face till he was through.

She had been told that Webster usually charged outrageous fees, money she didn't have. In her case, he had generously waived his fees and paid her other bills, too.

"Oh, I don't want your money," he had said, his eyes burning bluer than a laser, his voice scaring her a little. "Your case is unique."

She had given him pictures of herself. He had barely glanced at them.

"Oh, I won't need these."

"But I want to look like me…" Not that she had cared then all that much. She had been too ill.

He had turned away. "When you were a little girl, who did you want to look like?"

"My mother."

Webster had gone very still. "What was she like?"

"She sang. She was very beautiful. Everyone…loved her."

He had sighed a deep sigh. "Yes. There. You see?"

"No. You don't understand." She had stopped. She had never liked talking about her mother.

She hadn't told him about her early life, and he hadn't asked. She knew how she wanted to look, and it bothered her that Webster seemed so intent on his own agenda.

In the beginning Bronte had been too weak and too injured to tell Webster anything or to ask for anything. She had felt thankful that he seemed so directed and sure, that he saw her as a fascinating case. She had signed the informed consent without even reading it. She had been all too thankful that he let her retreat inside herself. Besides, she hadn't had anyone else she could turn to.

Slowly Webster had begun trying to perfect more than her face. He had given her a perfume that smelled of gardenias and insisted that she wear it. Like a robot with no will of her own, she had let him teach her to walk differently. What had anything mattered? He had changed her speech patterns. She was too skinny, but he had insisted she diet. He'd been bossy about her clothes also, as bossy as her long-dead mother, demanding that she wear clingy, silk dresses. The only colors he allowed her to wear were red and black. It seemed eerie that those had been her mother's favorites, too.

Bronte had begun to wonder a little about Webster's motives. She tried to reason with herself, knowing that surgeons were not wishy-washy people. Altering reality was Webster's job.

As it had been her mother's.

All of Bronte's doctors, even Webster's enemies, had been amazed by her quick recovery. Webster's nurse, Susan, the only member of his staff to ever see Bronte, was equally amazed.

Only Webster remained unsatisfied. "The nose isn't quite right. I think…just another session with the laser, my dear. We won't do much this time. Just shave the edge of a tiny scar. A little peel may work wonders."

"Webster, I'm tired—"

"Soon you can rest. I promise—just one more procedure."

He had refused to discuss the matter further.

Bronte was beginning to feel alive again, beginning to think that maybe she should have found the strength and the will to argue more. Now that she was no longer an injured caterpillar content to convalesce in her cocoon, she was weary of Webster's endless procedures, of the painful healing afterward.

She was growing tired of living with Webster. Sometimes she remembered old Dr. Montrose warning her not to go to Costa Rica.

"Miss Devlin—" dear old Dr. Montrose had hesitated "—do be careful. There are appropriate boundaries between a patient and a doctor—"

"Whatever do you mean, Doctor?"

He'd stared at her, groping for words. "What I'm trying to say…is that Dr. Quinn is not like other doctors. He seems so intense about you. I understand you're living with—"

"It's not like that."

"Forget it. I can see you're quite smitten."

"I am *not* smitten. It's quite the opposite. I don't care much about anything. And I have been told by so many that he has achieved miracles."

"Yes. *His* miracles. Not his patients' miracles."

Dr. Montrose's concern haunted her. Somewhere in the back of her mind, a vague foreboding had begun.

She was worrying more since their return from Costa Rica and their move to his charming house on his hundred-acre property in Connecticut. Except for those rare occasions when he took her to the opera, he had cut her off from everyone. Not that the physical isolation bothered Bronte. Bryan and she had lived on a small ranch several miles from Wimberley, a small town in the Texas hill country.

It was that Webster made her feel like a laboratory experiment. The snow had been deep in Connecticut, his house isolated on its hill. Even though she and Webster spent every night together and their bedrooms were side by side, he avoided her. It seemed strange that after every new procedure, when he studied her face and proclaimed his operation a success, he withdrew even more. And now that she was stronger and wanted to meet people, he didn't want anyone to see her.

Two days ago in his office, when he had once again insisted on shaving another scar, she had challenged him. "Susan says I'm pretty enough. I want a mirror. I want to decide. If I'm too pretty, I won't be me."

He had said nothing, but the fierce blue light that had burned in his eyes as he brushed the tip of her nose with a proprietary finger had silenced her.

Webster had removed all the mirrors at his farm.

Once Bronte had teased him that he was like a painter who wanted to realize his vision before he revealed his creation.

She was too upset to tease now. Last night at dinner she had asked him, "Has my face become your obsession?"

His blue eyes had stared straight into hers. "You flatter yourself."

"How come you scare me a little?"

"You are highly imaginative. You have suffered severe trauma. You are theatrical like…"

"Like…like what? Like who?"

He was silent. "Forget it." He stood up. Without another word, he strode out of the room.

She had watched his tall form move through the dark kitchen. Then the kitchen door had slammed, and he had disappeared.

Bronte knew Webster had gone to his study in the loft of his barn—a place that he always kept locked and had forbidden her to enter. It was this one mysterious place beyond that dark fringe of trees—like Pandora's locked box—that intrigued her more than anything on his farm.

Once or twice after dinner she had begged him to let her spend time with him in his study. Each time, he had refused, saying only that his experiments could mean a lot to other women, many of them more badly injured than she.

Once she had read him an unflattering article about his work from a newspaper. The writer had made the allegation that he had given several infamous criminals new faces.

"My jealous colleagues exaggerate my ability to

perform miracles,'' Webster had replied with uncharacteristic modesty.

But did they?

"A-a-a-a-choo!" She heard him pacing downstairs in the living room. When he got close to the stairway, where she was hiding, he saw her. "Bronte?" He expelled a long, nervous breath. "Bronte..."

"Yes?"

He relaxed visibly. Almost it seemed that, before he recognized *her* voice, he had thought she was somebody else.

Somebody whose existence electrified him.

She could not imagine Webster passionately involved with anyone.

"What on earth were you doing up there—hiding in the shadows?"

"I—I, er...just thinking."

When Bronte dashed down from the landing and into the living room, Webster's blue gaze sharpened. "Slowly!"

Instantly she obeyed, gliding toward him with long, graceful strides like a runway model.

"Better," he said. "Now where are they?" He forced a smile.

She arched her brows and innocently scanned the small tables and shelves.

He cupped his nose with his hands again to ward off a sneeze.

"I thought surely that just one small vase of lilacs could do no harm."

He sneezed again—this time so deafeningly her ears rang.

"Would you please get those damn flowers out of here!"

"All right." She seized the offending vase and rushed back upstairs, spilling water everywhere. Her hands were still sopping when she returned a minute or two later.

He made no comment this time when she remembered to glide down the stairs. He sank into his leather chair and opened a thin black volume on plastic surgery. Bronte had scanned the book once and read of several cases where the doctor had made mothers look like their twenty-year-old daughters.

Flipping the illustrated pages, Webster pushed his glasses up his nose and bent his sculpted, silver head so low over the book she felt completely shut out.

He was so self-contained. So utterly controlled.

At fifty, despite the deep lines in his face, Webster had an ageless brand of masculine good looks that were bone deep. His athletic physique was that of a man of thirty. He hadn't the slightest interest in clothes, but his wardrobe was stunning. Even at home he always wore custom-made suits and silk ties. Yet nobody ever called him. He never dated; he never spoke of other women. He was so different from the hard-living, hard-drinking cowboys who had been Bryan's friends.

Bronte left him to check on the chicken she was preparing for dinner and found it so tantalizingly brown and tender, the meat was falling off the drumsticks. She took the clay pot out of the oven to cool. Then she walked outside to the swimming pool and the sculpture garden.

Lightning flared above a nearby stand of towering maples and changed the sculptures to frightening, spidery shapes. Webster's isolated house, even the beautiful woods, had never seemed a sanctuary. The peace and solitude that should have comforted her made her feel isolated and alone.

She turned and saw that Webster was watching her from a lighted window, as he often did when he didn't think she knew.

His moving away quickly when she saw him made her uneasy. It was strange how his farm and his house felt so much like a prison. Strange how he seemed like her jailer instead of her doctor.

When Webster stepped out onto the porch and called her, she ran away from him.

She was hungry, but she walked farther than she'd ever walked in the dark, even though the air now felt dense and heavy with the promise of rain. Past the pool and the bizarre modern sculptures. Through the mysterious, aromatic pine forest. Down to the stagnant marshes that reeked of dead, wet foliage. Across the lush fields of corn and alfalfa. Through a field of waist-high clover that smelled fresh and green and moist.

She didn't stop till she got to the lane. Her bad knee was throbbing by then, so she stood for a while and watched the bright headlights of the cars whizzing past. Dark clouds were massing to the north, and lightning blinked behind them. She longed for the day when she would leave Webster and this farm forever.

But she had promised him she would wait—till he was finished.

And he had promised, too—only one more procedure.

Soon. No more than a month or so. Then she would be free. Reluctantly she turned and walked back to the house.

When she passed the barn, she lingered in the long

shadow of a maple and looked up at the brightly lit rooms of the loft where Webster worked. She heard the faint strains of the opera *Carmen*. The soprano was some new star. When Webster's tall shadow loomed against a window, Bronte bit her lips and stifled the impulse to go up there and confront him.

Instead she returned to her attic room, which was cold in the winter and hot in the summer but pleasantly cool that April night.

There she undressed and went to bed.

But she couldn't sleep.

Not after it began to rain and the branches of the large oak tree by her window scratched the roof of the house.

Not when the sensitive skin on her face itched and her bad knee continued to throb. Not when the lights from the barn twinkled through the raindrops. Not even when the lights in the barn went out and she heard Webster climb the stairs and close his door.

She felt uneasy as she listened to him undress. He had never made a pass at her or expressed the slightest sexual interest in her. Still, she didn't like living alone with him now.

Something was wrong, really wrong between them. At first she had been too ill to understand that theirs had never been a normal doctor-patient relationship.

Webster wasn't telling her everything.

Why had he helped her?

Why was he so possessive?

He was a brilliant doctor, but he was a less-than-insightful human being.

Maybe she had made a mistake to put herself so completely in his hands.

But she was in too deep to simply cut and run.

Still, the sooner she got away from him, the better.

Chapter 4

Jack hadn't expected to like France.

He'd been told that the French were snooty and rude. Not so. Except for his Parisian taxicab driver, who'd tried to short-change him and had insulted his French.

The French sure knew how to dress. Americans all ran around in their kindergarten clothes. Jack, whose idea of dressing up was to wear a tie or a corduroy jacket with jeans, was pretty casual himself.

The French ate well, too, if you had time for two-hour meals. They had excellent wines, so he'd been told. It had been a struggle, but so far he'd stuck to lime water.

He'd figured he'd get homesick. But Provence, with its limestone cliffs and clear cool springs and green rivers and woodsy smells and golden light, was just like the Texas hill country.

Not that he felt easy here.

Not this close to such dangerous prey.

Suddenly the world-famous model who'd been strutting back and forth on top of the ancient aqueduct like an angry cat paled. Then she whirled and made wild gestures in Jack's direction. ''Over there! Down there...!''

Damn! Damn!

Jack dove into brambles that scratched his face as the shoot's entire crew stared down into the trees.

Maybe she smelled him, Jack thought as he wiped blood off his cheek.

It wouldn't be the first time.

Chantal had strange powers, just like her sweeter half sister, Cheyenne, whose moods had made flowers bloom out of season. Cheyenne, whom he'd once loved...

Whatever. Quickly he hunkered lower in the dense foliage.

The air was cooler and smelled mustier under the trees. Contrasting shadows and light flickered over him.

A second or two later he aimed his binoculars back at the long-legged woman standing on the topmost limestone tier of the first-century Roman aqueduct. He had come all the way from south Texas to get a good look at her.

The woman atop the Pont du Gard calmed down. She wasn't quite as white underneath all those layers of professionally applied makeup. She wasn't pointing his way anymore, either. Still, the husky Italian photographer everybody called Edmondo had stopped the shoot and was demanding the rouge pot. The makeup artist was brushing the woman's high cheekbones frantically as Edmondo yelled that the light was fading.

Was she? Or wasn't she?

Jack squinted, focusing on the triangular face.

Damn. He needed to get closer, but the shoot was under tight security.

He felt pretty desperate. It was April. The four months Theodora had given him to find Chantal were nearly up. Things hadn't been going too well for him back at the ranch. For one thing, Theodora had aged greatly in the past five years. She had grown stooped, as if some weight rested on her heavily. Even though conditions were tough, he wasn't sure it was just the ranch bothering her.

Corn prices were up, cow prices were down, and they hadn't had any rain. The calf crop percentages were down as well. There had been more than the usual number of accidents and other problems, too. He and Theodora couldn't seem to get along even as well as they had in the past. She was determined to keep to the old ways, to the old ranch traditions, even though to survive and be competitive they needed to change. With workman's comp as high as it was, they needed fewer permanent cowboys and more contract labor.

More than one *vaquero* had hinted things had been smoother before Jack had come back. And even though Maverick had returned to the ranch as soon as he'd heard Jack was there, he'd been more of an aggravation than a help. He always sided with Theodora. He always found a way to lay every accident and every problem at Jack's door. Right before Jack had left for France, Maverick had noticed some cash shortages and taken the books to Theodora, who'd promised to show them to their accountant.

Theodora had ordered Jack home but had given him almost no support. One cowboy had been injured by a combine. Then the night of Jack's departure to France, when she'd sided with Maverick and blamed Jack for Caesar getting hurt in a tractor accident, he and Maverick had nearly come to blows. The truth was Caesar had gotten hurt due to his own damn carelessness. The only person who routinely took Jack's side was a distant cousin of Chantal's, Becky, but Becky lived in Houston and owned only a small percentage of the ranch holdings.

The dozen detectives Jack had hired to find Chantal had come up with zip. Then last Tuesday, when reaching for his wallet to pay for the more than twenty bags of groceries, he'd suddenly noticed Carla staring at the cover girl on a magazine.

Carla, who had begun to thaw a little, who even smiled at him every now and then, had quickly glanced away.

But not before he'd seen her tears.

Not before the model's glacial green gaze had riveted him, too.

He'd gone cold as he'd ripped the magazine off the shelf.

"No, Dad!"

Holding the magazine above Carla's outstretched hands, he hadn't heard the checker tell him how much he owed.

The man behind them slung a six-pack onto the checkout counter. "That's Mischief Jones. Get a load of those chi-chis. They say she prowls New York in her limo looking for men. She goes for dark young Latin types. Like you and me.''

Jack had flushed.

''We've gotta go, Dad.'' When Carla jumped and grabbed at the magazine, the model's face tore in half.

''That'll be an additional $5.59, sir.''

Jack's hand had remained frozen on his wallet.

Was she? Or wasn't she?

A powerful chill of recognition swept him.

The model had a classic-looking face. Her narrow, feline features were savage. She had huge slanting eyes, a delicate nose, prominent cheekbones and full red lips. She didn't look much like Chantal.

Yet he had known with an instinct that was needle sharp and true. His hand had shaken. He'd have given anything for a double shot of gin.

Chantal was alive.

And she was going to pay.

For what she'd done to him.

For what she'd done to Carla.

''It's not her, Dad!''

He'd stared at Carla. ''Yeah. Right.''

She'd screamed when he'd pitched the magazine into a grocery sack.

Theodora was always getting on his back because he never talked or explained himself to Carla. Hell, how could he when he was too afraid of damaging their new, fragile relationship? In the past she had always sided with her mother, making excuses for Chantal, saying she was perfect, blaming him for Chantal's neglect. Not being able to explain how he felt to Carla made him feel tight and all wound up inside.

When they had gotten back to the ranch and unloaded the pickup, he'd waited till Carla sulkily grabbed her sketchbook and raced outside to climb that damned tree of hers. Then he'd called his P.I. and asked him to check out the model.

B. J. Smith called him back within an hour. "Mischief Jones ain't as lily-white as she claims."

"So what did you come up with?"

"Not much. She became an instant celebrity four years ago when she hit Paris. Mostly because the most famous supermodel in the world, Beauty Washington, took her under her wing. But your girl's pretty wild."

"Tell me about it."

"Last spring at one of her parties, this friend, Beauty, fell ten stories to her death. Mischief got some bad press, but nothing was proved against her. The publicity pushed her to the top.

"Your Mischief's fed the press a clever line of crap from day one. She says her daddy is a French viscount. Wrong. The guy's dead, and so is his only daughter. Their château has been made into condos. She says she studied art history in Paris. Nobody over there ever heard of her. None of her other lies checked out, either."

"So whoever this lady is, she completely reinvented herself?"

"Yeah. By day she models classy clothes and lives like a queen. By night she screws bikers and losers she picks up on the street or in bars. She's got a soft spot for kids, though. Every single child model in the agency is crazy about her. Seems she wows them with presents from her shoots."

Chantal had always given Carla gifts instead of love.

"She's Chantal."

"You don't know that."

"I'm bringing her in, B.J."

"Hey—that could be dangerous. The lady has two bodyguards with records a mile long."

"My kind of guys."

"Why don't you just forget her? Theodora will come around."

"I have to because of Carla. It's hard to explain…"

Edmondo began barking orders, and just for a second Jack aimed his binoculars on him. Then the gorgeous young woman threw her head back so that her trademark masses of curling red hair tumbled down her back.

She was thinner. Much thinner. Bone skinny, in fact. But she had a long, swanlike neck and a sculpted, feline face. She moved like a cat.

Or a snake.

But this woman was different from Chantal. So different, he never would have known her…if he hadn't sensed her.

The woman thrust her legs apart, her stance that of a conqueror. Chantal used to do that. Right before she told him how much better she was than he.

Still, he had to get closer, much closer—to be sure.

Tonight he'd find a way.

Mischief had put on a CD of *Carmen*. But not even the soaring voice of Webster's favorite diva, Madame Devlin, could soothe her tonight.

Disappear or die.

Those were the same choices Mischief had faced five years ago in the barn. Only now the stakes were higher.

All her life other people had forced her to do terrible things. She hadn't wanted anybody to die that night in the barn anymore than she had meant to push Beauty. All she had wanted was what was hers.

The gilt-edged mirror loomed above the frightened woman in red. Feral green eyes devoured her own reflection. Dozens of Webster's facial creams, which were like a religion to her, lined the marble counter beneath the mirror, but Mischief had been too filled with dread to use any of them tonight.

A beautiful woman dies twice. A coward dies many times.

Webster had whispered those bitter truths to her after they'd made wild, vicious love the last time. He'd known those sentiments would fester and hurt far longer than his slap. Her terror of getting old only increased his power over her.

Mischief had the shower running in the luxurious marble bathroom in her six-room suite at the renowned George V in Paris. Madame Devlin's soprano voice swelled passionately. Thus, Mischief didn't hear the slight sound of a stolen key turning in the latch of her living room door.

Nor did she hear the hushed footsteps of a large man padding across her huge, elegantly furnished salon and bedrooms.

Mischief was naked beneath her red silk dressing gown with a golden dragon emblazoned on the front. As she stared into that misty bathroom mirror at her beautiful, triangular face, she did not see her beauty.

She saw only the faint, feathery lines beneath her eyes. Lines that would grow deeper and longer, and crueler. Until her lovely face would melt into those crevices like wax.

Mischief prized beauty because it was her source

of power. She had no other, for her father had taught her not to trust love.

Her father had said he loved her more than anybody in the world. But he'd lied.

He had had another little girl—a secret daughter, a usurper.

Chantal had been ten years old when she'd followed him to a strange shack in the marshes. She'd seen him hug that pretty witch, Ivory Rose. She'd seen him sweep another little redheaded witch girl named Cheyenne into his arms and kiss her and laugh with her as he carried her inside, where he stayed all night. When he had closed the door, night flowers had begun to bloom.

Chantal had vowed that night never to love any man again.

If she loved her new face, it was because it gave her fame and power over men. She loved the wild sex with boys who seemed to get younger and more in awe of her every year. She loved the limos, the clothes and the money. Or she would have loved such a life if the bastards who hounded her would leave her alone. And if she hadn't left behind a little girl she couldn't forget no matter how hard she tried.

Who was stalking her?

Beauty's big bad boyfriend who'd written Chantal threatening letters from prison because he blamed her for Beauty's death?

Rumor had it that José Hernando hadn't drowned in Costa Rica after she'd sicced him on her sister whom he'd almost killed. Had he figured out who Mischief Jones really was and where she was and sent his thugs after her?

Modeling was competitive. She'd made plenty of enemies getting where she was.

Then she remembered that last night in the barn...when she'd barely escaped with her life.

Whoever her stalker was, Mischief had damn sure felt him in Provence this morning.

But despite the dangers surrounding her, she was just as worried about the way her life was rushing by so fast, like grains of sand streaming through an hourglass.

Her beauty had been her ticket to the extraordinary life she had always wanted to live.

She was nearly thirty-five. Soon, too soon, she would look old. Her life-style was taking its toll.

She worked so hard and still she never had the energy to do all that was demanded of her. She had to wear the right clothes, entertain the right people. She loved the brilliant, glamorous life of Mischief Jones, daughter of a French viscount, internationally famous supermodel. Still, even though she was on top, Mischief could feel herself slipping.

All too soon, younger models would take her place.

Suddenly Madame Devlin's soaring voice stopped in midnote.

In the next instant a hard male drawl broke into Mischief's unhappy reverie.

"Chantal!"

Stunned, Mischief Jones whirled.

A tall, dark man stood in the shadowy doorway with the bedroom light behind him. He had massive shoulders and a dangerous face.

Her green eyes narrowed to slits.

Her husband.

Her heart beat madly. She felt herself blanch.

She had not expected Jack.

The long scratch that marred his tanned cheek made him look even tougher than usual. Tough the way she liked a bedmate to look. But too steely eyed. And too sober.

Like characters in a ballet, they stood poised, frozen, their gazes locked.

The roof of Mischief's mouth went dry.

"I thought they locked you up and threw away the key," she taunted in a low tone.

"You hoped."

Another piece of her past had suddenly caught up with her. So had more of her lies.

Jack would tell the world who she was. He would ruin her. *Who back at the ranch knew that he had found her?*

"Where are my bodyguards?" she whispered.

His slow, white smile was insolent, his laugh hard. "Those two overweight goons?"

Jack's educated voice was only faintly accented. If she hadn't known, she would never have guessed he came from squalor and whores and gang-infested streets or that he'd spent the last five years behind bars. He was tougher and harder than anyone she'd ever known. His memories were worse than most people's nightmares. He'd probably taken care of her bodyguards as easily as another man might knot his tie.

"Strip. I want to see you naked," Jack commanded in that dark growl that had once electrified her with lust.

Now, because there was nothing sexual in his request, she was momentarily at a loss as to how to handle him. If only he had been drunk. If only there had been even the slightest hint of a sexual demand.

In that other, almost-forgotten lifetime when they had been young, they had been good that way.

How she had despised and yet been fascinated by him when he'd been dirty and poor and illiterate. And wild. Uncontrollable. So wild, nobody had been wilder or made her feel wilder than he. He hadn't been afraid of anything. Not even of Theodora. Then he'd come up in the world. Gotten those damned college degrees. She had married him, so Cheyenne couldn't have him.

They'd had their darling little girl, Carla Ann.

Carla.

Carla, who had adored her. Carla, who would forgive her anything. Carla, who with her magic pencil could draw anything. Carla, who climbed trees and hid and did all the glorious things Chantal had done as a child before her father's cruel betrayal.

Oh, Carla.

Chantal remembered standing over the crib, willing herself to hate their little girl and then weeping uncontrollably at the thought of such a darling baby girl with downy red curls being born to a mother who hated her. She remembered how her hands had shaken as she'd lifted her precious baby into her arms and comforted her till she quieted. She remembered how only she had had that effect on the child. How, at last, she'd been first with someone again.

But not even her adorable little girl, not even Jack's proficiency in bed had been enough to satisfy her. She'd grown restless for more. For more men. For more of everything. Her dreams had been so much bigger than the ranch and motherhood.

Not once in the past five years had she ever allowed herself to think of Jack. Not true. She had thought of him the night she'd met his brother, Garth, at that film festival in Cannes. It had been weirdly thrilling to seduce the world-famous movie star even though his performance in bed wasn't even a close match to Jack's.

Still, her marriage was dead and cold. And even though she had missed her daughter unbearably, she had told herself Carla was better off without her.

"What do *you* want?" Chantal whispered. "Why are you here?"

Jack just stood there like he had when they'd been together in the burning barn. When he'd laced his large brown hands around her slim neck and tightened them very slowly, all the time staring into her eyes.

She hadn't been afraid even when his fingers had dug into her windpipe for that fraction of a second before he'd released her. He had a temper, but he wouldn't ever hurt a woman—even her. He would have let her go even if Carla hadn't wandered into the barn. But he had seen their child's stricken face. He had backed quietly away from her as Carla had hurled herself sobbing into her mother's arms. And Chantal had played the part to the hilt by screaming that he would have murdered her.

But Chantal hadn't run away from him. She'd run away from someone else, from that person who had set her up and sent Jack down to the barn that night, from that person who had tried to finish what Jack had lacked the guts to finish.

Jack's harshly carved face was silhouetted against the elegance of the Pompeian inlaid-marble wall.

Chantal shivered. His body was as heavy with muscle as she remembered. She knew the power in his hands. His black eyes burned her with a censorious and malicious fire.

Anyone else would have been afraid.

But Chantal's blood was pulsing with an unnatural, raw, animal excitement. Once she had liked his hating her and his wanting her at the same time. She remembered his rough hands on her soft skin. Maybe prison had given him a taste for the things she had always tried to push him to do.

"Strip!"

"Why? Do you still want me?" she asked.

His black glare flamed hotter.

She smiled. She kept smiling as she lowered the red silk dressing gown over her shoulder. The rippling silk felt cool and soft against her hot skin.

"Did you miss me?" she whispered. "You and I—we were pretty incredible."

"Shut up." His voice was deeper, gruffer.

"What was it like for a man like you—doing without for five years?" Her voice lowered huskily as she bared her breast and ran her fingertips over her nipple.

The color left his dark face; profound emptiness dulled his eyes.

"It beat marriage to you."

"I hope they hurt you."

"Oh, they tried." His dark face drained of color. He looked gray and sick suddenly.

"I wish I could have watched."

"Come here," he demanded, seething.

"Sure, baby," she purred, wanting to push him till he went wild.

At the last moment she rushed at him, claws extended, thinking she might somehow get past him. He grabbed her arm, shredding her dressing gown. And even as she thrilled to the brutal power of his hands on her skin, they gentled.

Just for a second she felt the old keen, wild wanting as his glittering gaze stared down at her naked body.

Then she read the true emotion in his eyes.

Too late she realized that he didn't desire her. That all he felt was cold, icy contempt. "Are you even human, Chantal?"

He continued in a strange, disembodied voice. "You have the body of a beautiful woman. But you're sick. If you weren't so dangerous, I might even feel sorry for you."

He'd told her once that for him their marriage had been like a roller-coaster ride. After a few cheap thrills, he'd been tired of it. He'd told her he'd only stuck it out because of Carla.

The last thing she'd ever wanted from any man was pity.

Suddenly Chantal could barely hear him. It was as though he were speaking from the bottom of the sea.

He forced her to turn around. She shivered as his callused palms traced down that jagged white scar on her back.

Then he released her and let her fall gently onto the Aubusson carpet.

And she knew.

Her fingernails, which would have clawed his flesh, raked the worn wool pile as she snaked away from him. He hadn't been sure who she really was. He was merely identifying her. Checking the scar on her left shoulder the way he'd check a brand to see if an animal belonged to him.

"Bastard!" she hissed, humiliated. "I wish you'd

burned to death in the barn that night. You were supposed to die then. So was I.''

"Get dressed," he snarled, helping her to her feet,
throwing her dressing gown at her. "You have a
plane to catch. You're going home. Back where you
belong. To Texas.''

Hadn't he learned anything? Hadn't he figured out
what had happened? If he took her back to the ranch,
she would die. But so would he.

"I'm not going anywhere with you."

"You're my wife—remember?''

"In name only. Our marriage is dead. I want a
divorce.''

"Ditto, honey. But first we go home—together.
You have a hell of a lot to answer for. We both do.
Carla, for one thing. It's time people down there know
what you are.''

Oh, Jack, somebody does.

As he pushed her into the bedroom, Chantal realized she needed to use her brains—fast.

On the edge of panic, she turned. "What about
Carla?''

"She can't get over you. She runs away. She
doesn't go to school. She's flunking math—''

I aced math. My daughter can't flunk—

"Carla blames… Hey, why am I telling you this as
if you care?''

Chantal saw two white-faced lumps sprawled beside her bed—her bodyguards. How had Jack done
that without making a sound?

"I—I do care about Carla. But she's better off with
me gone.''

"Carla won't go to school unless I chase her down
and put her in my truck and drive her. Carla and I

are closer, but she still blames me for your absence from her life. She doesn't say much, but without you there...she feels all alone.''

An odd desperation coiled around her heart as she thought of her little girl having problems. Of Jack dying. But fear for her own safety swamped all other anxieties. ''Okay. You win. I'll do what you want.''

Inside, Chantal was like a lava-filled volcano, ready to burst. She felt bad about Carla, but guilt couldn't compare to her fears and fury. She had a new life now. Big problems. Going back now would ruin everything. She felt crazy, absolutely crazy as she always did anytime anybody forced her do something she didn't want to do.

Jack was blind. Stupid.

Pretend. Pretend to go along with him.

She was moving past him into the bedroom, grinding her pretty white teeth, fighting for self-control as her wild gaze raked the silk draperies, the woodwork ornamented with gold leaf, the polished marble, seeking a weapon. The door to the terraced balcony was open, revealing its summer furniture and urns overflowing with red geraniums. Too far away. He'd catch her for sure. And the urns might be too heavy. Besides, the balcony overlooked a courtyard; she might be seen.

Nearer, she spotted the magnificent bookends on the antique table behind the sofa. They were made of heavy dark stone carved into the graceful shapes of big-eared Egyptian cats.

She lunged toward them, seizing one by the neck. As leather-backed books tumbled off the table, she whirled on one foot like a dancer and struck Jack square in the jaw.

She sidestepped gracefully as he toppled toward her.

She hadn't wanted to hit him. He had made her do it. He should have known better than to push her.

She knelt beside his massive, sprawled body to make sure he was unconscious and not...

With a fingertip she tenderly wiped away the blood that oozed from his mouth. There were deeper grooves running from his handsome nose to his well-remembered lips, a faint webbing beneath his black lashes. He, too, had grown older. He might have been happy if only she had not seduced...

But Cheyenne had stolen her father.

So she had stolen Jack from Cheyenne.

Suddenly the hotel maid assigned to her stepped into the room. "What are your men doing on the floor, *madame?*"

Mischief froze. Fear and guilty regret died instantly. She couldn't afford them. Couldn't afford to think about what Jack had said about Carla needing her, either. Couldn't afford to remember her own father abandoning...or Beauty's terrified face before she'd fallen...or the face in the barn that night....

Mischief had been forced to do all the things she'd done.

Forget the past. Forget Carla. Think.

She had to think. She stayed at the George V because of its excellent service. The hotel maid assigned to her was multilingual and impeccably trained. The traits that made her such a treasure would make her a perfect witness.

Mischief remembered the police and their questions after Beauty's death. The investigation had gone on for months. The newspaper stories had lasted even longer. She had to make up something that the maid would believe, so she could escape.

"Monique, this man is an intruder," she said softly in a robotic tone, forcing herself to let the bookend fall onto the carpet. "He attacked me. It was… terrifying." The stone cat landed with a dull thud. "Call the police, you little idiot! Now!"

This was Jack's fault. He had had no right to come here. No right…

He could have been followed.

She had to get out of here—fast.

All the designer clothes in Mischief's closet were either red or black. She ripped dress after dress off its hangers. Evening gowns as well as skirts were all thrown onto a heap onto the floor until she found…

With a smile she ran her hand down a favorite, black silk shantung jacket.

She got dressed quickly, methodically, in a severely cut suit that accentuated her voluptuous curves. She pinned a circle of diamonds onto her lapel.

When Monique wasn't looking, Mischief scooped up her purse and a long red scarf and walked out of the room, down the long corridor, letting the scarf whirl behind her so that it licked the carpet like a tongue of flame, letting it trail all the way down the wide, sweeping staircase that led to the public rooms and lobby that, with their rich old tapestries and paintings from the eighteenth and nineteenth centuries, were masterpieces of understated elegance. As she was.

Without bothering to check out, she stepped outside onto the tree-lined avenue, hailed a taxi and quickly vanished into the Paris night.

It was almost midnight. The city was dark and quiet

beneath a black sky as she sped past the Arc de Triomphe. Other cars glided past her cab on the wide avenue as silently as fish scurrying in an ebony sea.

She lost interest in the city with its lighted buildings and monuments and stared at her reflection in the window. In the dark glass, the tiny lines beneath her eyes were no longer visible. Her face appeared as flawless as it had five years ago after Webster's first procedure.

Not that she found pleasure in her beauty. She was filled with a deep and burning anger that was so all-consuming that it left no room for anything else. Why couldn't Jack have left well enough alone? Why had he cornered her? Why hadn't he seen that she couldn't allow him or that part of her life to threaten her again?

If he came back he would force her to—

Jack knew who she was and where she lived.

If he stayed sober, he would be relentless.

She would have to change all her carefully made plans.

Fast.

He was far more dangerous than the others.

He would come after her again.

If she didn't stop him, he would bring her down.

She didn't want to hurt him, but she would.

II

Chapter 5

A dark-faced Papual fertility figure smiled mockingly from its fastening on the wall beside a boldly modern painting by Basquiat.

Later Bronte would look back on this night and wonder how she could have ever been so naive.

But then her mood was almost as eager as a child's during that last hour of kindergarten before being released for a holiday.

A heat wave had struck the Northeast. The May evening that was to bring revelation, ecstasy and so much despair was a blistering ninety degrees.

Not that she and Webster felt the heat in the immense, cool, ivory-tiled master suite's spa. Swathed in white towels, she sat on a three-legged stool with her long legs crossed in a lotus position while he hovered over her with powder and rouge. She had been taking turns staring out at the pool and sculpture garden or at the muted television screen every time her favorite star, Garth Brown, appeared.

Webster had turned off the television sound, muttering, "What garbage!" after a story about an attempt on a supermodel's life in Manhattan began. Then he'd played a CD—Mozart's *Magic Flute.*

"Close your eyes," Webster commanded in a raspy voice, setting powder and brush on the pink marble counter. "No. Don't squint."

All day his mood had been tense and more autocratic than usual.

When she relaxed, she felt the tip of the eyeliner brush flow expertly across her lids.

His brush tickled, and she wiggled her nose. "When can I look?"

"Hold still." A few minutes later, he said, "There! Now you can open your eyes."

But when she did so, Webster's intent, almost-angry stare alarmed her.

He gripped the sides of her stool and leaned closer. His unsmiling face was taut; the lines between his keen eyes furrowed. "I can't believe—" He broke off, looking appalled, dazzled.

With shaky fingertips she felt the warm, baby-smooth texture of her cheek.

His hands shook more violently as he traced the same cheek with a finger. "Magnificent."

Curious for the first time, she said, "I want to see…"

His dark smile died. "First I want us both to fortify ourselves with a glass of champagne."

"Why?"

"There is a great deal about me you do not know.

Why indeed?'' he asked ominously. "The changes in your appearance are…radical.''

"But if I look pretty, why wouldn't I be pleased?''

"Because…'' His frown deepened. "Because…'' His voice was low and hard. "Go to your room and put on that red Dior I selected. And the perfume. Tonight I want you to look and be just like… Just perfect.''

"Webster, there's no need to make such a fuss.''

"Go!'' He waved her away impatiently.

She ran upstairs, wanting to get this unveiling over, wanting to get on with her life.

On her way back down, the phone rang. When he picked it up and said her name, Bronte stopped. He spoke in morose, cracked whispers. Still, she caught fragments of his side of the conversation.

"—I told you it's dangerous to call—''

"—yes, I saw it—''

"—the resemblance to you and—''

"—quite startling—''

"—upstairs—''

"—damn it—''

"—any minute…coming down—''

"—I don't give a damn about your husband—''

Only when he slammed down the phone did Bronte realize her heart was racing. With difficulty she resumed her composure and descent. She was halfway down the stairs when the telephone rang again.

Instead of answering it, Webster yanked it out of the wall. He was throwing it onto the couch and trying to untangle his legs from the wires when she glided through the doorway into the dining room.

"Webster, what's wrong?''

He whirled, gesturing grandly. "Nothing. Absolutely nothing. Where's the champagne?"

When she'd left the room, he'd put on a CD of *Rigoletto*. The passionate music made her remember her unhappy childhood, her beautiful mother, her own terrible self-doubts. Her first two lives. Her failures.

Jimmy's loss.

After her son's death she'd enrolled in a CPR class. Bryan had laughed at her for doing so. "A little late for that, Bronte, don't you think?"

She'd thought, he's right. She couldn't win ever again.

Bitter memories.

Don't look back.

Bronte smiled brightly, determined to put all that behind her. Webster hardly had drained a glass when he poured himself another. While the music soared, maneuvering toward a climax, Bronte sliced slim pieces of pink roast onto fine china plates.

He drank steadily through dinner. From time to time he would stare down the length of his gleaming table, his fierce blue eyes glowering moodily at her from behind the silver candelabra and its flickering red candles. Then he would look away as if deeply troubled.

"Webster, why are you so upset?"

"And why do you give a damn?" he growled.

What could she say when she understood him so little? She simply stared at him with compassion in her heart.

"I—I thought a woman like you could have no power over me. Not when she..." His eyes blazed. "But no..."

The soprano sang faster and faster, higher and higher.

Bronte recognized her mother's voice. Which was odd. Webster had never played any of her mother's performances before. She had believed he was only interested in the latest stars.

"She?"

"Forget it."

"I want to help you," Bronte said.

"You always want to help me," he said softly. "Damn it. You do everything I ask, don't you? You cook. You keep house. You're nice even when you are burdened with great pain. I've tried not to let it affect me. But I've never known anyone like you. And every day...as you grow more beautiful and look more like..."

Madame Devlin was singing the most haunting of arias.

Webster continued. "It would drive a sane man crazy—and I am hardly sane. To be in the house, night after night, alone with...with the daughter...with my goddess..." His eyes were wild as he sprang from the table. "Stay away from me. There's no help for me now—do you understand?" He heaved himself toward the kitchen. "No, of course, you don't. But, dear God, you will."

Madame Devlin's pure voice rose and held the final note in that last, dazzling crescendo. Then abruptly her angelic voice and the music ceased. But the silence that followed held even more dark, mysterious passion.

Suddenly Webster made an inarticulate, almost animal cry. Then he turned his back on her and left Bronte alone, staring at their ruined candlelit dinner.

When she heard the kitchen door bang, Bronte got up and, leaning over the polished table, blew out the candles one by one. She had found the opera disturbing, for it brought back the past. But she had found her conversation with Webster even more troubling.

For a moment she savored the darkness and the quiet of the dining room. Then she turned off the CD player and began to worry about Webster.

As always, he'd gone out to his study.

What was wrong?

She had thought he was cold, uncaring.

But he wasn't. He was afraid.

Of what, though?

Bronte's mind reeled. She knew what it was to be terrified. To feel all alone...and guilt stricken.

When she went into the kitchen with their plates, she nearly dropped them when she realized that the big carving knife with the sterling handle that she had used to slice the roast was gone. She rushed to the sink, but it wasn't there.

Then she remembered her mother's wild rampages after a bad performance. Had Webster taken the knife?

In a panic, Bronte rushed out into the sweltering night. A dog barked in the distance. Moonlight gilded the modern sculptures in the garden and made them appear to be twisted and oddly knotted as she raced past them.

Webster was nowhere to be seen until she reached the barn. Then she looked up and saw his black silhouette swell and then vanish against the blinds as he dashed back and forth furiously. The grotesquely elongated shadow of a huge knife arced and slashed. Next, the window shattered and a rectangular object fell and broke into pieces at Bronte's feet. He was playing music from the opera *Carmen*.

Wild panic surged through Bronte as she leaned down and picked up what was left of a broken frame and photograph of a girl with a lovely triangular face.

It was a face too like…

She recognized her mother's voice again, singing high and true—perfect as always.

No… No…

The world had suddenly gone crazy. Bronte was a child again, cowering in her mother's brownstone house during one of her rages.

When more glass broke, a thousand terrifying images flashed through Bronte's mind. Flinching at every violent, crashing sound, she forced herself to climb the stairs. For once, the loft door that Webster had always kept locked stood ajar. A narrow bar of pure yellow light spilled onto the first stair.

When she pushed the door wider, she nearly stepped on torn fragments of an immense photograph of the same beautiful girl who wore nothing but a silver fox fur. Her lovely cat-shaped face with its sculpted cheekbones and flowing spirals of long red hair had been slashed. Part of her lip lay in tatters. Her ample breasts had been shredded.

Webster raked a dozen framed pictures of her off his desk. His laughter was shrill when they smashed onto the oak floor.

Everywhere there were pictures of the same girl.

Then Bronte saw the huge poster of her mother costumed as Madame Butterfly.

This had something to do with her mother.

Bronte heard her mother's voice as she had heard it as a child, so many times, under glittering chan-

deliers with long gold mirrors reflecting the radiance
of her mother's exquisite face and slender figure in
glorious costume. The music and the voice surged
toward Bronte in waves, hurtling her backward in
time to her mother's brownstone where the original
painting of that poster had hung, where gigantic photographs of her mother had graced every wall. The
world had worshipped her mother's voice, her
mother's beauty.

Nobody had cared that Madame Devlin had been
dissatisfied with her child and unfaithful to her husband.

Bronte put her hands to her ears and forced herself
back to the present.

Webster had known who Bronte was from the first.

The likeness between the girl in Webster's photographs and her own mother was uncanny.

How?

Webster had known all along about her mother.

Why did this model have her mother's face? How?

One of the photographs in Webster's loft was
signed with the letters *M.J.* On another the model had
signed her full name—Mischief Jones.

In one Mischief wore a black Chanel gown. In another red chiffon. In another she was painted gold and
draped with gaudy silver jewelry. In one she stood on
the deck of a ship in front of a wind machine. But in
every shot, whether she was a waif or a siren, she
looked incredibly feral and boldly haughty.

She had red hair, and it was the same startling
shade as...

Mischief had slanting green eyes.

They were the same dazzling color, too.

Bronte was filled with a profound and growing confusion. Webster was watching her sympathetically. But comprehension dawned slowly.

Mischief's legs went on forever.

Just like—

Dear God. No!

Just like—her mother's. Just like her own.

Bronte sucked in huge lungfuls of air.

No! No!

What had he done?

She shook her head. He couldn't have... He wouldn't—

Bronte had longed to look like her mother. Until she had realized that it had been her mother who had longed for that. Not she.

As Bronte stared at the pictures, she struggled with a chaos of thoughts and long-suppressed emotions.

"Who are you obsessed with—my mother...or this model?"

"As a little boy, I adored your mother. She was like a goddess. I worshipped her. Then a woman came to me... I *made* Mischief Jones. I made you, too. I watched you at your mother's house. I followed you...before your accident."

"What?"

"Only you're even more beautiful than they were." His handsome face was strange and passive. "I never considered how your beautiful soul would enhance the perfect, ruthless facial structure so necessary for photography that *they* both had..." He swung around in a flash. He loomed over her, his thin face going in and out of focus.

Suddenly Bronte was absolutely certain. She didn't need a mirror. She knew what she looked like, *who* she looked like.

*I want to be me. Not my mother. Not this look-alike
Mischief Jones, either. I want to be Bronte Devlin.*

I don't want to be beautiful. I don't want—

"You are a goddess now," he whispered, sinking
to his knees.

For an instant the pain she felt in her heart was as
cold as if an icicle had pierced it.

She stared down at him hopelessly. "You never
cared about helping me. This was always about them.
Which one are you obsessed with?"

His face went haggard.

"Why, Webster? Why did you do it?"

He just stared up at her.

"For vengeance?"

A low moan came from him. The knife fell from
his hand with a clatter.

"Why?"

His gaunt face was gray, his blue eyes empty.
"I—I wasn't sure I even could. I tried before. But
this time, I used a three-dimensional CT scan. That's
why I was able to get the facial bone proportions the
same. I succeeded beyond even my wildest dreams."

As always, his plastic-surgery jargon was little
more than gibberish.

"When Mischief became a famous model, did she
jilt you? Did she crush your huge ego? Is this about
my mother? Or did you do it to ruin Mischief? Well,
if you did, I'll go to her and tell her that no matter
how you threaten her, I'll never try to take her place.
I'll make her know that all I'll ever want is to go
home to Texas and get my own life back."

Webster got up, rushed toward her and, grabbing
her arms, began to shake her. "If she sees you, you'll
sure as hell never have your own life back. Stay away

from her, do you hear me? Whatever you do, stay away from her. She's evil. Dangerous. She'll tear you to pieces. She'll destroy you—the way she destroyed me.''

''Why should I believe you? You think you're a god. The way you play with other people's lives makes me sick. Well, you can't play with mine anymore.''

Brave words.

''Don't go…''

Bronte felt hollow despair rising in her as his grip tightened.

''Bronte…''

Suddenly she was trembling as she stared at him and at the model's face behind him. And then at her mother's poster. Bronte's eyes glazed. ''Why? Why did I let you do this? I've been such a fool.''

Then Mischief's huge photograph with its slashed red lips blurred. So did her mother's poster. Bronte felt blank and empty. Almost like she had ceased to exist.

''Let me go,'' she said dully.

''Bronte, you've got to listen to me.''

Her confusion was replaced by rage and fear when his fingers dug into her shoulders.

''Get your hands off of me!'' When he just stood there, she pushed him away and ran, tears wetting her cheeks as she stumbled into the night.

He let out a cry of frustration.

''Bronte!''

At the sound of her name, she gave a sudden, anguished scream and ran faster.

"Bronte, I'm not a monster."

No. She was. She was the one with somebody else's face.

Chapter 6

Webster had replaced *her* face with another woman's.

"Oh God, oh God, oh God!"

And not just any woman's.

Bronte hadn't felt anything for so long. Now her feelings were swamping her.

She was shaking as she stared up at the Gothic turrets and gables, balconies and gargoyles that decorated the exterior of Mischief Jones's luxurious apartment building on Park Avenue.

"Not yet," Bronte whispered aloud to herself when one of Mischief's liveried doormen caught sight of her and waved, thinking he knew her. "I—I can't face her yet. Not when I don't even know who I am anymore."

Terrified, Bronte waved back at the doorman. Then she began backing away from the building. Not knowing where to go or what to do, she crossed the wide street and hurriedly walked two blocks to Central Park. She couldn't find a taxi so she strolled along Fifth Avenue.

Last night she had driven Webster's Mercedes to the train station and then taken a train to Grand Central. She'd watched the manicured Connecticut countryside give way to dirty, crumbling buildings spray-painted with graffiti. Then she'd caught a cab and checked into a nondescript hotel not far from the Museum of Natural History.

Why had Webster done it?

Bronte hadn't slept. She'd had nightmares about dozens of women, all who had the same lovely face she did.

Then she had a truly terrifying nightmare about her mother. Bronte had been a little girl again. She had sneaked into her mother's room and was standing in front of her gilt, floor-length mirrors, her young face garishly made up, her plump body zipped into a glittering gold costume. Then her mother had come in and had begun tearing the jewels and rich fabrics from her body.

Her mother had screamed, "Just look at yourself. You may be my daughter, but you can never be me! You're fat and pimply faced and...and just horrible!" In her dream, her mother's beautiful face had slowly melted into a death mask.

At first light Bronte had checked out of her hotel. Then she'd spent the next few hours wandering up and down Fifth Avenue, staring vacantly into shop windows. Finally she'd caught sight of her reflection and realized how much she really did look like her mother in the red chiffon gown she was wearing. New clothes would make her look more like herself, she'd decided, and she'd been the first customer to enter Macy's Department Store when it opened. There she'd stripped out of the evening gown and bought a pair of jeans and a white cotton blouse.

It had taken her that long to realize that she couldn't ever look remotely like herself again.

During her sleepless night in the hotel, she had carefully studied her strange and wondrously beautiful face in the hotel's many mirrors. Unable to accept that the incredible new face was really hers, she would touch her baby-soft flesh and then the cool mirror.

With such a face, it would be hard to hide.

How many others were there?

Where were they?

These questions haunted her.

Still, she did feel a little like Cinderella after the Fairy Godmother had magically changed her into a princess. Only this spell wouldn't end at midnight.

The slim, cat-like face with its delicately molded nose, with its tenderly voluptuous mouth and the seemingly high cheekbones was undeniably exquisite. A mad genius had taken her plain features and rearranged them to stunning effect. Her skin appeared fresh and golden, as if she'd bathed in honey. But while her bold features were smolderingly sensual, her huge green eyes made her look irresistibly innocent.

It was the face she had dreamed of having.

But now she would give anything to have her own face back.

Bronte didn't feel quite real. She wasn't sure who she was. And she was terrified.

Webster had told her numerous stories about nose jobs changing people's lives.

And she had this simply incredible new face.

Maybe Webster had made dozens of others.

"Oh God…"

Talking to God wasn't going to help. This wasn't *His* fault. This was Webster's.

Why had he turned her into a freak?

What could she do about it?

It was bad enough that she looked like her mother. But how was she ever going to work up the nerve to face the infamous Mischief Jones?

Webster's warnings haunted her.

She's evil. Dangerous. She'll tear you to pieces. She'll destroy you the same way she destroyed me.

Bronte had gone to the library and read about the woman. Her father was some sort of French viscount. Mischief had grown up in a château near Paris. After Mischief's meteoric rise in the fashion world, thanks to the help of an African-American model named Beauty, Mischief's sexual excesses had scandalized even the fashion world.

In Europe Mischief's lovers were older men who sported Italian suits and Riviera tans. In New York she went for young, leather-jacketed musicians and even younger Latins who hung out on street corners or bars at night. She was insanely jealous of younger models. When Beauty, her only friend, had mysteriously died, Mischief had been blamed.

Even though Mischief Jones didn't sound like a nice person, Bronte had tried to call her. When she'd failed to reach her, she'd gone to her building, but the mere sight of it had induced panic.

Bronte's plight wasn't made easier by the fact that

several male passersby on the street had propositioned her. Even though she had fluffed her hair so that she had as many spiraling red curls as possible to hide her face and was dressed plainly, everywhere she went, men stared at her.

Unused to so much attention, she didn't trust it.

In the hotel, the desk clerk had gasped, "Haven't I seen you before?"

She lowered her beautiful face. "No!"

"But aren't you—"

"Look, my name is Bronte Devlin. I used to teach kindergarten in Wimberley, Texas."

"I could swear…"

She was a freak.

This morning in the café where she had eaten a waffle and syrup, the waiter who had filled her coffee cup ten times had practically drooled with admiration every time he came to her table.

Suddenly, as Bronte was walking along the sidewalk, she felt a hot, prickly sensation race down the back of her neck. Next she heard hurried, yard-long masculine strides close behind her. When she tried walking faster and the purposeful footsteps quickened, she was terrified. Then she saw a cop nearby writing parking tickets and found new courage.

She whirled…and did a double take. Standing behind her in a black Stetson and a crisply starched, long-sleeved, white shirt was a man who looked almost exactly like her favorite movie star.

Garth.

No. This man was a bit broader in the shoulders, bigger boned. His skin was swarthier, his hair darker.

"What do you want from me, mister?" she demanded, shaken.

Bronte tilted her face to get a better look at him, remembering for some reason that Mischief had been attracted to dark Latin men.

As stunned as she, the man stopped. For a second she found herself staring into the fiercest black eyes—no, the most haunted eyes—she'd ever seen. His harsh features were tight with fury and disapproval.

He definitely thought he knew her. But he hated her.

Bronte's fear of him lessened because when he spotted the cop, he scowled at her and then veered quickly away. For a second she watched him race toward the street.

His boots and jeans and Stetson made her wonder if he was from around here. When she kept staring, he ducked his head quickly. Too quickly.

Who was he? The cop had scared him. Strange, since he didn't look like he'd scare easily.

Her confidence restored, she decided to give him a taste of his own medicine. "Hey! You there!"

When he didn't answer, she sidestepped so that she landed directly in front of him again. He had to either stop or run full-tilt into her. "You with the Garth Brown face and the linebacker's shoulders and the big black hat. And the attitude. I asked you a question, cowboy."

The tall cowboy opted for a collision course. When he hit her, his big hands clamped around her shoulders.

"Good morning to you, too, Mischief Jones!" he drawled through gritted teeth, despite his fury sounding pleasantly of Texas and wide-open skies.

His low tone was intimate as well as insolent.

His lips were so close, his warm breath tickled her neck and ear.

Bronte's racing heart jolted when the hostile stranger's hands yanked her closer. She had a vague impression of being slammed against a wall of muscle and bone as her injured knee gave and she swayed on her feet. When he caught her and supported her, his hands and body felt so electric that her skin tingled.

Was he one of Mischief's lovers? Or just a wannabe?

She went still as she considered his long brown body lying over her, his hands roaming…

No. Still, she felt an unwanted tremor as she pushed the embarrassing vision from her mind. Still, her skin tingled and she flushed hotter.

Every sound in the city seemed to die, and the strikingly good-looking stranger became everything.

She didn't want to know this man, nor find him the least bit attractive.

Not now when she was so mixed up.

She saw a man whose eyes were dark and cold. A man who, for his own reasons, had given up on life, as she had. All these things she saw and knew yet didn't see and know at all. And didn't want to know. But she understood him without understanding him. And she studied him with more than the casual interest she would normally give to a stranger.

Somebody had broken his nose. But she marveled at the beauty of his hard, carved face under the wide black brim as it came into focus against a blur of blue sky and green trees.

His hair was Indian black, his skin burned to a permanent bronze. Or maybe his white cotton collar merely made him look so tanned. Still, there was something exotic about him, something foreign. When she met the haunted blackness of his eyes again, a wild tom-tom started in her chest.

She had been numb, dead at the center for so long. Maybe it was only because he looked like a movie star she lusted after, but the powerful wave of emotion she felt scared her so much she wanted to run.

This man both attracted and terrified her. He was not at all like Bryan or the other men she had dated in the past. There was nothing laid-back or casual about him. He was chased by demons. As she was.

The old Bronte would have withdrawn and gone deep inside herself until he let her go.

Sunlight beat down on him, tingeing the edges of his broad Stetson with a halo of gold. He held her in a tight, relentless grip. She didn't like the powerlessness of being held nor the feeling that he could have let her go and she would have stayed there still because he was like a sexual magnet compelling her into his orbit.

She didn't move or utter a sound when he snugged her hips against his. Nor when she felt her breasts, heavy and swollen, mashed into his solid chest.

"I—I'm not Mischief."

"Who are you today then?" he murmured tightly.

Oh, just the daughter of the diva a crazy plastic surgeon worshipped and made your friend, Mischief, look like. One day when he was feeling creative, he made another one. That's me. But you should know more about all this than most people, since you look like somebody famous also. Oh, hey, did Webster Quinn get ahold of you, too?

The stranger's eyes blazed with even more fury

when the cop looked up from his tablet and edged closer.

"I—I know I look a lot like your friend," she whispered. Why was she explaining anything to him? The smart move would be to get away from him.

"Yeah. Just like her." He glared cynically from the cop to her, his hard, glittering eyes clearly skeptical.

"How do we know each other?" she whispered.

His hands tensed. "Don't play games, honey. Okay?"

"Okay. I'm fixing to tell you the truth. *My* name is Bronte Devlin."

"Sure." He towered over her. His shoulders were so broad and thickly muscled she couldn't see anything but him. Not even the cop.

"It really *is* Bronte Devlin," she persisted. "This is going to sound implausible, but…but I had the same plastic surgeon as Mischief—"

"Hey, stop it," he interrupted. "What do you think—that after Paris, I would come after you here and just let you say sorry, stranger, and walk away?"

"Bronte… My name…" Too late, she realized she really shouldn't explain anything.

"Yeah. Right. *Bronte.*"

For an instant she wished she could have taken his arm and led him to a café where she could ask him questions about his real relationship with her lookalike. In the next instant that was the last thing she wanted.

"Just let me go," she whispered.

"Sure…*Bronte,*" he said with biting sarcasm. At the same time he kept a wary eye on the bulky man slapping tickets under windshield wipers. Then the stranger stared back at her, his ruthless face growing colder.

"I'll scream…"

There was a quick glimmer of hot emotion in the stranger's eyes that he couldn't quite conceal. "You'd do it, wouldn't you?"

"What?"

"Get me locked up in a cage again."

She stared at him blankly.

"You're damned good at this new act of yours." He broke the tension between them by barking an order. "So—go!"

She almost didn't hear the low rumble of sound that followed. And probably he didn't mean for her to.

"Run while you still can, honey."

She had felt the threat in his words all the way to her bones.

At the sound of children's laughter, she turned and fled toward a nearby playground. For a terrified second she felt the familiar prickle of heat at the back of her neck and was terrified he might chase her.

But when she turned, she saw he was still standing where she'd left him, with the sunlight gilding his hat and his large hands thrust deeply into the pockets of his jeans. He was watching her as intently and coldly as before. Why was his mere gaze, even long-range, enough to heat her skin?

Was it because he thought he'd slept with her?

No man had touched her for so long. She'd been dead to all that. For no reason, she thought of large brown hands shaping her body. Her skin burned at the thought.

Suddenly she turned and ran faster.

The next time she looked over her shoulder, he was gone.

What the hell was she trying to pull? He needed a drink.

Jack's black eyes blazed with censure and anger.

He didn't feel anything.

Nothing was changed.

Hell, yes, she was different.

He'd felt different, too—from that first second when he'd seen her.

She'd looked ingenuous and charmingly afraid. She was so radiantly beautiful she could have startled a blind man.

How could he think that after the way she'd led the cops to him in Paris? The bastards had thrown him in jail for three damned days.

She was working a number on him, dazzling him the way she dazzled Carla, softening him. Why? It had been years since she'd bothered to try to attract him. And even back then, he hadn't felt anything close to this.

His mind spun back to when they were kids. He remembered his first *corrida*. Theodora had cleverly assigned Mario, who'd worshipped Shanghai, to look after him, but Chantal had seen to it that Jack'd been given a bad rope and Potro, the oldest, clumsiest horse in the *remuda*. Then she'd chosen her moment when they'd been running in deep sand and had spooked his horse. Potro had stumbled right in front of the herd. Jack had been pinned under Potro as several steers rushed him.

He had been terrified. Chantal had laughed. Potro had been lying in the sand and kicking for all he was worth, and one hoof had nicked Jack's nose and broken it before Mario had jumped off his horse and pulled him out of danger. That misadventure had made Jack the joke of the cow camp, after Chantal and Caesar had told and retold that story.

"Damn the witch!" Jack whispered, coming back to the present. She'd never been so stunning. Her frightened, doe-eyed gaze had never been so soft. She was completely different than she'd been in Paris.

Maybe it was the fact he'd been raised by a whore that made him so sexually aware of feminine wiles and so determined not to be seduced. But he'd noticed all of Chantal's new tricks, the way her fingertips had skimmed his flesh so lightly, the way she'd smiled tremulously, the way she'd softened her voice.

Bronte?

What the hell was she up to? She'd recognized him instantly and then pretended not to know him, pretended to be some Bronte person with a plastic surgeon. And all the time she'd reeked of gardenias.

He had to remind himself that he'd found her standing in front of her own apartment building, that he'd seen her doorman wave to her.

Damn. If only she weren't Chantal....

Bronte. The name was soft and feminine and romantic.

In the sunlight her long red hair seemed a dozen gleaming shades as it fell in silky coils down her back. She was so much more than beautiful. She would have been striking in a room full of beautiful women. She exuded sweetness and innocence as well as a smoldering, vitally alive passion. Hell, her jeans were so tight, every man on the street had stopped to stare at her backside and mentally strip her... including him.

No matter how beautiful she was now, she was bad news.

Still, Jack felt shaken from their encounter.

Till he remembered the cop.

Nobody, no matter how pretty or supposedly nice, was going to get him locked up again. He would die before he got himself arrested, handcuffed, searched, fingerprinted and photographed again. Nobody was going to strip him of his clothes and pride and cage him like an animal.

Jack was still shaking as he watched the incandescent creature he believed to be his wife run toward the playground under the trees. He wasn't sure what had scared him more—thinking she was going to set the cops on him again—or holding her.

Chantal had damn sure never felt so good before. All soft skin and molten green eyes. Eyes that had stared into him and shared his pain and other things for a second or two.

Damn her for doing that when he knew what she was. He didn't like the way he'd reacted to her physically, either. Holding her had made his palms sweat and his groin swell with a need he'd thought she could never arouse again.

He'd better not let it happen, or the witch would sense her power over him.

He knew it had to be the plastic surgery and the new skills that came with her career. She'd deliberately reinvented herself. Still, he was stunned that her act was so effective that she could seem like such an entirely different woman.

For the first time ever, her beautiful green eyes had

felt fresh and compassionate, pure and alight with disarming warmth and tantalizing tenderness instead of evil. She'd even drawn his pain out of him for a second or two.

But he knew she wasn't like that. He'd already given her way too many chances.

He couldn't allow himself to forget again how dangerous she was.

Bronte was shocked by her forward behavior with a perfect stranger.

Why did he have to look so much like Garth?

Forget him.

But no matter how much Bronte wanted to forget Mischief's lover, she couldn't seem to put him out of her mind.

Thus, as she stood in the quiet of the sun-dappled playground, seeming to watch children play chase and throw balls and swing and ride seesaws, she saw instead the enigmatic stranger with the dangerous face whose haunted black eyes had burned her. She smelled him still—his clean fresh scent that was all-male and so pleasingly outdoorsy.

He had made her feel bold...and different. And most of all alive.

Suddenly Bronte was glad he was gone. Glad New York was such a big city. Glad he had refused to tell her his name. Glad she would never see him again.

Still, the brilliant sunshine seemed duller without him. The park, which to stressed-out city dwellers might have been a green oasis in the middle of looming steel and glass, felt like a prison to her.

The sky was the same serene blue. The soft greens of the grass still blended with the darker greens of the trees and the gray granite boulders pushing up through the earth. The light breezes still carried the wild, sweet fragrances as well as city smells. Beautiful couples still threw Frisbees. But Bronte felt alone and lost and unable to find joy in the children's creative antics at the playground.

A solitary little boy with copper curls, who looked just as alone and left out as she felt, was digging in a sandpile with a blue shovel. For want of anything better to do, she sat down and watched him build mighty castles and towers.

An hour later, when he got up and began kicking them to bits, she decided to leave.

"Don't go. Stay and watch me dig, miss."

She hadn't thought he'd even noticed her.

"But you're done."

His green eyes widened.

He had Jimmy's eyes.

"I'm starting over, miss."

He had been playing by himself, pretending not to see her. As she met his urgent green eyes, she realized how much her being there had meant to him. She remembered how Jimmy had liked her to watch him.

The little boy smiled shyly.

Jimmy's smile.

He said, "Please stay. I don't like playing alone."

It seemed to her suddenly that she had been alone her entire life, except for those brief years when she'd been Jimmy's mommy. After the little boy's request to stay, nothing could have made her leave, for nothing mattered more than her staying there and watching him.

So fascinated was she by the child that when the back of her neck prickled, she didn't think of the stranger. She merely brushed her hand through her red curls.

"Okay. I like watching you dig," she said.

The boy laughed when she climbed on the rock wall and asked him what he was going to build next.

"Disneyland."

"That'll take awhile."

"I'm fast," he bragged shamelessly. "Better than any of the other kids."

She stayed there until his pretty, blond mother pushed a stroller up and declared it was time to go.

He protested as all boys do, saying he wasn't finished, but his mother took him by the hand and led him away anyway. While Bronte watched them go, he shot her a backward glance. Waving, she felt a longing to have another child and to be a mother again. She wanted to be loved...

No. Quickly, very quickly, she suppressed those thoughts.

To love was to risk.

Never again.

When the boy and his mother vanished and Bronte was alone once more, she felt the warm, prickly feeling at the back of her neck again.

For no reason at all she thought of the handsome stranger with the Indian-dark hair and Garth Brown's carved face.

Terrified, she turned, half expecting, half hoping...

She saw only thick forest and a quiet pond.

Then a breeze blew sand all around the boy's buildings.

Her terror died. But so did that strangely expectant rush of unwanted excitement.

As she headed back to the sidewalk, a tall, rangy,

big-boned man watched her. His smile came and went, and somehow his face was left harder and meaner afterward. His skin was brown and tough and so tightly pulled across his forehead that she could see the shape of his skull. Beneath his collar hung a bright red tie.

When she shivered, the cruel smile came and went again. Then he ducked out of sight. She had the uneasy feeling he had been watching her.

It took her a minute to remember and reassure herself that she was arrestingly beautiful now. That she had the face of two promiscuous goddesses.

As she hurried past where the stranger had stood, she decided that perhaps she had overreacted. She was not used to the kinds of stares and interest her gorgeous new looks or possibly Mischief's reputation aroused.

What if she were disfigured instead of arrestingly beautiful? Suddenly she remembered all the patients she'd met in Webster's clinic in Costa Rica and felt ashamed for feeling sorry for herself. So many of them had been permanently maimed. When she had been a child she had prayed every night to grow up and look like her mother.

Be careful what you wish for.

At least her health had been restored.

At least she was beautiful.

She remembered the way her mother had walked down the streets of New York—head held high, a supremely confident smile lighting her exquisite face. Madame had expected admiration, craved it, demanded it. Trailing along behind her, Bronte had shyly noted the awed stares. Nobody had ever looked at her back then except with kindly tolerance and pity.

And she had dreamed, oh, how she had dreamed of growing up and being lovely and glamorous, too.

Well, now, miraculously, she was.

Bronte felt strangely confident as she hailed a cab and told the cabbie to take her to lower Manhattan and Trinity Church. As her taxi fought its way into the stream of jammed automobiles and buses, she thought that, as always, everybody in the city seemed to be in a frantic rush.

There were so many people, so many cars—all going so many places. Maybe that was why she didn't notice the man who stepped out of the trees and hailed a cab as soon as she got into hers. Nor did she notice when his cab stopped half a block behind her when she got out at Trinity Church.

The vaulted interior of the church seemed medieval. After the rush of the modern city, the solemn quiet inside those cool stone walls soothed her. She hadn't been in a church since Jimmy's funeral. She hadn't been able to pray since that day, either.

Immediately she knew she had been right to come here. She felt different. More open. She was grateful for her life. Maybe this time she wouldn't feel so dead inside when she asked for help.

Wrapped up in her concerns as she was, she never heard a man step inside, or his hushed footsteps behind her.

When she sat down near the front of the church, he took a back pew.

When she laced her slim fingers together and lowered her bright head to try to ask God to help her to accept her new face and teach her to confront the challenges in her life instead of letting them defeat her as they had in the past, the man's cynical eyes turned to shards of black ice.

Chantal at prayer?

Chantal with a look of serenity on her face after she left the church?

The whole afternoon had been damned odd. His response to her had been odder.

From the moment Jack had spotted Chantal lurking outside her own apartment, looking like a lost child who'd forgotten her key, everything she'd done and everything she'd said had surprised him.

Still, when she'd left the church and headed back uptown in another cab, Jack had no choice but to follow her.

Not that he wasn't getting sick of their cat-and-mouse game.

First they'd had their little chat on the sidewalk and she'd pretended not to know him. Then she'd watched the kid with the blue shovel.

Next Chantal had gone to Trinity Church. After that she'd made a dozen calls from public phones. Where the hell was her limo? Last he heard supermodels lived on cellular phones.

What the hell would she pull next? he wondered, as raindrops began to splatter the windshield.

When her yellow cab reached fashionable Park Avenue once again, she jumped out a block or two short of her apartment. For a second she just stood there looking as lost and confused as that frightened child again, staring up at the black sky with those big eyes of hers and letting the rain soak her. Only when a laughing crowd of young people burst out of a fancy club across the street, their umbrellas exploding like brightly colored parachutes, did Chantal seem to decide what to do next.

She took a minute to read the neon sign above the exclusive bar. Then, after cautiously waiting for the light to change when there wasn't a car to be seen for a block, she ran lightly across the street and vanished into the club.

Jack felt a sudden, powerful thirst.

Why a bar?

She never went without sex long. No doubt this was where she picked up the men she took home.

Still, he was baffled.

So much about her seemed different.

Of course, he still wasn't used to her new face.

But she'd changed even more since she'd come back from France.

When he'd held her today, nothing about her except the color of her hair and eyes and her perfume had seemed like the old Chantal.

And what was she doing running around all day without bodyguards? How come she'd pounced on him like that and then acted terrified, all the while pretending not to know him?

He still couldn't get over the way she'd watched that little boy in the park, either. And Jack had never known her to pass out spare change to street people.

Hell, she'd stayed in the church for a damn hour, the whole time looking as pure and sweet as a troubled angel.

Nothing about her behavior today added up. She was like a completely changed person. If he hadn't stripped her naked in Paris and seen the scar, he'd never have believed she was Chantal.

All he knew for sure was that he was damned tired of trying to figure her out.

The bar would be dark and loud.

Before she could hit on a stranger or sic the cops on him, or he gave in to the temptation to drink, he'd grab her.

Chapter 7

Gone was the brave new Bronte who had emerged from Trinity Church. The Bronte who had felt spiritually inspired to accept her new face as a gift. And not to question it.

Panic surged in her as the rain beat down.

For rain always made her remember the day when she had lost everything.

Like a·frightened animal seeking cover, she darted inside the mobbed bar, racing past half-a-dozen round tables of solitary men in an attempt to vanish quickly into the bar's neon-lighted, smoky depths.

She didn't know this was a frequent haunt of Mischief Jones. That sometimes when Mischief was on the prowl she came here to find men. That usually she headed straight for the pool tables.

Bronte didn't feel the dozen pairs of wolfish, male eyes devouring her body as she slipped past them.

She was early, the men thought. *She must be hot for it.*

A new tension wired every single one in the bar when she walked straight past the pool tables, past the men grouped there. Automatically they stood a little straighter; they stuffed wrinkled shirts back into their trousers; they finger-combed their hair. They lit cigarettes or squashed them out.

Not that Bronte felt the electric expectancy of their mood. She was still trying to absorb what Webster had done. She'd been robbed of her own identity and given someone else's. Every time she thought of Mischief, she felt so guilty she was glad she hadn't been able to reach her. The last time Bronte had called, a woman had answered and said Mischief was expecting guests tonight and would be far too busy to see her.

"Tell her Webster Quinn…" Bronte had lost her courage. "Never mind. I'll call back later."

Bronte needed to make that call. Instead, oblivious to her many admirers, she went to the bar and ordered a margarita. When a dark hand shot out and manacled her wrist, she cried out. The face leering into hers was thin and brown. The man's overlong, chopped tufts of black hair hung over his wire-rimmed glasses. When he smiled, his leathery skin made deep creases on either side of his mouth. His teeth were as yellow as old piano keys, and his breath stank of stale beer and cigarettes.

She shrank from him.

"I missed you, baby. We had some good times together, playing pool and other stuff—remember?"

"I don't play pool."

"You ran the table." He slid his stool closer and

slapped a crumpled five-dollar bill on the bar. "This one is on me, Miss Jones. For old times' sake."

She pushed his money away, shaking her head so fiercely that raindrops flew at him from her red hair.

"I never saw you before in my life, and if you don't leave me alone, I'll call the police." She turned away as the bartender set a frozen margarita in front of her.

Other men with heavy-lidded, smoke-stained eyes and teeth to match noted the little exchange with surprise. The woman they knew usually wasn't so choosy.

Bronte was cold and wet. When she started to shiver, a thin-faced man with a wispy goatee decided to try his luck. Shuffling behind her, he grinned boozily as he held out a limp jacket with a trembling hand. The jacket reeked of sweat and bourbon and cigarettes.

"What you looking for, baby?"

She shook her head, hating her new face more than ever. "Go, away. Please."

Suddenly she crossed her arms on the bar and laid her forehead on her wrist. The bartender signaled the bouncer.

She knew she should get out of here.

But she wasn't ready to face the city. Or the rain. Or herself. Or her mother's face.

A few minutes later the band began to play, and the female singer, who wore a long black gown, began to sing a particular song from Bronte's past. The first husky notes from the sultry brunette made Bronte forget her new face and admirers. Her fingers clenched tightly around her empty glass. With green eyes frozen in pain, she slowly lifted her head to stare at the singer.

Out of nowhere came the memory of that hospital aide's remark when she'd been stroking Jimmy's cool, waxen face after they told her he was gone.

All your kid had was a nick in his temporal artery. Why didn't you just apply pressure, lady?

Of all the bars in New York, why had she walked into this one? No other song could have brought back such bittersweet anguish. Bronte used to dance with Bryan and Jimmy to that tune every afternoon. Jimmy had had only to hear it to come running into her arms, demanding to be picked up and whirled about their living room.

He had been so full of life.

Bronte's face drained of color. She tried to swallow, but her throat was too tight. She put her hands over her ears and squeezed her eyes shut, but time ticked backward anyway.

Then a frightening sound—a hoarse sob—rose from deep inside her. She knew she'd lost all control. For the first time since her accident, scalding tears streamed down her cheeks.

Helplessly, Bronte saw Jimmy smiling up at her from the kitchen doorway as he'd picked up his skateboard that fatal afternoon, laughing mischievously when she'd chided him for wearing such ragged jeans and begged him not to go out because even though the sun was shining, the sidewalk might be too slippery.

When the notes of the familiar melody faded between stanzas, Bronte wept even harder as she remembered how she'd found his board lying upside down in the muddy gutter. As she remembered Bryan trying to force his way into the surgery suite hours later to see his little boy after the doctor told him he was gone. Most of all she remembered the way Bryan had tried to comfort her at the funeral as the casket lid was closed. He hadn't understood why she'd pushed him away and refused to let him hold her that day and for weeks afterward. She hadn't understood why grief wasn't harder for him.

Not that Bryan had ever done more than gently criticize. Not that she had hated him for being able to go on. But she had cut herself off from him, and the palpable silence had created an ever-expanding void until every intimacy of their fragile marriage had been devoured by it. Finally, Bryan, who was needy himself, had lost patience and turned to someone who hadn't given up on life as she had.

The lyrics expressed a deep and profound sadness for the lives of men and women who had loved and dreamed and hoped, who had made promises they couldn't keep. For men and women who had loved and lost and could never be whole again. As the singer's voice rose and grew more passionate and pain filled, Bronte's heart swelled with her own private grief. She'd loved her son and missed him more than anything.

Shrieks of male laughter erupted from a nearby table.

Bronte was sobbing, with no thought for where she was or who she was, when the thin man with the black bangs and yellow teeth put a familiar hand on her shoulder.

"Miss Jones, I've got just what you need."

"Please, would you just leave me alone?" she begged.

But when her would-be companion edged drunkenly closer and dug his hand into her waist, she pushed at him. "Please, I'll scream if you don't—"

"You needa shoulder to cry on—"

She couldn't stop sobbing even when she felt the presence of another man behind her.

They were like sharks.

"She's with me," drawled a deep voice.

Bronte stilled as a wave of heat warmed the back of her neck. For no reason at all she conjured Garth Brown's face as she had so many other lonely nights. Her knees went shaky; her stomach knotted. Slowly, as if in a dream, she turned.

Never in all her life had she wanted to be by herself so much as she had a few seconds before. Suddenly, even though she was terrified of the stranger from the park who stood there with his movie-star face, and of those eyes that held the same kind of dark pain she'd known, never had she felt such a fierce need to be with anybody else.

How could she feel such a profound desire to touch or be held—but only by *him?*

No matter how much he looked like a certain screen idol, this man was a stranger.

He had been fierce and terrifying on the sidewalk.

He still was—with his ice-black eyes and harsh face. And yet she sensed that underneath his anger, he was kind.

This man was intense as Bryan had not been.

He was her double's lover.

Through the thick blur of her tears she made out the same broad shoulders and lean hips and crisp black hair. The same white shirt and jeans. The same wonderfully carved features, which were rugged and hard and yet beautiful, too.

His shirtsleeves were rolled up now.

Their eyes met and locked. He frowned as if she confused him, too.

He was clean-cut compared to the other man beside her. Still, she suspected he was by far the more dangerous.

She knew she should run.

Blindly, she tried to rush past him, but he caught her and yanked her into his arms.

"Hey, hey—truce," he offered gently. "Go ahead and cry it out."

"Let me go."

His hands fell to his sides. "Okay."

Again she knew she should run. But she hesitated. Involuntarily she found herself grabbing handfuls of his starchy shirt with shaky fingertips and burying her face against his chest.

The man with the yellow teeth scowled as she sought comfort from the stranger.

Through soft cotton she felt the man's muscles. His skin was warm, his heart steady. He was so tall and so powerfully built that he made her feel small and infinitely feminine.

Swallowing tears that were thick and salty, she lifted her cheek from his shoulder and attempted a fluttery smile. "I feel like a fool. My grandmother used to tell me there wasn't any use crying over things that can't be changed."

"Somebody told me that once," he whispered, pulling her closer so that she could bury her face against his broad chest again and make big, wet, wrinkly splotches on his shirt. "Go ahead and cry. Who knows—maybe your grandmother will be wrong this time.''

His hands stroked her hair as she wept. When she was done, she levered herself away from his lean body.

As soon as she was free of him, she felt his heated gaze. What little light there was came from behind him. His white shirt glowed pink from a neon sign, emphasizing the width of his shoulders; the rest of him was in darkness.

She knew she probably looked awful, that her face must be red and swollen. Even though his carved features were hidden in darkness, she sensed the return of his grim mood.

But his stillness told her that he understood her pain.

''What's the matter?'' he demanded.

''I was thinking about the past. About all that went wrong. I was blaming myself for what happened—as usual.''

''That's damn sure a new one.''

He thought he knew her. But he didn't.

''Maybe for you. Not for me.'' She lapsed into an uneasy silence for a moment. ''I'm sorry. I probably ruined your shirt. What are you doing here, anyway? I didn't think I'd ever see you again.''

''You wish, don't you, baby?''

He ordered a whiskey for himself and another margarita for her. He brought his glass to his lips. Suddenly he slammed his drink back down on the bar and sent it flying away with a violence that startled her. And yet he never took his eyes off her—as if he was more afraid of her than he was of the contents in the glass.

Her margarita was strong. Too strong. Even as she lifted her glass again, she knew it was unwise to drink more.

"Thank you…for holding me a while ago."

"No problem."

"I lost it. You were kind."

His brows arched cynically as he ordered a lime water.

When the band struck the opening bars of another sad song, the flashing strobe light became a glistening ball that splashed the room with a million diamonds. The song was too sad to sit through. And suddenly he seemed less dangerous than a whole lot of other things—like loneliness and her new face and the real Mischief.

"Dance with me," Bronte whispered, desperately draining her drink. When he tossed his lime water down and shoved back from the bar, she laid her hand over his.

The minute her shy fingertips touched his, a shudder passed through them both. His callused hand coiled tightly around hers. "Hey, what is this?" he demanded warily.

"I just want to dance. That's all."

His eyes burned her. "Sure."

He yanked her closer, but not that close. How could the merest brush of her body against his be so electrifying?

He felt it, too.

"You're in a strange mood," he murmured with sudden huskiness. And yet with fury, too.

"I've had a really, really rough day. Then you come along looking like…a movie star."

Once again his grip relaxed, his mood, too. "Just

call me Hollywood.'' His other hand slid around her waist, imprisoning her against his body. She didn't like the way his manner was overtly familiar, but then he thought they'd been lovers. He was in for a surprise. She'd lose him—later.

"Okay," he said hoarsely, angrily. "I'll dance."

He snugged her tight against his thighs and pushed his jean-clad leg between hers. His gaze darkened.

He was holding her too close. Too late she realized that her confusion had made her too vulnerable and too forward.

She grew even more alarmed when he began to sway with her to the hot, pulsating music. Belly-to-belly. Hip-to-hip. Beneath the whirling lights, they undulated to the throbbing tempo like a jungle couple.

Bronte had never danced like this in her life. Not even with Bryan. She knew she should stop.

"Not here," she finally whispered. He laughed harshly and pulled her closer.

"The dance floor is over there," she whispered weakly, pointing to the wooden square of parquet tiles near the door. "Not like this—"

"I'm surprised you give a damn."

Dear God. What was Mischief like? What things did this man believe she was capable of?

The song got sadder and the beat stronger, and her memories made her cling to him despite her fears.

"You know I never was much of a dancer," he murmured as he wrapped her in his arms and led her with heavy, long strides toward the dance floor. "Nobody taught me the finer things down in Mexico."

Mexico?

"I don't know any such thing," she said.

His hand slid up her shoulder to her throat. Then

he lifted her chin, forcing her face closer to his.
"You'd better watch yourself, baby. You used to
know not to push it. This could get dangerous."

He was so right. Too much was happening too fast,
but the two margaritas had gone to her head. So had
the music and the man. She felt alive. Achingly, pul-
satingly alive for the first time in years. Shy with him
and yet bold, too.

Too late she remembered that she was in a very
big city. That nice girls didn't drown their woes by
drinking in bars and then coming on to a virtual
stranger. A stranger who believed himself to be her
lover. This anger-filled man who thought he knew her
could be anybody and could want anything from her.

She felt hot.

He was hotter.

No matter how he might try to act like he wasn't.

She'd known so much pain. Was it so wrong to
dance one dance with a handsome stranger in a public
place?

The drums beat hard and fast, and as she melted
into his body, she felt the electric tension between
them quicken and wind tighter.

"Baby, you're playing with fire."

"Maybe you are, too."

"The difference is I have no choice."

"Neither do I," she said.

"We're crazy, you know that?"

"This city—what it does to people."

He'd lied when he'd said he couldn't dance. He
shimmied with her, dipping her so low her red hair
swept the floor and then easily pulling her up into his
strong, hard arms again. The steady friction of his leg

moving between hers caused the fierce explosive heat inside them both to flame hotter.

The music got faster.

Their bodies slowed.

Feeling the urge to touch him, she skimmed his face in the darkness with her fingertips. As she lightly traced the shape of his jaw, she heard his quick, indrawn breath.

"Don't push it." His voice was tight.

Her pointed nipples burned through her damp blouse and brushed his chest.

"I said stop," he whispered in that same urgent, tight tone. When she just stood there, swaying to the beat, his hands snaked into her wet, tangled hair, bringing her face and her lips within an inch of his.

When she wrapped his neck with her hands, she felt his pulse beating beneath her fingertips.

"You think you know all my weaknesses, and you're willing to use them against me. Since that first day when you called my mother a *puta* and threw that snake at me, you pushed. You knew I got started in the gutter, that I grew up with sex all around me. Sometimes my mother wouldn't even send me out when she had a customer. You knew I wanted to reject that kind of life, that I wanted my woman to mean more than just that. Still, you know I'm too damned primitive and too damned Mexican to ever be the kind of polished gentleman Maverick and his college friends were, the kind your mother wanted for you. You know I can't always cover my feelings with a civilized veneer. You knew that even though I'd lived so rough and wild, what I really wanted in a woman was gentleness and sweetness. So you've decided to tease me tonight and pretend—"

No. She hadn't known any of those things. She didn't know him.

"You probably even know I haven't had a woman since prison. I haven't even had a drink. That I'd get hot if you teased—"

Prison!

The cuffs of his long-sleeved shirt were rolled to his elbows. Too late Bronte saw the crudely tattooed hunting knife on his muscular forearm.

No commercial tattoo, that one. There was a raw, nasty power to it, a stark, unpolished simplicity. His tattoo had definitely been done on the inside.

He was an ex-con. He'd grown up in a whore-house. He thought she was Mischief Jones, a woman who thought nothing of picking men up on street corners and in bars.

He and she existed in totally separate realities.

And yet…they didn't.

"Wait…" Little by little, reality was filtering in as she studied the slightly crooked, dark blue lines of the knife etched into his brown skin.

"You asked for this, baby…"

The strobe lights flashed, momentarily illuminating his hard, dark face and then casting it into shadow. His insolent black eyes burned deeply into her, down to some inner core that was real and true. And yet in that same moment, when Bronte felt her soul bonded to his, she knew how darkly she was hated.

But the knowledge came too late.

He was over the edge.

So was she.

As his mouth loomed closer, she felt dizzily bewildered and yet on fire with need, wanting nothing more than the intimate wetness of his lips on hers.

He could be taking her to heaven or to hell. She wasn't sure which, and she wasn't sure she cared.

She felt alive.

So alive that the furious impact of his hard mouth upon hers staggered them both.

The music ended. Not that they noticed.

The next song was wilder.

Spontaneous combustion consumed them. He stopped dancing and fused himself to her. She felt the dance floor tilt, so she clung to him.

His hard hands tightened around her. Desire made her weak and hot. With a carnal moan, she parted her lips and let his tongue come in.

Swift hot blood pounded through her in a deafening roar, blocking out her awareness of everything except him. Somehow her passion was all mixed-up with his hate. For a timeless moment, neither of them could stop devouring the other's mouth and tongue. His leg was still between hers, pushing tighter, closer. She parted her legs. The flimsy barrier of their jeans might as well have been nonexistent. She felt the heat of his skin pouring into her.

She wanted more. More. More. So much more. Everything from him.

So did he.

His kisses made her tremble as he half lifted and half backed her forcefully into a corner. When he imprisoned her there, her hands moved urgently down his back, over his waist, pulling him closer—if that was possible. Then she threw back her head and let his lips begin a heated journey from her mouth down her throat and then lower down the front of her damp blouse to her berry-tipped nipples protruding against wet cotton.

When she felt the warm gentleness of his mouth sucking at her breasts above the cups of her lacy brassiere, she wrapped his head with her hands and combed her fingers through his thick black hair.

Yes. Yes.

No. No.

Heaven and hell.

Shrouded in darkness as they were, no one could see them.

The tempo of the music got wilder and wilder.

She had forgotten where she was. Who she was. She became the wild, dark creature he imagined her to be. Someone she had never been before.

His tongue flicked roughly, hungrily, lustfully at the tips of her nipples. His kisses were like lightning bolts—sizzling bursts of sensations followed each one.

Her breathing became choppy and loud. Tears of joy and tenderness filled her.

"Say my name," he commanded. "Say Jack."

Jack? Jack who?

Funny how all she could do was obey him.

"Jack…Jack…Jack…"

Everything he did, everything he said was so erotic and suggestive that her emotions and needs were spiraling out of control.

She didn't care who he was. Or where he'd been. Or who he thought she was.

Underneath all his anger, underneath the dark torment of his soul, she sensed someone who was fragile and sweet and dear. Someone who was hard on the outside but gentle and good deep down. Someone who had known the same kind of terror and emptiness and loss that she had known. Someone who needed the same things she needed.

Someone who had been dead and was now, at least for this instant, excitingly alive.

All he'd done was kiss her. But she already wanted him so much.

She wanted him—forever. With his eyes and mouth and hands and body, he spoke to her on some deep, nonverbal and nonphysical level.

When she finally opened her eyes, he was gazing directly into them. For a fraction of a moment she lost her soul in that look.

Then his expression hardened.

"Damn you," he said. "Damn you to hell and back, Chantal."

His words and his glare were more brutal than a slap.

She remembered her new face and his prison tattoo.

And to be terrified of him.

Chapter 8

"Damn you," Jack muttered thickly again as he tore his mouth from her wet, soft flesh.

She was moaning like an animal in heat. Sex alone could never have aroused him so powerfully. But the sad music had opened his shuttered heart and exposed his bruised psyche. Music always made him yearn for love.

She was so sweet he could still taste her. Still, it had been the combination of that song and her tears, as well as the luminous pain lingering in her eyes, that had melted his anger for that insane time. He had seen so much sorrow and uncertainty and regret in those shining eyes. So much regret. All the things he'd felt and known and understood.

He should never have held her or danced with her. But he'd seen how the sad song had affected her. Music had a way of making his feelings bubble to the top, too. Images, buried deep and long forgotten, had seared his mind with startling clarity.

But it wasn't just the music. It was her, too. Incredibly, she had made him feel again.

The swollen ache between his legs was so hot and fierce he could barely stand. But the inexplicable tenderness he felt for this vulnerable-seeming woman he believed to be his wife was way more dangerous than his desire.

Never had he felt half so much for her, but his anger at himself overrode all else now as he fought a losing battle for control.

He was a dead man. Way past any hope of resurrection.

Nothing is changed. Nothing.

"Why did you stop?" she asked, backing away and looking so scared and uncertain he wanted to take her in his arms and reassure her.

He caught the faint fragrance of wild gardenias.

"One of us had to. We're in public—a fact that probably turns you on."

"No. I—I shouldn't have asked you to dance. It's just so much has happened to me. I needed…" Again she spoke in that soft voice he'd never heard her use before, the voice that twisted him into knots. That made him want to protect her. "Why am I telling you this?" Then she wet her lips with her tongue as if to taste what was left of him on her mouth.

As a kid he'd watched whores do that in bleak, dusty streets. He'd watched his mother do worse in that narrow bed beside his.

Chantal's licking her mouth that way sent his male hormones into overdrive. He wanted nothing more than to slam her against the wall and push himself

into her and finish their rotten game. The same way
people did it every day and every night in the barrios.
Like animals.

Slam. Bam. No next time, ma'am.

"Damn it. Don't do that," he said.

"What?" she whispered looking nervous and
scared again.

"The tongue bit…"

Her eyes widened. She stopped instantly, afraid.

That darling face of hers was tearing him in two.
All he wanted was to hold her again, to savor the
sweet, strange feelings she aroused, the first sweetness
and tenderness he'd felt in years. The first he'd ever
felt from her.

She was afraid; he wanted to protect her.

Damn. Reality check. This was Chantal. She'd
slept with everybody. His friends. His enemies. Maverick. His cowboys. And that piece of slime who'd
died in the barn, whose body had been charred to a
crisp. She hadn't discriminated. Jack had stuck with
her because of some idealistic, perverse, bulldog determination to save her or to change her and make
their marriage work.

He'd spent five years in prison because of her.
She'd cost him his soul. She could have come forward. But, no, she'd been too busy jetting to Europe.
Too busy cruising for new lovers. He was through
with her forever.

This whole trick today was a brilliant piece of modeling or acting.

He had to get a grip—fast. Before he really started
believing there was a chance he could get from her
all those things that were even more dangerous than
sex—which was bad enough.

All he had ever wanted was to settle down with a woman he loved, have kids and work the ranch. But Chantal had been bored with all that. She had wanted sex from him, sure. The wilder the better. She had wanted him because she had thought he was low class. She had wanted lots of men. And maybe some part of him had thought he deserved no better than that.

Not that this beautiful girl with the loose, red tendrils falling against her rosily angelic face, this nymph in the damp white blouse and skintight jeans, seemed a thing like the old Chantal.

He knew he shouldn't stare, but he couldn't quit. Once, he would have sold his soul to have her kiss him like this. Instead, on their wedding night she had torn him with her claws and teeth—like an animal.

How the hell could she look like an angel when he knew how she'd lived?

He remembered how her face had been streaked with tears when he'd first come inside the bar. Damn it. He forced himself to remember the George V and how her eyes had glittered with hellfire when she'd smashed that black stone cat into his jaw.

How could she be so different? So different she seemed like someone else?

So different she could drive him crazier than ever before? Crazy with wanting, needing and hating—and all at once? New York City must have the finest acting schools in the whole damn world.

For his sanity's sake, he needed to get away from her.

But not for a second could he trust her out of his sight.

He needed a drink.

He didn't dare take one.

"How come you went to prison?" she asked fearfully in that soft, new voice that pretended to care.

"Oh, that's rich." Roughly he caught her wrists and yanked her toward the door.

"Where are we going?" she whispered, sounding frightened, as he tightened the grip on her hands.

"Home."

Her look of fear softened him.

Still, somehow he managed to make his voice hard and gruff. "Baby, you never used to go this far and say no."

She went as white as if he'd struck her.

"I'm not...who you think."

So sincere she sounded. So scared and uncertain.

A trick, he told himself. But when his hand clenched around her elbow, her low whimper of pain caught at his heart and gentled him.

He released her instantly. "I didn't mean to hurt you," he said, despising himself when his rough voice became velvet.

His obvious concern threw her off balance, too...as it never would have the old Chantal, who would have despised him even more.

"Look, this has all happened too fast. I like you...." She faltered. "I could like you a lot. At least I think I could. But this isn't what you think, and I've got something important to do now. I can't go anywhere with you. Not tonight, anyway. We need to slow this thing down. Maybe we could exchange phone numbers—"

"Phone numbers?" Careful to avoid her injured elbow, he circled her waist again and shoved her toward the door. "Cut the crap, Chantal, Mischief, whoever you say you are."

Still using that soft voice, she protested again. "I said I like you, but if you don't let me go, I'll scream."

"Scream and I'll give you what you gave me in Paris."

"Paris?" she squeaked, dumbfounded.

He kept half pushing, half hauling her through the cavernous bar.

Suddenly, in a milder tone, the kind she might use to calm a large, dangerous animal, she said, "You'd better let me go, or you're going to be in serious trouble. Look, I don't want this to get ugly. But you could end up in jail again."

"You get off on that, don't you?"

When she tried to twist free, he yanked her more tightly against his body. "I've been in trouble since the first time you sank your vicious little claws into me." He opened the door, pushed her out into the rain. He swore softly. "So what were you trying to prove back there by pretending to pray and to act so saintly in that church?"

His question made her whiten. "You were there, too? You've been following me all day?" she gasped, her pale face looking convincingly shocked. "I—I didn't see you."

"What did you think? Did you really think I wouldn't come after you when I knew where you were?"

The tears that glistened in her eyes only made her more beautiful as she began to struggle. When she opened her mouth to scream, Jack pinioned her against his body.

Two men stepped out of the bar.

Before she could react or make even the smallest sound or try to call for help, Jack's mouth crushed down on hers. His arms wrapped around her as he forced her against his long, lean body.

Again the taste of her both inflamed him and stole his wrath.

A cab skidded to a halt in front of the bar, spilling out a man and a woman, who rushed past them, laughing.

Only when the men and the couple had vanished did the pressure of Jack's mouth on hers ease. But by then, Bronte had sighed and raised her hands tentatively around his neck. Her breath was becoming uneven again, and she was gently quivering and going soft against him as she kissed him back.

Oblivious to the rain, he realized he could stop kissing her now.

Only somehow he couldn't.

Not when her fingertips were brushing the soft black hair on his neck, winding the short strands around her fingers. Not when the pain in his heart was dissolved by her tenderness. Not when his anger was gone, and so was her fear. Not when passion and new yearning for all that he had missed in his life consumed him.

He wanted more. Much more. Somehow nothing mattered but keeping his mouth fused to the soft, wet, responsive warmth of her lips.

Despising her, despising himself even more, he gave himself up and surrendered to what was the hottest, sexiest kiss he'd ever tasted. And the sweetest.

When he slid his tongue inside, she kissed him back with a silent desperation that matched his own, her small hands rushing over his back as she molded herself to him tightly.

He felt her fingertips slide from his collar up his neck to brush his damp face softly.

In the past she'd been wild and abandoned.

But never sweet and tender as she was now. She'd never sucked his heart out of him. She even tasted different.

In the past she would have bitten him when he kissed her. Now her gentle hand was gliding through his wet hair, stroking him in this new way she had never used before. Her mouth was warm velvet. She was moaning, and the emotional sound seemed torn from the depths of her soul.

Slowly and very reluctantly, he forced himself to let her go. But even as he eased her away, he found himself staring at her lovely face, his starved senses clamoring for more.

His confused gaze met and locked with hers. Even the way she looked at him was different. Her face was flushed crimson. Her eyes were as green as ever, but they didn't pierce him like cold daggers.

No. They were dark with fear and yet luminous and tender, too. Her cheeks were aflame.

Before today Chantal had never blushed in her whole damned life. Now she wouldn't quit.

He caught his breath. She made him feel young again, like he was a horny kid on the verge of falling in love with the innocent girl of his dreams.

His heart beat wildly as he remembered how delicious her flesh was to touch, how smooth and soft and warm.

What the hell was he doing? He knew any sexual involvement with Chantal was insane.

And this involvement was more than sexual. His needs were hopelessly profound. Longing with unkind intensity for what might have been filled him.

He brushed her hair back, saw the faintest trace of a scar at her hairline and was reminded of the plastic surgery she'd had, of who she really was and what she'd done.

Chantal had changed her face and let him rot in prison for her murder. She'd lived the high life while one dark night a gang of convicts had held him down and stripped him and tried to... Then Brickhouse had come at the last moment, and together, somehow, they'd fought them off.

But just barely. And all the while Chantal had continued her old tricks, but on a grander scale.

He remembered Paris. No matter how sweet she looked or acted tonight, she was the same.

"Damn it," he snarled, his voice harsh in his pain.

Remembering his purpose, he caught her arm, his hold as strong as a python's as he pushed her unresisting body toward the cab. After their kiss, the fight seemed to have gone out of her, too. She even opened the door and fell limply inside, without him having to force her.

He was about to slide in beside her, but she came to life like a dozing cat to sudden danger, slamming the door on his hand. Then, clubbing at the tips of his trapped fingers with her purse, she screamed, "Cabbie! This lunatic is trying to kidnap me!"

Pain knifed from his knuckles up his nerve endings as she squeezed the door harder.

"Let go, Jack," she pleaded. "I don't want to hurt you."

"She's my wife!" Jack yelled at the driver.

"I never saw him before in my life!"

"She's my wife, damn it!"

"I tell you, I don't know him!"

The cabbie, who had probably had more than his share of trouble with loonies, wasn't taking any chances.

He probably thought he could handle a tall, pretty girl.

But a powerfully built man with crazed eyes and hate-contorted features was a different matter.

"Step away from the car, buddy!"

"Hey, don't you dare drive off with my wife—"

"Please let go, Jack—"

The bulky driver stomped down hard on the accelerator and the cab shot forward into the darkness, swinging the door so hard onto Jack's hand that he fell back yelping in pain as tires spewed muddy water all over his jeans and boots.

He cursed violently and then stopped when he saw her beautiful, tear-ravaged face pressed against the back window. She was staring at him with those huge, bewildered eyes—as if she genuinely regretted hurting him.

Dear God. He felt all the pain and loss and longing in her soul as she stared at him.

His heart hammered in deep, aching beats. His palms were sweaty.

Damn her for making him feel so drawn to her all over again.

He tried to tell himself that she had sneaked up on his blind side because she was the only woman he'd held since he got out of prison. But that rationalization didn't play.

"Damn."

She'd outsmarted him again.

He opened and closed his bruised, aching fingers.

There were a few scratches on his knuckles, but no bones seemed to be broken.

At least all she'd hit him with was a purse. She probably could have crushed his hand with the door if she'd wanted to. But she hadn't. She'd begged him not to make her hurt him.

Begged.

In the past, Chantal had relished inflicting pain.

After Paris his jaws had been wired together for a month. He wouldn't soon forget the contorted, maniacal expression on her face right before she'd clipped him with that bookend.

Why was she so nice now?

Hell, he was through trying to figure her out.

He knew what she was and where she lived.

He'd catch her.

And when he did, she'd pay.

Chapter 9

She's my wife.

He had been so passionate and angry when he'd said that. So possessive.

And she…

She'd just met him.

She'd felt dead for years.

How could she feel anything for him?

But she did. Churning emotions.

Bronte was still hot and shaky all over. It was as if after being dead at the center so long, some pent-up life force had exploded inside her the moment she'd met him.

She was afraid of him and yet excited, too. She felt relief to know that she could still feel, that she was alive, and yet regret for all that had gone wrong before.

How was it possible that with a man she didn't

even know, she had felt something so rare, something so tender and fine and true?

It had been a gift.

A gift she wasn't really ready to receive.

Some irrational and wildly romantic part of her truly wished she had met him some other way. In some future time.

All he'd done was kiss her.

No. That wasn't all.

He'd stirred her soul.

He'd tried to kidnap her.

Because he thought she was his wife.

Stop defending him. He was Mischief's problem. Not hers.

Chantal? Mischief? Her mother? How many more...

When Bronte stepped out of the cab under the gold-tasseled canopy of Mischief Jones's apartment building, she was still stunned from his kiss and wrestling with her confused emotions.

Her stomach knotted.

Trembling, she brushed her knuckles across her lips. They felt raw and feverish.

Never ever had she been swept away so recklessly. He hated her. She had to remember that. He'd been rude and hostile. Maybe he looked like her favorite star, but he was dangerous.

No, *he* had a name. Jack.

Jack...

She had to put *Jack* completely out of her mind. Forever.

Right. Forget the unforgettable.

A limousine pulled up in front of her cab. A young blonde in white satin and wristfuls of diamonds got out and then helped an old man, who was probably immensely rich, out of the car, too.

As Bronte rummaged in her purse for cab fare, she knew she wasn't likely to forget Jack anytime soon. His effect on her had been more than anything she'd ever felt for Bryan. Maybe that was only because she was overwrought from all that had happened....

After paying the cabbie, Bronte strolled regally up the plush length of gold-trimmed, red carpet that led to the building's stone stairs. Her slim nose thrust self-consciously in the air, she moved with the hauteur and long-legged grace Webster had taught her.

Three doormen with gold collars and starched dickies rushed to help her up the stairs. A set of iron-grilled doors were thrown open for her.

"Good evening, Miss Jones. We thought you'd already gone up."

She barely acknowledged them. Stepping past them, she paused to clamp her purse shut and get her bearings.

"Some party you're throwing tonight," one of the doormen offered.

She didn't trust herself to speak for fear her voice might betray her. Instead she gave him a little condescending nod, the kind her mother used to give anyone she considered her inferior.

A second set of doors made of heavy glass and edged in polished brass were held open for her. Inside an opulent lobby of pink marble and crystal chandeliers, she felt even more like a fraud as two uniformed men waved her past security and video cameras toward a bank of elevators.

Her heart was racing like a rabbit's as she pushed the Up button and the doors opened.

The elevator was paneled in old mahogany that had been waxed till it glowed. Not that she had time to get used to the luxury. Within seconds she was whisked up ten floors.

When the brass doors opened into Mischief's opulent elevator vestibule, Bronte was hit by waves of throbbing music and high-pitched voices, punctuated by shrill laughter. The air itself seemed to pulse with frenetic energy. She saw the blonde and the old man again.

Mischief's dimly lit apartment, even the vestibule, was packed with the gaudily rich and the fun rich—famous actors and models, agents and photographers, as well as leading fashion editors and designers. Territorial people, fierce, self-absorbed people. Superficial people who loved fashion, who used clothes and interior design as an art form to define themselves and others. Rivals who fought like cats and dogs over every scrap of publicity, over every shoot, over every big-name model, every potential star, every assignment; petty people who pretended to love each other on nights such as this one, while they sought new means to gut each other professionally.

Naturally, nearly every woman was fashionably anorexic and dressed in some fashion absurdity with puffed sleeves or huge ruffles. Sexy nobodies had been invited to admire the rich and the famous. For how can one dazzle if there is no one to be dazzled?

Somebody had opened a vault. Slim wrists and throats and fingers flashed with fiery jewels. Everybody was drinking too much and shouting too loudly, each person wanting to stand out from the crowd.

Thankfully, nobody could hear half of what was being said, since the pulsing rock music drowned all of them out.

Bare-chested waiters with shaved heads and slave collars served sushi and champagne from silver trays.

When a thin man with intense gray-blue eyes and silver-rimmed glasses grabbed her elbow, Bronte had to fight the instinct to run.

As he leaned close and blew her a series of rapid-fire air kisses, the elevator closed behind her like a trap door. "Jeans? Ah, dah-ling, but *you* can wear anything."

Bronte smiled at him.

"You're looking so-o-o wonderful. Fresher, younger. Even better than you looked four years ago on our first shoot. You remember—the beaches? Normandy? You were so perfect. I'll never forget your skin, your neck, your legs…your breasts. And what we did in that cave. You have the most perverted sexual imagination of any woman I have ever met."

His voice was abrupt and yet speedy, but Bronte felt hot with embarrassment when his eyes flashed over her body and then stared pointedly at her breasts.

"You are still so exotic, so mysterious. And tonight you are quite exceptional. Simply sensational. If only I had my camera, I would ask you to strip for me the way you did that day in the cave—"

Bronte gasped.

"George…"

He shouted to the beauty who called to him, blew Bronte another series of air kisses and moved away.

Bronte had no idea who George was. He had made her blush and feel extremely uncomfortable.

A tall, African-American man with bronzed shoulders was staring holes through her. There was a disturbing blend of hostility and familiarity in his smoldering eyes as he set his tray of sushi down right beside her. Afraid he'd grab her or do worse, Bronte found an opening in the crowd and escaped.

When he tried to leap after her, a young woman threw her arms around him and licked his cheek with her long pink tongue. He was forced to stop. Bronte ran from them, knowing she was out of her element.

And always she searched the sea of garishly made-up faces and overdressed figures for a face whose savagely sculpted, cat-like features were identical to her own.

It was early, but the party's wild atmosphere held a dangerous, anything-goes edge. Bronte moved deeper into the starkly glamorous co-op. The apartment's trendy furnishings were in sharp contrast with the elegant French decor of the public rooms downstairs. Here the angular walls were covered in dark red and black silk. Heavy moldings framed high ceilings. The spare furnishings were a macabre blend of classic and modern. Huge paintings done in a style typical of Van Gogh were of tortured countenances and horrifying landscapes.

Candles burned from wall sconces and flickered in every window. Yet despite these bright, wavering flames that cast long dancing shadows, a feeling of soul-deep coldness permeated the rooms. The guests' cruel jokes bit without humor; their brittle laughter sounded cracked and cold. This was a house that exuded money, ambition and fine material things, but held no warmth or love.

In another room Catholic candelabra and antique silver picture frames covered the ebony surface of a miles-long grand piano. Dozens of pictures of Mischief wearing either red or black emblazoned the four walls. Above the fireplace was that last famous photograph of Bronte's mother, Madame, dressed entirely in red for her last performance as Carmen.

Bronte had seen most of these pictures before— only they had been slashed and had lain in curling fragments on the floor of Webster's study. Again she noticed how cold the lifeless eyes were as they followed her from room to room.

There were souvenirs from Mischief's shoots. Huge sabres and knives lay on tables draped in Indonesian fabric. Brass-handled daggers from Morocco filled another room covered by red satin wallpaper. Dead flowers were everywhere—both dried and silk— shimmering in the burnt orange glow of the candles.

When Bronte entered the last room, which had even higher ceilings, taller windows, towering oak bookshelves and a massive desk upon which sat a gilt phone, she barely noticed those details. Instead she caught the heavy scent of gardenias.

Like one caught in a spell, Bronte was suddenly held motionless, unable even to look away from the glare of green eyes.

A shock of recognition passed through Bronte's body. The woman in front of her had a fierce, triangular face. A face too like her own. Too like her mother's. And yet not like either of them at all. For this countenance was darker and crueler, like one of those weird, elongated reflections in a carnival mirror. And far, far scarier.

Against the candles, Mischief's shadow seemed to undulate in the middle of a brilliant kaleidoscope. Her dark brows lifted sharply and her lips curved.

As if caught in a witch's spell, Bronte could not move.

"What took you so long?" Mischief murmured from her stance near the fireplace. Her voice was low and deep and not at all friendly.

She wore a black silk pantsuit with huge cuffs and a wide belt and not a single jewel. She had a long, wonderful body. She was turning a wineglass around and around with her slim fingers, watching the flickering of candlelight in the bloodred liquid. Behind her, tall windows carved glittery, black rectangles out of the Manhattan sky.

Mischief had strange eyes. Eyes that drew one and yet repelled.

Webster had warned Bronte. *She's evil. Dangerous. She'll tear you to pieces.*

Bronte's boldness vanished. She felt tired suddenly, completely drained. Mischief had watched her move out of the elevator like the overconfident, naive little idiot she had been. Her ancient eyes had tracked her uncertain progress through each room with a deadly patience.

"I'm sorry. I don't know why Webster did this." Bronte's words sounded clumsy, ill thought out even to her.

"So, you're Madame's daughter." Mischief's voice was like ice and hideously calm. "She had a wonderful singing talent, but she was a very great actress as well. Do you have that special gift, too?"

"I—I don't know."

"Now is your chance to find out."

"I don't understand."

"I have a very special role in mind for you."

Bronte stared at her.

"My dear, the role you would play is…me."

"I—I just want to be myself."

"It would only be for a little while. I need to go away for a few weeks," Mischief said. "But no one can know I've left the city. Webster will escort you everywhere he normally escorts me. He tells me that you have made wonderful progress walking and that you will be able to keep my modeling assignments."

"I couldn't possibly do any of that. I—I just came by to tell you that I'm leaving New York. That you don't have to worry about me being Webster's pawn in whatever plot he's concocted, that I would never dream of trying to compete with you or hurt you in any way."

"You really don't have an inkling…I mean, about what this is all about." Mischief just stood there silently, like a spider in the center of a web. "Bronte Devlin, I need your help."

"Whatever do you mean?"

"It wasn't Webster's idea to give you your mother's face. It was mine."

Involuntarily, Bronte began backing away from her double. "I—I have to go. Now. I'm meeting someone."

"You're lying. Nobody knows you're here. You have no friends. No family. Webster made sure that you ceased to exist when you got that new face."

A premonition of dread struck Bronte as she turned to run.

But the black waiter with the smoldering eyes and the tattoo was suddenly standing in the door, his huge legs apart, blocking her flight.

"Shut the doors and get out of here, you big ape!" Mischief shrieked at him. And then she whirled on

Bronte. "Not so fast." Mischief's voice was sly as she slid toward her, a second glass of wine in her slim hand.

"I want to go home," Bronte whispered.

"In due time."

"Now!"

"Not till you listen to what I have to say."

Bronte felt some dark emotion that was as fierce and palpable as roaring flames.

"If it weren't for me, you would be a faceless monster. I, not Webster, paid for your operations. Now, I need your help…with a little project of mine. But first, why don't we relax and get to know each other? After all, we do have a great deal in common."

Bronte's heart was clamoring. "But—"

With a fluid gesture Mischief placed a wineglass into Bronte's shaking hand.

"I—I already had a margarita. Two in fact."

"Who's counting? The evening is young." Mischief's green eyes compelled her. "There's nothing faster than friendships made with wine. If you don't drink, I'll find a way to make you stay, anyway. And aren't you curious…to know why I did it?"

As if hypnotized by those cold eyes, Bronte nodded.

"Well, you just drink your wine like a good little girl, and I will tell you everything."

Bronte sipped, but something in the wine tasted so bitter that she gagged.

Almost immediately Mischief's face began to waver, as if she were under water.

"Enjoy," Mischief said maliciously.

"You were going to tell me… Where are you going?"

''Oh, I'll be back. We'll talk again…when you're in a more receptive mood.'' Mischief turned and walked away, her tall, black-clad body vanishing into the throng of revelers.

Bronte's thoughts seemed to fly around her like dark birds, but she couldn't organize them into anything coherent or call after her double. Suddenly the library tilted. The bookshelves leaned toward Bronte like the heavy limbs of trees. The candles seemed to be burning at a forty-five-degree angle.

When Bronte staggered, she barely made her way to the sofa before she fell. When she tried to get up, her brain would not tell the rest of her body what to do. Her legs and knees felt like they were made of spaghetti. Somehow she managed to reach across the desk and pick up the golden phone.

The desktop wavered. She leaned against the bookcase, and two biographies of her mother's life tumbled messily onto the desk.

One of them fell open to a picture of her mother's face. No. *Her* face. *Mischief*'s face.

No. No. With sluggish, clumsy fingers Bronte dialed the first phone number her dulled brain could remember—Webster's office.

''I'm sorry but this number has been disconnected.''

Dear God.

She slammed down the phone and dialed his house. No one answered.

Bronte felt sicker. She had begun to perspire so heavily her hair was plastered against her neck and face.

She put her hand to her damp forehead and would have wept, but she lacked the strength.

The receiver slipped through her fingers. The bookshelves began to spin. She fell to the floor and then
crawled back onto the sofa, dragging herself up with
her elbows as if there were no bones in her legs.
When she pulled herself into a sitting position, she
stared mindlessly down at her feet.

Around and around, her black leather pumps
whirled against the gleaming cherry floor and throw
rug. Her head fell back. The throbbing music died to
a whisper and then vanished altogether in a void of
utter blackness and silence.

She shivered, her body filled with an enormous las-
situde. She tried to keep her eyes open, but they were
like leaden weights, and the instant they closed, she
slid deeper into the whirling blackness, but so slowly
she had time to wonder with a sinking feeling of horror what Mischief had in mind for her.

A long time later Bronte was awakened by
screams. Webster was there, smiling grimly down at
her, a syringe in his hand. "It's all right," he said.
"I'm here."

But it wasn't all right.

She could see the fear in his eyes. And the fierce
determination in those of Mischief, who stood behind
him.

Bronte lost consciousness again. When she opened
her eyes once more, she had the vague feeling that
something awful had happened in the apartment.

Even though her mind was hazy with exhaustion,
she knew that Webster had been part of her nightmares. For no reason at all she remembered the huge
black waiter with the golden face. Groggily she remembered Webster's voice tangled with Mischief's

in a shouting match. Webster had wanted Mischief to release Bronte and abandon what he called her mad plan.

Then, suddenly, another dark figure had been there. Mischief had screamed. Bronte remembered Webster raising his hand to ward off a blow. No... He had leaned toward her with a syringe. She'd had a glimpse of a man's huge, bony hands. There had been a terrible fight, more screams. Webster had run.

Bronte was too confused to remember anything clearly.

Strangely, she kept seeing Mischief's white face, her neck twisted at an odd angle as she lay beside the library couch, her dead eyes staring wide-open at the spidery cracks in the ceiling with a look of horrible surprise, her long red hair flowing in a pool of dark purple liquid. Her face had been smooth, no lines marring its classical beauty, no expression of evil staining her loveliness, either. She had been wearing a black evening gown.

But when Bronte managed to sit up, she found that it was she who was sprawled awkwardly on the floor beside the couch. Her own clothes were gone, and it was she who was wearing a black evening gown with spaghetti straps. A wineglass had been knocked over, and there was a dark purple stain on the oak floor.

Bronte's skull throbbed as she clawed her way up the sofa. When she shook her head, her ears roared and her temples pounded, while bright stars whirred before her eyes.

She caught a shivering breath as she scanned the library for signs of violence and found none.

Where had everybody gone?

Was Mischief really dead?

Suddenly Bronte knew she had to get out of here before Mischief, if she was alive, or Webster returned. But when she lifted the telephone, there was no dial tone.

Most of the candles had burned out, and the vast, silent rooms were dark save for a tiny guttering flame in a candlestick or two.

Her heart beat wildly, in sharp contrast to her sluggish, heavy muscles. Her legs felt so numb and disconnected she could barely walk toward the library door.

When she finally opened it, she lurched into the next room like a sleepwalker and then into the next. Heading toward the elevators, she leaned on couches and tables and chairs, using them to keep her balance and to guide her.

But when she reached the massive oak doors to the vestibule, they were locked. Just as she was about to push against them, someone began to pound from the other side.

Terrified, she stretched onto her tiptoes and peered through the peephole and was riveted by a man's angry, golden face. She'd seen those fabulously sculpted, African-American features somewhere.

He was that waiter who had blocked her escape.

What did he want?

Like a child, she backed robotically away from the door.

She would lose, no matter what.

The waiter kept pounding, but the blows were muffled now.

A pulse in her temple beat a soundless rhythm as she sank to the wooden floor. Her sense of impending danger grew acute. She had to get out before he got in.

Fear propelled her. Using the same chairs and couches to guide her again, she stumbled back across the living room and out onto a balcony.

From the narrow ledge, she looked down and then rocked back dizzily. It was drizzling, but she was so glad to be out of the oppressive apartment that she welcomed the cool drops and lifted her pale face to the fresh, damp air. Uncaring that she was soon soaked, she continued to stand there, as if wanting to wash away some evil experience.

Her body weaved from the drug. Gripping the railing, she stared down to the faraway sidewalk, street and parked cars.

Two windows away on the same level as she, a metal fire escape gleamed wetly. She stared at it a long time, letting the rain soak her, until gradually she felt more alert.

But just when she decided she was strong enough to walk again, the lights went off in the apartment. She heard the creak of old wood flooring straining under pressure.

The pounding had ceased.

Was that waiter inside?

The single remaining candle was blown out.

The vestibule door must have been opened because cooler air raced against her damp skin. When the curtain billowed out onto the balcony and wrapped around her body, she screamed.

There was a crashing sound as a table fell over. A lamp smashed to the floor.

"Damn. Where are—" Suddenly a big-boned arm snaked out of the darkness and fastened around her

waist like a steel band, dragging her back inside. A
gloved hand cupped her under the armpit.

A circle of white light flashed on and off, blinding
her.

"Mischief Jones!"

"No, I'm not her."

The barrel of a gun dug into her scalp.

"Scream, and I'll blow your brains all over the
wall!" Another gloved hand closed around her windpipe.

Her assailant would kill her no matter what. He just
preferred silence. Well, she wouldn't give it to him.

In terror and fury she lashed out at him with her
feet and arms, clawing, scratching and kicking.

But the long, bony fingers around her throat tightened and dragged her down. Their bodies became en-
tangled. Twisting together, they crashed onto the
wooden floor. He ripped something from his neck and
wrapped it around her throat.

She fought, determined that her life would not end
like this.

But his gloved hands were a vise, winding the red
coil of silk tighter around her slim throat.

Tighter.

"No! No! No..."

Bronte didn't want to die. Not before—

She tried to scream, but the strong hands increased
their pressure.

He was pulling her down, down. Then she was
drowning, sinking into a deep pool of endless darkness.

III

Chapter 10

Jack pulled a white windbreaker over his head.

When his black head popped through the neck hole, his face was shadowed and tense. He thought of Carla, who wanted to be a spy.

He'd never make it as a P.I.

For one thing, a stakeout or surveillance or whatever the hell you called it was a hell of a bore.

Damned uncomfortable, too, in the rain.

Jack's stomach growled. He was starved, but he couldn't leave. His jeans were wet, so his legs were cramping. But he couldn't sit down. The best he could do was lean further into his doorway.

He needed to take a leak, too.

But worst of all, he was thirsty.

Because of the emotional havoc Chantal had wrought, he wanted nothing more than to drown himself in drunken oblivion. For three months he'd fought the urge, staved it off.

Damn Chantal for being so nice today. For pushing him closer to some dangerous edge.

In the past she'd always thrown his low-class background in his face; never for a second did she let him forget that he came from dirt.

Theodora had tried to tell him that he was as good as anybody. But that first week after she had brought him home, when he'd clumsily nicked an antique highboy with a spur, Chantal had snickered and reminded everybody that he was used to old milk crates for furniture. When he'd tracked mud all over an Aubusson carpet, Chantal had found his muddy boots and carried them downstairs and told everyone that he should be made to live in the barn, that he was used to dirt floors and mud like pigs were.

Because of her, he'd damn near killed himself to prove himself to Theodora. But deep down, he'd believed Chantal.

Still, he had always made *A*'s in school, even if it had meant staying up nights to study subjects he hated. He had pored over books about ranch management, too. He remembered Chantal taunting him that it was his Mexican blood that made him so stupid he had to study so hard. She'd laughed at his accent, so he'd spent years practicing with tape recorders to get rid of it.

"If you were me, you would just know stuff," she'd said imperiously. "You're crazy to care about feeding the poor. What real good will that do? They'll just breed, and then there will be more to be miserable."

He'd been cynical enough to see her point, and yet the problem was too real for him simply to ignore it the way she could. He was in awe of her, though——

because she had been born higher than he. Because she took as her due all the things he had struggled to acquire.

His fatal mistake had been marrying her.

She'd driven him to drink. Funny how it only took a beer or two to make him feel almost as good as she. But the feeling always wore off.

Jack knew she was probably planning to shred him. She was just making sure to sink enough tantalizing hooks in his heart that she could tear out. He knew it, and still tonight her soft-hearted gazes and passionate kisses had stripped his soul bare.

The sky was a nondescript gray-black, streaked with wispy clouds. The damp air was so still he could hear his own ragged breathing.

Where the hell was Chantal, anyway? His neck had a crick from craning his head back at such a sharp angle for so long. And if that wasn't bad enough, the mist and rain made it damned hard to tell what was going on up there.

But something sure was.

Shortly after Chantal had gone upstairs, her party had broken up. Which was damned odd, since the doormen had told him it had just started and her parties usually lasted all night.

Jack had stood in a cramped, dark doorway across the street and watched suspicious-looking shadows of a man and a woman loom against the windows. Then the place had gone dark and quiet. But he hadn't seen Chantal or the man come out.

Jack was about to go mad with curiosity. Suddenly the drapes billowed out of one of the windows, and a fragile-looking woman in a black evening gown staggered out onto the balcony. She would have fallen if she hadn't grabbed the railing.

Chantal.

Jack stepped forward, into the rain. Chantal stood there weaving back and forth like a reed in the wind, letting herself get as thoroughly soaked as he was. She looked so lost and desperate, again so unlike the arrogant, hateful woman he knew. Jack felt an odd, unfamiliar ache in his heart. Sensing she was in some sort of danger, he was already loping across the street when he heard her cry out.

The guttural sound was low throated, terrified. A scream was formed, then swallowed.

A man was on the balcony with her.

The bastard got her by the throat. His hand closed over her mouth. She fought him as he dragged her inside.

All Jack knew as he raced across the street was that if he didn't get up there fast, she would die.

He'd never been more scared.

Not even in prison when they'd held him down. When they'd ripped his uniform off and tried to force him to play the part of a girl. When he'd known that if they had, they would have damned him forever to hell.

The red silk was a vise squeezing her larynx.

Bronte's eyes bulged. Her splayed hands clawed.

Her assailant fell heavily on top of her, the silk tie an ever-tightening band, cutting into her slim throat and windpipe until she stilled.

Dimly, ever so dimly, Bronte felt the band loosen. Too soon. Her attacker stood up and began methodically wrapping the tie around his big-boned fist. Then he inserted the roll into his pocket, as if he considered his business with her finished.

He moved, and a silver light from the window touched his hard features. For an instant she saw brown skin stretched tight over a huge skull. He had a prominent brow, a cruel mouth. Then his face dissolved into the darkness.

Whole but disoriented, she was dizzily aware of his quick movements about the room as he doused furniture and drapes with some sort of fluid.

She caught the reeking scent of gasoline.

A match flamed.

Above its golden flare she saw a deep wrinkle in his brow. His quick smile came and went, leaving his face crueler than before.

He relished his plan to burn her alive.

Bronte heard clanging footsteps on the metal fire escape outside. The sound of breaking glass elated her. A man shouted to her.

Boots crunched over glass. In the library a table was slammed into a wall. Books fell and were kicked aside.

"Damn."

The match was shaken out, the vestibule doors thrown open.

As her assailant rushed out, a man burst into the living room.

"Mischief..."

Bronte's eyes opened. Her gaze clung to his.

"Chantal..."

Through mists of pain and terror Bronte felt a large, warm hand close gently around hers. Next she felt him kneel beside her and lift her wrist. Then the hand was softly touching her face, tracing the line of her cheek, wet with her tears, and finally examining her bruised throat.

Jack seemed huge. His rain-wet hair stood wildly out from his head. She saw the knife tattoo on his arm.

He was savage. But beautiful.

When his finger grazed her windpipe gently, she moaned.

''That damned son of a bitch—''

She whimpered; his voice softened instantly. ''Honey, try to put your arms around my neck.''

Bronte tried to, but she was too weak. She barely lifted her arms before they fell limply.

''Never mind,'' he whispered as he slipped an arm under her shoulders and another under her knees.

She lost consciousness when he picked her up and carried her into the elevator. As they descended, he held her against his massive chest. She regained consciousness for a moment, and it was as if she were falling...falling in an endless, black sky.

Then the elevator stopped, and she was aware of blazing chandeliers, of him carrying her across the opulent lobby, past a dozen curious doormen, fielding their disruptive, shocked questions while he demanded that they clear a path and open doors, that they hail a taxi.

Motion.

He was carrying her hurriedly down wet stone steps.

Out into a wild dark night that was misty with rain.

Then she was in a cab, snug and warm, and he was beside her, holding her head in his lap, stroking her tangled hair.

For an instant she held his arm still and traced the vivid, blue lines of his tattoo.

When she raised her eyes, his black gaze locked with hers.

"I'm sorry you went to prison. I would never hurt you."

He went still, as if the word *prison* alone could resurrect the most terrible ghosts.

She knew all about ghosts.

In a flash of white she saw Jimmy's face, her mother's, Bryan's, too.

The back seat of the cab seemed suddenly too impersonal. Bronte's heart thudded painfully. A compulsion to touch him seized her, a compulsion to smooth the lines from between his brows, to caress the unruly hair that fell over his forehead. To make him know by touch alone that she understood the darkness that lay inside him. But she was too weak to lift a fingertip.

Turning away from her, he stared moodily out the window. And she felt cut off from him again by the terrible hatred he bore for his wife.

As they sped away in the darkness, she began to drift again, but the currents were gentler now, because Jack was there.

The killer heard the Mercedes engine ping to life. He watched the good doctor back carefully out of his space.

He was glad of the early morning hour. The traffic would be lighter. He wasn't used to big cities.

He was glad it was still raining.

Good night for a bad accident.

After the killer eased his rental car out of the park-

ing garage, sirens sounded from the end of the street.
A dozen police cars flew up to the co-op's entrance
and squealed to a stop, their doors opening, slamming.

Rage—dizzying buzzes like sizzling currents—
charged through his brain, fracturing him. He took a
deep breath and concentrated while his windshield
wipers slapped back and forth.

Easy does it, cowboy.

He sped out into the misting night.

When none of the cops pursued him, he shot a
tense, lightning-fast smile toward his *date,* whose
long red hair fanned out over her seat. He remembered how she'd laughed at him when she'd told him
she'd found a new stud.

The killer chuckled.

"Bitch. Look who's propped up like a big dummy.
Look whose slim neck is as twisted as some dumb
chicken that got its neck wrung."

Chantal stared back, her icy eyes as big as green
saucers and frozen in that queer, unblinking stare.

"You ain't nothin' but a big broken doll now."

He smiled when he remembered how she'd kicked
and fought him. He wished he could've done it to her
one last time. Her fear had turned him on.

There were two of them.

Maybe he could have some fun with the other one.

The Mercedes swerved sharply to the right, speeding onto an exit ramp that led out of Manhattan.

Skidding on the rain-slick street, the rental car
veered across the same two lanes.

Webster Quinn was a boring target.

Men were no fun.

The smell and taste of a woman's fear gave the killer an erection.

When their hearts pumped wildly, his did, too.

When they died in his arms, his penis pumped as well.

Webster's stomach clenched when he saw the headlights behind him slew across two lanes and take the same exit ramp.

He was being followed.

Was it the same person who had broken into his car and stolen the before-and-after pictures?

While he'd been in Mischief's co-op and nearly gotten himself killed by Mischief's murderer, somebody had smashed his window and stolen Mischief's and Bronte's surgical pictures off the passenger seat of his Mercedes. He'd looked everywhere, but both manila envelopes were gone.

Mischief had asked him to bring them to her. She'd slapped him and screamed for him to go back down and get them when he'd arrived and told her he'd left them in his car.

Now somebody else had them.

Who?

That little mystery was the least of his problems.

A world-famous model had been murdered.

As her jealous lover, Webster could be a suspect.

Twenty party guests would be able to place him at the scene before she died.

He had to get out of the country—fast. With any luck, he'd be at his villa in Costa Rica by tomorrow, enjoying his tropical garden and waterfall in the mountains outside San José.

The traffic was heavy as Webster maneuvered the

Mercedes from lane to lane, speeding northward and finally along the tree-lined Merritt Parkway as fast as he could. But every time he checked his rearview mirror and saw the steady glare of those headlights, his heart thrummed faster.

Was the same horrifying bastard with the hideous smile, the one who'd strangled Mischief, on his tail?

Webster had tried to pull him off her, but the thug had punched him so hard that he'd been thrown halfway across the room. When he'd regained consciousness and staggered to his feet, the man had been pulling himself off Mischief's limp body.

When the guy had seen him get up, he'd lunged toward him with a maniacal smile.

Fortunately Bronte had cried out, and Webster had run.

Remorse struck him.

Why the hell had he played God? Why had he made her? At least he'd tried to warn her about Mischief.

He had no excuse. Mischief was a devil. She'd ordered him to do it.

His exit to Connecticut was next.

He was almost home.

There were no headlights in his rearview mirror now.

Just as he told himself he'd been paranoid, the little sedan was on his left, ramming him. Webster's steering wheel spun crazily. Fishtailing wildly, Webster pumped his brakes. The heavy car's tires squealed as the Mercedes whirled head-on into a van.

White streaks of paint that divided the lanes were rolling over and over, but the car landed upright. For a second he thought he was all right. Then the red car behind him rear-ended him.

Geysers of water and mist spuming around them, three vehicles skidded like out-of-control dancers onto the grassy median.

Back and forth Webster's windshield wipers swiped. Then the Mercedes hurtled into a pine tree. Webster was pitched forward. His forehead banged the steering wheel.

After that, all was still.

Webster was too numb to feel anything.

Then there was a muffled knock against his fogging window. A big-boned fist holding a jack crashed through the glass.

Briefly, in the white glare of headlights, a cruel smile lit the man's expressionless face.

Why was Mischief's murderer waving goodbye?

The face vanished. Webster heard breaking glass and an explosion like a bomb.

Flames filled the universe.

Clusters of people hung back in their cars, their worried faces brightening and darkening.

Webster tried to scream, but he couldn't make a sound.

They were shouting to him, but he couldn't hear them, either.

He was all alone, dying, already disconnected from them.

As he closed his eyes, the world seemed to dissolve a piece at a time until everything was still and blue and peaceful and painless.

Without breaking stride, the killer sauntered jauntily up to an old Volkswagen. The driver's baseball cap was turned backward. His jaw was slack as he gawked at the over-turned van and burning Mercedes.

The killer jerked the dented passenger door open. He was inside before the kid even knew he was there.

A gun was shoved under the baseball bill.

"Hit it, kid. Take off…slow. Real slow."

The killer turned around and watched the fire and wondered how long it would burn like that in the rain. He wished he could stay and see what was left of the bodies.

She wouldn't be much to look at now.

He should have felt happy.

But he hadn't been able to get the envelope with both women's medical records out of the car.

It wasn't over.

Jack had the other one.

Not for long.

No matter who she was, Chantal or her twin, she had to die.

Then the kid began to babble through choked sobs. "Just let me go, mister. Take my car. I don't want to die."

Tears streamed down his young, freckled face.

Fear.

The killer felt good.

"Shut up and drive, you blubbering sissy."

"You'll kill me."

The killer smiled. "Maybe." He twirled his gun with careless ease. "Maybe not."

Killing was an art.

He'd decide when it was time.

Jack cursed out loud as he stepped inside the bedroom of a charming, colonial, roadside inn with the sleeping woman in his arms.

He didn't want to stop. Not with the adrenaline pumping through him, wiring him. Not after he'd seen all those damned cops at the co-op. Not when his mood was to get as far from New York and whatever trouble was back there as soon as possible.

He had sensed a cold, deadly presence in Mischief's apartment. The fierce, sixth-sense premonition of danger had stayed with him. It was a gut-level instinct, something he couldn't put into words. Just a tightening inside him. But it was this instinct that had kept him alive in the barrio and alive for five years in prison.

This wasn't over.

That danger aside, he didn't want to spend the night with Chantal. He didn't want to share a strange bedroom with her. Nor a strange bed.

Not with her injured and higher than a kite.

Not with his own heart laid bare by her soft helplessness; not when he was so susceptible to her new tricks.

He'd wanted to drive south for at least another hundred miles. But Chantal had lain in the front seat of his pickup, shivering in her wet evening gown no matter how high he turned up the heater.

Sweat had poured off him, and not just because of the heat blasting out of the vents. Every time she dozed off, she'd awakened whimpering. He'd never seen such stark terror. The pupils of her eyes had been so dramatically dilated that they'd been all black with only rings of emerald encircling them. Her lips and skin were so bloodless she seemed only barely alive. Her fragility and terror scared the hell out of him.

Repeatedly he'd tried to reassure her. "Chantal, you're with me. You're safe now."

But were they?

"Chantal?" She had stared at him in dazed confusion, mispronouncing her name as if she'd never heard it before.

The things she said, the questions she asked made no sense. She was delirious. Finally he'd decided that he had no choice but to stop.

He'd bought burgers at a fast-food place, using the drive-in window so he could hold her head in his lap and stroke his hand through her hair. At the next corner he'd spotted a convenience store. He'd thought about buying beer, but he'd only jammed down the accelerator harder. Half a mile down the highway he'd found the inn. Weakening at the thought of spending the night alone with her, he'd made a U-turn and sped back to the convenience store, ripped the first case of beer he'd seen off a shelf and bought it.

He'd torn the carton open and pulled out a bottle, wanting to twist the cap off so bad he'd hurt. Then she'd moaned from the front seat and he'd driven back to the inn without touching the bottle.

Now he was in the tiny, dark bedroom, and she was shivering in his arms. She felt even softer and smaller and more helpless. Dear God...

Quickly he hurried across the room and laid her on the plump mattress of the high four-poster bed. She shuddered as her head fell back against the pillow.

He ripped the sheets back and tucked her into the bedding. But she continued to shake so violently he decided he had to get her out of her wet clothes.

Why had he let Theodora talk him into this?

''Undress!'' His whisper was brusque and hoarse. ''You're going to freeze to death if you don't. This is your own damned fault, you know—for standing out in the rain on the balcony.''

She pushed weakly at a spaghetti strap. Then her hand fell to the pillow.

Her eyes were green pools of terror. ''Can't. Oh, Jack...'' Her voice slurred.

A surge of guilt swamped him. ''Chantal...'' His voice was grave, kinder. ''Dear God, girl, take off your dress.''

''Can't, Jack...''

His mouth tightened as he studied the supple curve of her smooth shoulder. Stripping her in Paris had been easy compared to this.

While he fought his demons, she stared wildly, mutely, pleading.

Maybe if he didn't look at her. Without bothering to turn on the lights, he rolled her over and unzipped her gown. But the second his rough palms rasped against the damp skin of her spine, he began to shake. His hands skimmed the straps from her shoulders. The silk clung to her buttocks as he pulled it downward along her curves.

She mumbled unintelligible sounds as he peeled the dress all the way off, discovering she wore no panties. No bra. Nothing underneath.

He shut his eyes, but his fingertips read her like a blind man's. She had creamy breasts, an hourglass waist, shapely hips and slim, long legs. She was too thin. Still, he felt thrills of warm sensation from her satin-soft body.

He was dizzy by the time he draped her dress over a chair. She curled herself into a tight ball and snuggled under the blankets. Determined to drink till he drowned out the memory of her, he strode outside and brought in the case of beer.

He set the case on the table and stared at it moodily. Finally, instead of a beer, he grabbed a cold hamburger from the sack, devouring the grease-soaked bun and then the limp fries almost angrily. He wadded up the empty burger sack. Leaning back in his chair, he read every word on the carton of beer while she continued to moan and shiver beneath her covers.

"Shut up, Chantal."

More kitten-soft moans.

He grabbed the phone. The manager yawned and said the heat couldn't be turned on this time of year and that no firewood was available for the fireplace, either.

Chantal kept shivering.

Jack's gaze splashed across the hype on the beer carton. He licked his lips, but he'd been down that particular road to hell. Too many times.

Maybe he should fill the bathtub with hot water and place her in it, but the thought of carrying her naked body anywhere made him break into a cold sweat.

And the last thing he wanted to do was get in bed with her or hold her. When her teeth clicked together louder than ever, he got up and grabbed the case of beer. In a rage at himself, at her, he cracked open the door and flung the case outside.

Glass exploded against concrete. Unnerved, he slammed the door.

He sat down quickly and bundled her shivering body into his arms, all the time wondering if every single bottle had broken.

Then she moaned. When her soft gaze roamed his

face, he felt an unbearable rush of heat. She seemed so helpless and innocent that he forgot the beer. He swallowed, his heart threatening to burst.

Stripping off his own wet jeans, he slid under the covers and eased her into his arms, hoping his body heat would warm her quickly so he could soon escape.

At first all the warmth in his body, as he held her shivering in his arms, felt inadequate to help her. The hardness of his chest gave her no softness upon which to lay her head. His muscled arms made an awkward cradle. Not that she seemed to mind. She nestled against him, burrowing her silken head into the hollow of his throat. Snuggling against his chest, seeking warmth more than softness, she was instantly asleep.

No more moans. Only contented little sighs rose from her injured throat now.

His skin burned beneath the soft swell of her breasts. He felt even warmer where her hips joined his.

Naked male flesh against fragrant woman flesh. Sober as he was, the sensations were too vivid—the floral-shampoo scent of her hair too sweet, the petal-soft texture of her skin too tempting. Nipples taut as berries were glued against his chest.

He wished he was drunk now. Maybe then lying with her wouldn't saturate him with such pleasure.

Did he really have to go through with this? Take her home? Didn't he have enough battles to fight already?

Then he remembered the haunted look in Carla's eyes when he'd tried to help her with decimals three nights ago. ''My mother knows math. She'd come home if—''

He'd tried to stay calm. "Look, Carla, I know it's tough for you, not having a mom. Believe me, I know what that's like. But your mother and me…" What was the use of even trying to explain?

"Why do you drink?" she'd asked.

"I quit."

"You always start back. You used to get mean."

"I'm sorry. God, Carla, I'm so sorry."

She had thrown her arms around him.

He thought of the smashed bottles outside.

He was a drunk and a bad father.

Not anymore.

One day at a time. That was his mantra. Sometimes, like now, it got down to a minute at a time.

When Jack remembered what Carla had seen in the barn that night, he couldn't blame her for what she thought. But she didn't know what had gone down that night.

Somehow he had to bring Chantal home and keep her there until Carla and Theodora accepted him and saw once and forever how completely unfit she was as a mother or daughter or as his wife.

So he lay as stiffly as a post while Chantal slept, careful to keep his body rigid, careful to keep his hands to himself. But when she nestled deeper into the covers and her bottom rested against his thigh, he burned even hotter.

Motionless, soundless, sacrificial, he drew a tortured breath and then exhaled with a shuddering sigh.

He couldn't stand this.

He wanted to brush his lips against her hair, to kiss the velvet skin of her throat.

How was it possible to want a woman he hated?

Then she sobbed his name hoarsely, and he felt like he was flying to pieces.

The pillow crooked his neck at a bad angle. But she was so soft and warm curled against him. So he lay there as wide awake as a cat charmed by a bird. His mind hated her, but his body wanted her.

It seemed an eon before she finally stopped shivering.

He shot out of bed and stalked away. For a long time he stood in the door and let the night breeze cool and caress him. When he finally got a grip and began cleaning up the broken glass and pitching shards into a nearby garbage can, he discovered one unbroken bottle.

His seized the slim brown neck.

It was still cold.

Then Chantal cried out his name. He shut his eyes and flung the bottle at a nearby tree, hating the splintering sounds of glass breaking.

She was moaning when he stepped inside. He made sure she was okay and then went to the bathroom and shut the door. He sagged against it for a long time.

Then he stripped and took a long, icy shower.

His skin was blue, but he was cold sober when he stalked into the bedroom and got into his own bed. Next he called Theodora and told her he had Chantal. She was thrilled. She asked where they were. He asked about the ranch. She told him there was a problem with the sperm count of the new bulls. He told her to call the vet. Then he hung up.

He couldn't figure out the bull problem. He had had them tested at the cattle auction when he'd bought them. How could all eight be sterile?

He was too wired up to sleep, so he punched buttons on the television remote-control device and began to channel surf, determined not to worry about the bulls or Chantal.

But she moaned, her cries cutting him like a blade.

He swore softly and made the television louder.

He was all too human. He had needs, regrets. Not that he intended to reveal them.

Bronte was running through high-ceilinged dark rooms. Women imprisoned in square golden frames with golden bars across their faces were staring down at her with the trapped looks of exotic animals in cages, yet they did not try to save her from the tall, redheaded woman with the cat-shaped face and savage green eyes who chased her.

Then she saw that the women staring at her all had the same faces. And the same eyes as her pursuer.

Their faces were exactly like her mother's. Exactly like Chantal's.

Exactly like her own.

How many? How many were out there? Trapped as she was, in faces that weren't theirs? In lives that weren't...

Webster...

Next she saw a man whose skin was dry and dark and stretched too tight across his skull.

"Mommy?"

"Jimmy. Jimmy." Bronte stirred and began to thrash.

"Wake up," a terse male voice ordered.

"Jimmy?"

The leathery-faced man loomed above her. Gigantic hands stretched red silk around her neck and yanked.

She screamed.

"Hush up about Jimmy. It's me, Jack. I'm the only one here," that grimly melodious voice drawled. "You're safe."

Bronte's terror held her a moment longer in that state of tortured unconsciousness. Then, gradually, she grew aware of other voices that were distant, far-away. Rat-a-tat-tat sounds, too.

With painful slowness, Bronte opened her eyes.

The television was on.

Jimmy was gone. So were the triangular faces caged in golden frames. Her throat burned, and she remembered what had happened in Mischief's apartment.

Unfamiliar shapes came into focus. Bedposts with huge carved balls gleamed in golden lamplight. Unfamiliar sounds jarred her consciousness.

The television set cast bluish, otherworldly flickers into the room. Ancient-looking airplanes were bombing cities. Pilots in leather caps barked orders. It was a war documentary. The kind Bryan used to love.

On the double bed next to hers lay the silent viewer of this program. He was tall and massive, with only a thin sheet covering his lower body. His duskily tanned chest was exposed above crisp white sheets bunched at his waist.

His hair was blacker than Garth's, his shoulders broader. His dangerous, sinewy muscles rippled in the eerie bluish glow.

He hated her.

He had stalked her.

He had saved her life.

She remembered the gentleness of his warm hands when he'd undressed her.

But he could be so nasty and mean. He'd been to prison. He had that awful tattoo. And yet...

She knew without knowing how she knew that he would have fought to the death to save her. She had panicked when Jimmy had been hurt, and done nothing other than hold him in her arms. This man had nerves of steel and an incredible will. And he was kinder than he pretended.

She had lain beside him shivering on the front seat of his truck, staring up at his harsh, chiseled, dark face, which had whitened every time they met another car. Grimly he had tried to explain that she was Chantal West, his wife, and that he was taking her home to their Texas ranch. He had said he didn't want her back, but he had come for her because their little girl, Carla, wasn't going to school and wasn't passing math, and because of Theodora, her mother, who was growing old and wanted Chantal home for her thirty-fifth birthday. This birthday had something to do with who got control of the ranch, which was important because the ranch was in trouble.

Mischief was this man's wife. She had run away from him and changed her face so he couldn't find her.

Bronte had tried to tell him again that she wasn't Mischief, but he had refused to listen.

He had said she was going to live with him whether she wanted to or not—at least till Theodora saw that she wasn't fit to live on the ranch.

Bluish light flickered on black satin.

Her dress! Her black evening dress.

Every sensory receptor in Bronte's body went off as she eyed the glistening folds of cloth draped over the dinette chair behind Jack's bed.

She was naked. Completely naked. And he'd lain beside her. He probably thought nothing of it because he believed her to be his wife, a woman he had slept with for years and years.

Slowly she ran her hands beneath the soft cotton sheets till she touched bare nipples. With an indrawn breath she felt the curve of her belly and then lower.

He had stripped her. Then he'd lain beneath her as rigid and still as a statue, not taking advantage of her even though he'd been aroused and she'd been too weak to resist.

She remembered how wildly he'd kissed her in the bar. From the start she'd sensed a vein of ice in him that made being alone with him crazy and dangerous. Still, as Bronte's mind cleared, she knew she had to get away from New York fast.

Jack West, no matter how much he disliked her, thought he was her husband. He wanted his wife back.

Bronte was becoming quite calm. He was tough and frightening, but he was her only ticket away from the man with the big hands and tight brown skin. For now Bronte had to be Jack's despised wife—at least till she got better and could think of a superior plan.

"Jack?" Bronte whispered across the dimly lit room.

"Chantal?" he replied. "Feeling better?"

"A little."

His glittering, obsidian eyes were deep and dark and dangerous.

"So you finally admit who you are."

She shivered, momentarily afraid to lie. Then her coolheaded determination surprised her. "I should

have known that I could never ever fool you for long,
my own *dear* husband.''

His gorgeous mouth twisted. ''Stop it. I am not
your *dear* anything. You know as well as I do that
our marriage is a farce.''

His face was hard and set, his voice tight and dry.

Panic clawed through her. How could she know
anything about their marriage?

She squeezed her eyes shut. Turning away, she
stared at the wall quietly. ''Why did I ever marry
you?''

''You got pregnant—on purpose—or have you
conveniently forgotten about our daughter, too?''

''I didn't do that all by myself, now, did I, Jack?''

His heavy silence made her skin heat.

''No. You came to my bedroom, took off your
clothes and got into my bed. You were all over me
in the next breath. Hands and tongue everywhere. I
was drunk. You said she was mine.''

''Was I supposed to be eternally grateful you married me?''

His laughter was brutal.

These awful events had nothing to do with her. She
wasn't his wife. She was just using him. She didn't
care what he thought or felt.

For no reason, she remembered how gentle his
hands could be, and in a soft, thready voice, she said,
''Thank you for saving my life.''

Silence.

She held her breath and counted the cracks in the
wall. Why couldn't she just fall asleep and forget
him?

But she tossed and turned for what seemed like
hours. When finally she did sleep, she dreamed Garth

Brown was kissing her. Then the characters and scenery changed, and Garth was Jack.

When she awoke, the memory of Jack's mouth on hers brought new panic. The television was blaring. He had fallen asleep, his brown hand frozen on the remote-control device.

With agonizing care not to wake him, she pushed her covers off and eased herself out of bed. The room was icy, so she wrapped herself in a blanket.

Gently she tiptoed over to him and, loosening the remote from his fingers, shut off the television.

For a long moment she studied the rise and fall of his dark chest. The room was so quiet, she heard only his breathing.

Sleep had erased the deep lines of exhaustion from between his brows. His black, curling lashes were inky crescents against his dark cheeks.

Again Bronte remembered how helpless she'd been, how he'd saved her. How tender he'd been, even though he disliked her. Hot new tears brimmed against her lashes. She didn't want to feel anything for him.

But she'd nearly died. The shattering experience had left her ego about as sturdy as an eggshell. So, on a sudden impulse, Bronte leaned down and brushed her lips against his with a kiss that held both gratitude and gentleness.

She drew back, slightly dazed from the kiss.

At least he was asleep and would never know.

Suddenly she swayed weakly. The walls swirled. Nausea crushed out her next breath.

The memory of those horrible bony hands throwing her onto the floor made her dizzy. She was shivering again from the aftermath of terror and pain. She told herself she was safe with Jack. That as soon as she recovered from the aftereffects of the drug in the wine and the assault, she'd be fine.

Then she remembered her new face. Maybe the killer was still after her.

Jack's truck keys glittered on the table. Jack was connected to Mischief. Which meant he was connected to her killer, too. Some part of her longed to seize his keys and bolt.

When she took an involuntary step toward them, Jack's eyes snapped open. "What the hell?"

"I—I couldn't sleep."

He pinned her with his darkly glittering gaze. "Get back in bed and stay put."

Chapter 11

Where the hell was she?

Jack was anxious to hit the road.

The premonition of danger had stayed with him even though he couldn't justify it. There was no sign they were being followed.

Still, Jack felt grim as he sipped his strong black coffee. He snapped his newspaper shut, drummed his fingers on the steering wheel of his truck and glared at the door of their motel room.

He wasn't just worried about unseen dangers, either.

He worried about her.

He couldn't concentrate with her around. He hadn't been able to sleep much, either.

Last night all he'd thought of was her in the next bed. Every damn thing she'd done from the first moment she'd seen him in Central Park baffled him.

When she'd sneaked over to his bed, he'd breathed

in the dizzying smell of gardenias and tensed, fearful she'd claw him.

Instead she'd brushed her mouth against his with exquisite tenderness. Nobody had ever done anything like that to him. His life, for all its passion, had been singularly lacking in gentle affection. She was shy and enchanting and utterly different from the hard, calculating woman he'd hated.

Just remembering had him edgily aroused. When he'd gotten up this morning, she'd been asleep.

Shivering no longer, she'd been tucked warmly beneath her covers. He'd studied her boneless, outstretched arm, her wild spray of red hair. Damn, but he'd wanted to get in bed with her, to fall back asleep wrapped in the silken heat of those arms and legs. He'd ached for her to kiss him again as tenderly as she had in the night.

Fortunately, the maid sweeping broken glass outside had distracted him. He'd tugged on his jeans and rushed out to tip her. Then he'd gone to the tree and gathered up the rest of the brown slivers.

After that he'd gone shopping. When he'd returned, he'd half expected Chantal to be gone. She'd been sleeping still—her cheeks rosier than ever, her hair the same riot of red waves spreading across the pillows.

He'd barked her name.

The lazy smile she gave him made him so hot he'd rudely chucked two sacks of clothes at her and ordered her to dress.

The sun was well up and shining brightly on a tall stand of maple trees behind the inn. He was on his third cup of coffee when their door opened and Chantal stepped serenely outside, her slim hips encased in skintight denim.

He was one lousy shopper. The blue cotton blouse was at least a size too small. The sight of her slim, but voluptuous body in that snug outfit made him bolt his coffee so fast he scalded his throat.

When she glanced into the trash can and smiled at all his beer bottles, he ducked sheepishly, cowering behind his paper while she struggled with the heavy door.

He didn't help. She was breathless by the time she climbed inside the pickup.

Her floral scent filled the cab. He fought to ignore it just as he fought to ignore her. Which was hard when her pretty face was framed with that bright aureole of shimmering curls. Again he remembered how silky those masses had felt on his shoulders.

Damn. She was so sexy. She made him feel needy.

He *felt*.

Feelings.

They scared the hell out of him.

Especially where she was concerned.

Nothing's changed.

Trapped with her in the cab, he felt his mood darken.

Think of anything else…anything at all.

He pitched his newspaper over his shoulder. With no more than a curt grunt, he started the ignition and swerved out of the parking lot, tires squealing.

The foam coffee cup she had forgotten on top of the cab flew onto the parking lot.

"Who broke all those bottles?"

He flushed. "Who tried to strangle you?"

"I—I asked first."

"I bet it thrills you to see how close you came to driving me to drink."

"You?" Her quiet voice seemed to hold both surprise and concern.

His eyes narrowed on the gritty black surface of the highway as they rushed past the suburbanized farm town and its enormous white colonial houses, into rolling, green country.

"Who tried to kill you?"

"I—I didn't see him clearly."

"You must have an idea."

"I don't have a clue."

Her voice sounded so painfully hollow he felt sorry for her. Then he caught himself—this was no time for misplaced sympathy.

He bit his lower lip till he tasted blood. Okay. She wasn't going to talk. Forget her. Drive.

But he couldn't forget her. She was too damned different. So different it was hard imagining anybody wanting to hurt her.

With an effort he reminded himself of the long years of their hellish marriage.

It was easier to note how her blouse and jeans snugly molded her slim figure.

He'd bought a blue bandanna to match the blouse. She'd carefully tied it around her throat to conceal the dark bruises. Jack remembered how scared he'd been when she'd lain across his lap barely whimpering. A suffocating despair had gripped him.

Jack turned on the radio. Music was a dangerous distraction, but he needed to take his mind off those buttons, which were about to pop open. She was a little bigger at the top than he remembered. Why wasn't there one damn thing that was the same?

There was! He remembered the jagged white scar on her left shoulder.

"Can I have a sip of your coffee? I lost my cup," she purred as a news commentator began to talk about a plane crash in the Indian Ocean.

"Sure," he muttered. Despite his best effort to sound indifferent, his rough voice was charged.

His hand shook as he extended his white cup. When her fingertips brushed his, he jerked back, sloshing lukewarm coffee all over his jeans.

"Damn."

The music was country and western, his favorite. Old Hank was crooning a melody about lost love and new love with way too much passion.

"Oh, dear," she said when she saw Jack's soaked jeans. "Did I burn you?" She touched his damp thigh and gave him one of those dazzling, worried looks of hers.

He jumped, his heart racing. "As if you give a damn!" he shouted like a man in the last stages of lunacy.

She closed her eyes as they sped south. "I do."

"I'm fine."

"Why is it so important that I be home for my, er, thirty...fifth birthday?"

"As if you don't know." He twisted the dial of the radio.

"No, leave it on," she said. "I sort of like it."

"Since when did you ever like... Well, I don't."

Liar. She could tell it was one of his favorites. It opened him up to her.

He spun the dial.

Jack wished he could remove himself, erase himself, as he had that first year in prison. Then the music and the woman wouldn't be able to get to him.

Nothing's changed.

"My, my. Aren't we grumpy? You remind me of a five-year-old. My specialty…"

Since when? he wanted to thunder.

But she laughed, and the silvery sound pulled him out of himself. Did he only imagine she sounded short of breath? Leaning toward him, her lips sipped from the same place on the coffee cup where his own mouth had been.

What the hell was wrong with him—to notice her lipstick smudges on a white cup? He hated her.

He had sex on the brain, the way his mother used to.

Suddenly he wished he'd bought airline tickets. They had too many miles to be stuck alone in this tiny cab together. But flying with her after she'd hit him in Paris had seemed risky.

"It's going to be a long trip." He leaned forward, hunching over the steering wheel, staring moodily at the flying white center stripes and black asphalt.

"Are you always this scared around girls? Or is it just me?"

"I'm not scared." *Like hell, West.*

"Why don't you tell me what's happened since I've been gone?"

She met his dark glance shamelessly.

"Do you really want small talk? All right then. I served five years of hard time because of you. I chopped cotton from dawn till dark with my ankles chained to other men's. When I wrote a letter, it'd take me fourteen days to get a single page done 'cause every night I was so damn tired all I could write was

a line or two. I got stabbed. I nearly died, damn it.
There were days I wished I could die. Like the night
I nearly got raped...while you jetted around the
world!''

Chantal's eyes were brilliant in her white face.
''And the tattoo...''

''Oh, that. That was a gift from a buddy. I don't
mind it so much. He saved me from those other
guys.''

''Jack...'' Her voice was soft with remorse.

He gripped the steering wheel harder. ''Shut up.''

Jack turned the volume louder, so that the disk
jockey's voice drowned her out when she tried to
speak.

Five minutes later he spotted a roadside café. He
jerked the wheel hard to the right, sending the pickup
slewing into the parking lot. The horn of an eighteen-
wheeler behind them blared wildly. Brakes screamed
when Jack stopped.

More coffee spilled. This time all over her thighs.

She cried out. ''You drive like a maniac. And
you're rude and mean.''

''Because you drive me crazy.''

''This trip was your idea.''

He flung open his door. ''Get this. You and I have
nothing, absolutely nothing, to say to each other.''

She was dabbing at the coffee with a paper napkin
as she slid out. ''You want me to come home with
you, to live with you as your wife, but you don't want
anything to do with me. Have you thought this out at
all, Jack? Here we are, stuck in this truck for however
long it takes to get home.... Well, what's going to
happen when we have to live in the same house and
act like...husband and wife?''

The confines of the cab suddenly seemed stifling and close as he thought of those implied marital intimacies. Images of her naked body entwined with his, of her mouth parting in a gardenia-perfumed dark tormented him.

"That's why we're stopping now, girl. It's time I established some ground rules."

"I might want to establish a rule or two of my own," she said, shoving helplessly at her door.

"Very funny," he snarled as he came around and yanked it open.

He grabbed her arm and pulled her toward the restaurant.

But just the heat of her skin through her thin cotton shirt got him hot. After pushing her into the restaurant, he let her go.

She took one step across the threshold and froze. A dozen men had looked up and were staring straight at her. And why wouldn't they? She was drop-dead gorgeous. Her face was as beautiful as that mythic face of ancient Greece that launched a thousand ships. And not only her face. With every step, her hips swayed. Skintight denim seductively encased that curvaceous derriere and those forever legs.

A cowboy whistled.

She blushed.

Then she came running back to Jack, wrapping her arms around his waist.

"I don't want to go in."

"I'm hungry."

With an air of forced indifference, Jack shouldered his way through the door and led her to a booth near the jukebox. All the time, he was thinking that Chantal had never once run from male admiration and sought his protection like that.

The small café was reminiscent of restaurants from the 1950s, with old neon signs, plastic flowers and pool tables. The menu had low prices. Working men sat on stools and in booths, and more besides the one who'd whistled stared as she walked by.

But their stares just made her hold tighter to Jack. Watching her warily, he let her go and helped her into the red vinyl booth. He slid in across from her. After they ordered, she left him and went to clean up in the ladies' room.

Then she was back, and again, sitting across from her, he was as awkwardly spellbound as all the other men. He watched her every dainty sip of coffee, her every delicate bite of scrambled egg. Had she always been this sexy?

It had been a long time since he'd found such pleasure in just watching a woman, especially her—not holding, not even kissing, but simply watching.

Damn.

When she finished eating, she crossed her fork and knife across her plate on top of her two uneaten toast halves and beamed at him. "You said something about rules."

"Well, first, stop being so damned polite."

"So even that is a crime."

"Especially that."

"Did anybody ever tell you that you are rude and…" She looked away, out the window at a van flying north on the highway.

"And what?" he demanded, furious—and surprised, too—that he cared what she thought.

"And so insufferable. I—I see why Chantal, I

mean, I see why I left you. Why, any normal woman would. Didn't anybody raise you, Jack? What kind of mother did you have?''

His face blackened. ''You always did love throwing her up at me.'' Planting his elbows on the table, he leaned forward. ''Stop it. Cut that little-miss-purity act right now. You're not much better than she was, you know. She had to do what she did. You're not even normal. Our marriage was never a real marriage. At least I tried to make it work. You didn't.''

''Oh, right. You're the saint. The way you act, that's getting harder and harder to believe, Jack.''

''I was faithful. You weren't.''

''I wonder why.''

His mouth thinned. ''Because you're insane.'' Red rage washed him. ''And completely unreasonable.'' His hands knotted into tight fists. He made a low, animal sound and was further infuriated when she shrank from him.

''And did you ever hit me, Jack?''

''You begged me to,'' he exclaimed.

Her white face went still, her green eyes huge. ''Did you?''

Why was she forcing all the bitter memories?

Too vividly he remembered finding her naked just days after their marriage in the bunkhouse with Maverick's massive, square body sprawled all over her on that narrow bunk. Jack had wanted to tear them apart, to see blood run. Instead he'd just stared, dying inside.

Blindly he'd stumbled out and gulped in fresh air. He'd felt the same violent urges when he'd watched his mother with men, but he'd learned as a boy how to shut down. He hadn't laid a hand on his pretty wife. Not even when she'd taunted him later.

"You know the answer, Chantal. You were my wife. I didn't like finding you with Maverick, but I never laid a hand on you. After him, you slept with every man on the ranch. How many times did I catch you in some bushy ravine or cheap motel with a wrangler? You did it everywhere. You wanted me to find you. The only time I came near hurting you was that last night.... But I didn't. I couldn't. But I've been through a lot since then. Don't push me."

Her hand lifted and fluttered uneasily to her bandanna. Her eyes were wary. "Is that a threat?"

"You're damned right it is."

He wrapped his fingers around her wrists and pulled her halfway across the table.

Big mistake. Her lips were too provocatively near. He didn't know which was hotter, his rage or the carnal flame licking through him.

His voice dropped and became more intimate. "I don't want you back. I don't want you for my wife. But damn it, this time you're going to be—"

"Excuse me, dears," their plump, motherly waitress interrupted, probably because she sensed trouble. "Hate to bother the two of you when you look so...wrapped up in each other...like a honeymooning couple. But could I borrow your salt, dears?"

Chantal yanked her hands free.

"Sure," Jack snapped, seizing the salt and pepper shakers and slamming them down in front of the pushy woman. "Here. Take them." He grabbed the napkin holder and pushed it forward. "Take everything on the table, why don't you?"

"You were saying?" Chantal prompted too politely, rubbing her bruised wrists.

"This has gone far enough. We're in a public
place." He grabbed the check, crumpling the cheap
paper in his fist. "Let's get the hell out of here."

"Wait." From beneath lowered lashes she looked
up at Jack with that uncertain smile that made her
look younger and more innocent than she ever
had—even when she'd been a girl. "Jack, I want you
to know something. I—I'm not going to sleep with
those other men ever again."

Her sweetness only made his dark panic wind
tighter. "I don't give a damn."

"Jack, I—I give you my word."

His skin felt like it was stretched too tight across
his cheekbones. When he spoke, his voice was so low
she strained forward to hear.

"Which never meant a damn thing in the past."

Her lovely eyes were wide with amazement. There
was no way, however, that he could explain to her
that his plan was to convince Theodora and Carla
what an unfit wife, daughter and mother she was—so
they would want her gone as much as he did. He
wanted to use her to convince Theodora she had to
trust him to run the ranch till Carla was older.

"I've changed."

Nothing's changed.

"You damn sure have." He admitted that before
he thought that was the last thing he wanted to believe. "Your eyes are different. So damn different I
sometimes can't believe it's you in there. Even your
voice…"

Caution sprang into her eyes. Her incandescent
smile died. "How?"

"It's deeper. Huskier. Not so sly. Everything about you is different. The way you look at me. The way I feel, too. I keep asking myself why? How?"

"Five years—"

"No. Since Paris. In one month you've changed completely."

She swallowed hard. Then she licked her lips as if they'd suddenly gone dry. "I have a sore throat. Last night—"

"No. You didn't talk the same in the bar, either. You didn't act the same. You've got some hidden agenda. I can feel it in my gut."

"Jack, I—I hardly know myself…who I am. Ever since my plastic—" Her voice broke. She swallowed. Suddenly she seemed unwilling to discuss the matter further.

"Well, I'm on to your little act," he said. "Nothing you can say or do will ever make me change my mind about you. You'll be packing your bags soon enough."

"Look, Jack…" Without thinking, she touched his sleeve. "If we're ever going to get to Texas, shouldn't we go?"

Her fingers burned through his cotton shirt like a brand. When she leaned closer, the scent of gardenias enveloped him.

Damn her. Was she trying to seduce him? Here? In front of all these men?

"Rule number one." His voice grated harshly as he jerked his arm away. "No more touching." He stared at her slim, trembling hand as if it were an obscene object. "You got that?"

"No objection here."

"No more kissing, either."

He was staring at her lips as she swallowed hard.
"Fine."

"I know you sneaked over to my bed last night and kissed me."

"That…was an accident."

Her gaze grew intense and dark, and she blushed as if she was struggling to fight down some foolish emotion. But her acting embarrassed and shy about it didn't fool him.

"Don't do it again."

"Any more rules?" she murmured tautly, staring at her plate now.

"Separate beds."

"Separate bedrooms, too?" she suggested, the charming blush creeping across her cheeks as that damn voice of hers deepened and grew huskier.

Jack felt thoroughly aroused. "Damn it. Separate houses."

"Great." She wet her mouth with her tongue. Her eyes flashed with defiant fire when she dared a glance his way. He could tell she was remembering he'd told her not to do that.

"Don't do *that,* either."

"Just testing. I'll be good." But she twirled her pink tongue one last time, making her lips so wet they glistened.

"I'm so glad we agree," he growled.

"Oh, me too." She paused. "Is that it?"

"That about covers it." But as he slid his wallet out of his back pocket, she snatched the crumpled check from him.

"Just a minute," she murmured in a low, sensual tone. "Maybe I want to make a rule, too."

He glared at her. "No way."

"Marriage means compromise."

His scowl darkened. "How would you know?"

She ignored him. "Here's my rule, Jack. You can be your rude, hateful self just as much as you like—when we're alone. But in front of our daughter and everybody else, I want you to treat me with courtesy and respect. I don't want you taking sides and ganging up with anybody else against me. In short, I want you to pretend you are a loving and supportive husband."

A stream of vivid Spanish curses mushroomed in his brain, but he bit them back. "No way."

"No. You prefer to wallow in misery like it's a religion. You want to feel sorry for yourself and punish me forever. Our marriage is nobody's business but ours."

His voice was rough. "You never gave a damn about our marriage before."

"Well, I won't follow your rules if you don't respect mine."

His whole point in bringing her home was to show everybody how miserable they were together. "I can't act nice to you," he muttered.

"I'm sure it would be a challenge for a man with your temperament to be pleasant to anyone," she agreed. Her saccharine voice grated. "You could still try." She squared her shoulders, which stretched the buttons of her blue shirt dangerously. Then she leaned back against the red vinyl booth as if she were prepared to camp there forever.

"We're getting off to a rotten start."

"Because you're stubborn."

"Me?" He was determined to run the show this time. Determined to be so hateful she'd be worse than ever. How else could he rid himself of her? But if she started playing the loving wife, even in public...

A cowboy put two quarters in the jukebox, and a sad golden oldie enveloped them. The lyrics and the singer took Jack back to their youth. To that time before he'd know for sure what she was. The warm, husky voice and a slow guitar worked sensual magic. For an instant the music bridged the distance that held them apart. Sadness they shared. Despair as well. He wanted to take her in his arms, to start over, to build instead of destroy. Then his anger rose up and smashed even that tenuous link.

"All right," Jack growled, yanking the check out of her slim fingers. "Satisfied?"

Her charming smile touched off an alarm in him. "For now."

The lyrics told of a man who couldn't live without love and made him ache with an unnamed need.

Jack had sung that song about a million times. How come he couldn't listen to it now with her? He raced toward the cash register.

She'd agreed to his every rule. How come he felt like she'd won?

Hell, she won every time she got close. Every time her eyes dilated. Every time a flush rose in her pretty cheeks. Every time he heard a melody.

His hands balled and stretched. He wanted to crush her against his body and make love to her.

He'd grown up with sex all around him. Hard as he fought his growing hunger, he just felt hotter.

He caught her uncertain glance.

They faced a long day on the road together.

An even longer night.

Chantal knew his weaknesses, especially his sexual weaknesses.

When a man didn't want to want her, she loved the power game of seducing him.

Nothing had changed.

Everything had.

Chapter 12

Three hundred strokes.

She had counted every single one.

Slowly, sensuously, rhythmically, she pulled the brush through her long hair as she sat at the mirror, her back to Jack. Her manner was calm as she pretended an indifference to him that she was far from feeling.

Suddenly the back of her neck prickled. Next she felt a tingle trace the length of her slim, straight-as-an-arrow back.

She didn't have to turn to know that Jack's smoldering black gaze was devouring her.

Never had a motel room felt tinier.

Or so dangerously intimate.

Not even when she'd been married.

As the hour grew later and the night sky blacker against the windowpanes, the atmosphere between them grew increasingly charged.

A shiver passed through her. How could his mere gaze, his mere presence, make her feel so alive? And yet so threatened, too?

Her fingers clenched spasmodically on the brush as she set it down.

Her skin burned. And not just the dark bruises that circled her throat.

He was Mischief's husband, and, thereby, connected to her killer.

She was his prisoner.

But he had saved her, too.

If their first day together on the road had seemed interminable, what would tonight bring?

No touching, he had sworn threateningly.

But he wanted it.

So did she.

Even though Bronte sat as far as possible from him, even though she struggled to ignore him, she felt inexorably drawn.

Her flesh was weak.

There was one bed.

No couch.

So where was *he* going to sleep?

For now, Jack sat rigidly hunched over a desk beside the windows. She was perched before the small dressing table, her slim back to him, the double bed between them.

She couldn't seem to stay still, though. She picked the brush up again and slid it through her hair, this time tangling the heavy strands more than smoothing them. No sooner did she set the brush down than she began chewing a fingernail. She'd already gnawed two down to their bloody quicks.

''Would you quit?'' he demanded.

"Is that a new rule?" Her shiveringly soft question cut the silence.

The muscles in his jaw bunched.

She glanced at his mouth and remembered last night's tender kiss.

"Sorry." Her indrawn breath sounded faint. "You're right. Bad habit. I always get depressed and hate myself afterward."

He leaned over his map and pretended to ignore her.

Her gaze touched the raven darkness of his hair. She met his eyes.

He's not your husband.

He'll walk out of your life without a flicker of remorse.

He's not Garth Brown, either.

He hates you.

Use him. Don't think about him.

Suddenly she grabbed her purse and looked inside for an emery board. But as she rummaged, the soft leather pouch collapsed, spilling its contents. When her pen fell under the bed, rolling toward Jack, she gave a startled gasp. She couldn't help watching it in her mirror as it headed toward the scuffed toe of his boot.

Jack, who with a yellow marker was highlighting the shortest route to the ranch in a road atlas, jumped a foot when it struck him.

As if he felt her gaze, he leaned down, picked it up and made eye contact with her in the mirror.

With his glittering black eyes trained on her, Bronte felt caught in some cat-and-mouse scenario. He leaned back in his chair, his powerful, sinewy muscles rippling with tension in the artificial light. His savage countenance unnerved her.

She wished they were on the road. Then she could turn her back and distract herself with the constantly changing scenery.

He set her pen down too carefully on his desk. ''How come you're always looking at yourself in that mirror?'' His husky voice was precisely pitched and too controlled.

Because I don't see me. Because I see my mother. Or your wife. Or Mischief. Because I want to forget you.

''Am I?'' she queried innocently, swiveling on her flimsy stool. ''You do it, too.'' Her voice sounded false, too bright.

''Because I can't get used to your new face.''
Tell me about it. ''You will,'' she said aloud.

''Maybe. I don't know. You look younger.''

''The magic of plastic surgery.''

''Prettier, too.'' His lip curled cynically.

''How?''

''I don't know exactly. I just wish you didn't.''

''You love to hate me, don't you?''

''It's easier.'' He paused. ''That guy that tried to murder you must have hated you a lot. Who was he?''

His stare made her cheeks burn.

''Can't we be together five seconds without bickering?'' she asked.

''You used to love fighting with me. It turned you on.''

She turned her face away, her cheeks flaming again. ''Is that what you're trying to do, Jack, turn me on? For God's sake, we have the whole night to get through.''

"You think I don't know that?"

His fist slammed down so hard onto the wooden arm of his chair that his atlas crashed to the floor.

"Sorry. I shouldn't have said anything," she whispered.

When he grabbed her pen and bolted out of his chair toward her, she jumped up and scampered on bare feet to the bathroom.

His boots thudded heavily on the wooden floor as he stormed after her.

She barely managed to shut and lock the door before he hurled himself against it.

"Damn it, let me in! I was only going to return your pen."

Shaking, she leaned against the door. "Put it inside my purse—"

He beat on the door with his fist.

Sometimes two of her kindergartners had fought like this. But adults weren't supposed to...

"Jack, please, you're scaring me."

As the vibrations of his pounding raced through her body, she buried her face in her hands and wept. This wasn't her fault. Webster...

No use thinking of him.

Jack was her new reality, her new problem.

She'd only been with him a day. One agonizingly long day on the road. Now she felt like she'd been locked inside a powder keg.

How could she endure even one more night of this pseudomarriage? Of this tense, angry man who made her feel so scared...and yet so excited and bewilderingly oversexed too. Was she crazy? He was incredibly attractive, even when he stared at her with those

hot, brooding eyes and accused her of all those lu-
rid…

Bronte understood pain and betrayal, hurt and anger. On some deep level the pain that lay beneath his
hatred drew her and made her want to heal him.

Crazy thought. Crazy impulse. Bury them.

He had to be a lost cause. If not, why had Chantal
changed her face? Had this impossible man made her
so desperate she'd abandoned her child? Her mother?
Her home?

Why had Webster made Bronte look like this complicated woman? Had he worshipped her mother? Or
Chantal?

Bronte felt the mystery expanding and growing
more complex. She had so many questions. Already
her charade was far more difficult than she'd bargained for. Jack despised her so much he could barely
stand to be in the same room with her. He could
barely endure the most impersonal conversation. Yet
she sensed part of his anger had to do with a sort of
baffled self-disgust that he found her attractive.

His constant hatred laced with desire exhausted and
unnerved her. Never having been treated thus before,
she hadn't realized how stressful such a relationship
could be.

There were so many questions she wanted to ask
him before they got to the ranch, but each time she
was about to, she stopped, because she knew he'd just
bite her head off again.

Who lived at the ranch? What were Mischief's habits? Did Mischief ride? How well? Did she work? If
so, at what? Who were her friends? But how could
Bronte ask him anything without making him even
more suspicious?

Right now she had only him to fool. At the ranch there would be dozens of others. How many people lived there? What were their names?

She had a mother, Theodora. A daughter, Carla. A half sister named Cheyenne.

And all those unnamed lovers Jack had alluded to.

Bronte had yearned for a sister. She had been faithful to Bryan. She had never hated anybody in her life. How long could she possibly pretend to be this complicated woman? Mischief had given little away about herself in the few moments Bronte had been with her.

When Jack's pounding subsided to polite knocks, she wiped her tear-streaked face on a washcloth and opened the door.

She ignored the dangerous glitter in his eyes as she swept past him.

"I don't understand you anymore," he said.

How could he?

Hysterical laughter gurgled in her throat. She suppressed it. "Handle it."

"We've been married for years. We grew up together. But you're like a stranger. All day long I had this feeling that I have never been with you before. Why—"

"Handle it." Her voice sounded far colder and more impersonal than she really felt.

His dark gaze was leveled at her. "How, damn it?"

"This reconciliation was your idea," she reminded him in her calmest kindergarten-teacher voice.

"Not really." He grabbed her by the arm and spun her around.

Ah, that sullen, sensual, movie-star face of his. Not to mention his touch, which was all heat and sizzle.

Their gazes locked. Her nerves wound tauter. Suddenly she couldn't breathe. It had been years since she'd had sex. Forever.

Blood pounded in her ears like the roar of thunder.

"Remember rule number one," she whispered, her kindergarten tone shakier now.

"What?"

"No touching, wasn't that it?" She met his molten eyes.

"Yeah. Right. Right." Hardness edged his voice as he yanked her closer with surprising ferocity.

Her throat tightened.

So did his grip.

She went white when he snugged her against him. Whiter still when his hand slid roughly into her hair and a steel band circled her and made her his captive.

"You've never acted controlled or sweet a day in your life. Are you trying to make me love you and want you again? Is that why you're being so coy and ladylike—"

"No. I don't care what you think about me." *Liar.*

"No? Then why do you look so good? And feel so good?" His hand coiled a strand of her hair around two dark fingers. "Your hair is darker." His voice grew hoarse. "Thicker. Silkier. Even when you're quiet, I can't quit thinking about you. Even though you don't act bold the way you used to, you still…"

With the back of his hand he pushed the heavy lock back into place. His fingers were gentle against her ear and her cheek. Every nerve in her body was tingling in reaction to what he was saying and doing. She might have pushed him away, but she didn't. "Don't do this, Jack."

"You would never have said that in the past." A

derisive expression played across his face. "Is that your new come-on?"

She shivered. "I hate you when you're cynical and too knowing."

"I know you."

"Do you?"

"Hell yes." Angrily, he caught her closer, holding her arm so hard his fingers would leave dark marks on her flesh. "One day—almost two—and you're like a drug in my blood." He glared down at her with profound bitterness. "I crave the taste and feel and scent of you."

His rippling muscles and his hard-edged masculinity were like an aphrodisiac. She craved all those things, too.

"I want," he continued, "things from you I thought I could never want again."

Her arms curled around his neck in artless abandon. *What was she doing?*

"I felt dead to all women until I saw you in the park—"

"Oh, Jack…" Desire flickered through her—and a joy she had not allowed herself to hope for came back to her. Her blood pulsed.

He saw it. The urgency in her eyes was a reflection of his own.

His arms were iron bands crushing her to his chest. His brutal hands roughly forced her chin higher.

"I…I was scared of you that day. I'm still scared—"

"You're my wife. You're not scared. So don't play those games. You used to want it rough. You used to beg—"

"Not anymore—"

"Bullshit. You still like your sex hot and wild, I bet."

With genuine panic, she stared into his fiery black eyes. Her breath came unevenly. Then his searing mouth ground down on hers. She wanted tenderness, kindness. And yet... Instantly, a feverish hunger swept through her, too.

He was forcing her down.

"You've driven me mad for years, Chantal. You chased after every man on the ranch while I did without—"

Bronte slid her fingers into his black hair. "I swear I didn't. I wouldn't—"

"I loved Cheyenne. You seduced me and got preg—"

"I would never ever do something so awful." But she was quivering like a frightened animal as his long, lean, manipulating fingers molded her to his length.

"If I drank, it was because—" his lips devoured hers "—because I couldn't stand the thought of you with another man. I kept thinking you'd change, and now that you have..." His hands ripped at the buttons of her blouse.

She trembled as his hands roamed her, shaping her naked woman flesh to his. Trembled when his breathing grew loud and harsh and his fingers closed gently over her breasts. Trembled when his body heat fused to hers.

Bronte moaned and fought to escape his plundering mouth and hands. "Don't... We mustn't..." But her thickening voice rasped more faintly.

"No, love." He knelt, bathing her nipples with his tongue till they became wet, erotic pebbles.

With a sigh, she closed her eyes and was still. She

would be who he thought she was for now. But, maybe someday, she could be herself.

A long time later, when she had quickened under his expert titillation, he stood up and pushed his delicious tongue into her mouth. With both hands, he stretched her tightly against his body, so that her breasts flattened against his chest. In the next moment, he prized a muscular thigh between her legs. She gasped, thrilled by the raw sensuality of this intimate cue.

At least he thought she was his wife.

She had no such excuse.

Still, eyelids fluttering, she clung, craving the mindless glory that only total knowledge of him could bring.

It had been too long. He made her feel sweet and feminine, and thrillingly alive. He was brave, and his bravery inspired her.

She would despise herself in the morning.

He would despise her even more. When he learned the truth, he would hate her for that, too.

For eight years she had been married to Bryan. She'd hardly known Jack two days.

Never once had she felt such insatiable and exquisite sensual pleasure.

She stared into his eyes and felt she'd known him always, wanted to know him always. There was pain inside this man. So much pain. What else could he feel for a woman…if he ever let himself go?

Jack ripped off her jeans.

She should have fought.

Instead she stood statue still, scarcely breathing, sighing as he did things she'd never let any man do, feeling strange and shy, and yet fully roused, too. She sank to her knees and unzipped him with fingers that shook.

In seconds he was naked from the waist down.

His body was long and lean and brown. His rigid manhood jutted toward her mouth.

When she kissed his bare thigh, he caught her closer with a groan.

She shifted, self-conscious suddenly as she gazed up at him, her torpid eyes both questioning and languorous.

He bent over her, his rough hands stroking gently through her hair, his fingers sliding down her neck as he pulled her face higher, guiding her mouth to the source of his maleness.

What might have been wrong with any other man was right with him. Still, her lips parted with a startled breath as he pushed inside.

He shuddered when her lips and tongue began to toy with him. She was shy and timid at first. With a groan of unadulterated pleasure, he used his hands to move her head back and forth. He was staring down at her, his black eyes cynical and hard and unyielding, shocked that she could arouse him so.

Yet when he reached that shattering, hair-trigger edge of control, he pulled out. Lifting her swiftly, he carried her to the bed. Then he lay down on top of her.

His arms circled her. In the velvet blackness, her eyes shone as brilliantly as emeralds.

"One of us is crazy," Jack muttered against her ear.

"Both of us." Desire swept the last vestiges of her guilt and fear away on its burning tide.

She caressed his inky hair. The sandpaper roughness of his carved cheek rasped beneath her exploring fingertips. His body felt heavy and huge and hot, but she twined her legs around him to keep him there.

He kissed each black bruise on her slender throat. "I'll kill the next bastard who hurts you."

Then the hot moistness of his breath brushed her scalp. His mouth nuzzled her warm skin and his hands fondled her breasts. He traced his mouth across her nipples till little moans rose from her throat.

"Open your legs."

Mindless with pleasure, she arched toward him so he could enter her. Instead, he stroked her wetly with long, deft fingers till her muted cries died completely.

"How beautiful you are, how soft and warm and sweet." His rough drawl was lazy and low with reverence and wonder. "You aren't the same at all." Then gently he thrust inside her and was still, enveloped by her warmth. When he began to move with a slow, passionate rhythm, gradually her desire built. Faster and faster, like dancers caught in the same spell, their bodies twisted together, till she was so hot she felt ready to spark. But when he felt her fully roused, he slowed, smiling down at her, drawling sexy endearments.

"Now," she pleaded as she felt the flame at the center of her being ignite. "Now."

He slammed into her, and she was moaning and writhing and soaring as he exploded, and the hot torrent poured into her womb.

Clinging. Sighing. Dying.

Together.

Too soon, the rush of emotion was over.

She wanted to lie quietly, enclosed in his strong

arms until long after the trembling of their bodies ceased.

She thought he did too.

He finished and rolled off her.

Her lovely eyes snapped open. Fully conscious, she stared at his handsomely aggressive profile as he lay on his back and glared at the ceiling.

His posture was rigid, his utter coldness like a slap, shocking her to her senses.

If only he would take her in his arms again... She had felt so warm and tender and alive. Crazy thought. She didn't really want that.

He lay beside her like a stone figure, hating what they had done together she supposed.

When she foolishly raised a hand and gently touched his face, the muscles of his jaw flexed. Violently he flung her hand away.

"Don't make it worse."

She shut her eyes so she wouldn't cry.

She had not meant for this to happen. She had tried to stop him.

She should have fought harder.

This cold, dark man was not hers to love.

Whatever her regrets were, his were more profound.

His ravaged face spoke volumes. When he finally spoke, his voice was solid ice. "This doesn't change a damn thing."

But it had. For him too. No matter how he tried to deny it.

"I—I tried to stop you." Her fragile voice was thready.

"Yeah. Sure. You said no, but you egged me on—with your hot eyes and your soft, willing body.

With that new pretty face that made me forget who and what you really are. I told you you were good, didn't I? You should be, honey. You've had a hell of a lot of practice. How many men have there been since me?''

When her hand flew toward his face, he seized it.

"That's more like the old you," he spat.

A tear welled out of the corner of her eye and rolled into her hair. Every muscle in Bronte's body hurt. He wasn't her husband. How could his words cut so deeply, shaming her to the core? As if she'd actually done all those terrible things he accused her of?

"I'll never touch you again, Chantal."

Bronte's stomach tightened. She felt numb.

"Who wants you to?" But she did. God help her, she did.

She bit her lips, and with a moan, twisted onto her side. Jerking the covers up to her neck, she closed her eyes again.

He hurled himself out of bed.

Through slitted lashes, she watched him.

With cold insolence, he stared down at her body, molded by the thin sheet. She watched him dress with desolate fascination. Watched him snap frayed, cotton buttonholes over every button.

She felt his determination to hate her. She tried to summon hatred for him, too. Instead the emptiness surrounding her dully pounding heart expanded into an aching void.

He yanked on briefs and jeans. Finishing swiftly, he flexed his hands into knotted fists and then un-flexed them, as if every nerve in his body was lit by dark self-disgust and loathing for her.

"Jack?"

He jumped. "Damn it. I thought you were asleep."

"How could I possibly sleep after—"

"You always do. Tonight will be your last chance for a while because tomorrow's going to be longer than today 'cause I don't intend to risk another night in some motel room with you."

She curled her body into a tight, miserable ball.

He strode outside and slammed the door so hard the thin wall gave a convulsive shudder.

Or was it she who shuddered?

She didn't want to cry.

But the hot tears came anyway.

Later, when her sobs ceased, she knew what she had to do.

A red silk tie lay across the dusty, blue dashboard of the battered VW.

The killer got out and unzipped his fly.

Just as he frowned in tense concentration, a dark shadow appeared beneath *their* bathroom window across the highway.

Hot damn.

He whipped his rifle out of the back seat and raised his scope.

The bathroom window slid up.

A pair of pretty, long legs slid over the windowsill. Then a pretty, round butt wiggled in that golden square of light.

He got a hot tickle of lascivious excitement in his groin.

Get your head out of the window, bitch, so I can splatter your brains and red hair all over that wall.

A little song played in his head.

Kill. Kill. As fast as you can.

Yippee. He felt like a Wild West cowboy.

No way could he miss at such close range.

Her red head bobbed out.

His trigger finger quivered. She'd never know death was on its way. Her skull would pop just like a blood-filled watermelon.

He expelled a tense breath, took aim and squeezed the trigger. Damn! Suddenly Jack sprang out of the dark, quick like a cat, grabbing her and pulling her down into the dirt.

The bullet slammed into the wall. Pieces of wood splintered as a woman screamed.

The killer got off three more shots.

But his target was rolling over and over. When she got up and tried to scuttle away, Jack dragged her behind a tree by her hair.

Three motel doors opened.

The killer jumped into the VW and jammed his keys in the ignition. A minute later the center stripe was flying.

A hundred yards down the highway, he felt warm fluid gush between his legs.

Damn the bitch.

He'd peed on himself.

She'd pay for that.

He'd get up close to her. Take his time. Have some fun.

She'd die slowly while he came inside her.

Chapter 13

Bronte's heart was pounding so fast she had to think to breathe. Sharp rocks and tree roots ground painfully into her back. She couldn't move because Jack was sprawled on top of her, holding her down. The muscles of his arms and legs had her pinned helplessly. His breath rasped against her neck; his heart thudded like a voodoo drum. Worse, the bulge between his thighs was swelling bigger and bigger.

His angry gaze ran over her shrinking body with hot interest.

She closed her eyes in terror and despair.

Almost, almost, she'd escaped him—permanently.

Then he'd grabbed her and thrown her to the ground right before that bullet—

Bullet!

Again she felt the whisper of metal whizzing past her cheek. Again she saw pieces of wood splintering, felt flying slivers hit her face. Then Jack had her on the ground, and he'd rolled over and over with her. When she'd screamed at him to stop hurting her, he'd dragged her behind this tree and had thrown himself on top of her again, shielding her with his body.

"Get off me, you big lummox!" Bronte pushed at his broad chest with splayed fingertips.

He was enormous and as heavy as lead. All she could do was squirm helplessly under his long, muscular body as he looked up and peered past her toward that place where the gunshots had come from.

"Feels good," he growled, a nasty, tauntingly seductive sting in his low tone.

Instantly she was terrifyingly aware of the immense heat of his body, of the rippling muscles crushing her, of the rock hardness of his arousal. With an effort, she stopped moving and pushing at him.

"I said get off me!"

The expression on his face grew diabolical, so she quieted.

Jack didn't get up till he was good and ready. Then he stood up cautiously, brushed himself off, not caring that dust and small rocks rained down on her. When she tried to get to her feet, her ankle gave and she slipped back and fell heavily. She tried to get up again, but her arms were wobbly and her legs seemed to be made of jelly. Then Jack was there, yanking her up, his grip and expression so brutal that when she stared into his ruthless face, she screamed.

He clamped his hand over her mouth and slammed her against the tree. She fought him wildly, weeping and kicking. The rough bark tore her T-shirt and scratched her skin. He kept her pinned till she lost her strength and her hysteria played out.

"Hush."

When she finally quieted, sobbing still, but utterly exhausted, he removed his hand from her mouth. "You about done?"

"Did you see those bullet holes? Somebody tried to shoot me."

Perspiration stood out in beads on his brow, and his arms were damp with it. "I damned near got my ass blown off because of you."

"Is that all you care about?"

Other guests were outside their rooms shouting to each other, demanding to know what all the ruckus was about.

When Bronte started to answer them, Jack's big hand clamped over her mouth again.

"Shut up," he growled. "We've got to get out of here before the cops show up."

"I don't see why you're so afraid."

"You didn't spend five years in prison."

"I forgot about your record. This is all your fault, isn't it?"

His lips thinned. He grabbed her by the waist and hauled her bodily to his truck. "No, honey, it's yours. That trigger-happy slimeball is after you."

"No. It's not what you think."

"I'm sure it's a hell of a lot worse."

"Hey, you! Did you guys see anything?" a male voice called out to them from the dark.

Bronte whirled.

"Just get in the truck," Jack ordered.

"My things. They're all over the ground. I can't just leave—"

"Forget them."

His rudeness was making her mad. She'd nearly been shot, and he was blaming her!

When he opened the heavy truck door, she began to fight him again. He jammed her against the truck, imprisoning her with his body.

In that shadowy darkness everything about him—the muscles she felt bulging beneath his shirt and tight jeans, the hellish belligerence of his rugged features—shouted low class, barrio background, ex-con, dangerous.

"I—I don't want to go anywhere with you," she cried. "I'm sick of you."

"Ditto." Then with a dark scowl, he spanned her small waist with his hands and shoved her inside. He jumped in, too. She scooted across the slick seat and would have grabbed her door handle, but his hand manacled her wrist and yanked her back across the cab. "You gonna make me hog-tie you?" His voice was low and frighteningly intimate. He leaned closer, so close she felt that hot, unwanted prickle of awareness even before his warm breath hit the flesh of her throat. "Remember how you used to beg me to tie you?"

"No...." She didn't remember any of the sick, terrible things he was always alluding to. Shocked to the core, she didn't want to. She didn't want to have any more to do with him.

His face was an expressionless mask, his body perfectly still. With one hand he clamped her wrists together. His angry leer caused a freezing, burning sensation that held her motionless. "I could use my belt," he said. "I bet you'd like that."

"Just let me go."

His eyes smoldered for a long, charged moment, the dark irises almost entirely obliterated by the black of his pupils.

"Please," she whispered.

He released her wrists and started the ignition. "Stay put. Or I swear I'll do it."

"Jack…"

He turned. In the dark his heavy lids only half hid the blaze of those infinitely black pupils. With a lover's skill, he brushed his hand down the length of her arm. Then his fingers skimmed the undersides of her breasts, reminding her of the intimacies they had shared only a few hours ago. When he spoke, the chilling, sexual inflection was back in his husky voice. "Will you be good? Or do you want me to tie you? Like I said, I will…"

In that fraction of a second, before she got some of her nerve back and skittered to her side and began snapping on her seat belt, she began to burn with shame and some unnamed, never-suspected secret, sensual need.

A wild, thrilling shiver raced through her as she contemplated him tying her.

Then something cold curled deep inside her.

Terrified, she realized she didn't know who she was. Or what she felt for this man. Or where this dangerous relationship would lead.

He had bedded her. He had served time in prison for murder. What kind of man married a woman like Mischief? Even if he hadn't killed her, twelve people had believed him capable of it. Probably more than twelve. What else was he capable of?

Dear God. She had to get away from him as soon as possible.

Later, as Bronte stared moodily out her window at the flying scenery, she realized that if he hadn't yanked her out of that bathroom window when he

had, the bullet would have lodged in her brain instead
of that wooden wall.

Maybe he hated her.

Maybe she wanted to hate him.

But upon occasion, his timing was superb.

Jack's palms were embedded with gravel. His
whole body was sweaty and his gut ached—and not
from hunger.

He was in a state of acute agitation. Shock. He'd
nearly died this morning because of her.

She wasn't worth it.

He had to send her packing—*pronto.*

Jack's window was rolled down, but the warm,
early evening air that blew against his face and
smelled of grass and cattle neither cooled him nor
relaxed him.

His hands were clenched on the steering wheel. His
spine throbbed from sitting so long, driving so long
with her. He caught the scent of gardenias.

Texas.

The state was too damned big. At least it seemed
so today, even though he'd driven like a madman.

Forget last night.

Forget her.

Nothing's changed.

Yeah. Right.

Forget the best lay of his life.

It had been more than that.

No.

Forget the hurt in her voice and eyes afterward
when he'd been such a bastard.

Memories of her body joined to his flickered in and
out of focus.

Forget how he'd felt when he'd seen that bullet hole in the wall and realized how close she'd come to dying.

He couldn't forget. Especially when she was sitting beside him, still looking hurt and lost and scared.

Not when he could still remember so vividly the feel of her naked, silky skin under his callused palms. Not when he could still remember how she'd arched up to meet his every thrust, how she'd gloved him so tightly again and again, pulling him deeper and deeper, her thighs closing tight around his hips.

Damn it.

She'd felt so right.

She'd never felt like that before.

He'd been married to her for years.

But only this once had the blending of their bodies ever included their souls.

How could he think that?

Early this morning she'd looked so pretty when she'd come into the bathroom when he'd been shaving. Her hair had been a bramble bush of disorganized curls, but her eyes had shone with that special tenderness that tore his heart out.

She'd been wearing his T-shirt, and she'd looked so damned sexy he'd remembered that sweet kiss she'd stolen in the dark. He'd almost pulled her into his arms and done it to her again right there against the bathroom wall.

Instead he'd pushed past her and stormed outside. He'd slept in the truck. The next time he'd seen her, she'd been backing out of the bathroom window.

God, she had him on the ragged edge.

All day they'd been in the truck together.

It seemed to Jack like it had taken them forever to cross Texas.

But here they were, barreling down the last ten-mile stretch of narrow blacktop.

He hadn't used anything last night. She could be pregnant again.

He was a fool. The worst sort of fool.

The narrow ranch road had never seemed this endless.

He wanted to be alone.

He needed to think about the ranch. About what Theodora would do once she had her precious daughter back. Who would she choose to run things now? Chantal? Maverick? Or him?

All he could think of was Chantal.

When he'd said they were nearly home, she'd put her terror and hurt aside and stared out at the view of sky and pasture and oil wells. She was looking up at the huge black buzzards that spiraled over the open pastures, riding the wind currents on their wide, seemingly motionless wings. When she tired of the vultures, she smiled at the red Santa Gertrudis cattle grazing on the sparse brown grass growing between the oak motts and rusting oil tanks.

South Texas was a land of mesquite and sand, of prickly pear and chaparral, of vast sky and brush country, of cowboys and cattle. It was hardly beautiful. At least not to the untrained eye.

But it was home and, therefore, beautiful to Jack.

The subtle lure of this wild, flat land drew him back again and again.

Chantal had always hated the ranch.

Until today.

He remembered the last night in the barn. Somebody had hit him from behind with a two-by-four, locked him inside and set the building on fire.

Until today he'd always thought it was her.

Today she looked innocent and guilt free.

She laughed when a flock of flustered wild turkeys ran back and forth in front of the truck, their tails fluttering like ballerinas' skirts. Jack slowed his pickup as they waited for one turkey to get up the gumption to fly. When one did, they all sailed clumsily over the low fence to safety. All except one lost Tom. This big bird ran back and forth along the fence line, too stupid and frantic to fly.

"Oh, Jack," Chantal said in a worried voice. "Stop! I want to see if he makes it!"

"Since when have you ever given a damn about wildlife?"

Confusion and hurt filled her eyes. She swallowed and looked down.

If she kept up this act, she would thwart his plan to convince Carla and Theodora that she was the last thing they needed.

Even though Chantal had insisted on sharing the driving, Jack was bone tired. He was sick to death of thinking about her and all the consequences her return might have.

He wanted the ranch.

He wanted her gone.

What was he going to do about this wife he didn't want to want? This wife who was besting him on every front? He felt all mixed-up.

Chantal probably knew she had him.

No touching, she'd reminded him.

Hell, he'd devoured her.

Hell, every time he looked at her, he was hungry for more of the same.

Odd how he couldn't think of one time when it had ever been like this between them before. Never once had he kept on craving her afterward.

He'd grown up in Mexico, despised because his mother was a whore. Even when Theodora had brought him to the ranch, he'd still been an outcast. Prison had been even worse. He'd begun to wonder if he'd ever belong anywhere.

Making love to Chantal last night had been like finally coming home—for the first time in his life. Finally he'd felt like he belonged somewhere—to someone. He had no clue that sex could be more than the satisfaction of a bodily itch, that it could be the touching and joining of two hearts.

Damn her.

He despised himself for wanting that feeling again.

Sitting beside her in the cab all day, acting grim and sullen every time she asked him the least little favor or question, had been sheer torture.

He wanted her tonight. Every night.

She was on the run from a killer.

They both had more important worries than sex. She'd let him bed her, too. She probably wanted to wind him tighter and tighter before she played him for a fool. He remembered her malevolent expression right before she'd hit him with that stone cat.

That was the real Chantal.

He had to stay away from her. Period.

The closer they got to the house, the more he thought about their living arrangements. In the past, they'd shared the large bedroom at the back of the big house. It had a wide balcony and a view of the lawns and pasture that swept down to the bay. He'd been living in it these past few months.

Separate bedrooms, she'd said. Separate houses.

He shoved his booted foot down hard on the accelerator. Chantal shifted in her seat with a look of surprise when they stopped in front of the gate. He leaned out and punched in ten numbers on the tiny keypad beside the road. As the gate backed away in slow motion, she stared up at the fifteen-foot-high stucco arch with the huge gold letters that read El Atascadero as if she'd never seen it before.

A guard came out of his trailer and waved them through.

Jack nodded. "*Buenas noches,* Bucho."

She waved at Bucho, too.

In the past she'd never done that.

So why this fake friendliness now?

How come she gave that little gasp of surprise and sat up taller when they topped a low rise, and the big house loomed above a thicket of mesquite like a Moorish castle?

He remembered that same look of surprise on her face that first day in New York when she'd claimed her name was Brooke or Bronte.

"What's the matter?"

"Oh, nothing," she said quietly. "It's been a long time."

"What has you so all-fired eager? Your family? Or your lovers?"

Her chin inched up a notch, and a haunted vagueness came into her luminous eyes. Suddenly he felt guilty again as he took a curve too fast.

The driveway arced around a planting of tall palms, a majestic live oak and the bell tower. He braked near

the huge garage that stored tractors and cars and
housed his office. Bougainvillea, scarlet and dense,
bloomed from dozens of terra-cotta pots that marched
up the staircase to the main house. Wide concrete
steps that had been painted red led up to a screened
verandah. Another set of stairs led down beneath a
covered archway to the kitchen.

A short distance beyond the house a group of ragged, brown men stood in the deep shade of the palms.
When they saw Jack, the tallest waved his dirty straw
hat.

Good old Ernesto. He was an Indian of singular
stature. A born leader, he was at least six feet tall,
bullet-headed with a thatch of black hair, wide shouldered and reed thin. He swam the river at least half-
a-dozen times a year. Jack didn't remember the
others, but from the looks of the them, they'd probably walked all the way from central Mexico without
a bite to eat.

Jack could empathize. He'd never forget how it felt
to go hungry.

Desperate for work, they walked up from the border. The pipeline easement that ran north and south
across El Atascadero was their highway, at least till
they made it north of the Sarita checkpoint, where
their friends could pick them up and carry them to
the bigger cities and work in *el norte*. All over Mexico, at every post office, long lines of women dressed
in black, their bowed heads draped in shawls, would
be posting letters to these husbands and brothers and
sons who had to leave them behind for months and
years to work in *el norte*. Mexico's bad economy and
young and exploding population made such illegal
trafficking of human beings virtually a necessity.

Jack waved back to them. He'd deal with them later.

When Bronte saw them, her eyes grew huge with fear. Almost instantly, as she realized their desperate plight, her face softened, and with a timid smile, she waved, too.

When she grabbed her door handle, Jack caught her arm.

"Chantal…"

At his touch, stark pain glittered in her eyes. Then she composed herself and glared at his bruising hand. "Rule number one," she said very calmly.

His jaw clenched guiltily when he remembered what he'd done when she'd said that the night before. "Right."

With a supreme effort of will he relaxed his fingers. White-faced, she stared back at him.

"If you so much as look," he began, "at another man—"

"Why would you care? The only reason you're bringing me home is because of the precious ranch."

"That's right." But his scowl deepened, and his blood beat violently in his temple. Suddenly he wanted to make love to her again. Right here in the cab. He didn't give a damn about the ranch. He didn't care that they were parked in front of the mansion and that anyone could see.

"I don't care what you do with other men," he stated. "Or which one of your rejected lovers is after you."

She hesitated, somehow sensing the true emotion beneath his words. "Look, I said I wouldn't…" Her voice shook. Almost, she seemed to be a real human being in that moment. Though she tried to hide it, her hand trembled on the handle.

"You will!"

"Are you jealous, Jack?"

"Jealous? Of you? No way." But her question stabbed him as sharply as a well-placed needle. "Nothing's changed!" he persisted. "And you'd better stay away from Carla. I won't have you playing your new tricks on her the way you're playing them on me."

Bronte cracked her door.

"I'm not finished with you. Don't be playing your tricks on anybody else around here, either."

Bronte ignored him and jumped clear of the truck. When she raced past the house, toward the clump of men under the palms, he watched her with a growing wariness.

What the hell was she up to now?

At first the men seemed hesitant with her. Then shy smiles broke out on their young, emaciated faces. They gestured toward the kitchen. She nodded, obviously promising them food.

Never before had Chantal taken the slightest interest in the plight of the starving Mexicans. She called them wetbacks. Once she'd even called the border patrol.

His estranged wife was surprising him at every turn.

Jack hurled himself out of the car.

She was speaking Spanish. He caught an awkward vowel pronunciation he had never heard before.

Even her Spanish was different.

Her syntax was formal, textbook Spanish. She had the typical, bad gringo accent that she used to mimic.

Chantal had grown up on the ranch where everybody spoke Tex-Mex. *Pocho,* the Mexicans derisively called it. Her grammar was horrendous, her vocabulary local slang.

Jack had hardly had time to recover from her shocking kindness and bizarre Castillian phrases before Guerro, Jack's golden lab, bounded toward her, barking ferociously. The Mexicans all cowered around Chantal for protection.

As if Chantal would protect them. She hated dogs. Guerro had detested her since she'd run over him when he'd been a puppy and then driven away.

Jack rushed to stop his dog. "Guerro! Stay, boy!"

"Shh," Bronte whispered. She turned calmly from the men and faced Guerro as he lunged. "Nobody's going to hurt you, big fella."

The dog's ears pricked up in confusion. As she continued to croon, his barking softened to a low whine. Although the hair on his neck remained spiked, his tail began to wag.

She'd charmed him the way she and Cheyenne had once charmed snakes.

Bronte extended her hand toward Guerro, all the while smiling. "Come on, big fella. Let's be friends."

"When have you ever wanted to be friends with my dog?" Jack yelled, letting go of his fury now as she petted the big dog behind his ears, reducing Guerro to slave-like adoration.

As she'd reduced him to submissive adoration last night.

Jack felt rage as the stupid dog sloppily licked Chantal's long, slim fingers.

Bronte laughed when Guerro's tail speeded up. Then she looked up at Jack, her beautiful face pert with triumph. "Today I want to be friends. And Guerro is smart enough to know it—even if you aren't."

She shot Jack a smile that would have melted the layer of ice around any other man's heart.

Damn her. She used sex, her beauty, even Guerro to best him at every turn.

She laughed when Guerro's big tongue lapped her nose. Her shining eyes, her bright hair, her glowing face—everything about her caught Jack's heart and charmed and enraged him.

Bronte's smile died. "Jack, these men are very hungry. Do we have some food?"

"You know damn well I always feed these men."

In rapid Spanish he told the men food would be forthcoming, but they were all looking at her.

Then, swearing beneath his breath, he grabbed Chantal's arm. "I said no more tricks, damn you."

"What's wrong now?"

"These men! My dog! You never liked dogs."

"Why do you want me to be as mean and bad as you say I used to be?"

"You may have a pretty new face, but people like you don't change. Not down deep, where it counts."

"Okay. I'm a witch." She flashed the Mexicans an ear-to-ear smile. *"Bruja."* Her warm green eyes sparkled mischievously.

The men shouted, *"No. No, Señorita Angel."*

"These men are starving," she said. "And so am I. Why wouldn't you stop on the road when I begged—"

"Because I didn't know who might be following us."

Because I didn't want to risk another night alone with you.

"Can we eat now?"

"Yes," Jack grumbled.

"How generous of you, darling."

The endearment stung. He was about to lash out at her, but she was quicker. "Do you remember our last rule, Jack darling? *My* rule?"

Suddenly the very air between them was electric.

Don't call me darling, he almost yelled. But he didn't want to make the starving men think he was mad at them.

While he glowered, Bronte said to the men in her peculiar and yet endearing Spanish, "He's my husband. This is our second honeymoon. If he wants me back, you'd think he would at least try to be nice."

"I don't want you back."

Gray-faced, Jack stomped down the kitchen stairs. Fast on his heels, Bronte followed him.

Suddenly, finding himself inside the house with her, he thought of his bedroom upstairs. They were husband and wife. Everybody would expect her to move in with him. He thought of waking up every morning to the sight of fiery red hair on the next pillow. To the smell of wild gardenias. To the knowledge that her satiny warm body lay next to his. To the knowledge that she was always hot for it and available any hour of the day or night.

He wanted that.

No way.

She was the same with every man.

The ranch was a big place.

Where…?

Shanghai's cabin.

Jack had never set foot in it because he'd never felt strong enough to deal with his misgivings about his father.

Years ago Theodora had boarded the shack up.

"Till you're ready to get to know Shanghai," Theodora had said once. "Nobody's going to touch the old place till then."

"What about Garth?" he had asked.

"Garth's mother made him hate Shanghai. You know he thinks he's too good…"

The shack was badly in need of repairs. Pieces of stucco had fallen loose. The porch was sagging. There was no phone. The weeds around it were neck high.

Upon occasion Theodora had tried to shake Jack with guilt. "You ought to take better car of your daddy's place. He'd want—"

"I don't give a damn what he'd want."

Everything was different now.

The shack was a palace compared to the hovel Jack had grown up in. Dealing with his father's ghost was nothing compared to living with Chantal.

Before they reached the kitchen, he grabbed her in the dark hall and shoved her against the wall.

"Why are you bothering to pretend?" His eyes narrowed contemptuously into ice-black slits.

She tipped her chin up and met his gaze.

Ruthlessly he scanned her guileless features. Then his expression grew even darker. "You don't give a damn about those men."

She bristled with outrage. It took all his determination to ignore the quivering in her quiet tone. "Maybe if you weren't determined to see me as a monster, you'd see the person I really am."

"What's that supposed to mean?"

"You figure it out." She pushed him in the ribs and backed three steps toward the kitchen.

"And what the hell's the matter with your Spanish? You sound like you learned it in grade school instead of—"

"It's a bit rusty," she snapped hastily. "I took a class. To improve my grammar."

Before he could reply, Eva was there, her body huge and ponderous, her glowing skin as golden-brown as maple syrup, her stained white apron carrying with it the smells of the kitchen. Someone had told her Chantal had returned—looking different, it was true—but still the same woman underneath the changed exterior.

"Hello." Bronte smiled dazzlingly at the ranch cook.

Eva frowned in confusion.

"There're a dozen hungry men outside. They've walked all the way from Mexico," Bronte said pleadingly.

That stopped Eva dead in her tracks. Chantal had always scorned her in the past, as she had the poor starving Mexicans on their way north. Eva, who was loyal to the mistress and the ranch, had kept her distance and her silence when it came to the mistress's daughter.

Eva flushed. But as she studied Bronte's sincere face and then the sudden tightness of Jack's jaw, a puzzled look softened her huge dark eyes.

Eva had had a hard life. She'd married a gambler of roguish charm whose loser's luck kept them broke. Eva found her joy by savoring the little things. She could stand a full minute with one of her cats, watching a bee buzz in a red bougainvillea blossom; she could stand longer than that in front of her oven to enjoy the scent of fresh rolls baking. She had raised a houseful of children and had more than a dozen grandchildren.

She liked the sparkle of sunlight in dish suds as much as a grander woman might admire the fire of a diamond. She found joy in feeding hungry men. Her father had been such a man.

And Eva saw something shining in this girl's face that was as true and beautiful as the pure love that always radiated from her favorite granddaughter.

"Well, I'll be. You're the last person I'd ever expect a kindness from. But maybe you got more than a new face, after all."

"I'm sorry, Eva, if I was—"

"Don't." More softly, she continued, "Your mama. She's been mighty worried. She's got the whole world on her shoulders. I expect you'll be a joy to her. Won't she be, Don Jack?"

"Oh, don't ask his opinion," his wife said. "He's determined to hate me forever."

"He brought you back, didn't he?" Eva said, disappearing into the kitchen.

"Not because he wanted to."

"Oh, you know Jack, he only pretends he's made of stone."

Jack didn't like them talking about him like he wasn't there. Maybe he should find Mario and get some details on those infertile bulls. Then his stomach growled, and he remembered he hadn't eaten, either.

Jack shook his head. He was crazy to risk another minute in Chantal's bewitching presence.

Hell's bells. He stomped into the kitchen and opened the refrigerator. Just as he was about to grab a drumstick off a pile of fried chicken, Chantal reached past him and grabbed the entire platter.

He ate a peanut butter sandwich in silence, gloomily pretending to ignore the generous spread of fried chicken and potato salad and beans that she piled onto tray after tray, pretending he wasn't the least bit interested in having a piece or two or a bowl or two of the beans and salad himself.

She could have at least offered him something.

All he had to do was ask, of course, but pride stopped him.

The Chantal of old would have begrudged those pitiful men every single bite.

This Chantal—

She was the same.

Nothing had changed.

Chapter 14

"She's trouble with a capital *T*. Nobody wants that bitch back but you!"

"What I want counts, and don't you forget it. I run this place. I was running El Atascadero when the rest of you were in diapers or living thousands of miles away."

"I want her back, too!" The indignant, childish cry pierced the quiet as well as Bronte's heart.

A long, smoldering silence followed. Bronte's blood ran hot and then cold as she climbed the stairs. The family sounded every bit as difficult as Jack.

It wasn't long before the angry outbursts resumed. The name Chantal rang out several more times.

"She's my daughter. I, and only I, will decide if she goes or stays."

Bronte froze. What had she done? What was she doing, walking into this minefield that had nothing to do with who she really was?

To save herself from the man who'd tried to kill her, she'd told a lie, and then lived that lie for two days and nights. She'd even slept with another woman's husband. And now...

Why couldn't it feel like an adventure? Why did she feel ashamed and a little afraid?

She dug her fingertips into the waxed wood railing. How could she face them?

Jack's hand found the small of her back. None too gently, he nudged her up the stairs. "Go on. You might as well get it over with. They'll settle down once they've seen you."

"But—"

"It isn't like you to be afraid," he jeered. "I'm sure you'll probably charm the socks off them—the same as you've—"

She whirled, wondering what he meant by that.

For a heartbeat they stared at each other.

Even that brief glance at his dark, movie-star face and long lean body had her skin prickling hotly. He tensed, too, as if he couldn't look at her, either, without a similar unwanted reaction.

"You have a funny way of acting charmed."

"I didn't mean it like it sounded!" But his explosive denial came too quickly and was followed by a rush of color to his face.

It was chemical. Inexplicable. Unwanted by both of them. Unimportant. Still, she found him too sexy for words.

He'd been equally sexy this morning when she'd stumbled into him in the bathroom as he'd been about to shave.

He'd whirled, and she'd gasped, some part of her longing to rush into his arms and confess the truth, hoping he'd stop hating her and want her. "I—I thought you were outside. I didn't hear you come back insi—"

His shirt had been off and his jaw dark from a night's growth of beard. Standing there, he'd seemed a symbol of dark, seductive passion. Her mesmerized gaze had fastened on the network of muscles across his brown chest.

"I'm going," he'd growled as he'd grabbed his shirt and raced past her. He'd flung the door open and forgotten to close it in his haste to get away from her. She'd heard his truck door open and slam.

She'd gone to the doorway and paused, one palm on the edge of the door, the other on the doorjamb as she stared at his slumped form in his pickup for a long moment. Then, sorrowfully, she'd returned to the bathroom. That time her gaze had flicked to the tiny window, and she'd known she had to use it to escape. She'd decided to leave him because she'd started to care too much.

Playing his awful wife when she found him attractive was getting harder and harder to do.

"Keep moving." His cold smile jolted her back to the present.

Her head drooped. "All right."

The upper floors were as cool and dark as the kitchen. Everything seemed immense and strange. The angry voices were a low rumble now, each person straining to outdramatize the other.

"The men don't want Jack back. He's got them running scared with his constant talk about labor costs, spreadsheets and net profit. They've watched all the other big ranchers around here go back on the promises their granddaddies made to their granddaddies. They've seen whole families of loyal ranch hands kicked out of homes their families have lived in for fifty years, homes they thought they would stay in for another fifty.''

''The ranchers are fighting to survive. It's hard to give people rent-free housing forever these days.''

''We could subdivide a few acres, sell off some of that worthless—''

''Over my dead body!''

Then Jack's drawl sounded behind Bronte. ''High drama as usual. Funny how your folks can get along till you throw millions of dollars on the table or force them to face extreme economic realities. Every year is harder than the last one. I've been trying to make them see that things aren't the same as they used to be. That's a hard pill to swallow when you've been born and raised to do things a certain way. Then I go and bring you back from the dead to claim what some of them have been thinking might be theirs. So try to understand if they seem a little panicky, *darling*.''

Bronte's stomach knotted. ''How do you feel, Jack?''

''My only claim is through you, *darling,* so my opinion doesn't count. But it sounds like your aunt Caroline, Maverick, Becky, Cheyenne and Theodora are plenty steamed up.''

Bronte's pace had slowed on the stairs again. If only she'd been able to get away from Jack at the motel. These weren't her problems. This wasn't her life. He wasn't her husband. How long could she possibly fool Theodora and these other people? Why should she even try?

She walked slower and slower till finally, on the

second-story landing, Bronte came to a total stand-
still.

"Nervous? Or is it Theodora's renovations you
can't get used to?"

Renovations? Everything looked and smelled old,
Bronte thought.

"I'll go ahead," Jack said as he led her through a
series of cool, dark rooms lit only by the fading afternoon light.

"You remember how your mother is so tight about
spending her money?" Jack said. "Well, she's gotten
worse."

The rooms were large and grandiose, but boxy and
unimaginatively designed. In each, tall windows faced
east to catch the prevailing breezes. Wide doors
opened onto shady porches and balconies with views
of the ranch and the bay.

Her mother's brownstone had been grander. As
Bronte looked at the heavy antiques, at the sombre
family portraits, the drapes, the Aubusson rugs, she
tried to memorize every detail. At the same time she
struggled to act as if she were familiar with the house
and its routines.

Its strangeness oppressed her.

The house was dark and cold. Like her husband, it
seemed reluctant to reveal its secrets to her.

"I've fought Theodora on some of the changes.
But you know your mother. When she's set on a
thing, she won't listen."

Bronte nodded.

Jack pointed toward the fireplace, where the grim
portrait of a man with a long white beard hung.
"Your great-grandfather was just as stubborn. Still,
he was one hell of an empire builder even if he did

have a rather limited imagination when it came to designing houses. He wanted to build something grandiose to impress the neighbors. He had this big ranch; he wanted a big house. You can't do all that much with a house like this. Not when it's so pure Victorian. Theodora went absolutely crazy when I suggested tearing it down and building something modern. She's equally determined to keep the ranch and its traditions the way that old man said they should be.''

Bronte nodded.

''I've fought her pretty hard, but he rules from the grave. Trouble is, no man's vision is all that keen once he's been underground a spell. Things change. His ideas were good in his time, but we can't keep this place going by following a dead man's dictates. She doesn't want to be the one to sell even one acre of land and let the family or the ranch down. His traditions are both her legacy and her burden.''

''But if the others want to sell—''

''She's in control. She cares more about him than she does about the modern family. When a powerful, hard-willed man with a vision takes you out on horseback before dawn when you're barely four, it's easy to be brainwashed. It doesn't mean a damn to her that we've got the government breathing down our neck at every turn—about everything from endangered-species laws and regulations about beef to the ranch's ever-increasing tax burdens. But back to his house. None of the modern family likes living in this old white elephant, and it's proved impossible to remodel.''

For once Bronte agreed with him. The house was too big and drafty. Suddenly she wanted to open the thick draperies and the windows, too. She wanted to run outside into the evening light, to climb that magnificent tree out back and be free.

Even as she longed for freedom, the library door swung open and a tall, elegantly dressed man with golden hair loomed on the threshold. An inch or two shorter than Jack, he was dressed Western-style in jeans and boots and a snow-white Stetson, but his boots shone and his clothes were crisp and new. He was not nearly so formidable or masculine as the rougher-cut Jack. No, this man's features were somehow too properly in place, his teeth too straight, his ears too flat against his well-shaped head. Only there were lines of dissipation beneath his eyes, and his mouth looked a little hard as if his boyish charm was wearing a bit thin as he aged.

He frowned when he saw her. Even so, he took a few steps toward her.

Bronte shrank into the darkest shadows and tried to hide from him.

"Well, who do we have here?" Maverick's too-hearty voice bellowed when he caught sight of her lurking under the stairwell. "Come out of that dark corner so your favorite kissing cousin can welcome you home."

A stillness descended upon her.

Cousins. Childhood playmates.

Lovers.

A sickening knot formed in Bronte's stomach. Even if Jack hadn't stared warningly at her as he gripped her elbow and steered her past the flirtatious Maverick, she would have wanted nothing to do with this overly familiar cousin.

Everyone except a redheaded little girl stood up as she entered.

Bronte felt their eyes on her face, and self-conscious guilt burned inside her, eating away at her natural friendliness, causing her posture to stiffen. They thought she belonged here. But she didn't.

On one wall there were tall oak bookshelves, on an opposite wall ten male heads. To avoid the living people's stares, Bronte studied the stern, bearded faces that hung, painted and friezelike, in heavy golden frames.

"Unbelievable," the tall, slim, redhead who had to be her half sister, Cheyenne, said.

"It can't be her, Jack," said a plump girl with a pretty face and shiny brown curls.

"Believe me, Becky, she's Chantal," Jack said heavily.

Bronte felt thick waves of dislike radiating from everyone except possibly Cheyenne, who merely studied her disbelievingly.

"New face or not, it's her," Jack asserted. "So she's got this beautiful new facade. Take a good long look till you get used to it. I know I had to. Then it'll come to you that underneath, she's still the same. This shouldn't be such a shock. After all, you sent me after her."

For a second or two longer, everyone stood frozen like actors in a bad play. Then a small, dark figure with a halo of silver hair detached itself from the group and hobbled toward Bronte.

Jack leaned closer to Bronte. "Now don't you be playing your tricks on your mother, either."

Theodora's sharp, curious eyes assessed Bronte and then Jack. "Don't just stand there, Chantal dear.

Come over here where I can see you. I'm afraid my old eyes aren't what they used to be. Neither are my legs.''

Bronte turned quickly, but it took her a second to find the older woman's face in the gloom. She had instinctively aimed her gaze too high. The woman whose mere voice exuded raw power and authority was surprisingly small in size. Theodora had halted in the middle of a bar of purple light that one of the long, stained-glass windows splashed on the carpet, and in that merciless cascade, the lines on her weathered face seemed as harshly and unapologetically etched as those of a Plains Indian.

Although Bronte felt a strange reluctance to leave Jack, everyone gasped in amazement when she rushed to embrace the older woman.

Cheyenne quickly excused herself. ''I have to go.'' She made a hasty exit after a word or two to Jack.

Only the little girl, who was scribbling wildly on her large tablet again, failed to watch Bronte.

The undemonstrative Theodora hugged Chantal as fiercely as she herself was being hugged.

Jack stared at them in amazement as the embrace went on and on. Finally, several minutes later, Theodora shot Jack a smile. ''I never thought...I never dreamed you could find her.''

Then she hugged her daughter again.

Something wasn't right, Jack thought. Mother and daughter had never been like this.

''You wonderful boy. It's a miracle, Jack. Too wonderful to believe,'' Theodora continued.

Yes, it was too wonderful to believe.

''But you did it.'' Theodora gripped Bronte's hand. ''Welcome home, my dear. You are beautiful. Truly beautiful. But…your new face is going to take some getting used to. You are, as I'm sure you know, quite changed.''

''Yes. I don't feel quite like I'm me, either.''

''I've been lonely these past five years.''

''I…'' What could Bronte say? She knew all about loneliness. Suddenly she saw that pretending to be this woman's daughter was unforgivable. She had to tell her the truth. ''You know, I—''

Theodora's grip tightened. Before Bronte could confess, she rushed to speak. ''Everything I've ever endured has been worth it…to have you home. Safe and sound.''

Jack shifted uneasily. He was thinking of the heat and drought and bad cattle prices, of the faithless husband and the wild, hell-bent daughter this old woman had endured. Not to mention the ungrateful half-Mexican boy she'd adopted and educated even when everybody, especially he, had fought her every step of the way.

Jack was willing to hide his misgivings about the ranch's future and this reunion and give Theodora a moment or two to celebrate. Still, he noted Maverick's sulky glare and Becky's jealous glances and Carla's frown as she scribbled more frantically.

''You used to call me Mama,'' Theodora was saying.

''Mama.''

Suddenly, Carla shot the pair a furious, pain-glazed glance.

The bill of Carla's blue baseball cap was cocked at a defiant angle and turned sideways. She had a pugnacious nose, and her red hair was tied back in a tangled ponytail.

As the child stared at her, Bronte felt the years slide backwards, and an odd excitement began to churn inside her. Looking at Carla was like staring into a mirror when she herself had been ten. She saw Jimmy in the girl's face, too, and wondered if he wouldn't have looked something like her at the same age.

"Did you bring me a present?" Carla asked.

"I—I'm afraid I left New York in a hurry."

Without a word the little girl suddenly turned back to her drawing and began to chew her pencil tip.

Bronte flushed. "Maybe we could go shopping...together."

"You always brought me presents!"

"I'm sorry."

"Carla!" Jack said.

I have no right to be here. I don't belong here. These are real people. This is a real little girl. I've hurt her.

When Carla's pencil dug into the tablet again, her curly red tangles sparked like angry fire in the lamplight.

Just like Jimmy's had.

Carla's defiant eyes were like Jimmy's, too.

While Carla was pale, Jimmy had had rosy cheeks and a husky body. Jack's daughter was pathetically thin, and her jeans were so stained and rumpled Bronte wondered how long she'd been wearing them. And how long had it been since anyone had run a brush through that ponytail?

The child was *motherless*.

Bronte was *childless*.

They were a match.

No. Bronte was a fraud.

Maverick came up to hug and kiss her. As he bent

his perfectly combed, blond head to Bronte's, his firm
dry lips claiming hers in a perfunctory kiss, she
fought to squirm free. But Maverick caught her hands
in his own and slid them down the front of his body
in a too-suggestive manner. "We always were…kiss-
ing cousins," he whispered. "We shared a cradle, if
you know what I mean."

Panic mixed with fury as she pushed at him.

"You never used to be this way," he said, his
voice deceptively soft, his breath hot on her face for
a second before his mouth closed over hers again.

"Take your hands off my wife before I break your
neck."

Maverick released his supposed cousin in an instant. "I didn't mean anything. Why, hell, Jack, you
never used to care."

"Well, I care now. Come here, Chantal."

Bronte scuttled back to Jack, who ruthlessly studied
her innocent face before pushing her behind him.
"You probably love me making a fool of myself
over…"

She went white.

Jack jerked away from her. "I need some air."
From the door, he said with self-derision, "Sorry. I
almost lost it. I'd better check with Mario on how
roundup is going. See about those infertile bulls. And
the other stuff…while the rest of you enjoy getting
reacquainted." Mockery and tension underlined his
every word.

Then he stormed out into the hall, with Becky chasing after him.

And Bronte, her hands clenched at her sides, was
left to deal with *her* family.

"Where's Eva? I thought she made fried chicken,"

Maverick said, sliding his arm around Bronte and daring a flirtatious smile.

"Right here, Don Maverick." Eva padded breathlessly toward him, carrying a silver tray loaded with peanut-butter-and-Ritz-cracker sandwiches. Becky returned to the library, carrying a second tray with drinks.

When Bronte, anxious to rid herself of Maverick, rushed forward to help Becky, everyone watched her as, together, the two women set the tray down without spilling a single drop of iced tea or coffee.

When Bronte started lifting plates and glasses and cups, Maverick edged her away. "What happened to the fried chicken, Eva?"

"Why, your cousin, Doña Chantal, fed it all to those starving men from Mexico—"

"She what?" Maverick sounded both shocked and alarmed.

Feeling hemmed in by all their questions and stares, Bronte lifted another glass from the tray. "I'm sorry, Maverick. They looked so pitiful and hungry."

With a withering glare of sour disapproval, he reached for a sandwich. "This is stale and soggy," Maverick complained sulkily.

"I'm sorry," Bronte repeated.

Her apology brought a long, grumpy stare.

Stifling a nervous yawn, Bronte moved across the room to the largest chair. Sinking into it, she laid her head back.

Their gazes followed, and their mild surprise was now shock.

For one paralyzing second Bronte wondered what she'd done wrong now. Since she had no idea that Theodora was most particular about where she sat or stood in any room, and that she had a particular chair or spot everywhere, Bronte didn't know that she had chosen *her* chair.

Without a word Theodora sank onto the sofa near Bronte. "I'm starved," the old woman said mildly.

The moment passed.

Still, Bronte felt the tensions around her mounting. She kept making mistakes at every turn.

Suddenly she wished for her own face. For Wimberley. Why couldn't she be sitting at her old dinette set in her kitchen with her calendars and lesson plans thumbtacked to the walls, with Pogo purring on her lap?

She almost wished for the numbness and grief she'd felt after Jimmy's funeral and the divorce.

"I remember how you used to love iced tea," Theodora said rather too quickly. "Carla, I said come over here and greet your mother. You're so skinny, she's gonna think we've been starving you."

"I'm not hungry."

Bronte's throat went dry, but when she lifted a glass, she suddenly paused, wondering what Chantal put in her tea. Sugar or lemon? Neither? Maybe a diet sweetener?

Just as she was about to set her glass back down, Theodora quickly handed her a pink envelope and a slice of lime.

Bronte tore the envelope and squeezed the lime, thanking Theodora silently for the clue as the older woman poured bourbon from a silver flask into a glass of tea.

"Carla…"

Carla threw down her scratch pad. "I won't sit by her! You can't make me!"

As the child was about to stomp past them, she saw a teaspoon on the carpet. On her way out, she picked it up and tossed it onto the table at Bronte.

Bronte picked up the spoon and then set it back down. Very slowly she got up and gathered the little girl's sketchbook and pencils.

Time faltered as she saw her own features and Theodora's scrawled on the white tablet. Bronte traced the vivid black lines with a shaky fingertip. With what cruel and yet clever talent had her lovely face been distorted into a merciless caricature. Theodora's likeness looked even worse.

She held the drawing up so everyone could see it.

The library grew soundless. Other than the ticking of the grandfather clock and the guilty beating of her own heart, Bronte heard nothing.

"I have to go see about her," Bronte said quietly.

"Why don't you give her time?" Theodora asked. "We've hardly—"

Bronte clutched the tablet. "Because she's...my daughter."

"She's been drawing those awful pictures ever since you left. She doesn't mean to be so unfriendly. Carla was very excited when Jack called her earlier. She's been running out to the verandah every five minutes. But when she saw your truck, she hid the way she used to when you first came home from one of your trips, dear—"

"She's upset. I have to see about her—"

"Why don't you let Chantal go, Theodora?" protested Caroline's kind, cultured voice. "I'm sure Carla needs her more than we do."

"Oh, all right." Theodora arose and sat in her own chair. Like a willful child she drained her iced tea laced with bourbon. ''But come back as soon as you're done.''

When Bronte was gone everybody smiled.

She was beautiful, one of them thought warily. And sweet. Still, her departure was a relief.

It was time to finish what had been started five years ago in the barn.

It was too bad about this lovely girl.

It was too bad about Jack.

Sometimes unpleasant necessities had to be rationalized.

Who was she, anyway?

She didn't belong here.

The girl's existence threatened everything.

That's why she had to die.

Chapter 15

"Chantal!" Jack's rough voice barked as Bronte raced out into the hall after Carla, who was bounding upstairs to the third floor.

Involuntarily Bronte stopped, her eyes searching a wall of grim portraits till she found Jack's tall, familiar form leaning negligently against a doorjamb. Relaxed though he appeared, she knew he was anything but calm.

"I told you to leave her alone." There was steel in his low tone.

"I thought you left to see about the ranch."

"Believe me, there're always plenty of emergencies around here. They'll keep." He straightened into a taut, upright position. "I decided my biggest problem was you."

"Or maybe," she taunted, her green eyes shining at him in the dimness, "maybe you like being around me…more than you're willing to admit."

He tensed with indignation. "I do not!"

"I remember how you looked at me this morning, when I surprised you in the bathroom," she whispered.

"You should have knocked. You caught me off guard."

"Your shirt was off." Her compelling gaze held his. "You looked...very sexy."

"Shut up."

"You were just as nasty then as you are now. But you couldn't take your eyes off me then...any more than you can now."

"I said shut—"

"Why are you always looking at me like that, Jack? Like you're starved? Like you want to eat me alive? I bet you could be sweet...if you weren't afraid to be."

"Your imagination is working overtime."

"You've given it lots of material."

"Don't flatter yourself. There's way too much wrong between us for sex to cure," he muttered savagely.

"Maybe you're not so sure of your feelings as you pretend. And...if I took a shine to you...I'd want way more than sex. I'd want you to treat me nice...all the time."

"Nice?" he sneered. "You'd be bored with nice in two seconds flat."

"Try me."

He lowered his voice significantly. "Just stay away from Carla."

For an instant longer, he stared at her. Then he walked away from her down the stairs.

She hugged herself, her feet rooted in the thick carpet. For no sane reason a secret, breathless longing filled her.

He'd dashed out of the bathroom just as abruptly. He *was* afraid of her.

Why?

Maybe they didn't want to like each other or to appeal to each other. But maybe they did, anyway.

The front door slammed. She closed her eyes briefly against the aching emptiness that assailed her, knowing he had plunged out into the blackening night.

She leaned against the wall, alone in that dark hall.

This wasn't her life.

He wasn't her husband.

She felt ashamed that she'd lied to him. Ashamed that she'd slept with him.

Maybe their having sex had been wrong.

Maybe she wasn't who he thought she was. But her new emotions felt all too real.

Maybe she had a new face. Maybe she wasn't his wife. But he had saved her. And their sex had been wild and incredible, and unforgettable.

Everything that had happened, the whole fantastic situation, was totally out of control. But maybe that was the way life was. Maybe you had to take what came and make the best of it.

Maybe none of the other stuff had been her fault, either. Maybe it was okay that she hadn't ever been able to please her mother. Maybe she shouldn't blame herself for Jimmy's death so much, either.

Maybe things just happened. Bad things. Incredible things. But good things, too.

Like Jack finding her.

Maybe Jack was her new chance, her fresh start.

Maybe she was his.

Maybe they were both too blind and foolish to see it.

Suddenly she knew that if she didn't find the way to his stubborn, intractable heart soon, he was going to teach her an entirely new meaning for the word *heartbreak.*

Fight harder, she thought. *You've got to fight harder.*

Carla hunkered lower when she heard the whine of the screen door far below before the second door slammed. She watched her father storm down the steps and wondered why he was so mad. A few minutes later the trick stair near the third-floor landing groaned. Someone was approaching her bedroom on silent feet.

An angry flush crept up Carla's neck. Was it the impostor?

If so, what did she want?

Carla glanced up at the shelves stacked with lavish dolls and exotic stuffed animals and other useless gifts her mother had given her to buy her love. After a stretch of tense silence, Carla began scribbling again.

Who did this woman think she was fooling? Carla could see straight through her. Probably everybody else could, too. Except for Grandmother.

Why was Dad protecting her? Where was Mother? Had Dad really killed her this time?

Rage and fear engulfed Carla. Then she thought about how nice he'd been these past few months, taking her out with him to work cows, trying to talk to her, listening, too. He'd been nicer than she'd ever believed he could be.

Some people still said he was guilty of murder.

Lots of people hated him....

Later. She'd think about him later.

Carla wished she'd gone out and climbed *her* tree. Sick with worry about her mother, Carla made wild black marks on her sketchpad. Her red eyebrows screwed together. Her magic pencil froze. No!

This monster wasn't any good, either.

She ripped the sheet from the tablet and brought her pencil to her lips. It was very, very naughty, and she was ashamed of it for drawing so badly.

"I'll throw you on the floor and stomp on you till your lead is broken into millions of pieces," she threatened.

The pencil wiggled, frantic.

"Okay. One more chance. But just one."

When Carla began to draw again, the pencil shaped the hideous nose more adeptly.

Who was the woman her father had brought home? This woman whose hair and eyes were the right shade of red and green? Whose creamy complexion was flawless? Dad couldn't take his eyes off her; she did look exactly like the magazine pictures Carla had collected of Mischief Jones.

How was such a thing possible? Was she a clone, like the alien in *Starman* that had taken a single hair and made himself into a copy of the heroine's husband?

Carla had wished for a real mystery so she could be a real spy.

Be careful what you wish for.

Sometimes when Carla skipped school, she spent

the whole day by herself either under her bed or up in *her* tree. She could spy, and tell stories to her pencil, so it could draw its magic monster pictures.

El Atascadero was a big ranch. And it held lots of secrets. Secrets big people never told little people. Secrets Carla had to find out alone. Grandpa hadn't loved Grandmother. He'd kept a woman named Ivory Rose as his lover. Ivory had been a witch. That's why Cheyenne was her aunt but wasn't. Maverick was mad because he might not get the ranch if Mother was back....

So now the impostor was the biggest secret of all.

Carla was just a little girl.

She never said much, so the big people didn't think she knew much.

Except how to draw monsters.

Her monsters worried the big people. Whenever Dad saw one, he would get tight-lipped and act explosive. Once he had ripped up an entire tablet. Usually he didn't say or do anything. But even when he was nice, he scared her. She couldn't forget how he'd put his hands on her mother's throat that last night in the barn.

Grandmother didn't get mad about the monsters, though. But she had hauled her to a lady shrink. Carla had sat there in that big leather chair studded with gold buttons while Grandmother had told the lady shrink how she'd started drawing monsters after their barn had burned down and her daddy had nearly gotten burned up and her mother had disappeared.

"What really happened that night in the barn, Carla?" Dr. Lincoln had asked.

Horrible images had flashed in Carla's mind as she had stared silently and stubbornly past Dr. Lincoln.

Finally the doctor had told Grandmother the sessions were a waste of everybody's time and money.

Carla couldn't wait to get big enough to leave home. When she grew up she was going to be a spy and marry a spy. The ranch was boring. She wanted to travel all over the world. She wanted a glamorous life.

Like her mother's.

Her tree was the huge, old live oak her great-great-grandfather had planted nearly a hundred years ago behind the house.

Carla had planned her life in *her* tree.

Too bad her plans never worked out. Real life just seemed like a series of accidents.

She was always sifting through the mail looking for a letter or even a postcard from her mother. Even with Dad acting nicer, she had wanted her mother, too.

But Dad hadn't really wanted Mother back. He didn't like hearing that Carla looked like her, either.

When she grew up, Carla wanted to look exactly like her mother. Only she wanted to have lots of kids.

She would spoil them, too. She wouldn't just go off…

She didn't dwell on how staying home with her children would conflict with her career as a spy.

She left the window and her sketchbook and stretched back onto her bed.

Again she stared longingly at the high shelves that contained all the expensive dolls and stuffed animals her mother had given her. The house was ninety years old. Her walls had cracks and the room was shabby. But she hadn't let Grandmother change anything. She was staring at a crack that ran from the ceiling to the dull oak floor when a gentle tap made her spring up sharply.

"Carla?"

Carla clasped her fingers over her mouth and willed her to leave.

The door opened.

"You forgot your tablet." The impostor laid her tablet on a low, antique table.

"Go away. I don't want it."

"It's very good. Have you had drawing lessons?"

Nobody had ever complimented her monster pictures, especially not after she'd made that person resemble a monster.

Carla wadded her pillow up and then buried her face in it. "Go away."

"Why?"

"'Cause you're not her."

Silence.

Carla lowered her pillow and glared.

The woman sank down into a chair that needed a new slipcover and nervously studied the doll from China.

"Is my dad in on this?"

"No."

"You're lying to him, too, then."

"I'm going to tell him the truth."

"When?"

"Soon. When it's safe."

"Safe?"

"A man thought I was your mother and tried to strangle me."

She untied the bandanna at her throat, and Carla gasped at the black bruises on her neck.

"My dad?"

"No. He's been wonderful…at least in his own way."

"Then who?"

"I don't know."

"And Mother?"

The impostor went white. Then she turned and stared fixedly at the Chinese doll.

The silence expanded. Suddenly Carla was filled by a nameless, sickening panic.

Her nightmare was real.

Her mother would never come home.

In the next second she was denying her worst fears and telling herself the impostor was trying to trick her.

"She's dead, Carla."

"No!" But even as she denied it, Carla clutched her pencil so tightly that it snapped in two. "I don't want you here. I don't want to talk to you anymore! Not ever again!"

"Carla…" The impostor leaned down and picked up one end of the broken pencil. She said very quietly, "I know what it's like to lose somebody."

"Why don't you stop pretending you're so nice and just go away? Nobody wants you here."

Grief lapped around Carla like huge black waves. She stared helplessly at the woman who looked so heartbreakingly like her mother. "I don't want you here."

But the impostor sat down next to her, and her voice became grave and gentle, comforting, like her own mother's voice had never been.

"Years ago I—I lost… I probably shouldn't tell you this yet." The impostor's eyes were infinitely kind and sad and vulnerable, too. "Maybe we won't have all that much time together. You see, I know that if we did have time, we could be friends. Carla, I like children. I used to be a teacher.''

''I hate teachers,'' Carla said defiantly. ''They're stupid.''

''Well, I like children. And I'd like you…if you'd let me.'' She hesitated. ''What I'm trying to tell you is that my own little boy died.'' She grew paler than ever, and Carla felt a wave of pity.

''How old was—''

''Five. He died in my arms under a big ash tree in my front lawn. It was my fault. I—I didn't know what to do to save him. I just held him and rocked him and talked to him. Later, I found out that if I had only known some basic first aid… But that doesn't matter now.'' Tears brimmed on her lower lashes, and when she spoke again, her voice was thicker. ''So I know what it's like to feel all alone…the way you feel. The way your dad feels, too. You're both afraid to love.''

Silence.

Then slowly Carla asked, ''What was his name?''

''Jimmy. He had lots of friends. He liked to ride his skateboard and his pony.''

''I don't have any friends.''

''I could be your friend.''

Carla's lower lip trembled, and when she felt the woman's gentle hand ruffle her hair, she started to push it away. Instead, she sat very still, for the fingers felt nice. Almost they felt like a mother's touch.

''My dad hated my mother. They say he killed her. I used to hate him.''

''He didn't do it. I saw your mother in New York. Why…''

"She was scared of him. That's why she ran away and left me behind."

The gentle hand caressed in soothing, circular strokes. "Maybe neither of them could help any of that. Your father saved my life. Carla, people can behave very differently around different people. Maybe your mother and father did the best they could. Maybe they just couldn't get along. Have you ever met a kid at school that you couldn't like no matter how hard you tried?"

"Lots of 'em."

"Well, sometimes no matter how hard you try, you just can't make things work. But you have to go on. To new things."

"What's your real name?"

"Bronte. Bronte Devlin."

"I want you to stay, at least for a while."

"I will if I can."

The impostor was at the door. About to go, when Carla remembered her overdue math assignment.

"Hey! Are you any good with decimals?"

"Math was my favorite subject."

"Then you've definitely got to stay...at least for a little while."

It was dark, and the shadows were long and deep in the wide hallway. Exhaustion was sweeping Bronte when she reached her bedroom door. But when she tried her crystal doorknob, her hand froze as something smooth slid through her fingers and rippled silently to her feet. When she opened the door, a bar of golden light flooded the hall.

In the next instant she was on the floor screaming.

For the silky thing she had seen coiled around her ankles like a snake was a man's red silk tie.

Her heart hammered as she picked it up.

The silk burned her fingertips.

She remembered large bony hands wrapping a similar tie around her neck.

Who had left it here? Was it a warning?

Was he here, too?

The red silk blurred.

She lay against the wall, unable to see or hear. She curled into a tight ball and again screamed.

She had no idea how long she lay curled like that in the dark, but suddenly she heard racing footsteps.

When she opened her eyes, Jack's arrogant face loomed out of the darkness.

Even as she tried to scramble away, he sprang toward her, his deep voice a kindly rumble.

"It's only me."

White-hot anger seared through her that he could be so calm. "Did you do this?" She held up the red tie.

"No!"

When he slid his hand down her arms to lift her to her feet, she fought to twist away from him. But he pulled her up gently, swearing to her, again in that soothing, velvet tone, that everything was okay.

Tears pooled in her eyes; she began to tremble.

"Have I ever hurt you?" he asked.

She fought harder to push him away.

"Hey, hey. Trust me," he whispered.

"How can I trust you or anybody here?"

He picked her up in his strong arms, carried her into the bedroom where he laid her down on a black satin, quilted spread.

"The killer is here. In this house."

"Okay," he said, sitting down beside her, folding her hands into his. "You found a red tie. You're scared." He wrapped his arms around her. Jack's voice softened to a caress that felt like velvet upon her skin. "But you're okay now."

And for some reason his saying that with such conviction helped her regain her calm.

"I'm okay." She bit her lower lip. "I'm okay."

Jack's eyes narrowed thoughtfully. "You're sure?"

"As okay as I can be…knowing he's here. But don't you go anywhere."

"I'm here." His reassuring grip tightened.

"You hate me."

"I wish."

The shadows of the bedroom and the rich black of the satin spread made his white shirt seem whiter and his dark skin darker. His features were so rugged that his potent, masculine virility struck her like a body blow.

Suddenly Bronte was aware that she was alone with him in their bedroom. With a little moan she pulled loose from him and buried her head in a pillow. "How can I trust you?"

"It feels odd, doesn't it?" A fleeting smile broke across his face. His usual dislike for her had vanished.

Then a thin gasp from the stairs broke the fragile moment of intimacy.

His smile died.

Bronte turned from him to the still, misshapen figure in the darkness.

Theodora.

Jack's face hardened when he saw the glass in Theodora's hand.

"Is everything all right?" Theodora demanded. "I heard a scream."

Jack's grim gaze was glued to the amber contents of her glass. "Everything's fine."

"Then I'd like to see my daughter—alone."

Chapter 16

Bronte took a deep breath as she stepped inside the library. The red tie had her so scared, all she wanted to do was confess everything to Theodora. She wanted nothing more than to run away from her pretend husband and false life as soon as possible.

But when Bronte tried to shut the doors so she and Theodora could be alone, Jack barged inside, too.

"Jack, I need to talk to Chantal alone."

"Later."

"Why don't you just go?" Bronte demanded. "There is no reason for you to act like you care about me."

"You're a most unusual wife. Most women would want a concerned—"

"Jack—"

After both women asked him to leave again, he finally said, "Okay, I'll give you a minute."

But he immediately returned with a huge laundry

basket full of mail, which he noisily emptied onto a polished library table. Then he plopped himself in front of the mess and grinned.

Both women glared at him, appalled.

He just smirked at them as though he relished the chance to be perverse. Like most men, knowing he wasn't wanted made him more determined to stay.

"You could do that in your office," Theodora said.

"I could. But I know how tough you can be." He slit an envelope with a theatrical gesture. "She's had a scare. I'm not sure she's up to what you have in mind."

"I'm fine." But Bronte's voice was weak.

"You look as pale as that lampshade. As your husband, my job is to protect you."

"From my own mother?"

"If necessary."

"Jack, don't be ridiculous."

"Humor me, *darling.*"

As always his endearment had that cutting edge. Even though she was still scared, Bronte hated feeling safer because he was there. His stubborn insistence was hugely annoying. Determined to ignore him, she turned her back on him and sat down.

But she heard every single sound he made.

Her skin prickled every time he glanced her way.

Did he have to slash through those crisp envelopes so noisily? His chair groaned when he rocked back and forth on two spindly legs. He wadded up garbage, slinging each piece to his feet.

"Sorry," he whispered politely when an envelope struck her ankle.

He was as distracting as a splinter festering underneath a fingernail. No matter how hard she might want to pry him out, he delighted in wedging himself in more obnoxiously.

Bronte had come down to tell Theodora the truth, so she could be rid of him and all these lies forever.

Theodora drank steadily from her flask, scowling at him, too. But he cheerily dominated their conversation, reading newsworthy items to Theodora that she didn't care to hear. And, oddly, Bronte, who had been so anxious to talk to Theodora and escape this house and this man and this unwanted life, soon found herself fascinated as he talked to Theodora about ranching, their mutual friends, Mario, the jealous and problematic Caesar, cattle breeding and horse breaking, El Atascadero and town gossip. So fascinated that sometimes when he read something really funny, she actually forgot her fierce urgency to be gone and turned back to face him, laughing out loud.

Theodora relaxed, too, and began telling him what had happened while he was away. They discussed the bulls, and she demanded his opinion of that particular situation. Even Bronte could tell his answers and concerns were intelligent. When Jack mentioned that certain accounts were off, Theodora poured herself another drink and drank steadily in silence for a while.

Gradually Bronte relaxed. She forgot the red tie. When he read a letter from a Tad Jackson from Australia, describing the Aborigines' custom of sleeping naked together in a hole they dug, and then pulling their dogs inside on top of them as the night got colder, even Theodora looked interested. Tad wrote that the phrase "three dog night" referred to a very cold night indeed.

Bronte turned her chair all the way around so that

she could see Jack better. Slowly a man she didn't know began to emerge.

This Jack frowned at some of the things Theodora said, smiled at others, dismissed her next remark with no expression whatsoever. Gone was the angry, impossible man who'd hated Bronte these past two days and nights. Gone was the intense lover who'd made wild love to her and then despised her and himself for it.

This man was milder, lighter. He was quick and intelligent, well-educated. This man had a golden lab named Guerro, a willful daughter who spent her time spying on her family and the *vaqueros*. He had a family. A past. A life. Depth. Friends. And there was a fascinating richness and texture to his character.

But every time Theodora poured more whiskey from her flask, Bronte noticed how his hard features tightened, how he caught his breath or chewed his lip or stopped talking for a second or two.

She remembered the smashed beer bottles at their motel.

He had battles to fight, but he was a man of rare courage.

He had saved her life.

Even though he professed to want nothing more to do with her, he had come running when she had screamed a few moments ago. He had been gentle, reassuring. He was with her now....

She owed him.

No. She couldn't let herself think like that.

She wished him gone and herself alone with Theodora.

Still, a pleasant half hour passed before Mario interrupted them. Mario was a small, powerfully built

man with a white streak in his black hair. He was
most upset to have learned that Caesar had gotten
drunk and torn up a bar and was now in jail in Val
Verde where he was being held without bail. Bronte
gathered that Val Verde was a border town eighty
miles south of the ranch headquarters.

With a worried glance at Bronte, Jack picked up
his Stetson and excused himself. Theodora's gaze
sharpened on her daughter.

Bronte smiled, and for a few moments longer, the
surface politeness between them remained untroubled.
But with Jack gone, the tension level rose, and Bronte
soon felt a good deal more insecure about all the lies
she had told.

She was sure that somehow Theodora knew. Still,
there was no telling how long she might have waited
before confessing, had not Theodora made it easier.

"Jack is different with you. I've never seen him
joke or laugh around you before." Theodora poured
herself still another drink. When she spoke again, her
voice was deceptively soft. "My daughter put
lime...two slices...in her tea. She didn't use sweetener. She knew better than to sit in my chair, too.
Except for your face, you are nothing like her. I'm
surprised Jack can't see it."

"What?"

The two women stared at one another.

"So why did you pretend I was...your daughter?"

"Because I could expose you anytime...as I am
doing now."

"I don't understand."

"How could you? But soon you will. For years I
have sacrificed everything for the good of the ranch.
I lived for the ranch. Chantal didn't understand that.

She was my daughter, but she took after Ben more than she took after me. She opposed me on every important issue."

"Why did you want her back?"

"She is the next generation. The ranch should rightfully be hers. I had to know for sure what had happened to her. Where is she? And why do you look like her?"

"She's dead."

Theodora took this news calmly, with only the slightest tremor passing through her.

"She was murdered, and I'm truly sorry. Two days ago. The man who killed her almost killed me, too. That's why—"

"Did you see him?"

"I couldn't see him, but I'd know him if..."

"Did Jack see—"

"No. The man was gone when Jack got there."

"I was afraid of this." Again Theodora's voice was only a trifle thinner. "For five years I've feared her death. Chantal led a wild, fast life that could only end one way. Did you talk to the police?"

"No." Bronte got up. "The killer's dark. He has big bones. Large hands. Strong hands. He tried to strangle me with a red tie. That's all I know...."

"Sit down," Theodora whispered shakily. "I need to think."

Bronte sank back into her chair. "Nothing you say will make the slightest difference. I'm leaving."

"It's not that simple."

"I'm not your daughter. It was selfish of me to pretend I was. My only excuse is that I was so scared. I was hurt. Terrified for my life. Scared of my new face, too. Jack saved me, but I knew he wouldn't take me with him if I didn't lie. But I could have a real life of my own, you know. I used to be a kindergarten teacher. My real name is Bronte...."

"I accepted you, Bronte, knowing you weren't her...to get to the truth."

"Well, this is the truth. I'm not Carla's mother. I'm not Jack's wife. I don't belong here. This face you see—it's not mine, either. It's a cross between my mother's and your daughter's. And...there was a red tie on my doorknob tonight."

"There are millions of red ties in the world."

"But somebody here knew what such a tie would signify to me. I can't keep pretending I'm Chantal. I don't want to die."

"You've told me who you aren't. Now tell me who you are."

For a long moment, Bronte was silent. "My mother was an opera star. I was a teacher. I'm divorced. But who I am doesn't matter."

"Tell me what matters more."

"I'm not sure."

"I've seen the way you look at Jack. Doesn't he matter?"

Bronte's eyes filled with tears. "No! We've only just met. Nothing is real between us."

"He's in love with you, you little fool. And you're in love with him. Even I can see that."

"I don't care what you think you see."

"So, you're a coward? A quitter?"

"No!"

"What about Carla?"

"My little boy died...because I couldn't save him. I'd probably hurt her more than I could ever help her. She's not my responsibility."

"If you love Jack, she is. You pretended you were Chantal, but he reacted to *you*. He fell in love with you. He never loved Chantal. He married her because she seduced him and tricked him. He stayed with her because he's stubborn. He sticks with anything longer than anybody I've ever known. He served five years for her murder because everybody knew he hated her. He loves you."

"He acts like he hates me."

"He's never loved anybody else. If you leave him, I don't know what will happen to him."

"He's stronger than you think."

"Becky's after him."

"Becky?"

"Chantal's plump little cousin. She's even got a small stake in the ranch. She lives in Houston, but since Jack's been home, she's come down every weekend. She's always out at the pens. He lets her work the gates."

Jealousy filled Bronte at the vision of Jack and Becky together. Bronte lowered her lashes against her pale cheeks, so Theodora wouldn't see. "Maybe they belong together."

"She'll get him, but Jack doesn't want Becky. He wants you."

"No...."

"If you leave, you'll smash him to pieces. I'm going to tell you a few things about Jack, because I know he won't."

"Please don't—"

"Jack's tired. Real tired. When you get as old as I am, you'll know that a man can only fight so much, for so long. First, there was the barrio and the shame of being a whore's son. He's stuck on the notion that

his daddy deserted him without a backward thought.
His father was the most talented cattleman I ever
knew. He would have been so proud of Jack. Then
Jack married Chantal, and she was his whoring
mother all over again. He went to prison and nearly
died because of her. He's different with you. Alive,
almost human. If he loses you, he's going to start
drinking—''

"He'll hate me when he finds out I lied."

"Jack saved your life. Maybe you owe him the
benefit of the doubt. I bet he cares…enough to forgive."

Bronte thought of all the things they'd done and
said together, of the glorious sex they'd shared. All
he had to do was look at her and she felt special, like
she belonged to him.

Theodora rose and lifted a heavy book from a shelf.
When she returned, she sat closer to Bronte and
opened the huge photograph album. After the first
picture of Jack, Bronte had to see the rest.

The childhood photos were brown and faded. Jack
had grown up overshadowed by Maverick, who was
golden and gifted and beloved. In every picture Maverick sat on his horse ramrod straight, his handsome
chin high and proud, while Jack sat slouched in his
saddle, his dark head down, his overlarge cowboy hat
propped low over his ears. There wasn't a single early
picture of Jack smiling.

Silently Bronte flipped more pages.

"You say that the man who killed my daughter is
here," Theodora murmured. "If you don't stay just
for a little while and help us nail him, he might kill
Jack…or Carla. You don't know what he's after."

Bronte paused on a page. "I can't stay. Nothing

you can say will make me change my mind.'' But even as she spoke, she realized there was nowhere else she wanted to go. And out of that knowledge came the fierce longing to know if she really was so special to Jack.

No. She wasn't.

Wordlessly, Bronte flipped more pages. In all of them Jack was such an unhappy-looking little boy.

Soundlessly, she turned the final page and found herself staring at a black-and-white studio glossy of Garth Jones.

Her movie star.

She'd barely given him a thought in the excitement of the past few days. Garth grinned at her insolently. He had signed his name in a flourish of swirling black ink.

A fragile stillness descended upon Bronte. Garth Brown was connected to these people.

''What's his picture doing in here?'' she whispered. ''How do you know him?''

''Jack and Garth Brown are half brothers.''

''I—I didn't realize—''

''Garth is Shanghai's older, legitimate son. I think Jack's always figured that Shanghai didn't need him because he had Garth. Only Garth took his mother's side and never came near Shanghai or the ranch.''

Bronte hurt for Jack.

''Jack's never had anybody to call his own. Unless you change your mind, he never will. Stay.''

''I can't,'' Bronte said. ''I'm really really sorry, but I just can't.''

Chapter 17

Bronte closed her bathroom door and stripped out of the jeans and blue blouse she'd worn the past two days. Bubbles foamed in the bath tub.

She was leaving tomorrow.

In her mind's eye she saw again the yellowed photographs of Jack slouching and looking so forlorn. At the thought of leaving him forever, a surging ache rose from deep inside her.

She cared about Jack. Even though he wasn't hers to care about.

How could she have fallen in love in such a short time? When he had been so awful to her at times?

But so much had happened so fast. He had saved her. He had that way of looking at her. Was it really such a wonder?

A lonely old woman had asked her to stay, even though she knew Bronte was a fake. But it was the little girl with tangled red curls and sorrowful eyes—a child who looked so much like her own darling Jimmy—who tempted Bronte to stay almost as much as her love for Jack did.

Still, no matter how much she cared for them, they weren't hers to love. She wished Theodora hadn't told her about Jack's childhood or about his feeling put down by his famous brother and Maverick and Chantal. Seeing him as a vulnerable human being only made her feel more attached to him. She wished she didn't feel that, beneath his anger, his soul was bound to hers.

Dropping her towel onto the sheepskin rug, Bronte sank into a huge, antique, white bathtub with claw-and-ball feet.

Who was she?

She didn't know herself anymore.

There were too many riddles to be solved. Both in her own life and in Chantal's.

For now, Bronte wanted to take a long bath and go to bed. In the morning perhaps her resolve to go would be stronger.

The warm, foaming bubbles rose high against the porcelain sides. The water felt soothing after what seemed the longest day of her life.

The lights were turned off in the bathroom, but she didn't need them. Her body ached from the long drive. And her head from all the tension with Jack, as well as from what Theodora had told her.

Bronte couldn't quit thinking about Carla, who reminded her of Jimmy. Carla had Jimmy's pure sweet face and Jack's fierce pain and anger. The child was motherless, but she might lose her father, too.

Bronte remembered sitting out on the balcony of her own mother's brownstone, staring sulkily down

at the street because she hadn't wanted to be inside
around her mother or her mother's friends.

Bronte wished that she could stay and teach the
little girl to laugh and smile, to make friends—as
Jimmy had. For Bronte, who adored children so much
that she had made them her career, Jack's daughter
had added an appealing new dimension to her role as
Jack's pretend wife.

She couldn't stay.

Thank goodness, Jack had gone out with Mario.
Stunned and yet relieved by Theodora's acceptance,
Bronte hadn't wanted the map the older woman had
drawn of the house and the ranch. Still, Bronte had
brought it upstairs to study. Theodora had shown her
several more photograph albums as well. She had explained all the family portraits and the ranch's long
history. She had told her how each generation kept
the name West even if control was held by a female.
Theodora had written names of key employees on the
back of the map, too. She had told her about Carla
and how she'd been traumatized that last terrible night
in the barn, when she'd thought her daddy had murdered her mother.

In all the photographs, Carla's hair had been tangled and her clothes torn. She had stood apart, looking motherless and defiant and as heartbreakingly isolated as Jack looked in his pictures.

Bronte had poured over the pictures. But those of
Jack as a boy had tugged at her heart more than any.
He'd been so thin and dark. So much rougher and
poorer looking than Maverick and Chantal. In every
picture he'd glowered at those other, more fashionably dressed children, scowling just like Carla.

Theodora had described the appalling conditions he'd grown up in.

"I don't want to hear any more," Bronte had pleaded.

"His house was four pieces of tin stapled to pallets stolen from loading docks. You wouldn't believe the flies. He wore rags. He'd never been to school. He ate garbage. His mother slept with men in the cot next to his. Why, he was more wild animal than boy. But he took the best from both his parents—his mother's beauty and his daddy's brains and character. I brought him back, determined to tame him. He fought me every step of the way.

"The girls always chased Jack, but he distrusted his sex appeal. Then he married Chantal. She took lovers. Maybe because my solution to a similar problem was the bottle, he turned to the same solution. Every new lover made his drinking worse."

Theodora had gone on to other subjects, but Bronte had barely listened. Theodora had said that her grandfather had installed a bizarre and antiquated security system in the big house that had included safes under the kitchens and gun towers on the roof and a maze of underground tunnels to out buildings, where the family could hide from Mexican bandits.

She told her an old ranch tale about how this same grandfather, the ranch founder, Samson West, had been murdered by a hired hand. How the murder had been made to look like an accident with a rope and a horse. How Samson had been dragged to his death across the prairie.

Well, at least with Jack out of the house, Bronte could finally relax. She wouldn't think of murder or sex or her new face, or of anything else that had to do with this whole fantastic scenario. She would just enjoy being deliciously alone in the glorious antique tub filled to the brim with floating islands of silvery bubbles. Above the tub, steamy, delicious scents of lavender and gardenia blossoms wafted in the humid darkness toward the beamed, wallpapered ceiling.

Bronte's hair was twisted high above her head in a thick, clumsily shaped knot from which thick tendrils curled in damp strands against her forehead and neck.

Drowsily she leaned back against the tub. The warm water with its mounds of bubbles rose dangerously higher as she sank deeper. With a washcloth she lazily rubbed her neck, her shoulders, and dabbed at her flat belly.

She sank deeper still, wishing she could stay there forever. Thinking that if she only could, maybe she should stop worrying about Jack. Maybe then she could stop caring about the rightness or wrongness of leaving.

Deeper she sank, until even her ears were submerged. The walls of the bath and the bedroom were nearly two feet thick, so she didn't hear Jack's skeleton key turn in the bedroom door, which she had so carefully locked. She didn't hear his easy, long-legged strides as he crossed hard floors and Persian carpets. Nor did she hear him making boxes, taping them; pulling his suitcases out of closets. Nor did she know when he began opening and slamming drawers, emptying his clothes sloppily into the half-dozen cardboard boxes and suitcases, so that sleeves were left hanging out and thin black combs and shoes and socks thrown in on top of them.

She lay in a meditative trance in the semidark bathroom, a warm washcloth plastered across her eyes. Slowly, the tension from her long drive with Jack eased. Forgotten, too, were the bruises on her neck. Suddenly she was daydreaming about her other life. She was on her screened porch, listening to wind chimes, watching Jimmy climb on his first pony.

For a while she'd been happy. Had Jack ever known anything approaching fulfillment or peace?

Bronte never heard Jack's quiet approach when he'd finished emptying the drawers and closet. The well-oiled hinges made no sound as the big, white bathroom door swung halfway open. She didn't feel the whisper of cool air as he stepped inside.

But she smiled seductively.

Almost as if she sensed him, a bittersweet ache blossomed inside her.

The door opened into the shadowy bathroom.

One minute Jack felt cool and collected and very determined about packing his things and moving out to Shanghai's cabin as soon as possible.

In the next minute his gaze had sharpened with dark, laser intensity as he found himself captivated by the sweetest half smile on his wife's lovely face. His jaw tightened as he raged an inner battle with himself to go.

Her heavy-lidded eyes were closed, her lush, cupid mouth slightly open. In invitation. Or so it seemed. She seemed to glow in that semidarkness like the rarest of jewels. Like a desert flower beneath a moonless sky.

Her skin was creamy except for those cruel yellow-black finger marks on her slender throat. Softly swelling breasts with pert pink nipples broke the sparkling surface of the water.

He'd spent five years in a cell with nothing nearly as lovely or as alive to look at.

There had been graffiti on the walls. The stench of sweat and urine everywhere. He remembered the hellish loneliness of being caged. The hell of thinking he'd never get out. And then when he'd gotten out, he'd still felt as if invisible prison walls were encircling him, cutting him off from everybody else.

Blood pounded in his ears like primitive drums.

He was free now. Around her, he didn't feel quite so lonely.

Again he studied the purple ring around her throat. Odd how just the thought of her dying had made him feel more helpless than he'd felt even in prison when those men had held him down on cold concrete and tried to rape him.

Odd how those bruises brought back the pure, raw fear of being beaten; he felt some danger even here, tonight.

They were home.

He remembered her piercing screams, her claim that she'd found the red tie.

He believed her. He didn't feel safe.

Suddenly his pulse was beating violently, and he was frozen stock-still. He'd wanted her all day. Maybe that's why he couldn't tear his gaze from her lips and her delectably slim body, the body that was so tantalizingly exposed to his view by those drifting mounds of silvery bubbles.

A minute before, his big black boots had been planted on terra firma.

Now he was sinking into a vat of delicious femininity.

Of all the abominable luck.

Chivalry dictated that he withdraw silently.

But he hadn't learned chivalry in the barrio. He had learned other things, all the wild things that men like him, men who had an easy way with women, could do to pleasure a woman.

Hungrily, Jack's eyes wandered over her breasts and hips.

Even the sight of her slim toes turned him on.

Perhaps he made some sound.

Perhaps she just sensed him.

Or smelled him.

Whatever.

Her emerald eyes fluttered open.

And in those torpid orbs he saw some strange emotion as she slowly focused on his face.

Warmth flooded him.

Forgive me, he should say, like some elegant gentleman.

But he had bad blood. He came from a bad background. He was no gentleman.

She was no lady, either.

He should forget the boxes, his need to pack, and simply run.

Instead he shut the door behind him, shot the bolt and joined her in the humid darkness. His scuffed black boots were soon rooted in the soft sheepskin rug by the tub, and he couldn't quit staring at her. He'd spent the whole damned day dreaming about her.

When had he felt like this about a woman before? Not even with Cheyenne.

Never with Chantal.

But everything was different now.

In the velvet darkness, the warm invitation in her gentle gaze compelled him. As if in a trance, she got up slowly, the curves of her body glistening, bubbles threading from the silken tendrils of her hair and trailing down to her nipples.

"Hadn't you better go, Jack?"

Oh, yes.

But he lacked the will.

Or, rather, his will was to stay.

Like Venus rising from her pink shell, this flesh-and-blood creature was infinitely more beautiful and magical than Botticelli's love goddess. Her face was illuminated with desire and the need to be loved. At the same time she warred against those things, too. In her gentle eyes he saw wisdom and desire wrestle with a soul-deep pain.

Warm water splashed the cuff of his jeans as she lifted a long, shapely leg gracefully over the edge of the tub.

She reached for a thick, soft towel.

But he was faster, leaping toward her, ripping the terry-cloth rectangle from the bar, handing it to her.

She began to pat herself dry with the fluffy cotton. She made slower strokes across the curve of her belly.

Watching every stroke, he felt like a man felled by surprise from behind.

Then he groaned aloud, took the towel from her and began to dry her skin caressingly, like a man worshipping at the altar of his goddess.

Long before he was done, he dropped the towel, and his hands were all over her damp, velvet skin. So was his mouth. He pulled her against his body until

every muscular inch was pressed burningly against
her soft, naked flesh.

He was lost.

So was she.

She was moaning as he trailed fervent, destroying
kisses down her vulnerable throat. She turned her
head toward his, sighing. It was as if she couldn't say
no any more than he could to this dream...to this
miracle that they alone shared. To this coming home.

He tore off his clothes. His belt with the huge
buckle snapped through jean loops and clunked when
he tossed it to the floor. Next came his boots, his
jeans. She ripped the buttons of his shirt apart.

There was almost no light in the bathroom now,
and they were naked together like living phantoms in
some wondrous love poem. Her slick wet stomach
skin fit against his dryer flesh. Thigh to thigh. Only
the murmur of her husky love words, the light skimming of her fingertips and the spiraling warmth of
erotic feelings were real. Her smooth, soft woman
skin was real, too. Whatever was happening between
them was beyond either one of them to stop.

His tongue slid inside her mouth, and she made a
low, feminine murmur of desire. Her arms circled his
neck and tightened beneath his crisp dark hair.

The fire inside him burned out of control. This was
beyond hatred. Beyond love. Beyond anything he had
ever known. His fingers closed around the swollen
underside of her breast and his palm filled with her
soft flesh. Her nipples budded.

Were they animals, bound by instinct to couple on
sight?

Or simply too human?

Or just too damned lonely and too damned weak?

He didn't know. And he didn't much care as he sank to the sheepskin rugs and lay very still, staring up into her warm, glowing eyes as she began tearing off his shirt with eager, light fingers that thrilled him.

When she was done, he caught her by the waist and rolled her over, so that he lay on top of her. His hands slid into her hair. He seized her wrists, raised them above her head and pinned her on that litter of soft animal hides imported from Tad Jackson's sheep station in Australia.

She shifted, her whole body quivering as she arched to meet him, molding her body to his. The heat of her damp skin fused them even before he thrust into her.

Tightly sheathed, with his heart thundering in his chest, he stared deeply into her eyes and knew a mindless glory. Slowly their bodies began to rise and fall.

Perfect harmony. Perfect rhythm.

Man to woman.

Eternal. Forever.

She drew him deeper and deeper inside her.

He moved faster and faster.

Until their hearts beat like the wildest jungle drum.

Drinking in her exquisite beauty, drowning in it, he closed his eyes.

She was heaven.

Sweet precious heaven.

An angel.

Not wanting to look at her, he kept his eyes shut.

Blind as he now was, the sensations of touch only became more exquisite.

He wished he could be soft and gentle, but found he couldn't hold back.

If he was hungry, she was hungrier. One leg came up and wrapped around him.

They devoured one another, moving more rapidly in a fierce, fantastic rhythm that rocked them in flaming surges ever upward toward the shattering conclusion.

And afterward, when they lay panting and breathless together after that explosion and dying of selves, she touched her hand to where his heart throbbed beneath his ribs like it still might burst. Even later, long after their bodies had quieted and cooled, her hand remained over his heart. He closed his eyes and held her close, unable to let her go.

For that moment his isolation was gone. Usually only a drink helped, but she was better than liquor.

He didn't dare look at her. He was too afraid that she would see tenderness shining in his eyes.

He wanted to hate her. But even now when he was done with her, he burned for her on a soul-deep level like a man delirious with fever. Sweat popped out everywhere on him, drenching his head, his black hair, his shoulders.

Hatred was simple compared to this.

Then he forced himself to remember the long, dark years of their marriage. Her mockery of his low-class birth. His despair, black and bottomless, over her numerous infidelities. She had taunted him with man after man. Every time he had caught her with a new lover, she had said that he was a whore's bastard and had laughed at him for thinking he deserved a faithful wife. Later, of course, she had always apologized and promised she would never do it again.

He remembered the long, whiskey-filled nights, the sinking into that sour, bleary, soul-destroying oblivion. How he had hated himself and her when he'd awakened in filthy rooms with coarse strangers beside him. More than once he'd landed in jail.

The same determination in his character that had driven him to overcome the obstacles of his birth and achieve goal after goal had proved to be his undoing in his marriage to Chantal. He had stayed with her and put up with her abuse far longer than he should have. Foolishly, he had thought his patience might reform her. Once when he'd gotten drunk with a shrink in a bar, the bastard had told him that he was trying to save his mother by saving Chantal. Jack had given up after that.

Yes, he had hated her. But he'd loathed himself more. There had been other reasons he'd stayed. Maybe deep down he'd thought she was the only kind of wife who would have him.

How could he want such misery back?

Too much was riding on him now.

If he were to have any chance with Carla...

If he were to solve any of the very real problems of running the ranch, he couldn't let her do this to him.

How could he stop her?

"That was one hell of a performance," he growled, his voice bitter. "You knew I'd come. You were just lying in that tub with the light out and the door unlocked, waiting—"

"You bastard," she whispered with a strangled sob. Frantically she unlocked her legs from his waist. "Get off me, you mean-hearted bastard." She had used that word to taunt him in the past, but tonight her broken voice was stark, pain filled.

Her beautiful face made him remember her lovers,

and he was filled with the old, smothering darkness that made him crave liquor. "With pleasure, honey," he sneered.

Even though her eyes glistened with sorrow and her soft, stricken face tore him apart, his chiseled features grew fierce and dark and ever more remorseless.

She snatched her clothes from the floor and held them in front of her body. She grabbed some sort of crude drawing that had been lying under her bandanna.

"I'm leaving you! And I'm never coming back! I don't want to be your wife anymore!" Then she ran to the door, stumbling blindly.

Her hoarse sobs tore at him. Then he caught a glimpse of her back. Of her smooth, unblemished shoulders.

Unblemished.

No scar!

What the hell—

No wonder his mind refused to accept this Chantal who was afraid, who he could hurt with a cruel word or two.

This gentle woman was a stranger.

He didn't even know her.

She wasn't real. And if that was so, nothing they'd shared could be real.

His dark face turned to stone. For a moment he was too stunned to react. Then he felt a violent building rage as he listened to her pull on her clothes.

He grew too furious to trust himself to deal with her, so he didn't get up until she had finished and had run out into the hall.

Slowly, methodically, he dressed and finished

packing. Except for his record collection, he took every other item that was his.

He slung his guitar over his shoulder.

No way was he ever sharing a bedroom or a bed with such a liar again.

If she was a liar, what did that make him?

A damned fool!

Who was she? What was she after? Why did he even give a damn?

He saw her exquisite face beneath his on that rug, her hot emerald gaze, adoring him.

Even though he hated her, he still wanted her.

Way more than he ever had before.

Because she wasn't Chantal.

Chapter 18

By the time Bronte climbed the stairs to her bedroom again, she'd replayed the seduction scene on the sheepskin rug a thousand times.

One minute he loved her, the next he hated her. Who was Jack, really? What did he want from her?

He'd ripped off his clothes as if he'd die without her. Afterward he'd turned dark and hostile.

Her emotional turmoil had left her exhausted. All she wanted now was to do a free fall across her bed and sleep forever.

Hesitantly, she pushed her bedroom door open. Except for the faint glow of a night-light, the room was dark. Jack's cardboard boxes and his black guitar case were gone. She stepped inside and walked toward the bed.

That was one hell of a performance.

Scalding tears slipped from her eyes as his cutting words hurt her all over again. She was even worse than he thought. She had slept with him under false pretenses.

Suddenly her tearful gaze fell on a long, thin envelope lying on top of the black satin spread. Bewildered, she picked it up and read the name Chantal. The slanting handwriting was unknown to her. Still, her heart began to pulse when she tore the envelope open and shook several newspaper clippings and a piece of white, lined notepaper onto the bedspread.

A bold black headline blazed up at her: Supermodel Mischief Jones And Lover Dead In Two-Car Pileup. There was a black-and-white picture of Webster's burned-out Mercedes and several large close-ups of Mischief.

"No...." Bronte pushed herself away from the bed and sprang to a nearby lamp and then to another, snapping the little chains under the shades and flipping wall switches until the room was ablaze.

Then she sank onto the bed and spread the articles out before her. Lifting them one by one, she read in horror. The second clipping was Webster's obituary, the third Mischief's.

They were dead.

Murdered?

On the lined paper, a handwritten note in a childish scrawl read, "Nothing is what you think. Leave or die. A friend."

Bronte wadded up the clippings and the note, stuffed them back into the envelope and shoved them as far as possible under her mattress. Then she got up and began to pace back and forth.

Who had left the red tie and sent her these clippings?

Were they trying to warn her or to threaten her?

Without bothering to undress or brush her teeth, Bronte got into bed. She propped her pillows behind her head and stared blankly at the tall, shadowy walls.

Whole minutes ticked by. She felt too paralyzed to move.

When she began to shiver, she slowly drew the blankets and black satin spread on top of her. Then she wrapped her arms around herself.

But soon a coldness that had more to do with mindless dread than with the temperature of her bedroom seeped through. She couldn't stop shaking.

There were no stars. A thick cloud layer blanketed a moonless sky. A wild breeze tore through the brush and mesquite trees and prickly pear cactus that grew right up to the cabin.

Shanghai's dark, stucco shack seemed to reject Jack and his cardboard boxes just like the old man would have done. Jack's stomach twisted into a cold, hard knot like it always did when he thought about his father.

"I'm here to stay, old man. Whether you like it or not."

Jack forced himself up the stairs a step at a time, walking gingerly, testing each of the spongy boards before trusting his full weight on it.

When he'd crossed the porch, Jack set his guitar down and regarded Shanghai's cabin for a long, tense moment. It struck him as odd that Garth, the legitimate son, had never bothered to come home, not even for his father's funeral. Theodora had told him Garth was ashamed of his father.

When Jack swung his flashlight around, fleeting arcs of white light floated across the boarded-up win-

dows, broken shutters and the wooden door, which
had been nailed shut. There were holes in the stucco.
Still, compared to his mother's tin shack in Mexico,
where the floor had been dirt and the walls unsup-
ported by mortar or cement or nails, Shanghai's shack
looked sound. At least Jack's bed wouldn't float away
on a river of mud or a wall collapse the first night it
rained. He'd get the *vaqueros* up here first thing tomorrow to clean and patch the old place up.

As his flashlight bobbed, a white envelope gleamed
on the porch floor near the door.

Jack aimed the cone of light downward and then
knelt and picked it up. He read his name rendered in
bold, childish, block letters. Then he ripped it open.

A cryptic note read, "Nothing is what you think.
Un amigo."

Too true. Furious, Jack wadded it up and stuffed it
in his jeans pocket. He had to get inside and find some
place clean enough to throw his bedroll. Mario and
the men would be up at first light working cattle. He
had to supervise them.

Jack set his flashlight down and went to work on
the door, using his hammer to claw and rip at the
rusty nails that secured the boards across the doorway.
Panting heavily after removing the first board, he
heaved it into a clump of prickly pear cactus. Then
he began straining to remove the second board, prying
the nails out and letting them clatter across the uneven
planking.

He was about to set to work on the third board
when the snap of a twig a little distance from the
house penetrated his consciousness. When his gaze
flew toward the darkness, he sensed unseen eyes staring at him. He turned on his own light and waved it

across the trees. When nobody spoke, he decided it was probably a steer or a buck and went back to work on the third board, yanking at it till he was again drenched in sweat. Still it didn't loosen.

Chantal, or rather her lookalike, came into his thoughts in vivid, full-color images that he couldn't fully control. She was lying beneath him on a sheepskin rug, her green eyes hotly ablaze. Next he saw the shape of her body as she'd walked away from him toward Ernesto and his starving troop.

The visions blended into fantasy, and she was suddenly there with him in the darkness, sliding toward him, smelling of gardenias, her moist lips parted, inviting his kisses as eagerly as she had in the bathroom.

Jack swore and hurled himself at the third board in a frenzy, swearing a blue streak in Spanish and English when it still didn't budge.

"She's not worth it," an inner voice taunted. "Hell, she's easy—you can have her any old time. So what if she's a liar, take her till you get your fill."

Restlessly he picked up his hammer again and hooked two more nails, yanking them out and throwing them onto the porch with a vengeance.

He didn't want to think about her, but the more he tried to put her aside, the more he remembered how she'd felt like molten satin, how she'd quivered at his lightest touch. She'd never been so sweet. So perfect.

He thought of how she'd smiled at Carla. She'd been friendly to Eva and to Theodora. She hadn't even flirted with Maverick.

No wonder nothing about the new Chantal had added up.

The new Chantal.

For years he'd hoped and prayed she'd change, but she never had.

Until now.

The girl was beautiful, naive. She made love like an eager virgin. She made him feel special, cherished.

Jack was thinking about how different she was in every way when he heard another footfall in the dry yard.

His mind cleared instantly.

Somebody really was out there.

In a single fluid movement he retrieved his long metal flashlight. Another stealthy footstep sounded in the dry grass closer to the cabin. Again Jack felt the pull of an unseen gaze.

"Hey? Who's there? You'd better answer." He hunkered low and slipped off the side of the porch, dropping as stealthily as a shadow into the soft sand behind a mesquite trunk just as a man's heavy work shoe rang on the first step.

"Hey there yourself, Hollywood," boomed a gravelly, all-too-familiar voice.

"Brickhouse?"

"Did I scare you, my man?"

Jack flashed his light onto a wide, bronzed face, a pair of bold black eyes that crinkled at the unexpected brilliance. Damned if Brickhouse didn't have the whitest smile in the entire universe.

"Shut that damn thing off. You had some manners in the stir, boy."

Jack doused his light. In the next instant they gripped each other in a bear hug.

"Sorry about sneaking up on you."

"I guess I was a bit jumpy."

"This place is spooky, man. Whatcha out here all alone for, anyway?"

"Long story."

"Here. I'll give you a hand." Brickhouse picked up the hammer and attacked the board Jack had been working on.

"When did they let you out?"

"I been out awhile." Brickhouse set his hammer down and pulled out a bottle of bourbon. "I thought maybe we could celebrate."

"Let's get inside first."

Brickhouse went back to work. Two more boards fell at their feet. Soon they were inside.

Jack lit a Coleman lantern and set it on a dusty chest of drawers. Draperies of cobwebs hung from the ceiling. A mouse skittered frantically along one wall.

Except for the dust that covered the two single beds, the rag rugs and the handmade furniture, the cabin was surprisingly orderly. Dingy, red-flowered curtains hung at the boarded windows on sagging rods. There was a picture of Garth on the bureau.

"Who's that?"

"This was my old man's place."

Brickhouse picked up Garth's picture. "This you or your famous brother?"

"It's him."

Brickhouse blew the dust off the photo and set it back facedown. "The real thing?"

Jack was furiously wiping dust off a chest of drawers. When he'd finished, he opened a drawer. It was full of neatly folded shirts, but the next contained tidy stacks of bundled letters.

"Man, this is giving me the creeps," Brickhouse said from over his shoulder as Jack read the envelopes. "How come nobody cleaned his stuff out before now?"

"'Cause Theodora wanted me—"

Jack broke off. The third drawer contained bundles of yellowed letters tied with a red ribbon like those his mother had always worn. They were written in Spanish and addressed to his mother in Piedras Negras. Jack slowly sat down on a bed and read the first letter.

"Whose are those?"

"My father's."

"Oh, man, I'm going outside to get drunk. You ain't supposed to read dead people's letters."

Jack was glad to have the cabin to himself. His dark face became a mask as he silently skimmed a dozen or so pages. In every letter his father had begged his mother to let him come down and get his boy.

Shanghai had wanted him.

The same as he'd wanted Garth.

With an indifferent air, Jack pitched the letters back into the drawer. What did they prove?

He went outside and picked up his guitar and then his boxes. He began throwing boxes into the house. He untied his bedroll and pitched it across a bed.

But all the time his mind whirled. How come his mother had said his father hadn't wanted him?

The unsavory answer came.

His mother had used everybody—her customers, her landlord, her neighbors—for all they were worth. She'd extorted money from Shanghai. She'd forced Jack to beg and steal for her.

Jack couldn't blame her.

She'd lived on the edge. She'd had to survive the

only way she knew how. Why would a whore who exploited herself hesitate to exploit her son or the man who'd fathered him?

Theodora had tried to tell Jack the truth, but he'd been too damned stubborn to listen.

Maybe Shanghai would have loved him.

No.

This didn't mean anything.

He couldn't let it.

"What'd those letters say?" Brickhouse demanded when Jack stepped out onto the porch again.

"Not a damned thing."

"You're in a foul mood."

"Shut up."

"You're too uptight. Why don't you play something on that guitar of yours? Loosen up. I need to relax."

"I don't mind if I do."

Bronte's breath sobbed, her heartbeats hammered as she whispered a silly little prayer. She would suffocate if she stayed inside the big bedroom a second longer.

Opening and then closing her French doors firmly behind her, she stepped out on the wide verandah and began to pace back and forth just as she had inside.

Waist-high ground fog swirled up from the lawns, blanketing the shrubs and the potted plants eerily so that she couldn't see much from the balcony.

Webster and Mischief were dead.

She couldn't be sure that their deaths were not accidents. And yet…

Jack had saved her life and then brought her home. He had made love to her. He didn't want her to stay.

With a longing that bordered on pain, she thought of the hard, accusing way he'd looked at her and insulted her when he'd sent her out of the bathroom.

And the red tie on her doorknob?

Bronte couldn't forget that red tie any more than she could forget those large bony hands winding a similar length of silk around her neck and nearly strangling the life out of her.

Jack had saved her.

He didn't want her.

Still, every time she thought of him, she flushed with a strange heat that told her no matter what he'd said or done to hurt her, she wanted him.

To go or to stay…?

As Bronte moved away from her lighted doorway down the shadowy verandah, she felt torn between love for Jack and Carla and her terror. The mists swirled up and enveloped her as she glided in utter silence past a tall grouping of wicker chairs and tables and potted ferns that were clustered beneath a ceiling fan.

"Chantal." Caroline's voice was soft, but the slim white hand that snaked out of a shadowy wicker chair and captured Bronte's arm when she was about to pass was surprisingly strong.

"Oh!" Bronte gasped. Her heart tripped faster as she made out the familiar face and shape of the older woman in the darkness. "I—I didn't see you sitting there."

"You looked like a ghost yourself. I had to touch you…to make sure you were real."

Caroline's dark eyes were wide, too, but she was as lovely as she'd been in the library. Her thick, golden hair was loose about her shoulders. For her age, she was astoundingly beautiful. Her feminine, heart-shaped face was as unlined as Theodora's was wrinkled.

"I—I should have said something when you first came out, but you took me by surprise, too. You may remember that I come up here and sit quite often this time of night. I hope I didn't frighten you, my dear."

"No. I couldn't sleep. But I thought you lived in that other house at the end of the drive."

"I do. With Maverick. But as you know, I often have trouble sleeping. I walk from my house past my husband's grave and then down to the big house and around it and back. I often come up here and sit and stare out at the ranch awhile."

"You're not afraid...?"

"Of what?" She sounded surprised.

"Oh, I don't know."

"It's quite safe, really. There's a guard at the gate. Then there's nothing but empty pasture and brush country and the Gulf for miles and miles on all sides of us. We know everybody who lives out here."

"It just seems like such wild country. Especially at night."

"Nights always seem softer to me."

"It's so isolated and so near Mexico."

"Well, there are dangers. Just a month back a *vaquero* got his leg caught in a combine, and Jack had to apply a tourniquet and give him first aid for nearly forty minutes till he could be airlifted to a hospital in Corpus Christi."

Jack was fast on his feet in an emergency.

"Is he okay?"

"He's back at work. But things like that don't happen too often. So except for drug runners..."

"Dopers?"

"They're a dangerous bunch. You don't want to catch them by surprise. But that's not too likely. They want to get out of your way as much as you want to avoid them. For the most part the wetbacks are harmless, too. More pitiful than anything. Now, we do get more dope planes flying over us than we used to. A few years back—when you were still in Houston—a plane crashed near the big house. It was chock-full of marijuana. By the time Jack got to it, the pilot and crew had run off like they always do."

"What happened?"

"Jack called the DEA. They sent some officers down to pick up the pot. The plane was registered to a Mexican citizen in Guadalajara. Not that he'd claim it when Jack notified him. So Jack just lassoed the tail and hauled the plane up to the house. It sat around here for a month. Then he sold it."

"So stuff can happen."

"There's no doubt dope smugglers are a dangerous breed. I wouldn't want to surprise one. They've been known to shoot and ask questions later. So you do have to exercise some caution out here. But then, of course, you know that. You were born here. You didn't used to be afraid of anything. You just hated it out here because it's so boring. I never told you…but I used to sympathize when you'd say that and Theodora would get so furious. At least I had a life *before* I married. I never blamed you for wanting more than this."

Jack knew a powerful thirst as Brickhouse threw his head back and swigged lustily from his bottle. Brickhouse drank once and then again and again.

"You gonna stand there looking at me like you're dying of thirst?"

"Give me that bottle. If anybody ever deserved a drink, I do."

"It's about time...."

Jack lifted the bottle. "To you, Brickhouse. To us. To freedom. We should be happy men."

"I don't put much stock in happiness no more."

"Yeah. This is the only true happiness."

Jack took a long pull. He liked the way the bourbon burned all the way down and then made him feel a little light-headed, wild.

"No woman's ever going to own me again." Jack took another long pull. "No woman—"

"Sounds like she's on your mind, though." Brickhouse's gaze darkened. "I gotta talk to you about that girl you brought home."

"She's the last thing I want to think about tonight."

"You wanna hear something crazy, man."

"I said shut up about her."

"That pretty white gal—she ain't your wife."

Jack's face went gray.

"Here, man. I can prove it." Brickhouse pulled out two folded manila envelopes. "That same night you were in New York to get your wife, I was there, too. I had my own agenda. I hired on as a waiter at Mischief Jones's party. Some job. I served raw fish and watched rich, phony weirdos gobble it down like that slimy shit was good to eat. Then this girl who looked exactly like your wife showed up. She looked me straight in the eye like she knew me and was afraid of me. Man, if I hadn't seen them both together..."

The liquor filled Jack with a strange lightness of

being, making him feel loose, relaxed for the first time
in years. He wanted Brickhouse to shut up.

"Jack, there was two of them."

Jack closed his eyes and felt the light breeze ruffle
his hair and caress his face. He was so tired, and yet
his temples were pounding. The liquor that only moments before had had him feeling good and free and
happy, now made him feel tense and confused.

A strange mist was rising from the ground and
swirling around them, so that they seemed to be the
only two people in the world. But the stars had come
out above them, and when Jack leaned his head back
against the railing, he could see the constellation
Orion blinking down at him.

"You listen to me, man."

Jack saw Mischief Jones, her green eyes maniacal
right before the stone cat slammed into his jaw.

He saw the girl in the park again, her beautiful face
aglow, her eyes tender as she talked to a little boy.

Jack nodded dizzily as he threw his head back to
take another long pull from the bottle. But this time
Brickhouse's large fist closed over his wrist. He
grabbed the bottle and threw it out into the darkness.

Glass shattered.

Jack jumped up drunkenly. "Now what did you go
and do a damn fool thing like that for?"

"You've had enough, man. Damn it. Look at these
envelopes. I got them out of Webster Quinn's car.
Quinn was the plastic surgeon who turned your wife
into a goddess five years ago. He made her so beautiful she became a model. For some damn reason six
months ago he made this girl named Bronte Devlin
look just like her."

Another piece of the puzzle.

Bronte.

Jack sagged to the floor, the name striking him like a blow. With a shudder Jack was back in Central Park. The girl with long red hair and glowing green eyes had run straight into him when she'd seen that cop.

Foggily he remembered her exact words.

I—I'm not Mischief. My real name is Bronte Devlin.

Like a damn fool, he'd played along with her. Because of the cop. He hadn't believed her, though.

She'd been telling him the truth. In the park. In the bar.

She'd run from him. She'd been scared and sweet. And *different*.

Jack's hand shook as he aimed a flashlight at her before-and-after pictures.

"She was pretty messed up," Brickhouse said needlessly. "These were taken in the E.R. She damn near died."

The pictures made Jack sick. As long as he lived, he was never going to forget them.

"Quinn took care of her for six months. When she found out what he'd done, she ran straight to Mischief. I was there, see, 'cause your Mischief had something to do with my Beauty's death. I wanted answers. Only somebody else got the bitch first."

"What the hell are you talking about now?"

"It's a long story. Forget it, man. I saved your ass in the stir because I wanted answers about Beauty. Only you hated the bitch more than I did. Then somebody else got to her before either of us could."

Brickhouse's words whirled queasily in Jack's brain.

Her name was Bronte.

He'd made love to Bronte Devlin.

Bronte Devlin had tricked him and seduced him.

Why?

Jack's stomach wrenched, and he swallowed the bitter bile in his throat. She'd used him. She'd made him care. She'd opened him up to the kind of pain he'd been running from.

"She's okay, man."

"No." Jack's face was hard and set. A cold, killing rage filled him. "She's a whore. Same as all women. She's faithless. Like my mother was. Like Chantal. She tricked me. I don't give a damn about her. She doesn't give a damn about me. She's been lying and pretending the whole damned time."

"You're too drunk to think straight."

"And whose fault is that?" Jack stood up. With a sickening lurch, he lunged at Brickhouse. His aim was off, and he weaved off balance. Staggering, he pitched forward, straight into Brickhouse's strong, waiting arms.

"You can't hold your liquor anymore, white boy."

The sharp tone made Jack's thoughts spin in a red haze.

Bronte. Hot tears burned close to the surface.

Once he had yearned for love. The bitter years with Chantal came back to him. The hopelessness and despair of prison was with him again. Old memories. Bad memories. He had too many of them.

Then he saw Bronte's shining face as she'd looked at him before he'd made love to her on that sheepskin rug. There had been so much hope and trust and adoration in those eyes.

Dear God.

"Bronte," he rasped with a choked sob.

"You got it bad, man."

Jack's cold, black eyes glared at his friend. The expression on Jack's face was just shy of frightening.

"I don't give a damn about her. Not really."

"You're too drunk and too stubborn to know what you want, boy. I expect you'll know in the morning, though."

Jack closed his eyes. "Shut up then, so I can sleep."

Chapter 19

Gossip was flying about the ranch as wildly as light-ning in a summer thunderstorm.

Everybody knew long before Jack crawled off Shanghai's porch at dawn and splashed himself with an icy bucket of water that he'd brought Chantal home, only to desert her up at the big house and go and get himself roaring drunk with a fearsome, black prison buddy.

Everybody wanted to know what Chantal had done, or who she'd done it with, to drive Jack back to booze so fast.

Chantal had always been trouble, big trouble.

The bets were on that she'd done it with Maverick right under Jack's nose. The *vaqueros* as well as the foremen and their families couldn't talk about any-thing else except her numerous exploits, naming cow-boys, naming places. Next to hunting, Chantal's ex-

ploits had been everybody's favorite topic of gossip
for as long as anybody could remember.

Eva said Chantal was nicer now. She said the witch
had grown herself a heart.

Then why was Jack so sore?

The smarter hands were sorry she was back. Sorry
to hear that Jack had lost out to his demons. If Jack
was finished, so was the ranch. The old señora was
past her prime, and Maverick was no rancher. He'd
sell the place first chance he got to city folk. He'd
take his profits, fire the cowboys and live in Europe.

"Mark my words. The ranch is done for," said old
Joe Crocker. "So are we. Chantal's trouble. She'll
bring Jack down. She did before."

The sky was dark above the cattle pens. The dusty
air that floated above the herd held a dampness that
smelled tantalizingly of rain.

Every muscle in Jack's body ached, and his eyes
burned from too little sleep, too much booze and a
foggy tangle of lust and guilt. The sun seemed over-
bright and his spurs, chaps and boots too heavy. The
red bandanna tied like a mask over his mouth and
nose choked him almost as badly as the dust.

He was glad of the deafening sounds. Glad of the
horses that were neighing and sputtering and pawing
the deep sand. Glad of the cattle in full voice, bawling
up and down the register as gates sorted them into
different pens, separating mothers from calves, steers
from heifers.

Only the *vaqueros* were quiet. Especially Mario,
whose all-seeing eyes darted everywhere.

Jack knew that the men had their minds on more
than cattle, that they were curious about his love life.

Not that Jack planned to set the nosy bunch straight.
He'd stick to the business of branding and vaccinating
and neutering, of sorting and readying steers and bar-
ren cows. The hands had better do the same.

He scarcely noticed the smell of mesquite smoke,
burning hide and manure that rose with the dust to
his nostrils. His jaw was hard beneath his Stetson. His
brown hands were folded across his saddle horn, and
he slumped forward on Dom, studying the herd, fighting to squelch his visions of *her* as he concentrated
on each animal.

From long hours and long years of assessing animals on roundup grounds, he'd imprinted a picture in
his mind of the perfect animal. He was always looking for that exceptional heifer or bull that would stand
out from a thousand others.

"You look kinda green about the gills, Jack." Dr.
K. North, the ranch's veterinarian had to shout to
make himself heard. "You gonna sit in that saddle by
this here chute and cull cattle all the damned day
when you're sick as dog? You oughta be back in the
big house in bed with your pretty wife."

Bronte.

Jack's eyes narrowed; his lips thinned as he imagined her naked body tangled in cotton sheets, her red
hair spreading away from her flushed cheeks.

He saw her bewitching smile and look of stricken
hurt last night after...

Just thinking about her got him as hot and hard as
a brick.

Dear God.

Without half trying, she'd wound him around her
little finger.

She must despise him for bedding her and scorning

her twice. Who could blame her? Why should he care?

She was a stranger and a liar.

Maybe she looked like an angel.

Maybe sinking into her body had been as close to heaven as he was likely to get.

She was a fake.

If and when she knew where he'd come from and what he was, she'd find him as disgusting as Chantal had.

For a moment he forgot Bronte and remembered the poor, desperate wretch he'd once been. He saw his mother's emaciated face, the helplessness and pain in her huge, dark eyes as she'd lain in that oven-like hovel under a cloud of flies. When he hadn't been out stealing scraps of garbage to feed her, he'd been home fanning her hot face and swatting flies. There'd been a man who'd paid him to sing for coins the *norte-americanos* threw. Only the man had stolen the dimes and laughed when Jack had begged for them because his mother was dying.

Jack had prayed for a way out of that hell. He didn't deserve Bronte. Who was he fooling? He was a thief, trash, unworthy....

Still, he *had* to know for sure if she was as bad as he kept telling himself she was. He needed to go to her and talk to her. To ask her dozens of questions. He wanted to know who she was and what her life had been like.

Damn it, he wouldn't do that. Something was wrong with her if she was mixed up with Chantal. It'd be a cold day in hell before he set foot in the big house again. At least not till she went back to wherever she'd come from.

What would Theodora do to him when she figured out the girl was a fake? Jack's plan to manage the ranch till Carla grew up was coming apart at the seams. Well, he didn't have time to worry about that.

"The work getting to you, K?"

"No, sir."

"Then don't go sticking your nose where it don't belong." Jack's black mood caused his voice to come out harsh and loud. It was an effort to speak with so much tearing at him.

"That girl got you drinking again, Jack?"

"It was only a slip."

"More than a slip by the looks of you."

"I went a little crazy. But that doesn't mean… Damn it. I'm not starting back. Don't you go blaming her, either."

"That's a new one." K.'s voice was sassier than ever.

"What?"

"Your defending her."

"If you say so, old man."

"One day at a time, young feller."

K. was a reformed alcoholic himself.

"You got that right, K."

Then Jack touched his Stetson and gave a grim nod toward a particular shiny-coated, auburn heifer in the chute. K. North scribbled something on his papers, and Mario herded the prized animal into the pen for Jack's experimental herd.

Jack had been up since dawn, working cattle with Mario and Brickhouse and the rest of his men. He forced himself to sit straighter in his saddle even though he still felt queasy. Despite two aspirins, a violent headache throbbed behind his fiery eyelids. He had a hell of a hangover.

Four hundred bawling cattle didn't help his headache. Neither did K.'s reports that confirmed the bulls were indeed sterile. Since Jack had tested the bulls at the auction house, how was such an error possible?

Ranching in south Texas was a hard business. Over half the land of El Atascadero was heavy sand, dunes left over from the receding Gulf of Mexico. During times of adequate rainfall, cattle could survive on the rolling dunes amidst shin oak and mesquite. Ranchers could make a small profit. In times of drought, like now, making money was damn near impossible. Still, the problems Jack had experienced since he'd come home from prison were worse than the norm.

Somebody was setting him up. There was more to these problems and accidents than could be seen on the surface. How come every mistake could be laid at his door?

Somebody wanted him gone.

Who?

At two, when the day's roundup was half over and the cowboys broke for lunch, tension filled the cow camp. In a grove of mesquite and ebony trees, Mario had stretched a couple of tarps to make more shade. Rough wooden tables had been set up under them. A side of beef, slaughtered that morning, hung from a limb. The other half gave off the tantalizing aroma of barbecue as it cooked over an open fire.

The men kept to themselves, avoiding Jack. Not that he minded. His touchy stomach rebelled at the thought of ribs and sausage and sliced tenderloin, and he wasn't in the mood for conversation.

There were refried beans, tomatoes and onions. While the *vaqueros* ate heartily together of roasted calf testicles and saddle strings, which were long, thin strips of grilled meat pulled from the ribs, Jack sat alone and consumed only a bowl of rice and beans, and a platter of thin camp bread, which he washed down with five glasses of sweet tea.

When the men were done, Jack could feels their eyes on him. In the cattle pens beyond, the dust and bawling seemed to be more intense. Jack stood up to try to see what had the animals so riled.

White horns bobbed up and down like waves in a stormy red sea, but he couldn't figure out why they were so jumpy.

"The cattle and the men are getting restless," K. said. "Let's get back to it."

Jack sat awhile longer with K. in the deep shade of a live oak. Something didn't feel right.

Thoughtfully he watched his men set their plates down and start poking their branding irons back into the fire until the ends were white-hot. Still he hesitated before he gave the signal to go back to work.

Above the low murmur of the men's voices, Jack heard someone say something about marrying a ranch and getting more than he bargained on. Then Greg Cassidy's voice rose even higher. "I was glad she kicked the greedy bastard out 'cause it won't be long before she gets the itch and comes looking for it. You ever dipped your wick in that honey pot? She's juicy and tight, and she don't lay still. She kicks and screams and bucks better than the wildest bull I ever rode in a rodeo."

"If you ain't careful, she'll bite it off like a wildcat, Cassidy."

Violence swelled inside Jack even before the men laughed. In a blinding flash, he was on his feet and lunging toward them, swinging a fist into Cassidy's jaw and kicking a boot heel into his shin. Cassidy was taller and heavier, but he hadn't seen the blows coming. He reeled backward, sprawling clumsily into the dirt. Jack threw himself on top of him. Before Cassidy could get his breath, Jack rolled him over and planted a boot on his stomach and leaned heavily on it.

"You say one more word about my wife and I'll kill you."

Cassidy's eyes bulged.

"Enough," K. yelled. "Break 'em up...before somebody gets himself kicked to death."

Rough hands grabbed Jack's shoulders and pulled him off. He didn't fight the men who grabbed him, but his deadly expression didn't relax much, either.

"Get the hell off this place." Jack leaned down and picked up his Stetson. "And any other man who has something to say about my wife better get, too."

Bronte.

No wonder they wanted her.

Jack remembered her naked body and how soft and sweet she'd felt beneath his hands. He remembered the warm honey of her kisses. The kindness in her voice.

He wanted to hate her. He was determined to hate her. But the fierce emotion that made him want to kill any man who so much as thought about touching her was not hate.

The day got no better for Jack as it wore on; if anything, it got worse. Thunder rumbled. Not that so much as a drop of rain fell. At four, a gate latch broke, and one hundred cattle burst free, nearly crushing Mario as they stampeded into the brush.

When Jack discovered that the latch had been deliberately tampered with, he again sensed his unseen enemy. Thoughtfully, he ordered six cowboys to round up the cattle and secure the pen. Then he told Mario to tell Maverick he wanted to see him in his office.

Maverick sent word back that he was way too busy.

Doing what—making more mischief? Jack wondered. He damn sure hadn't showed his face at roundup.

Jack had been sitting in his tiny office off the garage for an hour, with bills, ledgers and spreadsheets stacked around him sky-high, when Maverick finally saw fit to show up.

He was wearing a white linen suit and a red silk tie.

"You wanted to see me?"

Jack's gaze fastened on the strip of scarlet silk. "Nice tie."

Maverick leaned heavily against the huge gun safe for a minute. Then he bent over and tossed aside several neatly labeled files that had been stacked on a chair. With a casual air, he sprawled lazily into the high-backed, leather chair, which was opposite Jack's desk. "Heard about the fight."

Jack ignored the comment. "Somebody used bolt shears on that latch today."

"Don't look at me. I wasn't anywhere near—"

"Maybe I could have used your help."

"That's a first." Their gazes connected and held. Jack handed him the accountant's latest monthly report. ''Somebody's stealing, too. Got any ideas who that might be?''

A cool recklessness flashed across Maverick's aristocratic features. ''You don't want my guess.'' As always, his voice was oddly pleasant to the ear. It was the well-educated voice of a gentleman, overlaid with the flat, casual drawl of a south Texas rancher. His air of utter assurance irritated Jack almost as much as it had when he'd been poor and illiterate and Maverick a snot-nosed, sissy brat.

Maverick's mouth curled with cynical humor when Jack remained stern-faced and silent. ''Because I'd say it's you.''

''Somebody's damn sure trying to make it look that way,'' Jack agreed tightly.

Maverick's eyes twinkled. ''Who was a thief in Mexico?'' Jack's tanned face darkened. ''Settle down. Bear with me now. You know, there's a saying that goes like this—if you hear hoofbeats in Texas, don't think of zebras. When I hear the word *thief,* I think of the only one I personally know.''

''I only stole when I had to—''

''How reassuring.''

Jack rose out of his leather chair. ''Now—''

''You asked!'' Maverick's full red lips parted in a cool smile. ''Why, everybody knows you only married my cousin for the ranch, not for Carla. I never shed any tears thinking about you losing Cheyenne, either. Cheyenne was too poor back then. You loved this ranch way more than any woman.''

That got him—the way Maverick knew it would. But Maverick didn't stop there. No, sirree. Jack was determined to grit his teeth and hear him out.

Maverick sat up boldly, pushing him to the edge,

going too far, the way he could sometimes. "From the second you set foot on this place, you wanted it. You haven't changed, either. Why else did you go after Chantal as soon as you got out of prison? Why did you bring her back?"

"You tell me."

"Have it your way. I think you're hiding something, Jack. Chantal's acting strange. She's nothing like she used to be. I can't put my finger on what's wrong between you two, but something damn sure is. Don't try to make me think she's gone sweet on you. She only married you because she got knocked up and nobody else would have her. She wanted me…way more than she ever wanted you…even after she married you. She told me so lots of times. You saw the truth for yourself that day in the bunkhouse."

Suddenly Maverick paled as Jack's features grew wolfish, and it was mighty satisfying to see just how fast his rival could wilt when he felt he'd overreached himself and was cornered.

"If she's sweet on me now, that's our business. You stay away from her."

"I never chase women. Unless they encourage… With her, I don't imagine it'll take too long.…"

"If you're smart, you'll ignore her encouragement," Jack warned icily. "Now, back to the subject at hand. Unless things change, this ranch is going under. Bulls are going sterile. Men are falling into combines. Money is missing.… Somebody's behind all this."

Maverick leaned forward. "I wonder who."

The anger in Jack's gaze matched the insolence in Maverick's.

"None of this was a problem till you came home,

Jack. That makes it easy, at least for me, to figure out what's going on. Not many of the men trust you. Why don't you quit trying to blame me? Why don't you take your bottle and crawl into some hole? Do us all a favor—stay there till you drink yourself to death. I'll take care of the ranch and Chantal.''

''You'd drive this place into the ground the same you did Caroline's. If you lay a hand on…my wife, I'll kill you.''

Maverick got up. ''I've heard enough for one day.''

''Ditto. But I warn you, I'm going to talk to Theodora.''

Maverick grinned nastily. ''I've got nothing to hide. You're the one with the record.'' At the door he paused. ''If you're gonna attack every man that wants to do it with Chantal, you're gonna have to wage a one-man war.''

''That's my business.''

Late that afternoon the wind was rising. Thickening dust whirled beneath a black sky. Wranglers were once more hard at work on the herd, which was newly secured in the largest and strongest of the holding lots.

Jack could have quit, but it wouldn't be good for his men's morale. Besides, he didn't want to chance a run-in with *her*. So he waved to his cowboys as he rode past them, shouting he'd double-check the pastures and make sure the sandy stretches and dense brush were clean of strays. Cows could be ingenious at hiding themselves and their calves in dense brush or a gully until the line of the corrida swept by them.

Jack rode for a mile or two without seeing a single animal. Soon he was alone in a particularly brushy pasture. As was his custom, he had one end of his rope tightly knotted to the pommel of his saddle, while its coils, tied by a horn string, dangled loosely at his knee.

He kept a watchful eye on the thick line of brush as well as on the heavy, dark clouds that skimmed low and fast across the blackening sky. Suddenly lightning flashed against the horizon, and a startled calf, small but feisty, spurted out of the brush and raced away from him.

Dom shot after the calf. Jack bent forward and kept the stallion's head high. He neither urged nor spurred. Dom flew, his tail flicking in the wind. Jack hung on tightly to the reins. Fire ant mounds and thick clumps of *zacahuista* sped past pounding hooves. Mesquite and huisache blurred. Soon the poor little calf began to tire, and inch by precious inch, horse and rider started gaining on him.

Jack slipped the horn string off his pommel. With Dom racing over the uneven ground, Jack took the rope coils and the reins into his left hand. With his right, he made a small loop that he whirled and sent flying, but it landed short and fell into the tall dry grass. Jack held on to the rope, dragging it.

Dom never slowed as Jack coiled the rope and made a second loop, this one larger than the first.

The calf was slowing as Jack aimed for his head and threw. This time the loop closed neatly around his neck, and with an expert flick of his wrist, Jack pulled on the reins and the rope at the same time. Dom reared, yanking the calf around, dragging him, snorting and bawling, till he faced them.

When Dom quieted, the calf stood still, staring at them, wheezing and wild-eyed, the rope still strangling him. Sweat poured off Dom's flanks. He was panting even harder than the calf.

Jack dismounted. The calf was so tired, Jack figured the best thing was to carry him back to the herd over his saddle. But when he knelt to loosen the rope around his neck, the calf bawled and began kicking. So Jack just picked him up.

By the time Jack reached Dom, the tired calf was struggling and squalling only a little. But just as Jack was about to grab the reins and slip his foot into the stirrup, a powerful gust of wind stirred through the brush. Then a zigzag of white-hot lightning struck a hundred yards in front of Dom.

Dom's eyes rolled backward. Jack jumped away as the stallion reared.

"Easy, boy."

Thunder roared.

Dom didn't scare as easily as most horses, but like all of his kind, his instinct was flight. He'd trample anything or anybody in his frantic desire to escape.

Thoroughly spooked, the stallion broke into a hard gallop.

Jack's loose rope tensed. A single coil that Jack had inadvertently stepped through when he'd jumped away from Dom snapped tightly around his booted ankle.

"Hey, hey. Easy, Dom..." A cold sweat broke out on Jack's brow. He fought to hold the calf and twist his foot out of the noose-like coil.

But Dom continued forward, carrying the rope with him, and the loop wound tighter.

In the next instant Jack's foot was jerked out from under him. The calf kicked him in the chest and sprang to the ground. Hopping and then falling, Jack shouted to Dom as he felt himself being dragged.

But the stallion just raced faster.

They say that your life passes before you as you die.

Funny how all Jack thought of was *her.* Again he saw Bronte's luminous face as she'd lain beneath him on the sheepskin rug. Again he heard her soft sigh of surrender when he'd pushed himself inside her and been gloved by her exquisite warmth. Her shining gaze had locked to his as completely as her body, giving everything of herself to him—even her soul.

As Dom neighed loudly and lunged forward, the rope tightened and Jack's body bumped backward.

From a gallop, Dom broke into a hard run, dragging calf and man through mesquite, granjeno and brazil.

Jack's head cracked against a sharp rock, and everything went black.

Chapter 20

The sky whitened. Thunder crashed.

Guerro whined plaintively, thumping his tail against Bronte's ankle and looking up to her for reassurance.

A wild wet wind fanned Bronte as she sat on the verandah sipping hot tea with Carla and Theodora. An even stronger gust lifted Bronte's hair off her warm neck and tugged at her skirt.

Lightning flamed repeatedly, the sky flashing in bursts of green and livid white.

Bronte's fingers tightened on the wafer-thin handle of her china cup. A sudden uneasiness struck her. Jack was out in this violent weather.

Theodora pushed her chair back. ''We'd better go inside.''

Guerro loped to the door and looked up at the door handle expectantly, as if to suggest the same thing.

''But Jack's still working cattle.''

"It won't be the first time he got a little wet," Theodora said.

Bronte set her cup down. She couldn't stop staring at the black sky. For a crazy moment she wanted to run out and search for him. Guerro padded back to her and put his head in her lap so she could idly stroke him behind his ears.

Why should she care so much about Jack? He wanted her gone. She would have gone, too; she would have left with Becky, who'd offered her a ride to Houston. Only Bronte had seen Carla sneaking out of an oak mott near the house with her lunch pail less than an hour after her orange school bus had driven away.

Bronte had told herself it wasn't any of her business if *his* daughter skipped school.

But an hour later she'd been standing under Carla's tree, coaxing her to come down. Then she'd driven the thirty-two miles round-trip to Carla's school and visited Carla's teachers and principal in an attempt to discover why she hated school. The reason had been logical; the solution was simple. Carla was unchallenged and bored.

So Bronte's excuse for staying was that a child's educational welfare was at stake.

Liar.

Maybe that was one of the reasons...

"How long do you think roundup will take?" Bronte asked casually.

"You never can tell," Theodora said. "Depends on how things go. I expect Jack'll put in a long day. One of the gates broke. Half the herd got loose. Jack's checking for strays. I reckon we ought to start dinner without him."

Bronte stood up slowly, her face brightening. Dom

was streaking toward them across the pasture.
''No...look. Over there.''

Thunder rolled.

Something wasn't right.

A sudden fear struck her, and she ran to the edge
of the verandah, with Carla and Theodora close at her
heels.

Dom was riderless.

He was galloping straight at them, dragging something so huge and heavy that it raked up spirals of
dust behind him.

''Dad!'' Carla yelled frantically.

Wild terror swept through Bronte as she remembered the story of Samson West being murdered and
dragged by his horse to his death.

With a shiver Bronte grabbed the railing to steady
her wobbly knees. Juan, a young *vaquero,* who was
mowing the lawn, killed the engine, grabbed a coil of
rope from his pickup bed and ran toward Dom. Juan's
lean, brown arm was soon expertly twirling the rope,
which fell in a perfect arc over Dom's head.

Enraged, Dom reared wildly. Juan dug his boot
heels into the dirt and hung on, all the time talking
in soothing Spanish until, finally, the stallion calmed
a little.

Her face drained of color, Bronte ran toward them.
Carla had seized hold of her hand, and Bronte hardly
knew what she did as she dragged the child in her
wake.

The rushing wind grew stronger around them,
pushing against them, carrying the dark, voluminous
clouds toward the house. The air blew damp and cool
against their cheeks now.

Lightning flashed in a series of whizzing, white
bolts, and Dom reared frantically again. Backing,

prancing like a heavy, graceless dancer, the stallion lunged up and down repeatedly, his flying hooves crashing into the dirt and then flying at Juan's black head again as the *vaquero* hung on.

The sky had been equally dark and the weather equally violent the day Jimmy had died.

Jimmy.

Samson.

Bronte felt as if she stood on the crumbling ledge of a bottomless, black abyss. One false step and she would lose her balance and be sucked into the void.

Not Jack. Please, not Jack, too.

Before Bronte and Carla could reach the horse and the filthy, torn object that lay tangled and lifeless at the end of the rope, the rain began to beat down in torrents. Instantly Bronte's hair and dress were sodden.

"Oh, Jack."

"It's just a calf, *señorita,*" Juan said, his black eyes gentle, his breathless voice kind. "His neck's broke. The rocks, the rope…"

She knelt beside the still little animal that had been choked to death by being dragged across the pasture. Gently she removed the rope from its neck and laid the twisted hemp on the ground.

"Where's Jack? Where is he? I—I've got to find him.…"

She stood up, but when she put her hand on Dom's slick reins, the stallion jerked his head away from her.

"He's too tired and wild to be ridden by anybody but Jack right now," Theodora said.

"Doña Theodora, she is right, Miss Chantal," Juan said.

"He could be hurt!" Bronte said fiercely.

"I'll go," Juan said. "You stay here with the old miss."

Bronte stared at them both. Her eyes grew dazed and unfocused as the rain gushed down.

"I have to go!"

Before they could protest, she blindly thrust her slim foot in the stirrup and swung herself up into the saddle.

Carla screamed, "Take me with you!"

"No!" Theodora tried to grab the reins. "You'll both break your necks."

Bronte reached down and pulled Carla up behind her.

"Hold on tight." Then Bronte dug her heels into the big horse's sides. Dom took off, streaking away from the house, into the storm that now fell in drenching sheets.

They were only a mile down the road when the sky whitened again, and a man screamed weakly, "Over here."

The sky went black again. The rain was so thick and violent, they might have still passed him by if he hadn't yelled a second time.

"Bronte!"

Her name.

He knew.

Bronte stopped immediately and dismounted.

Carla took one look at Jack, who'd been holding on to the fence as he hobbled back toward the big house, and then at Bronte. "I'll send someone with a truck." The girl sprinted away from them toward the house.

Jack's face was white; his eyes were ringed with black. His blood-soaked shirt clung to his shivering chest in ragged strips. A long laceration ran from his pale cheek down his jaw and neck, down the length of his torso.

She saw the clotted red line of gaping flesh. "Oh, Jack...."

He didn't smile when Bronte raced up to him and threw her arms around him. "You're wet and cold," she exclaimed. "Why, your skin's like ice. You're shaking. But you're alive. I was so afraid. I—I've got to get you home. Out of these clothes before you catch a chill." With gentle fingertips she probed the long wound. "It doesn't look too deep—"

He jerked away from her. "I thought you were leaving this morning. Why didn't you?"

The rain hammered them.

Rivulets ran the length of her cheek and dripped off her face like tears. "I was, but Carla..." Trembling from deep inside, Bronte took a step away from him. "She missed her bus. I drove her—"

"Quit playing the loving wife and mother. I know who you are now. You're not my wife. You may look like her, but—"

"I care about you, Jack."

"You're a liar, *Bronte*."

"I—I tried to tell you who I was. That day on the street."

"You should have tried harder. I nearly got my ass shot off. You played the part of my wife to the hilt!"

"I didn't ask to look like Mischief. I—"

"Shut up. I wouldn't believe anything you said now."

She had to give him time. She shouldn't be surprised that he was furious. Still, his scathing insults, the mockery and harsh tone hurt.

"You played me for a fool," he said. "You're

worse than Chantal. You don't give a damn about me.''

"How can I—'' Bronte broke off abruptly. "When I saw Dom dragging that poor little calf... Oh, Jack, I was so afraid it was you.''

"You don't know me. You don't know anything about me—how I was raised, who I really am. If you did—''

"Theodora told me. Everything. I'm sorry about what happened to you as a little boy. I'm sorry about Mexico. About your mother, too.''

His dark face tightened. "We've known each other less than a week. We're nothing to each other now. Strangers...who shared a bed.''

"Twice,'' she said softly.

His face looked startled for a second by the stark emotion shining in her too-brilliant eyes. Then he flushed darkly. "It didn't mean anything.''

"Speak for yourself,'' she said tonelessly. "I love you, Jack.''

"I don't want your love. I don't want anybody's love. You said you were leaving. So go! What the hell are you waiting for? I don't need you. I don't need anybody. Dom—''

"Jack...''

Jack gave a low whistle, and the big stallion ambled over as docilely as a lamb, trustingly sniffing his outstretched hand.

"It's about time you decided to settle down.'' Jack's voice was gentle now that he was speaking to his horse.

When he grabbed the long reins and put his good foot in the stirrup, Bronte hung on to his arm.

"No.... You're hurt. You can't ride. Carla's—''

He pushed her away. "You just watch me,

Bronte.'' With a groan of pure agony, he slung himself heavily into the saddle.

He gazed down at her in contemptuous triumph. "See?"

"Jack, I really do love you." She didn't know her eyes had grown huge.

He clicked his tongue, and his stallion wheeled away from her.

"Quit acting like you give a damn one way or the other," he shouted down to her. "Because I don't give a damn about you." He set his cold, insolent gaze on her one final time. "If I did, I wouldn't ride off and leave you all by yourself in this storm. On this road. Where anybody could come…and anything could happen to you."

More frightened by his callous indifference than she was of anything else, she took three running steps after him.

He scowled when he glanced over his shoulder and saw her still chasing after him in the rain. From under the brim of his hat, his eyes darkened when she ran faster.

"Jack!"

He raced away from her down the road.

Low clouds enveloped horse and rider, until they were almost completely hidden from her.

But she knew when he stopped.

She knew when he turned and saw that she was still coming toward him through the mist.

She could tell he was fighting a grim battle with himself. She understood, because it was the same battle she'd fought with herself earlier when she'd tried to force herself to leave him.

Even though he looked enraged, he must have been more moved by the fresh desolation in her eyes than he was willing to admit because suddenly, with a movement of his heels, he spurred Dom to a gallop and raced straight toward her.

Hooves splashed mud into her face and eyes.

Her scream of pure terror was cut short as Jack reached down and grabbed her by the waist and scooped her up. Without ever breaking stride, he slung her behind him.

Her legs clambered over the horse's back with fluid expertise. Quickly her arms circled Jack's waist, and she held on to him tightly, feeling foolishly joyous to suddenly find that he hadn't been able to gallop away and leave her as he'd so heartlessly threatened.

With a grim sigh, Jack turned Dom toward home. Bronte gasped with heady pleasure and buried her cheek against the middle of Jack's back and inhaled the musky warm scent of his damp shirt and skin.

When he felt her lips wantonly scorch his spine, he shuddered. Whether he knew it or not, whether he willed it or not, this was where she belonged and where she intended to stay.

Beside him. With him.

Always.

And she was willing to fight for their love and fight him every step of the way.

You can't win, no matter what you do.

Yes! Yes, I can! I have a new beautiful face. And this new, beautiful man. I am not an ugly duckling anymore. I am brave and strong.

As Dom walked back toward the house in the steady downpour, the whirling rain seemed less threatening to her than it ever had before.

Jack was alive and not too badly injured.

She loved him, and she was going to win him.

When the red-tiled roof of the mansion finally rose

over the tangle of mesquite, Bronte clung to him and pressed her cheek more tightly against his hard back. Again he trembled violently every time she touched him.

She wanted to share her life with him.

Not that she would tell him again just yet.

Not when he was so set against her.

Maybe, with such a stubborn man, it was necessary to play a rather perverse game to win him. She remembered her flirtatious mother playing hard-to-get with her many lovers. Always in the past, Bronte had spurned her mother's games. But she had her mother's face now. Perhaps just this once…

When Dom got to the drive that wound up to the house, Bronte jumped down and, with a pretense of spirited independence, ran from Jack toward the stairs.

Quick as a flash, Jack dismounted, too.

When she heard his boots ring on the concrete steps behind her, she tried to run up the stairs away from him, but he caught her slender wrist and spun her around.

His face was deeply lined, and his eyes were shadowed by fatigue. "Thanks…for coming after me," he said, his deep voice unsteady.

She swallowed, barely able to talk around the lump in her throat. "Jack…you—you should see a doctor."

"I'll be fine. I have to see about Dom now."

"I'll get Juan to do that. Your cut needs to be cleaned."

"I said no doctor."

"Then let me do it."

The muscles tightened in his throat. His expression grew fierce. "I said—"

She glanced up at him through her lashes, flirting

the way her mother had. "Why, Jack, did anybody around here ever dare to tell you that you're just about the most stubborn man alive?"

In his eyes, she saw some new emotion.

He looked away without answering.

She smiled gently—her own smile. "Well, I'm telling you then. I want to take care of you."

"There you are," a voice boomed. Maverick raced inside, drenched, grim-faced. "Carla sent me out to rescue you two."

Jack ignored Maverick and smiled at Bronte. "Looks like we did just fine without you."

"Thanks, Maverick," Bronte whispered softly, appeasing him. But she, too, was staring at Jack.

When his smile never wavered, she began to feel safe and warm. She almost felt she was beginning to belong in this house and to this man.

She was so beautiful that just staring at her made him feel euphoric.

And the minx knew it and was using it against him.

To shut her out, Jack closed his eyes and counted horses.

In the shelter of their bedroom, Bronte was gently bathing the jagged slash that ran from his neck to his midriff while he lay bonelessly sprawled in a large armchair. He didn't flinch even when the alcohol swabs Bronte dabbed at the cuts in his scalp and the long tear across his torso burned like hell.

Her breasts, swathed in damp, clinging cloth, pressed into his shoulder as she leaned over him, and her cool, trembly hands moved slowly through his thick, wet hair, down his neck and still lower.

He breathed in the dizzying smell of gardenias along with her own special scent and longed to touch that slim, luscious body that swayed so seductively over him.

The horses blurred, and she filled his imagination. *Bronte.*

Was it really so essential to his pride that he stay mad at her forever?

No matter how hard he tried to maintain a sour expression, he couldn't stop thinking about how joyous she'd looked when she'd found him hobbling along that fence line in the rain, and realized he was alive. The memory of her bright smile and soft hands stirred him so hard that his longing for her bordered on agony. He clenched his fists to keep from grabbing her.

What was the matter with him? He was a lowborn barrio bastard. She would despise him for that alone.

She had said Theodora had told her everything. That she knew about his past. That she loved him anyway.

She had lied to him.

He'd been a thief. Who was he to judge? Nobody was perfect. And when, oh, when had anyone ever acted like they cared so much about him as she had this afternoon? In his whole damned life there had never been a single soul before Bronte.

She was touching his chest with those infinitely gentle fingertips, tending him with such care.

All night he had lain on Shanghai's porch in a drunken haze, dreaming of her. Remembering how huge and powerful he'd felt when he'd been tightly sheathed inside her. Wanting to find and kill the bastard who'd shot at her. Knowing he'd either die or explode if he couldn't ever have her again. Telling himself he wanted her gone. Knowing the whole damned night that he wanted her forever. Feeling scared and sick that she might still be in mortal danger.

He had never wanted anybody the way he wanted her. That's why she'd driven him crazy by being so sweet and kind to him when he'd thought she was Chantal.

Maybe he should back off his stubborn tack and compromise…just a bit. If it was a bad idea, he could play the bastard again later.

Then she smiled at him, like a golden sunbeam shining through a dark cloud. One glance, and he felt like she was staring straight into his soul.

As if he had a choice.

His steely black eyes narrowed. "Come here," he whispered, tenderly.

"Who, me?" Her voice was soft as she backed a step or two from him—deliberately flirting.

But her eyes held the connection, and as she began to understand his change of mood, her smile got bigger and brighter. The silence that stretched between them grew as taut as his nerves.

His mouth stretched into a slow grin. "I want to talk to you, Bronte Devlin," he said huskily.

"Kiss me first."

"How—if you won't come here?"

Her lashes fluttered, allowing him a final glimpse of emerald irises clouding with desire before she obeyed him.

Gently he wrapped his arms around her slim waist. He felt warm woman skin burning through wet cotton. Her slender fingers curled into the mat of crisp, dark chest hair, and when her hand stirred there, he felt his heart pound beneath her lightly caressing fingertips.

Slowly, gently, she lowered her face over his.

He kissed her mouth as she had kissed him that first night—sweetly, tenderly.

He closed his eyes as she returned his chaste kiss, her warm lips lingering gently.

"Bear with me," he murmured. "There's something I've got to see for myself."

With unsteady fingers he unfastened the top three buttons of her damp blouse and slid the fabric downward to expose her left shoulder.

"I knew who you were right after we made love in the bathroom," he said. At the sudden huskiness in his voice she looked up, bewildered.

He brushed the creamy, smooth skin with a reverent fingertip. His lips tasted the same sweet flesh. Then he sighed, deeply content, and began to rebutton her shirt.

"Jack, why did you do that?"

He felt like a cowboy checking a brand.

"Maybe I'll tell you someday."

She was his. Only his. He felt a rush of unwanted emotion.

No. Not yet. He wasn't ready to feel so much or to admit so much. Not even to himself.

"But why—"

"Later. Right now all I want to do is kiss you."

"Oh, I love you so much. I didn't think I could ever love anybody again."

"Do you honestly mean that?"

"Yes. And I love having sex with you."

He chuckled.

"I want it all the time. Every time I look at you." She blushed shyly. "Nobody ever made me feel like that. I just hope you don't mind my saying it."

He looked down at her, his eyes dark with unnamed emotion. "I don't mind." What she said was too wonderful to believe. "I just hope you don't mind if I can't say it yet." His voice cracked. "I don't know what I think anymore," he added a long time later when she broke free and nuzzled her cheek against his muscular shoulder. "Or what I feel. It's too soon to make promises. I would if I could...." Gently he traced the lines of her face.

"You don't have to," she uttered whimsically. "In my real life, I was a kindergarten teacher. Big changes...take time. I learned a long time ago to celebrate the small ones. So I don't expect anything. I just want this moment. It's enough...your acting nice for a change...."

He laughed. "I'm sorry. The situation has been a bit complicated. It still is. Maybe more than ever. Theodora sent me after her daughter. My wife."

"She's dead."

"I know. That's not what I mean."

"Does Chantal still matter so much?"

"Not like you might think she does. No. In that way, there's only you. I swear. But there's more to this whole situation than I first thought."

"What do you mean?"

"I'm not sure. I have a bad feeling about all this. I think we'd better be careful. Somebody nearly killed you—twice. I don't think that was an accident. Then you saw that red tie...here. Chantal is dead. So is Webster Quinn. I think they were murdered by the same person who tried to kill you. Nothing's been right since I got out of prison. Money's missing. We've had too many accidents. And I want to know why. Somebody's after something. I have a hunch we're blocking them—"

The phone rang downstairs. A couple of minutes later Theodora's shadowy form stood in their doorway. She gripped the cordless receiver in her thin, shaking fingers.

"It's Mario."

Mario was on a cellular phone. Static popped on the line, breaking his voice into incoherent fragments.

"A plane…down…pasture…"

"Where?"

Static crackled. "Three miles…pond…south…big house."

Rubbing his brow, Jack moved away from her.

"Jack, what is it?" Bronte whispered, frantic.

He told her.

"Who would fly in this weather?"

Mario was talking to him at the same time, so Jack lowered his head and strained to listen.

A second later Jack put his hand over the mouthpiece and looked up. "Mario says it's a private plane. He's not sure whether the pilot and crew got out. I have to go check—"

"No!"

"The *vaqueros* are afraid to go anywhere near it. They've heard too many stories about ranchers getting plugged in the head by dope runners. Two weeks ago a Mexican *federale* was shot a hundred times in front of his house and then run over with a car. I've got to go myself—"

Theodora shook her head grimly.

"Jack, no. You're hurt," Bronte whispered. "If they're dope smugglers, and they're still there, they'll be desperate. Caroline told me how dangerous—"

"I'll be okay."

"Jack, no—"

"Hey, maybe we'll get lucky. Maybe we'll be able to sell the plane. It'd make up for those bulls."

"Don't joke…"

Bronte knelt down before him. She threw her arms around him, pleading silently with wide, terrified eyes that showed the intensity of her feelings for him more clearly than any words ever could.

She loved him.

His hard face softened.

There was a roaring in his ears.

His heart drummed.

Tell her you love her.

His mouth was dry.

He whispered a garbled curse, and then he wrapped his arms around her, too. If he couldn't say it, he had to at least kiss her, even with Theodora standing there.

Gently he cupped Bronte's chin and brought her sweet face to his. His mouth met hers with an aching tenderness that soon deepened into something more. Their kiss was timeless, and yet for him it was fresh and new. The building pressure inside him was soon more than he could endure. He was as hot as a capped volcano when he let her go.

"No more," he whispered dizzily against her ear. "Later."

"Promise?"

A harsh shudder rocked him. He stared past her. At Theodora.

"I love you," Bronte said.

"I don't deserve you," he murmured.

"Yes, you do."

"You're too sweet and fine for a man like me."

"I've been such a coward in my life. I admire courage more than anything. You're the bravest man I've ever met."

"Do you really mean that?"

"With all my heart."

"Oh, my darling," he groaned, resealing their lips and then tearing himself reluctantly away again.

"Take me with you." Her whisper was low and hoarse, thready with need.

He wanted to push Theodora politely out of the room, to take Bronte to bed, to have her naked underneath him, to explore her warm, womanly softness, to forget the dope plane and all the other dangers swirling around them, to forget everything except losing himself in this beautiful woman again. To hold her in his arms for hours afterward—as he had not done before.

Wind and rain beat at the windows.

"No way can I risk anything happening to you. You stay here. Take care of Carla." Then he kissed her softly.

When he opened the front door several minutes later, Jack still felt dizzy and disoriented from their final kiss. Gently, very gently he loosened his hand from her slender, clinging fingers. Hurling himself out of the big house, he dashed down the stairs into the wild, wet rain.

He didn't look back.

Not even once.

He had no way of knowing how soon he would lie dying in her arms and regret that he hadn't.

Chapter 21

Never had Bronte hated rain more than tonight. It fell in gushing torrents. The wind roared in the palms, battered the shutters and screamed around the house, howling in the eaves. Thunder rolled incessantly, and the sky flashed like strobe lights.

Numb with fear, Bronte hugged herself and stared at the huge, sparkling raindrops slashing the long windows.

Jack was out there. Hurt, half-dead with exhaustion, he faced God alone knew what dangers in that wild storm.

"Why doesn't he call?"

"You've asked me that at least a dozen times," Theodora said impatiently. "He will."

"How can you know that?"

"He always does."

"Anything could happen to him."

"Not to Jack."

Still, when the phone rang, Theodora jumped, too.

"There! I told you!" she said as Bronte rushed past her to the library.

"Jack…"

The tense, male voice identified himself as Sheriff Ortiz from Val Verde, Texas.

"You've got a problem. Two convicts busted out of our jail down here tonight. They're armed and dangerous. We spotted them by helicopter not ten minutes south of your house. Lady, you'd better get your guns and your ammo. Lock your doors and windows. Get that cousin of yours and Caroline and everybody else into the cellar of your big house. Y'all stay put, till my deputy gets there. It's gonna take him an hour."

"But Jack's—"

She was speaking to a dial tone. The sheriff had hung up on her.

When she explained what he'd said to Theodora, the older woman's black eyes turned chillingly cold.

"We don't have much time."

"What about Jack?"

"Get Carla down here. Tell her to turn the lights off, both inside and out. Tell her to phone Caroline. You and I'll get the guns. Get Juan."

Bronte screamed up to Carla, who had no doubt been eavesdropping because for once she came flying.

"One more thing…" Theodora said to Bronte as Carla dialed.

"What?"

"The guns are outside in Jack's office."

"We'd better keep one," Theodora said, seizing a handheld automatic from Juan's pile.

"What for?" Bronte whispered.

''Just in case...'' Theodora rammed bullets into the clip.

Bronte closed the steel door of Jack's huge gun safe as Juan rushed out into the wild night toward the house with the last sack load of pistols, revolvers, hunting rifles and shotguns.

Theodora offered her the loaded automatic, but Bronte, who was more terrified of the gun than the convicts, shook her head. ''You keep it.''

Bronte shut off the lights. With a pounding heart, she stepped outside.

Rain gushed from the gutters. Lightning streaked the sky.

Theodora followed as silently as a shadow.

A single light burned from a telephone pole.

Behind Bronte, Theodora lifted her automatic and took careful aim at the light. When she squeezed the trigger, the bulb exploded.

They were smothered in darkness as the rain beat around them as loudly as a drum. Bronte remembered how it had rained the night Jimmy died.

''We've got to make a run far it,'' Theodora said.

Sensing some uncanny difference in the atmosphere, Bronte hesitated. Suddenly the sky lit up again. She felt a gust of cool air as she raced out onto the drive toward the roaring palms. For an instant she was alone. Then thudding boot heels rang heavily on the asphalt drive behind her.

She whirled, only to be blinded by the rain. ''Theodora?''

Silence.

Then a deadly male voice came out of the darkness. ''It's me.''

A scream rose and died in her throat. Before she could run from him, a large, bony hand manacled her wrist. "You'd better be good after the trouble you've put me to."

She tried to scream again, but rising terror made her throat catch. "Where…Theodora…"

He laughed. "You stupid little fool—"

"What did you do to her?"

Lightning lit his bony face. He looked haggard; his cheeks were sunken as if he hadn't slept in weeks. Then he smiled, that terrible, long-toothed smile that she'd first seen in Central Park.

He'd been there.

"Central Park? You—you were there…when I watched that little boy dig…"

Had he been stalking her then, too? Or…had he been after Jack?

"Who are you?"

"Caesar."

"Mario's son?"

"Not anymore. He liked Jack better than he ever liked me. Always throwing that bastard up at me. I'm sick of people thinking he was better than me. I took *his* woman. Now you're mine, too. Say my name— Caesar. It turns me on when a woman says it."

When she shoved at him, he slapped her.

Dizzily she reeled backward, her neck snapping as her skull cracked against the rough trunk of a palm. He ripped her skirt from the hem to her waist. With a laugh he pushed his body against hers.

"You're shaking. I like that."

Recovering a little, she fought him wildly.

"There you go! Wiggle against me! Scream! I like 'em wild…and scared. It'll be your last chance to get off for a while!"

Bronte froze as his hand crawled up her thigh.

Tears streamed down her face as he unfastened his belt buckle.

When he leaned forward to kiss her, she flailed her arms. Twisting her head from side to side, she clawed his face. His muscular body pressed against hers with an ever-strengthening purpose. She felt his hot, beery breath too near her lips.

He was about to kiss her when a hard voice behind him snapped, "Where's Nick?"

He turned. "Dead. Shot through the throat just like you wanted."

"Finish her."

"Not till—"

"Now!"

"In a minute—"

From out of nowhere a spurt of orange fire blossomed with an ear-splitting crack. In the next instant the big hands probing her breasts and thighs were lifeless. Bronte's would-be rapist slumped to the ground.

"He won't bother you again," Theodora said.

Bronte looked down at him. A neat, black bullet hole gaped from his forehead like a third eye.

The automatic jerked in Theodora's palsied hand.

"Where were you?"

That voice behind them.... "Finish her."

Theodora's face wore a sad-sweet expression as she raised the gun again.

Bronte's blood turned cold. Her mouth went dry. "You!"

Theodora leveled the automatic at her heart.

"You're behind everything."

Still Theodora said nothing.

Bronte's teeth began to chatter. "But...why? Why

did you set Jack up? I—I don't understand. I thought you loved him.''

''You're going to have a tragic accident. I will say that I was trying to save you, but my hand shook. I shot you first. Then him. I'll be so very sorry.''

''But why?''

''It's a long story. Chantal lived recklessly, extravagantly. This ranch is worth millions and millions in land value alone…not to mention mineral rights. She wanted her part. She wanted me to break it up and destroy it. She didn't believe in the family or the ranch. She was no good…like her father who married me for money. She was always after me for money. Jack was just as bad…always wanting to modernize.''

''But—''

''The ranch doesn't belong to anyone. It's sacred. Chantal couldn't see that, and finally she was so desperate she began to threaten me. That last night before she ran away, when she came here with those two murderers—with that cheap thug, Nick Busby—I think she wanted them to kill Jack and me. She slept with the boy in the barn to push Jack to the limit. He did get furious, but in the end he lost his nerve and backed down. But by then I saw a way to rid myself of all of them. I hit Jack in the head with a board. I shot that boy who died in the barn…. I shot Nick, too. Only, he and Chantal got away. I set the barn on fire. If Carla hadn't opened the barn doors and gotten help, if they hadn't pulled Jack out, everybody would've blamed him….''

''You sent an innocent man to prison. Your adopted…''

''I liked him, but he was always trying to change things. I had to put the ranch first. Jack wasn't the only one who suffered. I nearly went mad these past few years, wondering where Chantal and Nick were, wondering what Jack would do if he ever learned the truth. Then Nick started blackmailing me. He told me Chantal was alive. When he confessed to the cops that he'd killed that boy in the barn, he was setting me up. I nearly died of fright. He thought it was a grand joke bringing all those cops down here...while he taunted me the whole time that he'd tell them the truth. Then Jack was free, too. I couldn't let Jack out of my sight for fear Nick would talk to him. Nick kept hounding me, threatening that he'd set Jack on me. I kept paying him.''

Bronte shut her eyes.

"Then Chantal called me. She needed money more than ever. Lots of it. Said she was coming here to get it, too. She said if I didn't give it to her, she'd go to the police, that she'd tell them I shot that boy. I didn't know who or where she was or what she even looked like. Then I saw a way to use Jack again...for the ranch's good, you see.''

"The good?''

"I couldn't let them destroy what all of us have given our lives to build.''

"But why me? Why kill me?''

"You saw Caesar. He couldn't hide out forever. He got himself locked up down in Val Verde to bust Nick out. Then he killed Nick. Caesar had bad, expensive habits. He'd do anything I told him to, as long as I paid him. He's always been jealous of Jack. If you die, I won't have to kill Jack. He'll never know....''

"I know everything, Theodora.''

Bronte was thrilled and terrified when Jack's disembodied voice came out of the darkness.

"Put the gun down, Theodora.''

Theodora swung around violently, staring in horror at the tall man in the blustery, rain-filled night.

"It's over," he said.

"Not quite, Jack."

He saw the insane hatred in Theodora's eyes and lunged.

In a blinding flash Bronte jumped toward Jack, trying to shield him as Theodora took aim.

But she wasn't fast enough.

A fiery spit of light exploded from the automatic.

Bronte screamed as Jack slumped toward her and fell unconscious to the ground.

The fabric of his shirt had been blown away. Theodora had shot him at point-blank range.

Bronte knelt, shielding his broken body from the downpour. His wet face was as pale as death.

She lifted him in her arms, but his head lolled just as Jimmy's had when she'd held him that last day.

Jack's eyes stared wildly, not seeing her.

"Jimmy...!" she screamed, for she imagined she was holding her dying son again.

No.... It was Jack....

She had to do something this time. Dimly she remembered what she'd learned in that CPR course. Desperately, mechanically, she wadded her shredded skirt and pressed it against his flowing wound.

"I need a blanket...something to cover him." She put her lips to his pale, purple-gray mouth and began to breathe for him.

"Breathe," she whispered. "Don't you die. Don't die, too."

"It's your turn to die now." Theodora lowered her gun to Bronte's temple.

The front door of the big house banged open.

"Grandmother!"

Framed in a square of golden light stood a little girl with tangled red hair. Maverick and Caroline raced out with shotguns.

"We heard shots—"

"Grandmother! What… No! No, don't! I—I saw you in the barn. I was spying that night. They told me to go the cellar, but I sneaked out. I—I remember what happened at the barn now…and it's not what you told me. I remember everything! You drove Mother away. She was scared of you! You tried to burn Daddy up!"

Carla streaked down the stairs toward them.

"She must've suppressed everything, all these years.… Those monsters she draws. I think she barely survived what you did that night in the barn," Bronte whispered. "If you shoot me in front of her, you'll destroy her, too. Are you going to kill that child? Is the ranch more sacred to you than your own flesh and blood?"

Theodora couldn't take her eyes off Carla. Slowly her ancient face crumpled with self-revulsion when Carla ran past her and threw her arms around Bronte and Jack.

"Daddy, Daddy.… I'm so sorry, so sorry I never wrote you. I read your letters before she sent them back. I read every single one."

The gun fell from Theodora's trembling hand.

Suddenly Maverick was there, picking it up. "Call 911. We've got to fly him out!"

Very slowly, with stooped posture and a shambling gait, Theodora turned away from all of them and shuffled toward the big house.

Hot, searing pain spread through his right shoulder, but Jack couldn't see or hear anything.

He knew *she* was there, gripping his hand, pressing something against his wound, pouring her warm breath into his aching lungs again and again.

He wished he'd looked back and seen her that last time when she'd stood at the door, watching until he'd disappeared in the rain.

Bronte loved him.

Something hard seemed to crack around his own heart. His chest throbbed.

He didn't want to feel such shattering need. He didn't want to want so badly to live. Not when his lifeblood oozed past Bronte's wadded skirt and flowed into the mud in thick red rivulets.

Not when he felt so weak and tired, and death yawned before him like a black chasm.

He loved her.

Why hadn't he told her when he could have?

The ranch didn't matter.

Nothing mattered but her…and Carla. He had always wanted to be part of a family. To have his *own* family. To be proud of the woman he loved.

He wanted to marry Bronte. He wanted her to be a mother to his lonely Carla. He wanted more children.

Their children. A whole houseful. He wanted to have a long, happy life with her.

Nothing was more sacred in Mexico than family. He had always envied people with families. But he was getting colder and sleepier.

A bubble seemed to close over him. Only dimly did he feel Bronte shudder. Her piercing sobs and Maverick's shouts grew louder. He barely heard them.

"I'm sorry, Jack," Maverick said. "I knew she was stealing. I knew what she did to those bulls, too. But I never thought…"

Jack wanted to look at Bronte one last time.

"Don't die, Daddy," Carla said. "Don't you leave me like Mommy did. I'll go to school. I just didn't want to because it was so easy. But Bronte told me I could go to a better school in Corpus. I'll be good if you get well. I'll love you forever. Only don't leave us."

"Open your eyes, Jack," Bronte whispered. "We love you. We need you."

It was too late.

He was too weak even to lift an eyelid.

He expelled a final breath, and the pain subsided.

Then he was free. Light as a feather. Floating above them. The rain stopped, and a warm lavender light pulsated around him. He was weightless. Flying. His being fused with that brilliant light. In the next instant he soared above that desperate little crowd huddled around his shattered body.

Higher and higher he rose, rushing far away from them.

Then, suddenly, a little boy with copper curls stood before him. He wore torn jeans, yet he glowed like an angel at the center of that blinding tunnel, blocking Jack's path like the fiercest sentinel. The boy had a skateboard tucked under one arm, but he held up his free hand and stopped Jack.

His strong, determined fingers closed around Jack's wrist.

Jack tried to shake himself loose. He felt an impatience to move higher, to fly faster, but the boy smiled a charming, lopsided smile and shook his head, pointing fiercely down to Bronte.

Slowly, Jack understood.

A leaden heaviness filled him. His shoulder began to throb again with splinter-sharp bursts of pain.

Then, hand in hand, the redheaded boy led Jack back through that glorious cavern of light.

Back to her.

Jack was on the ground again, helpless, his broken body pulsing as if metal blades stabbed him, his life-blood draining through her fingers.

"Open your eyes, Jack," she begged.

The boy squeezed his hand, and a new strength flowed into him.

Jack's inky lashes fluttered.

His soul had flown away when they'd locked him up in that cage and kept him there for five long, hellish years.

As he stared into Bronte's dazzling green eyes, his own soul rushed back to him.

"I love you," Jack whispered.

The boy looked from him to Bronte, his lopsided smile radiant. Then he was gone.

"I know," she said. "I love you, too. Don't try to talk."

Jack's perception of time was warped. How long he lay there swaddled in blankets and tarps, drinking in the sight of Bronte's exquisite, triangular face, he didn't know. He only knew she was beside him, holding his hand. He held her just as fiercely, determined never to let her go.

Then the helicopter was above them, a black, roaring, round bubble, its rotors sending out waves of blowing rain that beat down upon them. Everybody was screaming and running and ducking except her.

Then paramedics and cops jumped out, flung open a huge side door and scrambled anxiously toward him with a stretcher.

He heard one cop's voice, deep and calm. "Get him. Bring him in."

For once Jack wasn't afraid of a uniform. He knew he never would be again.

He was free of all the shackles that had ever bound him.

The rhythmic thumping of the rotors never slowed or stopped.

Jack and Bronte were airborn within seconds, circling overhead, rising above the big house into that violent night sky, like souls rising to heaven.

"A little boy led me back to you," Jack whispered, his voice low and choppy. "He had red hair. It was the same color as yours. He had your smile, too. And he looked a little bit like Carla."

Bronte's face lit with a tender, eager radiance that matched the little boy's. "That must have been Jimmy." Her eyes streamed with tears. "My Jimmy brought you back to me."

Epilogue

The bride wore white organdy; the groom wore jeans.

The redheaded flower girl wore jeans, too.

Bronte's feminine gown was styled with ruffles at the neck and hemline. She carried a bouquet of lily of the valley, gardenias and white tea roses. Her frequent smiles were as radiant as the golden sunshine outside.

The groom had pressed the razor-sharp creases into his jeans himself; his black, gleaming boots had been polished by the same hand.

The big house overflowed with guests and family. Carla wore a demure blouse of beige silk with her jeans, and her ponytail that was caught up in cascades of fresh lilies was neatly brushed for once. The pictures her magic pencil drew today were of flowers instead of monsters.

All the Jacksons were in attendance. Tad Jackson

had even come all the way from his home in Australia. Cheyenne and her husband had arrived from Houston, too.

Sterling-silver fountains bubbled with endless champagne, but the groom wouldn't drink anything but iced lime water. The wedding cake that had been flown in from Houston rose in graceful tiers nearly to the ceiling.

While members of the orchestra mingled with the wedding guests during the intermission, Madame Devlin's recorded voice soared to the highest rafters in the ballroom. Her daughter was as gorgeous as the diva.

Everyone was thrilled that Jack West, who had suffered poverty and unjust imprisonment, was marrying the beautiful daughter of the legendary opera star.

Except for Theodora West—who'd tied a rope around her neck and fired a single shot into the air, so that her beloved horse had bolted and dragged her to what she considered the most honorable death possible—everybody who was anybody had come to the wedding. Indeed, the same people who had followed Theodora's cortege and riderless horse to her grave site three weeks earlier had flocked to this wedding of the decade.

No one was listening to Madame Devlin, though. Nor were they paying much attention to the beautiful bride and handsome groom. No. The glittering throng had gathered at a far corner around Garth Brown, whom the groom had invited since his wife was an avid fan. The star had taken to his brother and was having the time of his life, autographing wedding napkins by the hundreds.

"You're being upstaged, Hollywood, by that scene-stealing, half brother of yours. At your own wedding reception,'' Brickhouse teased, lifting his drink as Jack pulled Bronte tighter.

''He's okay.''

''Yeah. He is,'' Brickhouse agreed.

No longer did Jack feel even the slightest bit jealous of his handsome brother. Instead he felt admiration and pride and joy at the fledgling bonds that had begun to form between them.

''You sure you don't want *his* autograph, Bronte?'' Brickhouse persisted.

''Why would I, when I am holding the real thing right here in my arms?'' Bronte whispered against her husband's lips.

''Why don't you go get her one anyway, amigo?'' Jack asked, for Brickhouse, he'd discovered, had been the one to leave the mysterious envelopes with the cryptic messages.

''Oh, I git you.'' Brickhouse smiled broadly. ''You two want to be alone…to get a headstart on your honeymoon.''

The three of them laughed. Then Brickhouse picked up a stack of napkins and headed toward the movie star.

''You stinker!'' Bronte's eyes shone. ''How come you didn't tell him you already had Garth autograph a dozen napkins for me?''

''Because I love you, Bronte Devlin West,'' Jack said, drawing her behind a potted palm. ''Because I want to kiss you…without him studying my technique. Because I don't want Garth to run out of napkins to sign any time soon and come over here and flirt with you again.''

''Jealous?''

''Never.''

''Liar.''

"I love you. And I don't feel like sharing."

Jack bent to kiss his wife, and, if ever a bridegroom had felt sheer joy to be alive and in love with his bride, if ever a man had passed beyond all doubt and uncertainty, it was Jack West on his wedding day.

Their mouths touched, clung. Time stopped, and they felt absolutely alone with each other even in that crowded ballroom.

It was a very long time before Jack let her go. Afterward Bronte stared up at him raptly.

"I adore you," he whispered hoarsely. "I wish we were already on our honeymoon so that I could make love to you for as long as I feel like it."

She could not speak, but her eyes said she adored him, too.

"You freed me from the past," he breathed softly. His gaze traveled across her face, as if memorizing every feature. "I didn't think I'd ever—"

"I love you, too. You and Carla gave me a new life. We have a future together now. I never thought…"

Jack knew she was remembering Jimmy.

"I'm going to give you children. Lots of children," he murmured.

"Jack…you…you already have."

"What?" His eyes scanned her slim waist.

She blushed and then nodded, smiling shyly. "I'm expecting your child."

Jack wrapped his arms around her.

"Don't squeeze…the baby."

The baby….

Jack remembered how quick-thinking and brave she'd been, how she'd sat beside him day and night at the hospital. How Brickhouse had been there almost as often. "I owe you everything. Even my life."

"No woman in the whole world is happier than I am."

He was going to have another child. With her.

Their child.

Bronte was exquisite. Her sweetness made up for everything. Jack would always love her. Even though Theodora had used him and betrayed him, because of Bronte, he believed in love and the goodness of life more than he ever had before.

Not that it was easy or pleasant for him to believe that Theodora had deliberately set him up. That she had sent him after Chantal. That, all the time, she had planned to use him to destroy her daughter a second time and then destroy him, too.

For the ranch.

She'd been crazy.

Forgive her.

Theodora had loved the ranch more than she could ever love anything or anyone, but at least, in the end, Theodora had set things right by changing her will and making Carla her principal heir. She had stated her wishes that Jack run the ranch, and he was thankful she'd written him a personal letter begging his forgiveness, too. As he had read her shaky handwriting and bizarre phrasing, Bronte had held his hand, and all his anger and bitterness toward her had flowed out of him.

At least Theodora had done right by him in the end.

That was all that mattered. He could live at the ranch he loved and manage it. Even Maverick seemed happy enough about the way everything had turned out. He had taken a job in Europe with an accounting firm, and leased Jack his land.

But the main thing was Bronte. He had always dreamed of having a family. Even in prison.

Now he had her. And their baby.

And Carla who was smiling and laughing and dashing after Cheyenne's son, Jeremy.

His wife and daughter and their baby were his new beginning.

Bronte was staring up at him with eyes so bright that they seemed to have invented the color green.

She was irresistible.

Gently, tenderly, Jack lowered his mouth to his bride's again. Her arms circled him, holding him close.

Marriage.

It meant family, love, and a houseful of children as well as a love that would last forever.

Their kiss went on and on.

Marriage.

The best part was that it meant having such a pretty, sweet wife to kiss every single day and night for the rest of his life.

"Bronte," he whispered a long time later.

"Yes, love."

"Who's going to tell Carla she's going to be a big sister?"

"You are. I'm going to break the news to your brother."

"You just want to make me jealous."

"And…are you…jealous, Jack?"

"No way."

"Liar."

Then he kissed her.

*   *   *   *   *

Face To Face

REBECCA YORK

To our mums,
Beverly and Fannie,
for nurturing us and our love of books.

Chapter One

Justine Hollingsworth could afford to play with the hired help. It was one of the perks of wealth.

Mike Lancer stood on the corner of Light and Lombard Streets, watching her retreating figure and wondering if it was remotely possible that she hadn't heard him call her name. She was less than fifty feet away.

Her pace didn't slacken as she made for the shelter of the parking garage. Maybe she hadn't heard him over the noise of the midday traffic that was mucking along through the fifth straight day of hard spring rain.

Dodging a double-parked delivery truck, he made it to the opposite curb in time to get splashed by a passing taxi. With a curse, he brushed water from the legs of his jeans.

"Justine Hollingsworth? Were you looking for me?"

The slender redhead didn't turn, and he felt a stab of anger.

He'd seen her leave his office building. Had she come an hour early for their one o'clock appointment, found the door locked and decided to pay him back by ignoring him? So much for the mysterious job she hadn't quite offered him— and the sizzle of sensuality that had crackled in the air of his office last Wednesday as she'd sat across from him. He felt like a film noir character—the detective who's taken in by the sexy client and then ends up floating in the harbor with a bullet in his back.

As he watched her duck under the garage's overhang, he

wondered if the gray light was playing tricks with his vision. Maybe it wasn't her. Her rain hat hid her wavy red hair, and he'd caught only a glimpse of her face. Then she turned the corner, and he got a good look at her elegant profile with its high cheekbones and dainty chin. It was the face that had regularly graced the *Baltimore Sun's* People and Places section since she'd married Kendall Hollingsworth and his million-dollar construction company eight years ago. Usually she dressed as if she'd just stepped out of a *Vogue* layout. Today she was playing it low-key, with hardly any makeup and a raincoat that shouted Value City rather than Nordstrom's.

Shoulders hunched, fist pressed against her mouth, she looked as if she was trying to hold back tears. Mike fought an unwelcome wave of concern. Had something devastating happened to her? Earlier in the week, he'd decided she could take care of herself, with or without his help. Now she looked fragile—a flower mowed down by a thunderstorm. The sight of her stricken face made it hard to remember that the attraction he felt for her was dangerous and that he'd be a fool to involve himself with the problems of a woman like Justine Hollingsworth—unless she paid him very well for his time and effort.

Mike's brows drew together in a scowl. He almost spun around and headed back to his office. He didn't need her money. Or the hot jolt of sexual voltage that had flared between them. Yet he quickened his pace to catch up as she entered the garage.

Before he'd taken twenty paces into the darkened interior, a man with unkempt hair and a dirty fatigue jacket materialized from behind a concrete pillar. In his late fifties with weather-beaten skin, the man could have been homeless, using the building for a shelter. However, instead of slinking into the shadows, he fell into pace behind Justine. Ten to one the guy was after her purse.

"Whoa, buddy. Don't even think about it," Mike growled, tensing his muscles and lengthening his stride. The man glanced fearfully over his shoulder. For a few seconds, they sized each other up in the murky light. Then the would-be mugger bolted, apparently deciding to cut his losses.

The delay had given Justine enough time to disappear from view. Listening intently, Mike glanced up and down the row of cars. Moments later, an engine started. Then a teal blue Taurus drove slowly toward him, with Justine at the wheel.

No way could she miss seeing him. He stood on the oil-splotched concrete, trying to look casual. Resisting the impulse to swipe back the dark hair plastered to his forehead, he felt his arms stiffen at his sides. Her eyes locked with his for a split second, and he thought he saw her react before she turned the car toward the parking attendant's booth. After paying the fee, she made a right turn onto Light Street.

Another engine roared. Mike barely had time to jump out of the way as a gray Pontiac Firebird with two men in the front seat barreled toward the exit. After a rolling stop at the gate, they, too, turned right. Mike wanted to think they'd simply happened along at the same time as Justine. His old cop's instincts told him otherwise.

As he climbed into his battered Mustang, he cursed the sixth sense that urged him to follow Justine into the downpour. Maybe he simply wanted to find out why she needed to yank his chain. Bending forward over the wheel, he squinted through the windshield. The rain was coming down harder, the wipers barely keeping up with the deluge. He almost lost the Taurus in the noontime traffic near Camden Yards before Justine turned north again and headed up Charles Street. She was driving as if she didn't know where she was going—or didn't care.

THE WOMAN in the blue Taurus brushed the back of her hand across her eyes and fumbled in her open purse for a tissue. On the street, she'd kept herself from breaking down. In the privacy of her car, she couldn't prevent the tears welling in her eyes from spilling down her cheeks.

Lord, what a wreck she'd made of her life—and all because she'd been naive enough to trust the wrong man. Now he was

trying to punish her for *his* mistake. Her hands clenched painfully on the steering wheel. Until two months ago, she'd been
reasonably happy with the niche she'd carved for herself.
She'd worked hard to get where she was, but everything was
tumbling down like a house built on shifting sand. She
couldn't even imagine the future. Like the past, it was
shrouded in mist.

Unbidden, the faces of her parents stole into her mind. As
she thought about them and what they'd meant to her, what
they'd taught her, she worried her lower lip between her teeth.
Lucky they weren't here to see what an unholy mess she'd
made of her life.

Trying to quell her painful thoughts, she lifted her gaze
from the bumper of the car ahead and peered through the rain
at her surroundings. With a start, she realized she had no idea
where she was, except that she was on a highway hemmed
in by high stone walls. She'd been driving for thirty minutes,
and she didn't have a clue where she'd been or where she
was heading.

It was symbolic, she decided. She didn't know where she
was going to end up—on this ride—or in her life.

Several trucks passed her, shaking her car and splattering
the windshield with dirty water. Slowing to a crawl, she wondered why she'd gotten herself onto a highway in this kind
of weather. An exit sign loomed out of the swirling mist
ahead. Falls Road. She turned off, breathing a sigh of relief
as the traffic thinned.

MIKE KEPT the Taurus in sight, noting with a kind of grim
satisfaction that he'd been right. The men in the gray Pontiac
were also taking the same tortuous route through the city.

Coincidence? He'd given up on that concept years ago,
growing up on the streets of East Baltimore. He glanced at
the bigger car's license plate. It was smudged with mud. Not
improbable in the rotten weather, but damn convenient. He
could barely read an 8 and an *H*. Inching closer, he tried to
make out more.

SHE WAS ABOUT to turn on the radio, hoping music would help change her mood, when she caught an unexpected flash of movement from the corner of her eye. Glancing to her left, she gasped. A large gray car had crept up alongside her on the narrow road. It was in her lane, edging over, crowding her toward the shoulder.

Was she going too slowly for the driver? Hoping the fool would pass, she eased up on the accelerator. The other car dropped back, as well, pushing her farther toward the right. Her chest tightened and her hands gripped the wheel tighter. Sparing another quick glance to her left, she saw a man staring at her from the passenger seat of the other vehicle. The expression on his face made her blood run cold. In the split second when their eyes met, she knew he was enjoying her terror.

Her right tires sank into the shoulder, making her car list dangerously to the right, and suddenly she needed all her skill to keep the car on the road. Everything was happening so fast she barely had time to react. The car started to slide. She stabbed at the brakes and knew she'd made a mistake. Lord, what were you supposed to do in a skid?

Frantically, she tried to turn into the direction the wheels were taking her, but the power steering didn't respond properly. The road took a sharp turn, and she felt herself hurtling toward disaster.

MIKE HAD DRIFTED BACK a couple of car lengths, watching with narrowed eyes as the Pontiac followed Justine onto Falls Road. When the car crossed a bridge, he caught a glimpse of the creek that meandered along the thoroughfare. Usually the water was all but invisible; now it was swollen to an ominous torrent.

A passing van going too fast for the road conditions drenched his windshield with a curtain of muddy water, reminding him that the winding road was treacherous in bad weather. Momentarily blinded, he hunched forward and tapped the brakes. When the obscuring sheet drained away, he realized he'd lost his quarry around a bend.

Taking a chance, he speeded up as he rounded the curve. The Pontiac was pulling rapidly away, and Justine was on the shoulder. Good God, had the other car shoved her off the blacktop? He couldn't be sure; he hadn't seen. But, regardless, Justine was in trouble. For an endless moment, the Taurus clung to the gravel. Then it hit a ramp, hydroplaned and jumped the guardrail, heading toward the rushing creek.

He glanced from the car to the water. It was flowing at least five feet above normal level. And Justine's car was making straight for it.

HEART RACING, she jerked the wheel the other way. But nothing she tried had any effect on the car. It barreled toward the creek; then for several heart-stopping seconds, it was airborne. Time seemed to slow to a series of freeze-frames. She was trapped in an endless ride of terror as the vehicle nosed over a small rise and plunged down a steep incline.

Nothing lay in the car's path to slow its momentum. A scream rang in her ears as dark water rushed up to meet her. Then a sudden impact slammed her forward against the steering wheel, and the world went black.

MIKE WAS ON THE LINE with 911 when Justine's car went over the embankment. He barely had time to choke out the location of the nearest cross street before the Taurus plunged into the foaming current.

"The car's in the water!" he shouted to the dispatcher as he screeched to a halt, perilously close to the roadway, and threw open his door. The voice on the other end of the line was still asking for details, but he barked out only one more sentence. "I'm going in after her."

Rain sluiced over his head and shoulders as he vaulted the guardrail and slid down the muddy bank, following the path of the car's destruction through honeysuckle vines and tall grass.

The vehicle was a hulking, indistinct shape in the mist. When he drew closer, he saw that it rested at an angle, nose down in lapping waves.

Mike waded into the shallows of the rain-swollen creek, judging the strength of the main current. He quickly decided it was strong enough to sweep him away if he wasn't careful. His eyes riveted on the evil-looking water swirling above the level of the car windows. Then he looked at the car. Inside he could see a mop of red curls slumped against the steering wheel, and the water level was rising quickly inside the vehicle. Damn. She must have gone in at the wrong angle for the air bag to deploy.

Tossing his leather jacket onto the bank, he waded farther into the icy cold. The current seized him, and he grabbed a tree limb to keep from being carried downstream. He grimaced as the numbing cold rose to his thighs, his hips, his waist. Letting go of the limb, he reached for the car's door handle, thankful it was within his grasp. As he transferred his hold, he found that the door was locked.

He pounded on the window, calling her name, but she didn't move, didn't respond. Back braced against the side of the car, he reached down and scrabbled along the creek bed with his fingers, loose gravel biting into his flesh, until he found what he was looking for—a good-size rock. Yanking it free of the muck, he smashed it against the window. The safety glass held. He angled his body away to get more leverage, horror gripping him as he saw Justine's face submerge. She didn't even struggle.

Bringing his arm down in a mighty arc, he slammed the rock against the glass again. The window imploded, showering the interior of the car with tiny pellets.

Reaching through the ruined window, he tipped her head back and held it above the water. Her eyes were closed, her face pale as marble except for the streak of red slashing across

her forehead. When he tried to pull her from the car, he realized the seat belt was still locked in place.

With a curse, he dived inside, pushing between her slack
body and the steering wheel. Working by touch, he found the
metal buckle and released the latch. Then he retraced his path,
pulling the unconscious woman with him through the window
and into the flooded stream.

She was a dead weight in his arms, threatening to drag
them both under. Tightening his grip, he held her above the
water as he contemplated the treacherous ten-foot stretch of
surging creek between him and the shore. With a technique
he'd learned at the police academy, he shifted her to a shoulder carry. Still, negotiating the torrent was a lot harder than
his solo journey to the car. His muscles ached from fighting
the current. His body was numb from the cold, and his jeans
felt like metal weights on his legs as he pulled Justine through
the rushing water to the bank.

His jacket was lying where he'd dropped it on the shore.
Spreading it out, he laid her down, put his ear beside her nose
and felt her chest. She wasn't breathing, but her heart was
still beating. Her lips and cheeks were bluish gray.

He tilted her head back to open her airways and checked
to make sure that her mouth was unobstructed. Then he began
mouth-to-mouth resuscitation, concentrating on forcing air
past her icy lips while he slowly counted off the seconds.

He tried to think of her as an anonymous victim. But fear
twisted his stomach into a tight knot. When she'd sat across
from him in the office with her skirt hitched up to display her
well-shaped legs, he'd wanted to touch her. God, what a way
to get his wish. Trying to keep his mind blank, he continued
methodically blowing into her lungs and compressing her
chest.

Somewhere in the distance, he heard the wail of sirens.
Then Justine coughed, and all his attention narrowed to her
pale face. The blue tinge was gone.

"Thank God," he whispered, gently turning her to her side.
She sputtered and coughed up river water.

"That's it," he encouraged as she began to breathe on her own. "That's it."

Above him on the road, tires screeched to a halt. Two men with a stretcher slid down the bank. One of them brushed past him and knelt over Justine. The other draped a blanket around his shoulders, and he realized as he climbed unsteadily to his feet that he was soaked to the skin, covered with mud and freezing cold. Shivering, he pulled the blanket tighter.

"Can you make it back to the ambulance on your own?" asked the paramedic who'd given him the blanket.

He stared at the flashing light. "Don't worry about me."

"You could go into hypothermia, buddy. And you need a typhoid shot. You'd better let us take you to Mount Olive and check you out. You can ride in the second ambulance."

Resigned, he glanced back at Justine. Her eyes were open and tracking him. He wasn't sure what he expected to see in their blue depths. Certainly it wasn't what he found, a mixture of gratitude and longing that shattered him. In that moment, he wondered how badly he'd misjudged her.

JACK ORDWAY, Jackal to his friends, swore loudly as he craned his neck out the window of the gray Pontiac.

Lennie Ezrine, the car's driver, clenched his teeth to keep from delivering the bitter rejoinder quivering on the edge of his tongue.

Up on Falls Road, traffic had slowed to a crawl, though not because of the rain, which had finally stopped. Drivers were gawking at the ambulances pulled onto the shoulder and the car half submerged in the roiling water of the Jones Falls.

At the next intersection, Lenny turned onto a residential street and pulled into a driveway. After backing rapidly out again, he made another slow pass at the accident scene. This time, he could see two men carrying a woman on a stretcher toward an open ambulance door.

"You stupid shit," Jackal muttered.

Lennie had taken enough abuse. "You were the one who

told me to edge her over. You thought it was funny when she looked like she was gonna freak!''

''Yeah, well, it sure as hell ain't my fault she went into the creek.''

''Or mine neither. How was I supposed to know her damn car would go over the guardrail?''

Jackal didn't answer as they followed the ambulances down Falls Road.

''Heading for Mount Olive,'' Jackal guessed. ''That's the closest hospital.''

''Yeah.''

''We better make sure.''

Lennie nodded tightly. They were both in trouble, unless they could cut their losses. ''She buys the farm, and we never get what we need.

''The stuff's probably at her house. All we gotta do is get the maid and the handyman out of the way so we can toss the place. And if we don't find what we want, we bug the phones so we can follow along on the conversations.''

Jackal's eyes widened. ''You really think we can get away with that?''

''Why not?''

Jackal chewed on that for a while. ''Okay. I guess you're right. Any way we can do it—just so we get results.''

Chapter Two

The phone rang, and Maggie Dempsey, housekeeper in the Hollingsworth mansion for more than a dozen years, rushed to the receiver. "Hello?"

"This is Mount Olive Hospital," a man said on the other end of the line.

It was the second call from the hospital. The first had sent her into a tailspin. Hoping against hope, she'd tried to contact her employer to inform him of the accident. But the Alaskan outfitters had relayed what she'd expected to hear: Mr. Hollingsworth was hunting at a remote mountain lake, and he'd left strict instructions not to be disturbed. Did she want to authorize a special flight into the camp?

Maggie had learned the consequences of disobeying instructions, and she'd respectfully declined. But what if Mr. Hollingsworth came home and demanded to know why she hadn't told him that his wife was in the hospital?

Sweating, Maggie had compromised and phoned Estelle Bensinger, the snooty executive assistant who ran Mr. Hollingsworth's office. Estelle thought they were on the same side, but Maggie didn't trust Mr. Hollingsworth's secretary any more than she trusted his wife. But at least she'd shifted responsibility to someone else.

"Why are you calling? Is Mrs. Hollingsworth all right?" Maggie asked the man from Mount Olive.

"She's feeling better."

"Thank the saints," Maggie breathed, hoping she sounded sincere.

"She wants you to bring her a nightgown and toilet articles."

"She does?" Maggie's brow wrinkled. "But I already brought down some things—a nightie and some clothes she can wear home from the hospital."

There was a slight hesitation on the other end of the line.

"Must be a mix-up. We don't have them."

Fretfully, Maggie glanced toward the window. It had been dark for several hours, and her night vision was so bad that she never drove after sundown. Yet there was no question of denying the request. She'd have to get a ride.

"I'll be there as soon as I can," she allowed.

"This time, make sure you come to the nurses' station."

After hanging up, Maggie went in search of Frank, the handyman who took care of the garden, repairs and heavy cleaning on the Hollingsworth estate.

He wouldn't like coming back on duty after his supper, but that was just too bad. They both had it good here, with high pay, medical insurance and a snug roof over heads. They could even eat steak every night for dinner if they wanted, and nobody would be the wiser. In fact, Maggie had thought many times that she was a darn sight better off than when she'd been married to Patty Dempsey, ex-fighter and ex-con. She'd been lucky to get this job, and she was going to hang on till retirement. Whatever it took.

SHE AWOKE from a drugging sleep that seemed centuries long. Yet some self-protective impulse kept her lying very still, wishing that the comforting blackness would swallow her again.

Her brain felt as if someone inside her skull was banging on a kettledrum. Every time she tried to move, her body ached, but it wasn't physical pain that kept her quiescent. It was the fear of some unknown yet terrible threat lurking at the edge of her consciousness, ready to spring if she gave the slightest sign that she had returned to the world.

She knew, however, that she couldn't simply lie here forever. Wherever *here* was. Holding her breath, she cautiously opened her eyes. The first thing she discovered was that the man in the sopping wet T-shirt was gone. He'd been holding her, his strong arms a shield from the terrible cold. She remembered his lips on hers. And his dark eyes, so close, so full of worry. She'd wanted to reach for him, but she'd been too weak to lift her arm. She didn't even know his name, yet with him gone, she felt a stinging sense of loss.

She heard her own ragged sigh in the silent room. Where was she, anyway? She could see plain walls, plain curtains and metal furniture. The serviceable theme was repeated with the crisp white sheets on her hospital bed.

She let that sink in. She was in a hospital.

Yet she didn't know the reason, and her heart started to pound. Raising a hand, she ran her fingertips lightly over her face. Her forehead and cheeks were abraded.

Gingerly, she moved each arm and leg. They were stiff, but nothing seemed broken. And she wasn't attached to any kind of machine. She was breathing on her own.

Breathing. Why should that be a problem? As quickly as the question formed, the answer danced away from her.

In sudden panic, she tried to locate a call button near the bed, but the mechanism eluded her. Feeling trapped, she pushed herself up, then gasped at the sharp pain that stabbed through her head. The room began to spin, and she gripped the sides of the bed, willing the dizziness to subside. When the vertigo finally eased, she drew in a deep breath, staring at a framed reproduction of the Mona Lisa on the other side of the room. The subject of the famous portrait smiled back benignly, increasing the feeling of unreality hanging in the air. She realized she knew the name of the woman in the picture—but she didn't know her own.

In growing terror, she scrambled for the combination of sounds that would deliver her identity. Her name. She had to know her name! But her mind drew a blank. Frantically, she looked around the room, and to her left saw an open bathroom door. Swinging her legs over the side of the bed, she slid to the tile floor and managed an upright position. It was a small victory. Concentrating on each tiny step, she shuffled to the washbasin and leaned against the cold porcelain for support. After switching on the light, she stood, barely breathing, summoning the courage to study her image.

In the end, there was no other choice. The woman staring back at her uncertainly was wearing a silky white gown with tiny lace trim. She was in her late twenties or early thirties with a wild wreath of red hair, blue eyes and skin that probably looked healthy when it wasn't marred by abrasions and a large bruise that spread across her forehead.

Objectively, nothing about the collection of feminine features was threatening. Yet as she peered into her own haunted eyes, she felt as if a chasm had opened beneath her and she was dropping toward the center of the earth.

A cold sweat broke out on her brow. "Who are you? What's your name?" she demanded in a quavery voice.

No answer came, either from the image in the mirror or from the depths of her soul.

A strangled sound welled in her throat. How could you forget your own identity?

Her temples pounded as she tried to remember—anything. But her personal memory started with the moment she'd awakened in the hospital room. No, with the man in the wet T-shirt. He came before the hospital. But she didn't even know the date, the day of the week, the year.

The vacuum gnawed at her; it grew inside her mind, threatened to sweep away all traces of sanity.

"Please. Somebody help me," she sobbed.

No one answered. Her legs were trembling so hard she would have toppled over if her fingers hadn't clamped the cold washbasin in front of her. Hours, or perhaps only minutes, later she turned on the tap and splashed cold water onto her face. It stung her damaged flesh, but it made her feel more alert.

Looking around the little room, she spotted a bar of soap still in its wrapper. Perusing the label brought back a measure of reassurance. She could read. She recognized the brand name. For that matter, she recognized a hospital room when she saw one.

She straightened her shoulders. She might not know her identity, but she sensed that it would take a lot to make her fall apart completely.

With renewed purpose, she reentered her room. A private room. Expensive. Who was paying? she wondered.

After finding a robe in the closet, she eased into the dimly lit hall. A man in a green uniform was cleaning, his dry mop moving noiselessly over the tile floor. The nurses' station was in the opposite direction. It was empty. So it must be night-time or early in the morning when the patients were asleep and the staff was skimpy.

Hanging on pegs behind the desk was a row of clipboards. Patient's charts. Turning, she noted her room—321. The chart with the corresponding number was within easy reach.

As she picked up the folder, the name on the outside leaped out at her, and she realized she must have the wrong chart.

Mrs. Justine Hollingsworth. Experimentally, she tried it aloud. Not hers. Even if she couldn't dredge up her own name, it should *sound* familiar. But Justine Hollingsworth struck no chords.

With a grimace, she checked the room numbers on the chart and her door. They were the same. But someone must have mixed up two patients. She shouldn't be prying into this woman's records. Yet morbid curiosity made her scan the sheet. Justine Hollingsworth had been in an automobile accident on May eleventh and diagnosed with a closed head injury. She'd been unconscious for two and a half hours. Then she'd awakened and had had a conversation with the attending physician—a Dr. Habib. Now she was under observation.

She sighed. Some observation. The only living soul she'd

seen since she'd awakened was the janitor. However, the information on the chart supported her conviction about the mistaken identity. She certainly hadn't spoken to a Dr. Habib. Or anyone else since she'd arrived.

A flash of movement made her look around guiltily. A woman in a white uniform had come out of one of the rooms, seen her with the clipboard in her hand and was hurrying forward. The nurse's name tag said she was Mrs. Maxie Folkherst.

"Good. You're awake again," the nurse said.

"Again?"

"Are you okay? You really shouldn't be out of your room, Mrs. Hollingsworth."

"No." The denial came out as a wispy gasp. Her hands began to tremble, and the chart tumbled to the surface of the desk.

Mrs. Folkherst was all solicitude. "Let me help you back to bed and call Dr. Habib. He'll want to talk to you again."

Her head spun. "Dr. Habib," she repeated, trying with every ounce of concentration to put a face to the name. Nothing came, and she felt a shiver sweep across her skin as her mind snatched at the only explanation she could conjure. All this—the hospital, the chart, the name—was a colossal conspiracy designed to drive her crazy.

The paranoid thought made her laugh aloud, and the nurse gave her a sharp look.

"I promise not to get hysterical," she managed to say, drawing herself up straighter. "I'm sorry. There must be some mistake. My name isn't Mrs. Hollingsworth."

"It's okay, hon. You'll feel more like yourself in the morning."

Not here I won't.

Her gaze darted up and down the dark hall and fixed on an exit sign. "I have to leave."

"But your husband isn't home yet, Mrs. Hollingsworth," the woman said with gentle firmness. "I'm sure he wants you to stay with us for a few days."

"My husband?" *What husband?* That must be the strong, sexy man in the dripping T-shirt and the muddy jeans. "Where is he?" she asked.

"Away."

She probably looked stricken because the nurse responded with a reassuring little pat on her shoulder. "He'll be back soon."

She let that comfort her. He hadn't left her to fend for herself. He'd be back.

Kindly, the nurse led her to the room where she'd awakened. As she stepped through the doorway, every instinct urged her to run headlong for the exit, to escape from this nightmare. Yet she knew she wouldn't get far on her wobbly legs. And her legs were the least of her problems. Where would she go?

Her head swam with confusion. The name—Justine Hollingsworth—sounded wrong. But the man felt…right.

Feeling numb, she sank to the edge of the bed, her jaw clenched with the effort to keep from whimpering. When the nurse shifted her legs and tucked the covers around her icy body, she didn't protest.

Eyes squeezed closed, she heard the sound of rubber soles receding. Then she was alone again. But she couldn't cope with being alone. Fear seeped into every pore, like floodwater soaking into a low-lying field. She had no defenses. And she knew the rising tide would swamp her.

Blindly she reached out for a mooring. Then *he* was beside her in the dark, a comforting presence come to rescue her from madness.

Do you need me?

Oh, yes. Yes, please.

Perhaps it was only a fantasy. Perhaps if she opened her eyes, she would see that he wasn't there. But as she lay shivering and alone in the dark, her need made him real.

Are you cold?

Yes. So cold.

Let me warm you. He was beside her on the bed, holding

her the way he had before, his voice deep and reassuring, his
body solid and warm. *I'm here,* he whispered. *I'm here.* He
said it over and over, easing the dreadful tension, lulling her
into a strange kind of peace. And finally she drifted into sleep.

THE MOMENT MAGGIE stepped from the garage to the service
porch, she knew something was wrong.

"Someone's been in here," she hissed.

"You're crazy," Frank snorted as he followed her across
the sun room.

Trying to prepare herself for the worst, Maggie sprinted
into the kitchen and stopped short. Every cabinet and drawer
was opened, much of their contents strewn across the floor as
if a tornado had swept through the room.

For several seconds, she stood staring at the mess with
Frank right behind her. Then Frank lumbered around a pile
of scattered spaghetti and reached for the phone. Maggie
moved almost as quickly to slap her hand down on his—hard.

"What are you doing?" she demanded.

"What do you think, woman? Calling the police."

"We can't."

"Why not? Mr. Hollingsworth will be furious about this."

"Frank, think. We've both worked here for years. We
know how much he hates the law messing in his business."

"That's true." Frank nodded slowly. "He solves his own
problems. But what are *we* gonna do?" he asked, looking in
dismay from her tense face to the ravaged room.

"Clean up."

"But—"

"You want to call the police, you take responsibility."

Frank looked unhappy.

"You find out where they broke in, and fix it up," she
said. "I'll start cleaning. And until Mr. Hollingsworth gets
home, one of us stays here."

"Yeah. Okay," he agreed.

With a sigh, Maggie started on a tour of the house. The
kitchen was in the worst shape. The only damage to the living

room was the pile of sofa and chair cushions in the middle of the rug. And the office had hardly been touched, thank the saints. The worst surprise was in Mrs. Hollingsworth's bedroom and her walk-in closet. Maggie stared in horror at the clothing, cosmetics and contents of drawers and shelves scattered everywhere. Mother Mary, how could she put everything back in the right place?

As she surveyed the damage, another thought struck her. Snatching up a phone book lying in a heap of papers on the rug, she called Mount Olive Hospital. When a woman's voice answered, she asked, "How can I find out if a patient received the things I brought over to her?"

"You could check with the nurses' station."

Ten minutes later, Maggie had the information, but it didn't make her feel any better. There had been no problem with the first bag she'd brought. Sitting down heavily on the bed, she squeezed her hands into fists. The call had been a trick to get her out of the house. If she'd had her wits about her, she would have phoned the hospital before rushing down there again. Now she'd have to pay the price for her stupidity.

"JUSTINE?"

She ignored the thickly accented male voice coming from a few feet above her head.

"Mrs. Hollingsworth, I know you're awake."

The man's tone was kind but insistent. "You can't hide forever. Please open your eyes."

There really was no alternative. She obeyed and found herself staring into a round, brown face. Behind horn-rimmed glasses, the eyes were dark and liquid. Sympathetic. Or perhaps that was what she wanted to think.

"I'm Dr. Habib. We met earlier. Do you remember?"

"No."

Over his shoulder, morning sunlight streamed into the room. It did nothing to dissolve the choking knot in her chest. Under the covers, her hands clenched at her sides.

"I'm not Mrs. Hollingsworth." She made an effort to keep her voice steady. "Why are you calling me that?"

"I see your memory has not returned," the doctor said, his voice matter-of-fact. He was short and round, his body poured into an expensive-looking suit. "I know that must be upsetting."

She gave a little ironic laugh.

"Do you remember what happened?"

She shook her head.

"You were in an accident. Your car went off Falls Road and into the water. The Jones Falls is at flood stage." He paused, giving her time to assimilate the information.

She felt her features freeze into a mask of shock.

"Let me make you more comfortable." The offer came from a moon-faced nurse standing behind the doctor. According to her name tag, she was Mrs. Janet Swinton.

Lord, she'd have the staff memorized before she knew her own name.

Mrs. Swinton came forward and touched a button, raising the head of the bed. "Better?" she asked.

"Yes."

Dr. Habib continued. "You were rescued by a passing motorist and brought to Mount Olive Hospital."

A motorist? The man with the T-shirt and the muscles. Last night, she'd imagined him cradling her trembling body in his arms, shielding her from the abyss.

"Who is he?" she managed to ask.

"Someone named Mike Lancer."

"Mike Lancer," she repeated. It was a strong name, strong like the man. But he was a stranger. And apparently *not* her husband. In the dark, she'd conjured his comforting presence, but she couldn't rely on him now. She had to rely on herself.

She fought to stay calm, to collect data, search for clues that would explain the bizarre misunderstanding about her name. "I was driving Justine Hollingsworth's car?"

"Uh...no." For the first time, the physician looked a bit uncomfortable. "Apparently you had a rental."

"Then I had Justine Hollingsworth's purse. Her identification?"

He spread his hands apologetically. "I'm sorry. The river was moving very fast. Everything inside the car was swept away."

She gave him a sharp look. "Then why are you so convinced of my identity?"

"Mr. Lancer recognized you."

She searched his eyes for signs of duplicity. Listening to his outlandish story, it was hard not to come back to the conspiracy theory she'd dismissed the previous night. Only this time, she wondered if the man she remembered as her savior was part of the plot. She fought the tightness in her throat. "Let me get this right," she enunciated carefully. "I was driving a rental car. I had no identification. But someone I know just happened along?"

The physician favored her with a little smile. "You're a well-known member of Baltimore society."

"I look like Justine Hollingsworth?" she clarified.

"Yes. Except that you've cut your hair. In recent months, you and your husband have attended a number of charity events. The Mount Olive Ball, for example. And the fund-raiser for the aquarium. Your picture has been in the paper."

"And that special feature on the Channel Eleven evening news that they shot at your lovely St. Michaels vacation home," Nurse Swinton added brightly. "Your husband made a very substantial donation to the hospital fund. Which is why we're taking such good care of you."

Habib gave her a quelling look. "As you're well aware, we take excellent care of *all* our patients, Mrs. Swinton."

Color rose in the woman's cheeks. "Yes. Of course. I only meant…"

The exchange barely registered with the patient sitting in the hospital bed. She was trying to imagine herself at a glittering media event or owning a vacation home. The picture simply didn't fit her image of herself. She sucked in a little breath. What image? She didn't have an image.

"Unfortunately," the doctor continued, "Mr. Hollingsworth is on a hunting trip in Alaska and can't be reached until he returns to Anchorage. But we contacted your housekeeper, Mrs. Dempsey. She brought several nightgowns for you to wear and some other personal items."

Silence filled the hospital room while the patient tried to come to grips with a truth that was becoming harder to deny.

"I have amnesia," she finally blurted out, feeling like the main character in a bad suspense movie. Only no one had bothered to give her the script.

"Amnesia. Yes, that appears to be true," Dr. Habib agreed as if he'd been reluctant to put a name to her affliction and was grateful she'd relieved him of the onerous task. "I'm sure it must be unsettling—not remembering your past."

She gulped. "Yes. Why did this happen to me?"

"We're not sure. You apparently hit your head against the steering wheel."

She nodded tightly. Now that the doctor had apparently decided to speak frankly, he went on for several minutes with technical information about brain tissue and neurological trauma. Most of it eluded her, but a pertinent phrase penetrated her numbness.

"In addition to the inability to remember your personal history, you might have other problems, as well."

"What other problems?"

"Well, you might have trouble remembering information that's told to you."

"How long will I be this way?"

"We can't be sure. Each case runs its individual course. You could regain your memory in a few days. Or…"

"Or what?"

"It could take time."

She shuddered, reading between the lines. She might never recover. That's what he meant. The possibility was so frightening that she thrust it from her before it could suck away what remained of her sanity.

"But we're here to give you all the help you need, Justine," Dr. Habib concluded on an upbeat note.

Justine. That damn name again. It set her teeth on edge. She sat very still, afraid that if she moved, she might shatter.

"Don't call me Justine."

Habib gave her a paternalistic smile. "It's your name."

She looked down at her hand, watching the fingers pleat the rough fabric of the hospital sheet. "What if it upsets me?"

"I'm sorry."

Her eyes darted around the room and settled on the reproduction of the Mona Lisa she'd seen on the wall the night before. "If you have to call me something, call me..." She might have said Mona. Somehow that didn't seem much better than Justine. But Lisa sounded...more familiar. "Call me...Lisa," she almost shouted.

Habib looked startled. "What?"

"Humor me. Call me Lisa," she said with more force than she'd mustered since the beginning of the strange interview.

The physician started to say something, then he shrugged. "If that makes you feel more comfortable. But really, it's best if you try to work toward the familiar."

"Lisa," she insisted.

"All right. We can...uh...do that for the time being." He shifted his weight from one foot to the other. "I have some good news that should cheer you."

"What?" she asked cautiously.

"Our staff physician did a thorough examination when you arrived in the emergency room. You have no broken bones or major physical trauma."

She nodded.

"And your pregnancy is intact."

"Pregnancy?" she gasped, her throat squeezing closed.

Chapter Three

"Are you telling me I'm going to have a baby?"

"Yes," the doctor said. "You're about two and a half months along."

Tiny shivers raced over her skin. She stared at Dr. Habib, unable to absorb this new shock that was somehow greater than all the rest.

"No. I can't be." The denial rushed out of her as if saying it quickly would make it true.

"In your present state, the news could be a little disturbing," the doctor allowed in a soothing voice that chipped at her uncertain mental health. The bland look on his face was the last straw.

"Stop it!" she screamed. "Stop being so damn calm and reasonable. My whole world has fallen apart! I—I—" She stopped simply because she wasn't sure what to say.

Dr. Habib took a step back. "I see you're upset..." He hesitated. "Mrs....ah...Lisa, why don't I give you some time to adjust, and we'll talk later."

She nodded tensely, wanting nothing more than to see him vanish. No, she wanted this whole nightmare to vanish.

"You just take it easy, and we'll be in with breakfast in a few minutes," Nurse Swinton added soothingly.

Dr. Habib and the nurse stepped into the hall, no doubt to hold a whispered conversation about the deranged behavior of the patient.

With a little moan, she slumped against the raised head-board. Eyes closed, she clutched the bedding, doing her best to hold tight to reality. Yet reality had no meaning. Pregnant. She couldn't be.

Trying to read the signs of her body, she cupped her hands under her breasts, testing their weight. They were full and rounded, but she had no basis for comparison. She hiked up her gown, peered down at her middle, and with shaky fingers, she stroked her hand across the ivory skin. Did her abdomen curve outward the barest amount?

Again she touched her breasts, gliding her thumbs gingerly across the pale nipples. They were prominent and tender, al-most the way they felt before she got her period. She clutched at the tiny bit of self-knowledge that had popped into her mind. Yet she didn't know whether it was real memory of her own body or merely something she'd read in a magazine.

Her heart was slamming against the inside of her chest. All at once, she knew that she couldn't stay in this place, couldn't wait for the next startling revelation from Dr. Habib. What would he tell her next? That her husband was running for president of the United States and she'd better not screw up his chances for election or maybe this was like that movie where a devil-worshiping cult helped the Prince of Darkness impregnate an innocent woman. What was it called? Some-thing about a baby...*Rosemary's Baby.* Yes, that was it.

The crazy idea sparked a hysterical laugh. Then the worst thought of all shot through her mind. Habib and Nurse Swin-ton had destroyed her memory with drugs, and they were holding her here against her will. They wouldn't let her go until—she felt a surge of panic and struggled to suck in a breath—she docilely went along with the fable that she was Justine Hollingsworth.

The last vestige of rationality fled. Terror gripped her and wouldn't let go. She had to escape, had to find someplace safe. Someplace where she could get back her memory, where she could start to string one coherent thought after another. Figure out what was going on.

In that moment of terror, she wanted Mike Lancer, the man who had looked as if he cared about her, to stride through the door and whisk her away. But he wasn't coming. She couldn't count on him any more than she could count on the doctors and nurses here.

With a furtive glance toward the hall, she slipped out of bed, tiptoed across the room and quietly shut the door. Then she opened the closet. Inside were clothes she didn't recognize—a classically styled aqua silk shirtwaist and a matching tailored blazer. There was no purse. No identification. Quickly she searched the jacket pockets and found two folded twenty-dollar bills that might have been tucked away for an emergency. They'd have to do.

Imbued with a sense of purpose, she pulled the nightgown over her head and reached for the undergarments folded on a narrow shelf in the closet. The panties and bra were thin and silky. They didn't look or feel like the sort of things she'd pick. But then, neither did the dress, really.

The panties rode low on her hips. The bra was a little tight, but her pregnancy could account for that. She was adjusting the waistline of the dress when a flash of movement made her turn.

Nurse Swinton had opened the door and was standing there uncertainly, a tray of food in her hands, a startled expression splitting her moon face. "Mrs. Hollingsworth, what are you doing?"

Lisa froze.

The nurse spoke firmly. "Please get back into bed. I'm going to call Dr. Habib."

She had no intention of obeying. With a violent shake of her head, she went down on her hands and knees and retrieved the aqua pumps sitting side-by-side at the bottom of the closet.

Clearly giving up on further protests, the nurse silently backed out of the room.

Lisa knew they would cut her off at the pass if she didn't escape in the next minute. Clutching the shoes, she made for the hall. But it was already too late. Nurse Swinton had jettisoned the tray and was heading back toward her room. Dr. Habib was right behind, his hand pressed close to his side. But she saw what he was trying to hide—a hypodermic needle.

She screamed as her tormentors bore down on her. Flinging the shoes at them, she ran. She made it as far as the next room before strong hands grabbed her shoulders and wrestled her against the wall.

"No. Let me go," she cried out.

An orderly pushing a gurney stopped in midstride. Patients came out of their rooms to stare at the spectacle.

"Help. Please, somebody help me."

But none of the onlookers sprang to her defense.

She tried to fight, striking out wildly with her fists, hitting Swinton's shoulder, knocking off Habib's glasses.

"Mrs. Hollingsworth," the nurse gasped, "you'll hurt yourself."

Relentlessly, they moved her down the hall and back into her room. Then a jab stung her upper arm, and she knew she'd lost the battle and probably the war, as well. She tried to hold on to consciousness, but it slipped though her fingers like water through a sieve.

ESTELLE BENSINGER'S long fingers drummed against the receiver as she impatiently waited for the supervisor to answer the call. Normally she was bedrock-steady, but the events of the last twelve hours had crumbled her composure.

Finally, a woman's voice came on the line. "This is Mrs. Swinton, nursing supervisor. Can I help you?"

Her angular features sharpened. "I'm Estelle Bensinger. I want a status report on Mrs. Justine Hollingsworth."

"Are you a relative?"

"No, but I *am* Mr. Hollingsworth's executive assistant." Estelle put as much authority into her voice as she could muster. As Kendall Hollingsworth's office manager, she screened his calls, answered his correspondence, scheduled his meetings, researched his associates and competitors and performed other duties, as required. Like her boss, the head of the K.H. Group, she was accustomed to people jumping to her commands. This morning, she only hoped she didn't sound too eager.

Rocking back and forth in her custom ergonomic chair, Estelle listened to the nurse.

"Mrs. Hollingsworth has suffered a mild concussion and minor abrasions. She is listed in stable condition."

"Are there any serious problems?"

"We're not allowed to release those details," Nurse Swinton clipped out.

Estelle tried several more interrogation techniques but kept coming up against a brick wall. Then the nurse abruptly said she had to attend to a patient and hung up.

Estelle rubbed the tension lines in her forehead as she tried to regain her usual composure.

She'd been on the wrong side of thirty with no hope of marriage when she'd won the plum job as Kendall Hollingsworth's executive assistant.

God, what a man he'd been back then. High-energy. Strong. Self-confident. The distinguished dark hair with a touch of gray and his conservative good looks hadn't hurt, either. They'd simply added to his aura of power and wealth.

She squeezed her eyes closed, trying not to think about subtle differences that only a wife or mistress or longtime private secretary would notice. It was more soothing to remember the good times, when everything was clicking along. She'd been his unflappable, reliable assistant for almost ten years. They'd been a great team despite his marriage to Justine. As far as she was concerned, Justine was trouble from the top of her salon-styled red curls, to the toes of her five-hundred-dollar Italian shoes. For at least a year—maybe longer than that—the marriage had been on the rocks. Anybody could see she and Kendall were all wrong for each other, that their breakup was only a matter of time. So why hadn't Justine left town the way she was supposed to?

"Oh, God, what do I do now?" Estelle muttered. For starters, she needed more information. Like what, exactly, had put Justine in the hospital. An accident or…something else? If the answer was something else, would Justine be foolish enough to tell her doctor the whole truth?

MIKE LANCER BRUSHED several wayward yew needles from his dark hair and sighed. Since five that morning, he'd been stationed in the bushes of a small park in Catonsville, waiting for Mr. Clyde Patruski to take out his trash.

Mike was stiff and bored, and he had to take a leak. But he wasn't about to leave his hiding place until Patruski showed.

It wasn't until seven twenty-two that the barrel-shaped Patruski emerged, carrying a green thirty-gallon trash can. With a smile of satisfaction, Mike began to snap pictures of his quarry muscling the can down seven steps and then twenty feet to the curb. As a dividend, he got several shots of the jerk picking up a tricycle from his front walk and slamming it onto a neighbor's lawn. So much for the story that Patruski had wrenched his back so badly on a work assignment that he was incapable of doing more than shuffle from the sofa to the bathroom. When Able Exterminators showed the man the pictures, he'd be smart to drop his medical claim against the company—if he didn't want to face a charge of insurance fraud.

As Mike slid behind the wheel of his car, he breathed out a long sigh. After reading Patruski's case file, he'd have bet money that the guy was faking the extent of his injury. But up to now, Patruski had been careful not to do anything in public that would give him away. He'd even had a neighbor kid unload grocery bags from his car. A week of shadowing him had netted nothing suspicious. Mike had to admit, it had been one of his better ideas to watch how Patruski got his trash to the curb.

Whistling the theme song from *The High and the Mighty,* Mike headed toward the beltway and then to I-95. But, the jaunty notes of the song tapered off and finally stopped as he neared the Russell Street exit. Truth be known, he hated this kind of two-bit assignment. He'd take a good murder investigation any day, except that there weren't enough of those to pay the rent. A private eye had to fill in with what he could get.

At 43 Light Street, he stopped in the newly opened lobby café for a large cup of coffee, then took the elevator to the office he'd been sharing with Jo O'Malley since last November. Formerly the sign on the door had said O'Malley and O'Malley; now it read O'Malley and Lancer. He'd begun taking over some of Jo's business after she'd been shot by a couple of thugs trying to steal some of her husband's custom-designed electronics equipment. He and Jo liked each other and worked well together, and when she'd gotten pregnant, she'd asked Mike to come in as a partner. Since she'd gone part-time, he'd been carrying the major caseload.

Sipping his coffee, he leaned back in his desk chair and started listening to his messages. Three years earlier, he hadn't been sure he could make it as a private detective, not after resigning from the Baltimore police force under pressure. As far as the powers that be were concerned, he was a bad cop who'd taken the easy way out—which was hardly a great recommendation for getting jobs in the metro area. But he was good at his work, and the clients kept coming. And he had the satisfaction of helping people who had nowhere else to turn.

After noting a phone number from a child-custody case, he jabbed at the button on the answering machine and waited for the next message. It was from someone who identified himself as Dr. Habib at Mount Olive Hospital and who spoke with an East Indian accent.

"Mr. Lancer, I was told you were the man who rescued Mrs. Justine Hollingsworth from the Jones Falls. Mrs. Hollingsworth appears to be suffering from amnesia and is having some difficulty coping with her lack of personal memory. Your account of the rescue would be helpful." He ended with his phone number.

Mike sat forward. Since the accident two days ago, he'd been trying—and failing—to put Justine Hollingsworth out of his mind. He pictured her again, first as she'd looked outside the parking garage, then on the bank of the rain-swollen creek, her face white as death, her red hair streaming, her body limp as a broken doll. Her eyes had focused on him with an unnerving intensity that had made him want to scoop her back into his arms and damn the consequences. Almost but not quite, that look had held the power to wipe away everything else he remembered about her.

The doctor said she had amnesia. That certainly put an interesting twist on things. Could this very convenient illness possibly be real? He was listening to the tape again, trying to read between the lines, when a noise in the waiting room made him twist around.

Jo was standing near his door, looking disheveled but cheerful. A royal blue diaper bag was slung over one shoulder, and a molded-plastic infant seat, complete with a two-month-old sleeping occupant, dangled from her other hand.

Mike grinned at the peacefully sleeping baby. "Getting Scott started in detective business early, huh?"

"I hope he's going to be an electronics genius like his father. It pays a heck of a lot better."

"Tell me about it."

As he watched her carefully set the baby carrier on the rug in her own office and crack the door, a stab of envy took him by surprise. She had it all—a husband who loved her, a child, a job that she could shift into low gear while she concentrated on domestic life. Did she know how lucky she was? Mike struggled to contain feelings that rarely got the better of him. If things had worked out differently, he might have had a wife—even a family—by now. Below the desk, the hand resting on his knee clenched.

On her way back to his office, Jo scooped up the pile of mail he'd stepped over in the front hall. Sitting down, she set a couple of envelopes on the edge of his desk. "So what was that intriguing phone message I overheard? Are you working for the famous Justine Hollingsworth?''

''She interviewed me for a job, but she didn't get around to telling me what it was.''

''Hmm. Did you really rescue her? How come I didn't read about it in the paper?''

''Maybe the hospital kept it confidential. We're talking about a socially prominent woman who wouldn't want that kind of publicity.'' Keeping his voice carefully neutral, Mike briefly related the details of the accident and his suspicions about the guys who'd been following her.

''It's possible they deliberately ran her off the road,'' he concluded. ''Or they could have been trying to scare her and screwed up. Or maybe they were only trying to pass illegally.''

''But you don't think it was a coincidence,'' Jo clarified.

''At this point, I have no way of knowing. I'd like Justine's take on it. But if she really has amnesia, maybe she doesn't remember the accident—or why she wanted to hire me in the first place.''

''Why do you think she's faking?''

He sighed. ''It could be a ploy, an expedient way to duck out of a bad situation. What if she has a secret she doesn't want her husband to find out? Amnesia gives her some breathing space.''

Jo continued to sort through the mail. ''I suppose you didn't talk to the police about seeing the other car following her?''

He ticked off three very good reasons on the fingers of his right hand. ''The license number of the other car was smeared with mud. I can't prove I saw anything sinister. And they're going to wonder why I'm dragging the name of a well-known citizen into the mire. So going to the police will only set me up for a hostile interrogation. I think my best bet is to forget Mrs. Hollingsworth ever contacted me,'' he muttered, tipping back his chair again and trying to appear relaxed. But he suspected from Jo's expression that she could read the tension in him.

"It's not that easy," she said.

He sat up straighter. "Oh yeah?"

Jo passed a piece of mail across the desk to him. It contained a brief note explaining that Justine Hollingsworth wished to retain his services—and a check for five thousand dollars.

Chapter Four

Benita Fenton took the stairs to the second floor like an ancient train chugging up a mountain track. Every step was an effort. At the top, she held on to the railing and gasped for air. It had been four months since her quadruple bypass. She was only seventy, but she felt more like a hundred. Ed had turned his study into a temporary bedroom until she got better—if she ever did. The operation might give her a few more months, a few years at the most. Regardless, she was going to have to suffer through whatever time she had left.

Today was May twelfth—Andrea's thirtieth birthday—and Benita was determined to visit her daughter's room. She moved slowly down the hall of her Philadelphia row house. The floor squeaked, the carpet needed replacing and the roof leaked in a few spots when it rained really hard. But they didn't have the money for repairs.

When Benita reached the last room on the left, she pulled a key from her pocket and unlocked the door. The musty smell made her cough, but she stepped inside, anyway. Her eyes watered as she looked around the sanctuary that had remained virtually unchanged from what it had been when Andrea was a teenager, except back then, clothes and shoes had been slung carelessly around the room. Lord, they'd had some real knock-down drag-out fights. Andrea had been determined to show her independence. Benita recalled that she had been just as determined to make her daughter toe the line.

Then Andrea had taken off for good—and left an empty place in Benita's heart.

Benita's gaze swept over the room, letting the familiar furnishings comfort her. The canopy bed; the flowered, handmade quilt; the Billy Joel poster on the wall; and the tray of eyeshadows, lipsticks and nail polish on the dresser. A fine layer of dust lay over everything like a blanket. Several industrious spiders had taken up residence in the corner where three Barbie dolls sat. The room hadn't been touched for over six months, since she'd started having chest pains. Now she had a compulsive urge to clean, to make the mirror above the vanity sparkle in the morning sun, and to wash, starch and iron the faded pink-checked curtains that hung limply at the window. But her days of compulsive housekeeping were over.

Benita pulled out the photo album from below the nightstand and sank onto the bed. As she turned the pages, she tried to recapture the joy she'd felt when they'd first brought little Andrea home. They'd waited so long for a baby.

Pictures of Andrea in the bath…in a pink snowsuit that clashed with her carrot-colored hair…in her first frilly dress for Christmas Eve—she'd looked like an angel come to earth. Benita's heart clenched at the memories. She'd tried her best to bring up the perfect child. It was a parent's responsibility to keep her offspring out of trouble and make sure she was a credit to herself and the community. She'd heard Pastor Downing say that dozens of times. So why had she been punished all these years for doing her duty?

Her fingers traced the edges of Andrea's confirmation picture. The girl had been so obedient when she was little, but from the time she'd turned fifteen, they'd fought over everything from her funky wardrobe, to curfews and drinking. Then, at two o'clock one rainy morning, Andrea had screamed that she hated everything about her life—even her first name, which she said she wasn't going to answer to anymore. Benita's own nerves had been at the breaking point. Angrily, she'd lashed out at her ungrateful daughter, blurting out the truth about Andrea's birth.

The next morning, Andrea had taken two suitcases of clothes and moved to a friend's apartment.

At first, Benita's pride had kept her from calling. Then when she'd wanted to mend the breach, she found that Andrea had withdrawn the ten thousand dollars from her college savings account and left town without leaving a forwarding address. She'd never given up hope that she'd see her daughter again, but now…well, it might never happen. Benita might be dead in another month—or week.

Tears were streaming down her face as she closed the album. "Dear Lord," she whispered. "Please, let me see my baby again. Please, before I die."

WEARINESS DOGGED Mike as he stepped into the twilight of the parking garage. With his thoughts focused inward, the cars on either side of him were reduced to shadowy blurs. He knew his exhaustion had as much to do with being stuck in the middle of the Justine Hollingsworth case as it did with his early-morning stakeout. He knew that he was too tired to make a snap decision about turning down five thousand dollars. Keeping it would mean he wouldn't have to worry about his share of the office rent or the rent on his apartment for several months.

It would be smart to get some sleep. But as he headed toward his car, he decided to drive to Mount Olive Hospital—not home. Maybe if he looked into Justine's blue eyes again, he'd know the truth.

The noise of stealthy footfalls snapped his attention back to his surroundings. Someone was keeping pace behind him. With a sudden movement, he pivoted and found himself facing the guy with the weather-beaten skin and the fatigues who'd been following Justine two days earlier. The one who'd run away when Mike had confronted him.

They stared at each other, both tense, both ready to take appropriate action. Whatever that was. The scent of unwashed skin and cheap wine drifted toward Mike, and with a sudden, unbidden stab of anger mingled with pain, he wondered if this was how his father had ended up—a drunk on the street with no family and no friends.

The derelict moved from one foot to the other, his rheumy eyes regarding Mike with a wildly changing mixture of emotions—fear, determination and anger warring for dominance, with no clear victor.

The safest thing would have been to walk away. Mike stood his ground.

"We met the other day. Something I can do for you, buddy?" he asked, subtly shifting the initiative from the other man to himself.

The stranger licked cracked lips, took a step back.

"What's your name?" Mike hoped the abrupt question would elicit an unguarded answer.

"Gary." The man looked surprised that he'd answered.

Mike gave him an encouraging smile. "Well, Gary, what can I do for you?" he repeated.

"What happened to—"

Before he got any further, a car backfired somewhere out on the street. Gary dropped to a crouch on the oil-stained floor, his head bent, his hands and arms a protective shield. A high, keening wail came from his lips. "Noooooooo."

"Take it easy," Mike said, moving closer. "It's just a car."

"Make it stop."

"It has."

But Gary was in a world of his own. His eyes were wide, darting from side to side as if he expected enemies to emerge from the shadows. Scrambling up, he backed toward the wall, and from somewhere in his dirty clothing, he pulled a wicked-looking knife.

Mike wasn't a fool. He didn't move any closer. "It's okay," he tried in a reassuring voice. "Put the knife down, and we'll talk."

"Noooooo." With surprising agility, the frightened man turned and fled.

"Wait!" Mike shouted.

He could have saved his breath. The vagrant vaulted over

a wall that separated the ramp from the parking deck and dropped to the next level of the garage. Mike heard footsteps pounding on the metal steps but when he reached the door to the stairwell and threw it open, the area was deserted. He debated going down, but he knew Gary had a tremendous head start.

Slowly, Mike walked back to his car, his brow furrowed. Gary was mentally unbalanced. That much was certain. And he'd been following Justine the other day. Did *this* encounter have something to do with her?

Mike unlocked the door of his Mustang and slid into the driver's seat, his mind replaying the bizarre encounter as he started the engine. Gary's terror when the vehicle had backfired had been tangible. He'd been reacting as if he'd been under fire.

Just what he needed. More questions.

Putting the car in gear, Mike left the garage and headed toward Mount Olive Hospital, determined to get some answers.

SEVERAL BLOCKS from the garage, Gary sucked in great drafts of air as he staggered along the sidewalk. His lungs burned, and his side ached, but he kept moving. Had to get away.

He risked a quick look over his shoulder. Stupid jerk! He'd made a bad mistake. He balled his hands into fists. Every time he tried to…tried to… He shook his head in frustration. One moment a thought would be there, the next it would skitter out of reach.

With an anguished sigh, he turned onto a narrow street lined with ancient row houses. Some had been demolished, leaving gaps in the ranks like teeth plucked from a decaying mouth.

"Can't let 'em find me," he muttered under his breath. "Gary made a mistake. Sure as hell made a mistake."

One of the houses ahead had boarded-up windows. With a stolen pair of wire cutters, he'd made a hole in the chain-link fence guarding the backyard. Then he'd put the edges back together nice and neat, so nobody could tell. He was good with his hands. He could do stuff. Like in the old days when he'd lived in a house. With…her.…

A wave of anguish rolled over him, and a longing so palpable that it made his chest ache. He stopped and leaned against the wall, gasping, his eyes squeezed shut. When he could go on, he darted across a trash-filled gap in the row and made for the fence.

Almost there. Almost safe. He stopped to look over his shoulder to make sure nobody was watching. Then he squirmed through the fence, put the pieces back together and crossed the tiny yard. He didn't rest until he was in the basement stairwell.

Safe. In his snug little foxhole. He'd fixed it up nice and comfortable. And safe. Sinking down on the bed of newspapers and old blankets, he hooked his arms around his knees and rocked back and forth.

He'd given Mr. Private Detective the slip, all right. And the rest of 'em. The police, too. They didn't even know he had a beat-up car stashed a couple of blocks away with license plates he'd lifted across town. His transportation might look as though it belonged in a junkyard, but it ran good. And it was full of gas. He could go where he pleased anytime he wanted.

But he'd made a mistake today. He should've known better than to trust that detective. Should've known the guy would be on the other side.

"Stupid jerk. Gary made a mistake," he muttered, "Gonna get himself killed if he don't watch out." With shaky fingers, he felt inside his shirt. The knife was there. Just where he'd put it. Pulling it out, he cradled it in his lap. He was good with a knife. An expert. "That guy gets in my way again, I'll cut him good. Cut him good, for sure."

SHE WAS GETTING USED to it. The sensation of waking—the feeling of hope blooming like a small, bright flower unfurling in a protected garden. This time would be different. This time she would remember everything. Her life. Her job. The people she loved. Were they looking for her, worried about her? And what about the father of her child?

Oh, God, the father of her child.

She tried to wrap her trembling fingers around the flower, being careful not to crush the tender petals. But it was too late. The frigid wind had already blown into the garden, snatching the blossom from her grasp.

Her memory was no more than a pitifully short stretch of hours. The time since she'd first awakened in this hospital room and been told that a stranger had pulled her from a rain-swollen creek. The history of her life prior to that moment was a great yawning void.

Fear rose in her throat again. By an effort of will, she stopped herself from screaming. From deep in the recesses of her soul, she called forth the moral fortitude she instinctively knew she possessed. Until now, she'd been like a boat in a storm, helpless to fight the elements tossing her about. The only way she was going to survive was to stay calm and roll with the swells. From now on, she vowed, she was not going to lose control. *She would not.*

The resolve brought a measure of serenity. Lying very still, she opened her eyes a slit and examined her surroundings. To her vast relief, she was in the same room. Same walls, same furniture, same picture of the Mona Lisa. At least they hadn't moved her to the violent ward.

On the other hand, a trim-looking nurse was sitting in the corner of the room reading a magazine.

She longed to postpone the moment of reckoning, yet she'd learned there was nowhere to hide, either from the nurse or herself. So she stirred slightly in the bed.

The woman was instantly alert. "Mrs. Hollingsworth."

She grimaced, saw the nurse's gaze zero in on the movement. Under the covers, she pressed her palms against the mattress. This time she wouldn't make a big deal about the name. This time she'd go along with the program. Because they wouldn't let her out of here if they thought she was loony.

The woman watched her closely. "They told me you'd rather be called Lisa. Would you like that better?"

"Lisa would be fine, thanks," she said politely, surprised at the vast relief she felt.

"Why do you like the name?"

She pushed herself to a sitting position, making time to answer while the woman raised the head of the bed.

"It sounds real," she responded lamely. "I can't explain why.... Uh, are you a private duty nurse?"

"Yes. Dr. Habib thought it would be a good idea to have someone here when you woke up. Are you feeling any better?" she asked brightly.

Lisa considered the answer carefully. "Well, I still can't remember anything about my past. I'm sure you can understand how frustrating that is. And I find that I'm overreacting to things," she added for good measure.

"That's typical with a head injury."

"It is?"

The woman looked a bit puzzled. "Didn't the doctor talk to you about that?"

"We haven't talked much." Lord, had she forgotten something important? Vaguely, she recalled him telling her she might have trouble remembering things.

"Yes, well, why don't I let Dr. Habib know you're awake? Will you be all right by yourself?"

"Of course."

The woman left. That was a small victory. They trusted her to be alone for a few minutes. Actually, it was less than a minute before she caught a flash of motion in the doorway. Looking up, she expected to see the short, brown-skinned doctor, but it was someone else entirely.

A man in a worn leather jacket, faded jeans and a dark T-shirt. He stood in the doorway, filling the space, his left shoulder braced against the frame. His deep-set brown eyes regarded her as if he wasn't sure he'd be welcome.

The universe seemed to tilt. It was *him*. He'd been im-
pressive in her memory, but memory didn't compare to the
physical reality of the man.

The quizzical expression on his face said they must have
some kind of relationship. It shifted to a look that told her he
was trying to gauge her mood. She found she was going
through the same exercise.

The first thing she decided was that he was making an
effort to appear casual, with one hand thrust into the pocket
of his jeans. Yet she sensed his underlying wariness, and a
current of man-woman awareness that zinged from him to her
and back again. Dr. Habib had called him a passing motorist.
Had he deliberately misstated the situation to see how she'd
react?

She wished to heaven she weren't sitting in a bed, wearing
a nightgown. It took an effort to stop herself from looking
down to see if her nipples showed through the thin fabric.
Feeling them tighten, she plucked at the covers, dragging
them higher to cover her bodice.

His lips twitched as he caught the movement. They were
well-shaped, sensual. She didn't want to concentrate on his
lips. Yet she found no safe focus. Everywhere her gaze rested,
she liked what she saw. His features were craggy and honest,
in a basic sort of way, as if he came from sturdy working-
class stock. His dark brown hair was in need of a trim. His
shoulders were broad, his hips narrow and his legs long. She
guessed he didn't make a living sitting behind a desk.

But she didn't want guesses. She wanted to know all about
him. For the first time since she'd awakened in this room, she
was more interested in someone else than in herself.

She sensed she was teetering on the edge of some important
truth. The frightening part was that she didn't know whether
it was good or bad. Even worse, she knew she couldn't discover it by herself. She needed him. The way she'd needed
him last night, whispering gentle words in her ear, keeping
her safe in his strong arms. The memory of her fantasy made
her face hot.

"I know you," she said in a husky voice.

Something blazed in his eyes.

"Are you my husband?" she blurted out.

His grim laughter filled the room, and she felt her skin go from hot to flaming.

Chapter Five

"I'm…sorry," she stammered, momentarily bewildered and stunned. Too late she remembered the doctor had told her the man who'd rescued her was not her husband. But things had a way of getting muddled in her brain. Lord, what a mistake. "You have me at a disadvantage."

"That wasn't my intention," he demurred.

She tilted her chin up. "I take it you're not Kendall Hollingsworth."

"Hardly. I'm Mike Lancer."

"Mike Lancer," she repeated. It seemed to fit. She had the sudden image of a crusader trapped in the wrong century. Partly it was the name, of course. It was easy to picture someone named Mike Lancer wearing armor and charging full tilt on a warhorse with a lance at the ready. But it was more than that. It was the solid, steady aura that surrounded him. And the knowledge that he'd saved her life. "You're the man who pulled me out of the river."

"Yes, I'm also a private detective. You sent me a retainer in the mail. I got it this morning."

"I hired you? To do what?" Silently, she fought off disappointment. She'd been clinging to the hope that he was someone important in her life. Instead, they had a business relationship. Still, she knew she hadn't mistaken the sensual pull between them. It went both ways.

"You came to my office last week and said you were

considering hiring me," he continued. "We never got around
to discussing the particulars."

"So you didn't just happen to be driving by when my car
went into the water."

"I was following...you."

She had the feeling he'd changed his mind about something
in midsentence. "Why?" she probed.

"I saw you on the street outside my office. When I called
to you, you ignored me."

"I wouldn't do that," she said with conviction. He was
damn hard to ignore. More than that, she couldn't imagine
being so rude. "I must not have heard you."

"On the way out of the parking garage, you stared right at
me, Mrs. Hollingsworth, but you didn't slow down." His dark
eyes bored into her.

"Don't call me that name." She wasn't sure why, but it
was achingly important that he, above everyone else, believe
she'd somehow gotten swept up in another woman's bad
dream.

"Why not?"

She started to reach toward him, as if touching him might
convey the bewilderment and upset she felt at being identified
as this Hollingsworth woman. Then, embarrassed, she let her
hand fall back. Midnight fantasies notwithstanding, she
couldn't expect him to understand. All she could do was repeat what she'd said to the doctor and nurses. "It doesn't
sound familiar. It doesn't feel right. What they've told me
about her life seems totally alien. I can't be her."

He crossed his arms and continued his unnerving scrutiny,
and she sensed he was struggling to maintain his cool demeanor.

"I asked Dr. Habib and the nurses to call me Lisa," she
said, her voice suddenly defiant.

"How'd you come up with that?"

Feeling foolish, she pointed toward the picture.

He looked from her to the portrait. She knew she was

blushing again and wondered if he caught even a little of the desperation behind her choice of name.

"I called your house," he said patiently. "Mrs. Justine Hollingsworth hasn't been home since your accident. Her staff thinks she's in the hospital. Her housekeeper brought down that nightgown you're wearing. It fits, doesn't it?"

She nodded tightly.

"You're a dead ringer for the missing Mrs. Hollingsworth."

She let out a long, frustrated sigh. "I can't explain why I look so much like her. But…but…why would I feel that people are trying to push me into someone else's life? Dr. Habib. The nurses. You."

He spread his hands. "Because there's something in your life that you don't want to face."

She studied the tight line of his lips, the disapproval in his eyes. What had she done to rattle this supremely confident man? Made a pass at him? Or was it the other way around?

"What did Justine Hollingsworth do to offend you, besides not saying hello when you saw her on the street?"

"Nothing," he shot back so quickly that she was sure he was lying.

She sat very still in the bed, fighting a silent war with herself. When he'd first appeared in the doorway, she'd hoped he'd come to rescue her from the prison of her mind. No, more than that, she added with bitter honesty. Last night when she'd been so alone and afraid, she'd made up a little fantasy that he was someone who cared about her. That if he took her in his arms, soothed his hands across her back, he'd ward off the terrible forces that threatened to annihilate her. Clearly, it wasn't going to happen.

Yet he'd said he was a detective. If he wasn't here to comfort her, maybe he could help her. She didn't want to be Justine Hollingsworth. But it could turn out to be true— whether she liked it or not. With a tight feeling in her chest, she acknowledged that she might be fighting the association because she didn't like the person she'd become. What if she'd once been the nice, innocent woman whose reactions seemed so genuine to her? What if, over the years, she'd changed into someone she was trying desperately to deny?

"I'm in trouble," she whispered. "Even if I can't remember what it is."

His features softened for a moment, giving her a little spark of hope.

"You must have some thoughts about why I came to your office in the first place. I mean, why does a married woman usually hire a detective?"

He shrugged. "The standard motives. Money. Sex. Revenge. Fear."

She cringed. So much for imagined hope. "Could you be more specific?"

"Well, you could be pretty sure that your husband is having an affair. Maybe you want to know whether he's getting ready to divorce you. Or you may want to make the first move—get the goods on him so you can get the best possible settlement."

She wished she hadn't asked. "You're not painting a very pretty picture of my domestic life."

His tone gentled a little. "There are other possibilities. Something from your past could have come back to haunt you. Someone could be blackmailing you, or harassing you, and you want ammunition to get them off your back."

A frightening scenario leaped into her mind. Oh, Lord, what if this had something to do with the baby? Was Kendall Hollingsworth the father—or was it someone else?

She pointed toward the chair the private duty nurse had vacated. "Why don't you sit down and tell me some things I don't know about Justine."

His expression was unreadable, his eyes hooded as he turned the chair to face her and made himself comfortable. "Okay, you're thirty years old—an age where women make reassessments of their lives, by the way."

She nodded.

"You come from Philadelphia." When she didn't comment, he continued. "You went to college at the University of Maryland—before you dropped out to get married. I assume you don't get along with your parents. They didn't come to your wedding."

"Maybe they're deceased."

He shrugged. "You got kind of wild in your teens. Beer. Pot. Sex. You might even have tried coke."

She cringed, then told herself that he was talking about someone else.

"In college, you met a guy who was different from your crowd. He was earnest. Hardworking. Putting himself through school. You were attracted to him. People who knew you then said you were crazy in love. He wanted to marry you when he finished school and had enough money to support you. Then you met Hollingsworth while you were working as a waitress at his country club and realized you liked life in the fast lane. For the past eight years, you've been one of Baltimore's wealthiest socialites."

"How do you know all that?"

He gave her a little shrug. "You'd be surprised at how easy it is to pick up information."

He couldn't be describing her. "Isn't there anything good you learned about me?"

"You and your husband give a lot of money to charity. You serve on a number of honorary boards. Your radar detector keeps you from getting traffic tickets."

She seized on that. "The day of the accident, I was driving a rental car. Why?"

"Maybe you were trying to give somebody the slip." He cleared his throat. "I didn't exactly follow you out of the garage. I was following the two guys in a Pontiac who were already tailing you."

She tried to absorb this new revelation. "You're sure they were following *me?*"

Methodically, he explained. "You took a circuitous route through the city. They stayed right behind you all the way. I dropped back a couple of hundred yards on Falls Road. When

I came around a curve, you were on the shoulder heading toward the Jones Falls, and the Pontiac was speeding away.''

She felt goose bumps rise on her skin. She couldn't remember the accident, yet she could imagine her terror as the car slid toward the water. Not only for herself, but for the baby. She'd been shocked to learn she was pregnant, but now the power of her concern for her baby stunned her. There was no reason the baby should be any more real to her than the rest of this nightmare she seemed to be living; she didn't look pregnant, feel pregnant or even know how she'd gotten pregnant. Still, the prospect that her child might be in danger brought feelings of outrage and an instinctive protective need welling from some unknown place deep inside her.

Disturbing thoughts spun through her mind. What if her life with her husband was so empty that she'd sought refuge with another man? What if her husband had found out and wanted to get rid of her and the baby? She squeezed her eyes shut, unable to imagine herself engaged in that kind of betrayal.

"Who do you think those men were?" she asked.

"I don't know. Maybe I can find out."

"You think they caused the accident?"

"It's possible they were trying to frighten you."

"What did I do to them?"

His voice turned husky, as if he'd heard the bleakness in her tone and was offering comfort, but it was comfort given grudgingly. "It may not be anything you did. They could be trying to get at your husband through you."

Somehow, his speculation brought a measure of relief. Perhaps her troubles weren't something she'd brought on herself. "Why did they wait until he was in Alaska on a hunting trip?"

"He's away? Interesting. That gives him an ironclad alibi."

Once more she sensed a spark of sympathy. Lord, what she wouldn't give to have this man in her corner, not because she was paying him, but because he cared about her.

"I'd appreciate any help you can give me," she whispered.

He looked directly into her eyes. "It would make it easier if you could dredge up some pertinent memories—you know, give me something concrete to go on."

"Every time I wake up, I pray my mind won't be a blank—that I'll know my name. That I'll remember the important things. You've told me facts, but they're as sterile…as a gauze bandage fresh out of the wrapper. What you've said doesn't make me *feel* anything. Nothing's changed. I'm still struggling with the unknown."

"Well, then, it seems I have my work cut out for me." He looked as if he was already starting to formulate plans. At least she could hang on to that.

"Thank you."

When he rose, she stretched out her right hand as if to seal their agreement. For a moment he hesitated, then his palm clasped hers. His hand was large and warm and steady, the way she remembered. Hers shook slightly. The contact between them—not only his flesh against hers, but the locking of their eyes—stretched beyond the limits of social custom. She wanted him to feel something positive in the touch. She couldn't guess what *he* wanted, why he kept his palm pressed to hers.

For a second, she forgot why they were holding tightly to each other. Then he broke the connection and jolted her back to reality. She watched him closely, noting that the color in his cheeks had deepened. At least she had the satisfaction of knowing she wasn't the only one affected. What would he do, she wondered, if she asked him to spirit her out of the hospital, whisk her away from this horrible mess, in the same way he had pulled her from the river? That was asking too much. But maybe she could persuade him to do something that could prove even more valuable.

"Change your assumptions," she whispered.

"What?"

"Work from the premise that I'm someone who stumbled into another person's life."

He looked startled. And there was something else in his

eyes, as well, a flare of warmth that made her insides turn liquid.

"Please don't discount it as a possibility. Don't write me off as an empty-headed socialite who screwed up."

He hesitated a moment, his jaw tight, but finally he agreed. "Do you have a card, if I need to get in touch with you?"

Silently, he withdrew a case from an inside pocket and set a small white rectangle on the night table. Then he was gone. And she was alone again.

The hand that had clasped his slipped under the covers and pressed against her middle. Somehow, through some terrible cosmic twist of fate, she'd gotten trapped in Justine Hollingsworth's life. Regardless of the reason Justine had hired him, it was she herself who Mike Lancer was going to help. He was going to get her—and her baby—out of this predicament.

The notion comforted her for less than a minute before she ruthlessly told herself to put things into perspective. Mike Lancer had saved her life. He was the only thing she remembered from before the hospital. She was more than a little desperate, and she'd let herself get fixated on him. On his masculine strength. His tempting sexuality. Surely her reaction to him was natural in her fragile state. But it was also dangerous. Because in the end, as she'd known all along, the only one she could depend upon was herself.

Chapter Six

As he stepped into the hall, Mike flexed his fingers, remembering the touch of the woman who called herself Lisa. Her hand had been small and warm in his. The pleading look in her eyes as they'd held on to each other had almost melted his heart. Almost.

He knew more about Justine than he'd told her. Enough to know it would be suicidal to get involved beyond a superficial business level.

Despite that, as he strode toward the elevator, he couldn't get her image or her final heartfelt plea out of his head. She'd looked vulnerable and sexy in that simple nightgown, with the covers pulled up around her so he couldn't see her breasts. Either she was an excellent actress or she was so frightened and upset, she didn't remember how to be arrogant.

It was hard to deny that she believed what she was telling him, and he felt a stab of guilt that he was walking away. Slowing to a halt, he considered going back.

"Mr. Lancer?"

He became aware that someone was calling his name. When he looked up, he spotted a small, rounded man motioning him toward the nurses' station.

"Yes?" he said, approaching the man.

"I'm Dr. Habib."

Mike recognized the name from his answering machine.

"I'm glad to meet you." The physician held out his hand,

and they shook briefly. "It was very heroic of you, plunging into that flooding creek to rescue Mrs. Hollingsworth," he said.

Mike shrugged. "Anybody would have done it."

"I think not. Thank you for coming down to the hospital. I understand you're a private detective?"

"Yes. I'm working for Mrs. Hollingsworth."

The physician looked surprised. "Did she hire you before or after the accident?"

Mike went through a quick mental debate and decided to fall back on the standard explanation. "I'm afraid our business is confidential."

"I was hoping you could help us come to some conclusions about her memory problem."

"You're convinced it's genuine?"

"Oh, yes. She's finding her condition very distressing. She's particularly disturbed by—" he hesitated, as if he, too, was dealing with questions of confidentiality "—her name. She asked us to call her Lisa."

Mike cleared his throat. "Can amnesia radically change a person's personality?"

Habib looked thoughtful. "Under certain circumstances. For example, if Mrs. Hollingsworth were playing a role in her everyday life, she could have lost the memory of that behavior."

"You'd be seeing her real self now?" Mike clarified.

"Yes. However, the trauma of her present predicament could bring out tendencies toward, uh…radical modes of coping."

"Like?" Mike pressed.

The doctor looked a bit uncomfortable with the direction of the conversation. "Earlier, she became quite agitated and we had to sedate her."

"Oh." A wealth of implications simmered in Habib's comments. Mike found himself wondering if there was some way to sneak a look at her chart.

"I was hoping you could give me some insights, but I seem to be doing most of the talking," Habib observed.

Mike didn't bother to explain his talent for getting people to open up. Part of his technique was simply to assume their cooperation. "I'm sorry I couldn't be of more help to you," he murmured. "But feel free to call if I can be of assistance."

The doctor said goodbye, and as Mike turned toward the elevator, his mind was playing with the tantalizing premise that Justine—Lisa—had proposed. What if the frightened, sensitive-looking woman in the hospital bed really wasn't Justine Hollingsworth? She looked the same—except for the shorter hair. If she wasn't Justine, who the hell was she? Even more pertinent, how and why had the real Mrs. Hollingsworth conveniently disappeared?

Were the two women part of some weird conspiracy? What if Justine had decided to disappear and had hired this other woman—this double—to take her place? Then the double had gotten into an accident and ended up with amnesia. What a mess for Justine. And for the double.

The whole scenario was pretty farfetched, but he'd heard of stranger things. And he wasn't in a position to exclude any angle. Even as he considered the outlandish scenario, he felt a curious spark of hope ignite inside him. If she wasn't Justine, if she wasn't Kendall Hollingsworth's wife, then he might be free to— His body reacted, and his blood began to simmer. He knew he was treading on very dangerous ground.

TAPPING HER low-heel pump on the portico of the Hollingsworths' palatial Mount Washington home, Estelle Bensinger waited for someone to answer the doorbell. She'd been here before to retrieve files from Kendall's private office and on other occasions to attend cocktail parties given for clients and associates. Then there was that day last year when she'd slaved eight hours to install software on Kendall's home computer, for all he'd appreciated it. And the weekend she'd had to reinstall almost all the programs because Justine had fooled with the machine and managed to screw up everything.

But no matter why she came, Estelle always felt the pull of the stately two-story mansion with its eight-acre partially wooded grounds. She'd imagined herself mistress of the house. Wiggling her toes in the plush carpet of the enormous master suites. Having mocha almond coffee and chocolate croissants in the formal dining room. Working out with her hunky personal trainer in a fully equipped gym, or taking a skinny-dip in the indoor pool that Kendall would build for her. She was normally a practical person, but the daydreams of enjoying all the decadent pleasures that money could buy had made Estelle shiver with secret longing.

The door wedged open to reveal the lined face of Maggie Dempsey. When Estelle had first entertained the fantasy of living here, she'd taken the time to cultivate the woman's friendship. After all, they had a lot in common. They were both overworked and underappreciated—and they shared a dislike for the present Mrs. Hollingsworth.

"Ms. Bensinger, this is a surprise. Are you needing something?"

"Yes. For Mrs. Hollingsworth in the hospital."

"Didn't the things I took over last night suit her?"

By an effort of will, Estelle kept her face neutral. She should have checked on that. "Who knows?" she temporized.

"All right. You see if you can please Her Highness. If you don't need me for anything else, I'll be getting back to my work."

Work, Estelle thought. She could hear a TV tuned to an afternoon soap opera. Maybe it was in the kitchen.

She breathed a little sigh as she climbed the stairs to Justine's room. Her past investment with Maggie had paid off. The housekeeper had practically invited her to search the upstairs suite. Of course, if she took too long, the woman might get suspicious. But efficiency was her forte. And with any luck, she'd find the ticking time bomb Justine had hidden and be out of the house before Maggie's favorite soap-opera heroine delivered her sobbing last line.

IN THE DARKNESS, Lisa shifted her position yet again. The green numbers on the clock told her it was ten fifty-eight. She'd been trying to get to sleep for an hour and a half and wasn't making any progress. The four walls of the hospital room seemed to press in upon her. Once again, her eyes flicked to the drawer of the bedside table. With a sigh, she gave in to the compulsion she'd been fighting all evening and pulled out Mike Lancer's unadorned business card. Turning it in her hand, she pressed the crisp edges against the pads of her fingers. She didn't look at the card. Instead, she pictured Mike's face—the assessing brown eyes, the square jaw, the sensual lips. He'd sent her a whole packing case full of mixed messages. Yet she wanted to believe that by the end of their conversation she'd convinced him to be on her side.

The door to her room opened and a man in a white hospital coat stepped inside. His footsteps were almost silent as he came toward her bed. She cringed, although she didn't know exactly why she was frightened. He looked well-groomed, and he smelled of expensive after-shave. Wordlessly, she closed her hand around Mike's card.

"I'm sorry if I've alarmed you," he said in a voice that had a distinct Latin accent.

"What are you doing in my room?"

"I'm Dr. Ray." He paused, watching her expectantly.

"Do I know you?"

"We've met at some of the hospital charity events, *señora*. I was hoping I might be a familiar face." He moved into the shaft of light from the street lamp outside, and she gazed into his deep-set eyes. Like his hair, they were dark. But his most distinctive feature was his pockmarked skin.

"I'm sorry. I don't recall you."

"A pity. I heard about your accident. I was making rounds, and I thought I'd stop by to see if there was anything I could do."

He continued to watch her intently, and she felt a little shiver.

"I should have come by earlier," he said. "But I'm so busy during the day."

"It's kind of you to visit." She knew she sounded insincere.

"Perhaps I can help jog your memory. Let's see, do you remember the cocktail party at your husband's office when he was celebrating the San Marcos contract?"

"Celebrating what?"

"A big business deal. You served champagne. And wonderful focaccia."

She shook her head She didn't know this man, but she was sure she didn't like him.

"Well, I'll see you again if I have the chance."

"Yes," she managed to say.

"Buenas noches, señora."

He exited as quietly as he'd come, and she was left breathing unevenly and wondering if the encounter had been a weird kind of dream.

She sat very still watching the numbers change on the clock, trying to come up with some sort of association. Hollingsworth's office. The San Marcos contract. But her memory of the man and the occasion was as blank as everything else.

Her fingers closed convulsively, and she realized she was still holding Mike's card. She thrust it into the shaft of light where the doctor had stood. After Mike's office number, his home number was listed.

It was after eleven. Was he awake? she wondered. Even if he was, it was clearly too late to call. Yet, as she stirred restlessly on the hard mattress, she knew that she was going to do it, anyway. He was the only individual in her limited memory to whom she'd related on any kind of personal level, and she needed to hold on to that human link. At least that was an edited version of what she felt. She wasn't going to think in terms of compulsion or the way their eyes had locked and held as he'd clasped her hand this afternoon.

After dialing, she leaned back against the pillows, closed her eyes and pressed the receiver to her ear.

He picked up on the fourth ring. "Hello?"

Her throat clogged, and she couldn't speak.

"Hello, is anybody there?" He sounded annoyed.

Before she lost her nerve, she cleared her throat. "It's Lisa," she answered in a shaky voice, glad he couldn't see her face. When he didn't respond, she continued, "You know. The woman in the hospital. The one accused of being Justine Hollingsworth. Guilty until proven innocent."

"You make it sound like a life sentence."

She wasn't sure what to answer. Maybe calling him had been a mistake. Silence stretched across the phone lines.

"I know it's late. I'm sorry to bother you," she finally said.

"No. I keep pretty irregular hours. What can I do for you?"

What indeed.

"I need to talk to someone familiar."

"You've remembered me from before the accident?" he asked sharply.

"No. I mean..." She paused again, knowing it would be folly to bare her soul to this man, deciding to risk it, anyway. "I told you, I feel lost—alone—isolated from everything that's normal. Trapped in a space where there isn't any past— or—or any future." She swallowed. "When I saw you standing in the doorway this afternoon, I had a feeling of connection to you. Or maybe it's just that I'm hoping you can help me," she added quickly as she wondered why she'd given so much away.

"How do you mean, 'connected'?" he asked warily.

"When I woke up in the hospital, you were the only memory I had." As soon as she'd said that, she knew he'd take it the wrong way, so she rushed to explain, "I mean, your mouth on mine. Your hands."

Oh, Lord. She was glad he couldn't see the hot flush spreading across her cheeks. She heard him suck in what sounded like a strangled breath.

"After…after you pulled me out of the car. When you saved my life. I didn't thank you for any of that."

"No need."

Oh, yes, there was need.

"Could we pretend we're friends?" she asked softly, surprised again at her boldness.

"That implies we've known each other long enough to get acquainted—beyond one afternoon swim, that is."

"Well, you seem to know a great deal about me. More than I know about myself," she murmured.

"After I left your room, I was trying to imagine what it would be like if my past were a blank."

"It's…frustrating."

"It could have its advantages."

"Why?"

"People carry around a lot of baggage. It would be nice to be free of some of it."

She wanted to ask what he'd like to forget. His childhood? A woman? Instead, she pleated the sheet under her left hand. "Is there anything you're willing to share?" she asked softly.

"There's not much to tell."

"Are you married?" Now why had *that* popped into her head?

He cleared his throat. "No."

"Why not?"

"Is this a survey for a dating service?"

Once again, she was glad he couldn't see her blush. Somehow, the conversation kept getting off on the wrong track. Floundering for something safe, she tried, "Uh, where are you—what room of your house? Apartment?"

"Apartment. I've got the top floor of an old row house. I'm in my bedroom. Propped against the pillows."

"Oh."

"I'm working late on my laptop to fill out a report for an insurance investigation."

Immediately, an image of his long, jean-clad legs leaped into her mind. His shoes were off but not his socks; his feet were crossed comfortably at the ankles, the way he'd sat in the hospital chair. His face was relaxed. His dark hair slightly mussed. She went back and edited a bit, putting a little smile on his face, pleased with the picture.

Was he still wearing his dark T-shirt? Or had he changed into pajamas? Almost at once, she canceled that notion. He didn't seem like the type for pajamas. It was easier to envision him sleeping naked or in a pair of briefs. She found herself wondering whether his broad chest was smooth or covered with hair. Hair, definitely, she decided. It would be dark, like on his head. Was there a lot, or only a sprinkling? In her imagination, she let her gaze drop lower. Shocked by her recklessness, she made an effort to pull her mind back to more acceptable images.

"I'd like to picture the room," she said in a husky voice.

"It's big," he answered. "With high ceilings and the kind of fancy woodwork that would cost a fortune today. The best feature of the room is the turret. It's got a window seat. But most of it's piled with stacks of magazines and videotapes."

"What kind of tapes?" She wanted to know more, and to keep listening to the sound of his voice. There was something heady about the secret warmth of talking to him like this in the dark. It was liberating. For a few minutes, they could be a man and a woman exploring possibilities. Was he feeling it, too? Did she hear it in the slight rasp of his voice, or did she only imagine what she wanted to hear?

"I collect old movies."

"I'm picturing plants in the window."

"Nope. Occasionally, a client gives me one, I forget to water it and it dies. I'm not very domestic," he added.

"You need—" She stopped short. She'd been about to tell him he needed a wife. To change the subject, she grabbed at his earlier comment. "How come you're working so late?"

"I've been busy, and I hate paperwork. But this report is due in the morning."

"So I guess you haven't had time to investigate Justine Hollingsworth's case."

He paused, and she was immediately sorry she'd asked the question. She should have known it would shatter the intimacy. "Actually, I checked out the license plate on the rental car you were driving. The vehicle was assigned to the Atlas office on Lombard Street."

"And I rented it in the name of Justine Hollingsworth?" She held her breath, waiting for the proof of the identity she didn't want to claim.

"I don't know." He sounded like a man who'd been cheated out of a poker jackpot.

Her brows wrinkled. "Atlas wouldn't show you the records?"

"The manager claims the paperwork's been mislaid."

"What do you mean, mislaid?"

"There's supposed to be a folder for each transaction. The one for that particular car is missing."

It was hard for her to get out the next question. "Are other folders for that day lost?"

"He wouldn't tell me. But I got the feeling yours is the only one. It's just a hunch, but I'm good at picking up nuances."

She stared into the darkness with unseeing eyes, wondering if the turn of events could possibly be a coincidence. "Why didn't you tell me about this?" she accused.

"I don't stop and report every little piece of information to a client. It's better to wait until some sort of pattern emerges."

"Better for whom?"

"In this case, for you. You haven't learned anything conclusive. All this has done is upset you."

"Yes," she admitted, her voice quavery.

He sighed. "It's late. You should get some sleep, but I don't want to leave you like this."

She gripped the phone more tightly, wishing he were beside her in the dark, wishing his arms were around her, warm and protective. The fantasy was even more potent now that she'd met him. And she couldn't help wondering how things would be if they'd met under different circumstances.

"You know what I feel like?" she asked suddenly. "Like I'm trying to claw my way out of an Alfred Hitchcock movie."

"Which one?" he asked, his voice taking on a note of tension.

"*The Man Who Knew too Much.* No, *Marnie,*" she answered. "She had amnesia, didn't she? And Sean Connery was determined to find out who she was."

"You remember Hitchcock plots?"

"My memory's selective. It's kind of like an old patchwork quilt, with a lot of the squares in the middle missing. The pattern's best around the edges."

"We...I used to watch a lot of Hitchcock movies."

"Who is 'we'?"

"Me and my college roommate. The way I remember it, Marnie didn't have amnesia. She was hiding her background from Connery," he added, speaking brusquely.

"Are you sure?"

"It's a tricky plot. He catches her stealing from him, and the only way he won't turn her in is if she'll marry him, but she's afraid to have sex. Finally, he gets really frustrated and, uh...forces himself on her."

Lisa felt a cold shiver sweep across her skin. In the darkened room, she curled to the side and burrowed lower under the covers so that only the top of her head and her face were visible.

"Of course, since the film was made in the sixties, we don't get to see the gory details."

"She tries to drown herself," Lisa whispered. The scene was starkly etched in her mind. Marnie floating facedown in a swimming pool. Only it wasn't simply a movie. It was her own near death in the creek, and she could feel the cold water lapping over her.

"He saves her life," Mike added.

"Like you saved mine."

He didn't answer. She was vividly aware of the other reason she identified with the movie. She felt shaky and scared, and the need to confide in him built inside her until finally, the pressure was too great. "I'm afraid of sex," she admitted with a ragged little gulp.

"You?"

Explicit pictures flashed in her mind. Pictures she didn't want to see. "I—I keep trying to…to imagine what will happen when Kendall Hollingsworth comes back and wants to—to make love to his wife. And I won't be able to respond because—" There were a number of things she could have said. She could have told him about the baby she was carrying. Or she could have described her fear of being vulnerable to a man she didn't know and didn't want to know. But even over the phone, she couldn't cross that line.

Several seconds of silence passed during which she sat in the dark listening to her heart pound.

"Maybe it will be okay," he finally said, his voice surprisingly husky.

She might have screamed that this wasn't what she wanted to hear. Not from him. But she'd promised herself not to give in to hysteria again. Instead, she forced her voice to sound normal. "Yes, well, as soon as you find out anything about the car, please let me know. And, uh, something else. A Dr. Ray came to my room a little while ago. He acted like he knew me and Hollingsworth."

"And?"

"It was a strange encounter. Could you check to see who he is?"

"Sure."

"Mike—"

"What?"

"Thank you for keeping me company for a little while." Before she said anything else embarrassing, she set the receiver gently onto its cradle.

FOR ALMOST A MINUTE after hanging up the phone, Mike sat staring across the room, wishing the conversation hadn't gotten quite so personal, especially that it hadn't taken its last, disturbing turn. He didn't want to talk to her about sex. Or making love to her husband. Or her most private fears.

Hell, he wished he could stop picturing her the way she'd looked that afternoon…in that revealing nightgown…before she'd pulled up the covers to hide her breasts. But he'd seen their rounded curves through the gauzy fabric, and the hardened tips of her nipples.

Gritting his teeth, he brought his attention back to the computer, and finished his insurance report. Then he printed a copy and switched off the laptop, setting it aside to get up and stretch. It had been a very long day.

With a deep sigh, he stripped off his clothes and pushed the computer and his case folders to the unoccupied side of his wide mattress. Piling work on the bed was a habit he'd formed since he'd started keeping the irregular hours of a PI. It was also a sure sign that he wasn't entertaining any overnight company.

He really should do something about that. Then he wouldn't be so fixated on tender, tempting Lisa.

No, he admonished himself. He'd better keep in mind that she was probably hard-bitten, savvy Justine Hollingsworth. But the image of Justine kept fading into the far more appealing vision of Lisa.

Annoyed with the turn his thoughts were taking, he pulled aside the covers with a snap of his wrist and slipped between the sheets. Then he shut off the light, determined not to lose any sleep over the woman, whatever the hell her name was.

Within five minutes, he was breathing deeply and evenly. While he knew how to govern his waking mind, he had no control over his subconscious or over his reaction to his late-night exchange with Lisa.

One moment, his body was relaxed, his mind drifting in the first stages of sleep. The next, he was caught in the snare of a dream. He was standing beside a river flowing high above its normal banks. The Jones Falls.

His head thrashed against the pillow, both his body and mind balking at the direction his subconscious was carrying him. With a feeling of inevitability, he stared down at the water. It looked different somehow. It should be muddier, more turbulent. But it was a clear, transparent turquoise like water in a swimming pool, so that he could see every nicely rounded rock on the bottom. And the current was lazy, not swift. He looked up, expecting to see a car plunging down the embankment. But there was no car. Instead, the woman he'd come to meet was floating facedown along the surface of the water, her arms spread out to her sides, her wild red hair drifting like the fronds of an exotic plant.

Fear rose in his throat. Fear that he'd arrived too late. Kicking off his shoes, he dived in after her, flipped her onto her back and pulled her toward the bank.

Then she lay on a bed of soft green moss, parts of which were covered with a quilt in a wedding ring design, only many of the squares were missing. She wore a thin gown. It was wet and plastered to her body, so that nothing was hidden. Not the tight, hard buttons of her nipples. Not the triangle of red hair at the junction of her thighs.

He forced his gaze to her face. The color was washed from her skin. Her lids were closed. She wasn't breathing. And he understood on some deep, primitive level that if he lost her, he'd lose part of himself.

Frantically, he went to work, clearing her throat and tilting back her head. But when he lowered his mouth to hers he felt her lips warm instantly. Her body came to life, and so did his. Desire, hot and unchecked, flooded through him.

"You're playing games. You don't need rescuing," he grated.

"Yes, I do. We both do."

He nodded. He'd known all along that he wanted her, known he was playing with fire if he got involved. He drew back, but her hand came up to grip his shoulder. Her eyes were open, and this time he was the one drowning—drowning in their crystal blue depths.

"Who are you?" he demanded, angry at her. Angry at himself for wanting to hear the answer.

"Lisa," she whispered, her voice pleading for understanding.

He gave a low laugh. "Wishing won't make it so."

"I'm not Justine. She has nothing to do with me."

"Prove it." He challenged her.

"You'll give me that chance?"

He nodded tightly. Instantly, he knew he'd made a mistake. But it was too late. She cupped her fingers around the back of his head and brought his mouth down to hers once more. It was a gentle persuasion, yet he couldn't break free from her hold, not when she'd kindled a fire in his belly.

As his mouth came down hard, her neck arched, silently pleading for him to increase the contact. He angled his head, ravaging her mouth, pressing his body to hers. And she responded with feverish movements of her hips and torso. Still, he might have pulled back from the brink. It was her wild, pleading little sobs that sent the inferno inside him raging out of control.

His hands tore at her gown, and, in the blink of an eye, they were both naked—heated flesh to heated flesh.

"I want you to need me as much as I need you," he ground out.

"I do."

He didn't believe her. Didn't believe that anything good could come of surrendering to this wild, hot passion. Yet he'd gone too far to pull back.

She was ready for him. More than ready. Urgently, she guided him to her, and the pleasure was so intense he was helpless to do anything but drive for release.

It was over very quickly. His body jerked. His breath came in a great gasp. Then he was awake, his flesh sticky, the bed covers in a tangled mess around him. He squeezed his eyes shut, but he couldn't shut out the woman in the dream. Who had he been making love to? Justine…or Lisa?

IT WAS FIVE in the morning when Estelle Bensinger pulled into the parking lot at Mount Olive Hospital. With the overnight bag gripped tightly in one hand, she strode through the lobby, as though she had an engraved invitation. A little digging had revealed that after a recent downsizing, the hospital was running understaffed on both the evening and swing shifts, and the security department had suffered the biggest hit. Her plan was to sneak into room 321 and get some answers from Justine, without anyone knowing she'd been there.

After taking an empty elevator to the third floor, she checked the wall map and started down the hall toward the nurses station. The ward was quiet but for the sound of a television coming from behind a partially closed door. Behind the counter, a nurse didn't even look up as she walked by.

Estelle figured she deserved a break. She'd nearly had a heart attack when Maggie had barged into Justine's room to complain that a special news report had interrupted her soap opera. What a time for some plane to crash in L.A. She'd barely escaped getting caught with her hand in a bureau drawer and had been forced to abandon her search with only a carry case full of silk nightgowns, French-cut underwear and a frumpy blue dress Justine wouldn't be caught dead in. But at least she'd come away with one startling piece of information. Maggie had told her that Justine claimed to be suffering from amnesia.

Damn the Hollingsworth bitch. What game was she playing now? Where had she hidden those documents she never should have gotten her hands on in the first place? What if they'd been in the car when she'd driven into the Jones Falls?

Estelle clutched the overnight bag as she stared at the closed door of Justine's hospital room. The lights were off, and she couldn't hear any conversation or TV. She reached for the knob, but a tap on the shoulder sent her spinning around.

"I'm sorry. Do you have a pass?"

"Do I need one?" Estelle asked innocently.

"I'm afraid so. You're not allowed here after visiting hours without one," the battle-ax of a nurse warned.

"But I've brought some more personal items for Mrs. Hollingsworth. And I'm sure she'd love to visit with me for a while."

"You can come back tomorrow. I'll see that she gets the things."

"How is she doing? Has she regained her memory?"

"You'll have to talk to her doctor about that."

Estelle weighed the odds of getting any useful information out of the woman, then decided that the probabilities weren't good enough to take the risk. With a little shrug, she handed the bag over and retreated down the hall.

Chapter Seven

As Dr. Habib entered the room, Lisa searched his face, trying to read the verdict before he spoke. After three days of exhaustive and sometimes painful tests, he certainly should be able to tell her something.

"All our tests confirm that you're in good physical health," he said.

"The baby, too?"

"As far as we can tell."

"Well, I can't wait to leave the hospital."

His expression changed from encouraging to grave. "I think under the circumstances it would be better if you stayed with us for a while."

"What circumstances?" she shot back. "You've done every medical test known to man."

He shrugged. "Not quite. But we have tried to be very thorough."

She plowed ahead. "And you've found out that I'm fine. How can you keep me here?"

"It's the logical course of action," he answered reasonably. "Your husband's away. You'd be alone except for your domestic help. My recommendation is that you check yourself into the psychiatric ward where our staff can help."

"No."

"I can't insist, of course. But if you leave the hospital, it will be against my advice, and I'll note that on your chart."

She had to hold tight to the edge of the sheet to keep from jumping from the bed. "I'll, uh, think about it."

He smiled encouragingly. "We have your welfare at heart."

Her answer was a slight nod as she struggled to keep her expression blank. But behind her staring eyes, her mind was racing. What if she did sign herself into the psychiatric ward? What if Kendall Hollingsworth came home and decided she was an impostor?

"You're *sure* of my identity?" she asked.

"Well, you have B positive blood, which is a fairly rare type. And you match Mrs. Hollingsworth on other important blood factors, as well."

"But that's not conclusive," she insisted.

"What would convince you?" the doctor asked, his tone maddeningly reasonable.

"DNA testing."

"I can initiate that process. An analysis will take over a month."

"Then get started, please. Do you need to take more blood or can you use some from the half gallon you've already drawn?"

"We have what we need."

He sounded agreeable enough, but then the uncertainty wasn't driving *him* crazy. Nobody was pressing to lock *him* in a psychiatric ward.

Feeling sick and shaky, she waited for Habib to leave. As soon as she heard his footsteps receding down the hall, she opened the drawer beside the bed and pulled out Mike's card.

When he hadn't called, she'd decided their phone conversation the night before had made him uncomfortable. And she'd vowed not to let things get so intimate again. But now Habib was trying to railroad her into a padded cell, and she had nowhere else to turn.

Mike picked up on the third ring. "O'Malley and Lancer."

She swallowed hard. "Mike, I—I'm glad I caught you in. It's Lisa."

"I told you I'd get back to you if I found out anything on the rental car. Or Dr. Ray," he added brusquely.

"Who is he?"

"There is no Dr. Ray."

"What?" She was already feeling shaky. The news made her head start to throb.

"There's no listing for him. Are you sure you have the name right?" he clipped out.

"I—that's what I thought I heard." She pressed fingertips to her pounding temple. Lord, *now* what kind of tricks was her mind playing? She wished she could picture the expression on Mike's face, the expression that went with his curt voice. Was he defensive because he hadn't learned anything? Or was he more uncomfortable about their late-night chat than she'd thought? In either case, he was cold and distant, and she might have hung up if she'd had any other alternative.

Instead, she hurried on. "I—I have a kind of urgent problem. Dr. Habib doesn't want to send me home. He says there's nothing physically wrong with me. But he's pressuring me to check into the psychiatric ward." Her voice faltered. "I...don't want to do that. I'm afraid if they get me in there, they'll never let me out." She clutched the phone, wondering why she felt compelled to share her deepest fears with this man.

"Yeah, that's scary," he said after several seconds.

Moisture clouded her vision, and she tried to blink it away. "He says if I check myself out of the hospital, it will be against his advice."

"Oh, yeah? Well, you need another opinion. Someone who's qualified to make that kind of judgment."

"A psychiatrist? I don't know one. I can't simply pick somebody out of the phone book."

"I've got a friend named Abby Franklin. She's a psychologist with a private practice here in my building. Jo O'Malley, my associate, and I have used her a number of times. She's good. Do you want me to see if I can arrange a consultation?"

"Yes. I'd really appreciate that."

"Sure. And listen—I'll let you know as soon as I hear anything on the car. I've been busy with some other cases."

She supposed it was a good sign that he was bothering to explain why he hadn't called. But he didn't prolong the conversation. Two minutes after she'd first picked up the phone, she was alone once more with her brooding thoughts.

"LISA? I knocked, but I guess you didn't hear."

"Yes?" She paused in the bathroom doorway. She had exchanged her gown for bra, panties and a soft blue knit dress that Kendall Hollingsworth's secretary had brought to the hospital—bless her heart. What a relief to get out of her sleepwear—even if the bra was a bit too tight.

The dark-haired woman standing in the doorway looked to be in her early thirties. "I'm Abby Franklin," she said, holding out her hand.

"Dr. Franklin. I didn't expect you so soon." They shook hands briefly.

"I had a cancellation this afternoon, and Mike said you were anxious to see me."

"Yes. Thank you."

"It's a beautiful day. There's a little garden where we could sit and talk, if you like."

Lisa contemplated her all-too-familiar surroundings. "I feel like I haven't been out of this room since Columbus discovered America. But are you sure they'll let me go down in the elevator? I might run off," she added with a slightly bitter note in her voice.

"I stopped at the nurses' station and told them I'd be interviewing you. You've been here five days?"

"Yes."

"So how's it going?"

"Frustrating." Lisa slipped on the sandals Hollingsworth's secretary had left.

The doctor nodded sympathetically.

They didn't speak again until they reached a small, walled garden at one side of the sprawling hospital complex. Lisa took a deep breath of the warm, flower-scented air. It was like breathing freedom. She stooped to pluck a sprig of grass from between the paving stones, then followed Dr. Franklin to one of the comfortable patio groupings tucked under the shade of a spreading dogwood tree. She smoothed her fingers along the blade of grass as she studied the other woman. Dr. Franklin looked compassionate. Yet it was frightening to think that her future could be resting in this woman's hands. What if she agreed with Dr. Habib?

"Mike thinks highly of you," Lisa said.

Dr. Franklin smiled. "At 43 Light Street we're a very close-knit group. We've come to rely upon each other. Professionally, and personally."

"That must be wonderful."

"Yes. But we should be talking about you. How do you feel?"

Caution was the safest policy, but so much was bottled up inside her that Lisa found it almost impossible to hide her real feelings. "Physically, I feel okay. Mentally, I feel like I've lost control of my life. Only I don't know what my life is supposed to be. Dr. Habib told me there's no way to know when I might get my memory back. Can you tell me anything more definite?"

Dr. Franklin grimaced. "I wish I could."

Lisa flapped her arms in exasperation. "This is all so unreal. Particularly since everyone keeps insisting that I'm Justine Hollingsworth."

"Mike told me you disagree."

"What else did Mike tell you?"

"Not much. I know about the amnesia. I know he rescued you. I don't understand why you're so opposed to the identity. At least it's a place to start."

"It never sounded right. And the more I know about Mrs. Hollingsworth, the less the identity fits. I can't picture myself jilting someone I loved to marry a wealthy man. Or spending my time at a bunch of social events. Maybe the truth is, I robbed a bank or murdered someone."

"Are you worried about that?" the doctor asked gently.

Lisa laughed self-consciously. "Well, I've had a lot of time to speculate about why I was running away. Do you think I can't remember because I don't want to?"

"That could be a factor, although you did have a head injury. But let's go back to something else you said. Why do you think you're a fugitive?"

She crumpled the blade of grass in her hand. "Why hasn't anyone inquired about me?"

"Let's assume for a minute that you're not Justine," the doctor postulated. "Perhaps you're from out of town. You could have flown to Baltimore and rented the car you were driving. Your family could have left a message for you at the motel where you were staying."

"So now they'd be worried sick."

Dr. Franklin shook her head. "Perhaps nobody's tried to contact you. You could be on vacation and nobody's expecting you back for a while."

"Or I could be running away from the father of my child." She stopped abruptly, looked down at her middle and then back at Dr. Franklin. "If you read my chart, you know I'm pregnant. Unfortunately, I don't have any idea who the father is. Suppose we're married. Suppose we're not. I wasn't wearing a wedding ring," she concluded helplessly.

"How do you feel about the pregnancy?"

"At first, I was stunned. Now...well, the baby's become the only thing that I know for sure is real." It was true. At first, she'd found it hard to believe in the pregnancy. But it had become important to her—maybe the thing from her past that was most important. For a moment, she pictured herself cradling a child—her child—in her arms. But the terrible uncertainty of her situation intruded, and the half-formed image evaporated. "If I'm in a fix, the baby's in worse trouble, because she, or he, has to depend on me. I mean, what do I do for a living, if I'm not Mrs. Hollingsworth?"

"What are you good at?" the psychologist asked.

"I think I know something about computers. There was a

program on the Learning Channel about surfing the Internet. I had a feeling I'd done that."

"Well, that's unusual. From what I understand, only a small percentage of Internet users are women."

Encouraged, she added another fact. "I'm getting good at reading faces, too. When I look at Dr. Habib, I know he wants to cover his ass—as Mike would probably put it."

Dr. Franklin chuckled. "Yes, Mike's very direct."

They shared a little grin.

Then the psychologist asked, "What do you see in my face?"

Lisa answered with the first words that came to mind. "Compassion. Open-mindedness. I think you want to help me."

"I do."

"So, do you think I belong in a psychiatric ward?" she asked in a rush.

"No."

The relief was so huge it made her giddy. "Thank God," she breathed. "But how do you know I'm not putting on some kind of act?"

The other woman laughed. "I can't be absolutely sure. But I certainly don't think you would have asked that question after I'd given you the go-ahead to leave, if you *were* putting on an act."

She flushed. "Right. That was somewhat rash of me."

"I'd recommend a change of scene for two reasons. The hospital isn't helping your mood. And if you *are* Justine, familiar surroundings might jog your memory. Do you remember anything from before the accident?"

Her brow wrinkled as she tried to give an answer that would make sense. "No. But when I wake up, I always have a strong sense of loss, like something important has slipped through my fingers. It's hard to describe…I feel like if I could only remember my dreams, I could connect them to my life. But they vanish the minute I try to hold on to them."

Dr. Franklin waited for her to continue.

"It gets worse. I—I'm left feeling relieved and…and at the same time frustrated. I know that must sound terribly muddled. Does it make any sense?" she asked anxiously.

The other woman nodded. "Your dreams may turn out to be important, a way to get in touch with your past."

Lisa gulped. "I'm pretty sure that part of the reason I'm not remembering is that I'm afraid to find out who I am. Or what happened to me."

"Don't push yourself too hard. Memories will come when you're ready. Maybe when you leave the hospital."

"I don't want to go to the Hollingsworth house. I realize I'm making assumptions from pitifully little information, but I don't think I'm going to like the people who live there."

"Perhaps Mike has painted a picture of Justine that isn't entirely accurate. We know he doesn't have the whole story. You have to keep an open mind."

Lisa nodded, wishing she could believe the therapist's optimistic assessment.

"What if you could make things turn out any way you wanted?" Dr. Franklin asked.

"I wish I could go home with Mike." She sucked in a breath, aghast at what had popped out of her mouth.

The doctor covered her hand. "He's a very appealing man. It would be easy to think of him as more than a friend. Especially when you're vulnerable and want someone to lean on."

Lisa shook her head. "It was a stupid thing for me to say. Even though I have a pretty good idea where it came from."

"Where?"

"When I woke up in the hospital, he was the only person I remembered. It was a very…strong recollection. Very… physical."

"He saved your life."

"I guess I want to think it, uh, created a kind of bond between us. But it wouldn't be smart to get involved with him. I'm a married woman, until proven otherwise. Then there's the baby." She gave Dr. Franklin a quick glance. "I don't want you to tell him about my being pregnant," she murmured.

"Why?"

"I want him to hear it from me." She kept her eyes lowered, unable to meet Dr. Franklin's gaze.

"But not right away?" the therapist guessed.

Lisa nodded tightly.

"Well, I respect your desire for confidentiality, of course."

"If he knows I'm pregnant, that will give him more reasons to dislike me," she whispered.

"He has no reason to dislike you."

"Maybe not me. But he doesn't have a very high opinion of Justine Hollingsworth."

"How do you know?"

"It slips out from time to time. He's made me sure I don't want to be like her." Lisa gripped the edge of her chair. "Does my keeping the baby confidential change your opinion of me?"

"Remember that honesty is always the best policy."

She lifted one brow, smiling, "You have a charming way of not answering questions when you don't want to."

Dr. Franklin spread her hands wide. "My professional training."

"Well, I'm glad you had time to see me so quickly. I feel a little better, now that I know I'm getting out of here."

"Only a little?"

"The idea of stepping into Justine Hollingsworth's life terrifies me. I wish I had some kind of proof that I'm not her."

"I think you have the strength to deal with either outcome."

Lisa let that sink in. She didn't feel strong, but she would try.

"Do you have any questions?"

She nodded gratefully. "Yes. Why are my emotions so...out of whack? It's like everything is...magnified."

"That can happen with a head injury. Also, with pregnancy. It's hard, but try to step back when you feel you're getting close to the edge."

She nodded, then asked one more question. "Do you know someone named Dr. Ray?"

Dr. Franklin frowned in thought for a moment before shaking her head. "Why?"

"He came to my room one night and acted like he knew me."

"Late at night? Could it have been a dream?"

"I guess I could have made him up." She sighed. "If I did, I wish I knew why."

The psychologist waited expectantly.

"No more wishing," Lisa said firmly.

"Don't be too hard on yourself. Give yourself time to heal."

"Time may be a luxury I can't afford."

TOO EXCITED TO RELAX, Benita Fenton lay on the narrow bed in Ed's den thinking about the article in the paper. She almost never read the sports section. Who cared whether the Phillies won three in a row or if the Flyers fired their coach? So it must have been fate that Ed had left the newspaper open to section D, page 3, on the dining-room table. The headline had jumped out at her as she started to clean up the dinner dishes. It read: Travis Stone Receives National Courage Award. Stone, the feature explained, was a former baseball player who'd fought a heroic battle with leukemia and won.

But it was more than his years of Major League accomplishments or his recent medical triumph that brought tears to Benita's eyes. His unwed mother had been tricked into giving him up for adoption when he was only a few hours old. And a Baltimore agency called Birth Data, Inc., had helped him track down his blood relations in order to save his life with a bone marrow transplant. A grateful Stone had taken over the funding of the charitable foundation, and many of the services were free to those who couldn't afford to pay. Birth Data, Inc., had become one of the most well-respected agencies in the region for reuniting adoptees with their birth parents.

Benita had recalled how Andrea had gone ballistic when she'd learned she was adopted, accusing her parents of lying to her for seventeen years. Benita had dug in and defended her position, saying she'd done what she thought was best. However, she'd come to regret having hidden her daughter's illegitimate birth from her. Andrea had stomped out of the house vowing to find her real mother.

What if she'd contacted Birth Data, Inc., as part of her search?

With shaking hands, Benita had picked up a pair of scissors, clipped the article and put it with the birth certificate she kept hidden in her jewelry box—the one with the names of Andrea's birth parents, Hallie Albright and Garrett Folsom. For years she'd pretended those people didn't exist. Now they could be the key to finding her long lost daughter.

First thing tomorrow, she'd call that agency. Then she'd tell Ed.

MIKE PUT DOWN the phone and sat staring out the office window. When he hadn't uncovered anything more on Lisa's rental car or the mysterious Dr. Ray, he'd approached the problem from a different angle. He'd contacted security at BWI, National and Dulles Airports and paid for a sweep of the parking facilities. The man at BWI had struck pay dirt. Justine's Mercedes was in the garage. According to the parking ticket on the dashboard, it had been there since May eleventh, the day the rental car had gone into the Jones Falls.

Mike scrawled a circle around the license number he'd written on the notepad. If Justine had wanted someone to think she'd skipped town, leaving her Mercedes at the airport would be the perfect ploy. Lisa could have been hired by Justine as a body double, then had her luck run out when the two thugs who were after Justine forced her car into the river.

On the other hand, suppose the real Mrs. Hollingsworth had taken a flight to parts unknown. And Lisa—or whoever

she was—had come to Baltimore on the same day and rented
a car. She'd been upset about something, driven around aim-
lessly and ended up in deep water, her purse swept away by
the current, leaving her with no identification. But she looked
enough like Justine Hollingsworth to be her twin sister.

Mike's stomach muscles clenched as he tried to picture
Lisa and Justine, tried to figure out if they were really the
same person. What if this very appealing woman with amnesia who kept insisting she wasn't Justine Hollingsworth was
telling the truth? What if she'd had the bad luck to get caught
in the middle of someone else's problems? Suppose she really
was the sweet, vulnerable, frightened woman she appeared to
be. Suppose she was in trouble and needed him... And suppose she was as attracted to him as he was to her. Against
his better judgment, he allowed himself to contemplate the
tantalizing possibility.

The cynical side of his nature wanted to dismiss the whole
line of reasoning as hopelessly farfetched. The other more
incriminating scenario he'd cooked up was equally plausible.
But his softer side urged him to keep an open mind. Until he
had proof of Lisa's identity one way or the other, it wasn't
fair to condemn her, or to insert her into the middle of some
criminal plot. And after all, he'd promised her he wouldn't
make assumptions.

He considered calling Abby Franklin to find out how the
interview had gone. Instead, he dialed Lisa's room at Mount
Olive Hospital. "It's Mike," he said in an upbeat voice.

"Oh, hello!"

She sounded pleased to hear his voice, with no hint of
recrimination that he'd been curt with her earlier.

"I want to thank you for recommending Dr. Franklin," she
said.

"What did she say?"

There was a slight pause on the other end of the line. "A
lot of things. The bottom line is, she thinks I don't belong in
the hospital. I'm planning to sign myself out."

"That's good." He hesitated about two seconds, then

asked, "Do you want me to drive you home, to smooth out the introductions to the Hollingsworth staff?" At least he'd have a chance to do some snooping around the house.

"Would you? I've been dreading going there alone."

"What time should I pick you up?"

"The sooner the better."

"I could get there by five."

"I'll be ready."

Mike hung up, fighting a mixture of anticipation and anger at his own rash behavior. Was he making use of an opportunity to poke around Justine's mansion? Or was he getting sucked in by sweet little Lisa?

Chapter Eight

Mike struggled to keep his expression neutral. This woman couldn't be Justine Hollingsworth. She looked too young, too subdued, too modest in an unassuming blue knit dress that brushed softly against her knees. And too pretty, which seemed to him a strange observation, since Justine was known among the wealthy crowd for her sleek good looks. But this woman had a different kind of beauty. Even with the ugly yellow of healing bruises on her forehead, there was a dewy quality about her that Justine had probably outgrown in grade school.

"All set?" he asked, his voice a little husky.

"No. But there's no point in putting it off."

Her voice had that soft lilt he remembered from their late-night phone conversation. It had turned him on then. It was having the same effect today. Pivoting on his heels, he led the way to the parking lot so that he wouldn't have to watch the feminine way her hips swayed when she walked.

A few minutes later, sitting in the car with her beside him, he caught the scent of lemon. Probably from her shampoo. It was less distracting than the feeling of nervousness emanating from her.

"You'll be all right," he said.

She swallowed, glanced at him and turned toward the window. He got the feeling her attack of the jitters had as much to do with being alone with him as anything else. When had Justine ever been shy around men? he wondered.

He had the sudden impulse to reach out and cover her small hand with his. But in the close confines of the car, that was much too intimate a gesture, so he kept his hands wrapped around the steering wheel.

"Where do I live?" she asked.

As he pulled out of the parking space, he told her, "In Mount Washington near Western Run Park. You've got an estate off Old Court Road."

They turned left out of the lot. From the corner of his eye, he watched her stare at the substantial houses with their wide lawns. There was plenty of opportunity for sight-seeing with the traffic moving in fits and starts.

Lisa gestured apologetically at the double line of cars. "I guess I should have left after rush hour, but I couldn't wait to get out of there."

"I understand."

He took his eyes from the road for a moment, then had to slam on the brake as the pickup truck ahead of them screeched to a halt. The end of the pickup's skid was followed by an audible clunk.

Lisa gasped. "A dog. I think I saw a dog run into the street in front of that truck."

The pickup pulled over the white line and tore off down the nearest cross street, giving them a clear view of a black and brown German shepherd lying limply in the middle of the road.

Lisa made a strangled noise. Unbuckling her seat belt, she hopped from the car. Oblivious of the honking horns from the line of traffic behind them, she knelt in the street beside the injured animal, stroking his head and talking softly. The only thing Mike could do was join her.

More horns honked.

"We have to get him out of the street," Lisa said.

"Yeah."

Carefully, she worked her hands under the animal's shoulders. Mike took the dog's back quarters. A teenage boy who had been watching from the sidewalk came forward to support the middle. As gently as possible, they lifted the animal and moved him to the grass strip along the curb. He lay limply under the shade of a maple tree, panting.

Several other neighbors had seen the accident, and a stout woman came forward to announce, "That's Bruno. He belongs to the Caseys. Must have jumped the fence again."

"Tell them what happened," Mike ordered.

The woman hustled off.

"Hey, buddy, get your damn car out of the middle of the road," someone shouted angrily from the line of vehicles stacked up behind his Mustang.

Glancing toward the street, Mike bit back a sharp retort. "I'll be right back," he told Lisa.

She nodded without taking her attention from the injured shepherd. "It's all right, Bruno," she murmured as she smoothed her fingers over the black ruff. "You're going to be all right."

Incredibly, the animal gave a feeble wag of its tail.

Transfixed, Mike stood and watched, until another frustrated commuter gave him a sharp reminder of the traffic piling up. Striding to his car, he started the engine and pulled into the nearest empty driveway. Then he hurried back to the strip of grass. Lisa was still totally focused on the injured dog. When her hand slid along one back leg, the animal yelped, and she winced, as if she were the one in pain.

"Good boy," she said, her tone soft and soothing. "I know that hurts. Your leg is broken. But the vet can fix it."

Watching her, Mike sensed that her desire to help the animal was purely instinctive, as instinctive as her knowledge of how to give comfort. Her actions were spontaneous, her words genuinely spoken. Certainly, the dog seemed to understand that he was in good hands, Mike thought, seeing the animal's tongue lick Lisa's fingers as she scratched his head.

A gray-haired man in slacks and a plaid sport shirt lumbered up the sidewalk toward them. "Bruno. Oh, no. Bruno," he gasped. When he reached the group, he dropped to his knees beside the shepherd.

At the sound of his master's voice, the animal lifted his head and wagged his tail again.

"Mr. Casey? Did your wife call the vet?" Mike asked.

"Yeah. He's expecting us." Casey stroked his pet.

"Rita says the guy who hit him took off like a bat out of hell. Thanks for stopping."

"Anybody would," Lisa protested. "I think the truck just clipped his leg. I hope so, anyway."

Casey went on as if she hadn't spoken. "Damn. This is my fault. There's a low place in the fence, where a tree limb fell. Bruno got out before."

Mike watched Lisa pat the man's shoulder, ministering to him the way she had to his injured pet. The whole scene was so foreign to his image of Justine Hollingsworth that he felt disoriented.

Mrs. Casey pulled up in a station wagon, and Mike helped Lisa and Mr. Casey lift the dog onto a blanket in the back. As the vehicle maneuvered into the line of cars and drove away, Mike slipped his arm protectively around Lisa. Her body trembling, she leaned heavily against him.

"Come on." He led her toward his car, and she shuffled stiffly down the sidewalk to where he'd parked between a high wooden fence and a bank of forsythia.

She climbed in and sat with her eyes closed and her head thrown back, looking small and fragile and very sad. "That poor dog," she whispered.

Then, to Mike's great dismay, she burst into tears.

She started to cover her face with her palms, but he reached across the space between the seats and pulled her into his arms. Her fingers gripped his shoulders as her anguish poured out in great sobs that racked her body. There was nothing he could do but hold her and offer gentle words. After a little while, he sensed she was struggling to regain control.

"It's okay," he murmured. "He's going to be okay."

With a final gulp, she fumbled in her pocket. Pulling out

a tissue, she blew her nose. "I hope so. I'm sorry I got so emotional."

"Don't worry about it."

She looked down at her hands. "I kept thinking how helpless he was. All he could do was lie there in pain and wait for someone to rescue him."

"We did."

"He made me think about…about what happened to me…. Mike," she said, her voice cracking, "what would I have done if you hadn't come along to pull me out of the river?"

"Someone else—"

She cut him off with a quick shake of her head. "I'd be dead."

"Don't think about that."

"I can't turn off my thoughts. Or my emotions. You saved me. But…I'm not *me* anymore. I don't know who I am. And it's so awful."

She raised her eyes to him. They were large, and pleading for his understanding.

"You're going to be fine."

"You can't know for sure. I think I was acting like me when I was helping the dog. How I felt when I saw him lying there came from somewhere deep inside. But how can I be sure?"

He couldn't cope with either the hopeless look on her face or the aching feeling in his chest. He needed to make her whole. He needed to ease his own pain, as well. Somehow, the logical way to accomplish both was to gather her close once more.

This time she gave a little sigh of contentment as she came into his arms, her body molding itself to his. She pressed her face to his shoulder, swaying her forehead against his shirt. He felt her inhale deeply and reacted with a shiver that swept across his skin. He knew she felt it, because she raised her head and looked into his eyes, her gaze seeming to search his very soul. Her lips were only inches from his. They trembled slightly, parted, spoke his name so faintly he barely heard. Yet he caught the intensity of feeling.

He answered her in the same breathy whisper. "Lisa."

Neither of them moved. Then the most natural thing in the world was to lower his mouth to hers. For a startled moment, he realized what he was doing, and he intended to pull back. But she made a muffled sound that shattered his resolve, a sound of suppressed longing that zinged along every nerve in his body. It was too late for second thoughts. For any thoughts. Since he'd seen her sitting in her hospital bed, he'd wanted to kiss her. And so he did. Greedily, he angled his head, slanting his lips over hers for the most intimate contact, and she opened to him as she had in his dream. Her name was a groan deep in his throat.

If the kiss started with finesse, it rapidly progressed with a frightening lack of control. Her greed matched his. As did her restless drive to explore—to know. He felt like a skydiver without a parachute. Only the contact of his mouth with hers would keep him from crashing.

He couldn't catch his breath, even when his lips left hers to trail a hot, wet line across her jaw and down the beautiful curve of her throat to the wildly beating pulse point at its base. Her pulse kept time with the pounding of his heart. And the way she gasped his name over and over was a rich erotic counterpoint.

With some part of his brain, he knew they were parked in a stranger's driveway. But the fence beside his window and the tall bushes on the other side of the car gave the illusion of privacy. Yet the setting was almost irrelevant. Right now, he wasn't sure he would have been capable of acting differently, even if they had been sitting in the middle of the traffic lane.

Desperate for contact, his fingers glided up and down her ribs. When she sighed out her pleasure, his hands stole inward to cup her breasts. They were rounded and full in his hands. And when he stroked his thumbs across the nipples, he found them hard and tight with arousal. Like his body.

"Oh, Mike, that feels good. Oh, so good," she gasped, arching forward into his hands, driving him to a new level of excitement. "I've wanted…" The exclamation ended on a tiny sob. She turned her head and captured his mouth with hers again. He tasted carnal desire. He tasted need that matched his own.

Her dress had become an intolerable barrier. If it had opened down the front, he would have attacked the buttons. Instead, he skimmed his hand up the smooth curve of her leg, profoundly grateful that she was wearing only sandals and no panty hose. Pushing her skirt upward, he stopped to admire her delicate knees before homing in on the silky skin of her inner thigh.

Her legs parted, and she moved restlessly, invitingly. There was no doubt that she wanted his touch as much as he wanted to stroke her. He reached higher toward the heat radiating from her core.…

And he froze as he heard a thump against the side of the car. They both jerked their heads toward the window.

A man in a business suit stood holding a briefcase in his hand. He was glaring at them.

"I'm afraid this is private property," he growled. "You'll have to find somewhere else for your little party—before my kids come out to play basketball and see something they shouldn't."

Mike felt his face redden. It had been a long time since he'd been caught making out in a parked car. From the corner of his eye, he saw Lisa frantically tugging at her skirt.

The homeowner marched past them and up his back steps. They were alone again, but Lisa didn't meet Mike's gaze as he started the engine and gunned it toward the street, tires squealing.

The traffic had abated somewhat. They drove for several blocks before she finally spoke in a strangled voice.

"I'm sorry. I didn't intend for that to happen. It appears my mother didn't raise me to be a lady."

"It was my fault as much as yours," he muttered, feeling like a jerk for letting things get out of hand.

After that, they rode in silence. From the corner of his eye, he saw her sitting stiffly in the seat, her arms folded protectively across her chest. She was motionless and looked as though she was struggling not to cry. He had to tighten his hands on the wheel to prevent himself from reaching over to touch her yet again.

IT TOOK an enormous amount of willpower to keep the tears in her eyes from spilling over and sliding down her cheeks, and giving away more than she wanted to reveal. Lord, it was hard to imagine a more mortifying scene—unless the home-owner had come by a few minutes later. When she felt in greater control, she stole a quick glance in Mike's direction. He was watching her. For a split second it looked as if he was going to say something. Then he firmly returned his attention to the road, leaving her glad that he was giving her some privacy, yet frustrated that he hadn't said anything. She'd been longing for some sign that he cared, but she hadn't been prepared for a white-hot flare of passion. She ached to know what he was feeling, but she knew he wouldn't welcome any questions. Even if she was brave enough to ask.

Maybe later, when she was alone, she could think about the pleasure of their lovemaking. While it had ended before either one of them was satisfied, it was by far the best thing that had happened to her in the short span of her recollection. But at the moment, it didn't make her feel better—or safer. She'd been trying so hard to keep Mike from knowing how vulnerable she was to him. Now her chest squeezed as she thought about how easily she'd given away her feelings. Yet what she wanted with all her heart was impossible. In fact, she didn't dare put it into words. At least while Mike was convinced she was married to another man.

Would it make a difference if she could prove she was free? The way he'd kissed and caressed her said there was hope.

A half smile began to form on her lips, but it was replaced almost at once with a rueful grimace. She was carrying another man's child. She wasn't free in any sense of the word. Not now, and almost certainly not when she remembered who had given her this baby.

But what if she never remembered?

Tears formed in her eyes. She mustered all her willpower to hold them back. Lord, she should have exercised more control. Only, she'd been hurting, and she'd reached for Mike. She hadn't realized what would happen, how quickly pain could be transformed into passion. It was a little like an alchemist turning lead to gold. Yet neither she nor Mike knew what to do with the riches. One thing was certain, though. She no longer could pretend that his saving her life was the only thing that drew her to him.

Lisa was unaware of the passing scenery. The daffodils and tulips in people's gardens sped by in a blur before her unseeing gaze. Then, all at once she realized Mike had turned the car between two stone columns, marking the beginning of a winding driveway flanked by graceful pink dogwoods. When they rounded a curve, Lisa stared in astonishment at an enormous two-story white house with a broad portico that looked as though it could have been transplanted straight from a southern plantation. Attached to the side was a four-car garage.

"Justine lives here?" she gasped, looking from the mansion to the wide lawn and carefully tended flower beds filled with perfectly coordinated white tulips and purple hyacinths.

"Not too hard to take, is it?" Mike retorted.

Before she could frame a reply, he pulled around the cobblestone circle to the front entrance, stopped the car and climbed out.

She was left staring at his back as he rang the bell. Then he stepped aside, and she saw a middle-aged woman in the doorway. Her salt-and-pepper hair was cropped short, her face was round and her plump body was clad in a black uniform with white trim. She looked about as friendly as a pit bull.

Taking a deep breath, Lisa climbed from the Mustang.

Mike made the introductions. "This is Maggie Dempsey."

"Mrs. Hollingsworth," she said in a voice that sounded artificially formal.

"I've been asking everyone to call me Lisa."

"Aye. They said." Mrs. Dempsey was perfectly polite while managing to convey disapproval.

Lisa stood uncertainly in the driveway. More than ever, she sensed that coming here was a mistake. She pictured herself leaping back into the car, throwing it into gear and driving away.

"How are you feeling, ma'am?" the housekeeper asked, as if she'd remembered it was her duty to sound concerned.

"Fine," Lisa answered automatically. "Do I call you Maggie or Mrs. Dempsey?"

"Whatever takes your fancy."

"All right then, Maggie, why don't you show me around."

The woman looked surprised by the choice of names. Wrong again, Lisa thought. She could see Mike watching the exchange, but she wasn't going to ask for his help.

"Thank you for bringing my things to the hospital, Maggie," she murmured.

"You're welcome."

Maggie looked away suddenly, and Lisa wanted to ask if the housekeeper had resented the extra duty.

Mike followed behind at a little distance, carrying Lisa's overnight bag. She knew he was interested in finding out how she interacted with her employee. She wanted to tell him she was as uncomfortable as Mrs. Dempsey apparently was.

The housekeeper led them into a wide hall with marble floors and flowered wallpaper. Then she stopped short, as though suddenly unsure of how to proceed.

Lisa realized the burden of smoothing the way was entirely on her shoulders. "Pretend I've come for a visit," she suggested. "Show me what I need to know to be comfortable here." She didn't add that the task was probably impossible; she could never be comfortable in such a pretentious place.

"Uh, this is the living room." Maggie gestured toward a large room done in pale white upholstery with a celery-colored rug.

Lisa wrinkled her nose, unable to imagine having selected such a color scheme or such stiff furnishings. It was the same in the relentlessly Chippendale dining room and the enormous ranch kitchen, where the counters appeared to be made of granite and the refrigerator was faced with maple panels so that it blended with the cabinets.

"Is everything all right?" Maggie murmured.

Lisa tried to take it all in. "Of course."

The woman seemed to relax a notch as Lisa went past the well-equipped home office, peering in quickly to see the personal computer and a row of filing cabinets integrated into a wall of bookshelves. Next, she peeked into the powder room off the side hall; it was large enough to hold a committee meeting. Only the sun porch across the back of the house, with its casual wicker furniture and enormous ferns and hibiscus, appealed to her.

A muscular man dressed in green overalls, who looked to be in his sixties, was watering plants and removing their dead leaves, which he stuffed into a small plastic bag. He stopped pruning and looked at her, as if he expected her to say something.

"You also work here?" she inquired.

He laughed as if she had told a particularly funny joke. "You know I do. Been taking care of the house and grounds ever since the place was built. Before you moved in," he added, as if he'd never considered the lady of the house a permanent fixture.

Lisa silently agreed with him—at least, as far as *this* lady was concerned. "I'm sorry. I'm sure you've heard about my memory loss."

"None of my business. I just do my work."

"May I know your name?"

"Frank."

"Well, Frank, for the time being, you'll have to pardon my little oddities."

He grunted and went back to work. Since she was all out of sparkling conversational gambits, she hurried out of the room.

They reached the front hall again, where Lisa gestured toward the huge vase of flowers on the sideboard. "Those are beautiful," she tried. "Did Frank pick them?"

"No, they're from Mr. Hollingsworth's business partner, Mr. Realto."

"Oh."

"He called several times to find out how you were."

Lisa nodded, wondering if she should send him a thank-you note. Her gaze fell on the overnight bag sitting in the hall, and she realized that sometime during the guided tour, Mike had disappeared. When she glanced out the window, she saw his car was still in the driveway.

"You go back to work," she told Maggie. "I'll be with you in a while."

The housekeeper hesitated, then started toward the kitchen. Lisa stood in the hallway, considering. Mike could be anywhere in the house. He could even be outside admiring the grounds. But she didn't think so. She was beginning to get a pretty good idea of how his mind worked. Quietly, she headed for the office. When she pulled open the door, she wasn't surprised to find him standing in front of a filing cabinet, riffling through the folders packed into one of the drawers.

Chapter Nine

It was a moment before he turned to look at her. When he did, his face was a study in composure.

"What are you doing?" Lisa demanded. Maybe it was irrational, but she felt betrayed. If he'd told her what he was going to do, it would have been different. But there'd been no discussion. She'd let him bring her here, and he'd lost no time in taking advantage of the situation.

"I'm doing the job you hired me for," Mike said casually. She couldn't match his nonchalance and heard her voice rise as she asked, "That includes going through the Hollingsworths' personal papers?"

"That includes finding out whatever I can about your problems." His eyes held an unspoken challenge.

She wanted to look away, but she held her gaze steady. "Did you offer to take me home so you could snoop around the house?"

"Partly. If you don't like it, I can return the part of your retainer I haven't spent on the investigation. That's most of it, actually."

Feeling trapped, she drew in a sharp breath. If he left, she'd be on her own in this house that was virtually enemy territory. But that wasn't the only reason she swallowed her pride. She needed to know someone was on her side—him, specifically. And she wanted him to understand that intuitively. But he was going to make her say it. "No. I don't want you to quit."

"You want me to keep working for you?" he clarified.

She longed to have him put it in personal terms. Didn't the kiss change anything? "Yes," she managed to say.

"Then let me do my job."

"Mike, please…"

"What?"

They stood tensely on either side of the room.

She swallowed. "We're both on edge about what happened…when we were alone. And…well, coming here to this house isn't making it any easier. I shouldn't have—"

"No." He cut her off, but as he continued, he wouldn't meet her gaze. "You didn't do anything wrong—or that I didn't encourage. So stop blaming yourself, and let's just forget about it."

Forget about it? Impossible.

What she wanted to say was, Mike, don't shut me out. But she didn't say it for two very good reasons. It wasn't fair either to make herself dependent on him, or to make him feel responsible for her problems.

Instead, she said nothing, simply stood with her hands clenched at her sides, and stared at him.

He gestured toward the files. "I need to know what was happening in your life before the accident. And you can't tell me."

"Not *my* life. *Her* life."

"Whatever."

"Are those Justine's files? Or her husband's?"

"His."

"Then why are you looking through them?"

"I told you, he could be the source of *her* problems."

She couldn't muster an argument. Swinging away, she found herself facing the computer. It was a top-of-the-line model, she noted, with a tower processor and a seventeen-inch screen. Sitting down, she booted the machine and scanned the Windows menu. There were several software packages—including a check-balancing program, a word processor and a selection of games.

"You know how to use the computer?" Mike asked.

"It would seem so."

"You're familiar with Windows?"

"Yes."

He looked surprised. "So which program do you want to access?"

"Finance."

"Smart girl."

A warm flush spread through her at his casual praise, and she chided herself for being so easily affected. Ridiculous that his opinion should matter so much. "I mean, it sounds the most familiar," she murmured.

Before she could test her theory, she heard someone in the hall.

"Where is Mrs. Hollingsworth?" an authoritative female voice demanded.

Maggie's muffled answer was followed by high heels clacking across the marble floor of the foyer. The door to the office flew open, and Lisa turned to find herself confronting a woman whose face was as homely as her tailored suit was businesslike. She seemed to assume that her very presence would elicit a response.

When the presumed Mrs. Hollingsworth didn't comply, the woman switched tactics and inclined her head toward Mike. "Who are you? What are you doing here?"

"Mike Lancer." He didn't answer the second part of the question. And he didn't offer his hand.

"Lancer." Her voice held an unmistakable note of derision. "You're the private detective Mrs. Hollingsworth hired before her bout with amnesia." As she spoke, the woman's gaze shot from Mike to Lisa and back again.

Neither of them offered what appeared to be the expected clarification.

"You seem to know a lot about what's going on," Mike countered. "Who are you?"

"It's my job to know what's going on," she clipped out.

"I'm Mr. Hollingsworth's executive assistant, Estelle Bensinger."

"So why aren't you at the office taking care of business?" Mike asked with what sounded to Lisa like more than casual interest.

"I came to offer my assistance in helping Mrs. Hollingsworth get settled after her hospital stay," Estelle answered, her tone of voice matching the stilted cadence of her words.

Mike gave her a half smile. "Then I'll get out of your way."

Lisa felt her throat close. Until he'd said the words, she hadn't let herself contemplate coping with this house of strangers on her own. She sensed Estelle was watching her with keen interest, so she made an effort to address Mike as if he were simply working for her.

"Well, thanks for giving me a ride," she said.

He didn't seem to have any problem manufacturing an easy tone. "Sure thing."

"You'll be in touch if you dig up any more information?" she got out, an edge of panic in her voice.

He nodded.

Their eyes met. A moment of silence passed during which he looked as if he was sorry he'd brought up the subject of leaving. Or was she making that up? Lisa wondered as she watched him exit the room and cross the hall.

She had no time to consider what to do next. The moment Mike was out of the house, Estelle firmly shut the office door and pivoted, looking ready for a confrontation. Lisa took an involuntary step backward.

"I don't know why you came up with this new ploy, but you can stop the playacting now," Estelle said. With her no-nonsense business suit and grim face, she could have played a warden in a woman's prison movie.

"I'm not acting."

Estelle snorted. "You expect me to believe you don't remember *anything?*"

"I don't have to explain myself to you," Lisa countered with what she hoped sounded like conviction.

"That's not true. You can't change the rules in the middle of the game."

"What game? I don't know what you're talking about."

The woman ignored her comment. "Why did you go to the trouble of renting a car and changing your hairstyle if you were only coming back here?"

Why indeed? Lisa wanted to scream out her frustration with the whole absurd mess. Instead, she murmured, "I can't help what happened to me."

"What about our deal? What have you done with the damn folder from Kendall's files?"

Lisa stood very still, fighting a sense of vertigo. Every time she thought her situation couldn't get any worse, a new crisis arose like a monster from the swamp. Now what? Should she insist she didn't know what file Estelle was talking about? Or should she play along in hopes of gleaning information? The latter course was tempting but dangerous.

Temporizing, she shrugged. "My circumstances have changed."

The woman's mouth tightened into a dangerous-looking slash. "For all I know, you have that tape recorder in the stereo unit activated."

"I don't." Lisa felt her heart pounding as she tried to make sense of this weird encounter. Suppose Estelle had come here to size up the situation and report to her boss? Suppose she was laying a trap? That might explain what was going on.

"I guess you think you hold all the cards," Estelle said.

"No."

Abruptly, the secretary's manner changed, perhaps, Lisa thought, because she realized she was getting nowhere by being a bully. "Let me shut off the computer for you. You don't want to make Kendall angry by messing up his files." Deftly, she leaned over the desk and exited the Windows program.

"Thank you," Lisa managed to say, not bothering to explain that she could have done it herself.

"You don't have much time left before the manure hits the fan," Estelle said in a conversational tone as she straightened. "So think about getting over your amnesia and calling me before it's too late."

"What—what do you mean?"

The woman smiled without warmth. "I won't take up any more of your time. If you want to tell me where you hid those papers, you know where to reach me." Then, as Mike had, she turned and left Lisa standing in the middle of what she'd come to think of as enemy territory.

Shaken, Lisa reached out to steady herself against the edge of the desk. What precisely was going to happen when, as Estelle put it, the manure hit the fan? And exactly how long did she have before it happened?

The housekeeper's voice coming from the hall made her jump. "Do you want me to show you the upper floors?"

Lisa closed her eyes. It would be wonderful if she could simply ask Maggie what in the world was going on. Like, for instance, who was plotting with whom? And who was spying on whom? But she couldn't ask, couldn't afford to arouse any more suspicion. Not when she had no idea who was friend or foe. The only person she could rely on in this house was herself.

Lisa composed her face before stepping into the hall. "Thanks, but I'd rather look around upstairs on my own," she told the housekeeper.

"You know your way around?"

"I'll figure it out."

Climbing the stairs, she stifled the impulse to glance back and see whether Maggie was following her progress. When she reached the second floor, she saw that the housekeeper had carried the overnight bag into one of the bedrooms.

Steeling herself, she stepped into the room and was pleasantly surprised. Downstairs, Justine had clearly felt compelled to decorate in a style that befitted the grandeur of the house, either to suit her or her husband's taste. Here, however, she had chosen a country French motif, with rich, light-colored wood, simple rugs and matching curtains, and a bedspread with a tiny yellow and blue pattern. It was a place where Lisa could feel content. More than that, it was a place in which she *wanted* to feel safe, to crawl under the covers and pull them over her head.

The image brought goose bumps to her skin. She'd been so convinced she wasn't Justine Hollingsworth, but perhaps she had been fooling herself all along only because she wanted so desperately to be someone else.

Like a madwoman, Lisa rushed across the room and threw open the first door she encountered. It led to an enormous walk-in closet stuffed with enough clothes to fill a small department store.

"Princess Di, move over," she muttered. She could picture herself in a number of the more conservative outfits. Others seemed much too dressy, or too revealing.

After closing the bedroom door, she grabbed a narrow skirt and coordinating blouse. When she tried to put them on, she found it was impossible to zip the skirt all the way up, and the blouse was too tight across her breasts. She wanted to shout that these were not her clothes, yet the snugness proved nothing. Although she hardly looked as if she was carrying a child, she couldn't be certain that pregnancy hadn't already changed her body.

But the size of her feet wouldn't change, would they? Kneeling, she began to inspect the lines of shoes on two narrow shelves. Most had three-inch heels. When she slipped on a pair of white pumps, she felt as if she were tottering around on stilts. Did she really go in for these ridiculous things?

She tossed them onto the shelf, and slipped back into the thong sandals that felt much more comfortable. Then, since she'd already discarded her dress, she indulged herself and selected a jade green knit shirt and a pair of loose-fitting tan shorts with an elastic waistband.

Struggling for a sense of calm, she drifted across the bedroom and stood at the window to look out. The estate grounds were so extensive and so heavily wooded around the perimeter she couldn't see any of the neighboring homes, which only increased her feeling of isolation. Her gaze swept the wide lawns and neatly clipped shrubbery. Not her taste, she decided. If she could have any kind of garden she wanted, she'd go in for more flowers. Annuals like snapdragons and petunias in bright colors, clumps of perennials to provide a changing panorama throughout the growing season.

Hmm. Did that mean she knew something about landscaping? Maybe she had a flower garden at home. Wherever home was. The mere thought of home and family and a pretty little garden where she might spend the weekends puttering or chasing butterflies with her little girl—or boy—brought tears to her eyes.

"Oh, baby," she whispered, pressing a hand to her middle, "I don't think we belong here. I really don't."

A moment later, she clenched her teeth, struggling against giving in to self-pity. Dr. Franklin had said being pregnant— or the bump on her head—could be making her emotions so volatile. Regardless of the cause, she hated being at the mercy of her feelings.

Swiping away the moisture from her eyes, she brought her mind back to the scene below. Seconds later, she thought she saw a flash of movement at the edge of the garden. Going very still, she stared at an evergreen that appeared to have swayed. Was there a glimmer of contrasting color in the green foliage?

Lisa's heart started to pound as she imagined someone creeping through the shrubbery to spy on the house. Never taking her eyes from the evergreen, she waited several minutes. But nothing further happened, and she breathed out a little sigh. Maybe she'd seen a bird or a squirrel. Or that man Frank could have been in the garden pruning the bushes. Or maybe…

Before she could stop herself, her mind conjured a comforting fantasy, the one she kept reaching for whenever she was afraid. It was Mike. He'd changed his mind about leaving, and he was sneaking back to the house. He was going to take her away. Her chest squeezed painfully. She clung to the fancy for almost a minute, even though she knew it would get her nowhere.

With a grimace, she turned from the window. She might be jumpy as a cat on a trip to the vet's, but she had more important things to do than imagine either intruders or a knight in shining armor in the Hollingsworth garden. She had to look for clues to her identity—before it was too late, as Estelle had kindly told her.

THE MAN who had been staring at the house stood with the back of his fatigue jacket pressed against the wide trunk of an oak tree.

"Stupid jerk," Gary muttered, his voice low and full of self-accusation. "She was standin' at the window. She could have seen you. Now what are you going to do? Run back to your hidey-hole?"

He waited, every muscle in his body tense, expecting to feel a heavy hand clamp down on his shoulder and haul him into the open. He wanted to sink down until as much of his body as possible was in contact with the ground. But he knew that if he moved, they might see him. So he stood glued to the tree while agonizing seconds ticked by.

Nothing happened. Still, he remained in the shadows. The only part of him that moved was his hand. It inched toward the knife thrust into the waistband of his trousers. When his fingers closed around the handle, he breathed a little sigh. In that moment of peace, he tried to collect his scattered thoughts.

His junk car was stashed in the woods a quarter mile down the road where nobody would find it. He remembered that part. But the rest of it? He had come here to…

Sweat beaded his upper lip as he strained to make his mind function. He'd made plans. But they'd skittered out of reach like a crab scurrying across an empty beach.

A tear slipped down his cheek. He wanted to scream. But he gritted his teeth and stood with his hand clenching and unclenching on the knife handle until a measure of calm returned. He had made it this far. They hadn't found him. That was the important part. He could wait for the rest of his plan to come back to him.

Chapter Ten

Everything was so neat. Lisa continued to search through Justine's suite, thinking it looked as if someone had purposefully straightened up before her arrival.

She wondered if the mysterious folder Estelle had demanded was hidden somewhere up here. Whatever was in it must be damning in some way to Kendall Hollingsworth.

Stepping into the sitting room, she began opening drawers in the chest under the television set. The most interesting thing she discovered was a leather photo album decorated with gold scrollwork. Meticulously mounted in paper sleeves, complete with captioned dates, were pictures of a woman who looked so much like herself it made her gasp.

"Oh!" Now she understood why nobody believed her protestations. She and Justine looked like twins. Were they sisters...or was she herself really Justine Hollingsworth?

Mouth dry, she sank onto the love seat and stared at the face that looked so like her own. The woman in the pictures had the same blue eyes, the same red hair, the same cheekbones, the same chin. The creamy skin. And yet...there were subtle differences. Justine had the thinness of a woman who controlled her weight with an iron will. Her hair was long, and it was carefully arranged with a casual wildness that looked affected. Her nails, where they were visible in the photos, were long and dark—the hands of a pampered woman, someone who shunned labor, not someone who fantasized about puttering in a garden.

The earliest pictures dated back more than eight years. Justine was always with the same man. Lisa could only assume that he was Kendall Hollingsworth. Her hands shaking, she studied his face, trying to imagine kissing him. No spark of recognition flared within her as she stared at his sharp eyes and contemplated his narrow lips. All she felt was a kind of revulsion.

Her skin grew clammy, and she made herself stop focusing on him. Instead, she tried to evaluate the two people in the picture as a couple. In the early pictures, Kendall and Justine were smiling and relaxed, at ease in each other's company. But the last few pages of the photo album conveyed a different impression, as if simmering tension existed below the smiling facade. Or was she imagining things—looking for a reason for Justine's disappearance?

She shivered as the implications of the word *disappearance* sank in. She couldn't account for what had happened any other way. If she wasn't Justine, then the woman who lived in this house had vanished into thin air. Estelle had made it sound as though Justine had run away. But she could just as easily have been kidnapped—or she could be dead.

Lisa grew cold as an image formed in her mind. An image of a woman who looked very much like herself lying pale and still in the woods—or trapped behind the wheel of a sunken car. Shoulders hunched, she rubbed her arms, willing away the chill. For all she knew, Justine was on a Caribbean island soaking up the sun.

She went back to flipping the pages with morbid fascination.

Knowing she must face the enemy, she shifted her attention away from the woman, to the man whose image made her so nervous. She tried to be objective as she compared the way he looked in the earlier pictures to those labeled with more recent dates. He was older than Justine by maybe ten or fifteen years. In the first photographs, he'd been fit and tanned, with a full head of wavy dark hair tinged with gray. Moreover, he'd radiated the maturity and confidence of a man who was sure of his place in the world.

That impression remained intact over the next seven years of photos. But in the pictures at the back of the album, Hollingsworth seemed to have aged overnight. His hair was much grayer and receded from his broad forehead. Also, his body wasn't quite so trim; in fact, a slight paunch marred the waistline of his expensive slacks. More lines fanned out around his eyes, and his mouth appeared tense and drawn with suppressed worry—or anger.

Lisa didn't like that mouth. Again, she couldn't stop herself from shuddering as she imagined it coming down hard on hers. She tried to reason that she was manufacturing an irrational fear of the man. That she didn't know enough about him to be so frightened. But the pep talk didn't help. Quickly, she slammed the book of photos closed. Still, the daunting image of Kendall Hollingsworth lingered in her mind.

Her hand slid down to cover her abdomen. "The man in those pictures isn't your father," she whispered with conviction. "He just can't be."

Even as she uttered the heartfelt assurance, she admitted that she had no way of determining whether or not it was true. Feeling ill, she closed her eyes and sat very still. In fact, she had no way of knowing whether any assumption she'd made since waking up in the hospital was valid. As she'd told Dr. Franklin, the only thing about her that was irrefutable and verifiable was the existence of the baby inside her. Her child.

"We're in this together," she said softly. "I know it's scary. But no matter what, I'll make sure everything works out for both of us. If Mike can't…or won't help us, I'll get us out of this myself. I promise."

She took a deep breath and let it out slowly. It was foolish to keep holding out hope that Mike would rescue her. Again. He had no obligations to her—beyond the simple fact that Justine had hired his investigative services. Yet he must feel something for her, otherwise he wouldn't have lost his head and kissed her as if they'd been alone in a bedroom instead of sitting in a car ten feet from a public street.

The image brought a tiny smile to her lips. And without warning, she was lost, swept away by the memory of the passion—and the pleasure—that had surged between them. Lord, the taste of him. The feel of his hands. Her breath quickened, and her body felt hot and tingly and suffused with yearning. She longed to lose herself in the sweetness of being with him once more. In her mind, she transported them to a different setting. A walled garden with beds of scented flowers and a gently bubbling fountain....

But she soon found it impossible to remember the fleeting moment of happiness without recalling the mortifying interruption. The memory of the man banging on the car window made her cheeks heat, and not from pleasure. Getting caught had been bad enough, but the worst part had come when Mike had slammed the car into gear and driven off, tires squealing, and she'd sat there beside him almost able to see the wall he was erecting between them.

The wall meant rejection, and it had hurt. It *still* hurt. Her hands opened and closed helplessly as she experienced the pain all over again. It was worse that the rebuff had come on the heels of an intensely erotic encounter, but it would have hurt regardless of the circumstances. With no memory of any family or friend, Mike was, quite frankly, the most important person in her life, the person with whom she felt the strongest ties, the person who had known her longer than any other— known her from the moment he'd saved her life. The idea of being cut off from him—worse, that he had deliberately shut her out—was nearly unbearable.

And yet, clearly, she had no right to make any demands on Mike. It wasn't his fault that she felt so attached to him, that his face was imprinted on her mind forever as her first and most powerful memory. Yes, he was obviously attracted to her, but that didn't mean he had any desire to be emotionally involved with her. And, after all, how could a man be emotionally involved or committed to a woman who didn't know who she was? Even if she and Kendall Hollingsworth had never laid eyes on each other, she certainly carried the evidence of some intimate relationship.

"I'm sorry," she whispered to the baby. "I'm so confused. I know none of this is your fault, and I swear I'm going to love you the very best way that I know how. But, baby, I do wish everything weren't so complicated."

Sitting very still, she tried to let the connection to her child bring her comfort. She didn't know her past, but she could at least imagine her future with this child. A dreamy smile flickered on her lips as she pictured herself in a comfortable rocking chair, nursing an infant at her breast while a tiny hand curled around her finger. The soothing image held until she tried to imagine where the chair was exactly. What did the room look like? If she tried hard, she could put herself and the baby in a sunny room with a crib and a white dresser and blue-and-white-striped curtains at the window. But she knew that she'd made up the whole thing. Because there was no way she could already have started decorating a nursery.

The conviction made her heart squeeze. She longed to think about nice normal things a mother could enjoy with her child. Yet even that was denied her. At least until she had her memory back. But what if it never returned? A wave of fear swept over her as the possibility of never knowing her past took hold in her mind. The idea was so terrifying that she'd tried not to think about it. Yet it might be the reality she'd have to live with for the rest of her life.

Her hands clenched the fabric of the sofa cushions as horror threatened to swamp her. She was saved by Maggie's voice coming from the hallway.

"Mrs. Hollingsworth, are you hungry?"

With a grateful glance toward the door, she called, "I'll be right down."

In the bathroom, she washed her face and brushed her hair. When she stepped out of her room into the hall, she almost smacked into Maggie, who was standing directly beside the door.

"You didn't have to come up." Brushing past the woman, she headed for the stairs.

The housekeeper trailed after her. "It's late, and I'll be off duty in an hour. I came to ask what you'll be wanting to eat."

It was a perfectly plausible explanation, yet it didn't sound like the whole truth. She felt as if Maggie was spying on her—for Hollingsworth, perhaps, or even Estelle—and it only upset her further not to know if the notion was true or pure paranoia.

"Really, you don't have to bother with dinner. I can fix something for myself."

"I'd rather you didn't—" The woman broke off abruptly, looking as if she wished she'd kept her mouth shut.

"Why?"

"It's not my place to say."

In the front hall, Lisa turned and faced the housekeeper. "Since I'm having memory problems, it would help if you didn't find it necessary to hide basic facts from me."

Several hushed moments ticked by. Lisa hoped they made the housekeeper more uncomfortable than they made her feel.

Finally, Maggie spoke. "Last time you were in the kitchen, you were making cheesecake, and you didn't, uh, screw on…I mean, the top came off the blender. Cream cheese and sugar sprayed all over the place. You threw, uh, you stamped out of the kitchen, and left the mess for me to clean up."

"Well, I guarantee I won't blame my failings on you." *Even if I am Justine,* she added silently, heading down the hall in the direction of the kitchen. When she reached her destination, she stopped short, staring at the closed wood cabinets. She had no idea what was beyond any of the doors.

Maggie watched her surveying the room, a wary expression on her face. Why was the woman so tense? Lisa wondered.

"Pretend I've been hired to help out with a party, and you're showing me where to find everything," she said as Maggie came up behind her.

She knew the woman probably thought she was crazy.

After a slight hesitation, Maggie began to open cabinets

and drawers and gesture toward the neatly arranged contents. "Well, here are the baking pans...the saucepans...the big pots. Knives, cutting boards, colanders, casseroles."

It certainly was a complete collection, Lisa thought. And expensive. Even the spices were in alphabetical order.

"Everything is so neat," she said.

"Decide on anything you'd like to cook?" Maggie inquired, her voice faintly edged with sarcasm.

"Pasta sauce." Lisa pulled down cans of Italian plum tomatoes.

"What seasonings do you want to use?"

"Basil. Thyme. Bay leaf."

"What about oregano?"

"I don't like oregano." She went very still as she realized what she'd said. It was true, she wasn't partial to oregano, but she hadn't known it until the words had popped out of her mouth. Just as she hadn't had a clue about what to cook until she'd spotted a can of tomatoes in the pantry.

"Should I fix a salad?" the housekeeper asked.

"Yes. Thank you."

"Is watermelon okay for dessert? I got some from Graul's."

"Fine."

Lisa hummed as she sautéed onions, then stirred the tomatoes into the pot and began to add seasonings. With a teaspoon, she tasted the mixture. It wasn't quite right, so she put in more thyme, along with salt, pepper and a little sugar.

Maggie interrupted her salad preparations to try the sauce. Her skeptical expression turned to one of surprise. "It's good. Have you been taking cooking lessons?"

"I don't know. I don't think so. Cooking feels natural." Lisa glanced up to find the woman looking at her intently.

"You're different."

"How?"

"You're...nicer."

"Thank you," Lisa murmured. She would have liked to believe that she'd taken a step toward winning the housekeeper's loyalty, but she was pretty sure it wouldn't be that easy.

Maggie turned abruptly and bustled away to the pantry.

In forty minutes, the simple dinner was ready, and Lisa felt a tremendous sense of accomplishment. She had discovered another ability in addition to her apparent knowledge of the computer. If worse came to worst, perhaps she could support herself as a cook.

Lisa looked toward the formal dining room, with its long table and dozen chairs. "Where do I like to eat when I'm here by myself?" she asked.

"Sometimes I bring a tray to your room."

"And other times?"

"You like the patio."

"That sounds pleasant."

Maggie produced a tray, while Lisa fixed plates of pasta and salad.

"I made a pitcher of iced tea," the housekeeper said.

"Maybe I'll have milk."

Maggie looked incredulous. "You hate milk."

"My tastes have changed," Lisa murmured. Actually, milk wasn't what she would have chosen, but she was thinking about the baby. In fact, probably she should make an appointment with Justine's gynecologist for a prenatal checkup. Then a new thought struck her, and she went very still.

"Do you know the name of my dentist?" she asked Maggie.

"Dr. Bishop. His phone number is in your phone book. Do you have a dental problem?"

"No. I just wanted to check on something." Lisa felt a surge of disappointment as she glanced at the clock. Eight-thirty. Dr. Bishop's office was undoubtedly closed. But she was going to call first thing in the morning, because she'd thought of a way to settle the question of her identity one way or the other—by comparing her teeth to Justine's dental records.

ENOUGH TORTURE for one night.

Mike lifted his gaze from the computer screen and rubbed his eyes. He'd spent all evening trying to transcribe a week's worth of chicken-scratched notes—which ought to teach him not to let his work pile up—and he'd reached his limit. After saving the file, he leaned back in his chair and stretched.

No use pretending he was concentrating on work. He knew damned well where his head was. He kept picturing the defenseless look on Lisa's face that afternoon when he'd announced he was leaving.

Hell. He'd known how stupid it was to get any more involved with her. So why the devil had he kissed her?

The answer was instant: because of the way she'd fussed over the injured dog and cried in his arms. Comforting her had seemed the most natural thing in the world. Then, comfort hadn't been enough for either one of them. Unbidden, the passion of the kiss came back to him in a blast of heat.

Surging off the bed, he began to pace the length of the room. A short while later, he tried working at the computer again. But even that reminded him of Lisa—her sitting at the computer in Kendall Hollingsworth's den—and he went back to pacing. He cursed himself for missing an opportunity. The moment he'd stepped out of the house he'd realized his mistake. He should have stayed while Lisa accessed the financial program—if only to see if she was bluffing when she'd said that she knew how to use the system. If she did know how, then he could have collected some very useful information. Obviously, his judgment was warped.

Maybe he'd go back tomorrow and ask her to try.

The instant the thought occurred to him, Mike stopped pacing, squeezed his eyes shut and clenched his jaw. Wrong decision. What was he doing, thinking up excuses to get closer to her? Every time he drew a line and said he wouldn't cross it, he somehow ended up on the other side.

Scowling, he strode down the hall to the kitchen and yanked open the freezer. Shuffling through the assortment of

TV dinners, he settled on spaghetti and meatballs, and stripped off the cardboard carton.

Inside was the familiar metal pan covered with foil. He'd been fixing these things for himself since he was seven. Back then, he'd been lucky to find anything in the apartment to eat since his old man habitually drank away most of the grocery money. Mostly he and Mom ate off of the tips from her waitressing job—and the uneaten food she scarfed from customers' plates when the manager wasn't looking. What kind of person would he be now if he'd had a normal family life? he wondered, not for the first time.

He sighed, annoyed that he was letting his mind wander over old pain. All that was way behind him. The scholarship he'd won to the University of Maryland had been his ticket to salvation. And he'd never gone back to the old neighborhood except as a police patrolman. Still, he sat surrounded by old memories and more recent reveries until the timer signaled him that dinner was ready.

At the dining-room table he peeled back the foil and burned himself from the steam. But his angry curse wasn't evoked simply by physical pain. He was cursing the foolish yearnings of his soul. He'd been disgusted enough with himself in the car, but walking into the Hollingsworth mansion had brought home a basic truth: Justine was married to Kendall. She belonged to someone else, and it didn't matter what Mike Lancer wanted. He'd never been the kind of person who stole anything, even if he was starving. And he wasn't going to start by stealing another man's wife. So if Lisa and Justine were the same person—and he had no proof that they weren't—he had no right to her. And that was all there was to it.

LISA STEPPED onto the flagstone terrace covered with a green-and-white-striped awning. A light breeze ruffled her hair, and she caught the scent of lilacs. Maggie, who had followed her outside, switched on a set of soft outdoor lights, and Lisa took in her surroundings—a wrought-iron table and chairs were at one end, a conversation group at the other. Probably, Lisa thought as she eased into a cushioned chair, these outdoor furnishings cost more than most people spent on their indoor furniture.

She couldn't picture herself actually living in this opulent setting, yet, as long as she was here, she could think of no reason that she shouldn't enjoy the tranquillity of the garden. It seemed to be having a positive effect on her appetite already. For the first time in days, she actually felt hungry.

She'd polished off most of the spaghetti, when her hand froze on her fork, as something flittered delicately at the edge of her vision. The evergreen branch she'd watched from the window swayed slightly. Again.

Trying to look nonchalant, she turned her head as if surveying the whole quiet twilight setting. She looked at the evergreen, but saw nothing special about that particular tree. In fact, as she watched, the wind picked up and began playing with shrubbery all over the yard.

The breeze sent a sprinkle of goose bumps over her skin. "Stop being paranoid," she ordered herself as she sipped her milk. But she suddenly found it hard to swallow.

Something wasn't right.

She started to push back her chair, when a furtive sound reached her ears. Straining to identify the source, she was sure she heard the crunch of stealthy footsteps on gravel deep in the shadows.

"Frank? Maggie?" she called, her gaze sweeping the garden that, only minutes ago, had seemed an oasis of peace and stillness.

No one answered. The hair on the back of her neck stirred, and in the next instant, she jumped to her feet, taking a stumbling step backward.

But it was already too late for escape. A man stepped out of the bushes and came toward her. Circling the table, he put himself between her and the house.

It was then that she saw the glint of metal and realized with a burst of terror that he was holding a knife.

Chapter Eleven

If she could remember her past life, Lisa thought, it would be flashing before her eyes. Instead, in a few terrifying seconds, she took in every detail of the knife-wielding intruder before her.

He was old and breathing hard, sucking in air as if he'd been running—or as if he was as nervous as she. She caught a scent of wine about him, saw that his skin was leathery and that he was wearing a dirty fatigue jacket and torn baggy pants.

His rheumy eyes sought hers, and she was transfixed by the odd assortment of emotions she saw cross his features, mostly fear and perhaps apology. He held her motionless with his gaze. She knew that only seconds had passed since he'd stepped from the shadows into her line of sight, but it felt like aeons.

By a tremendous effort of will, she managed to squeeze a few words past the painful constriction of her throat. "Please. Don't...hurt...me."

He shook his head. She didn't know whether he was agreeing with or dismissing the plea.

He licked his cracked lips, glanced furtively toward the house and then back to her. When he spoke, his voice was harsh, grating. "You're one of them."

One of *whom?* What part had this maniac given her in his paranoid delusion? She'd already had enough roles to play, none of them of her own choosing. "Please, leave me alone…"

He took another one of those heavy breaths, his gaze probing hers. "I can't. Got to tell you—" He stopped abruptly.

"Tell me what?"

His expression turned fierce and desperate. Without warning, he lunged forward.

Lisa's reaction was reflexive. Her hand shot out and snatched the paring knife off the watermelon plate. As she brandished it in front of her, the intruder went from bold to cowering in the space of a heartbeat.

"No…not you…" His body shrank into a protective crouch, arms curving above his head. From one second to the next, the balance of power had shifted. Now *he* was the terrified one.

"You frightened me, but I don't want to hurt you," Lisa whispered. "Who are you? What are you doing here?" Then, as a sudden thought occurred to her, she asked, "Do you know me?"

He looked up, his gaze darting around, scanning the area for the enemy, no doubt.

"Please," she said. "If you know something that can help me, tell me. Please."

"Too dangerous. They'll find out."

"Who?"

"The bastards who want to hurt me. Hurt you."

Her throat was so tight she could barely speak. "For Lord's sake. Tell me what you know!"

"I shouldn't have come here." His gaze shifted to the house. "Is he here?"

"Who? Hollingsworth?"

Instead of answering, he jerked around and ran, zigzagging across the lawn, his body low to the ground.

"Please! Wait! Who are you?" Lisa shouted at the receding figure. He didn't turn, didn't answer, he just fled.

She was left standing on the patio alone, wondering if her fevered mind had conjured an apparition. Yet no apparition could leave the smell of cheap wine and unwashed flesh hanging in the air.

"Lord, help me." She didn't realize how loudly she'd spoken until Maggie appeared on the patio, her features contorted with alarm.

"What's wrong, Mrs. Hollingsworth?"

Lisa's hand opened, and the knife clattered to the tabletop. She grabbed the edge of her chair to keep from falling over. "A man—"

"Where?"

"He came from the bushes. He went back there." Lisa made a gesture toward the conifers where the intruder had disappeared.

Maggie took several steps forward and peered into the shadows. "I don't see anyone," she said in a doubtful voice.

"He was here. Don't you smell him?"

The housekeeper sucked in a draft of the evening air. "I can't tell."

"He was standing right in front of me! He had a knife."

"You were holding the knife," Maggie muttered.

"For self-defense. He had one, too. It was a lot bigger." Frustration churned inside her. She wanted to press her hands over her ears to block out Maggie's objections. Instead, she took several shaky steps toward the lawn.

"I believe you, Mrs. Hollingsworth."

But Lisa knew the woman was only trying to placate her.

Sinking to her knees, she began to crawl across the two-inch grass where she thought he'd stepped off the patio.

"What in the world are you doing, ma'am?"

Ignoring the disdainful voice behind her, she searched along the ground. For endless moments she found nothing. Then, changing direction, she found a place where the neatly cut grass was mashed flat.

"Over here!" she called.

Maggie hunkered down beside her as she pointed at a double row of indentations in the lawn. They led to the clump of evergreens where the intruder had disappeared.

"There. See?" she breathed triumphantly. "His footprints. He's got big feet. Bigger than mine."

Maggie looked pointedly from the large footprints to Lisa's size-six shoes. "Maybe Frank—"

"It wasn't Frank! He wasn't anywhere around when I came out. And the grass wouldn't stay flattened like that for very long."

Maggie gave a little nod, conceding the point.

"He was an old man—or maybe he only looked old. He was wearing a fatigue jacket and smelled like he hadn't had a bath in months…" Something in Maggie's expression made Lisa trail off, then ask, "Have you seen him around here before?"

The housekeeper's look became guarded. "No."

Lisa was almost certain Maggie was lying. "Call the police," she said.

"I wouldn't do that if I were you."

Lisa's head came up. "Why not? I want to know who was trespassing here and why."

"Mr. Hollingsworth doesn't like the law messing in his business."

Lisa felt a wave of cold sweep across her skin. "Why not?"

Maggie ignored the question. "Frank will have a look around." She'd spoken as if it were the end of the discussion, but Lisa wasn't about to let it go.

"Does Mr. Hollingsworth have something to hide?"

Maggie shrugged. "That isn't any of my business."

Lisa bit back a sharp retort.

Maggie continued, "All I know is that he got mad as a hornet when Frank called the police after some tools disappeared from the shed."

Lisa studied her pinched face. "This could be a little more serious than stolen tools."

"I'll do what you say, but I'm not going to take responsibility." The housekeeper pursed her lips. "Did *you* recognize him?"

Lisa shook her head. She sensed that Maggie could tell her more, but no additional information was forthcoming. Finally, she turned away. She could defy Maggie and call the police, but she knew the action would be reported to the master of the house. She didn't know Kendall Hollingsworth, didn't understand his rules, and she was already dreading meeting him. She didn't want another strike against her when he returned.

Feeling like an animal boxed into a corner, she walked stiffly toward the house. As she passed the tray on the table, she glanced at the discarded plates. A little while ago, she'd been hungry. Now the pasta and salad felt like rocks in her stomach.

Without a word, she stepped inside. Maggie was only a few paces behind her.

"Do you want me to bring the tray up?"

"No."

The curt syllable hung in the air. All she wanted was to close herself in Justine's bedroom and pretend she was in a nice, normal environment—like a plush hotel.

Halfway up the steps, she thought of telling Mike about the intruder. By the time she reached the landing, she'd already changed her mind. What could he do—come running over with a flashlight and shine it on the footprints? They'd be gone before he arrived. She sighed. If she couldn't call the police, there was no point in calling anyone. Time enough to tell Mike when he phoned her—if he phoned her—with the information about her rental car.

She closed and locked the bedroom door, then stared at it. It would never keep the man out if he broke into the house. With her insides shaking, wishing she'd brought the knife upstairs, she dragged the desk chair across the rug and tipped it so that the backrest was under the doorknob. For long moments she stared at the barrier, feeling a mixture of fear and chagrin. Probably the chair wouldn't help keep anyone out, either. But it made her feel a little better. A very little.

Clammy and cold with raw nerves, Lisa headed for the bathroom, thinking that a hot shower might warm her up and

soothe her. She sat on the edge of the tub and began to remove her sandals, but, as she looked down, a flash of metal
under the edge of the French provincial vanity caught her eye.
Kneeling on the tile, she fished out a lipstick, then, bending
to look beneath the vanity, she found a small hairbrush, a
motel shower cap, a quarter and a nail file—all concealed to
anyone who wasn't on hands and knees. They weren't dusty,
so they couldn't have been on the floor for long. Still, they
seemed totally out of place in this excessively neat house,
which was run by an obviously meticulous housekeeper.

"Odd," she mused aloud. Then, addressing the owner of
the room, added, "Did you drop your cosmetics case in your
rush to disappear off the face of the earth?"

The absent Justine didn't reply.

Lisa stowed the articles in the lower vanity drawer. Then,
stripping off her clothes and stuffing them into the hamper,
she turned on the shower. Ten minutes under warm water
with spicy-smelling soap and peach-scented shampoo made
her feel better. Her improved state lasted long enough for her
to blow-dry her hair, pull on an oversize T-shirt and under-
pants and climb into bed. Then her mind drifted back to the
events in the garden, and her fragile contentment vanished.

The scruffy man in the fatigue jacket had acted as though
he knew her—or at least the Hollingsworths. But *what* did he
know?

"Has he been snooping around here before?" she asked
the absent Justine. "Is that why Maggie was acting so
weird?"

Her mouth twisted in a wry grimace. At the moment, she
was the one acting weird. Talking to the woman who lived
in this room—which was maybe the same as talking to herself. Either way, she didn't care. It helped to hear the sound
of her own voice. She couldn't bear the silence.

Knowing she wasn't going to get to sleep anytime soon,
Lisa decided to do some more investigating. Quietly, she got
out of bed and went into the sitting room where she began
to go through the end table beside the sofa.

Apparently, Justine liked to take home menus from expensive restaurants. A dozen of them were stuffed into one of the drawers. Underneath the pile, Lisa's fingers encountered a leather-bound book. The gold letters on the cover said Addresses. Eagerly, she began to thumb through the pages. Most of the entries were old, many of then crossed out entirely.

When she came to the L's, her breath caught in her throat. Mike Lancer's name was at the top of the second page. And it wasn't a new listing. He'd been in the book long enough for his address and phone number to have changed four times. The first two entries placed him in College Park, Maryland. After that, he'd moved to Fells Point, then St. Paul Street, where, she assumed, he must still live.

Lisa ran her finger down the list of addresses. "So, Justine...you've known him for a long time," she said aloud. "Funny, Mike didn't mention it. Does that mean he thinks that I'm you and he's waiting to see if I—I mean, *you*— remember him? Or is he hiding his relationship with you from *me?*" In either case, how big a fool had she been to let herself be so vulnerable to him?

She snapped the pages closed and tapped the book against her palm, contemplating this new piece in the puzzle of Justine's life. She thought about calling Mike to demand an explanation but if and when she brought up the subject, it would be face-to-face.

As she slipped the address book into her purse, she suddenly felt bone-weary, drained of both physical and emotional energy. A quick glance at the clock told her it was one-thirty in the morning. She'd been running on adrenaline for hours. Maybe, just maybe, she was tired enough to forget about the alien surroundings and the man in the garden and go to sleep.

On unsteady legs, she wobbled to the bed. When she turned off the light, she felt a surge of panic at letting herself relax in a stranger's room. But moments after pulling the covers to her chin, she slipped into blessed slumber.

STRANGELY ENOUGH, she knew she was dreaming. She was lying in Justine's bed, but she wasn't alone in the room. Mag-

gie, Estelle, Mike, Kendall Hollingsworth and the intruder
from the garden were all gathered there. Only, the disreputable
derelict had metamorphosed into someone who looked like
Charlie Chaplin playing the "little tramp." She watched them
all warily, waiting to find out what would happen. On balance,
she was more frightened of Kendall than of the tramp, which
seemed awfully strange. After all, Kendall was supposed to
be her husband.

Estelle leaned over the bed. "Where are the papers?" she
demanded.

She stared at Estelle. "I don't know about any papers."

The secretary snorted. "You're lying."

"Give us the papers," the others chorused as they formed
a circle around the bed.

She shook her head helplessly. "I can't."

Estelle regarded her with narrowed eyes, then turned to
address the others. "We can't let her get away with this."

She tried to sit up, but Mike moved closer and put a restraining hand on her shoulder. His touch was gentle, yet it
held her in place while Maggie, Estelle and the tramp began
to search the room. Hollingsworth strode to her side and
looked at her appraisingly. When she cringed against the pillows, he grinned. Then he silently turned and joined the
searchers. At first, the process was orderly: the foursome
opened drawers, sorted through their contents, carefully closed
them again. But when they found nothing, the pace quickened. In a frenzy, they began to rush around the room, roughly
sweeping everything from shelves and emptying bureaus. She
watched as a lipstick, a quarter and an address book rolled
under the vanity cabinet in the bathroom and vanished from
sight.

"Look what you've done," she shouted.

But nobody paid any attention.

"Help them," Mike whispered. "Help yourself. Give them
the papers."

"I can't," she protested, watching in dismay as the crew

tore madly through her—or were they someone else's?—belongings. Somewhere in the house, a clock struck, and everyone in the room went still.

"Saints preserve us," Maggie croaked as a towel slithered through her fingers and pooled on the floor.

"You're a fine one to talk!" Kendall shouted, tossing a pair of shoes onto the rug.

The housekeeper glared at him. "Get out of here. All of you get out so I can put this place to rights before the master comes home."

The order didn't make much sense, since the master was one of the people who had made the mess. But like everyone else, he obeyed the command, fading through the wall like a piece of trick photography. For a long time, Maggie stood there, looking disinterested. Then she began to pick up the clothing scattered across the floor.

"Do you want me to help?" Lisa asked.

"No. You go back to sleep," the housekeeper replied.

Obediently, she closed her eyes.

Lisa's eyes snapped open. With an unsteady hand, she fumbled for the light, blinking against the glare as she surveyed the room that had been torn apart. Incredibly, it was as neat as it had been when she'd climbed into bed. The mess was gone, along with the early-morning visitors. She was alone, drawing in shaky breaths as she huddled under the covers.

Chapter Twelve

Lisa struggled to bring the dream into focus, hoping that somewhere amidst the disjointed rantings of her subconscious a clue to her real self might lie hidden. Eyes closed, she tried to fix each detail in her mind. The tramp. Mike. Kendall Hollingsworth. Maggie. Estelle. A hash of fantasy and reality.

Sitting up, she craned her head toward the bathroom. In the dream, she'd been able to see the vanity, but actually, it was hidden from view around the corner, which could be why the things that had rolled underneath had escaped Maggie's housekeeping efforts.

Of course, it was ridiculous to think the items had gotten there during a search. She had no reason to believe that the room had been ransacked as it had been in her dream, no reason at all even to entertain that notion—except Estelle *had* come asking about a folder of missing documents and she had brought clothes for Justine to the hospital—clothes undoubtedly taken from this room....

Once the thought entered Lisa's head, it was impossible for her not to wonder if, indeed, someone had carelessly destroyed the room looking for the same papers Estelle so badly wanted. She could easily see Maggie putting everything back in order—everything she could find—so that "the master" wouldn't know she'd allowed an intruder to get into the house. Or perhaps it had been Maggie herself who had done the searching.

Frighteningly, incredibly, it was starting to make sense. Unable to stop what her mind had begun, Lisa took the speculation a step further. Having to clean up an unexpected mess could explain why Maggie had been so nervous about showing her around that afternoon. She could have been waiting for her—*expecting* her—to notice that some things were out of order. Unfortunately, Maggie's behavior was only conjecture. For that matter, so was any speculation about someone's going through the house. But the papers were real. At least Estelle thought so. And both Estelle and Kendall Hollingsworth wanted them.

Lisa's pulse pounded as she considered the possibilities. If Justine had stolen valuable documents and stashed them in her bedroom, they might well have been found already, not by Estelle, but by one of the other players. But what if Justine had been smart enough to pick a better hiding place?

After a quick glance at the clock, Lisa climbed quietly out of bed. It was four in the morning. She could probably do a lot of snooping before Maggie or Frank got up. If they caught her walking around, she'd say she couldn't sleep and was using the time to get reacquainted with her surroundings.

Pulling on a robe from the closet, she tiptoed over to the closed door that connected her room to the other master suite. It seemed to her that Justine's most secure hiding places would be in Kendall's room. Or his office.

With a shudder, she turned the knob. She'd deliberately stayed out of his bedroom on her tour of the house because she didn't want to get that close to him—even in spirit. The very idea of being vulnerable to Kendall Hollingsworth made her queasy. But he wasn't here, she reminded herself as she opened the door.

For a minute, she stood quietly, breathing in the faint smell of cigar smoke. Then she turned on the small lamp on the bureau. In the warm glow everything was solidly masculine, with heavy walnut furniture and a plaid pattern repeated on the rug and wallpaper. In the center of the wall facing her was a king-size bed. She'd wanted to believe that Hollingsworth and his wife kept separate rooms because they didn't have a sexual relationship, but the covetous look in his eyes in the photographs she remembered told her otherwise. More likely, he enjoyed the luxury of maintaining two ostentatious master suites.

Lisa stood looking at the wide bed, feeling her stomach tie itself into knots. Presumably, Hollingsworth had been celibate on his hunting trip. When he came back, would he be eager to exercise his marital rights? Would he want his wife even if she didn't remember who he was?

Her reaction to the sight of his bed was the same as it had been to his pictures. Her skin grew icy, and she rubbed her hands over her arms, moving the sleeves of the robe up and down. If he were a gentleman, he'd leave her alone. But nothing she'd learned about Hollingsworth made her think she could count on that. He'd stolen another man's sweetheart. He didn't want the police on his property, probably because he was engaged in something illegal. And he didn't trust his wife.

Would he be surprised to find her at home instead of in a car at the bottom of the Jones Falls?

She pictured him grabbing her, slamming her down on the bed, taking out the latent anger and frustration she'd detected in the pictures on the closest available target. The images were so vivid that a sick tide rose in her throat. For a moment, she imagined it already had happened. She tried to catch her breath, feeling as if she were being swept through a long, swirling, terror-filled tunnel.

Light-headed and unprepared for the strength of her reactions, she grabbed the door frame. She had to get out of here. Had to get away.

Backing out of the room, she closed the door, leaning against the wall as she struggled to bring her breathing back to normal. It was several minutes before she felt well enough to remove the chair propped against her door and step into the hall. For long moments she stood listening. Finally, on silent feet, she tiptoed down the stairs.

By the time she reached Hollingsworth's office, the inexplicable terror had receded, though her heart was still beating much faster than normal and her hands shook slightly as she turned the doorknob. After closing the door behind her, she flipped on the desk light. Beside it was the computer.

Maybe she could save herself some time, she thought, by poking through the files.

Sitting down in the desk chair, she booted the machine. Then, as she'd wanted to do earlier, she accessed the financial program. But the results were disappointing. The data had been erased from every file. At least it appeared to have been erased.

"Or maybe you don't know as much about computers as you think you do," she muttered to herself.

Frustrated, she glanced around the room. Back to plan one—searching for papers.

Experimentally, she pried at the edges of the carpet, but they were firmly attached. Turning over the chairs, she checked to see if anything was taped to the bottoms. No luck. Nor was anything fixed to the bottoms of the desk drawers. She even checked some of the file drawers, although she was sure Justine wouldn't be *that* bold. After a half hour's careful search, she was still empty-handed—and she was running out of both time and places to look.

The office was designed for practicality, with touches of elegance like the expensive pen and pencil set on the desk, the Casablanca ceiling fan and the wood panels on the front of the filing cabinets. Matching wood shelving marched up the walls on either side of the windows. On the lower levels were books on engineering and business management. Above them were leather-bound sets like the complete works of William Shakespeare, Charles Dickens and Theodore Dreiser, of all people. They looked out of place among the well-used engineering volumes.

Was Kendall's taste in literature really so elevated? Suddenly it occurred to her that, if he never read the books, they'd make the perfect hiding place. Pushing a chair toward the wall, she climbed onto the seat and pulled down *David Copperfield*. When she opened it at random, the spine of the book was stiff, and she suspected it had never been read. Encouraged, she began removing each of the volumes in turn. Ten minutes into the search, she began to wonder if this was another dead end. Then she extracted *The Merchant of Venice* and saw a manila envelope sticking out from behind the next volume.

With a giddy feeling of triumph, Lisa replaced the books and brought the envelope to the desk. She was about to read the contents, when a sound in the hall made her go rigid.

The doorknob turned.

"Who's in there?" a raspy voice called.

She almost shoved the envelope into the first hiding place that came to hand—the desk drawer—but then realized she might never get it back. For a frightening moment, she didn't know what to do. Then, quickly, she tucked the evidence under her robe and held it in place with an arm pressed against her chest.

Before she had time to look up, the door swung inward, and she was staring down the muzzle of a shotgun.

"On your feet!"

"Don't shoot," she quavered, scrambling up.

"You," Frank, the handyman, growled. Then he called over his shoulder. "It's her."

His face angry, he addressed her again. "What the hell are *you* doin' sneakin' around like this?" At least he lowered the gun barrel.

"I'm not sneaking. Put that thing away. You could hurt somebody," Lisa countered.

"You gave me and Maggie a start. We thought—"

"—someone had broken in," Maggie chimed in as she stepped through the doorway.

"Like they did before?" Lisa questioned.

"How do you know—" Maggie stopped abruptly.

Lisa tried to mask her look of victory, but it was gratifying to have her theory confirmed. "Suppose you tell me who was snooping around before I came home from the hospital."

Maggie looked frightened. "I don't know. They didn't touch Mr. Hollingsworth's office. Mostly it was your room and the kitchen."

"The guy in the fatigues who came at me with a knife?"

Maggie shrugged. "It could have been him."

"What does he have against the Hollingsworths?"

"I wish I knew."

"Then you've seen him around here before?"

Maggie blanched. "I'm not sure."

"Yes or no."

"I may have seen him."

Lisa pressed her advantage. "What happened the night the house was broken into?"

"We didn't see. Somebody called and said they were from the hospital, that you wanted some things brought down right away. When Frank and I got home, we found a blooming mess."

"Who called? A man or a woman?"

"A man," Maggie muttered.

"Thank you for informing me," Lisa said.

"Are you going to tell Mr. Hollingsworth?"

"I don't know." She was pretty sure she wouldn't. But it wouldn't hurt to hold the threat over the housekeeper. "Does Mr. Hollingsworth have any enemies?"

"I—I wouldn't know."

The faltering answer made Lisa press harder. "If you don't want him to hear about the break-in, tell me what you know!"

Maggie paled.

"Did he talk to you about someone?" Lisa tried.

"No. But one night he had an argument with Mr. Realto." The housekeeper looked as if she wished she'd kept her mouth shut.

"The man who sent the flowers, Mr. Hollingworth's business partner?"

"Yes."

"What were they arguing about?"

"I don't know."

"Business?"

Maggie shrugged.

Lisa stared at the woman's downcast eyes, suspecting she had gotten all she was going to get. Pulling her robe tighter, she pressed the envelope more firmly to her body, and exited the room. She heard Maggie and Frank turn but didn't spare a backward look. Walking with studied care, she made quickly for the stairs, but her heart was pounding so hard that she felt dizzy.

Once inside her room, she stood with her back braced against the door, picturing Frank and Maggie coming after her with the gun. She had to remind herself that they hadn't really been after *her*. They'd thought someone had broken in. Again. Maggie said it was a man who'd called to draw her and Frank out of the house, so the culprit couldn't have been Estelle. What about one of the men who had forced her off the road, or the business partner—Realto—with whom Hollingsworth had argued? She'd pressed Maggie pretty hard. Probably she'd made an enemy.

With a decisive click, she locked her bedroom door, then carried the envelope to the bed, where she fluffed up the pillows and made herself comfortable. Yet her hands still weren't quite steady as she began to inspect her booty, which turned out to be photocopies of engineering specifications and construction plans for a project from the K. H. Group. That must be Hollingsworth's company.

"You understand these?" Lisa asked Justine as she began to examine order forms for steel beams and other materials. Why had Justine taken this stuff, anyway?

She was flipping back and forth between the spec sheet and the schematic, when her hand went very still. She didn't know about Justine, but she was having no problem reading the highly technical information. Wasn't that a bit unusual?

Unfortunately, an answer popped into her head. If Justine had worked in her husband's business, she could have acquired considerable technical knowledge. Suppose she'd found the proof she hadn't wanted to find—that she really was the woman who lived in this house.

With a grimace, she tried to convince herself that she'd drawn the wrong conclusion. From the remarks Mike had made, she gathered Justine hadn't worked after her marriage. Yet she could no longer rely on the truth of anything Mike had said. Not until she found out what his name was doing in that address book, with four changes of addresses.

Her lips pressed into a firm line, she went back to examining the papers. After a few minutes, her vision blurred, and she realized her brain wasn't in any shape to cope with so much detail.

Well, now she had a legitimate reason to contact Mike, she decided, not bothering to square the conclusion with her previous assessment of his honesty. She would show him the papers and ask what he thought. Then, perhaps, she could introduce the topic of the address book.

How long had he known Justine, and what exactly was their relationship? Silently, she admitted that she wanted answers to those questions as much as to any of the others tormenting her. She knew her feelings were confused, that reason and emotion were playing a tug-of-war inside her. She didn't have the right to quiz Mike about his past—if it had no bearing on her present problems.

How could she expect honesty from Mike when she wasn't being honest with him? she asked herself abruptly. She was hiding something from him, all right. She was keeping her pregnancy a secret, and she didn't like being the kind of person who lied even by omission.

Oh, she could come up with excuses. She was frightened and alone and attracted to the man who had saved her life. Perhaps her amnesia or her head injury was affecting her judgment. But really, she could think of no reason that pardoned her behavior. The next time she saw him, she was going to share her secret.

LISA AWOKE with a start to find herself sitting in bed with the light on. Her arms were folded tightly across her chest, and she remembered she'd been clutching the envelope of construction specifications.

But the envelope was gone.

With a gasp, she sat up straighter. A shaft of sunlight knifed though a crack in the curtains, and a glance at the clock told her that it was almost one in the afternoon.

Frantically, she searched the top of the bed, hoping to find that the papers were under the covers. When she couldn't locate them, she climbed out of bed and hunted across the rug. But the envelope had vanished.

Maybe it had never existed. Had she dreamed she'd found it, as she'd dreamed about the people rummaging through her room?

No, she vividly remembered Frank stepping into Kendall's office with the shotgun leveled at her.

She glanced toward the door. She'd locked it last night. But Maggie certainly would have a key.

Damn. She should have hidden the envelope. Now it was too late.

Still angry with herself, she began to get dressed. Brushing her teeth, she remembered there was something else she had planned to do that day. She pulled out the address book, and called the dentist's office. In a voice that quavered, she said she was Justine Hollingsworth and asked to come in and see her records.

The receptionist's answer was a crushing anticlimax. "I'm sorry, Mrs. Hollingsworth," the woman apologized. "Dr. Bishop is out of the office this morning, and you'll need his authorization. Can you call back after three?"

"Yes," Lisa replied before hanging up. She'd been so sure she'd have the answer to her identity this morning. The hours before three o'clock stretched ahead like an eternity.

With a sigh, she descended the stairs, relieved when she stepped into the kitchen to find it empty. Yet as she fixed herself breakfast, she kept thinking how quiet the house was.

If Frank and Maggie weren't here, anyone could have come in while she was sleeping. And surely bedroom locks were easy to pick.

Insecurity made her find a tray and carry her juice and cereal upstairs to the bedroom. As she ate, she thumbed through the address book, wondering what kind of response she'd get if she phoned some of the women listed. Nobody had called to chat since she'd gotten home. Perhaps these were women who worked with Justine on volunteer committees, not close friends.

When Lisa was finished eating, she eyed the phone again. Despite her decision of the night before, she was nervous about calling Mike. And when she finally mustered the courage to dial his number, her bad luck held; she got the answering machine. Not wanting to say too much over the phone, she left a brief message. Then she carried her breakfast tray down to the kitchen.

Grocery bags that hadn't been there a half hour ago sat on the kitchen counters and on the floor in front of the refrigerator. A noise in the back hall made her glance up quickly to see Frank striding through the doorway with two more bags in his arms. Maggie followed a few seconds later with two satchels labeled Graul's, which she carefully set beside the sink.

Lisa gave them both a long look. Maggie brushed past her to open the freezer.

"Are we having a dinner party?" Lisa asked as she looked at the mountain of supplies. *Did you take some papers from my room?* The question screamed in her mind, but she didn't ask.

"Not likely. Mr. Hollingsworth is coming home today," Maggie tossed over her shoulder.

Lisa felt the bottom drop out of her stomach. "Today?"

"That's right. I keep forgetting, you don't remember," the woman answered sarcastically. Apparently, the nighttime encounter in the office had been a declaration of war.

"What time?"

"Before dinner."

Lisa nodded and backed out of the room. Lord, she'd been hoping she had a few more days before she had to face her so-called husband.

A cold sweat beaded on her skin as she stepped into the hall and heard the sound of a car in the driveway. She expected to see Hollingsworth emerge from a Jaguar or some other equally luxurious car. To her vast relief, the vehicle was Mike's old Mustang. Climbing out, he trotted toward the house.

Before Maggie had a chance to interrupt them, Lisa sped across the marble floor and pulled open the door. Mike's hand was hovering at the bell. When he saw her, he went very still.

She was so glad to see him, it took a great deal of effort to keep from throwing herself into his arms. The look in his eyes made her think he might be fighting the same impulse. Or perhaps she was reading too much into the tension etched on his face.

"Come in." She took a step back.

He followed her into the hall at the same moment that Maggie appeared around the corner. She looked inquiringly in Lisa's direction.

"You can finish unpacking the groceries," she said stiffly.

"Very good, ma'am," the housekeeper replied like a bit player in a drawing-room comedy.

When she'd disappeared, Lisa whispered, "She's been keeping tabs on me."

Mike nodded and ushered Lisa into Hollingsworth's office. She would have preferred some other room, but this was probably the most private place. Unless she took him upstairs, and she could just picture Maggie gleefully reporting to Hollingsworth that "your wife entertained a male friend in her bedroom." If she was last night's thief, she could cap her success by handing him the papers his wife had stolen.

"You don't trust her?" Mike asked in a low voice after he'd shut the door.

"I don't trust anybody."

"Good, because…I'm sorry, there's no other way around this…I have a piece of information you're going to find disturbing."

Lisa tensed, waiting for the bad news. Mike took her gently by the shoulders, pitching his voice low as he spoke. "Yesterday I asked a friend of mine who's a mechanic to check out the car you were driving. There was a hole in the power-steering line. It could have gotten punctured by accident—maybe even when you plowed into the river. Or it could have been put there deliberately."

Chapter Thirteen

Lisa shivered. "You're saying somebody tampered with my car? They wanted me to have an accident?"

"I can't be sure."

"But you think so."

"I'd rather err on the side of caution. If somebody went after your car, and you escaped, they might want to get a little more personal now that you're back home."

All at once, her encounter last night in the garden leaped into her mind. "Somebody was here," she said quietly. "Yesterday evening, while I was eating dinner."

His eyes were instantly alert. "Are you okay?"

"Yes. It was an old man with a knife."

Mike's hands swept up and down her arms as if to assure himself that she was unharmed.

"He didn't hurt me. He ran away when I picked up a paring knife from the table."

"Good."

"Maybe not. He said, 'You're one of them,'—or something like that. I think he believes he knows me. Or Justine. He could be somebody with information about her. Or he could know who I really am," Lisa added.

Mike frowned. "Was he wearing a fatigue jacket?"

Her eyes widened. "You know him?"

"I saw him in the parking garage the day of your accident. He could have been in the garage waiting for you."

"Or for Justine," Lisa reminded him.

Mike made an impatient gesture. "Whatever. The point is, he could be the one who tampered with your car."

"Or the person who broke into the house while I was in the hospital."

Mike looked startled. "How do you know somebody broke in?"

"I tricked Maggie into admitting it last night. I got another lead out of her, too. Hollingsworth had a fight with his business partner. Someone named Realto."

Mike pulled out a notebook and wrote down the name.

"Can you find him?" she asked. "Or the vagrant? I'm almost sure Maggie's seen him around here before."

"I'll try to find the old guy, but he could be anywhere in the city. If he doesn't want to be found, it might be pretty difficult. Did you call the police?"

"Maggie discouraged me."

Mike snapped the notebook closed. "Oh, yeah?"

"She said, 'Mr. Hollingsworth doesn't like the law messing in his business.'"

"Great."

"Something else. Last night I found some papers Justine apparently stole and hid from her husband. Now they're missing."

"Where did you find them?"

"In an envelope behind those books." She pointed to a line of Shakespeare's plays near the top shelves.

He raised an eyebrow. "Kind of a lucky guess on your part."

"Yesterday after you left, Estelle—Hollingsworth's secretary—demanded the papers."

Mike's eyes narrowed. "How did she know about them?"

Lisa shrugged. "I haven't figured that out yet. But I, uh, realized it would be stupid for Justine to hide them in her room—or anywhere obvious. So I started thinking about where Hollingsworth wouldn't look. That's how I happened to search behind the books he probably never reads."

"Now the evidence is missing?"

"Yes. I took the envelope to my room. But I was exhausted and fell asleep. When I woke up, it was gone."

Mike swore and looked toward the closed door. "You think the housekeeper took them?"

"When I finally woke up, it was almost one o'clock, and she and Frank were out getting groceries. I guess anyone, from the men who were following me the other day, to the guy in the fatigue jacket, could have come into the house."

He snorted. "You must sleep pretty soundly."

Defensively, she replied, "I've hardly slept at all since I woke up in the hospital—except when Habib drugged me."

He conceded the point with a sigh. "What was in the envelope?"

"Engineering specifications for a construction project."

"You're sure?"

"Yes. I could tell that much at least. They must be important, or why would Justine have hidden them?" She looked down at her hands. "I feel like a fool for letting them slip through my fingers. Or maybe you think I'm making them up."

He didn't say anything for several moments, and she suddenly wanted to get out of the room.

She took a step toward the door, but he blocked her path. "Don't leave."

"Why?"

"I don't think you're making them up."

"That's something, anyway."

She saw his throat move as he swallowed hard. It was only a small gesture, but it broke loose more words locked inside her.

"Mike, I don't want to stay in this house!"

"You live here."

"Do you really believe that?" she demanded.

He looked perplexed, a man being forced to challenge basic assumptions. Several heartbeats later, he answered. "I don't know. If you're not Justine, that makes things a hell of a lot easier for me. I haven't felt like I was on very strong moral footing lately."

She kept her gaze steady. "What do you mean?"

"I'm not in the habit of making love to other men's wives."

MIKE WATCHED Lisa's reaction to his words closely—saw her surprise, saw her blush.

"Lisa," he began, then saw her expression change again at his use of her chosen name. Her relief was almost tangible.

When he'd driven her "home" yesterday, he'd wondered if he really was doing the right thing, but he'd tried to ignore the nagging doubts. Now the defenseless look in her eyes melted through another layer of his resolve. Honesty forced him to admit that nothing about Lisa reminded him of Justine—except her physical appearance. Everything under the surface was different, so different that it made complete sense to him that she was someone else who had gotten snared somehow in the middle of Justine's problems.

"I've been doing a lot of thinking," he admitted. "There are things we ought to get into the open. Things I haven't exactly handled...honestly."

"Like your name in Justine's address book?" she questioned softly.

Mike felt his cheeks grow hot. "You found that, too?"

"Since you left yesterday, I haven't had much to do besides search this place—or sit around asking myself questions."

They stared at each other across three feet of space, and he saw his own feelings of relief, as well as his wariness, reflected in her gaze. He waited, barely breathing, wondering if the gap between them would widen or close. When he couldn't stand the separation for another heartbeat, he took a step closer. She moved toward him at the same time. Then his arms were around her, and she let out a deep, shuddering sigh.

"Mike."

His embrace tightened. It felt completely natural to hold

her in his arms, and he wished things could be this simple, this uncomplicated. A man and a woman who needed each other, who belonged together, despite all the evidence to the contrary. She moved her cheek against his jaw, and he worried fleetingly that his beard would scratch her tender skin. Like putting his brand on her, he thought, conceding that there were other ways in which he wanted to claim her as his own, wanted it more than he'd like to admit.

"I'm so confused," she breathed.

"So am I."

"You? You're not the one in trouble."

"Trouble is relative."

"I don't have a past. I'm frightened of the future. I shouldn't be dragging you into my problems."

"You're not dragging me."

She relaxed against him, and he knew she'd needed his reassurance.

"I can't help myself. This feels right. It feels good," she added as she ran her hands over the strong muscles of his shoulders.

"Oh, God. I want you to understand what I've been going through," he grated. "I don't have any rights in this situation. You're supposed to belong to someone else. And I've been fighting that. And fighting my basic instincts. Do you understand?"

"Yes." She clasped him tighter. "Too well. You don't know how much I wish I could give you some kind of proof that I'm not Mrs. Anybody."

He knew she felt the ripples of reaction he couldn't hide. She tipped her face upward and their eyes locked. Then his lips brushed hers. A very light touch, yet the contact set a shiver across her skin.

"I might not remember my past," she murmured, "but I'm sure no man ever...ever affected me this way. When I'm with you like this, I can't think about anything but getting closer." The last part came out on a little sob.

His hands moved up and down her back, pressing her

closer, molding her body to his. "When I found out about the car, I had to come over and make sure you were all right," he told her. "No. That's not exactly true. I was looking for an excuse to come back."

"Oh, Mike."

His mouth came down on hers, taking what he'd been wanting for an eternity. She kissed him with the same intensity and he knew that any confessions he might make were less important than the need simmering between them. Carnal need. And something more—the need to mate, to bond. They'd aroused each other to fever pitch the day before. In seconds, they were back at the same level of hunger. She made little noises deep in her throat as she moved against him.

His hands slid to her hips, pressing her tightly to his erection.

"Not here," she whispered.

"Where?"

She drew in a shaky breath and looked wildly around, like a sleepwalker who suddenly wakes and realizes where she is and what she's been doing.

"Mike, we can't. I mean, I promised myself I'd tell you…things. But not here. Take me away from this house. Please. Before it's too late."

But it was already too late. Outside, tires screeched as a Mercedes pulled up behind Mike's car in the driveway. They both turned guiltily toward the window as the car door shot open and a man bolted out.

"Oh, Lord, it's Kendall Hollingsworth," Lisa gasped.

"You know him?" Mike asked sharply.

"I recognized him from the pictures in Justine's photo album."

Hollingsworth was wearing a knit shirt and jeans. His graying hair was a beat too long. And his lined face was tanned. For a moment, he peered at the Mustang that was probably occupying his favorite parking place. Then he looked toward the house. Through the windowpanes, Mike saw the other man's gaze scanning Lisa and himself standing with their arms around each other, and he saw Hollingsworth's face cloud with anger. The irate man strode toward the front door, and a couple of seconds later, it slammed open. Hollingsworth blew into the office with hurricane force.

He gave Lisa a scathing look before rounding on Mike.

"What the hell are you doing here with my wife?" he demanded.

"I'm working for her," Mike answered coolly.

"Working? Is that what they call screwing these days?"

Mike's hands balled into fists, but he kept himself from slugging the offended husband. "You've got the wrong idea," he growled. "Mrs. Hollingsworth—"

"—has had the hots for you since you tutored her for that college biology lab," Kendall interrupted. "I knew you'd eventually show up in her life again. She has a nasty habit of getting what she wants."

Mike saw Lisa's mouth drop open, then her eyes riveted to his face, which he was certain had guilt plastered all over it.

"Y-you said," she stammered. "That…that story you told me in the hospital…about Justine being engaged to a guy in college." Her eyes were very round. "That was you."

"Unfortunately, yes," he admitted.

"You should have told me. I would have—"

"You would have what? Put me through the wringer all over again?"

"No," she denied. "I would have understood why you've been sending me such mixed signals. I can't remember the past, but *you* can. You weren't playing fair."

"Are *you?*" he shot back. "Wasn't there something important you wanted to get off your chest?"

Hollingsworth was listening, too, but Mike focused on Lisa. Her face drained of color, and he took that as evidence of guilt. What had she wanted to tell him? That this whole amnesia thing was a performance she'd made up to protect herself? He should have kept Justine's penchant for deception in mind before he'd gotten swept away by wide-eyed, innocent Lisa.

He didn't want to be confused. Or uncertain. If anybody knew who this woman was, it should be Kendall Hollingsworth.

Her gaze was fixed on Mike. He wasn't sure what would have happened if he'd been alone with her at that moment. He was prepared to tell her anything she wanted to know in exchange for her confession, whatever it was. Then he'd get the hell out of this mess—for good. But the initiative was no longer in his hands. Hollingsworth had apparently heard enough.

"Were you with her last night?" he grated.

"Of course not," Mike retorted, angry that he was being accused of something he hadn't done. Lucky the husband hadn't arrived fifteen minutes later.

"Get out of here," Hollingsworth ordered. "And stay away from my wife."

"I'm not—" Lisa began.

Hollingsworth's deadly glare made her close her mouth. "You and I have unfinished business. But I'm not going to talk to you in front of an audience."

Her gaze shot from Hollingsworth to him, clearly pleading with him not to leave her here. The terror in her eyes nearly made Mike forget the excellent advice he'd given himself moments before. For a blinding instant he almost grabbed her by the hand and pulled her out of the room, out of the house, away from the angry man who looked as if he wished he were holding a shotgun. But the impulse died as quickly as it had been born. He himself was the one who had no rights in this situation.

"I'm sorry," he said. Sorry that they'd gotten caught. Sorry that he'd let himself get emotionally involved up to his eyeballs.

She didn't answer, but he could feel her gaze on him as he left the room. His anger with himself didn't allow him to look back. Nor did he glance through the window as he climbed into his car and jerked it into gear.

Yet nothing could erase the terrible look in her eyes that was part fear, part accusation. Ruthlessly, he tried to push the image aside. Justine Hollingsworth could take care of herself. She would always come out on top. But he couldn't quite make himself believe it.

STARING AT Mike's retreating back, Lisa struggled to make her brain absorb what she'd just learned. But the information was still too new. Too raw. Too overwhelming. All along, she'd sensed that there was some hidden undercurrent in her relationship with Mike. Something he didn't want her to find out about Justine. Well, he'd just dropped it on her like a case of explosives and left her to cope with the aftermath.

She had no time to cope with anything, though, before Hollingsworth's voice knifed through the thickened atmosphere of the room.

"So," he said tightly.

The syllable hung between them like an indictment. Staring at the closed door, feelings of abandonment and desolation washing over her, Lisa couldn't reply.

When the silence stretched on, he barked, "Turn around and look at me!"

For a split second, she pictured herself dashing toward the door. The notion was immediately followed by the image of Hollingsworth's grabbing her shoulders and hauling her back. She could almost feel his hands on her, and it made her cringe. She'd gotten the shakes simply from contemplating a confrontation with this man. And here he was, large and intimidating. Worse, in his mind he had good reason to be angry.

"Dammit! Answer me!" he shouted.

Forcing composure into her features, she turned to face him, though she wasn't able to meet his gaze for more than a couple of seconds at a time.

He snorted in disgust. "I leave for a little vacation and

come home to find my wife in the arms of her old lover. Now, you tell me—what have you got to say for yourself?''

Fighting to control the shaking of her voice, she replied, "A lot of things have happened this week."

"Oh, yes. An accident. And amnesia. And your ridiculous insistence on being called by another name. I don't know what your game is, Justine, but it won't work on me. Your doctor might have been willing to play along. I'm not."

No, she thought, he definitely wasn't the kind of man who'd play games of someone else's choosing. Nor could she envision him indulging his wife, no matter now injured she may have been.

"You talked to the hospital before you came here?" she asked.

He nodded. "And Estelle."

Lisa drew a ragged breath. "And you're convinced they're right and I'm lying."

His eyes raked her face, her body. "I don't need anybody else to convince me. I've lived with you for eight years, and I damn well know who you are." With a sneer, he added, "Butchering your hair and letting yourself get fat is hardly what I'd call a creative disguise. But then, you never did have much of an imagination, did you?"

Neither did he. At least, not enough of one to see her as anyone but the woman he'd expected to find. And it was eminently clear that he didn't like that woman. The edge of violence in his voice made Lisa's insides quake and her legs feel like water. Still, she tried with increasing futility to keep the fear out of her voice.

"It was a mistake to come here," she said. "I'm sorry your wife is missing. But I'm not her."

He uttered a harsh laugh. "Is that supposed to be an excuse for you to climb into bed with Mike Lancer?"

She lifted one shoulder in a tiny shrug. "What's the point in denying anything? You won't believe me."

"You've got that right. Not after the hot little scene I

caught through the window. The two of you looked like you were about to rip each other's clothes off.''

She blushed. He was too close to the truth for comfort.

''I told you, if I ever found you with him again, you'd be sorry.''

She couldn't disavow the embrace, but she wasn't going to admit to the marriage. ''Justine hired Mike before she disappeared.''

''To do what—give her a jolt in the afternoons?''

Was that part of it? Lisa couldn't help wondering. She now knew with certainty—and with a vague, undoubtedly irrational feeling of betrayal—that Justine and Mike had been lovers in the past. More than that, Mike had loved her. He had made plans to marry her when he graduated from college. Justine had hurt Mike badly by dumping him for Kendall Hollingsworth, which went a long way toward explaining Mike's wariness. He was afraid to let himself trust Justine again. And Lisa could hardly blame him.

''She hired him to do some investigating,'' she said.

Hollingsworth scowled a warning. ''Stop talking about yourself in the third person. It's getting on my nerves.''

''But I'm not—'' The protest died under his angry glare. Biting her lower lip to keep it from trembling, she looked away.

''So,'' he continued, ''when did you get together with him again?''

Anger warred with fear as she replied, ''He fished me out of a river. Or didn't the doctor tell you how I ended up in the hospital?''

''I heard the story.''

''It's no story. Two men forced my car off the road. My *rental.*''

''Why were you driving a rented car?''

''I don't know…. Do you?''

''What's that supposed to mean?''

''What do you know about the accident?''

The dangerous glint in his eyes told Lisa that she may have

gone too far. His voice, when he spoke, was frighteningly quiet.

"My dear, I think you may possibly have lost your mind."

Lisa wasn't sure what he would have said or done next if the phone hadn't rung. Her gaze shot to the desk before she realized that the sound was coming from a cellular phone that Hollingsworth pulled out of his pocket.

He flicked it open and pulled up the antenna. "Yes?"

Someone on the other end of the line started to speak, and Hollingsworth turned his back. As the conversation continued, he stepped into the hall and shut the door. A few moments later, she saw him through the window, standing in the driveway, rocking back and forth slightly on his heels. The person on the other end seemed to be doing most of the talking. Then he rang off and strode rapidly back into the house.

"I have to go out," he announced.

"Don't let me keep you."

"I won't. But don't get any stupid ideas about splitting. You'd better be here when I come back," he added, making his meaning perfectly clear, "because I want some answers."

"You haven't been listening. I've given you all the answers I can."

"I don't think so."

"I don't have any reason to stay in your house."

"And *I* don't have time for an argument. I have to leave, but I'm not going to let you take advantage of me again. If you run away, I'll find you."

She swallowed, somehow knowing he would.

His expression changed, and he gave her a malicious grin. "And if by some remote chance I can't find *you,* I'll go after Lancer. I'll make sure your boyfriend is very sorry he tried to pick up where the two of you left off."

Chapter Fourteen

The implied threat hung in the air.

"Do you understand?" Hollingsworth asked, his voice stabbing at her.

Woodenly, Lisa nodded. She'd come here to find out if she was Justine, believing she could leave anytime she wanted. In her wildest dreams, she hadn't imagined that her actions could put Mike in danger.

What in God's name was she going to do? Could she risk calling Mike to ask his advice? Would he even take her call?

"And don't you dare call your lover!" Hollingsworth added, chilling her with what seemed an uncanny ability to read her mind. It chilled her further when he added, in that steely tone, "Because, I promise you, I'll know."

She didn't doubt him. Didn't dare. Nor did she doubt that he had both the power and will to carry out his threats. His face was a twisted mask of venomous fury, and she knew she'd been right to fear this man. She couldn't begin to envision what living with him would be like.

"Got that?"

"Yes," she managed to say.

He stared at her for a full thirty seconds, his expression now reflecting obvious pleasure at his victory. Then he walked out of the room.

"Ms. Dempsey," he bellowed from the front hall.

"Yes, sir," Maggie replied almost instantly.

"I expect Mrs. Hollingsworth to be here when I get back. I'll hold you and Frank responsible if she isn't."

"Yes, sir."

The front door slammed behind him, and Lisa felt the sound reverberate through her. She was cold to the bone, shaking like a leaf and giddy. If she didn't sit down soon, she was going to fall down.

The moment she saw Hollingsworth's car pull from the house, she left the office. She kept her eyes straight ahead as she made for the stairs and willed her legs to carry her up the carpeted flight. She walked directly to her room, but as soon as she closed the door behind her, she felt her knees buckle and had to grab the back of a chair.

Her gaze flew to the phone. She could disobey orders and leave a message at Mike's office. But what if all calls from the house were being monitored? Her actions could get Mike killed.

Sinking onto the couch in the sitting room, she cradled her head in her hands. A hysterical little laugh bubbled out of her when she realized she wasn't going to get over to the dentist's office, after all. Hollingsworth had said he thought she was losing her mind. He was too close to the truth. How could anyone hope to stay sane with shock piling upon shock? The revelation about Mike and Justine would have been the final straw. Except that there was so much more.

She concentrated on breathing deeply until the hysteria passed. The only thing she knew for sure was that she couldn't stay in this house. She'd felt trapped from the moment she'd stepped across the threshold. She should have left while she could. Now she'd have to wait and try to sneak out in the middle of the night.

But where could she go with no money and no identity?

Well, at least she could solve one of those problems.

Rising from the couch, Lisa crossed to the bureau and began to rummage in one of the drawers. She'd discovered that Justine kept stashes of cash on hand, which had remained despite the break-in. When she'd found the money, she had decided she wasn't going to touch it, but present circumstances forced her to rethink that decision.

In a box of designer panty hose, Lisa located one hundred forty dollars, all in twenties. She stuffed the cash into the pocket of her slacks. Then, from the bottom drawer of a jewelry box, she withdrew ten one-hundred dollar bills and tucked them into a purse taken from the walk-in closet. Eleven hundred and forty dollars ought to take her somewhere—anywhere—out of Kendall Hollingsworth's reach.

How long would he be gone? she wondered. And would he be in any better mood when he came back? Either way, Lisa figured it wouldn't be good news for the woman he thought was his wife.

THE LUXURY CABIN CRUISER was moored at one of the docks on the far side of Baltimore's harbor. Estelle had always thought of it as a nice little retreat, a place to which she and Kendall could slip away for a few hours together. It was off the beaten path, yet close enough to downtown that they could pop over for a long lunch.

Today, when he'd called and asked her to meet him, she'd suspected it wasn't for a lovers' tryst. After hanging up, she'd thought about going home, packing a bag and taking a very long vacation. But she'd never been good at saving for a rainy day. Without the cash she'd been promised, she wouldn't get very far. So she'd simply have to tough things out for the next few hours, and hope plan B clicked into action.

With hands that trembled, she set two glasses on the galley counter, a whiskey glass for Kendall and a tumbler for herself. He always drank scotch. She never touched anything stronger than a wine cooler. But if she had been a drinking woman, this would be a good day for it, she thought as she poured white wine over ice cubes, added soda and took a swallow.

Estelle was fumbling for the makings of Kendall's drink, when the boat swayed. Panic seized her, and she almost dropped the bottle of scotch. Quickly, she finished her preparations as heavy footsteps crossed the deck.

"Kendall?" she called.

"Were you expecting someone else?"

Blood was pounding in her ears, but she forced herself to turn slowly, extending a hand with the glass of whiskey. "You need a drink."

"Later."

She saw the embittered look on his face and struggled to keep her own expression friendly. But she knew the smile she gave him was stiff. "Welcome back," she managed to say.

He set his briefcase on the table. "You've been busy while I was gone."

"Nothing I couldn't handle."

"Perhaps you'd like to tell me why you were making copies of the San Marcos confidential files."

She felt her heart skip a beat then begin to race. "That's ridiculous. You keep those records locked in your safe. I would never—"

"Cut the innocent act."

He moved purposefully toward her. She retreated until her hips pressed against the sink.

"Who are you spying for?" he growled.

"I don't know what you're talking about. You've got to believe me."

Kendall's large fingers dug into her shoulder, and she winced. She'd seen him manhandle Justine, but he'd never touched her like that.

"No mistake, Estelle. I had a surveillance system installed when you were in Atlanta last month. The guy reviewing the footage called a little while ago. I've got you on videotape with your hand in the cookie jar."

"Jesus, no," she gasped, struggling to get free.

"Do the ethics of stealing confidential information from your employer bother you?" he asked sarcastically.

Her lips moved, but no words came out.

As quickly as he'd pounced, he released her, and she stumbled against the counter, rubbing her shoulder.

An instant later, he faced her, a videocassette in one hand, a gun in the other. He was angry, and she could almost feel him drawing energy from her fear.

Putting down the tape, he reached for the glass of scotch and drained it in a couple of swallows.

Light-headed, she struggled to keep her expression blank.

"You'd better start talking, and I mean now. Who hired you? Realto? Or someone else?"

"I..."

"Talk."

God, if only Justine had played fair. But the bitch had left her twisting in the wind.

"Your wife," she whispered.

LISA SAT on the love seat in her room, trying to choke down the dinner Maggie had brought, her ears peeled toward the front door. When it opened, every muscle in her body tensed. The sound of voices in the hall was followed by heavy footfalls coming up the stairs. Automatically, she looked at the clock. Six-thirty. He'd been gone for hours.

Hollingsworth stepped into the room, and Lisa was shocked by the change in his appearance. He looked weary, his shoulders slumped, and his hair was mussed. He gave her no more than a quick glance as he crossed to his own bedroom, went inside and closed the door. She could hear him emptying change and keys. Then the toilet flushed. Water ran. When he opened the door again, he was drying his face on a blue towel. After pitching it in the general direction of her hamper, he lowered himself into the chair opposite her.

His presence made her heart hammer. At least he hadn't claimed the other end of the love seat, Lisa thought, wishing she'd been eating in the dining room when he appeared. Here in the bedroom, there was no place to take refuge if things went the wrong way.

Picking up her glass of orange juice, she took several tiny swallows to moisten her throat.

He cleared his. "I'm sorry."

She blinked, certain she couldn't have heard him correctly. "Sorry? About what?"

"Being on a hunting trip when you had that accident. You always hated my hunting trips."

Wary of his solicitous tone, Lisa frowned. She pictured him rehearsing the line all the way home. It sounded stilted enough. And she didn't believe it. Yet, under the circumstances, it would be worse than stupid to provoke a return of his anger.

"It wasn't your fault," she said carefully.

He seemed to relax a notch and started to speak again, but at that moment, Maggie appeared at the door.

"Come in," Hollingsworth called in response to her deferential knock.

The housekeeper swished into the room carrying a tray with another dinner plate. However, instead of orange juice, he'd apparently requested a bottle of scotch and an ice bucket along with his fried chicken, green beans, mashed potatoes and gravy.

"Thank you," he murmured. "I won't be needing you for the rest of the evening."

"Yes, sir."

Maggie left rapidly. She probably knew enough to get out of the way when her employer was drinking, Lisa thought as she watched Hollingsworth drop ice into a short glass and slosh in amber liquor. He belted back the first glass, then poured himself another. From the looks of him, she'd be willing to bet that he'd had a few on the way home.

With any luck, at this rate, he'd pass out before he finished eating.

He polished off the mashed potatoes on his plate and poured more liquor into his glass. Stretching out his legs, he drank the scotch, studying her across the coffee table between swallows.

The silence lengthened between them. Lisa consciously kept her palms pressed to the sofa on either side of her, fearing that if she moved at all, he'd see her shaking.

At last, he said, "If you've really lost your memory, you've got to be wondering about the two of us. As lovers, I mean."

She swallowed painfully. "I was hoping we could worry about that later."

"I'm not worried. I've been thinking about you the whole time I was gone. Absence makes the heart grow fonder."

His meaning was very clear.

In a small, breathy voice, she said, "I—I hope you're not planning to do something we'll both regret."

"It was too late for regrets when I came home and found you with Lancer."

So his apology had all been a facade. He was still blazing angry.

Feeling her throat clog, Lisa started to rise. But before she could escape, Hollingsworth was out of his chair, fairly leaping across the coffee table, shocking her with his speed and agility. As big as he was—and half-drunk, at that—he shouldn't have been able to move so quickly.

He came down on her hard, knocking the air from her lungs. As she struggled for breath, he pressed her into the sofa cushions. His face was very close. She smelled the liquor on his breath and turned her head to the side, but he put his hand under her chin and brought her face back to his. Then his lips covered hers in a hard kiss that was more punishment than passion.

"No—" She tried to twist from his brutal hold, but his free hand held her fast, clamping around her arm.

"Please! You're hurting me."

"Relax, honey. You always did like me to be a little rough. Don't you remember?"

"No! Don't do this!"

The protest was lost on him. His touch was devoid of all tenderness as his hand moved to her breast, squeezing painfully. Her gasp made his chest rumble with laughter.

"That's right. Let me know how much you like it."

"No! I don't like it. Let me up!" She was caught in a nightmare. A nightmare that was doomed to repeat itself over and over. For a confused moment, she imagined it was another man on top of her, another man she was trying to push away. The image blurred, lost in a haze of light-headed terror and bewilderment.

Then Hollingsworth spoke and she knew who he was.

"Close your eyes and pretend I'm Lancer."

"Don't—"

She might have saved her breath, for all it affected him. If she screamed at the top of her lungs, would Maggie come? She doubted it.

Hollingsworth grabbed Lisa's leg, straightening her body so that she was sprawled along the length of the short couch.

When she lashed out with her foot, he growled a warning. "Do any damage, and you'll really get hurt."

Then his body shifted, and he groped for the placket at the top of her knit shirt. The buttons popped, and the fabric tore.

From the moment she'd seen his picture, she had imagined his touch with deep, abiding distaste. But she hadn't imagined rape. Against her leg, she felt the hard length of his erection and knew he meant to use it as a weapon.

In total panic, she reached behind her, frantically searching the surface of the end table for something she could use in her own defense. She almost sobbed in relief when her fingers closed around the neck of the candlestick lamp. But when she pulled it upward, it only moved a few inches, then seemed to stick.

Oblivious to her struggle, Hollingsworth tugged at the waistband of her slacks, and she felt them moving relentlessly lower. She yanked at the lamp, and it came free with a jerk. Her arm completed the arc, and she brought the shaft down on Kendall's head.

He grunted, then abruptly went still, his weight pressing her down.

She wriggled out from under him, pulling up her slacks as soon as she was free from his grasp. For several moments, she sat huddled on the coffee table shaking uncontrollably and sucking in great drafts of air. Realizing she was still holding the lamp, she let it slip through her fingers. It hit the rug with a dull thunk.

She knew she had to get away before the madman on the sofa grabbed her again, but she wasn't sure she could stand. And she could see he wasn't moving.

Lord, what had she done? Reluctantly, Lisa forced her gaze to the top of Hollingsworth's head, where the lamp had connected with his skull. A red stain was spreading through his graying hair.

"Kendall?" she whispered.

He didn't move.

Heart in her throat, she knelt beside him and felt for the pulse in his neck. To her relief, it was strong and regular.

Pushing herself to her feet, wobbling slightly, she made her way to the dresser and grabbed the purse in which she'd put the money she'd found. Turning, she started to flee, then stopped dead. She had no keys. No car. No means of escape.

A picture flashed in her mind of Frank and Hollingsworth tracking her across the lawn, shotguns in hand, and the image was followed swiftly by the taste of bile rising in her throat. She glanced toward the couch. Hollingsworth was stirring. She had to leave now or it would be too late. And the solution to her problem was really quite simple: she would take Hollingsworth's car.

She crept into his room, looking to see where he'd emptied his pockets. In a little hall that led to his closet, she spotted an antique dresser, his change, keys and wallet strewn across the top of it. She was reaching for the prize, when the door between the rooms flew open. Hollingsworth swayed in the doorway, his face red with effort, his eyes glinting with emotion that went far beyond anger.

With a sob, Lisa snatched the keys.

"What happened?" he asked in a woozy voice, wincing as he fingered the top of his head. He winced. Then his gaze traveled the room and zoomed back to her.

"You hurt yourself," she answered. And as far as she was

concerned, it was true. She'd only hit him because he was going to rape her.

His eyes closed, then snapped open again. "Christ. You whacked me, and I saw stars." Again he touched the bump on his head, this time more carefully. "You bitch." He moved to block her escape route, raising his hands with fingers spread to grab her.

She took a step back and then another, her knees coming up against the edge of the bed.

"Gotcha!" Lurching forward, he lunged for her.

She dodged out of the way, and he swayed on his feet. She thought he would fall, but he made a quick recovery, and moving faster than she anticipated, grabbed for her again. His fingers grazed the hem of her shirt, and for a terrible moment she thought she was done for. Then he overbalanced and pitched forward, catching himself on the edge of the bed. Apparently, the effort was too much, and he sank to his knees, clutching at the spread, pulling it askew.

Darting around him, Lisa pounded down the stairs, thanking God that no one was standing in the front hall, waiting to block her exit.

It was dark outside, but she didn't stop until she was away from the glow of the porch light. Her lungs burned as she dragged in several deep breaths. The keys were in her hand, but she'd left the purse with the money in the house. Yet there was no way she was going back inside.

The car was a little farther along the driveway. She ran to it, yanked open the door and slid into the driver's seat. It was too far back for her to reach the gas pedal. She fumbled frantically, trying to locate a lever that would move her forward. Every few seconds, she glanced toward the house, expecting to see the enraged man she'd left upstairs barreling through the door with a gun in his hand.

Finally, she found the release mechanism, and the seat shot forward. She bumped against the wheel. More precious seconds ticked by as she eased herself to the right position.

The sound of the engine coming to life as she turned the

key in the ignition was the sweetest music she had ever heard. But she wasn't home free yet. Footsteps thudded to her right. With a moan, she glanced toward the window expecting to see Frank. Her mouth fell open when, instead, she beheld the tramp who had come at her with the knife. The man must have been lurking again—waiting for her.

Careening across the lawn, he made for the car, waving his arms for her to stop.

Not on your life, she thought as she tromped on the accelerator. The car shot forward just as the man stepped into the driveway. Into her path.

Yanking madly on the wheel, she swerved into the bushes. Branches scraped her left fender, and the tire bounced onto a hidden curb, making the car tip at a crazy angle. She missed the man by inches, then fought to bring the vehicle back to an even course. But the tramp surged forward, trying to block her path again.

His eyes were wild, his face contorted, as he shouted something at her. With the windows closed, she couldn't hear the words and didn't want to.

"Get away," she screamed as she lurched down the driveway, hunching forward so she could make out the dark shapes of the trees. "Get away. Get away. Get away." The words became a chant. She strained to see in the darkness, barely avoiding a stately blue spruce as the driveway twisted and turned. Several hundred yards from the house, she realized that she hadn't turned on the lights. With a whimper, she searched for the right knob and found it.

The road leaped into focus, and the trees receded into the background, speeding past on either side, dark and indistinct shapes. She couldn't believe it was over. She kept expecting the tramp to loom out of the shadows.

Mercifully, no one stepped into the path of her headlights as she wove her way down the endless driveway. She considered it a stroke of luck when a glance at the console beside her seat told her that Kendall had left the portable phone in the car.

Her luck changed, though, when she reached the end of the private road. Illuminated by a set of floodlights, the gates were firmly shut across the blacktop. For à split second, she thought about trying to crash through. Then reason overruled panic, and she slammed on the brakes.

Chapter Fifteen

On a sob, Lisa jumped from the car and ran toward the gate. Floodlights perched atop the entrance posts blinded her, and she shaded her eyes to locate the metal latch that held the gates closed. Fumbling with the catch, unaware of the whimpering noises coming from her throat, she unlocked the gate and swung it open.

Behind her, footsteps thumped against the hard surface of the driveway. She didn't wait to see who was coming. She simply ran for the car.

With hysteria not far off, she jumped into the Mercedes as a figure appeared in the darkness, his arms waving.

"Wait! Justine! Wait!"

Teeth chattering, she choked back a scream, slammed the car door closed and pressed the gas pedal to the floor.

Left or right? She hadn't a clue where she was, anyway, so it didn't matter. She chose left and zoomed away from the open gates.

She'd gone three hundred yards, when headlights filled her rearview mirror. Glancing between the dark road ahead and the mirror, she couldn't tell if the vehicle behind her had followed her through the gate.

Lisa turned onto a side road. The other car followed, picked up speed. She increased the pace. Ahead, a traffic light turned yellow. Stepping on the gas, she shot through the intersection, watching the signal turn red as she passed. Moments later, a van on the cross street started up, and the vehicle behind her was blocked.

Praying the light was a long one, she turned up another side street, then another…and another. Wooded lots crowded close to the narrow road on either side. When she saw a winding driveway, she pulled in past the first bend, shut off the headlights and waited, her heart pounding.

Seconds ticked by. She saw, through the trees, the lights of several cars pass, and each time, she reached for the door handle, ready to jump out and take her chances in the woods. But no one stopped. After fifteen minutes, she allowed herself to believe she had, indeed, escaped. Relief trickled in slowly, followed swiftly by utter exhaustion. She slumped in the seat and, without pause for thought, reached for the phone and dialed Mike.

Her breath rushed out in a heartfelt "Thank God" when she heard his voice, but then she realized she was talking to an answering machine, and disappointment swept over her. She had nowhere else to turn. Still, if she was found dead in the car, she wanted someone to know what had happened. So when the beep sounded, she began to speak.

"Mike, I-I'm in H-Hollingsworth's car," she began, fear making it hard to breathe—or speak. "I—I stole it. I had to get away. H-he tried to— He attacked me. I—I hit him, and I think he's—"

The phone clicked. "Lisa. Where are you?"

WRONG STREET. She wasn't up here. Lennie Ezrine screeched to a halt, then whipped the Pontiac around in a tight U-turn. Beside him, Jack Ordway sat with his meaty fingers wrapped around the butt of a revolver.

"You lost her," Jackal muttered.

"She's around here somewhere," Lennie insisted with more confidence than he felt. Damn, the bitch had sure picked her moment—with him taking a piss in the woods.

"You shoulda stayed in the car," Jackal growled.

"Oh, come on!"

"Well, you shoulda run the red light back there."

"And smashed into that van? Then we'd both be screwed."
From the corner of his eye, he could see Jackal squeezing his
fingers around the gun butt. "Put the piece away," he
snapped, "and get on the scanner. She makes a call from the
car phone, we've got her."

Jackal laid the gun on the console and turned on the scanner bolted to the dashboard.

Lennie made a turn down another residential street and
crept past the long driveways. Mouth set in a grim line, he
bit back the curses seething behind his lips. Jesus, if they lost
track of her now, what the hell were they going to do?

The green numbers on the display changed, and the monitor crackled, bringing in various conversations. Some jerk
was talking to his broker. A woman threatened to ground her
kids if they didn't clean up their rooms by the time she got
home. Talk about pissing away money. She could tell them
the same thing for free in five minutes.

The scan continued.

"Wait. Stop," Lennie ordered, recognizing her voice from
the phone calls she'd made that he'd monitored.

Jackal adjusted the volume, and the voice came in louder.
Lennie slapped his palms against the wheel. "It's her."

"Yeah, but where is she?"

"She'll give herself away," Lennie answered as he turned
down another street. Maybe they'd even hit it lucky and find
her while she was still talking.

"MIKE! Oh, thank God," Lisa cried. "I thought you weren't
home."

"I was screening my calls. Where are you?" he repeated.

"I'm in the car. I don't know where. Mike, I think somebody was following me."

"Hollingsworth?"

"I don't know."

"You lost him?"

"I hope so."

He was silent for several moments, then said, "It's easy to monitor a call on a cellular phone."

She sucked in a breath. "Somebody could be listening?"

"Maybe. I don't want to take the chance. Do you remember where we rescued the dog? Don't say the name of the street!" he said quickly. "But do you know where we were?"

"Yes."

"Can you find the place again?"

She peered through the trees toward the road. She might as well be in the middle of the north woods. "I think I can find it if I can figure out where I am now. I'm all twisted around."

"I'll meet you where we saw the dog."

"What if I can't...can't get there?"

"Ask directions at a gas station. Or ask for a map." His voice was calm and practical, steadying her. "If you run into any trouble, call me. I'll be right there." He gave her the number of his car phone and made her repeat it.

"Thank you," she breathed.

"I'll be on the road in three minutes. Don't give your location unless I tell you to."

LENNIE'S EYES NARROWED when the line went dead. He'd been hoping for more, but they were still in the game.

"That son of a bitch Lancer is smart," Jackal said.

"Yeah, but his girlfriend can't be more than a few blocks from here."

Jackal hunched forward, peering into the darkness. "Last time we followed her, she got lost. Maybe she'll have to call him for directions."

"Yeah."

"Why'd she change her name to Lisa?"

"Guess we'll have to ask her about it when we find her." Jackal laughed, an evil sound.

"She's got to be heading for a main road," Lennie muttered. "Too bad she knows we spotted her."

"So what? That won't do her no good when we catch up."

"Unless Lancer gets to her first."

Jackal fingered the gun. "He won't expect company."

Lennie made a disgusted noise. "I hope you're not planning to plug him on a city street."

"Do you think I'm dense? After we deliver her to the boss, we'll take Lancer somewhere a little more private."

"Fine by me." Lennie headed for the nearest gas station, hoping his quarry wasn't too far off target.

THE SECOND she hung up the phone, Lisa began to shake. She'd told Mike she could find the place they'd agreed to meet, and, reassured by the sound of his voice, she'd believed she could do it. But sitting there in the dark, alone, hounded by fear of being followed, she wanted only to curl up and cry. She wanted Mike to come and get her. She wanted him to make her safe. She wanted…him.

For long moments, she stared into the darkness, trying to steady herself. If she didn't get a grip and start moving, whoever had been following her might find her before she could meet Mike. She could end up back where she'd started—or worse.

Starting the engine, she backed out of the driveway. Less than five minutes later, she was at a major intersection with a gas station. She parked close to the office door, went inside and bought a map. Concentrating on the task instead of her fear, she found her present location. Then she was able to plot a course.

She arrived at the spot where the dog had been hit before Mike. Pulling to a stop on the shoulder, she put the car in park, then, with the engine running, slouched in her seat and trained her eyes on the traffic passing by. Again and again she had to remind herself that nobody else knew this location. She was safe. Yet she couldn't stop picturing a big gray car with two tough-looking men—one grinning wickedly at her out the window—blocking her escape. The image was so powerful she thought it might actually be real, her occluded memory giving up a piece of reality to fan the flames of imagination. As if the flames needed fanning.

It seemed an eternity before she saw Mike's familiar Mustang pass her. She straightened in the seat, and, with tears of relief blurring her vision she watched as he made a U-turn and pulled up alongside her.

She was about to jump out, but he motioned through the closed car windows for her to stay put, then opened his door and stood up long enough to scan the block in all directions. Lisa looked, too, and saw no other cars. When she met Mike's gaze again over the roof of the Mustang, he gave her the high sign to hurry.

Scrambling out of the Mercedes, she yanked open the Mustang's door and climbed into the passenger seat. She barely had the door closed when Mike said, "Hold on," at the same time he hit the gas and took off down the road.

The next few minutes left her too breathless to speak, which was just as well, for she was sure anything she tried to say would be incoherent. When Mike made a sudden sharp turn up a side street, she braced herself with a hand on the dash. He made several more quick turns, zooming through narrow residential streets until, finally, he turned left onto a well-lit, multilane road. There, he slowed to a reasonable pace.

With heart still pounding, Lisa saw Mike glance several times at the rearview mirror. His features, illuminated in snatches by the streetlights, were taut. He looked haggard and worried…and furious.

After several blocks, he said, "No one's following us."

But they were. She could feel them. They were out there, looking for her, and they wouldn't give up until they found her.

"Are you all right?" Mike cut into her thoughts.

"Yes," she whispered. "Just…scared."

"What happened?"

Her lower lip trembled. "Hollingsworth got a phone call and went out. When he came back, he…he'd been drinking.

He seemed better, though—better than when he left. Less angry. He kept drinking until…until he grabbed me.''

Mike swore, the fury she'd seen in his face surfacing in a flash. But it wasn't directed at her; he was angry on her behalf, and that made all the difference in the world.

His touch was gentle when he lifted a hand from the steering wheel to finger the front of her shirt where the placket was torn. "Did he hurt you?" he asked.

She looked down at the damaged fabric, remembering Hollingsworth's hands on her flesh. Shuddering, she replied, "He was—he was going to rape me. But I—I got away."

"Christ, Lisa…"

"Take me somewhere safe," she pleaded.

His hand reached down to cover hers where it clutched the seat. "I will," he said. "Tell me how you got away."

The heat from his hand seeped into her cold flesh, warming her. "I knocked him out with a lamp. Then I stole his keys. He came to and almost grabbed me again. But he was still groggy, and…and I got past him."

Mike was silent for several long minutes, his knuckles white as he gripped the wheel. When he spoke, his tone was controlled. "Why didn't you leave when he went out?"

Lisa dragged in a deep breath. "He told Frank and Maggie to guard me. And…and he said if I ran away and he couldn't find me, he'd come after you."

"You believed him?"

"He meant it, Mike. I know he did."

Mike fell silent again. Lisa considered telling him about the tramp who'd tried to prevent her escape that evening. But she was suddenly unsure of herself. He was sitting rigidly in his seat, both hands now fused to the wheel. She cast several glances at his harsh profile. It might have been carved from granite.

He wasn't an easy man to read. And the task was made harder because she had to rely entirely upon intuition and what little she'd learned of him in a week's time. Intuitively, she felt as if she knew him very well indeed; she knew he was an honorable man who she could trust with her life. Practically speaking, she didn't know him well at all. At the moment, she had no idea what he was thinking or feeling. And that scared her. A lot.

It also made her frustrated and upset with herself. Clearly, he was a private man—in some ways, a hard man—who didn't share his thoughts or feelings easily. She knew she shouldn't take it personally or assume that his withdrawal meant he was rejecting her. Yet, when she looked at his shuttered features, she couldn't quite prevent the feelings of loss and abandonment from creeping in to haunt her.

Despair settled over her, and the feeling grew as she watched street signs flash by. They passed some enormous mansions, then a long section of old semidetached houses. The semidetacheds gave way to block after block of four-story row houses with marble steps leading to their front doors. Mike turned right, into an alley, then right again into another alley that ran between two sets of skinny backyards. Halfway up the block, he parked.

He didn't touch her as she climbed from the car, or as they walked through the narrow, fenced yard to the back door. Silently, he turned the key in the lock and ushered her into a dimly lit hallway, then preceded her up two flights of worn stairs. Still without speaking, he unlocked one of two apartment doors on the landing, and pushed it open.

She hesitated, unconsciously hugging herself against a sudden chill as she looked from the open doorway to him.

"Come inside," he said, his tone low and strained by some emotion she couldn't guess.

Stepping across the threshold, she watched him throw the bolt behind them. The living room was in shadows. Only a dim bulb glowed from a table lamp near a window on the far side of the room. In the shadowy light, his tension was almost palpable. Down on the street, an occasional car passed, a distant reminder that the world had not shrunk to the two of them standing in this unfamiliar, dark room.

When she couldn't take another second of his silence, she

asked, "Do you think it was my fault—what happened to-night? That I provoked him?"

"Jesus! Of course not," he exclaimed.

"Then…what's wrong?"

He cleared his throat, yet when he spoke, his voice was gritty. "I should never have left you with that bastard. If I hadn't, none of this would have happened. You wouldn't have been in danger. You wouldn't have had to…to fight off a rape." His voice cracked. "Lisa, I'm sorry."

She couldn't tell him it was all right that he'd left. It hadn't been all right. It had been awful. Still…

"It's true, I was scared," she whispered. "But even I couldn't have imagined that he'd be as…wicked as he is."

Mike continued as if she hadn't spoken. "When I left, I told myself you were Hollingsworth's wife. That you'd made your bed, and you could lie in it."

Her breath caught. "You want to think the worst of me?"

"No. Maybe. Or maybe the worst of myself." He shook his dark head. "I don't like wanting something I can't have. I never did. My only excuse is that I was trying to protect myself." He ran a hand over his face, then back through his hair. "I haven't let a woman get under my skin since Justine left me. You scared me. You were my most compelling fantasy come true. Justine coming back to me. The old Justine, before she changed." With an angry gesture, he added, "But I couldn't trust it! And I couldn't defend it morally. I didn't *want* to be attracted to you. I didn't *want* to like you…. But I couldn't help myself."

Lisa stared at him, wide-eyed. "Oh," she whispered, and a wealth of feeling accompanied the syllable.

He took her by the shoulders, turning her so they were face-to-face. "Since I've been old enough to make decisions, I've lived by certain rules, and they almost always worked. But you make me want to forget all the rules. All I can think about is wanting to make love with you."

Those words and the horrible, haunted look on his face made her heart turn over. Suddenly, the basic equation between them changed. She wanted to heal him. She wanted to love him. Nothing was as important as giving him everything she could. Nothing except...

Lisa hesitated, knowing she had to tell him about the baby, knowing she had to tell him *now*. In another minute, it would be too late. But if she told him, would he still want to make love with her? Or would his code of honor insist that he couldn't make love with a woman who was not only pregnant with another man's child, but who didn't even know who the man was?

She knew the answer. And she couldn't bear it, couldn't bear even the thought of him turning away from her yet again. She needed him as much as she suspected he needed her, and neither dishonor nor disloyalty entered into it. She had no history, no memory of any man she had loved, and she might never remember. Unless she was to go on for the rest of her life alone, she had to begin again somewhere.

Fate had given her a place to start—here, with this man standing before her, watching her with such intense longing in his deep brown gaze. She couldn't deny either of them this chance to heal, to love, to begin life anew.

WHEN LISA TOOK a step toward him, Mike went very still. With effort, he managed to remain still as she laid a hand against his cheek. But a tremor raced through him when her fingers trailed down his neck, down his arm, then back up again, her hand coming to rest on his shoulder.

Pressing her face against his shirtfront, nuzzling his chest in a way that made him stifle a groan, she whispered, ''All right. I look like Justine. Everybody seems to agree and, having seen her picture, I can't deny it. But you know me well enough to tell the difference.''

With his arms plastered to his sides, he muttered, ''What do you mean, I know you well enough?''

''You know *me*. The woman you followed on a rainy afternoon. The woman you fished out of the river. Think about it. Do I talk like Justine Hollingsworth? Do I move like her?''

Lifting her face to look at him, she let her body rest lightly against his. "More important, what do you feel when you're with me?"

He swore softly. "I've never felt anything like this."

She gazed at him with her lovely blue eyes full of hope and longing. "Mike, be honest with yourself—and with me. In your heart, do you really believe I'm Justine?"

It was as if he was being tested—faced with salvation packaged to look like his worst nightmare. He could turn away, let his head overrule his heart, let his fear overcome his instincts, and go on living behind the brittle wall of pain and loneliness he'd built over the past eight years. Or he could trust his instincts, and believe what his senses told him was true. Suddenly it occurred to him that he'd be out of his mind to let this chance pass him by. Because, God knows, he'd never have another one like it again.

"No," he said softly. Then, louder, "No, I don't think you're her." With a low sound of suppressed need released, he wrapped his arms around her and crushed her to him. "Lisa," he whispered as his mouth covered hers.

He kissed her hard, a desperate kiss filled with hunger, and with every second that passed, his conviction grew stronger. It had nothing to do with reason or common sense, nothing at all to do with evidence or mental guesswork. It had everything in the world to do with instinct. He simply knew. The woman in his arms, all soft and warm, couldn't possibly be the same woman who'd teased and baited and ultimately betrayed him all those years ago.

His senses only confirmed what his heart already knew. He'd never tasted a mouth so sweet, or one that melded with his so perfectly. He'd never smelled this woman's scent, or run his hands over these same lush curves. She was no one he'd ever touched before. She was new to him.

She was Lisa. And loving her was like waking up from a bad dream to discover that the world was bright and shining and full of promise. Some inexplicable twist of fate—a good twist, for a change—had given her to him. And nothing between heaven and earth was going to persuade him to let her go. Ever.

He tried in every way he knew to tell her that. Feasting on her, angling his head one way and then the other, deepening the kiss as if she were the source of all life. His hands moved feverishly, across her back, down her spine, to her hips, molding their bodies, sealing them with heat. She met his hunger and his need, her mouth surrendering to his, her hands clutching at him, pulling him closer. The tiny, whimpering sounds she made fueled his passion, urged him to take it all, everything she had to give.

And he did. During that one endless kiss, he touched her everywhere—breasts, hips, the warm, secret place between her thighs, claiming her body through the barrier of her clothing until she was liquid in his arms. Her knees buckled, and he took her weight against him, slowly easing her down to the rug. They swayed together, clinging, hands and lips moving urgently—touching and kissing everywhere they could reach.

He let her go long enough to struggle out of his shirt, then to strip hers away along with her bra. Then he gathered her close again, feeling the hardened tips of her breasts graze his chest, moving from side to side to increase the pleasure for both of them.

"Oh...oh, Mike," she whispered, her warm breath brushing his neck below his ear.

"I want you naked in my arms," he growled. "Naked under me. So hot you can't think about anything but what we're doing."

She moaned softly. "I'm already so hot I can't think about anything else."

"Good. I plan to keep it that way."

He was as efficient in removing the rest of her clothing as his trembling fingers would allow. She helped him, her own hands shaking as much as his. When they were both naked, lying side by side on the carpet, he let his gaze rake her body from head to toe, let himself revel in the sight of her lush breasts, and her white, nearly translucent skin that felt like silk to touch. The narrow waist, the sensuous curve of her hips, and the smaller curve of her belly came together to frame the nest of red curls at the juncture of her thighs. His gaze lingered there for a long moment, his blood pounding hotter at the thought of what was to come.

When he finally lifted his gaze to meet hers, he saw in the muted light that she was blushing. She started to roll toward him, but something in her eyes—a trace of nervousness or fear—made him hold her back with a hand on her shoulder.

Softly, he asked, "Are you frightened of me?"

"No," she replied, her blush deepening. "Only afraid that you won't like what you see."

"Oh, sweetheart," he murmured, "you couldn't be more wrong." Stroking her from breast to thigh, he added, "You're beautiful—soft and lush and so damn sexy.... I wouldn't change a thing."

Her gaze made a slow trip down his body, then traveled the same path back up to meet his once more. "Neither would I," she whispered. "Only..."

"Only what?"

"Being with you...like this...it's new to me."

He thought about that for a moment or two, then asked, "Do you have any memory of ever making love?"

She shook her head a little. "Not really. Only a sort of vague sense that I have, but nothing specific." Then, with a flicker of dismay crossing her brow, she said, "Oh, Mike, I don't know if I'm any good at this. But I want to be. Tell me what you like."

If he hadn't already been convinced that she wasn't Justine—and seeing her luscious and totally unfamiliar body had given him all the physical evidence he could have wanted— he would have been then. Justine had never shown so much as a scrap of self-doubt and, indeed, had always acted just a little bit like anyone she took to her bed was damned lucky. Certainly she'd never put anyone's pleasure above her own.

A slow smile formed on his lips. "I like this," he said, pulling her to him. "And this…"

Taking her mouth in another hot, deep joining, he moved his hair-roughened leg between her smooth ones. At the same time, his hand found her warm center, fingers parting the folds.

Her hand splayed across his hips, fingers digging into his flesh as he stroked her, her mouth tearing away from his as she drew in ragged gulps of air.

But it was his own breathing that went ragged when her hand found his sex, her fingers exploring gently, curling around him.

"Oh, Lisa," he groaned, hips straining toward her.

"And this," she said. "You like this."

"Oh, yeah. And these," he murmured as his lips and teeth nuzzled at her breasts.

"Please. Now. Please," she begged, her hand guiding him to her.

He covered her body with his, whispering her name, spreading her thighs wide, his mouth finding hers as he probed for entrance. Then she seemed to blossom open, and he was sliding inside her, and she was taking him in, hot and full and deep.

She gasped his name, fingers clutching his back, hips tilting to take him deeper.

"That's it, sweetheart," he murmured close to her ear. "That's right. Let me know how you want it. Show me…"

His hips began a slow rhythm, his hands beneath her hips angling her body until her response told him that he'd found the right spot. He let her set the pace, let her responses guide him, moving faster now…and faster…until she was nearly frantic beneath him. Until he'd lost all sense of deliberation or control and was aware only of the unbridled desire driving him. It was a purely intuitive move when his hand slid upward to find her breast, his fingers capturing the nipple and squeezing it gently.

She surged against him, and the high, keening noises she'd

been making suddenly dropped a couple of registers. He felt the first quaking spasm hit her. He let it take him. Let it carry him over the edge until he felt the hot convulsion begin deep in his belly. Then they were both lost. The climax washed over them in one long, voluptuous wave, locking them together to ride it out, rippling back and forth between them, until, at last, it left them spent and breathless on a newly discovered shore.

LISA WAS STILL QUIVERING with aftershocks when Mike rolled to his side and folded her into his arms. She burrowed closer, not at all ready to be separated from him even by a few inches. She felt shattered—and not merely from the storm of physical pleasure but from the gift he'd given her: he believed, *truly* believed, that she wasn't Justine. Finally, she'd convinced someone—the most important someone. And, in convincing Mike, she realized, she'd also convinced herself. She hadn't been fully aware of how terrified she'd been that she might be Justine. Seeing—*feeling*—Mike's utter certainty that she wasn't…well, the relief was nearly overwhelming.

Yet, so was the confusion. If she wasn't Justine Hollingsworth, who was she?

At the moment, in all honesty, she didn't have the energy to care. She knew enough about herself to feel satisfied with the sort of person she was. And lying safe and warm in Mike's arms in the afterglow of passion, she found it impossible to be worried about much of anything. Surely she could put aside worry for one night. Surely she could begin again tomorrow—this time with Mike's full support—to unlock the door to her past.

For an instant, a tendril of fear curled through her at the thought of her pregnancy. Would unlocking her past destroy the present? Would some previous commitment make it impossible for her to fulfill the commitment she felt she'd made to Mike?

She refused to think about it. Tomorrow would be soon enough.

Wiggling onto her side, Lisa pressed a kiss to Mike's shoulder, loving the salty taste of his skin. In response, he kissed the damp skin along her hairline.

"I should have taken you to bed," he said quietly.

She smiled. "I couldn't have walked that far."

His chest rumbled with the sound of soft laughter. "I'm not sure I could have, either."

"I'm still too limp to move," she sighed. "Can we camp out here?"

She heard the smile in his reply. "Maybe you were a Girl Scout when you were a kid."

"I think the Scouts discourage this kind of behavior."

He laughed outright at that. "Well, at least let me make us more comfortable." He reached to the couch and pulled down a pile of pillows and cushions and an afghan, fashioning a makeshift bed on the rug.

Snuggling at his side beneath the afghan, she murmured, "You don't look like the crocheted granny-square type."

"My seventy-year-old landlady made it," he replied. "She'd be mortally offended if I stuffed it in the closet."

Lisa contemplated the notion of Mike Lancer worrying about a little old lady's happiness. "You want people to think you're tough. But you're not—where it counts."

"Don't tell anybody, okay?"

"Why not?"

"Tough is safer," he muttered.

She moved so that she was cradling his head against her breasts, realizing quite well that he'd tried to play it safe with her—and failed. She also realized that, at this moment, she held his complete trust in her hands. It was both a gift and a burden. She wanted to protect him, to be the one who made him happy—forever. She could only hope that whatever fate had plucked her out of her old life and plunked her down in this new one would allow her the time she needed to show him that his trust was not misplaced.

Quietly, she repeated his words, "Tough is safer. How did you come up with that philosophy?"

His hand trailed lazily down her arm as he replied. "My dad was a mean drunk. He was meaner if you let him know you were scared."

"Oh, Mike."

He murmured something against her breast that she didn't catch, then said, "I survived."

"Didn't your mother stand up for you?"

"In the beginning. By the time I was six or seven, she'd given up." He grunted softly. "I think she ran out of lies to tell in the emergency room for how she got the broken ribs—or arm or nose."

"Good Lord," Lisa breathed. "Why didn't she leave him?"

"I spent a lot of years asking myself that same thing—until I became a cop. By the time I'd been on the job six months, I'd lost count of how many domestic disputes I'd covered. And I'd stopped blaming my mother for what she did or didn't do."

It didn't surprise her to hear he'd been a policeman; it seemed to fit his personality exactly. Afraid to hear the answer, Lisa asked anyway, "Wasn't there anyone else you could turn to?"

Mike let out a heavy sigh, his breath warm against her skin. "I had some friends at school. But nobody I trusted enough to bring home."

Lisa's fingers toyed with the silky dark hair at the back of his neck.

"And I did have one teacher," he continued. "A gym teacher in junior high who took an interest in me. I thought it was because I was good at sports. But years later, when I thought back on it, I wondered if he knew something was going on at home. Anyway, he seemed to understand that I needed some kind of outlet. He got me started walking, which turned out to be not just an outlet but a means of escape."

"Where did you go?"

"Everywhere," he said. Shifting her so that she was tucked against his side, her head on his shoulder, he held her close as he continued. "Starting from home, I'd walk to Dundalk Marine Terminal and watch them unload cars from ships. Or to Greenmount Cemetery and try to find the headstone with the oldest date. And Herring Run Park—that was one of my favorite places. When I got sick of looking at East Baltimore, I started taking buses across or up town. I'd go someplace like the zoo in Druid Hill Park, then walk home."

"But you were only…what? Eleven or twelve? Wasn't it dangerous for you to be out in the city, all alone?"

He gave a short laugh. "Not as dangerous as being home with my father. Besides, I was always pretty much on my own."

Lisa bit her tongue so as not to speak the words that came to mind—that she found the notion of a little boy being on his own worse than appalling.

Perhaps in response to her horrified expression, he hurried on. "By the time I was sixteen, I knew Baltimore like the back of my hand." He snorted softly. "Of course, by then, I wasn't walking because I was afraid of my father. I was bigger and stronger than he was, and if he'd hit me, I'd've hit him back. But I kept walking, anyway. Still do it, almost every day."

He took a breath as if to speak, then hesitated. Finally, he said, "Walking is how I met Justine."

A sudden chill ran through her. Justine wasn't at the top of her list of favorite topics. But Mike was.

"Oh?" she prompted.

"Hmm." He drew back a little and looked at her—checking her out, she thought, to see if she minded hearing about his past lover—the lover who'd jilted him and who was the cause of her own current woes.

She gave him an encouraging smile. "Go on."

He snuggled her against him again. "We were both at the University of Maryland, living on campus. She walked every day, too, and we kept seeing each other, until one day we started walking together."

It sounded harmless enough, she thought. A perfectly normal way for young people to meet.

"Walking led to talking," he said. "Pretty soon, I was helping her with her science classes, and she was helping me with French. If it had been up to me, it probably would have stayed at that. Hell, she was beautiful and had a great sense of humor, and she was popular as hell—and I figured I didn't stand a chance. But one day, she said she was tired of waiting for me to ask her out, so she'd decided not to wait anymore. She asked me to take her to a showing of *North By Northwest* at the student union." He paused, casting her a downward glance. "I'm kind of a classics buff."

"I figured that," Lisa said softly. She'd noticed the framed posters of *Citizen Kane* and *Psycho* on the living-room walls. Oddly, they struck a chord inside her. Somehow, she felt that she could have remembered plots, even minute details, of dozens of old movies—if she'd tried. At the moment, she was too tired to bother.

Stifling a yawn, she said, "Go on."

His hand came up to her chin, and he tilted her face to his. "You're falling asleep," he said, planting a kiss on her forehead.

"No," she protested. "Tell me more."

"Not tonight." He smiled. "If you're determined to get the rest of the story—and God knows why you'd want to, 'cause none of it's what I'd call riveting—you'll have to wait for the next installment."

"It's riveting to me," she whispered. "Mike, how long were you and Justine together?" she asked softly.

"We had two great years before things fell apart. But we're not going to talk about her anymore tonight."

He lowered his head and kissed her, then his lips moved against hers in a whisper. "You need to sleep."

Unfortunately, she had to agree. Her eyelids were leaden, and even the thought of sleep brought her close to the edge of it. Close enough for a quick flash of memory to slip through her guard—a piece of the waking nightmare from earlier that evening. She gave a little shiver.

"It's all right," he said. "I'll keep you safe."

She sighed. "I know."

He kissed her again, then trailed a line of kisses down her neck to her breasts, kissing each one in turn before working his way back up to her lips. There, his mouth settled for a brief but tender moment. Their lips parted with a soft, moist sound, then he pulled her tightly beside him. Eyes closed, she listened to the reassuring beat of his heart, strong and steady. Her last conscious thought was that his living-room rug was the most comfortable place she'd slept in her short but eventful life.

FAINT GRAY LIGHT came through the window when her eyes fluttered open. For several disoriented moments, she wondered why the mattress felt so hard. Then she realized where she was, and that Mike was beside her.

His body was levered up on one elbow and his hand was on her shoulder, lightly shaking her. Suddenly, she became aware of the tension radiating through him.

The smile faded from her face. "What's—" He cut her off with a finger pressed against her lips. For a moment, she was confused. Then she heard it.

Outside in the hall, a floorboard squeaked—the sound of someone moving stealthily. It was followed by a gentle twist of the doorknob, then the indistinct jingle of keys.

Chapter Sixteen

Lisa lay rigidly, trying to imagine who was on the other side of the door.

Mike whispered urgently in her ear, pointing toward an overstuffed chair by the window. "Get behind there. Now!"

Pulling the afghan around her, she scrambled across the room. From her hiding place, she saw Mike moving in a blur. He appeared simultaneously to douse the lamp, grab a hiker's walking stick that stood by the coatrack in the corner, and position himself by the door. Naked, he looked like an ancient Greek athlete about to compete in some arcane sport.

She held her breath as a key slipped into the lock. Nothing happened, but she heard a muffled curse on the other side of the door. Then the intruder tried another key. This time it turned, and the door opened a crack.

Peering around the corner of the chair, Lisa watched the crack widen. To her horror, the first thing through was the long barrel of a gun. It was followed by a hand and the rest of the gun, then an arm, and finally a man who moved on silent feet.

Mike yanked him across the threshold with one hand while using the other to bring the walking stick down on the back of his neck. With a muffled groan, the intruder crumpled to the rug. Before Lisa had time to sigh in relief, another figure leaped into the room, weapon drawn.

Lisa screamed. Mike sprang aside as a low thunk sounded,

followed by the splatter of plaster falling from the opposite wall. Lisa realized immediately that the long barrel on the gun was a silencer, and that the assailant was aiming again for Mike.

Mike used the stick in an upward sweep to knock the gun from the second man's hand. The weapon sailed across the room. Recovering his balance, the man sprang at Mike. They went down in the pile of discarded clothes, thrashing about as each tried to get the upper hand.

Still clutching the afghan, Lisa made for the corner where the gun had landed. It took several frantic seconds of searching before her fingers closed around the cold metal. When she turned, the men were rolling across the floor, trading blows like sailors in a saloon brawl. Except that one of the combatants was naked.

Mike landed on top. He slammed the other man's head against the floor. The man only grunted, then reversed their positions.

Lisa saw blunt fingers press into Mike's windpipe. He tried to pry them loose but couldn't. As she watched in horror, his face began to turn red. Nearly wild with panic, she tried to get a clear shot at the intruder but was afraid she'd hit Mike.

Then, suddenly, she realized that she didn't have to shoot anybody. Heedless of the afghan that had slipped to her waist, she raised the gun in the air and fired. It didn't make much noise, but it was enough to attract the assailant's attention. His head swung toward her, his eyes bugging out.

She smiled grimly. "That's right. Next time I'll blow your head off," she snarled, advancing with the gun leveled at him, hoping it was too dark for him to see how badly she was shaking.

Her commando act worked. As the man's attention focused on her, Mike broke free. He landed a blow on the other man's chin. Then another. And another. The intruder let out a strangled sigh and went slack.

Mike was out from under him in an instant. "Keep them covered," he growled.

Lisa sagged against the chair, dropping her hold on the afghan to wrap both hands around the gun. But her effort to keep it steady was futile; she was shaking all over.

Mike darted to the closet and emerged with a roll of heavy tape. He closed the front door, then used the tape to bind the two unconscious men's wrists and ankles. For good measure, he sealed their mouths and left them trussed up and lying strewn about like logs washed up on a beach.

Lisa, who had never felt closer to collapse, marveled at Mike's cool common sense when he stooped beside each captive in turn and rummaged through their pockets until he found their wallets and located identification.

"Lennie Ezrine," Mike muttered with a nod toward the larger of the two intruders, the one he'd knocked out first. "And this one's Jack Ordway."

"Hollingsworth said he'd send someone after me," Lisa whispered, her voice shaking as badly as the rest of her.

Mike snorted with disgust. "Lucky, it's so hard to get good help these days." Dumping the wallets on top of the two unconscious bodies, he stood up, rubbing the knuckles of his right hand against his left palm. Then he crossed to her and pried the gun loose from her frozen fingers.

He led her around the corner into a dining alcove. A square pine table and two chairs filled most of the space. Mike put the gun on the table and turned to her.

"You hurt yourself," she said, taking his hand and running a gentle finger over the reddened knuckles.

"I'll be all right." He gathered her into his arms.

She clung to him, still trembling. He felt so good, his body so strong and lean and healthy. "I put you in danger. If they'd…hurt you or—"

"Stop it," he admonished gently. "It's not your fault you've stumbled into Justine's mess."

"It may have been hers to begin with, but it sure seems like my mess now."

Beneath her cheek, his muscled, hair-dusted chest rose and fell in a heavy sigh. "Until we figure out who you are—or where Justine is—yeah, I'm afraid you're right. And I should have realized it. I should have taken you somewhere else.'' He gave a self-deprecating grunt. ''So much for keeping you safe.''

''But you did keep me safe,'' she whispered. ''If I'd been alone, still driving around in the car, when they found me—''

His hands tightened on her back. ''Don't think about it.''

''I knew they were coming. In the car, on our way here, I could *feel* someone out there, looking for me. And I knew they wouldn't give up.''

''Did you recognize them?'' he asked.

''No.'' She looked up at him, frowning. ''Should I?''

''They're the creeps who followed you out of the garage next to my office. The same ones who drove you into the Jones Falls.''

She shuddered violently, burying her face against his neck. ''I don't remember anything from before the accident.''

The barest trace of humor crept into his tone as he said, ''So, Annie Oakley, you don't know if you've ever fired a gun.''

She shook her head. ''No, but it felt…odd. Foreign. I don't think I have.''

''Well, whether you have or not, you did exactly the right thing with it. You were very brave.''

''I didn't feel brave. I felt terrified.''

''I've never seen it written that you can't be scared and brave at the same time. But I tell you what—'' he leaned to glance around the corner into the living room ''—unless you want to face them awake again, we'd better split.''

Another violent shudder ran through her. ''I don't ever want to see them again—awake or otherwise.''

He grunted softly. ''Right. So let's get—''

''Mike, tell me the truth,'' she interrupted. ''They meant to kill me, didn't they?''

He studied her for a moment, and she could see that he didn't want to answer.

''I can't be sure,'' he said finally. ''But my guess would

be, yes, they were sent to kill you. Sweetheart, I'm sorry, but nobody uses a silencer unless he means business."

"Where can I go?" she whispered. "Until I know who wants me dead—or who wants Justine dead—it doesn't seem like anyplace is safe."

"I'm working on that," he said. "But first things first. I'd like to wake these bastards up and see what kind of information I could get out of them. But they might have backup outside, waiting. I want to get you away from here—fast."

She nodded. "Okay."

He gave her shoulder a reassuring squeeze, then left her while he went into the living room. Lisa took a small step forward to peek around the corner, her gaze following Mike as he began picking up couch pillows.

"Are you going to call the police?" she asked.

"Not from here," he replied.

She watched as he carefully retrieved her bra and shirt from under one of the combatant's feet. Shuddering as he held out the garments to her, she said, "I can't wear them."

"Then you'll have to borrow something of mine." He dropped her unwanted clothing, grabbed her sandals off the floor and led her to his bedroom. There he found sweatpants and a dark T-shirt for her and jeans and a shirt for himself. The clothes were far too big, but she didn't mind. They smelled like him, which gave her a sense of feeling safe and cared for.

"Afraid I can't lend you shoes, unless you want to play Bozo the clown."

Nodding, she slipped into her sandals. As her thoughts started to clear, she began to wonder who, indeed, had sent the two men tied up in the living room, and who exactly they'd come seeking. It was reasonable to assume they were after Justine, who apparently knew she was being followed and had escaped.

But it was also possible that the attackers had been looking for *her*. She knew next to nothing about herself. Before her accident, had she been involved in something that would make her a target for murder? Recent events led her to believe that anything was possible. Even that she could be running away from the father of her baby.

That thought led to speculation about a messy divorce and a wildly possessive husband. Or maybe a man married to someone else, who was driven to the point of madness because she'd refused to have an abortion. She couldn't envision herself having an affair with a married man, but at this point, it would be foolish to discount any possibility.

Sitting on the edge of the bed, she pressed her fingers to her suddenly pounding temple. "Mike, how did I look when you saw me on the street that first time? I mean, did you have any clue about my state of mind?"

He stopped in the act of loading a clip of bullets into a gun he'd taken from a bureau drawer. "You looked upset. Why?"

"I'm trying to figure out what I was doing in Baltimore with a rental car—or why I was in your office building. I mean, since I wasn't there to see you."

"Good question, but save it for later," he ordered gently. "We've got more pressing problems right now. Let's go."

The gun was in his hand as he preceded her down the hall and past their still-unconscious visitors. As they approached the front door, Lisa heard a thump. Both she and Mike froze. His gun came up into firing position. Another thump sounded—closer this time.

Mike grimaced. "Newspaper. Christ, if he throws it against the door, one of our visitors could wake up." Tucking his gun inside his jeans at the small of his back, he opened the door and stepped quickly into the hall. "We're going out, so I'll take it," he said to the delivery boy. Before the sleepy-eyed kid got a step closer, he drew Lisa by the hand into the hallway with him, and closed the door behind them with a quiet click.

After handing over the paper, the boy trudged back down the stairs, and Mike gave the paper to Lisa. "Here. Carry this."

She hugged the paper to her in an unconsciously protective gesture as Mike pulled out the gun. He motioned her to be quiet, and they stood listening to the delivery boy's steps as he descended the stairs. After the back door banged shut behind the boy, Mike led the way downstairs and into the yard. In the early-morning light, Mike's gaze darted up and down the alley, his attention on full alert. He held the passenger door of the Mustang open for her, then closed it after she climbed inside.

As he swung into the driver's seat beside her, she turned to toss the paper onto the back seat, but a headline on the front page caught her eye, and she stopped cold.

"Oh, my God," she breathed.

"What's wrong?" Mike asked.

"He's…dead," she managed to say, nearly strangling on the words. "But he…he can't be!"

"*Who's* dead?" Mike pulled the paper toward him. "Holy mother of…Millionaire Developer Kendall Hollingsworth Found Dead," he said, reading the headline aloud. As she listened in shock, he quickly summarized the story. "It says his housekeeper found him unconscious with a lump on the back of his head. His wife is missing and…*shit*. She's wanted for questioning."

"But, Mike, he was alive!" Lisa exclaimed. "I swear he was! He was alive enough to walk across a room and try to grab me."

Mike's dark brows were drawn together in a ferocious scowl. "Sweetheart, I believe you. But I think we'd better find someplace less public than this alley to figure out what happened."

As he drove slowly between the backyards, Lisa fought off the feeling of unreality that threatened to swamp her. None of this could be happening. But every few seconds, when the surreal sensation numbing her brain let up a little and reality seeped in, she knew that it was, indeed, happening.

It didn't seem matters could get any worse. She didn't know who she was. Didn't know where she lived or even her real name. About the only facts she did know were her height, weight, hair and eye color, blood type...and that she was pregnant. She'd been mistaken for some woman who had disappeared into thin air and who was married to a monster. A man who had tried to rape her and who was now dead. And the police thought she might have killed him.

"Are you taking me to the police station?" she asked in a small voice.

Mike gave her a startled glance. "No."

"Maybe you should."

He made a right onto a one-way street. "Why? You're not Justine."

"What if I was the last person to see him alive?" Feeling sick, Lisa picked up the paper and began to read. "It talks about his wife being treated for amnesia, and—" She sucked in a sharp breath.

"Read it to me," Mike insisted, his gaze flickering between the empty, predawn street and the rearview mirror.

"Are we being followed?" she asked.

"I don't think so. It would be hard to follow anyone this early in the morning and not get caught. Keep reading."

Lisa went back to the article. "They got a quote from Maggie Dempsey. "'I was working in the kitchen when I saw Mrs. Hollingsworth through the window," the housekeeper told reporters. "I thought it was strange that she was outside after nine o'clock in the evening. So I called to her, but she didn't answer.'""

"You were with me at nine o'clock," Mike said. "I looked at the clock on the dashboard right before we went inside my apartment. It was eight-thirty."

"But Maggie says—"

"She saw *someone*," Mike finished the sentence. "What if it was Justine?"

Lisa stared at him, her mouth slightly open.

He explained. "Justine's been hiding out all week. Her car was at the airport, remember? Suppose she came back last night. Suppose she wanted to get back at Hollingsworth for all the times he raped *her*. Suppose she killed him.''

Lisa let out a long breath. ''Only, I'm the one who's going to take the blame.''

Mike's face was grim. ''We've got to find out who you are. And prove that you're not involved in any of this.''

''But, Mike, I *am* involved,'' she insisted. ''For heaven's sake, I hit the man over the head!''

''In self-defense,'' he muttered. ''And if you *had* killed him, it still would have been self-defense.''

His calm assurance didn't stop shivers from racing over her skin. ''If Hollingsworth was dead last night, he can't be the one who sent the men this morning,'' she said.

Mike shook his head. ''He could have set something in motion before he died—like yesterday before he came home from his trip. Hell, he could have set it up weeks ago.''

Lisa gave a little nod. Wrapped in the shock of Kendall Hollingsworth's demise, she hadn't been paying attention to where they were going. When Mike made a right into an alley, she sat up and took notice. He pulled to a stop behind an aging brick row house and parked.

She gave the alley a nervous once-over. ''Where are we?''

''A friend's house.'' Hesitating, he explained, ''Pat's a bit strange, so be prepared.''

''How do you mean, 'strange'?'' she asked.

Lifting one shoulder in a shrug, he said, ''Rough. Keeps to himself. I arrested him a long time ago for petty larceny. When he got out of jail, he was nailed for an armed robbery he didn't commit. I caught the guy who did.'' Again, Mike shrugged as if to say what he'd done was no big deal. ''He does me favors from time to time.''

''And what favor are you asking today?'' she asked.

''I want to make some phone calls.''

''To the police?''

''I think we'll wait on that one until I've got you out of town. But I'm interested in the question you asked a while ago—about what you were doing in my office building. You didn't come to see me, but you must have been there for *some* reason. Somebody in one of the offices must have seen you. And they might know who you are.''

Lisa's eyes widened, a spark of hope flaring inside her.

Mike nodded. "Exactly. We've got a couple of lawyers, an architect, Dr. Franklin, a herbalist…''

He went on to name several dozen others. None of the names were familiar, but, she thought grimly, that didn't mean a thing.

Suddenly, a crash from somewhere nearby made her jump.

"Probably a rat in a trash can,'' he muttered. Still, he waited awhile before getting out to reconnoiter the alley.

When he was satisfied that no one was watching, he ushered her toward a door covered with peeling black paint. He knocked and, after a short time, the door was opened by a middle-aged man with broad shoulders, wearing a green plaid shirt and jeans.

"Mike!'' The man's lined face creased in a smile.

"Sorry to bother you so early, Pat, but I need your phone.''

"Sure, come on in.'' The man led them down a hall. "I just got off work, so you didn't wake me up.''

"Still working at High's?''

"Yeah, it's good. Too bad more ex-cons don't have a Mike Lancer to find 'em jobs when they get out of the joint.''

Lisa's gaze flashed to Mike as they entered a dark sitting room with faded overstuffed furniture. So, he'd done a little more for Pat than keep him out of prison. Is that how he thought of her—as simply another Red Cross case?

Dismissing the notion as implausible, given the night before, Lisa turned her attention to her shabby surroundings. From the sofa, a gray tabby looked at them curiously.

"Lisa, this is Pat Lemon,'' Mike said.

Lisa murmured something polite and shook the man's hand. He seemed nice enough, and he certainly seemed to like Mike. But the seedy, worn-out surroundings only added to the surreal, almost grotesque feeling of the morning.

"Can I get you anything?'' Lemon asked her. When she

shook her head, he ambled toward a flight of stairs, telling Mike, "I'll be working on my crossword puzzle if you need me."

After watching her taciturn host depart, Lisa perched on the sofa. When the cat moved two feet to curl next to her, she began almost unconsciously to pet it. And as Mike plunked down in a decrepit armchair beside the phone, picked up the receiver and began dialing, she went on stroking the purring animal, the soothing action helping to control her mounting tension as she listened to Mike's conversations.

A few people he tried didn't answer, but when he got someone on the line, he always started by mentioning the article in the paper about Hollingsworth, then asking if anyone had seen the woman in the picture. Lisa knew from his expression that the answers were negative.

After a dozen calls, he replaced the receiver with a sigh. "Sorry, I thought it was a good idea."

She spoke past the tightness in her throat. "It made sense to try."

"I want you out of the city," he said emphatically, picking up the phone again and punching in another number. Almost immediately, someone answered. "Jenny, it's Mike," he said. "I've got a problem."

Lisa listened, her anxiety growing, as he launched into a more detailed explanation about her amnesia, the murder and her being wanted for questioning. As she took in the earnest, worried expression on his face, she realized he fully intended to solve her problem. He really meant to find out who she was, and she had no doubt that he would move heaven and earth to do it.

Which made her aware in a way she hadn't been before that she absolutely had to tell him about the baby. It couldn't be put off any longer. And not only because he had a right to know. How could she expect him to do his job without all the information? Her pregnancy might be a major clue in leading him to her identity.

She'd intended to tell him that morning—perhaps over

breakfast together. But events had precluded breakfast and had certainly left no time for intimate chats about her condition. Now, the more she thought about it, the more difficult telling him seemed.

Last night it had all been very clear. As far as she was concerned, there was no man but Mike in her life. She loved him, and she longed to tell him she would love him forever. Yet, in the light of day, she faced the truth that she had no right to make such a promise, not without knowing what her previous commitments might be.

Moreover, she had no idea how her revelation would affect Mike's feelings about her. It didn't seem possible that he could have made love to her as he had and not love her. Even so, what if he *did* love her? How would he feel when he learned she was pregnant with another man's child?

Betrayed. Angry. Hurt. The words flashed into her mind, and she reluctantly had to accept that they could be accurate. Given his emotionally impoverished background, falling in love with Justine must have been an enormous step for him. Probably for the first time in his life, he'd dared to be happy. And it had lasted for two years. Justine's betrayal had made it almost impossible for him to trust a woman—particularly one who looked so much like Justine. It wouldn't take much—no, not much at all—to destroy his trust once again.

Lisa huddled on the couch, petting the cat, steeling herself to tell Mike about her pregnancy. Her attention snapped to the present, though, when she heard him ending his conversation with the woman to whom he was speaking.

"I really appreciate this, Jenny," he said. "We'll be there in about thirty minutes." He hung up the receiver and gave her a thumbs-up sign. "We're all set. You can stay at Jenny's while I canvass my office building with your picture."

Lisa nodded. "But, Mike, I have to—"

"The only thing you have to do is stay out of harm's way." He gave her a warm smile. "Now, let me handle this, okay?" Standing up, he walked toward the door, calling over his shoulder, "Come on."

Filled with all sorts of new trepidations, Lisa followed.

When they were back on the street once more, she started again to tell Mike that she was pregnant.

Before she could speak, he gave her a quick smile, saying, "Let me tell you about Jenny. She's a computer programmer." He paused for an instant, then added, "She's blind. But she insists on being self-sufficient. She lives by herself in an old farmhouse outside the city, in a little town called Elkridge. It's pretty isolated. Perfect for us. There isn't a chance anybody will think about looking for you there."

He shot her an expectant look, as if he was waiting for approval, and Lisa obliged him with a nod. She wasn't worried about the location; she trusted his judgment. There were other things about the arrangement, however, that bothered her.

They were on a major highway now, heading out of the city, and Lisa kept her gaze directed straight ahead as she said, "You didn't tell Jenny that I'm suspected of murder, did you?"

"The article doesn't say that," he replied.

"Why else would I be wanted for questioning?"

"First, they want Justine—not you. Second, they want to talk to the dead man's wife because she's missing. Hell, they could be thinking she's dead, too." He reached over to squeeze her hand where it lay clenched on her lap. "So try not to jump to conclusions. When I get you settled, I'm going to call a contact I've got in the department."

Lisa stared out the side window at the flat, marshy stretches of land flashing past. "Jenny could get in trouble for letting me stay with her, couldn't she? She and you both could be…what's it called? Accessories?"

"Lisa, stop it. Nobody's going to get in trouble for helping you, because you didn't kill anyone."

"Suppose I did," she insisted. "Suppose he had a brain hemorrhage or something."

Mike let out a sigh filled with exasperation. "Then, like I said before, it was self-defense. Sweetheart, you've got enough other things to worry about. Don't make yourself sick worrying about something that isn't going to happen. You're not going to get charged with a murder you didn't commit.''

Lisa wasn't at all sure he was right that she wouldn't be charged with murder, but he was certainly right that she had enough other things to worry about and that worry was making her sick. At least, *something* was making her sick. She felt awful, dizzy and exhausted and decidedly queasy. Was it only shock and worry? Or was morning sickness finally rearing its ugly head?

Wouldn't that just be the perfect way to break the news that she was pregnant—to throw up all over his car.

It soon became impossible to think about telling him anything. She couldn't talk without wanting to vomit. She considered it a blessing when Mike switched on the radio to a light rock station, making conversation unnecessary. For the remainder of the trip, Lisa concentrated on taking slow even breaths and studying the unremarkable horizon.

It wasn't long before Mike slowed the Mustang at a gravel driveway leading to a Victorian farmhouse perched atop a hill. The house was surrounded by a stand of huge spreading maples, covered in new, pale green leaves, and stately old hemlocks. A couple hundred feet away was a big red barn.

As Mike pulled the car to a stop by the front porch, the door opened. A slender young woman came out and made her way to the railing, tapping in front of her with a long white cane. Her brown hair was pulled back into a single braid. Her gaze, Lisa noticed, was directed toward the car as if she could see it.

Mike rolled down the window. "Okay if I park in the barn?"

"Sure," the woman called back.

Mike drove through the double doors and cut the engine. As they started walking toward the house, Lisa felt shyness and anxiety wash over her at the impending meeting with Jenny, and it occurred to her that, since waking up from the accident, she'd felt the same way each time she'd met a new person. It wasn't only a matter of nerves made raw from recent events. It was the notion of facing a stranger when she was a stranger to herself. Halfway to the house, Lisa's steps faltered. She didn't know if she could face this woman who Mike thought of as a friend and who was clearly important to him.

It was as if he knew what she was going through when he put his arm around her waist and tugged her close in a brief hug. "It's okay, Lisa," he said. "Jenny's the last person on earth who'd give you grief."

His lips curved upward in an encouraging smile, and she offered him a tentative smile in return.

"That's my brave lady," he said, then leaned down to give her a quick kiss. And just before they reached the porch, he murmured close to her ear, "Promise me you won't tell Jenny I was fighting burglars at dawn bare-ass naked. She might think it was…you know…undignified."

Despite herself, Lisa giggled.

He missed her grateful look as he mounted the porch steps, saying, "Jenny Larkin, I'd like you to meet Lisa. Lisa, this is Jenny."

"It's nice to meet you," Jenny said, her blue gaze appearing to follow the progress of their footsteps up onto the porch.

"Thank you for letting me come here," Lisa returned, stopping beside Mike. "But I'm worried you could get in trouble if the police find out."

Jenny didn't answer. She was frowning slightly, her head tipped to one side. "I've heard your voice before," she said.

For an instant, Lisa simply stared at her, confused.

"Say something else," Jenny said as she made small circles with the tip of her cane on the porch floor.

Lisa cleared her throat, feeling extremely self-conscious. "Um…what should I say?"

"Anything."

"Uh…" Nervously, she scrambled for something reasonably coherent. "I've had some upsetting things happen lately. I guess it started with my car going into a river."

Jenny's features, which were small and regular and pretty, softened in a sympathetic look. "I know this is awkward, but I identify people from their voices. Try telling me that you have an appointment with Mrs. Stone."

"I have an appointment with Mrs. Stone," she managed to say, feeling her throat constrict. Had she spoken those exact words before?

"I'm almost certain you were in my office," Jenny said. "We talked to each other."

With her heart suddenly racing, Lisa whispered, "What office?"

"Birth Data, Inc."

She blinked, at once bewildered and unbearably excited. "I—I came there? What is it?"

Before Jenny could speak, Mike answered the question, and his voice was strung with tension. "It's a family-search organization for adopted children run by Erin Stone. She was one of the people I called this morning, but she didn't answer."

"You wanted to locate your birth parents," Jenny added.

Dumbfounded, Lisa glanced from Jenny to Mike, then back to Jenny. "I'm adopted?"

"I presume so," Jenny replied.

Her knees buckled. Suddenly, as if the ground had opened under her feet, Lisa felt herself falling. Mike moved quickly to catch her, his arms coming around her waist from behind.

She could hardly breathe, but as she leaned against Mike for support, she managed to get out a few words. "Do you know my name? Do you know who I am?"

Chapter Seventeen

"The name you gave was Leigh Barnes."

"Leigh Barnes," Lisa repeated, squeezing her eyes closed. She waited for the magic door to open. Any second now, it would all come back to her—family, job, home, the father of her baby. But the place in her mind reserved for such memories was still only empty space. Nothing. Not even a hint of anything familiar.

The disappointment was so acute, tears filled her eyes, and she had to fight hard not to cry. She let Mike guide her with an arm around her waist into the house. Jenny followed. Lisa crumpled into a corner of the sofa, sinking deep into the fluffy cushions.

"Did you remember something?" he asked.

She shook her head.

To Jenny, he said, "Are you sure Lisa is the same woman you spoke to?"

Jenny's brow wrinkled. "I thought so. It was last week. Ellen, our receptionist, was on lunch break, so I talked directly to Leigh Barnes." Closing the front door and propping her cane against the wall, she crossed to the sofa and sat beside Lisa. "I'm sorry. I shouldn't have been so quick to speak."

Swallowing the tears clogging her throat, Lisa replied, "It's not your fault. I could be the person you met, but I simply don't remember."

Outside, a horn honked. "That's my ride," Jenny said. "I can tell them I'm not going in to work today."

"No," Mike countered. "Better follow your normal routine, in case anybody's nosing around Light Street."

She looked torn. "I hate to leave you like this."

"Go on," he said gently. "We appreciate what you're doing for us."

"Yes," Lisa added.

With what Lisa thought was remarkable confidence, Jenny rose and crossed to a small table by the door. She picked up her purse and the white cane—one of the only clues that she was blind—then said, "Make yourselves at home. There's an extra house key in the drawer beside the fridge. If you want to get some sleep, the guest bedroom is on your left at the top of the stairs. But please don't move any furniture, or leave anything lying around where I might trip over it."

"We'll put everything back where we found it," Mike assured her.

After Jenny left, Lisa sat with her head cradled in her hands. Grimly, she tried to push her thoughts through the blank wall in her mind. "Leigh Barnes," she repeated over and over. All she got for her efforts was a headache.

The sofa beside her sagged, and she let her hands fall from her face as Mike sat and pulled her into his arms.

"Don't make demands on yourself that you can't fulfill."

"How did you know what I was doing?"

He laughed. "If I were you, I'd be giving myself a migraine trying to crash through the memory barrier."

"I hated being called Justine—I mean *hated* it—enough that you'd think it might force me to remember who I am. If amnesia is part physical and part emotional trauma, it makes me wonder what on earth happened to me. I guess it was so awful that I've blocked out everything."

He stroked his knuckle against her cheek. "At least you know why you picked the name Lisa."

She managed a smile. "Yes. Leigh. Lisa. It must have sounded familiar."

"And you know why you were in Baltimore at 43 Light Street." With one arm still around her shoulders, he stretched for the phone sitting on the table next to the sofa. "Let's see what Erin Stone has to say. I'll try her again at home. Maybe she was in the shower earlier." Mike punched in the numbers, then gave her a quick nod at the same time she heard the faint "Hello" come through the receiver.

"Erin, it's Mike," he said. "Sorry to bother you so early, but I have an urgent request...."

It was quickly obvious that things weren't going the way he had anticipated. "But this is a matter of life and death," he argued. "I want to prove Lisa had no motive for assaulting Kendall Hollingsworth, except that he was trying to rape her." After a pause, he sighed. "Okay. I appreciate your position." He put his hand over the mouthpiece and spoke to Lisa, his expression exasperated. "Erin's sorry, but information on clients is confidential."

"Let me talk to her," Lisa said. Mike handed her the receiver, and she took a deep breath. "Mrs. Stone?"

"Yes," a pleasant voice answered.

"I'm sorry to bother you at home. I'm at Jenny Larkin's house because two men came into Mike's apartment this morning and tried to kill us."

The woman on the other end of the line sucked in a startled breath. "Mike left out that little detail."

"Yes, well, a lot of frightening things have happened recently, starting when the same two men ran my car into the Jones Falls. I would have drowned if Mike hadn't been there to pull me out. The problem is, I woke up from the accident with amnesia. I don't remember a thing—not even my name, much less where I live, where I work...nothing. My purse was lost in the accident, so I don't have any identification. When we got here this morning and Jenny said she'd met me in your office, that was the first clue I've had to my identity." Lisa heard the desperation in her own voice as she finished. "So you see, Mike wasn't exaggerating. It truly seems to be a matter of life and death."

A short pause ensued. When the other woman finally answered, her tone made Lisa want to cry again.

"I don't know what to say. God, what you've been through sounds dreadful! But, well, I can only hope you'll understand why our files are closed. Information about adopted children and their birth parents is very sensitive."

"But you may be the only one who can help me!" Lisa said, impatience getting the better of her. "What if I came to your office? If you recognize me as Leigh Barnes, would you release the file?"

This time the pause was longer.

"Yes. All right," the woman said finally.

"Oh…" Lisa bit back a sob. "Thank you. You don't know…" Her hand sought Mike's, which was resting on her shoulder, and gave his fingers a squeeze. Then, she asked, "Did I fill out some kind of form?"

"Yes."

At the positive response, Lisa asked the question burning in the back of her throat. "Could you give me one piece of information? Did I say I was married?"

"I believe you said you were single."

"Thank you," she breathed.

"Let me have the phone." Mike took the receiver from her trembling fingers. "Erin, I don't want to bring Lisa to Light Street. Whoever sent the thugs to my apartment might have the office staked out, too. Could you meet us, say, at that little coffee shop near the Walters Art Gallery? …All right. Noon. Yeah, that's fine."

Replacing the receiver in its cradle, he was silent for a moment. The lines of tension in his face mirrored the strain in his voice as he spoke. "Well, what's the answer to the question? Are you married?"

She shook her head. "No."

"Thank God." He grabbed her hand, clutching it tightly.

This was it, she thought. There would never be a better time to tell him. "Mike…" She drew a slow breath, trying to calm her churning stomach. "I wish it were as simple as my not being married. But it isn't."

He uttered a humorless laugh. "I'm just glad to hear my worst fear isn't going to come true—that I don't have to turn you over to some other guy."

"No, but…there are other complications."

Leaning away from her a little, he gave her a sharp look. "You remember something you're not telling me?"

She shook her head. "Not on a conscious level."

"Then are you trying to say that last night didn't—" he broke off, his gaze falling from hers "—that it didn't mean something to you?"

Her eyes misted. "Oh, Mike, of course it did. It meant the world to me. I love you. Or I wouldn't have made love with you."

He gathered her close. "Lisa—"

"Oh, Lord, I shouldn't have told you that."

"Did you mean it?"

"Yes, but I'm not free to say it."

"You're afraid there's some other man in your life."

"No. I mean, that's not the point. The point is that I'm…I'm pregnant."

He suddenly went rigid and very still. "You're what?"

She didn't repeat it. She knew he had heard.

Several dreadful moments went by in utter silence.

Rising, he took a couple of steps away from the couch and turned to look down at her. "You knew that last night?"

Heart pounding, Lisa nodded. "Dr. Habib told me."

"So why didn't you tell *me?*" he demanded.

Sighing raggedly, she said, "At first it was too personal. Then I tried to tell you a couple of times. I was going to do it right before Hollingsworth came home from his hunting trip and found us in his den."

An injured look crossed his features, but he quickly regained control. "But it slipped your mind last night."

"I wanted you so much," she whispered. "Mike, last night we needed each other—you know it as well as I do. And I was afraid if I told you, you wouldn't want to make love with me—that you would think it was wrong or…I don't know…dishonorable.''

"Well, you got that right.''

"But don't you see,'' she pleaded. "It *wasn't* wrong or dishonorable! I have no idea who the father of my baby is, and I might *never* know. Should I have to go on for the rest of my life without anyone? Or condemn my baby to having no father just because I'm waiting for my memory to come back?''

"So, what if you don't remember?'' he countered. "It's only been a week. It's not at all unlikely that either you'll find out who you are or that somebody is looking for you—and that he'll find you.''

She gave her head a quick shake. "It wouldn't matter. Mike, I love *you*. I could never go off with some man I didn't even know, much less love, no matter who he is or what he's been to me! It would be like promising eternal fidelity to a total stranger! No. Worse than that. It would be like keeping a promise that some other woman made!''

In the silence that followed, Lisa saw Mike waver, saw the longing in his eyes war with the anger and pain of what she knew he perceived as her betrayal. But the battle was over quickly. Anger and pain won. He turned away, walking over to stand at the window, his back toward her.

She stared at the rigid set of his shoulders. "Mike, please,'' she begged. But he didn't turn around, and she knew it was hopeless to try again. The wall was in place between them, more impenetrable than ever.

Had she lost him forever? The possibility brought a strangled sob to her throat, and tears soon followed, hot and heavy. Scrambling off the sofa, she dashed toward the stairs, but with tears blurring her vision, she was clumsy. She slipped, banging her knee against a stair tread.

Ignoring the pain, she pushed herself up and kept going. In the guest room, she shut the door and threw herself on the bed, where she curled into a ball and cried. She needed Mike there, on the bed with her, holding her, telling her everything would be all right. But she knew he wouldn't come, not now. And maybe never.

LENNIE SQUINTED as he emerged into the watery sunshine outside police headquarters.

Beside him, Jackal breathed a long draft of warm spring air and let it out slowly. "I need a drink," he muttered.

"Later," the high-priced lawyer snapped as he led them rapidly down the block.

Lennie had never met the guy before, but he'd been impressed at how fast he'd gotten them sprung. As they turned the corner, Lennie saw a black Lincoln that looked as out of place in the neighborhood as a champagne bottle in a cooler of beer.

"He wants to talk to you." The mouthpiece gestured toward the sedan, then walked away.

Lennie peered at the car but couldn't see through the privacy glass. Wiping his sweaty palm on his pants, he reached for the handle and opened the door. The man in the back seat looked as though he was on his way to a board meeting. A uniformed driver sat behind the wheel, eyes straight ahead.

Lennie eased into the back seat. Jackal took the space by the window and closed the door. The air inside the luxury sedan was heavy with the aroma of expensive after-shave. Probably fifty dollars a bottle.

"I hear you had considerable difficulty this morning," Señor Realto observed in his slightly accented English.

Lennie hesitated, afraid to trust the man's mild tone.

"Yeah, but it wasn't our fault," Jackal jumped in. "We woulda put Lancer away and grabbed the broad—if the son of a bitch had taken her to bed instead of screwing her on the living-room floor."

"He heard us at the door," Lennie added.

"Heard *you*," Jackal pointed out, to Lennie's disgust. "You were the one with the lock pick."

The car pulled away from the curb and nosed into traffic as Realto said, "There's no point in assigning blame."

Relaxing a little, Lennie said, "Thanks. And thanks a million for springin' us so fast."

Señor Realto nodded, his expression completely neutral. The man was always hard to figure. He was from some banana republic, and he only came to Baltimore a few months a year. When he was around, he paid real good—if you did your job and kept your mouth shut.

"Tell me what happened, *por favor*," Realto asked.

"Lancer was ready for us when we came in the door," Jackal whined. "It was just bad luck."

"*Sí*. But I'd like to hear about it."

As they drove up Fayette, Lennie answered questions. No, they hadn't squealed to the cops. Yes, as far as they knew, the woman was still with Lancer. No, they didn't know where he might have taken her.

"I think it's time for me to handle things personally," Realto murmured.

Lennie breathed a sigh of relief. He and Jackal were off the hook. This job had been bad news from the start. He wished they'd never picked up Miss Rich-Bitch's trail at that parking garage the week before. They'd known she had an appointment with Lancer, but they hadn't expected her to be driving a rental. Or to go into that Birth Data office. They'd been playing catch-up ever since.

The Lincoln stopped in back of an abandoned warehouse.

"Where are we, anyway?" Jackal asked.

"You'll be safe here," Realto said in a tone that sent a warning shiver up Lennie's spine.

The chauffeur pressed a remote control. The door opened and closed again as the car rolled into a dimly lit space.

Realto stepped out, then turned to look at them. His voice still bland, he said, "I'm sorry I overestimated your abilities, but I've learned when to cut my losses."

Jackal's "Hey, wait—" turned into a gurgle as a slug from the chauffeur's gun tore into his chest.

Lennie knew he didn't have a chance. Heart pounding, he leaped for the open door. He was half out when the bullet caught him, making a neat hole in the side of his head.

LISA HAD NO NOTION how long she'd been crying when she heard Mike's footsteps in the hall. Quickly, she wiped her hand across her eyes.

"You have an appointment with Erin Stone," Mike said through the closed door. "She's breaking her rules for you, so let's not keep her waiting."

Lisa struggled to pull herself together. A box of tissues sat on the bedside table, and she took one and blew her nose.

"Lisa, did you hear me?"

"Yes."

Her knee throbbed as she stood up and limped to the door. She hesitated before opening it, her hand on the doorknob, not wanting to face him. But it couldn't be avoided.

She found him looming in the hall, arms folded across his chest like protective armor. Ducking her head, she scooted past him into the bathroom. She stared at herself in the mirror. The woman who stared back looked awful, eyes puffy, skin splotchy, and splashing cold water on her face didn't help.

Trying not to limp, she met Mike at the front door. His expression was stony. He left her standing on the porch to go retrieve his car, and he didn't speak as she climbed in beside him. The silence continued during the ride into the city. She wanted to say something, to make him understand why she'd done what she'd done, but it was clear that he was in no mood to listen. So she simply stared straight ahead, wishing she had some makeup or, at least, a pair of dark glasses to hide her blotchy face.

They drove back through the city the way they'd left, and at some point Lisa realized Mike was looking for a parking place. She noticed a coffee shop on the next corner and assumed it was their destination. Her stomach, which had been none too stable all morning, began to churn once more with nerves over the impending meeting. A meeting that quite literally could determine the rest of her life.

Straightening in her seat, she cleared her throat. "Thank you for bringing me back to town. You can let me off at the corner. I guess you'd better return the balance of the retainer to Justine. I-I'll pay you back the rest as soon as I can. How much did she send you?"

"Five thousand dollars."

Lisa gasped.

"I'm working for her until further notice," Mike said, skidding to a halt behind a car pulling into traffic from a parking spot at the curb. He slipped his Mustang into the vacated spot, saying, "I think my expenses on her account were legitimate."

Lisa frowned, confused. His tone and expression told her that he was angry, but if that was so, why wasn't he doing as she'd asked, dumping her out at the corner?

"Do you have any money?" he muttered. "Anywhere to go?"

"I found some cash in Justine's bedroom," she replied. "But some of it's in the pocket of the slacks I was wearing last night and the rest is in the purse I left at Hollingsworth's. But, Mike, that doesn't matter. Mrs. Stone is going to tell me about Leigh Barnes, and it certainly looks like that's who I am. I presume I have a job—a home. Somewhere."

When he didn't respond, she cleared her throat again and said, "Maybe the best thing for me to do is contact the police."

That got a reaction.

"Like hell," he stated flatly. "You're not in any shape to answer a barrage of questions from a hostile interrogation team. Kendall Hollingsworth was an upstanding citizen, and they'll be under pressure to name his murderer. Right now, all they've got is you."

Lisa winced at hearing the truth put so bluntly.

His expression was still dark and brooding, but his tone

less angry as he said, "Listen to what Erin has to say before you make any decisions."

"Won't it look bad that I'm hiding out?"

"Not if we can figure out who killed Hollingsworth—or, failing that, where Justine is. Or who you are."

Lisa noted his use of the word *we* but didn't dare speculate about its implications. Before she could ask how exactly they were going to solve a murder, Mike got of the car, fed a couple of coins into the meter and started toward the coffee shop. Lisa followed as fast as her injured knee would allow her to hobble.

Mike waited for her at the entrance of the small shop and held the door for her to enter. As they stepped inside the almost empty restaurant, she saw an attractive, dark-haired woman sitting in a booth near the back. She had seen them, too, and was looking toward them expectantly. With Mike following her, Lisa started down the narrow aisle, toward the woman who was presumably Erin Stone. As she approached, she was relieved to see a spark of recognition in her eyes.

"How did you hurt your leg?" she asked as they drew near her table.

"Oh...I tripped on the stairs." Lisa slid onto the opposite bench, casting a quick glance at Mike, who seemed to hesitate before sliding in next to her.

"I guess it's badly bruised."

Her hand fluttered in a dismissive gesture. If Mrs. Stone wanted to assume that was why she'd been crying, so much the better. She was acutely aware of Mike's shoulder and arm brushing hers. Tension was radiating from his body. It took more energy than she was capable of mustering at the moment to put the distraction entirely aside as she asked, "Mrs. Stone, are you reasonably confident that I'm Leigh Barnes?"

"Please, call me Erin. If you're a friend of Mike's, there's no need for us to be so formal." She smiled. "And, yes, I'm sure you must be Leigh Barnes. You look like her, and Jenny's right, you sound like her."

Lisa squeezed her eyes closed and uttered a sincere "Thank

God.'' Then, looking once more at Erin, she said, ''Since I woke up in the hospital, people have been trying to convince me that I'm Justine Hollingsworth.''

Erin opened a briefcase and pulled out a slim folder. She was about to hand it to Lisa, when a waitress appeared.

An eternity seemed to pass while Mike ordered coffee. Lisa shook her head. She couldn't have swallowed a thing; her stomach was roiling.

When the waitress left, Erin passed the folder across the table. Pulse pounding in her ears, Lisa scanned the information. She was thirty years old. She lived in Philadelphia.

The waitress came with Mike's order and left again. Lisa kept reading, vaguely aware that Mike didn't touch the coffee.

''I'm an architect?'' she asked, incredulous. From the corner of her eye, she saw Mike's startled look.

''That's what you said. Do you have reason to doubt it?''

''No, it just seems...unusual. But I guess it explains why I know how to operate a computer—and how to read construction specs.''

As her eyes scanned down the page, more facts leaped out at her. High school. College. Childhood illnesses. Her adoptive parents, Sheila and William Barnes. They were both deceased, according to the information she'd written. But the words might as well have been about someone else.

''None of this means much to me,'' she admitted to Erin. ''Did I tell you anything about myself? About why I came in?''

Erin threw Mike a quick glance. ''I have notes from our conversation. But it's all extremely personal information.''

Mike stood up instantly. ''I'll make myself scarce.'' Before Lisa could stop him, he strode away.

She wanted to call him back, didn't want to keep any more secrets from him. But she wasn't sure he wanted to know more about her than he already did, which appeared to have been too much. She watched him exit the restaurant and head in the direction of his car. Then, with a sigh, she turned back to Erin.

Erin pulled several typed sheets from her briefcase and ran her eyes over the contents. "Some of this will be disturbing."

"Please, just tell me."

"You came to us because you were pregnant."

"Yes, the doctor at the hospital told me that."

"You said you wanted to know your heritage and your medical background so you could do the best for your child."

Lisa leaned forward. "Did I mention the baby's father?"

"Leigh—"

"Call me Lisa. I'm comfortable with that. Leigh still sounds foreign. Maybe I'll stick with Lisa permanently."

Erin nodded. "You said the father of your child is a man you met professionally. When you told him about the baby, he insisted that you get an abortion."

Lisa blanched. "I could never have an abortion."

"That's what you told him, and he threatened to get you fired. Apparently, he has some pull with your boss."

"Oh."

"You said that if you had to, you'd find a job in another state. That was another reason you came to Baltimore. You sent résumés to several architectural firms here, and you had interviews scheduled."

Feeling giddy and extremely unwell, Lisa pressed her fingers to her forehead. "Too bad I don't remember a thing about designing buildings," she muttered. "Did I happen to say if I had any money saved?"

Erin looked unhappy. "You mentioned some medical bills you're paying off."

"Oh, Lord." Under the table, her fingers clenched together as she wondered how she was going to support herself, let alone a baby. She didn't know. She didn't know how she was going to manage anything.

It was the final straw. Her stomach lurched in complete revolt. Suddenly, the smell of coffee and food wafting through the restaurant became nauseating, and she knew no amount of steady breathing was going to help.

"I'm going to be sick," she managed to say hoarsely, struggling to slide out of her seat.

As she bolted from the booth, she saw Mike coming through the door. Mortified, she darted to the back of the shop and shoved open the door marked Ladies. She just made it into one of the stalls, where she heaved into the toilet.

Several minutes later, she was sponging her face at the washbasin when the door opened and Erin came in.

"Are you all right?" she asked kindly.

"Embarrassed," Lisa murmured. Cupping her hands, she took a sip of water.

Erin looked at her sympathetically. "Morning sickness is part of the package."

"This is the first time for me. At least, it is as far as I know." A sudden, unbidden thought chilled her to the bone. Her head came up sharply. "Oh, Lord, what if it isn't? What if I've got other children who don't know where I am? What if—"

"Lisa, stop," Erin ordered firmly. "You'll make yourself crazy. If you do have children, the chances are excellent that they're being cared for and will be perfectly fine until you can get back to them."

Staring at Erin's reflection in the mirror above the sink, Lisa caught her breath, then let it out slowly. Erin was right, and as she became aware of how extreme her reaction had been, a little of the anxiety seeped out of her.

Erin continued on a sensible note. "If it will make you less worried, have a doctor examine you. She can tell whether you've ever delivered a baby. Maybe they even did an examination at the hospital while you were unconscious, to see if your pregnancy was threatened by the accident, in which case, all you have to do is call and ask." She concluded with a little shrug and a reassuring smile.

Lisa sighed. "Actually, I'm not sure I even want to know right now. I've already got more to worry about than I can handle—like, for instance, how I'm going to take care of *this* baby. It seems, with what you've told me, that I may be unemployed.''

"Well, I have some ideas about that, too." Studying her, Erin said, "You look better. Are you ready to go sit down again?"

"I think so."

They left the ladies' room and began walking slowly back toward the table.

Halfway there, Erin said, "Birth Data, Inc., is part of a larger organization called the Stone Foundation. It was started by my husband, Travis Stone. We have many different programs, and I think we could help you."

Lisa shook her head. "I don't want to take anybody's charity."

"Would you take a job with us?"

She gave Erin a surprised look. "I—I suppose so, but...well, what sort of job? I don't remember any of my technical background."

Erin stopped beside their table. "I can arrange for aptitude tests. Then we'll have a better idea of what you've studied and where your interests lie."

Lisa's spirits rose a little. She might never be an architect again, but then, she had no memory of being one before. The important thing was that she'd have a job. Erin was offering her the chance to solve one of the many, seemingly unsolvable problems facing her. It felt good to be able to take positive action.

"Yes," she said. "That sounds fine. Thank you."

Erin slid into her seat. "It must be awful losing your entire memory—and on top of everything else! I can hardly imagine what you've been going through."

Looking down at the tabletop, Lisa fingered the spoon lying beside Mike's abandoned coffee as she muttered, "I have the feeling I don't want to remember the shambles I made of my life. If only I could—"

"Lisa."

She jumped at the sound of Mike's voice beside her.

"I'm sorry," he said. "I didn't mean to startle you."

Her hands fluttered at her waist. "It's okay. I just didn't see you."

"Are you all right?" he asked, glancing briefly at Erin, then back at her.

"As well as can be expected, I guess." She searched his gaze, wary of the urgency she saw reflected there. "Why? What's happened?"

"I have some news." His voice was grim.

The knot in her stomach tightened in anticipation.

"I checked in with my office from the car phone," he said. "There's been another murder."

Chapter Eighteen

Lisa could hardly bring herself to ask. "Who?"

"Estelle Bensinger."

She pressed her hand over her mouth. "Oh, Lord."

Holding her gaze, Mike went on. "She was found floating in the Inner Harbor—with a bullet in her back."

Lisa stared at him in numb silence, trying to grasp the implications of this latest catastrophe. The jingling of the bell above the shop door failed to break through her daze, but the sight of a uniformed policeman coming through the doorway yanked her back to the present with a snap.

"Oh, no," she gasped. "Mike…"

At her stricken look, he glanced over his shoulder. Then, without hesitation, he took her hand and pushed her into the booth, sliding in after her until she was tucked between him and the wall, their backs to the door.

"Sit tight. He's probably just getting a cup of coffee," he hissed as he cupped his arm around her shoulder.

She huddled next to him, heart pounding, her gaze riveted on Erin, whose eyes followed the policeman's progress. Lisa expected that any second the officer would stride over, grab her by the shoulder and whip out a pair of handcuffs. Several horrible minutes passed before she saw Erin's tense features relax.

"He's gone," she said. "Mike was right. He only wanted a cup of coffee."

Lisa let out the breath she'd been holding. Without thinking, she turned her palm up to clasp Mike's hand and lowered her head to his shoulder. "Thank you," she whispered.

His acknowledgment was little more than a grunt, and it made her remember that she didn't have any right to lean on him. Straightening, she detached her hand from his, her cheeks growing warm under Erin's curious gaze.

"I hate feeling like a fugitive," she said, her voice strained and ragged. "What if I just go home? To the address I listed on my application." As soon as she'd said it, she thought, wait a minute, bad idea. Given the new knowledge of Hollingsworth's and Estelle Bensinger's murders, it seemed almost certain that the two men who'd broken in that morning had been looking for Justine, not her. But suppose they'd been sent by her baby's father—the man who'd threatened to get her fired. Philadelphia would be the first place anyone wanting to harm Leigh Barnes would look.

"No, forget it," she said.

"Right," Mike agreed. "You're in danger. And the only thing we know for sure is that whoever's after you isn't Kendall Hollingsworth. He's dead. So is his secretary. It seems pretty clear to me that Justine is high on the hit list. And even if they realize you aren't Justine, they might *still* follow you home because they think, by now, you know too much." Mike shook his head slowly. "The way I see it, you have one choice. You've got to lie low for a few days until we figure out who's behind the murders."

He was right. Lord help her, she knew he was right. But she wasn't only terrified for herself and the baby. She raised reddened eyes to Mike. "They know you're helping me. Maybe they wanted to kill you this morning, too."

"I can take care of myself," he repeated his earlier assurance.

She dragged in a shaky breath, knowing there was no use arguing with him. But he wasn't the only one she was endangering.

"I can't go back to Jenny's. I can't put her in jeopardy, too."

"There isn't a snowball's chance in hell that anybody's going to know you're there," Mike assured her. "The only way they'd know is if they followed us, and you can damned well bet I'm not going to let that happen. I'll drop you off. Then I'll show up at the office, so anyone keeping tabs on me will see I'm alone."

She didn't bother arguing. She knew it wouldn't do any good.

"I hate to leave you like this," Erin said.

Gathering what wits she had left, Lisa asked, "May I take my folder? Maybe looking at it will trigger a memory."

"You can take the copy. I need the original."

Lisa folded the papers and put them into her purse. "Erin, you've been a tremendous help. I can't tell you how it feels to know that I *am* somebody. I may not remember my past or my current life, but having facts about them makes a big difference."

"I'm glad." Erin handed Lisa a business card and started toward the door. "Call me if there's anything else I can do."

Lisa watched Erin's departing figure, then, as Mike rose to leave, dragged herself after him to his car.

Dropping into the passenger seat, she leaned back, exhausted. From the corner of her eye, she watched him drive. His eyes seemed fixed on the road ahead, yet every few moments his gaze flickered toward her.

"Well, are you going to tell me about your lover?" he finally asked as he wove though the traffic.

She stared at his hands. They were clamped around the wheel so tightly that the knuckles were white. "I still don't remember anything," she said. "According to Erin Stone, I don't have a lover."

"So it was an immaculate conception?"

She folded her hands in her lap. "It seems I was involved with someone who didn't like the idea of fatherhood. He wanted me to have an abortion."

She saw his jaw tense, and a second or two later, he said, "You can force him to cough up child support."

Lisa shivered as she recalled Erin saying the man had threatened to get her fired. "I don't think so."

A few minutes of silence passed before Mike spoke again, his tone reluctant and a little bitter. "Did you love him?"

She wanted to say, no, she hadn't. The best she could do—with honesty—was, "Erin didn't say. I guess I didn't tell her."

Silently, Lisa wondered if she could have slept with a man she didn't love. She hoped not. Yet she also couldn't imagine falling for the kind of person who would have tried to force her to have an abortion.

"I only know one thing for sure," she whispered. "I love this baby."

She waited tensely for Mike to say something. When he didn't respond, she gradually felt herself giving in to numbing fatigue. Letting her eyes drift closed, she allowed sleep temporarily to bury some of her anxiety.

MIKE DROVE toward Jenny's house, trying to ignore the woman sleeping next to him. But his eyes kept wandering from the road to her. She was slumped at an angle, so he couldn't see much of her face, only the gentle curve of her cheek and the small slope of her nose. He wished he didn't find them so appealing.

What a sucker he was. Twice in his life he'd let himself care about a woman, and both times, he'd been screwed. Used. Taken in. Whatever he called it, it amounted to the same thing: it hurt. Bad. Bad enough that he couldn't shrug it off or push it away or pretend it didn't exist. But this time, he admitted, was worse than the last. This time, he cared more about the woman.

Which was maybe why he was so angry. Where the hell did Lisa get off, thinking it was okay to make love with him without mentioning that she was pregnant? Despite her rationalization, somewhere, someplace, she did have a past, and it did matter. She couldn't simply ignore it.

He couldn't ignore it, even if he did understand her argument that she might never remember her old life.

Unfortunately, he also couldn't ignore the overwhelming tenderness and protectiveness that he felt toward her. It had been bad enough, knowing she was lost, without a memory, while people were running her off roads and trying to rape and kill her. It hadn't helped to get to know her, to find out she was as warm and loving as she was bright and engaging. But, ironically, knowing she was pregnant was the final straw. It made everything he felt about her a thousand times worse.

He wanted her, wanted to be with her, wanted to protect her. And nothing he told himself about how she'd betrayed his trust made a bit of difference. Yeah, he was angry and hurt. But he was old enough and mature enough to realize that his anger and hurt were mostly leftovers from Justine's betrayal; they had little, if anything, to do with Lisa. And if the man who'd fathered her baby was really the bastard it sounded like…well, she was probably right, he didn't matter, and she was better off not remembering him.

Mike clenched his teeth. He couldn't walk away from her. Not now. Not, at least, until he knew she was safe. Then…hell. Face it. He didn't know what he was going to do.

IN THE SMALL WAITING ROOM at Birth Data, Inc., Benita sat nervously next to Ed, twisting the strap of her oversize purse. Ed hadn't wanted her to make the two-hour car trip from Philly to Baltimore, but she'd insisted with as much of her old energy as she could muster. Finally, when he'd realized that taking her where she wanted to go was the only way to give either one of them any peace, he'd agreed.

When the office door opened, she looked up eagerly.

"I'm Erin Stone," a slim young woman said. "Can I help you?"

Benita started to push herself to her feet. Ed levered an arm under her elbow to help her. "I'm Benita Fenton. And this is my husband, Edward. I called you about my daughter."

"Oh, yes."

"We drove down from Philadelphia to give you a special picture of her that I had made. I thought it might help you find her."

Mrs. Stone nodded, although she looked a little puzzled. Benita figured she was wondering why anyone would come so far to deliver a photo in person. Benita didn't want to explain herself. She'd been seized by a terrible urgency that if she didn't get the ball rolling right away, she wouldn't live long enough to see her daughter. She hadn't even been able to tell Ed. She sure couldn't tell this stranger, no matter how kind she looked.

"Why don't you come into my office?" Mrs. Stone suggested.

Benita shuffled after her, with Ed silently bringing up the rear. When they were all seated, Benita unsnapped her purse and brought out a large envelope.

"After I wrote to you, I sent Ed to the library to do some research." She gave her husband a little smile. "He found out about a new technique, where they take a picture of a missing child and somehow they put it into a computer. They use the computer to add years to the person's face. Make them look the way they would now."

Mrs. Stone nodded. "Yes, I've seen it done."

"Well, I found a place that would do that for me. And I wanted to bring you the picture of Andrea as soon as possible." Opening the envelope, she looked at her daughter's face, amazed once more at the transformation. It was her precious Andrea, but she looked so grown-up. Passing the altered photo across the desk to Mrs. Stone, she said, "Isn't she pretty?"

"Oh!" Mrs. Stone gasped, her eyes widening.

"What's wrong?" Benita asked worriedly.

"This is your daughter—Andrea?"

Benita gripped the arms of her chair. "Tell me! Has something terrible happened to her?"

"I—I don't know," Mrs. Stone began, then quickly continued. "I talked to a woman this morning who contacted us to help find her birth parents. She looks like this enhanced photo of your daughter." She picked up a folder from her desk and hastily scanned the contents. "But according to the information she gave us, she was adopted by Sheila and William Barnes."

Benita suddenly felt hot all over. Leaning forward in her chair, she said, "If she looks like my Andrea, I've got to see her. Right now. I'll know if I see her." Her voice rose in panic. "You are going to give me her address and phone number, aren't you?"

Ed slung an arm around his wife's shoulders. "Honey, take it easy. You know what the doctor said about getting over-excited."

Her heart was pounding against her chest like a kettledrum, but she shook him off. "Ed, don't fuss."

"Mrs. Fenton, does Andrea have any distinguishing marks?" Mrs. Stone asked.

Benita frowned. "Marks? I'm not sure.... I... Oh, yes. There's a scar—about three inches long, I'd say, on her right thigh. You remember, Ed, the time when she was nine. She fell on a soda bottle and broke it. I'd never seen so much blood. Even when it healed, you could still see that scar." Benita began to sweat, the beads of moisture rolling down her face. "Mrs. Stone, you've got to help me find her."

"I'll do my best."

Benita gave her a weak smile that turned into a grimace as a sudden crushing pain spread through her chest, up her neck and down her left arm. With a low moan, she slumped in the chair.

"Oh, my God!" Ed gasped. "It's her heart. Mrs. Stone. Please, call 911. We need an ambulance."

LISA WOKE to an odd combination of sensations—warmth and contentment mingled with small physical discomforts. Grimacing a little at the crook in her neck, she realized vaguely that she was curled against Mike with her head on his chest, one hand hooked over his shoulder and the other gripping a fistful of his sweatshirt. His arm was curved around her hip.

Enveloped by his warmth and his familiar scent, she thought hazily about the taste of him...and the feel of his hands on her body. She snuggled closer, then lifted her mouth for a kiss, sighing in anticipation of feeling his lips cover hers.

Instead, she felt every muscle in his body go rigid. Her eyes blinked open in time to catch a yearning look on his face, but his features quickly became an expressionless mask. And suddenly she remembered. She wasn't supposed to be in his arms. He was furious with her over her lie of omission.

Her face turned hot with embarrassment, and she quickly looked away. Sitting up slowly, she said, "I'm sorry. Why didn't you wake me?"

"You needed some sleep."

"I need..."

"What?"

She wanted to say "you." Instead she said, "Courage." Tears hovered behind her eyes. Lord, she was turning into an automatic watering system. Press an emotional button, and she cried.

Opening the car door, she made for the house. But her knee had stiffened since she'd whacked it, and she stumbled. Mike caught her.

"I'm okay." She waved off his help.

"You should have put ice on that knee."

"I wasn't thinking about it."

She took another step and winced, and he swung her into his arms.

"Mike, you don't have to carry me. I can walk."

"Shh." He ignored her weak protest, carrying her across the gravel driveway toward the porch.

Closing her eyes, she anchored her arms around his neck and pressed her face against his shoulder. He shifted her weight as he searched for Jenny's key in his pocket. Pushing open the door, he crossed the living room and stood in front of the sofa for several seconds without setting her down, as if he was reluctant to let her go. Finally, he lowered her to the sofa. She stared up at the wet patch where her face had been pressed against his shirt. He followed her gaze, looked momentarily embarrassed, then seemed to snap into another gear.

"Ice," he said.

"What?"

He cleared his throat. "Ice. For your knee."

"Oh." She looked at her leg, feeling helpless and hating it. "I guess."

He turned and strode into the kitchen, where she heard him yanking drawers open, rummaging through them and slamming them closed.

Slipping off her shoes, she stretched out on the couch and tried to focus on her surroundings. The room was sunny and welcoming. Jenny's home was very appealing, with lots of warm colors, handmade pottery and paintings on the wall.

As Lisa studied a pink and green Mexican bird on the mantelpiece, a fantasy began to play through her mind: she and Mike were a married couple and this was their house. She'd hurt her knee, and he was worried. He'd gotten very protective since she'd told him that she was pregnant....

The fantasy spun out pleasantly for a few minutes, then came to an abrupt halt when Mike returned with a towel-wrapped bundle of ice.

"Are you all right?"

She nodded.

"Your face is flushed."

"Hormones, I guess."

He sat beside her, and she thought for a minute that he was going to roll up the leg of her sweatpants—*his* sweatpants.

"Um..." He hesitated.

Rather than wait for him to ask her to perform the task, she simply reached down and did it. She tried not to wince as the fabric grazed her knee. Her skin was marked with a large purple bruise.

"You'd better put this on," he said, carefully handing her the towel without touching her hand.

She gingerly set the lumpy compress in place. "That should help. Thanks."

"Uh-huh."

"Why did you leave the police force and become a private detective?" she asked.

He looked startled. "What kind of question is that?"

"A personal question."

Standing up, he crossed the room. "Then why are you asking?"

She regarded him steadily. "What do I have to lose? Of course, you don't have to answer if you don't want to."

He hesitated briefly, then spoke in a flat tone. "I was set up to take the fall in a drug bust that went bad. I resigned rather than go through a bunch of garbage with Internal Affairs."

Lisa frowned. "Set up? By whom?"

"A faction I'd annoyed."

"A faction? You mean in the department? Policemen do that to each other?"

"I made some enemies in high places. Questioned authority. That kind of thing."

Lisa was indignant. In fact, it stunned her to realize how angry she was about the injustice done to him. She had to work hard to tamp down her anger in order to speak.

"Is that why you didn't want me to turn myself in?" she asked.

"Yeah. Most cops are okay. But they can get overzealous when they're being squeezed for results. "

"Then aren't you taking a chance by harboring a fugitive?"

"I'm used to taking chances."

On some things, she wanted to say.

Their gazes seemed to touch over the invisible wall that stood between them. The telephone made them both jump.

Mike answered it. "Yes. She's here." Handing her the receiver, he said, "It's Erin. Do you mind if I listen in?"

She shook her head, then spoke to Erin, her voice shaky. "I didn't expect to hear from you so soon. Have you found something?"

Mike moved rapidly out of her line of vision. In the background, she heard him pick up an extension.

Erin asked, "Does the name Andrea Fenton mean anything to you?"

Lisa closed her eyes and tried to think. "Andrea Fenton... No."

"A Mrs. Benita Fenton is trying to locate her adopted daughter who ran away from home ten years ago. This morning, she brought us a computer-altered picture showing how the girl probably looks now."

Confused, Lisa said, "I thought you did searches for birth parents."

"That's usually true. But in this case, Andrea hasn't contacted the family since she left home." Erin paused. "Lisa, the picture looks startlingly like you."

Lisa drew a sharp breath, then grabbed her purse off the floor where she'd dropped it and pulled out the papers Erin had given her that morning. With trembling fingers, she found the application she'd filled out the week before. Swallowing hard, she asked, "Can you tell me if Andrea's birthday is May 12, 1966?"

Chapter Nineteen

"Yes," Erin answered. "That's right. May 12, 1966."

Breathless, Lisa said, "That's the date I put on my application."

"It's Justine's birthday, too." Mike's voice carried a trace of excitement as he spoke from the extension.

Lisa felt the hairs on her neck stand up and gooseflesh race down her arms. When Erin told her she was adopted, she'd wondered if she and Justine were twins, but it hadn't seemed likely. Now it seemed not only likely but probable.

"Mrs. Fenton was quite upset," Erin continued. "She, um, had a heart attack in my office, which makes her search a matter of some urgency."

"Oh, no!" Lisa gasped. "Is she all right?"

"She's in the hospital, in stable condition."

"The poor woman!"

"Erin," Mike cut in, "do you think Lisa may be this woman's daughter?"

"Fenton isn't the name I gave for my mother," Lisa pointed out, looking at the application she was clutching. "I put that my mother was Sheila Barnes. And my father was William Barnes."

"You could have given false information," Mike said.

His words brought a stab of pain. She realized immediately that he was implying she might have deliberately lied—after

all, she'd lied to him. But she couldn't allow his lack of faith
in her to get in the way of her quest. With effort, she spoke
in a reasonable tone. "What would have been the point of
my doing that?" When he didn't reply, she suggested,
"Maybe Mrs. Fenton is Justine's mother. Maybe Justine ran
away from home and changed her name."

Mike uttered a harsh laugh. "Sure. Why not?"

"Well, there may be a way to find out," Erin said. "Mrs.
Fenton told me her daughter has a three-inch scar on her right
thigh."

Fumbling to tug her pants down below her hips, Lisa
thought how absurd it was that she had to look—how bizarre
it felt not to know her own body. Exposing her right thigh,
she examined the skin. It looked and felt smooth as she ran
her fingers from hip to knee.

"I—I don't see any scars," she said, readjusting her clothing. "I guess it could have faded since Mrs. Fenton last saw
it. But I just don't see why I would have put Sheila Barnes
on my application if my adoptive mother was Mrs. Fenton.
It doesn't make sense. I mean, if I was really interested in
locating my birth parents, it would have been plain stupid not
to provide accurate information."

"That's certainly true," Erin agreed.

Reluctantly, Lisa asked, "Mike, did Justine have a scar?"

He was silent for a moment, and, when he did finally answer, his tone was gruff, as if he didn't want to admit he
knew the answer any more than she had wanted to ask the
question. "No. At least I don't remember one."

Lisa sighed. "Of course, that would have been too easy.
Erin, what else did Mrs. Fenton tell you?"

"When she first contacted us," Erin replied, "she sent a
copy of her daughter's original birth certificate."

Lisa's fingers tightened on the receiver. "With my birth
parents' names?"

"Well…Hallie Albright and Garrett Folsom. They're your
birth parents—if you're the Fentons' daughter, or if you and

Justine are sisters and *she's* their daughter. Or if, somehow, you're their daughter's sister. But if you're Justine's sister, and Justine *isn't* their daughter, that would mean there are three of you, wouldn't it? God, Lisa, I'm getting as confused as you must be about all this.''

"Erin, I don't know what to say. Hallie Albright and Garrett Folsom aren't any more familiar to me than Sheila and William Barnes were. But I guess that doesn't mean anything.''

"I can tell you're upset,'' Erin said. "I'm sorry. I was hoping the information might help you remember something.''

"I was hoping so, too,'' Lisa murmured. "And I really do appreciate your help. I keep expecting one of these pieces of information—a name, a date—to trigger my memory, and for it all to come flooding back, but it doesn't happen.'' She gave a small, humorless laugh. "I guess a lightning bolt will have to strike me first.''

Erin had to ring off then, when her next appointment arrived. Dazed and slightly giddy, Lisa didn't move until she'd heard Mike hang up the extension, then, with a sigh, she carefully replaced the receiver.

She should be excited, hopeful, about the new information. She had names to work with now—lots of them. And a birth date. But the date was only a spot on the calendar. And the names meant no more to her than the label on one of Justine's designer dresses. Less. She'd heard of some of the designers. The thing that bothered her most, though, was the near certainty that she and Justine shared some familial connection. How could she feel excited or hopeful about being related to someone she found just short of loathsome, from the way she decorated her mansion to the way she had treated Mike?

She glanced up to see Mike standing in the doorway, watching her with an unreadable expression on his face. One more reason to dislike Justine, she thought. For she was certain that it was the memory of Justine's betrayal, more than anything she herself had done, that had turned him away from her. He was afraid of being hurt again, and so he was making himself as inaccessible to her as a stranger.

He shifted his weight slightly. "I'd better get down to the office."

She felt a hollow place open in the region of her heart. She had the terrible feeling that if he left now, she would never see him again.

"You look like you're suffering from information overload," he said.

"Yes." Sitting up a little straighter, she tried to dispel her dark thoughts. "Erin's given me some facts, but they don't touch me inside, where it counts. It's a weird feeling."

Mike took a few steps into the room. "Will you be all right by yourself?" he asked.

"Yes," she lied, figuring she'd better start remembering how to be independent. "It's probably better, anyway. I—I need to sleep."

Mike paused by the couch. Their eyes locked, and the moment stretched. She felt her heart pound as they regarded each other. She waited for him to say something, but he remained silent, his eyes and hers the only point of contact. Then he broke the connection. Giving her a brief nod and a mumbled "I'll see you later," he walked out the door. And she was left sitting on the couch, alone.

BY AN EFFORT OF WILL, Mike kept his mind on business as he drove into downtown Baltimore. As soon as the autopsy report on Hollingsworth was available, he was going to call in a favor and get the results. Meanwhile, he wanted to find out what was happening with the two guys he'd left on his living-room floor. And he intended to accomplish both tasks without giving away the information that he had the prime suspect stashed in an Elkridge farmhouse.

The prime suspect. He didn't call her by name. Not even in his thoughts. He was trying hard not to feel anything about her. But unwelcome emotions like longing and need and compassion kept sneaking past his defenses. When they did, he felt his heart twist.

As he parked and walked out of the garage across from 43 Light Street, he couldn't stop picturing her face as he'd left Jenny's house. There were dark smudges under her eyes, her skin was pale and her mouth was pinched. He knew she'd wanted to ask him to stay, that she was afraid of what might happen in the next twenty-four hours. Probably even more afraid of the future. But she hadn't said a word. That had taken a kind of courage most people didn't possess. He admired her for it. He admired her for a lot of things.

HAND PRESSED against the knife under his shirt, Gary edged toward the side of the parking deck where he could watch the detective head for his office. Lancer was alone. So where was Justine? Or was it Leigh? He wasn't sure about her name anymore. But it didn't matter so much, he reassured himself.

She'd come running out of the house last night and he'd tried to catch her, but she'd gotten away in the car. This morning he'd been hoping he'd find her with the detective. Keeping low, Gary crept toward the car and took a quick look in the back seat. Empty. The girl wasn't hiding in the car.

Sinking to the oil-stained floor, he cradled his head in his hands. Sometimes when he tried real hard, he could make his brain work almost as good as it had before he'd gotten all messed up. He knew he could do it. He'd done it before. Like when he'd gone back to that no-good lawyer who'd helped screw up his life.

The guy was old and sick now. In a nursing home. Maybe, Gary figured, the lawyer had felt sorry about what he'd done all those years ago. He *should* be sorry. But it didn't matter anymore. The important thing was, for the first time, the old goat had given him some answers. Enough information for him to come to Baltimore and start nosing around.

A shiny sports coupe pulled in to park in the same lane of

cars as Lancer's Mustang, and a man got out. Gary went very still. It was another guy he'd seen at the Hollingsworths' estate a couple of times. *Señor* something or other. Mostly he didn't drive himself around. Usually he was sitting in the back of a big black car with a chauffeur in the front.

So what was he doing down here alone? Did he know where to find Leigh?

Maybe, Gary thought. And maybe he ought to follow him. Yeah, that was what he should do, all right.

THE DOOR TO O'Malley and Lancer was unlocked. When he entered the waiting room, Mike could see Jo sitting at her desk, talking on the phone. She gestured toward his office, indicating that someone was inside. Apparently, whoever it was wanted privacy, because the door was closed.

The cops?

Trying to keep cool, he planned what he would say to them. He also prepared for a fight, in the event that it was another pair of goons.

When he pulled open the door, the breath froze in his lungs. She was sitting in the easy chair in the corner, looking very much the way she had when he'd left her a half hour ago— dark circles under her eyes, pale skin, and tension lines around her mouth. What struck him hardest, though, were the ways in which she *didn't* look like the woman he had left sitting on Jenny's couch. The differences were indefinable, yet, to him, couldn't have been more obvious. He wondered how he ever could have been fooled.

"Justine. Where the hell have you been?"

The slender redhead gave him a cool smile. "Minneapolis. I got in last night." At his surprised look, she shrugged. "It seemed as good a place as any to lie low. But I've been keeping tabs on the situation."

"How?"

She brushed a hand lightly across the front of her tight blue skirt. "Maggie told me about the woman's accident and amnesia when I called, pretending to be one of my friends from the country club. After that, I got some information from the hospital. How does my double fit into the picture? Did you bring her in to pinch-hit for me?''

Without answering, Mike crossed to his desk and sat down. He couldn't take his eyes off her. Couldn't stop his brain from cataloging the subtle differences between her and Lisa. Justine was polished in a way Lisa would neither care nor seek to be. Thank God. Justine was hard, even cruel, where Lisa was soft and warm and almost too sensitive for her own good. Justine looked like a woman with an agenda. She also looked too damned skinny. And he could think of a lot of other ways to describe her, too, none of them flattering.

"No," he replied to her question. "She got tangled up in your life by accident." Pausing, he added, "She's most likely your twin sister."

It was with considerable satisfaction that Mike saw Justine's face go even paler.

"That's impossible!" she snapped.

He shook his head slowly. "It isn't if you're adopted and your birth mother had twins."

She stared at him, her composure slipping another notch. "I am adopted. But I—I didn't know there were…two of us." Giving her head a quick shake, she spoke briskly, "But at the moment, I've got other things more pressing to worry about than some long-lost sister."

"Apparently." Mike picked up a pen from his desk and pulled a pad of paper in front on him. "You say you've been keeping tabs on the situation around here. So you know Kendall is dead?"

"Yes. That's why I'm in your office. As his widow, I'm going to inherit a sizable fortune. And I wouldn't want my stand-in to get the inside track."

Mike's voice turned steely. "But you were content to let her cope with the chaos you left behind."

She lifted one slender shoulder in a delicate shrug. "She gave me some breathing space."

How could he ever have been so entranced by her? It didn't help much to remind himself that he'd been young and immature. He felt he should have seen the seeds of callousness and avarice in her from the start. But then, those seeds had been buried beneath the shining surface, and he hadn't had enough experience with intimate relationships to know how to see beneath that surface. When Justine met Kendall Hollingsworth, the seeds had sprouted, taken root and grown like weeds to choke out anything that might have been worth having. God, how she'd changed.... God, how lucky he felt to be free of her.

Slowly laying his pen on top of the pad of paper, he spoke in a glacial tone. "What do you want from me, Justine?"

She shifted in her chair so that her skirt rode up a little farther, giving him what he guessed was supposed to be a tempting view of her legs. "You're the best, Mike," she said. "I know you can protect me—while I probate the will." At his complete lack of response, she added quickly, "When the will is settled, I'll be able to pay you a lot more than that measly five thousand."

"I thought the fee was fair."

She lowered her lashes and smiled. "There could be substantial fringe benefits."

He didn't want to hear about them much less accept them, but this wasn't the time to say so. He kept his expression carefully neutral.

"I've missed you," she said. "You and I had something good together. And now...well, with Kendall gone..."

"You and I could pick up where we left off," he finished for her.

"I knew you'd understand."

He understood, all right, and it made his stomach turn.

"I, uh..." She fidgeted a bit with the strap of her purse. "I know something you'll be interested to hear."

"Yeah?"

"It was Kendall who had you framed in that drug bust. He's the one who got you off the police force."

Caught off guard, Mike couldn't hide his surprise. "*You* knew?"

"Mike, I learned about it last year, but there was nothing I could do then. I'm telling you now."

And he was supposed to thank her? Clearly, she thought he should be grateful for the information.

His face hardened once more into a mask. "Tell me exactly why you came to me a couple of weeks ago," he said.

She squirmed a little in her chair. "It's complicated."

"Let's start with some basic information. Do you know who killed Kendall and Estelle?"

Her head jerked up, and she met his gaze directly, her eyes wide with astonishment. "Estelle's dead?"

She wasn't faking it, he decided. She really hadn't known.

"She was found floating in the Inner Harbor this morning," he told her. "With a bullet in her back."

Still holding his gaze, she whispered, "Kendall could have killed her—if he knew she was helping me."

Mike frowned. "Let me get this right. You and Estelle were working together on something?"

She nodded. "We had a deal. She took some papers from Kendall's office for me. Stuff about his San Marcos construction project with Johnny Realto that I could use as insurance."

Lisa had asked about Realto, Mike remembered, but when he'd checked, the man's name hadn't come up in connection with the K. H. Group. "Explain it to me—slowly," he ordered.

Justine brushed away an imaginary stray hair from her face, and he noted that her hand was trembling.

"Realto's a silent partner," she said. "I think he lives in Miami."

"Why would *you* need insurance?"

She flushed. "Okay. I was stupid enough to sign a prenuptial agreement. If Kendall wanted out of the marriage, I would only get a minimum settlement.''

"He wanted a divorce?'' Mike asked, understanding a little better why she hadn't been perfectly straight before. Kendall was her trophy husband, so to speak. If he didn't want her anymore, it meant that she was a failure.

"We weren't, uh, getting along all that well,'' she murmured. "I didn't know if I could hold it together.''

"Why would Estelle want to help you? Wasn't she his devoted executive assistant?''

Justine gave a harsh laugh. "Sure. And his mistress. I've known that for years, but I didn't care because it took some of the sexual pressure off me. It turns out the two of us weren't enough for him. He was cheating on her, too.''

Mike digested the information quickly. "Let's go back to the papers.''

With a sigh, Justine explained, "They're construction specifications for the housing projects Kendall is building in San Marcos. Realto has government connections down there. He arranged to have the inspectors pass on stuff that's not up to code. The partnership was saving millions of dollars by cutting corners.''

"So you could have put Kendall in jail by spilling the beans,'' Mike concluded.

She nodded.

"And Realto.''

"Yes.''

"Well, that would certainly piss them off—if they found out.''

A look of genuine fright crossed her features. "Yes, that's why I hid the specs before I left. I was afraid if Kendall caught me with them, he'd kill me then and there.''

"So why did you come back last night?''

She shot him a quick glance. "I got nervous wondering what that woman who looks like me might be doing in my house. I couldn't stand it anymore. I had to make sure the specs were safe. And they aren't. They're gone, Mike, and I'm scared.''

He watched her try to control her features. She was right, Hollingsworth would have killed her if he'd thought she was going to expose his scam. But the danger hadn't ended with Hollingsworth's death.

"Help me, Mike," she said in a small voice.

"I'll try," he answered, not for old times' sake or because he still wanted what she might deign to give him. He'd do it because, at this point, helping Justine meant helping Lisa.

"But this time I need the truth. Did you kill Hollingsworth?" he asked bluntly.

She drew back, indignant. "No."

"Where did you go last night after you left the estate?"

"I have a room at the Hyatt Regency."

That much he could verify. He wished her vow of innocence could be proven as easily because she could be lying through her teeth, and he wouldn't know it.

THE RINGING OF THE PHONE catapulted Lisa from a restless sleep, dogged by nightmares. Her eyes snapped open, and she was overwhelmed by a crushing feeling of loss.

Mike. Where was Mike? For an instant, she didn't even know where she was. Then the phone rang again, and suddenly the details of Jenny's living room swam into focus.

She sat up and reached for the receiver, scattering the Birth Data, Inc., papers she'd been studying before exhaustion had claimed her.

"Hello? Mike?"

No one answered.

"Hello?" she tried again.

There was no reply except the moaning of the wind outside. It had begun to blow since she'd fallen asleep.

"Is anyone there?"

The line went dead, and she was left clutching the receiver. Carefully, she replaced it in the cradle, her still-foggy brain wondering vaguely who had been on the line. Wrong number or someone expecting Jenny?

Then all thoughts of the phone call evaporated as an image from the nightmare she'd been having flashed into her mind: a man with a charming smile. Yet the smile sent a chill up her spine.

She went very still, knowing with inexplicable yet terrifying certainty that she was teetering on the edge of something dangerous. Dangerous but significant. Lord, what was it about the man in the dream? It seemed suddenly that she'd been dodging him every time she woke up.

Her breath came rapid and shallow as she started to banish his face from her conscious thoughts, back to the place where she'd been hiding it. But something stopped her—the question leaping into her mind: Where would the image of that man's face take her? If she dared to go.

For a moment or two, she hesitated, frightened, trembling, the image still swimming hazily in her head. She felt repulsed by him, and her entire being revolted at getting any closer. But she'd reached the point where not knowing her past was a suffocating burden, much worse than anything she imagined she might learn. She knew she had to look, had to know. And the sooner, the better.

She pressed her hand to her face, hiding behind the screen of her fingers. Then, heart pounding, she concentrated on pulling the dream into her mind, reeling in the details.…

It had started at dinner in a restaurant with starched white napkins and gleaming cutlery. She was with a good-looking man. He was paying close attention to her, lavishing compliments on her. He had conservatively cut brown hair, laugh lines around his eyes…and strong, blunt fingers that she found appealing. He was older than she, more experienced, and she was flattered that he wanted to get to know her better. They talked about the contract her company had with his firm. And she nodded when he gave her advice, thinking how clever he was and how much she could learn from him. After dinner, they danced....

Sitting on Jenny's couch, Lisa began to tremble. The bad part was coming. She could feel it as every nerve in her body grew taut in anticipation. At the last minute, she tried to back out, tried to stop what she'd started. But then, abruptly, the choice was taken from her. The dream—the memory—sprang into her mind all at once, and in all of its hideous detail....

"I'll walk you to your room," her companion offered.

"You don't have to."

"You shouldn't be alone in a big city hotel at this time of night."

She opened her door, and he slipped inside with her.

"Hank, I have to catch an early flight."

He didn't listen. Reaching for her, he pulled her into his arms and ground his hips against hers.

"Hank, no."

"Don't tell me no. You've been sending me signals all week that you want to go to bed as much as I do."

"But I don't know you well enough—"

"We're going to get to know each other a lot better, honey."

She tried to break free from his grasp, but his arms tightened around her, and his mouth came down hard on hers. Frantic now, she pushed at his chest but he grabbed both her wrists in one of his hands.

"I know you're a nice girl," he soothed. "I know you have to pretend to resist. But you're as hot as I am, aren't you?"

"Let me go. Please. If I gave you the wrong impression, I'm sorry."

"Stop playing games. Relax and enjoy it." The advice was punctuated by his free hand closing over her breast.

She gasped. He cut off the sound with his lips. Then her back was pressed against the bed, and he was on top of her, pushing up her dress and tugging at her panty hose. He tore the clothing from her lower body and thrust painfully inside her, his hips pounding against her until his body convulsed....

OUTSIDE THE FARMHOUSE, thunder rumbled in the distance as Lisa sat hugging her knees and rocking back and forth on the couch. Choking sobs rose in her throat and escaped. And as the scene that had taken place on that hotel-room bed gradually receded, the door to her past swung open. Unlocked by the shattering encounter she'd been struggling so hard to repress, her memory flooded back, full force.

She sucked in a breath, drowning beneath the deluge. Lightning seemed to crackle inside her head, and each flash was a new memory that made her slender frame shiver and her teeth chatter with reaction. *This* was what she had prayed for. Yet she felt that the onslaught might tear her apart.

Recollections shook her body: the important contract she'd won for Williamsburg Architects; the business trip to Chicago to work out the details with Fairland International; Hank Lombard, the contract manager who'd been so enthusiastic about her work. They'd gotten along very well—until he'd pushed his way into her room and forced himself on her. What had she told Erin—that the father of her child had threatened to get her fired if she didn't have an abortion? Lord, it was true. He could, and probably would, do it. He and her boss at Williamsburg were longtime friends. So she'd taken a month's vacation—to try to find another job.

How helpless she'd felt. How powerless. Leigh Barnes. The brainy architect who didn't have a clue about men.

A sick feeling rose in her throat, and she pushed it down. With shaking hands, she reached for the Birth Data, Inc., application. She'd been pouring over the form, memorizing her birth date, her street address, where she'd gone to elementary school. But the entries had only been words. Now like magic, they'd become real.

Tears welled in Lisa's eyes and ran down her cheeks. She wasn't Benita Fenton's daughter at all. She was the much-loved daughter of Sheila and Williams Barnes. Yes, she remembered her adoptive mom and dad and the wonderful, loving home they'd provided. They'd been too old to adopt through an agency, so they'd found a lawyer who knew about a pregnant woman whose boyfriend had been shipped off to Vietnam. She'd always known she was adopted—and very precious to her parents.

They'd been so proud of her. She smiled as she remembered things about them: Dad teaching her to ride a bike and, later, getting her one of the first home computers on the market. The whole family gathered around the Christmas tree, eating cookies and hanging decorations. So many good memories. And a few that were painful.

Dad had died five years ago. Mom had broken her hip and gone into a nursing home, and she'd passed away last year. That was why Leigh—she—was still paying off medical bills.

Wiping tears from her face, she laid the application carefully on the coffee table, then sat back to draw a slow, deep breath. Now she knew. The worst—and the best.

MIKE COCKED HIS HEAD as he heard someone rush into the outer office. Then a loud, urgent knock sounded at his door.

"Come in," he called.

Erin tore into the room and stopped dead, a look of relief spreading across her face when she spotted Justine. But the look rapidly gave way to confusion. "You aren't Lisa," she said.

Justine straightened in her chair. "I'm Justine Hollingsworth, if that's what you mean."

"When I saw you, I thought—I hoped you were Lisa." She turned to Mike and raked her hand through her hair. "God, I'm sorry. After the Fentons left, I was doing some research on Lisa's birth mother—trying to contact the hospital where she was born. I should have put her file away, but I didn't think anything would happen."

"Slow down. Tell me what you're talking about," he suggested.

Erin drew a steadying breath. "I usually grab a bite at my desk, but Travis was downtown and asked if I wanted to go out to lunch. When I came back, Lisa's folder was missing."

He frowned. "Did anybody else put it away?"

"No." She shook her head. "Jenny thinks someone may have been in the office. She isn't sure because she was in the bathroom for a few minutes."

Fear clutched at him, making his voice curt as he asked, "What was in the folder?"

"The application Lisa filled out. My notes." Erin hesitated. "And the phone number at Jenny's."

Mike swore. "Anybody with a computer directory could figure out where she is."

"Call her. Make sure she's all right."

He was already reaching for the phone. He dialed, waiting tensely for the numbers to go through. When they did, all he got was a weird-sounding busy signal. "She may be talking to someone," he muttered, although he had no idea who she might call. "Or the line has been disconnected."

Erin waved an arm in a helpless gesture. "Mike, I'm so sorry."

"Not your fault. How could you imagine that your own office wasn't a safe place to leave papers?" Unlocking his bottom-right desk drawer, he pulled out his gun. He stood up and strode toward the door, saying, "I'm going out there."

"What about me?" Justine called after him. "We're having a conference."

"Not anymore."

"But *I'm* the one who paid you!"

Over his shoulder, he tossed, "I'll send you a refund." Then he slammed the office door closed behind him.

SHE HAD FOUND a kind of peace. Lisa sat alone with her memories for another hour. But, gradually, the desire grew to share the news with someone. With Mike. A little smile played around her lips. She could finally come to him whole and complete. She could tell him who she was, that she'd had a safe and happy childhood, that she'd done some good things in her life, that she wasn't a money-hungry, manipulative female who would use a man, then leave him for greener pastures.

She could tell him all those things—if he ever forgave her.

Her smile slowly faded. Who was she kidding? Mike was probably never going to forgive her or trust her again.

Something scraped against the window to her left, and for an instant, she froze. When she looked to the window, she saw that it was a tree branch swaying in the wind. The sky was darkening fast—the storm was getting close. She'd hardly been aware of it.

With a little sigh, she rose from the couch and wandered into the kitchen, where she set the ice pack in the sink and picked up the mug of soup she'd made after Mike had left. Earlier, although she hadn't felt hungry, she'd forced down a few swallows by reminding herself that she needed to eat for the baby.

The baby. It didn't matter how her child had been conceived. She'd come to terms with that, she recalled, before the accident. She remembered her doctor giving her the results of the pregnancy test, remembered being upset at first—and scared. Most of all, she remembered wishing her parents had been alive, because she'd never needed them more. But in all her turmoil and upset, she'd never once thought of rejecting the baby. Really, it had been easy to accept the life growing inside of her. In her mind, the baby had nothing to do with Hank Lombard. It was *her* child.

Outside, the wind tore at the trees, and a clap of thunder shook the old house. Lisa stood holding the soup mug, staring blindly at the magnetic braille calendar on the front of the refrigerator. As the thunder receded, she heard a noise somewhere behind her.

She jerked around, and her eyes flew to the window over the sink. It was open. Lord, she'd been so lost in her own world, she hadn't even thought of closing up the house.

She set the mug down and reached for the window, then froze, her hand halfway there. This time she was sure she heard something that didn't sound like any noise a storm might make. Thinking Mike had come back, she started to call his name, but then realized he wouldn't steal into the house unannounced.

Sliding open a drawer, she began to look for a knife or something she could use as a weapon, but only came up with dish towels. Trying to stay calm, she opened another drawer.

But it was already too late. She knew someone was in the room before she turned. Someone who smelled of expensive after-shave.

"Close the drawer and turn toward me slowly," a voice grated. When she hesitated, a large male hand clamped down on her shoulder and spun her around.

Chapter Twenty

A scream rose in her throat and bubbled out.

"Quiet! Don't move, or I'll kill you."

Lisa looked at the gun in his hand, then back at his eyes. *He'd do it,* she thought wildly. *He'd kill me without a moment's hesitation.* His eyes looked malevolent, boring into her, and…and she'd seen them before.

Staring at him in terrified confusion, she tried to remember: dark eyes and hair, temples flecked with gray and a complexion pitted with acne scars.

"Dr. Ray," she breathed. She'd come to think the late-night encounter in her hospital room had been a dream. But the man holding the gun to her ribs was all too real.

He smiled. "Yes. You remember our brief visit. But Ray is not my name. I'm Juan Realto. Johnny to my friends. But then, *señora,* I wonder if you do not know already who I am."

Lisa could hardly breathe, much less speak. Gasping, she managed to say, "Kendall Hollingsworth's partner?"

His eyes narrowed. "So you *do* remember me."

His tone was mild, even casual, but his look was fierce. Lisa realized dimly that her responses were critical, but she had no idea what he wanted to hear, what would satisfy him.

Trembling all over, she gave her head a tiny shake. "No. I—I only remember you…from the hospital. But Maggie said

Señor Realto sent me flowers, and…and when I—I asked who…who that was, she told me.''

He seemed to consider her answer, then he smiled again. ''I must say, *señora,* either you are telling the truth, or you missed your calling as an actress.''

''What do you want?'' she whispered.

The smile left his face. ''I want the documents Estelle Bensinger took from Kendall's files.''

''I don't have them,'' she whispered.

''You are lying,'' he said. ''I see it in your eyes.''

''N-no,'' she stammered, ''I only know there are some papers that Estelle wanted back from Justine. She came asking for them the day I left the hospital. She wanted them badly, but I…I didn't know what she was talking about. Because I'm *not* Justine. My name is Leigh Barnes. I swear it!''

He gave her a long, hard stare. Her heart pounded so hard she thought she would collapse, and she gripped the counter behind her for support as she waited for his verdict.

Finally he said, ''I believe you are not Señora Hollingsworth. But, unfortunately for you, I had a talk with Señorita Bensinger, and she told me everything—everything except where the stolen papers are now.''

''But I don't have them!'' Lisa insisted.

''Señors Ezrine and Ordway weren't so sure.''

''Ezrine and…'' Frantically, Lisa tried to think who he was talking about. ''The two men who tried to kill me by running me off the road.''

Realto scowled. ''Their orders were only to frighten you. *Pero* you do not have to worry about them anymore. They are gone, and I am here. Now we are going to see if pain will force you to tell me what you know. And if you know nothing more…'' He shrugged. ''*Sí, es la vida.* That is life. I must make certain that you cannot tell anyone else about my business dealings with my late lamented partner.''

He was going to kill her. He'd tortured and killed Estelle— Lisa was sure of it—and now he was going to do it to her. It didn't matter whether or not she was Justine. It didn't matter whether she told the truth or lied. Either way, she was going to die.

Realto gestured with the gun. "Into the living room where we can be more comfortable."

She couldn't fight him. Nobody else knew he was here and nobody was coming to save her. For a moment, despair overwhelmed her terror, and she nearly broke down in tears. Then she thought of the baby, thought about the injustice of her child's life being taken away before it had been given the chance to grow.

And she thought of Mike—of never seeing him again. Never loving him again. He was hurting so badly, thinking she'd selfishly made a fool of him. What if she never had the chance to convince him otherwise?

It could all end here. Unless somehow she found a way to stop this criminal lunatic.

In a flash, Lisa achieved a clarity of thought she hadn't possessed since the accident. With steely resolve, she let her shoulders sag, as if in defeat, and started walking toward the living room. But as she passed through the kitchen doorway, her hand shot out and gave the door a hard slam backward. The ploy took Realto by surprise, and the heavy wood hit him in the face. A split second later, the gun went off, several slugs tearing through the wood inches from her.

But she was already running full tilt for the front door. When she threw it open, the wind whipped her hair around her face and shoved her sideways. She pelted down the steps and across the yard, trying with every ounce of inner strength to ignore the shooting pain in her knee and simply run. At first, she had some dim idea of disappearing into the woods, but she quickly realized she wasn't going to make it. She could hear Realto behind her, breathing hard and cursing angrily, the wind carrying his words away on a high, keening note.

It was hopeless to think she could outrun him.

Veering left, she made for the barn, hobbling now in pursuit of a place to hide. As she yanked open the door and crossed the threshold, the gun cracked again. Two more shots. Did he have two left, she wondered, or was that only in the movies?

Near the door, a pitchfork stuck out of a bale of hay and she snatched it, then searched wildly for cover. With only seconds to spare, she made a dive for a dark corner.

TREES BENT and swayed along the roadside as Mike raced toward Jenny's house. When he turned into the driveway, lightning streaked across the sky and raindrops began to splatter his windshield. If he made it to the porch without getting soaked, he'd be lucky.

Halfway up the winding driveway, he heard the blood-chilling sound of gunfire. Outside.

"Oh, God..."

Pressing the gas pedal to the floor, he reached for the car phone. He'd stashed Lisa here to keep her away from the law—but saving her life was more important. Dialing 911, he quickly got the Howard County Police and requested help; at the same time, he swerved to a halt at the top of the driveway. When he grabbed his gun and jumped out, the first thing he noticed was the barn door was open. He was sure he'd left it closed. But what if he guessed wrong about where to find Lisa? Quickly he glanced at the surrounding woods. There were empty. No sign of movement. Eyes narrowed, he headed for the barn.

OUTSIDE, the storm broke, sending a torrent of rain onto the barn's metal roof. Lisa heard water begin to drip onto the concrete floor somewhere to her right.

In the cool darkness, she crouched behind a stack of hay bales, curling to her side to make herself as small a target as possible. Her knee throbbed abominably, and she rubbed it with one hand, the fingers of her other hand clutching the pitchfork.

Footsteps pounded on the concrete floor, and she felt every muscle in her body tense.

Realto's voice sounded, harsh and grating. "There is no way out, *señora*. I have you trapped. The longer you make me look for you, the angrier I will be when I find you."

Tough. Let him be angry. He couldn't be any angrier than she was.

"Come out, *ramera*. Whore."

Lisa gripped her makeshift weapon with both hands. It was hardly a match for Realto's gun, but it was all she had. And the long, pointed prongs could be lethal—if she had the opportunity to use them. It was either kill him or let him kill her baby, and, between those two extremes, there really was no choice.

Through the open door, a bolt of lightning split the sky. Hard on its heels, thunder shook the old building to its foundation.

Please, God, she prayed silently. *Let me save my baby. Give me the chance to be a good mother.* Paradoxically, alongside those prayerful thoughts, Lisa contemplated the best way to inflict damage with her dubious weapon.

Rain drummed on the roof. More drops found their way to the floor. Thunder clawed at the eaves, drawing her gaze upward. She scanned the rafters high overhead at the same instant a bright streak of lightning illuminated the shadowed space.

Her heart skipped a beat, then thudded painfully in her chest when she made out the profile of a man creeping across the loft. Realto had climbed a ladder to the second floor.

But no! Recognition sizzled through her like an electric charge. It wasn't Realto. It was Mike.

Gun drawn, he moved stealthily through the shadows. Could he see her from up there? She wanted to let him know where she was, but she didn't dare move.

Somewhere close, Realto was on the prowl again. She heard his footsteps crossing the floor and knew he wasn't bothering to hide his whereabouts. Why should he? He was confident of how this game of cat and mouse was going to end.

Waiting for him to pounce was agony. Worse, though, was watching Mike as he edged closer to the rim of the loft, closer to making himself a target. She wanted to scream at him to stay back, and she prayed as hard as she'd ever prayed in her life that he would be careful. That he wouldn't get killed trying to save her, because she'd never be able to live with it if he did.

Frantic for his safety, she scrambled furtively in the straw looking for something to throw to divert the gunman's attention. She found several loose clods of dry earth, and her hand closed around them, testing their weight. Then, cautiously, she lifted her arm, aiming at the boards of an open stall on the other side of the barn.

She was about to fling the clods, when metal clattered in the loft above, ringing clearly over the drumming rain. Realto whirled, lifted his gun and fired. Mike shot back, but the killer ducked into a stall and got off two more shots. Lisa watched in horror as Mike grunted and staggered backward.

Seeing him go down, something seemed to break loose inside her. She launched herself, half-crazed, pitchfork in front of her like a bayonet, at Realto's back. But before she reached her target, inexplicably, she was flung aside.

The pitchfork went flying, and she landed in a heap on the straw, gasping for breath and utterly confused. Then, as she struggled to a sitting position and looked to see what had hit her, a hysterical sound—half scream, half laughter—escaped her. It was the tramp. The man in the fatigue jacket who'd been dogging her steps everywhere she went. Like a ghost or some grotesque kind of guardian angel, he'd materialized again, out of nowhere.

With a savage howl, he spun Realto around, knife in hand. The knife flashed as the tramp's arm came down, and the blade plunged into the side of Realto's neck.

For a split second, Realto went rigid, his eyes wide with shock. With a clunk, the gun fell from his hand. Then, with an eerie gurgling sound, he crumpled to the barn floor and lay still.

"You miserable scum," the tramp snarled, yanking the knife from his victim's neck.

Lisa hadn't a clue if the tramp was truly her guardian angel come to save her from certain death, or if he would go for her next. She didn't wait to find out.

Springing to her feet, staggering a bit as her injured knee rebelled, she looked frantically for a ladder up to the loft. When she spotted it at the other end of the barn, she ran toward it, leaving the vagrant crouched over Realto.

Gritting her teeth against the pain in her knee, she climbed up the rungs and made for the place where she'd seen Mike fall. He was sitting against a stack of hay bales.

"Mike! Oh, Lord!" she cried as she came down beside him.

His skin was gray and his breathing ragged. "Lisa..." He tried to sit up straighter, gulping air to speak. "Lisa, are you all right?"

"I'm fine." Anxiety strained her voice. "Where? Where are you hurt?" she demanded, feverishly running her hands over his chest, horrified at the amount of blood soaking his shirt. When she touched his shoulder, he winced.

"Oh, God, I'm sorry," she said. "Please don't die. I love you." She pressed her palm against his chest, wishing she could enfold him in her arms but afraid she'd hurt him worse.

His hand came up to cover hers. "I'm not going to die," he said, his voice a little steadier. "It hurts like hell, but it's not fatal. Knocked me over, though. Musta' hit my head. Clumsy." He gave a low grunt of disgust. "Just give me a minute. I'll be okay."

She wanted to believe him, wanted to believe he wasn't simply trying to reassure her as he quietly bled to death. Even as she watched, the blood continued to spread steadily across his shirt.

In the background, Lisa heard the wail of a siren.

"Are you sure you're all right?" Mike asked urgently, his eyes searching hers.

"Yes," she replied. "He didn't touch me."

His head fell back against the hay bales, relief momentarily wiping pain from his features. He sat with his eyes closed, his fingers wrapped tightly around hers, while Lisa listened tensely to the sirens getting closer.

Shaking his head as if to clear his thoughts, Mike opened his eyes to look at her. "What the hell happened after Realto nailed me?"

"That vagrant...you know, that man who—"

"The smelly guy in the fatigue jacket?" Mike's eyes widened. "He's *here?*"

She nodded. "He came out of nowhere. Just...jumped out of the shadows with his knife. I had a pitchfork, and I was going to try to stab Realto with it, but before I could, the tramp attacked him."

Mike started to say something, but suddenly the sirens screamed into the yard with a vengeance. Mere seconds later, the barn was filled with the sound of running feet.

Lisa cringed, huddling toward Mike.

"It's okay," he said. "I called the police when I drove in and heard gunshots."

Below them, she heard a man's voice snap, "What's going on here, buddy?"

Nobody answered.

Wincing, Mike pushed himself away from the hay bales and edged forward.

Lisa reached to stop him, but he shook his head urgently. "Got to tell them who's up here—before we get shot."

Numbly she listened while he shouted down, "This is Mike Lancer, private detective. I called the police. I'm up here with Lisa...Barnes."

He shot her a quick glance, and she guessed he was asking for approval of his choice of her name. She shrugged a little and nodded. It hardly seemed to matter.

Moments later, a face appeared over the edge of the loft.

It belonged to a uniformed officer, who quickly took in the situation.

"You okay?" he asked Mike.

"I'll live."

The uniform nodded. "An ambulance is coming. It won't help the guy on the floor, though. He's dead."

"The tramp stabbed him," Lisa said. And because she felt she owed the man a considerable debt, whoever he was and whatever his intentions toward her, she added, "He saved my life. The man who's dead—Juan Realto—was going to shoot me."

The cop's expression remained noncommittal. "Well, the guy's not saying anything. We're taking him in."

Drawing a deep breath, Mike started to get up.

"Mike, wait." She tried to stop him. "Let somebody help you."

But he waved her away. As he struggled to his feet, she could see he was determined to leave the loft under his own power. Heart in her throat, she watched him make his way awkwardly down the ladder, using one hand to grasp the rungs. At the bottom, he moved aside so she could follow, and she scrambled down as quickly as her knee would allow.

When she reached the ground, she turned to see that Mike was even paler and his forehead was beaded with sweat. He leaned heavily against one of the support posts, cradling his left arm against his body.

"Mike, you need to lie down," she said.

"No," he insisted. "I need to talk with the police. *Now,*" he added sharply.

Another officer strode through the door and approached them. He stopped in front of Lisa. "Is your name Justine Hollingsworth?" he asked.

Shaking inside, knowing she had no choice but to face this moment and get it over with, she met the officer's gaze directly. "No, my name is Leigh Barnes. I live in Philadelphia, and I work for Williamsburg Architects. I only look like Justine Hollingsworth.'' She didn't add that the resemblance was most likely due to their being twins.

The officer raised one eyebrow in a skeptical look. ''Do you have some identification?''

She hesitated, then admitted reluctantly, ''No. But if you talk to Erin Stone at Birth Data, Inc., she will identify me. I can give you her phone number and address.''

''What she said is true,'' Mike put in. ''And if you go to the Hyatt Regency in Baltimore, you'll find Justine Hollingsworth herself.'' When he caught her shocked glance, he nodded. ''She came into my office this morning and told me where she's staying.''

The officer's skepticism cracked a little, took on a mildly perplexed cast. But his confusion soon passed. ''Where were you last night between five and eight o'clock?'' he asked her.

Before she could reply, Mike snapped, ''You don't have to answer. You can demand that an attorney be present.''

She pressed her lips together and kept silent, although it seemed like postponing the inevitable. She didn't look at Mike, was afraid she'd come apart if she did. She had to get through this. And, Lord, she'd just escaped death, surely the worst was over.

It wasn't.

''You're going to have to answer sooner or later,'' the policeman said. ''You're under arrest for the murder of Kendall Hollingsworth. You have the right to remain silent. Anything you say can and will be used against you in a court of law. You have the right to an attorney…''

The rest of the words went by in a blur. This wasn't happening. It couldn't be. Not after everything else.

Mike shoved away from the post. ''Wait just a damn minute. You can't—''

''An arrest warrant's been issued,'' the officer cut him off. At the same time, he pulled out a pair of handcuffs and reached for her hands.

She croaked out a few words. ''No. Please. I didn't kill him.''

"Yeah, well, you'll get your chance to prove it," the officer said.

Lisa's gaze sought Mike's, her eyes filled with desperation. But he looked pale and sick and as helpless as she.

Sinking back against the support column, he rasped, "Lisa, don't say anything without talking to a lawyer first."

"I don't know any lawyers," she said, her voice a thready whisper.

"I do." He heaved a breath, squeezed his eyes closed. "Don't worry. It's going to be all right."

But it wasn't. Somehow, she knew it wasn't. When she'd gone into the river and hit her head, something had changed in the universe, and since then, nothing had been right. And at the moment she was thoroughly convinced that nothing would ever be right again.

It was too much. Far too much. She was beyond upset, beyond anger, beyond feeling anything.

She stood quite still while the officer snapped the cuffs around her wrists. The metal was cold against her skin.

Dimly, she was aware of Mike arguing with the policeman, and soon other officers came to intervene. She didn't hear what they said. She was somewhere else, floating out of her body, away from this place, this time, her conscious mind in a state of total shutdown—her only defense against the unendurable.

As the officer led her out of the barn, her feet moving automatically one in front of the other, she vaguely registered the rain pouring down to soak her clothing. It was cold. Cold like the handcuffs.

Cold like the bleak, empty future that stretched endlessly before her.

Chapter Twenty-One

"It's going to be all right." Mike's last words to her rang in Lisa's head as she lay on the narrow bunk in her tiny cell. She was trying hard to believe it but without success.

She scarcely remembered the process that had brought her here. She did remember being shuffled through several police stations, somehow landing in the Baltimore City Jail. She also recalled a judge pronouncing her a flight risk and refusing bail. Mostly, the past twenty-four hours were a blur. She thought she might actually have slept through a lot of it.

Amazingly, it seemed she'd slept through the night, as well, although conditions weren't conducive to rest. The place was hot, airless and crawling with bugs, and the smell was enough to make her gag. Still, she'd awakened somewhat revived—physically, at least. The problem was, the emotional turmoil that exhaustion had staved off had come flooding back.

At the moment, despair threatened to sweep away her sanity. Squeezing her eyes closed, she shut out the grimy walls covered with hateful messages scribbled by previous prisoners. But the imprint of the lumpy bed against her back was a constant reminder of her circumstances.

Despair gave way to fear. Not only for herself. For Mike. The thought that he might be in the hospital was driving her crazy. After all, the last she'd seen of him, he was dripping blood and close to collapse. She had to content herself with the knowledge that he'd been well enough to make a phone call, because he'd sent Laura Roswell to see her.

Laura had come early, announcing she was a colleague of Mike's and an attorney. Lisa had asked her immediately how he was, but all Laura could tell her was that his arm was in a sling. Then she'd forced Lisa to go back over the gory details of the past incredible week. Next, she'd demanded the police show her the autopsy report on Hollingsworth. Unfortunately, it named the cause of death as respiratory arrest brought on by a subdural hematoma resulting from a blow to the head. It hadn't helped Lisa's case at all.

At that point, Laura had advised her to tell the police everything—from the time of the car accident, to her escape from Hollingsworth's estate. The police were unimpressed. They had only her word that she'd been attacked. Given the autopsy report and her admission that she'd hit Hollingsworth, she was still the prime suspect. Moreover, they had checked the Hyatt Regency, and Justine wasn't registered, which reinforced their notion that *she* was Justine.

Laura Roswell had left saying she would make it a top priority to get Lisa some positive ID. Because, if she wasn't Justine, the only motive she would have had for hitting Hollingsworth was self-defense. Armed with every phone number and name Lisa could remember, starting with her colleagues at Williamsburg Architects, Laura had promised to make phone calls that afternoon. "Meanwhile," she'd told Lisa, "don't worry."

Easier said than done.

Lisa shifted a little, trying to get comfortable on the hard cot. The frustration of not being able to help herself was enough to make her scream. She wanted to be doing something. Anything! And the only thing she could do was lie here. And wait. And worry.

Down the hall, the heavy door to the lockup squeaked as it swung open. The sound was followed by purposeful footsteps drawing closer. They stopped in front of her cell, and she saw a prison guard and Ben Brisco, one of the detectives who'd interrogated her. Ben was tough-looking, but he wasn't as hard-nosed as Munson, the other officer who had questioned her.

"You've got a visitor," Brisco said.

Lisa sat up, her hopes surging. "Mike?"

"No." Brisco hesitated for a second, and she thought he was going to say something else. But all he said was, "Sorry."

Lisa's spirits plummeted. "So, who is it then?"

Brisco's reply was laconic. "You'd better see for yourself."

Sighing, Lisa sat up. She was hot. Mike's sweats that she'd put on yesterday morning were undoubtedly starting to smell, and she felt in dire need of a shower. Hardly a state in which to receive visitors. She didn't even have a brush for her hair. She winced as she stood up. Her knee was better, but it stiffened when she wasn't using it.

"You okay?" Brisco asked as the guard unlocked the cell.

"Mentally or physically?" she muttered, unable to keep the sarcasm out of her voice.

He muttered back, "Keeping you here isn't my idea."

She shot him a surprised look. Did she actually have an ally in this hellhole?

He gestured for her to precede him down the hall. They waited while the guard unlocked the gate, then he ushered her to one of the interrogation rooms. With the guard stationed outside, Brisco motioned her through the open door of the windowless, gray cubicle containing three metal chairs and a table that had seen better days.

But when she stepped into the room, it wasn't the decor that riveted her. It was the auburn-haired woman sitting with her hands clasped on the scarred tabletop. The woman was a copy of herself. Except that her hair was carefully coiffed, her makeup in place and she was wearing a blue silk blouse instead of ill-fitting, dirty sweats.

Lisa felt as if she'd had the breath knocked out of her, and she grabbed the back of a chair for support. For a full minute, she couldn't speak. Finally she managed to wheeze, "Justine?"

The woman raised her chin, and Lisa gazed into blue eyes that were mirrors of her own.

"That's right," the woman answered. Her voice was cool, but her wide eyes and pale, drawn expression told Lisa she was not unaffected at meeting her double.

With a scrape of metal against tile, Lisa pulled out the chair she was holding and dropped into the seat. Maybe, she thought, if she'd always known she was a twin, this experience wouldn't be so shattering. As it was, she'd had only the pictures in Justine's photo album as evidence of their similarities. And looking at a picture was nowhere near as unnerving as this.

"Wh—what are you doing here?" Lisa breathed.

Justine waved an impatient hand, looking as if she wished she was anywhere else on earth. "Mike made me come."

Before Lisa could comment, Brisco said, "Mike found her. After she left his office yesterday morning, she checked out of the Hyatt, where she was registered under another name, and checked into the Harbor Court."

Justine shot the detective an angry glare. "Do you really have to be here? I've already given you my statement, admitting I was at my house the night Kendall was murdered. That's all you're going to get."

"You were there?" Lisa gasped.

Tearing her heated gaze from Brisco, who remained steadfastly present, Justine looked at her. "I must have arrived after you'd gone. Kendall was already decked out on the bedroom floor."

Lisa frowned. "So, if you were there, why didn't you stay? Why did you wait for Maggie to find him dead?" And as a stunning thought hit her, she whispered, "Or did you kill him?"

"No, I didn't kill him," Justine muttered. "Although there've been times..." Recovering her composure, she shrugged. "I didn't stay for the same reason I went away in the first place. I needed some breathing space."

Lisa's jaw went slack. "And I gave it to you? How long have you known what was happening to me?" When Justine didn't reply, she guessed, "From the beginning?"

Still no reply.

Anger overriding shock, Lisa fixed her sister with a burning look. "I think you owe me some honesty, don't you?"

Justine tried to stare her down—and failed. Her gaze slid away. "Okay," she said, grudgingly. "I've known since the day after the accident. I called Maggie, pretending to be a friend of mine from the country club. She started babbling about your car going into the Jones Falls."

"And you let me go through hell, tangled up in your life, without saying a single word."

The slender shoulders rose and fell in a shrug. Justine fidgeted in her chair. "I was scared, all right? Is that so hard to understand? You saw enough of Kendall to know what he's like. I'd done something I knew would make him angry, and I was scared he'd find out. So I let you cover for me. And...well...I'm sorry."

She wasn't sorry, Lisa thought—at least not for what she'd done. She was only sorry that she'd been caught.

Lisa stared, repulsed, yet unable to look away from the woman she was forced to believe was her own flesh and blood. It was beyond her comprehension that one human being could use another as callously as Justine had used her.

She didn't know what to say. Truly, she didn't have *any-thing* to say to Justine, which saddened her deeply. She'd found a sister only to discover they didn't have a single thing in common.

No, that wasn't true. Incredibly, by some bizarre cosmic twist, they'd both been attracted to the same man. The difference was, she loved Mike. Lord knows what Justine had felt for him—but surely it wasn't love.

Lisa was saved from having to speak when Justine continued, her voice low and a little shaky. "You can't imagine what living with Kendall has been like. What did you have with him? A couple of nasty hours?"

"About that," Lisa whispered. "He was awful."

"Yes, well, try multiplying those hours by eight years." Drawing herself up, Justine made a fuss of straightening her skirt and tucking in a stray hair, but her hand was shaking, and her trembling lips and little frowns kept ruining her cool demeanor. "He was wonderful to me," she continued, "when he wanted a pretty young wife. By the time I found out what he was really like, it was too late."

"You could have left," Lisa said.

Justine uttered a short, harsh laugh. "Oh, sure. And he would have stood back and let me, right?"

No, Lisa realized suddenly, he wouldn't have. Kendall Hollingsworth wouldn't have let anything he considered his possession get away from him. She'd heard him order her not to leave and set his housekeeper and handyman to guard her. No, he would never have allowed Justine to walk out on him.

"I thought I could handle him," Justine murmured. "But I was wrong." She shot Lisa a quick glance. "Maybe if you'd had to live with him for all those years, you'd have done the same thing I did."

Lisa doubted it. Yet, slowly, she was beginning to understand how desperate Justine had been. She knew about desperation. Was learning more about it every day. More than she'd ever wanted to know. But she didn't think it was possible that she'd ever be desperate enough to let another person suffer on her account, while she sat back and watched. At least she hoped she'd never sink that low.

A loud knock at the door cut off Lisa's thoughts, and Detective Munson burst in. He looked from Lisa to Justine, his gaze stony and unrevealing.

"Okay," he said to Brisco. "I'm ready for them."

"Ready for what?" Justine demanded.

He focused on Lisa as he replied, "There's a crazy man in custody. The one you say stabbed Realto."

"He did!" Lisa insisted for the dozenth time.

Munson gave her a long look that made her wish she'd hung on to her self-control. "Yeah, well, I'd like confirmation."

Lisa seethed. Brisco and Laura Roswell had explained that since Mike had been on his back behind a bale of hay, she and the tramp were the only witnesses. "Why don't you get confirmation from the man who had the knife? Ask *him* who stabbed Realto."

It was immediately obvious that Munson wasn't about to answer questions asked by prisoners. Before he could repeat his order for her and Justine to follow him, Brisco stepped in.

"The guy clammed up on us as soon as we got him to the station house. Wouldn't even say what he was doing at the farm. Just sat for hours with his mouth shut. Then he started saying he was willing to make a deal. Said he'd write out a confession—if we let him talk to you."

"But *I* don't have to talk to him." Justine stood up. "I'm free to leave whenever I want."

Brisco gave her a look that put her back in her seat. "By admitting that you were at the estate the night your husband died," he said, his voice ominous, "you cast doubt on the identity of the woman who struck him."

Justine's composure slipped a notch. "But it wasn't me."

"So you said. But if we put you and Lisa in a lineup, I bet your housekeeper won't be able to tell you apart."

Another notch down, Lisa thought. Yes, underneath all that polish and silk, Justine was really frightened. Only, for some reason that Lisa didn't know—and didn't particularly care to know—Justine was driven beyond reason to try to hide her fear.

"Mike didn't say this would happen," she snapped. "He told me it was perfectly safe for me to come down here."

Brisco shrugged. "If you cooperate with this investigation, you'll be less likely to end up behind bars. Leave now, and I won't guarantee that you won't be picked up again within the hour."

Justine's face went pale, and in another minute, Lisa was certain the sophisticated facade would be in tatters.

Brisco seemed to sense it, too, because his tone was mild as he said, "The sooner we clear things up, the sooner you can go. Okay?"

Munson gestured impatiently. "Can we get on with this?"

Lisa was as uncertain as Justine about seeing the tramp, but she'd go along with almost anything that got the guy to talk.

Munson led the way down the hall to a large room, where behind a glass window two uniformed guards stood on either side of the vagrant.

He was dressed in a jailhouse-orange jumpsuit, which, although ugly, was a distinct improvement over his former attire. Moreover, he'd showered. His previously matted hair was clean, and standing out in clumps around his head. He was sitting with his arms folded, a stubborn mien deepening the lines on his weather-beaten face.

His head jerked up expectantly as the door opened. When he spotted Lisa and Justine, his hard expression melted, taking on a dreamy softness.

Lisa shrank back, confused. This man had followed her, come at her with a knife and killed Realto. He was dangerously unpredictable.

At a nod from Brisco, the two tough-looking guards left.

"Okay, Gary," Munson barked. "We've filled our end of the bargain. Now tell us about Realto."

The man called Gary ignored him. All his attention was focused on her and Justine.

"Please," she whispered. "Tell them what happened."

He spoke as if he hadn't been listening. "You're here. Two of you are here. But where's Andrea?"

"I told you, we don't know," Brisco answered calmly. "This is the best we can do."

Gary sighed. "I guess I got to be grateful for that. Here I am with two of my baby girls. Leigh. No, you want to be called Lisa. And Justine."

What on earth was he talking about? As his gaze narrowed on her, Lisa took an involuntary step back.

"How do you know who I am?" Justine croaked.

His face fell, his disappointment so acute Lisa felt she should be able to touch it.

"Don't you understand?" he pleaded. "You're my girls. My baby girls. Mine and Hallie's."

Lisa's mouth fell open, and for an instant her heart stopped. *This* was Garrett Folsom? A quick glance at Justine confirmed that her sister was equally shocked. Together they listened, speechless, as the peculiar man continued.

Head hanging low, swaying back and forth, he muttered, "I should have married her before they shipped me off to Nam. Brains got scrambled over there. Posttraumatic stress syndrome, they call it." His head snapped up, his gaze shooting from Lisa to Justine. "No shame in that, you know. No shame."

Light-headed, Lisa wobbled on her feet. She barely noticed when Brisco eased her into a chair.

Justine's reaction leaned toward outrage. "You can't be serious!" She looked down at the disheveled man as if he'd just crawled out from under a rock. "You're claiming to be my father? Why—do you want money?"

"Money?" He looked bewildered. "Don't need money."

Lisa pressed her hands together on the table and tried to remain very still, tried very hard not to become hysterical. How many shocks could one person absorb? Whatever the number, she'd passed it. Justine, her sister. Now, this man saying he was her father. Hers and Justine's and…and somebody named Andrea.

Andrea…*Fenton?*

Lisa gasped. "Wait! Do you mean there are *three of us?*"

He gave her a beatific smile. "Yes. Three little girls. Three little babies Hallie gave me." His smile faded. "But by the time I got back from Nam, you were all adopted and nobody would tell me nothing. Social Services kept saying it was better that way—'cause of, you know, my stress syndrome."

And with a hint of the bulldog determination that she herself had witnessed, he added, "But I didn't give up. I kept trying. All these years. I finally got the lawyer fellow who arranged the adoption…he's in a nursing home now…I got the names of your families from him. That's how I knew Justine was in Baltimore. And Leigh was in Philadelphia." He shook his head sadly. "Can't find Andrea."

Not twins but triplets. Lisa drew a ragged breath—at the same time, Justine, sitting beside her a few feet away, also heaved an unsteady sigh. Lisa met her sister's gaze. They studied each other for a moment, and Lisa saw that Justine was no more able than she to cope with this.

Justine sighed again and looked away. "Well, this is all perfectly unbelievable. And, frankly, I've got more important things to worry about than long-lost relatives."

Fortunately, Brisco rescued them both from having to respond to Garrett Folsom's desire for a family reunion.

"You were following Lisa around because she was your daughter?" Brisco asked.

Gary nodded vigorously. "Leigh…I mean, Lisa and Justine. See, I was trying to help! Like when I got those papers…you know, those papers? I got them the night Lisa fell asleep, and I put them in a safe place."

"*You* took them?" Lisa and Justine cried in unison.

He grinned. "Sure. I've got 'em. Got the folder from the rental car company, too. Yes, indeed, I do. Nice and safe."

"You mean, from Lisa's rental car?" Brisco asked.

Gary bobbed his head. "Saw the company sticker on Lisa's car. Knew where to go. Waited 'til late—real late—then got in and went through the records. Matched up Leigh's name…Leigh Barnes…that's her right name, you know. I'm sure it is. Yes. Matched up Leigh's name with her car's tag number."

The detective frowned. "But why did you take the records?"

Gary drew back. "To keep Leigh safe, of course."

Brisco shook his head over Gary's muddled logic. Rather

than seek further clarification, the detective steered the questioning back to the previous topic. "Tell me more about these papers you took from Leigh. Are you talking about the ones Justine got from Kendall Hollingsworth's files and hid?"

Gary frowned. "Don't know where they came from. Just know Leigh found them in Justine's house." He looked at Lisa. "You fell asleep, and I was afraid somebody would take 'em. You know that housekeeper is pretty nosy. Can't trust her. So I grabbed 'em for safekeeping. Been watching over you," he said smugly. "You and Justine. I can slip in and out of that house when old Maggie is asleep."

Justine made a strangled noise.

Lisa held her breath when Brisco finally asked what was to her the most important question.

"Did you kill Realto?"

Gary looked incredulous. "Of course. What did you think?"

"Just tell us why you did it," Brisco suggested.

Gary snorted in disgust. "Don't you understand anything? He was going to shoot my girl. Shoot Leigh. Couldn't let him do that." He gave Lisa a beseeching look. "I'm not bad. Really. Never got a chance to prove I could be a good father. If Hallie hadn't died—God, I wish she hadn't died—her and me would have kept the three of you, and things would have been different." His gaze shifted between Lisa and Justine. "Don't hate me. Please don't."

"I don't hate you," Lisa answered automatically, with no real idea what she did feel. At the moment, she didn't think she would ever be able to accept this man as her father. She'd had a father, a very good one, and William Barnes could never be replaced.

Still, the truth was unavoidable; Garrett Folsom was her flesh and blood—the man who had given her life. And despite the fear he'd engendered in her with his bizarre behavior, he had saved her life. More than once.

Again Brisco relieved her from having to commit to anything definite.

Clearing his throat, the detective told Gary, "It will help Leigh if you tell us what happened at the farm."

Gary sat up straighter. "I want to help her. I do."

"Come on then," Munson said, putting his hand on Gary's shoulder. "Let's go do it."

Hesitantly, Gary rose. "Where are we going?"

"Where you can write down what happened," Munson answered, guiding him toward the door.

"But I want to talk to my girls some more."

"Later."

Gary threw Lisa and Justine one last look as he left the room. "You understand?" he asked urgently.

Lisa nodded, even though she wasn't sure what he'd meant.

"What's going to happen to him?" she asked Brisco when the door had closed.

The detective said, "He'll probably go to a veteran's hospital."

Justine pushed back her chair and stood. "I can't take any more of this. I've got to get out of here."

"I don't think so." Brisco took a step to the right and blocked her path. "I think you're going to sit tight right here while I make a phone call to my lieutenant."

"And then what?" she snapped.

"We'll see."

Folding her arms tightly around her waist, Justine fell back into her chair and stared at the wall. Her light, rapid breathing was the only sound she made. Lisa was sure she was wishing she'd never come back to Baltimore, much less to the police station.

"And me?" Lisa asked. "What's going to happen to me?"

Brisco sighed. "Sorry. I don't know. It's not my call."

It was what she'd expected. Yet the thought of going back to her cell made her throat tighten and her eyes sting. The detective opened the door and stood holding it for her. She rose slowly and started to leave.

"Wait."

Justine's voice stopped her at the doorway.

Lisa gave her a questioning look.

Justine studied her intently, a slight frown flitting briefly across her brow, her expression filled with indecision. Finally, the frown disappeared and she spoke bluntly. "You do know, don't you, that Mike is in love with you?"

Lisa stared at her, her lips parted slightly in shock. "Did he tell you that?"

Justine gave a delicate snort. "He wouldn't tell me anything if I tried to torture it out of him. No, he didn't tell me. It was obvious."

Not knowing what to think—and more than a little wary of believing her—Lisa asked, "Why are you telling me this?"

Justine looked at her for another long moment, and slowly, a tiny crack appeared in her armor—a softening of her mouth, a trace of warmth creeping into her eyes. Quietly, she said, "I don't know. Maybe because I owe him. Maybe because I owe you both. Maybe because I know him well enough to guess he hasn't said a thing to you about how he feels." Drawing a deep breath, she straightened, and the armor was suddenly intact once more. "What you do with the information is your own business. But, honey, I'll tell you this—the pastures don't get any greener anywhere else. And men don't come any better than Mike Lancer."

Lisa's mouth curved into a small, sad smile. "I know."

Chapter Twenty-Two

The instant Lisa stepped into the hall, she heard angry male voices coming from the other end of the corridor. Her heart skipped a beat, and her head turned sharply to look—because one of those voices was gloriously familiar.

"All I'm asking is that you *listen* to me!" Mike shouted, shaking a manila folder under the nose of a uniformed guard. A white sling cradled his left arm, but otherwise he seemed—and definitely sounded—healthy.

"And all I'm asking is that you follow procedures!" the guard shouted back at him.

"Dammit! I want Lisa out of jail!"

"And I'm telling you—"

"What's going on here?" Brisco started toward the two arguing men, giving Lisa all the excuse she needed to follow.

Mike whirled at the sound of Brisco's voice. "Ben! Thank God! I'm trying to get this—" He broke off, and Lisa saw his gaze swerve past the detective and come to land on her.

With Justine's startling revelation still ringing in her head, her instinct was to keep walking until she was in his arms. But uncertainty brought her to a stop several feet short of him.

Her eyes searched his features but found nothing on which to pin her hopes. He had dark shadows beneath his eyes, stubble across his jaw and he looked worried, exhausted—and furious.

"Your shoulder…?" she began. "Are you—"

He waved aside her concern. "It's fine. Nothing serious." His gaze raked over her once. "Are you all right?"

She nodded.

"What have you found out?" Brisco asked.

Mike's gaze flashed to the detective, but instead of answering the question, he said, "Don't take her back to her cell. She didn't kill Hollingsworth."

Brisco hesitated. "Mike, you know it's not up to—"

"I can prove it."

The two men appraised each other in silence, and as the moment stretched on, Lisa could feel the tension rising.

Finally, Brisco relented. "Okay. Let's hear what you've got to say."

Hope surged inside her, and her gaze automatically sought Mike's. She wanted so badly to go to him. But she didn't. No matter what her untrustworthy sister had said, she had to assume he was here because he'd agreed that first day in the hospital to help her—and Mike Lancer kept his promises. To read anything else into his presence was wishful thinking. Lisa reminded herself of that as she followed Brisco into another ugly interrogation room and sat down at the table.

Brisco closed the door behind Mike, then walked to the head of the table, where he straddled a chair. "All right," he said. "What've you got?"

Mike plunked the folder he was holding onto the table and took the chair across from hers. Giving her a quick, inscrutable glance, he spoke directly to Brisco, "I got a second opinion on Hollingsworth's autopsy report."

Brisco's look was wary. "Something wrong with the first one?"

Mike's features twisted in derision. "Tappenhill signed it."

"Oh, Christ."

Lisa caught the look the men exchanged, and it brought her to the edge of panic. Was she going to be tried for murder on the basis of a report done by an incompetent? Hands clenched together in her lap, she listened closely as Mike continued in clipped phrases.

"So, we start with the assumption that Tappenhill's report is a piece of trash," he said.

"I'm listening," Brisco muttered.

"Last year I did some divorce work for a Dr. Paul Meyers. He's in pathology at Johns Hopkins. He told me that if I ever needed his expert opinion, I had it. Between midnight and two this morning, he gave me a crash course on the interaction of certain drugs."

"And…?"

"Hollingsworth was already a dead man walking when he was hit on the head. The blow isn't what killed him."

Lisa sucked in a sharp breath.

Brisco cocked an eyebrow. "So what did?"

"You're gonna love this. Just listen. Hollingsworth was on Capoten for his high blood pressure. I've confirmed that with his physician." Mike pulled out a sheet of paper from the folder and handed it to Brisco. "The police pathology report states that Hollingsworth had lithium in his system—a drug regularly prescribed for bipolar disorder. But according to his medical records—" another sheet appeared and was passed across the table "—he's never been diagnosed with or treated for any mental condition."

Brisco studied the sheets, then looked at Mike. "And?"

Mike handed him several more sheets. "These are copies of pages from the *Physician's Desk Reference* and some pharmacology texts, documenting that lithium in combination with Capoten produces toxic effects. The time of onset of symptoms varies from one to six hours, which would have given Hollingsworth plenty of time to get back from his meeting with Estelle Bensinger before he bought it."

"You're getting ahead of me," Brisco muttered. "Slow down."

Lisa stifled a groan. In the past two minutes, the tiny spark of hope she'd felt hearing Mike tell Brisco he could prove her innocence had grown to a blaze. She could hardly contain her eagerness for him to get on with it.

"Estelle Bensinger," Brisco repeated. "The dead woman."

Mike dragged in a deep breath and let it out. "Right. Hollingsworth's secretary—and mistress. I'll get to their meeting in a minute." Handing over more papers, he continued, "These are copies of several articles found in Bensinger's apartment about the consequences of combining lithium and ACE-inhibitors like Capoten. And don't ask me how I got them."

Brisco gave him a jaded look. "I don't want to know."

"Two weeks ago, she obtained a prescription for lithium from a physician in Washington. But only a small amount is missing from the bottle found in her medicine chest. Probably only the quantity that went into the drink she served Hollingsworth when he met her on his boat."

"Boat?"

"He owns...*owned* a cruiser that's docked at the Inner Harbor. She didn't have time to clean up from their little rendezvous before she was killed, so the glasses were still on the counter. I had the residue from both glasses analyzed. The lab confirms the presence of lithium in the one that contained scotch—which is what Maggie Dempsey, the Hollingsworths' housekeeper, swears Kendall Hollingsworth drank exclusively."

"Wait a minute." Brisco held up a hand to stop the onslaught of information. "How do you know they met on his boat the day he died? Our investigation didn't turn that up."

That's because your colleagues weren't trying to find out who really killed Hollingsworth—Lisa almost said the words aloud. If she hadn't been so ecstatic over the mountain of evidence Mike had amassed to absolve her, she easily could have been furious at the police for their smug assumption that they already had the killer behind bars. Cautioning herself not to get too ecstatic too soon, she couldn't quite hold back a sound of excitement. It came out as a tiny whimper.

Mike's gaze snapped to her, and he frowned. "You okay?"

She nodded, her eyes shining. If ever a woman had wanted a hero, he was it. She knew he must see her love for him written plainly on her face—she couldn't help it—and when his frown deepened to a scowl, a shard of pain lanced her. That scowl took the joy and hopefulness right out of her and made the thought of freedom nowhere near as bright. She listened with leaden spirits as Mike turned back to Brisco to finish making his argument.

"You know Bensinger and Hollingsworth had been having an affair for years," he said.

Brisco nodded. "Yeah, we got that."

"I checked out all their regular hangouts. They were both seen boarding the cruiser Monday afternoon, before he died. She got there a half hour before he did. I've got witnesses who are willing to sign statements."

Brisco was clearly amazed. "How the hell did you manage all this—" he flapped the papers in his hands "—in twenty-four hours?"

Mike combed his fingers through his hair, heaving a deep, tired sigh. "I've had a lot of help." Shrugging his good shoulder, he added, "I also have a record of Hollingsworth's phone conversation with a detective agency he employed, in which he's told about a videotape of Estelle Bensinger removing a folder from his confidential files."

"Where did you get *that?*" Brisco asked.

"From the same company that was videotaping his office."

"Christ." Brisco studied him for a moment, then shook his head. "I told those bastards they didn't know what they were losing the day you left the job. I like being proved right."

Lisa watched Mike's neck and cheeks turn ruddy, and she was a little surprised when he didn't try to deny Brisco's praise.

"Thanks, Ben," Mike said. "Your confidence means a lot to me. But I'm not in this for myself. I'm only here to prove that Lisa didn't murder Kendall Hollingsworth." His lips thinned to a grim line. "The point is, Estelle Bensinger had a motive for killing Hollingsworth. She also had the weapon that killed him, the knowledge to use it and the opportunity.''

Brisco gave a low grunt. ''Too bad Juan Realto drilled her a couple of hours later.''

''You've got confirmation on that?''

''Yeah, the ballistics report came back. The bullet they took out of her was fired by his gun. No doubt about it.''

''Ben, I want you to turn Lisa loose.''

Brisco shook his head. ''Mike, you know I don't have the authority.''

''Dammit!'' Mike's fist hit the table with a bang, the anger and frustration Lisa had read on his features erupting.

''Take it easy,'' Brisco said. ''You've made your case, and it's damned convincing. Now let me put the cards on the table, and we'll see how it plays.''

Mike stared at Brisco in silence, his nerves visibly stretched to the breaking point.

Lisa knew that she, too, was on the verge of exploding, and she was awed by Mike's self-control. Her own was rapidly deteriorating. Finally, she couldn't prevent herself from reaching across the table to place a hand on his arm.

She felt the muscles in his forearm tense beneath her touch.

''Thank you,'' she whispered. And she managed a grateful smile that he didn't return.

His eyes searched hers, his dark gaze smoldering with emotions she couldn't begin to read. Finally, he gave her a single nod, then looked away.

She withdrew her hand, fighting back tears, and turned to Brisco, who was busy politely ignoring the private exchange taking place. When he caught her gaze, he motioned toward the door. She nodded, and, without further speech, he ushered her out of the room and back to her cell.

AN ETERNITY. That's how long it seemed to Lisa that she sat cross-legged on the bunk in her cell, literally biting her nails. In fact, it was five hours. She looked up at the sound of approaching footsteps. Brisco appeared with a guard in front of the bars—and he was smiling.

"You're free to go," he said as the guard unlocked the cell door and opened it.

She squeezed her eyes closed against sudden tears, relief pouring through her so strongly it made her giddy. "Thank God."

"And Mike Lancer."

"Yes, and Mike Lancer," she murmured, rising.

Brisco led her through the locked gates and dingy corridors to a large room where guards were supervising prisoners visiting with friends and relatives. A row of tables bisected the room, divided by bars separating the free from the incarcerated.

Lisa searched for Mike, but he wasn't here. A little desperately, she asked Brisco, "Have you seen Mike?"

The detective shook his head. "He stayed until we found out the charges were being dropped. That was around two. I don't know where he went then." His tone was apologetic. "I had to wait for the paperwork before I could release you."

She nodded. "I understand."

She also thought she understood why Mike wasn't here. He'd fulfilled his obligation, gotten her cleared of the charges and now she was on her own. He could hardly have made it plainer if he'd said it to her, face-to-face.

"Where are you going?" Brisco broke into her thoughts as he led her to the jail's front entrance.

"I was staying in a Sheraton in Towson," she replied, swallowing the lump in her throat as she tried to return her mind to practical matters. "My things are all there. But I don't know if they're holding my room—or, for that matter, how I'd get into it without the key or some ID." Her hand fluttered in a helpless gesture. "I guess I'll have to convince them that I am who I say I am." In Mike's borrowed clothes and with the grime of the Baltimore City Jail clinging to every pore in her body, it seemed unlikely to her that she'd succeed.

"I'll call and talk to the manager," Brisco offered. "I'll make sure you get your key."

She gave him a grateful look. "I'd really appreciate it."

"No problem. Do you have money?"

"No." Heat crept into her cheeks at the admission. That she had come to this, that she could be standing in a jail in a strange city, penniless and wearing borrowed clothes was beyond humiliating. Her voice was scarcely a whisper as she explained, "My wallet, credit cards, money…everything was washed away in the accident."

Before she could argue, Brisco took out his wallet and handed her two twenties.

"Oh, I couldn't—"

"Sure, you can," he insisted. "I wouldn't be able to sleep tonight if I put you out on the street without a cent."

"Thank you," Lisa whispered, wadding the bills into her clenched fist. "I'll pay you back."

He gave a brief laugh. "Well, you know where to find me. Look—I've got to get going, but I'll call you a cab before I leave. Just wait out front for it."

Thanking him again and saying goodbye, Lisa stepped through the main door onto the sidewalk. She was shocked to see that it was still daylight. The sun was just dropping below the tops of the tall brick and gray stone buildings, bronzing their surfaces in amber tones.

She waited ten minutes, standing on the busy city street, disoriented and dirty and saddened beyond anything she'd ever experienced. Probably it wasn't really cold outside, but she stood shivering in the light wind. When the cab arrived, she slumped in a corner of the back seat and gave the driver the name of her hotel. As the vehicle made its way through the bustling downtown traffic, she stared out the window, oblivious to the passing scenery.

She was back to square one. The place she'd been last Tuesday morning when she'd left Erin Stone's office in tears.

No, that wasn't quite true. She'd acquired two identical sisters, one of whom she happily could have done without and one of whom she probably would never meet. She'd also acquired a biological father who was well-intentioned but who needed more than therapy. For her baby's sake, as well as her own, she thought it might be better to forget she'd ever learned of her blood relations.

Which left her and the baby with no family at all. Oh, she had friends. Some very good ones, she remembered. Melody and Esther would stick by her, but they weren't going to raise her baby with her. In all ways that counted, she'd be on her own.

She also had to find a new job, even if Hank Lombard didn't get her fired; her firm did too much business with his for her to be able to avoid him. Under ordinary circumstances, she wouldn't have doubted her ability to find a good position. But how would prospective employers respond when she told them, as she surely would, that she was pregnant?

Still, there was something worse than financial uncertainty, she thought sadly. Since her parents' deaths, she'd thought she felt as lonely as a person could feel. She'd been wrong. She still missed her parents dreadfully, yet she had memories of them, a lifetime of having known them and their love, to comfort her.

She had no memories of a lifetime with Mike to console her. She'd wanted a partner, a friend, a lover. She'd wanted a father for her baby. Somehow, she'd known intuitively, even in those first foggy moments she'd laid eyes on him, that he could fulfill her needs and desires as no other man could. It was agony to know she would never hold him again. Never feel the strength and vitality of his body pressed to hers. Never feel his tenderness—or his passion. Never hear his laughter. Having tasted what love between them would be like, she had to accept that there would be no more.

Tears threatened to spill down her cheeks. She would have to thank him, of course. He'd moved heaven and earth to get her out of jail, and he'd saved her life, several times over. She couldn't simply leave town without acknowledging her debt to him. If he didn't want to see or talk to her, she would have to find some other way to tell him how grateful she was.

And then she would have to tell him goodbye.

At that moment, riding silently in the back of the shabby yellow cab as it headed out of the city, Lisa knew what it felt like to have a broken heart. The pain stabbed at her and she fought to hold herself together for just a little longer.

The cab dropped her at the Sheraton and she went to the desk, where, to her relief, the manager met her with the key to her room. Blushing at the curious looks of the hotel staff and guests in the lobby, she hurried onto the elevator.

With a prayer of thanks that no one was in the hallway on her floor, she walked quickly to her room and opened the door. Stepping inside, she was struck for a moment by the eerie feeling that she'd been gone only since that morning. There was her suitcase on the bed, her blue linen suit hanging in the open closet, her bottle of Chanel No. 5 on the bureau...her sneakers, her briefcase...all of it exactly as she had left it. How odd that nothing had changed when she would never be the same again.

Closing the door behind her, she went immediately to the bathroom, where she stripped off her clothes, turned on the shower and stepped under the stream of nearly blistering hot water. When she'd lathered and scrubbed everything once, she started over and did it all a second time.

The steam still billowed around her when she belted a terry cloth robe around her waist. A knock at the hotel-room door brought her out of the warmth and security of the bathroom.

Unable to imagine who it could be, she peeped through the security viewer. In the next instant, with her heart racing, she had the door unlocked and open.

"Mike!"

"Thank God," he said. "You made it out here all right."

Stunned by the sight of him, she could only manage a nod.

"I went home to shower and shave," His tone was gruff, businesslike. "I planned to be back at the jail when they released you. But I sat down on the couch to eat a sandwich, and that's the last thing I remember. I fell asleep.''

"You looked exhausted," she said, thinking that he still did, despite the clean clothes and shaven face. Much as she'd like to reach out to him, she had to hold back her hands. Mike had come here as a detective closing a case, not as a man claiming a lover.

His arm was still in a sling. Shrugging his good shoulder, he said, "That's no excuse. I should have been there to get you. I'm sorry.''

She shook her head. "The last thing you need to be is sorry. I owe you a lot more than a nap.''

He scowled. "You don't owe me anything.''

"Mike, I owe you my life," she said with quiet insistence. "What you've done for me went way beyond the call of duty." Her gaze fell to the floor. "I'll never be able to thank you enough.''

He was silent for a moment, then spoke in an oddly strained voice. "Lisa, we have to talk.''

Her gaze flew to his. From the look and the sound of him—all those harsh lines in his face and brusque, short words—it wasn't anything she wanted to hear. Yet she couldn't help hoping that it might be.

"Okay," she whispered.

"Can I come in?''

She nodded, then stood aside to let him pass. Bolting the door behind him, she turned to find him standing stiffly a few feet away. He was half turned away from her, his right hand shoved into his back pocket.

"Lisa," he began, then hesitated, casting a quick, sideways glance at her. "Or I guess I should call you Leigh, shouldn't I?''

She shook her head. "No, I'm going to keep the name Lisa.''

"Oh? Why?''

She tightened the belt at her waist. "You'll think it's silly.''

"No, I won't. Tell me." His voice was quiet, more encouraging than it had been a minute ago.

"Well…" She lifted one shoulder in a tiny shrug. "I woke up in the hospital, and I wasn't Leigh Barnes anymore. I was Lisa. Now I remember who Leigh Barnes is, but I feel like a new person—I guess that's the best way to put it. Leigh and Lisa combined." Feeling horribly exposed, she gave him a fleeting glance. "It probably sounds totally schizophrenic."

"No," he said softly. "In fact, it makes a lot of sense." He paused for a moment or two, then said, "Tell me what brought your memory back."

"It was a dream," she replied in a scarcely audible tone. "After you left Jenny's yesterday afternoon, I fell asleep on the couch. I dreamed about something that—" She stopped abruptly, the words lodged in her throat. She wasn't ready to tell him about the dream, not when she had no idea why he was asking. "It was something that happened a couple of months ago," she continued. "It was…very bad. I've dreamed about it ever since it happened, but yesterday, the phone woke me up in the middle of the dream, and I remembered enough of it that I was able to force myself to remember all of it. Once I had, the rest of my memory…well, it just sort of switched back on."

"I wish it hadn't happened like that—when you were alone," he murmured. "And I hope not everything you remember is bad."

With her gaze directed at her fingers, which were twisting the belt of her robe into knots, she replied, "No, most of it is very good. I had a wonderful childhood with terrific parents. They weren't rich, but they gave me love and security and good values." She wanted to tell him more but didn't know if he wanted to hear. He was standing there so rigidly. He kept asking questions, but she still didn't know why he was asking them. With each answer, she felt more defenseless, more raw. Why couldn't he say what he'd come here to say and then leave?

He heaved a sigh. "So, what will you do now?"

She frowned, still unable to summon the courage to look at him.

"What are your plans?" he prompted. "Are you going back home soon, or will you...still be looking for a job in Baltimore?"

This was it. This was where he would extricate himself from whatever claims of dependency he felt she had on him.

Swallowing against the tightness in her throat, she said, "I suppose I'll go back. It seems like—" she drew a jerky breath "—like the logical thing to do."

A quick glance caught him staring fixedly at the blank TV screen across the room.

"Do you..." He stopped midsentence. "I mean, is there anyone special waiting for you?"

"No, it's only me...and the baby," she said softly.

He sucked in a deep breath, held it for a second or two, then let it out. "What if...what if I asked the two of you to stay?"

Her head snapped up, her gaze flashing to his face. Slowly, his head turned toward her, and their eyes met. Gone was his harsh mask and the guarded look. His features were open, vulnerable. His eyes, as they searched hers, were soft and warm with some emotion she was afraid to name.

"You *want* me to stay?" she asked, hope swelling inside her.

He nodded once.

"Here? With you?"

Again, he nodded. "Here. With me."

"Mike—" Lisa's hands flew to cover her face as a sob escaped her. "Oh, Mike, I...I thought you were getting ready to say you wanted me to leave. At the jail...you looked so angry. I thought—"

"God, Lisa, didn't you realize...? Sweetheart, I wasn't angry at *you.*"

Suddenly he was right in front of her, drawing her close against him. Even with only one arm, his embrace was solid and secure. He spoke with his lips buried in her damp curls.

"I was angry at the cops, at Justine…at the world in general. When I saw you, all I wanted to do was grab you and run, get you out of there and take you someplace I could hold you. It was hard enough even speaking to you without— If I'd touched you or held you…Lisa, I'd have lost it. And I *couldn't* lose it. I had to keep it together to get you out of there. I'm so sorry, sweetheart. I didn't realize how you'd take it."

With her face buried against his neck, Lisa sobbed, "Oh, Mike, I'm sorry, too. I know I hurt you, and I know I should have told you about the baby in the first place. But I was confused and worried and frightened, and I wasn't thinking straight."

"It's okay, sweetheart," he told her. "It doesn't matter anymore."

"But you were so angry." She gulped. "When you walked out Jenny's door to go back to the office, I thought I'd never see you again."

His arm trembled as it tightened around her. "You looked so sad. So…lost. But I felt used and manipulated in a way I hadn't since…since Justine. The only way I could deal with it was to tell myself that I'd be better off without you. Except I knew I wouldn't be. Deep down, I knew you weren't really trying to deceive me. I was only lying to myself, and the only excuse I've got is that I was mad…and scared."

She lifted her head to look at him. "Scared?"

"Damned right," he muttered. "I was scared as hell of how much I love you and how bad you could hurt me if you wanted to." Before she could speak the words on her lips, Mike raised his hand to her mouth. "Let me finish. When I got to my office, Justine was there." He laughed harshly. "Seeing her made me realize how different the two of you are. Not that I didn't already know it, but…well, let's say I gained a perspective I'll never lose."

And Lisa saw clearly that it was true—he wouldn't ever confuse her with her sister again. "She did something for me too."

"Did she?"

She nodded. "Justine told me that you were in love with me. I can't say that I like her very much, even if she is my sister. And I like her even less for what she did to you. But I think she's sorry for what she did—to both of us. I also think she's scared and I'm *certain* she had a very bad time of it with Kendall Hollingsworth."

His puzzled expression deepened to confusion. "Why are you defending her?"

Lisa shrugged. "I guess I'm hoping that if you stop judging her so harshly, you'll judge yourself less harshly, too. You blame yourself for being taken in by her, but your only sin was to trust the woman you loved. And that's no sin at all. She may even have loved you, too, but she was immature and impulsive. I'd bet anything that's how she decided to marry Kendall Hollingsworth—on the spur of the moment. I'd also bet she regretted it like mad almost as soon as she'd done it."

"And I bet you're right." He sighed. "You're a smart lady, Lisa Barnes. Which is only one of the many reasons that I love you." His hand came up to lie against her cheek, his thumb tracing the line of her lips as he whispered, "Marry me, Lisa."

She sucked in a sharp breath, her heart racing.

"I want to hear you say yes."

"Yes," she breathed. "Oh, yes!" She threw her arms around him, barely remembering to be careful of his shoulder. "I love you so much."

"Lisa…"

He lowered his mouth to hers for a searing kiss that promised much more. But when his hand slid up her ribs to find her breast, she drew back, gasping for breath.

"Mike…wait. I have to tell you something first—about the night the baby was conceived."

She saw a shadow flicker in his eyes. "Lisa, you don't have to—"

She smoothed a finger across his furrowed brow. "I do."

Her voice dropped to a whisper as she told him of her job as the only female architect at Williamsburg, how she'd struggled to win a position on the liason team, and finally of that fateful night in Chicago.

She paused for breath, glanced at Mike to see that he was watching her closely, then lowered her gaze once more. "I tried to fight him off, but I couldn't."

"Lisa…"

"Mike, it's okay. It's what I dreamed about at Jenny's, and when I woke up, instead of pushing it away like I'd been doing, I *made* myself remember it. Because somehow I knew I had to if I was ever going to remember anything else. That night was…it was the worst thing that's ever happened to me. But I faced it and it's over. He hurt me, but I survived. And I've got this baby that I do want very, very much. That's why I was at Birth Data, Inc. I wanted to learn my baby's heritage."

His hand stroked her back, caressing, soothing. "You looked so upset that day."

"I guess I was feeling pretty down, wondering how I was going to cope with being a single mom and working."

He kissed her cheek, her hair, then her mouth, gentle kisses, tender and healing. "I don't have much experience with happy family life. But when I said I wanted you, I meant the whole package." His voice broke a little. "I swear to you, Lisa, I'll do my damnedest to be a good father to your child."

She gave him a smile full of love. "I know you will."

"It'll be so good—the three of us together. Or the four of us, if you want."

"I want," she whispered. "I want your babies, too. But mostly—" She gasped as his mouth found its way to the base of her neck and his teeth nibbled at her shoulder. "Oh, Lord, Mike, mostly, I want you."

"You've got me," he growled. "For keeps."

His lips joined hers in a passionate kiss, and as he slowly began to walk her backward toward the bed, she realized that they were alone, and safe, in a snug bedroom where they wouldn't be disturbed. Finally, she was free to show him exactly how much she loved him.

When the backs of her knees bumped against the mattress, she lifted her gaze to find him smiling at her, as if he had come to the same conclusion. While he fumbled one-handed with the knot of her robe, she lifted one finger and gently traced the arch of his cheek, the curve of his lips, the line where his dark hair met his brow. Then she traced the same path with her lips.

"Damn," he muttered, giving up on the knot. "This sling is a nuisance."

"Not to worry," she said. With a provocative smile, she untied the knot and let the robe slide off her shoulders to pool around her feet. His heated gaze raked over her, and she felt her nipples harden against the silk of her nightgown as if he'd touched them.

He sucked in a quick breath, lifting his hand to cup her breast. "So sexy. So beautiful," he murmured.

She leaned into his touch, yearning for more. Still, she was determined to continue what she'd started. The first time, he'd undressed her, and he'd made it a delicious, carnal experience. This time, she wanted to do the same for him.

Reaching for the top button of his shirt, she began the task, and she continued to make it an erotic journey punctuated by lingering kisses and tantalizing touches. By the time she had him naked—but for the sling and his shirt, which she left unbuttoned and spread open across his muscled chest—they were both at fever pitch.

When it looked like he was about to lose all restraint and take control, she pushed him gently down onto the bed to lie on his back and lowered her body onto his. He gasped as he slid inside of her. For a moment, her eyes closed and she gloried in the feel of him filling her completely. She opened her eyes to find him smiling, then his hand slid down to curve gently over her abdomen, and she went very still. The smile left his face, and his eyes held hers as he spoke on a husky, solemn note.

"Years from now," he said, "when we talk about the time you got pregnant, this is the night we'll remember. This is the night we made this baby—together."

For the space of several heartbeats, she couldn't speak, could only gaze down at him in wonder. How had she gotten so lucky? She didn't know, but she would be grateful for the rest of her life to whatever god or fate had brought her to him.

"Oh, Mike," she whispered, tears glistening in her eyes.

His fingers laced together with hers, clasping hers tightly. "Ah, sweetheart," he said, his hips moving beneath her. "Don't make me wait any longer. Do it now."

Her eyes locked with his as she began to move. He let her set the rhythm. As the pace quickened and her own pleasure surged, she found exquisite joy in watching the mounting tension in his face.

"This is the way it's supposed to be, isn't it?" she whispered, her eyes never leaving his.

"Yes, this is the way it's supposed to be," he repeated a little later, cradling her against his side.

Epilogue

"More peppermint tea?"

Lisa smiled as Benita Fenton offered to pour her another cup. They were sitting in the older woman's Philadelphia home, Benita nestled in a wing chair, an afghan spread over her lap. Her health was still delicate, but lately, she'd made remarkable strides.

Lisa shook her head. "No, thank you, I'm fine. You sit still and let Andrea and me take care of the dishes."

Benita sighed. "I hate being waited on. Especially by two women with bellies out to here." She held her hand out in front of her, slightly exaggerated, to indicate the state of Lisa's pregnancy—and her daughter's, which was a little farther advanced.

Lisa joined her sister in clearing dishes, thinking that it had been five months since her fateful encounter at the Jones Falls. Over the course of those months, she'd been busy getting married and settling into happy domestic life with Mike and had all but forgotten her living nightmare.

The biggest surprise had been getting to know her sister, Andrea. Erin Stone had found her living with her husband and son in New Jersey. Lisa had welcomed Erin's offer to set up a meeting. Erin had also helped to facilitate a reconciliation between Benita and her daughter. In fact, when Andrea had learned about her mother's precarious health, she'd been determined to mend the breach that had kept them apart for so many years.

Lisa followed her sister to the kitchen and began loading dishes into the dishwasher. In the living room, she could hear Gordon, Andrea's husband, telling Mike about the relative merits of various mutual funds. She sighed. The guys were never going to be best buddies, but Mike had claimed he was learning something. With Gordon's advice, they were starting a college fund for the baby.

"How was Gary when you saw him last week?" Andrea asked, her voice low to guard against her mother's overhearing. Any mention of Garrett Folsom sent Benita through the roof, and no amount of reassurance would convince her that the man posed no threat to her relationship with Andrea.

"Better, I think," Lisa replied. "The doctor says the new medication is helping."

Both she and Andrea had been visiting their father regularly at the veterans' hospital in Baltimore. At first it had been so strange, thinking of him as her father. But as time went on, she was getting comfortable with him.

"I like to listen to his stories about Hallie," Andrea murmured.

Lisa nodded, pouring detergent into the dishwasher and closing the door. "Me, too. I loved my parents dearly, but I can't help wondering how things would have been if Hallie had lived and she and Gary had married."

"Different, that's for sure," Andrea said. "Maybe Justine would have turned out okay."

Lisa sighed at the mention of her other sister. The black sheep of the family, without doubt. When she'd left Justine sitting at the table in the Baltimore City Jail, she hadn't expected—or particularly wanted—to see or hear from her again. It had shocked both her and Mike when Justine sent them a wedding present, then months later a beautiful handmade quilt for the baby. So, who knew what might happen? Lisa had given up making predictions.

Andrea, who hadn't yet shown any interest in meeting Justine, glanced over her shoulder as she hung a dish towel on the rack to dry. "Mom was strict," she said. "And I turned into the epitome of the rebellious teenager—impulsive, inconsiderate, willing to do anything for the sheer risk involved. After I ran away, I was sorry, but I didn't know how to come back."

Lisa made a sympathetic noise. "I had some impulsive tendencies, too, when I was that age. But I was lucky. My parents knew just where to set the limits without making me feel trapped."

"I thought a couple of times that I'd wind up either in jail or dead," Andrea muttered. Then, laughing, she added, "Who would have thought I'd end up married to a stockbroker."

"You never know," Lisa agreed.

The back door banged, and Tony, Andrea's four-year-old, came in from the backyard with his grandpa. Lisa watched her sister kneel to hug the boy. Soon, she thought, she'd be holding her own baby—and she could hardly wait.

"We've got to get going," Andrea told Tony. "Go give Grandma a big goodbye kiss."

"I don't wanna leave!" Tony protested.

No, Lisa thought with a smile, not when he had two new doting grandparents who had to be restrained from overindulging him.

"If you're a good boy, we can come back and see Grandma and Grandpa next Sunday," Andrea assured him, which seemed to satisfy the youngster.

A half hour later, having said their goodbyes, Lisa walked with Mike to the car to begin the ride home to Baltimore. He slid an arm around her expanded waist as they walked, and she rested her head against his shoulder.

"I heard Gordon talking your head off," she murmured.

He chuckled. "Gordon's a little talkative, but he's part of the package."

She stopped walking. "What package?"

"My ready-made family," he said, his voice thick. "I never had one. Now I've got you, and this little one—" he patted her swollen belly "—and I've got your sister and her husband and the Fentons. Before it's over, God help me, I might end up with Justine, too."

"God help us both," Lisa sighed.

"If it happens, it happens. After all, she's part of the package, too." He gave her a tender look as he spoke in a husky tone. "Sweetheart, you've brought me so much."

"Oh, Mike." Lisa put her hand on top of his where it rested on her abdomen. She didn't think he'd ever be entirely comfortable revealing his deepest feelings. On the other hand, he hadn't seemed to feel the need to retreat behind his wall of reserve since the night he'd asked her to marry him. So, again, who knew what might happen? With Mike, anything was possible.

The baby started to kick, and she knew Mike felt it, because he grinned at her.

"He's getting stronger every day," he said.

"*She's* getting stronger every day," Lisa corrected. It was an ongoing mock battle between them, although neither of them really cared whether their baby was a girl or a boy.

Their baby. The child they'd made together that night in the hotel room. Mike had fixed the memory in her mind for all time.

Rubbing his hand gently against the mound of their child, he said, "Seems to me, early indications are that he's going to keep us busy."

"I expect *she* will," Lisa said, a frown flicking across her brow. "Andrea warned me that the first few months with a baby can be pretty rough. No sleep, no social life. No sex."

"I promise you, we absolutely will *not* let that happen," he muttered.

"Mmm. And it doesn't exactly get easier."

His eyes held hers. "We'll do it together, Lisa. And we'll make it good."

"Yes, I know we will," she whispered. And it was true. Because if she'd learned anything during her ordeal, it was that she could get safely through the fires of hell—as long as she had this man at her side.

Heart of the Jaguar

LINDSAY McKENNA

To all my wonderful readers
who have been with me over the years.
You *are* the greatest!

Prologue

"Oh, hell...I'm dying...."

The thought slammed through Captain Mike Houston's spinning mind and then, in disgust, he uttered the desperate words out loud. Sliding his long, muddied fingers along his camouflaged right thigh, he looked down to see bright red blood spurting like a pulsing fountain. A bullet had ricocheted off a tree and nicked his femoral artery, and he was bleeding like a butchered hog. Instinctively, because he was trained as a paramedic, he put direct pressure on the wound with his dirty hand.

Lying in the midst of the Peruvian jungle, Mike knew there wouldn't be any rescue coming. No, the helicopter he'd been in had been shot down by Eduardo Escovar's drug cartel mercenaries, who were intent on hunting him down and murdering him. As far as Mike knew, he was the only survivor of the flaming wreckage. The redness and blisters on his forearms, the tightness of his face, told him he hadn't gotten away without being burned. Gasping, he threw back his head. Sweat trailed down the sides of his hardened face as he began to feel each single beat of his heart in his heaving chest.

Though he'd leaped from the falling bird before it hit the triple

canopy of trees, Mike knew his Peruvian army team hadn't survived the attack. The helicopter had been hit by a rocket at five
hundred feet and had slowly turned over on its side like a
wounded, shrieking eagle, twisting around and around until it hit
the thick jungle cover.

In the distance, he could hear flames from the downed aircraft
still snapping and popping. He heard the excited voices of Escovar's men as they searched through the jungle, hunting for any
survivors. It was only a matter of time now, actually. A pained,
one-cornered smile twisted Mike's mouth. Helluva place to pack
it all in: in his mother's homeland. She was Quechua Indian and
had been concerned when he was assigned by the U.S. Army to
teach Peruvian soldiers how to begin ridding their land of the
cocaine lords. She'd wept in his arms, pleading with him not to
go down there, that he'd die.

Well, it looked like she was right. Mike scowled. At twenty-six
years old, he didn't want to die. Hell, he'd barely lived yet. He'd
only been an Army Special Forces officer since he graduated from
college at age twenty-two. He had his whole career—his whole
life—ahead of him. But as he lay in the shallow depression, the
surrounding green, leafy jungle effectively hiding him, the soft,
spongy ground beneath him damp with rotting vegetation, he began to feel light-headed. That was the first sign of shock, he noted
coldly. *Pretty soon I'm going to dump, my blood pressure will
drop through the floor and I'll lose consciousness and die.* It
would be like going to sleep.

Still, he'd been in so many close calls over the years as he'd
directed Peruvian army teams against the continuing battle with
drug lords in the highlands of this jungle country that he believed
he might have a chance. He had luck—his mother's Indian luck.
She prayed for him constantly. It made a difference.

He could feel his heart thudding hard in his chest. And, he
became aware of the pulse of blood through his body. The sticky
red substance had completely soaked the material around his thigh.
He tried to put more pressure on the wound. No, he thought
gravely, this time there would be no help, no helicopter coming,
no relief to make up the difference. He knew that the copilot had
gotten off a mayday message shortly after they were hit because

he'd heard him scream out their location as the out-of-control helicopter plunged toward earth. But who knew if anyone had picked
up the transmission? There was little chance of a rescue being
organized.

The heavy jungle growth felt comforting to him. In his green-
and-tan camouflage uniform, he was well hidden. With a mirthless
smile, Mike lay on his left side, placing his arm beneath his head
like a pillow while his right hand closed more firmly over his hard,
massive thigh. It was only a matter of time. Escovar's men were
local villagers. They knew how to hunt and track. They'd eventually pick up his trail. He hadn't been able to hide his tracks this
time. Usually, he was just as good as they were in hiding his
whereabouts, but not on this misty, cool morning. Blinking through
the sweat dripping off his bunched brow, Houston looked up
through the wide, wet leaves.

Humidity lay like a blanket above the canopy. On most days,
sunlight never reached the jungle floor. His eyes blurred briefly
and everything went hazy. The beat of his heart became pronounced. As he lost more blood, his heart pumped harder, trying
to make do with less. It was a losing battle. His mind was shorting
out, too. He wondered if he'd bleed to death before the cocaine
soldiers found him. He hoped so, because what they'd do to him
wouldn't be pretty. He laughed to himself. The Geneva Conven-
tion didn't mean a damn thing down here. Its declaration of the
rights of prisoners was a piece of paper in some far-off land. Here,
the law of the jungle prevailed. Any prisoner taken could expect
horrendous, painful torture until death released him from the agony. To torment one's enemy wasn't just permitted, it was a right.

Pain throbbed up and down his leg. He had to try and get his
web belt around his thigh and make a tourniquet. Mike laughed
at himself once again. Why the hell was he trying to save his own
miserable life? So Escovar's men could finish him off, an inch at
a time? He kept his hand gripped on his thigh. *No belt. Screw it.
I'll die instead.* He shut his eyes, the black, spiky lashes resting
against his ashen, glistening features. Ordinarily, he looked like a
Peruvian Indian, his skin not copper colored, but a dark, dusky
hue that hinted at the *norteamericano* blood interfaced with Indian.

He spoke Spanish and the Quechua language as easily as he did English, thanks to his mother's influence.

"Never forget your upbringing, Michael!" she would remonstrate, shaking that small, brown finger in his face. "Your father might think you're all *norteamericano,* but you are not! Your heart belongs to my people. Your spirit belongs to the Jaguar Clan in the jungles of Peru. Never forget that."

Mike chuckled softly, his face pressing into the scratchy leaves and branches where he lay. He was weakening further. In spite of the humid hell that surrounded him, he felt cold, and he was dying of thirst. Oh, for a drink of water right now! Somewhere in his hazy mind, he knew he was going to go through every classic symptom of shock as the blood leaked out of his body. For a moment, he felt lighter, the heaviness of his body, the belts of ammunition he wore criss-crossed around his chest no longer pulling him downward. Despite his tightly shut eyes, he saw the dull, whitish yellow glow of clouds that always embraced the jungle. The light always reminded him of his mother's belief that the clouds were actually the veil between the worlds. On this side was the "real world," she'd told him, when he was a child on her knee, listening as she spun story after story of her Indian heritage. But the other side...ahh...that was the world of the shamans and the Jaguar Clan. It was a world full of magic, danger, mystery and terror. Only trained medicine people could go between the worlds and come back alive from the experience. Anyone else foolish enough to try it would die.

I'm dying now. I'm going between the worlds. Part of him, the *norteamericano* side, laughed derisively at the thought. But his mother's Indian blood, that part of him connected deeply with Mother Earth, believed it. Until now, Mike hadn't really thought much about his mother's belief system. In these moments before his death, her words were more important to him than he'd ever realized.

Mike heard the shout of a soldier no more than a hundred feet away from where he lay. He knew he'd done a bad job of hiding himself beneath the damp, rotting leaves and branches that filled the shallow depression he'd dug, but his leg wound had taken most of his attention. Now consciousness was draining from him. His fingers began to slip away from his wound and he felt the pulse of warm blood spreading across them. He didn't have the strength to hold pressure over the bullet hole in his thigh any longer.

He was breathing shallowly now. His heartbeat was growing weaker. He was dumping. His blood pressure would plummet any second now, and he'd die. Opening his eyes, he saw nothing but that humid, moist veil to another world. Funny, he couldn't see anything else anymore. He supposed that was part of dying. Blinking away the sweat running into his eyes, he realized he no longer felt its sting. Yes, he was definitely going through the dying process. He began to lose his fear of being discovered. Absorbed by the white-and-gold light that now surrounded him, he realized the cold that had been flowing up his legs and into the center of his body had stopped. He blinked again.

A voice inside his head told him to look down at his arm, which was flung out before him. He shifted his gaze slightly across the surface of the ground, thinking he would only be able to see the white light. But he could make out his darkly haired arm, the camouflage material torn away, leaving the lower part exposed.

His vision was changing. As if he were looking at his arm through a microscope, Mike saw each black hair and his darkly tanned flesh beneath. His focus moved to his large-knuckled, heavily scarred hand. Suddenly, he felt something shift within him.

The feeling wasn't that noticeable, just a vague sense of readjustment. Mike wasn't sure what caused it, but there was a rumbling feeling in his chest, like a heavy truck grinding up a steep hill in low gear.

Sounds blurred around him. The drip, drip, drip of water falling from the leaves was amplified, while the shouts of the soldiers dissolved. Mike felt oddly uncomfortable, but his pain was nearly gone. Even the throbbing sensation in his leg had disappeared.

Puzzled, Houston blinked and continued to stare dazedly at his outstretched arm. The sight of it was his last hold on reality, he figured. Pretty soon, his vision would dim and he'd be gone—forever, this time. He felt lighter and lighter, all the noises and the pain slowly dissolving. He felt as if he were whirling and the sensation made him dizzy as it became more and more profound. His gaze clung to his dirty, bloodied arm, as if he were trying to absorb one last reminder of his physical body before he died. A part of him didn't want to die. It was his Indian spirit fighting, he guessed.

All of Mike's focus was drawn to the dark hairs that carpeted his forearm. Suddenly some of the hair began to turn a deep gold color. The black hairs remaining took on the shape of black crescent moons all over his now golden-haired arm. What the hell was going down? He didn't have the strength to utter the question. His mind spun. He couldn't think straight any longer. He watched, mesmerized, as his forearm continued to change. Gasping he saw his long, callused fingers transformed into claws. He was no longer staring at his hand, but the huge paw of a big cat! What was happening? Was he hallucinating? That was it. He was hallucinating just as he was dying.

A new strength began to flow up his right arm, a startlingly powerful, pulsing sensation of life triumphing unexpectedly over death. Groaning, Mike rolled onto his back. He closed his eyes, unable to comprehend this strange new feeling. As the warmth and power tunneled up his right arm and flowed into his thickly corded neck and head, he felt changes. Unusual changes. He felt his teeth elongate in his mouth. Strangely, miraculously, he began to regain his senses.

His left arm began to feel like his right one. Then his torso felt like it was shifting—expanding here, narrowing there. The warmth flowed down into his legs and he felt them change shape, too. He was dying, that was all. Dying. But if this was death, why was his heart beating so powerfully in his chest? He opened his mouth and took in a deep, ragged breath. Air flowed into his lungs, life-giving and galvanizing. *What's going on?* His mind wasn't working right. His senses were suddenly, inexplicably acute. Even more so, his sense of smell was heightened. He could scent the soldiers and detect the direction they were coming from. Even better, he could hear them as he'd never heard them before.

Mike rolled onto his stomach. He shouldn't have been able to due to his wound, but he did. The jungle had taken on different colors to him—not the shades he was used to seeing. Soft light surrounded every leaf, branch and tree. Everything was connected by that river of slowly moving light.

The first soldier was nearly upon him. Mike crouched and waited. Anger tunneled through him as he saw the man lift his rifle and quicken his pace toward where he lay hiding. The soldier was dressed in camouflage fatigues and heavily armed, his black eyes narrowed with a sort of savage pleasure. There was no denying his murderous intent, and Mike sensed this intruder into his domain had tortured many victims and enjoyed their pain, their screams. Blinking, Mike saw a dark gray color around the man. It wasn't at all like the clear, unbeguiling light he saw around the plants and trees. No, this man's light was murky. *Evil.*

Instinctively, Mike crouched, every fiber of his being set to defend himself. He didn't know where the strength came from, but he felt his hind legs tense, lower slightly, and then he lunged out of his hiding place, his body a projectile, his claws aimed at the man's exposed neck.

The soldier shrieked and tried to halt. Too late! Everything went black in front of Mike. As he slashed savagely at the soldier's neck, he heard the man's scream die in his throat. Within seconds, three more soldiers arrived. Though Mike did not see them, he heard their choking cries and screams of surprise, felt the powerful, flowing movement of his well-muscled, sleek body. The only thing he knew was that his life was at stake and he had to kill them before they killed him.

Once the killing was over, he felt blackness rimming his vision, the gold-and-white light rapidly beginning to fade. With a groan that seemed more like a low growl to his ears, he felt himself running, or more appropriately, loping. He could feel the slap of leaves against his body, but he couldn't see anything! His energy began to seep away. Strength left his legs, flowing up through his torso. He felt the damp earth beneath his hands and he suddenly collapsed onto it with a groan. The light was gone; the darkness rapidly moved toward him. He was dead. He was sure of it as he lay there on the jungle floor, covered in the humid mist that divided this world and the next.

Houston regained consciousness slowly. Prying his heavy lids open languidly, he stared upward. He lay on his back, hidden by the thick, luxuriant growth around him. Yes, he could see the dark silhouettes of the trees outlined in the mist. But something was different. What? His mind was groggy and he was having trouble remembering much of anything. Above the dense, humid white clouds above the canopy, the sun had shifted. It was almost dusk, he realized.

Little by little, strength flowed back to him. He groaned and rolled slowly onto his left side. Recalling his deadly wound, he propped himself up against a tree and groggily looked down at his right thigh. Blood was everywhere across his lower body. Yet where was the wound? Weakly lifting his hand, his fingers trembling badly, he tried to find the rip in the material where the bullet had entered. There was none. Frowning, he tried to think. It was impossible.

Was he dead and just didn't know it? Looking up, he realized he felt different, but very much alive. He dug his fingers into the damp, rotting leaves to assure himself of the reality of his surroundings. As he continued to stare down at the place where his wound should have been, he realized something else had changed. The entire front of his uniform was splattered with blood. He hadn't been wounded in the chest. What would cause blood to cover the front of shirt? Moving his hand slowly up his wrinkled, muddy uniform, Houston realized the blood had dried, stiffening the fabric. The metallic odor clung nauseatingly to his flaring nostrils.

How did he get covered with so much blood? It couldn't be his own. His mind railed at the illogic of it all. Lifting his head, Mike slowly tried to absorb everything around him. Yes, he was still in a jungle. The same one he'd crash-landed into, as far as he could tell. Monkeys screamed in the distance, their howling somehow comforting him. A few colorful parrots flew above him looking for a night perch before dusk ended in darkness.

As his gaze dropped from the jungle around him to his left arm, hanging at his side, he felt a jolt. There were gold hairs on his arm. Gold and black. He frowned, thinking he was seeing things. Using what little strength he had left, he lifted his arm and stared at it. What the hell? His vision blurred and then cleared once again. There, on his forearm near his wrist, was an irregular patch of gold hair with two black crescent-moon shapes. This couldn't be real, he reasoned. As he moved his fingers across the patch of hair, his heart thudded hard, once, in his chest. It was fur. Soft, short, thick fur, surrounded by his own hair. But as he explored it, it disappeared beneath his fingertips.

Overwhelmed, Houston leaned his head back against the tree and drew several deep breaths of air into his lungs. His senses were no longer as acute, but he heard voices not too far from where he lay. Escovar's men? Snapping his eyes open, Mike waited. For some reason, he didn't feel danger. That was silly, too. Just moments ago, several of Escovar's men were going to kill him. Confused, Mike narrowed his eyes and gazed toward the sound.

An aged white man, barefoot and wearing dark blue pants, with a jaguar skin draped over his shoulders, appeared out of the jungle in front of him. Houston raised his eyes to the gray-haired man's bearded face and met his crinkled gray eyes. The old man nodded in greeting and exposed strong white teeth in a welcoming smile. The man's two cohorts came toward Mike, an African man and a young Indian girl with willow green eyes.

"I was told you were out here," the old man said, leaning heavily against a staff that had brightly colored macaw feathers attached to its top. He touched the claw necklace around his neck and chuckled. "I see your guardian has left you your life, hombre. We will take you back to the village. You will be safe with us. Come...."

Chapter 1

"Mike? Mike, it's time to get up!"

Groaning, Houston turned on his side, jamming his face into the feather pillow. Damn, he thought groggily, he'd had that nightmare again. A flashback really, the same one he'd had a hundred times before...

"Mike?"

"Uh, yeah...I'm awake...." he muttered.

Where was he? Rolling over, he forced his eyes open. The plain timbers of the Santa Fe architecture of the room met his eyes, reminding him he was no longer in the jungle. The sounds were different here. He heard the crow of a nearby rooster and the soft snort of some horses in a corral. As he blinked the sleep out of his eyes, he heard the lowing of cattle, too. Oh yeah, he remembered suddenly. He was staying at the Donovan Ranch near Sedona, Arizona. Helluva long way from his normal digs.

He shoved himself upright in the old brass bed, the covers falling away to expose his naked chest and upper body. When he got the chance, he never slept with clothes on—even pajamas—preferring nakedness instead. All too often in his work he had to sleep in his fatigues, ready to leap up and start moving at a moment's notice. In fact, sleeping in a bed was a luxury for him.

Savagely rubbing his face to wake up, Mike felt the stiff prickle of beard beneath his fingers. He'd had that post-traumatic-stress-disorder dream again, reminding him of who he really was, of what made him different from other men, other human beings. Scowling, he shook his head and sent the fragments of memory back into the depths of that cauldron, his subconscious. *More like Pandora's box with an ugly twist,* he thought with a sleepy grin.

What time is it? he wondered, shoving his feet from beneath the covers and placing them on the cool cedar floor. The clock on his bed stand said 0800.

Dr. Ann Parsons had called him from the next room, he realized belatedly. The alarm clock must have gone off and he hadn't heard it. *Damn.* He'd promised Morgan Trayhern that he'd meet him at 0800 to get the details of his next mission. Grunting, Mike launched himself out of bed and stretched. He liked the feeling of each group of muscles in his body bunching, stretching and relaxing. Arcing his arms over his head, he closed his eyes and appreciated his physical strength. It was one helluva body, one that had more scars on it, had taken more blows and survived more than most.

Exhaling loudly, he ran his fingers through his military short, dark hair and headed to the bathroom that adjoined his room. As he padded across the pale gold floor, he remembered his nightmare. A smile cut across his thinned lips as he opened the door to the shower and turned it on. Nine years had passed since that incident in the jungle, and at thirty-five years of age, he still dreamed about that miraculous, life-changing event.

As he stepped into the pummeling stream of hot water for his morning shower—another luxury—the steam roiled in clouds around him reminding him of the endless twisting clouds that haunted the jungles of South America. He grabbed the soap and began to briskly wash himself. There was nothing like a hot shower to get the blood flowing and wake him up. For the first hour of the morning Houston was a bear of sorts, until he was fully awake and had poured a cup of good, black espresso down his gullet. Then and only then was he human and not growling or

snarling at everyone. Mike had a reputation of being a grizzly in
the morning.

Soaping his left arm, he blinked away the water running in
rivulets across his face. Grinning, he studied the burn scars on his
darkly haired arm, reminding him of his escape from the flaming
copter that had been shot down. Various white scars from shrapnel
that had exploded from the craft after it had crashed were also
visible reminders of that day he'd faced death and won.

But he no longer saw a tuft of gold fur with black crescents
across it. Scrubbing his arm, Mike turned his face into the stream
of hot water. That old shaman from the village, Grandfather
Adaire, had informed him that Mike's guardian had guided him
to rescue Mike and care for him. It took nearly a week of rest in
that remote jungle village known as the Village of the Clouds
before Houston had been in any shape to decide whether he
wanted to live or not.

Mike recalled how his men at the military barracks just outside
of Lima called him *El Jaguar,* or the jaguar god—the man who
had returned from the dead. Jaguars were believed to be the only
animal able to do that, according to legends about them that
abounded throughout South America. Everyone had thought Mike
died with the other men of his squad in that crash. But he hadn't.
And he never told anyone of his strange adventure through life,
death and life again. They'd have called him loco—crazy. No one
would ever know the truth of what had really happened out there.

Only that old shaman, his white hair sticking out around his
head like a hen's nest, seemed to know exactly what had happened. Mike had been too weak to question him. Inca, the young
Indian girl from Brazil with the willow green eyes and long black
hair, had fed him nourishing soup, kept him warm and tended him
hourly in a hut near the shaman's dwelling in the village. For that
entire week, Inca had cared for him like he was a newborn baby.
She was only eighteen years old, an orphan who had been adopted
by Adaire and his wife, Alaria. Every time Adaire dropped by to
see how well Mike was recovering, the old shaman would laugh
the laugh of a man who knew an inside joke. Only Mike didn't
know the joke and the shaman didn't seem particularly desirous
of letting him in on it.

After washing his hair, Mike quickly rinsed, shut off the shower and climbed out. Rubbing himself briskly with a thick, white, terry-cloth towel, he reveled in the sensations it created across his goose-bump-covered flesh. Funny, but since that incident nine years earlier, he'd become far more aware of his body than ever before. He had walked away from his experience in the jungle with a sense of pleasure about his tall, strong physical form that he'd not had previous to his brush with death. Sometimes he felt like a great, giant cat stretching. And if he ran, he could feel the joy of blood pumping through him, the incredible power in his muscles. It was a euphoric sensation, one that he'd come to enjoy.

Hurrying through the rest of his morning duties, Mike quickly dressed in his camouflage fatigues, put his spotless, shining boots on and placed his beret in the left epaulet of his blouse. Taking one more look in the steamy mirror, he saw staring back at him a man who looked like one tough hombre, in his opinion. His blue eyes were large, though more often they were narrowed, focusing on something that would catch his wary attention. Tiny white scars stood out against his recently shaved jaw. The many lines at the corners of his eyes and the slash brackets on either side of his pursed mouth shouted of his military hardness. He was a major in Special Forces and damn proud of it. He'd survived thirteen long years in the Peruvian jungle, where life was often snuffed out in a heartbeat by vengeful drug lords.

Glancing at the watch on his hairy wrist, he realized he'd better get a move on. He'd just hurry out to the kitchen, grab his very necessary cup of espresso and gulp it down before meeting Morgan. And he was anxious to get to that meeting for another reason beside the fact that he was late. Though Mike had enjoyed the peace and quiet of this ranch, he had discovered other, greater benefits to staying there—such as spending time with the good doctor. Dr. Ann Parsons had been assigned to tend to Morgan and his wife's recovery, while Mike had been assigned to keep guard. And he certainly hadn't minded working with the pretty M.D.

Even better than seeing his boss today, Mike decided as he opened the door to his bedroom, he'd get to sit and look at Ann once more. Smiling to himself, he realized he was looking forward to that pleasure most of all. Even though she also worked for

Morgan at Perseus, a high-level, supersecret government entity, he wouldn't see her after today. Houston wanted to take every opportunity to absorb her beauty before they parted ways. Sighing as he walked down the gleaming hallway, he knew he could easily fall in love with Ann. If he allowed himself to. The price that they'd pay, however, would be too high. Besides, his keen interest in her was only one-sided. Yes, they'd shared a number of heated, promising kisses over the last two months, but she wasn't really interested in him as much as he wished she were. Ann was afraid of commitment, Mike realized. Why, he didn't know.

The memory of her sweet, soft mouth beneath his made him go hot with yearning all over again. Ann enjoyed their stolen moments together, there was no doubt. So why did she keep pushing him away? He'd seen the desire in her thoughtful blue-gray eyes after one of their torrid, hungry kisses. Had felt her tremble deliciously in his arms. The hunger in her eyes went all the way through him. So what had stopped her every damn time? Mike was confused. He'd tried to get Ann to open up, to talk about it, but she wouldn't. It was like hitting a damn brick wall. But he didn't press Ann any longer. Because although this was the first time in a long time he found himself wanting a woman, being with Ann wasn't a game with him, either. Mike didn't see her as a one-night stand or someone to amuse himself with while he was here in Arizona. He, too, was wary of having a relationship and he knew he couldn't have things both ways. But what really did he want with her?

The realistic side of him told him that even though he could fall hopelessly in love with her if he threw caution to the wind, their relationship could go nowhere anyway. Not with his jaded past. Not with his dangerous present and future. His heart ached. He reluctantly admitted that he'd felt a lot of things for Ann over the past two months and there wasn't a damn thing he could do about it. Maybe, Houston ruminated sadly, it was just as well she kept her distance from him—for whatever secret reasons she held. Anyone he had ever loved had died. It was that heartbreakingly simple. A fact. And he had no desire to see Ann die. *Hell...*

More than anything, Mike respected Ann. She had started out as an Air Force flight surgeon and her training also included work as a psychiatrist. Now a medical doctor for Perseus, she was very good at what she did. Her work with Morgan had often placed her in danger; she was frequently assigned to fly in and pick up wounded mercenaries when they got into more trouble than they'd bargained for. Mike decided that maybe Ann had made a pact with herself a long time ago not to get involved with military types. Oh, he didn't blame her there. Hell, a military man could be alive one moment, dead the next. And where did that leave the woman who loved him? Alone, without the man she'd hoped to have around for a long, long time. Her lover gone—forever.

Too bad. She's a looker. Tall, leggy, self-confident, she had a gutsiness he admired. There was nothing about the thirty-two-year-old doctor that didn't appeal to him. Pity she didn't see him in the same light. Maybe her womanly instincts warned her how different he really was. Maybe she was picking up on his secret life and it was scaring her away from him....

Mike turned the corner and headed to the kitchen. Hell, any woman who took one look at his hard-bitten, scarred countenance and heard of his fearsome reputation would run the other way. He was one mean son of a bitch and he had his actions in Peru to prove it.

Down there they called him the jaguar god because he seemed to have nine lives like the most powerful hunter in the South American jungle—the dreaded, mystical jaguar. The drug lords feared Mike and they damn well should. Those bastards had destroyed his mother's helpless people, and as long as Houston could take a breath into his body, his whole life would be geared to eradicating them from Peru.

Maybe that's why no women wanted to become involved in a long-term relationship with him. They wouldn't be the focus of his life or his attentions. Houston couldn't blame them. Still, he'd miss Ann Parsons like hell. Her soft, exploratory kisses, the hunger she sparked in him would be no more. It was a damn shame. For she was a woman who could not only turn his head, but even make him consider devoting a little time to her instead of the one-man war he waged continuously against the cocaine lords....

When Houston reached the kitchen, he heard voices. Groaning inwardly, he realized it was Ann's honeyed, cultured tone and

Morgan Trayhern's deep, probing voice. Mike was so late the meeting was already underway. As he headed for the espresso machine, he heard them in the living room talking animatedly, like the good friends they were. Ann had worked for Morgan almost from the time he'd created Perseus many years ago. It was then he saw the note beside the tiled sink, next to the espresso machine. "In case you oversleep," it said in Ann's "doctor scrawl." No one could read her writing but him, and he'd teased her about it mercilessly during the eight weeks they had been at the Donovan Ranch baby-sitting Morgan and his wife.

Mike hurriedly snapped on the machine. Ann had ground the coffee, put it in the small basket and filled the steel container with fresh water that would soon be boiling, ready to percolate his desperately needed espresso. A mirthless, one-cornered smile cut into the hard planes of Mike's face. Though Ann didn't like him to the degree he fancied her, she had a good heart. She'd even taken pity on the likes of him.

Houston poked his head around the entrance to the living room of the cabin he was staying in on the ranch. They'd agreed to meet at his cabin and he saw Morgan, dressed in a pair of jeans and a red plaid, flannel shirt, sitting at the end of a leather couch, near the open fireplace. Ann stood in front of the blazing flames, which brought out the red and gold highlights in her shoulder-length, sable hair. She was rubbing her long, thin surgeon's hands together vigorously, warming herself.

Mike was chilly, too, but it was wintertime in Arizona, so what did he expect? When Ann lifted her chin and her blue-gray eyes met his, he grinned a little sheepishly.

"Morning," he rumbled.

"Is it? You haven't had your coffee yet, Major Houston, so I know better than to engage you in polite social conversation."

His boyish grin broadened in embarrassment. He saw Morgan frown and look first at Ann and then at him.

Houston nodded. "Yeah, you're right, Doc. I'm just an old, snarly jaguar before I get my espresso. I'll be in shortly. A good fairy all but made my java for me and it'll be ready pronto." He winked at her. "I owe you, Ann...."

"Take your time, Mike," Morgan murmured with a forgiving

look. He lifted a heavy white mug from the coffee table and took a sip. "Today we're not in a hurry."

Mike saw Ann's eyes sparkle mischievously even though her face had a deadpan expression. As he stepped back into the kitchen, he remembered the blush that had spread across her long, sloping cheekbones when he'd winked at her. She always reacted to his playful charm with some discomfort. He wondered why and lamented once more that Ann had never opened up to him about her past or why she couldn't fully embrace him now. Her kisses said one thing, the fear he saw in her eyes quite another.

Damn, but the woman was pretty. Did she realize she held his heart in her hands? Did she want today to be goodbye? He'd dreamed torrid dreams of loving her completely. The closest they had come to that was the day they had shared a picnic down at the creek. He'd accurately read her desire that time, and when he'd kissed her, she'd asked him to touch her intimately, to explore her with his hands.

In the molten heat of the moment, as he'd stretched out on the blanket beside her, she'd frozen. Mike had sat up, for he had no desire to push himself on her. She had apologized and quickly pulled her blouse back over her shoulders, before getting up and hurrying away. Her face had been flushed and he could tell she was embarrassed by her behavior.

It was so frustrating! Everything about their relationship was on again, off again. She wanted him. She was afraid of him. Or maybe she was afraid of herself? Mike pondered that angle as he waited for his espresso to brew.

Ann was a type A personality who didn't know how to rest or relax. She had to be doing something every single minute of her day. In his book, people like that were running away from something. So what was Ann running from? Sighing audibly, Mike scowled. If only she'd lower those walls she held around herself and talk to him. If only...

The aromatic odor of the espresso drifted toward him as he stood expectantly over the machine. Ann had often made a wry face at his need to drink only black, thick espresso, but hell, in South America it was the drink of choice, besides maté, Argentina's national drink. He'd been raised on espresso since he was a small kid, following his mother into the kitchen as she made her own cup each morning.

Picking up the note with his scarred fingers, he shook his head. He couldn't figure Ann out. Most of the time around the ranch she pointedly ignored him. His job was to run patrols and keep Morgan and Laura safe from possible drug-cartel attacks while they holed up and tried to heal from the kidnapping ordeal that had torn their lives apart, quite literally, at the seams. Ann had come because she was a qualified psychiatrist and Laura's state had been rocky and unstable at first.

Mike ran his fingers across the ink on the note. Since she'd been staying at the hideaway cabin on Oak Creek with her husband, Laura spent an hour in therapy every day with Dr. Parsons, and Mike wasn't surprised that Ann had helped Laura Trayhern tremendously. God knew, he wanted to feel the effects of Ann's undivided attention on him. Grinning darkly, he told himself that he'd change, too, if given the chance to be the center of *her* focus. But thus far, Ann evaded him whenever possible. So why did she obviously enjoy his kisses so much when he eased her into his arms? He could feel all her walls melt away as they kissed.

Was Ann prejudiced against his skin color—the fact that he wasn't a pure white, Anglo male with all the trimmings? Perhaps she couldn't bring herself to admit it to herself, much less him? Questions, so many damn, unanswered questions. And today was the last day he'd ever see Ann. His heart squeezed with pain. With need.

As he poured the espresso into a small, delicate white cup with his large hands, he sighed in frustration, mentally preparing himself to shift gears and talk business with Morgan Trayhern. At least Ann would be in the same room with him and he'd get one last moment with her. He felt like a man being sent to the gallows and having his last wish fulfilled, but hell, there was no love life for him where he was heading. None at all. The only thing waiting for him was a bullet or a machete with his name on it. No, Peru was his hell. Whatever small piece of heaven he'd been afforded had died years earlier, and Houston knew that with his karmic track record—the many men he'd killed over the years—heaven wasn't about to grant him a second chance at anything. With a careless grin, he shrugged his shoulders as if throwing off the grief and chains of the past, and headed toward the living room.

Chapter 2

Mike sauntered into the living room after taking his first, rejuvenating sip of the dark, fragrant liquid. He chose a leather wing chair opposite Morgan, in front of a coffee table littered with magazines. Ann was holding her own cup of coffee between her hands, standing with her back to the snapping, roaring fire. She refused to look him in the eye, some of the flush still lingering on her cheeks.

"I overslept," Mike growled in Morgan's direction, studying his boss's somber features. The man who had hired him was internationally famous. Morgan headed up Perseus, a high-tech mercenary operation consisting of men and women, mostly from the military, who were hired to perform dangerous missions around the world. Though Perseus was privately owned by Morgan, there wasn't a government in the democratic world that didn't hire his renown services. Like Morgan, whose honesty and strong military background kept this clandestine ship of state running smoothly, his people were the best at what they did. Most people, when they heard the word *mercenary*, thought of a turncoat bastard who had no allegiance except to the bottom line: money. Not so at Perseus. Trayhern's reputation for integrity was well known by almost every government in the world. He and his team were revered for coming to the aid of those who were in trouble and, for whatever reason, were without their country's legal or political protection.

Because Trayhern had been wronged by his own country, had been labeled a traitor and been in hiding for nearly half his life before his name was cleared with the help of his wife, he knew the disastrous results of not being able to reach out to some powerful entity for help.

As Mike leaned back and relished each sip of his espresso, he noticed once again the white scar that ran from Morgan's left temple all the way down his recently shaved cheek to his jaw, a mute testimony of his surviving on a hill in the closing days of the Vietnam War. There, he'd been a captain in the Marine Corps, and responsible for a company of men that had been wiped out and overrun by the enemy. Only he and one other man had survived. And then his troubles had really begun. Now that he was nearing fifty, Morgan's black hair was peppered at the temples with silver though his square face was still hard, shouting of the rigid discipline of his military background. Because he was a hero in Houston's eyes, Mike had agreed to act as Morgan and Laura's bodyguard during this rather bland two-month stay in rural Arizona.

"You ready to talk?" Morgan asked him with a slight grin. "Ann's been warning me about you being snarly without your espresso."

"Yeah," Mike rumbled, "she might as well have set up an IV and poured it directly into my veins this morning. Sorry I overslept." He glanced at Ann, who refused to meet his gaze. Mike was too much of a gentleman to say *why* he'd lost so much sleep last night. The reason was that he'd cornered Ann and asked her why she was evading him. It had turned into a frustrating, angry confrontation and he'd ended up silencing her with a kiss—a kiss that had nearly been both their undoing. Ann had almost lost control of herself. He had felt her unraveling in his arms. And that's when she'd pushed him away. It had been a miserable night for them, he acknowledged. She'd cried and he'd held her. Yet as he rocked her in his arms, she'd still refused to give in to him and talk about why she kept him at arm's length. One thing he knew for sure, she didn't trust him. That hurt Mike deeply and his heart ached with sadness.

Cocking his head in Ann's direction, he saw a slight, strained smile cross her full lips as she lifted the cup and took a sip of her coffee. Her eyes were still puffy looking this morning. He wondered if she'd cried more after tearing out of his embrace and fleeing to her room last night.

Morgan nodded. "It was a good day to sleep in." He picked up a file and handed it across the pine coffee table to Mike. "Here's your pay and a little extra bonus for taking this mission on. I know you didn't have to."

As the manila file slid into his fingers, Mike placed his cup on the table. Opening the folder, he saw a check for thirty thousand dollars, plus papers detailing all his duties over the last two months.

His brows raised. "This is a little much, boss."

Morgan grinned and crossed his legs. "I know soldiers like you don't enjoy baby-sitting jobs like this one. But you knew the drug lords involved, and you knew their habits and techniques. I know you'd rather be down in the Peruvian jungles chasing them than sitting up here for two months playing watchdog." He motioned with his finger toward the check Houston was holding. "I'm grateful you took the mission, pabulum or not, Mike. That's our way of thanking you."

Houston had heard several times from Ann how generous Trayhern was with his employees, as well as the charities they supported. Now Mike was getting a firsthand taste of it. "Hell," he muttered, "this is almost a year's army pay for me."

Chuckling, Morgan nodded. "It probably is. There's a first-class airline ticket there also, reserved under your assumed identity of Peter Quinn. You've got a flight out of Phoenix at 1500 hours today aboard Veracruz Airlines. They make a fueling stop in Mexico City and then you fly directly into Lima."

The man was excessively generous, Mike decided as he found the airline ticket. He frowned as he saw another check beneath the ticket. Setting the folder down in his lap, he muttered, "What's this?" His eyes widened considerably. It was a check for a hundred thousand dollars, made out to the Sisters of Guadalupe Clinic in Lima, Peru.

"Laura was telling me how, in your spare time, you work with two old French nuns down in the barrio, the poor section of Lima, using your paramedic skills alongside the nuns' homeopathic treatments. She said you'd established the medical clinic eight years ago to help Indian children who couldn't afford medical help." He waved his hand toward the check Mike was holding. "That's a donation to your clinic, Houston. Laura hinted that the clinic was usually running on hope and faith, and that you could use a lot more supplies." His eyes grew thoughtful. "Maybe this will keep the wolf...or jaguar...from your clinic's door for a while."

Mike swallowed hard, his Adam's apple bobbing as he held the check. The paper felt as if it were burning his fingers. "This..."

"Speechless for once?" Ann teased with a soft laugh.

Mike twisted his head to look up at her. That unreadable doctor's facade generally in place on her oval face was gone. He waited for such moments because her openness gave her unusual features a warm attractiveness. Her nose was long and thin and had obviously been broken at one time because there was a slight bump on it. She was narrow all over—narrow oval face, narrow hands and skinny but shapely legs. Her eyes were one of her finest features: large, intelligent and widely set. Her mouth, which was now curved gently, hinted powerfully to him of her soft, vulnerable side. Mike hungrily absorbed her countenance, and he managed a slight grin. Ann was trying desperately to be civil to him.

He saw the darkness in her eyes and could feel her fear. Was she as sad over their parting as he was? His heart said yes. Although his intuition didn't make sense at all to him, now was not the place or time to pursue it. He was sure Morgan didn't know about Ann's on-and-off relationship with him over the past two months, and he'd keep it that way—for her sake.

"Yeah, you're right—I usually have a comeback for almost everything, don't I?"

Ann nodded. "Without fail, Major Houston. One of your most reliable traits."

"I'll take that as praise, not an insult, Dr. Parsons." A little of her old, teasing self was resurfacing, and Mike was glad. The last thing he wanted was to make Ann feel bad, and he sure as hell had managed to do that last night. Before he left, he knew he'd have to draw her aside, privately, and apologize. He didn't want their friendship to end on a bitter note. Ann deserved better than that and so did he.

She shrugged her shoulders delicately. "Take it any way you want, Major. I'm always open to options."

How he wished she really were! Laughing deeply, Mike returned his attention to Morgan. "This is unexpected."

The warmth in Morgan's eyes belied the expressionless mask he usually wore over his features. "Needed, according to Laura," he said. "I like to help out the less fortunate. God knows, I was one for long enough, Mike." He scowled at the memory of the atrocities he'd suffered.

Mike stared at the check. "Thank you. You have no idea how *much* this is going to help. I was trying to figure out a way to keep the clinic open. I'm afraid our little charity isn't seen as very worthy by the rich and powerful in Lima. The children are dark-skinned Indians, not poor little Anglos in need. Believe me—" his voice shook with sudden emotion "—this is going to help more than you'll ever know." Mike vaguely recalled talking to Laura about his clinic once, a fleeting conversation he'd completely forgotten about. The woman didn't forget anything! And she was just as generous and giving as her very wealthy husband.

"We're glad to do what we can, Mike. From now on, your clinic is on *our* donation list. The sum might go up or down a little, but at least you'll know that every January, you'll be receiving enough money, I hope, to keep those doors open to the Indian children and their families." Leaning forward, Morgan took a second manila file from the coffee table and handed it to Ann. "Here are your marching orders, Ann. You were asking me where I was sending you next. Well, take a look. I think you'll be pleased."

Ann smiled warmly at Morgan as she took the file. "Thanks. I love new missions."

Mike saw how comfortable Ann and Morgan were with one another and realized they almost had an older brother–younger sister relationship. It was obvious Ann loved Morgan and re-

spected him. Hell, who wouldn't? Still, Mike felt a twinge of longing because he wished Ann would bestow such a warm, trusting
look in his direction. But he knew that would never happen after
today, and he found himself lamenting that fact far more sharply
than he should. Such was the effect the good doctor had on him,
although she pretended to be oblivious of the way he mooned over
her like a jaguar did over a lost mate. Mike suspected Ann really
missed nothing. She was a trained therapist. She was taught to
observe nuances of body language, tone of voice and subtle expressions. No, she knew he was powerfully drawn to her, but she
wasn't interested, that was all. And although that left him confused
and frustrated, he realized it was for the best. He wasn't exactly
the kind of man who could give her what she needed, in light of
his own past.

Sighing, Mike leaned back in the chair, stealing a moment to
watch Ann unobtrusively. He rarely got such a chance, and since
they were parting today and he'd never see her again, he wanted
to take this opportunity to absorb her into his heart one last time.
In some ways, he was like a greedy thief, and he felt a little guilty
about it.

Ann chuckled as she placed the coffee cup on the dark wood
mantel above the fireplace. "I hope it's a warm place, Morgan!
I'm freezing here." She opened the file in her hands. "Hawaii or
Australia would sure be nice," she hinted with a smile.

"Oh," Morgan murmured, "you're going someplace warm, all
right, but neither of those countries."

Ann picked up the airline ticket and opened it.

Mike saw her broad brow wrinkle instantly. And then she
snapped an unsettled look in *his* direction. He almost asked why,
but then she pursed her lips and began sifting through the rest of
the papers, reading intently.

"Morgan," she protested in a strangled tone, "what's going on
here? This isn't an assignment for another mission." Ann stared
accusingly at Houston again. "These are orders to go down to *his*
clinic in Lima and help him out for six weeks."

"Yes," Morgan murmured, sipping his coffee contentedly, "it
is."

Stunned, Houston looked at Ann's upset features and then at

Morgan. "What?" He couldn't have been hearing right. His heart pounded briefly in his chest as he sat up at full attention. Ann was coming to Lima with him? The news staggered him. Elated him. Worried him. He saw the undiluted fear in Ann's eyes as never before. His hands wrapped around the arms of the chair. What was going on here?

Waving her thin hand across the file, Ann sputtered, "Morgan, this isn't a mission assignment. This—this is—charity work!"

"It's a mission," Morgan soothed. "A very important one. Laura and I think you're the perfect person to help Mike get this little clinic up and running." He smiled slightly, satisfied with his plans. "As a matter of fact—" he glanced down at the gold Rolex watch on his wrist "—there's a load of medical supplies being trucked from Mesa, Arizona, over to Sky Harbor International Airport in Phoenix right now. Ann, you will be responsible for over fifty thousand dollars' worth of medical supplies once you two land in Lima. And then I expect you, with your usual precision and organizational skills, to take the six weeks and get Mike's clinic up to full speed like it should be."

Gasping, Ann shut the folder with finality. Her eyes flashed. "You *planned* this, Major Houston."

Mike's mouth dropped open and he quickly snapped it shut. "Now, just a minute, Ann," he muttered as he unwound from the chair and stood up, "I didn't know anything about this." And he hadn't. But he felt her anger directly. Those gray-blue eyes of hers turned icy cold when she was upset. Disliking the fact that he was being accused of something he was innocent of, he looked at Morgan. "Tell her, will you?"

"Mike knew nothing about this, Ann. It was actually Laura's idea. We spent several evenings planning it out, making the necessary phone calls and getting everything lined up."

Glaring at Houston, Ann closed her fingers tightly over the folder. "Morgan, one thing I learned about this Peruvian cowboy in the last two months I've spent here is that he's a master of manipulation."

"Oww, that hurts," Mike protested. Not that it wasn't true. "Sure, I rob Peter to pay Paul, so to speak, in order to get the money I need to finance our military efforts down in Peru, but—"

"You've got a mind like a steel trap," Ann accused in a low voice. "You probably purposely dropped the information about your clinic to Laura because you know she has such a soft heart for people who are in trouble or need help."

Anger stirred in Houston. One thing he didn't like was being wrongly accused. He saw the desperation in Ann's eyes and heard the raw pain in her voice. He was receiving so many confused emotional signals from her that he didn't have time to sort them all out. Keeping his voice soothing, he rasped, "Look, Ann, I had *no idea* when Laura buttonholed me about a month ago, and nosed around about what I did down in Lima, that she'd take the information and do something like this with it."

"Ann, calm down," Morgan said in his deep voice. "This isn't a prison sentence."

"Really?" Ann glared steadily in Houston's direction.

"Really," Morgan repeated. He sat up and placed his cup on the coffee table in front of him. "Why be so upset? It's spring in Peru. It's warm. It's a beautiful country and Lima is one of the most sophisticated and affluent cities in South America. I've arranged everything for you. There'll be a van waiting at the Lima airport. The medical supplies will be loaded into it and Mike can drive you to the clinic. There's another car there waiting for you. It was bought earlier and registered in the clinic's name, since the clinic's got a nonprofit status. You can use it to drive back and forth to the nice apartment we've rented for you." He smiled at her. "For once you aren't going to be flying around in a helicopter with a flak jacket and helmet on, wondering if you're landing in a hot fire zone. This is a pretty safe assignment. Quiet. Probably pretty boring, but I'm sure it will be immensely satisfying to you emotionally. It isn't that you don't like children. I know different."

Houston prowled restlessly around the perimeter of the living room. He watched Ann give him livid, stabbing looks of raw accusation every now and again, despite the fact that Morgan had an incredibly soothing effect on her—any woman, in fact. Mike wished he had the skill, but didn't. "Look," he protested in frustration, "if Ann doesn't want to go, there's nothing I can do about that. But maybe I can take the edge off things a little bit for her." He leaned down and picked up the thirty-thousand-dollar check.

''Here, put this with the rest, since you're going to have to put up with me six weeks longer than you thought.'' He handed Ann the donation and the personal check Morgan had written out to him. He could see the fear deep in her eyes. Anger warred with sadness and heartbreak within him. Trying his best to gather his strewn emotions, he rasped, ''You want to run a clinic, it takes money. So here it is. And if you're pissed off and distrusting of me and my intentions, well, that's okay. I know the truth—I had nothing to do with this assignment of yours. I won't be around the clinic that much to be a pain in the ass to you, anyway. Fair enough?'' He put both checks in her hands. Her gaze wavered as she met his hard, angry eyes.

Houston turned, shook Morgan's hand, thanked him and left. He needed to get out of the house and calm down. As he went out the front door, the coolness of the Arizona morning hit him. Throwing back his shoulders, he descended the wooden steps quickly and headed toward the corral. *Damn! Everything's screwed up. Everything!* As he took long, steady strides, Mike rubbed his aching chest.

But although this wasn't how he'd planned things to go with Ann, a tiny part of him was euphoric that she would be coming to Lima with him. He would have more time with her, even if the opportunities to see her would be severely limited down there. As he halted at the corral, where twenty Arabians were feeding, he placed his elbows on the uppermost rung of the pipe fence. The metal felt cooling to him, to his smarting anger and frustration.

Closing his eyes, Houston tried to wrestle with all his emotions. Ann thought he'd set this whole thing up. It was obvious she hadn't believed Morgan when he'd explained that Mike had nothing to do with it. Her anger was real. And so was that terror banked in her eyes. Closing his fists, Mike took a deep, unsettled breath of air into his chest. No matter how hard he tried, he couldn't erase the sweet power of Ann's mouth upon his, her incredible, hungry response to him. But although her mouth, her body signaled one thing, her mind held sway over her actions. What a helluva fix he was in now! More than anything, Mike wanted to somehow convince Ann that he was innocent of dragging her on this assignment. Judging from her anger, she probably wasn't going to give him an opening very soon to explain. Maybe, on the flight down to Lima, she'd cool off and he could reason with her. He hoped so. Or maybe Morgan could soothe her because Mike certainly couldn't!

"Morgan, I don't want to go down there," Ann declared.

He shrugged and sipped his coffee. "Calm down, Ann. This is an excellent assignment." He smiled up at her drawn features. She looked cornered but Morgan didn't really want to let her out of this one. Worried that Escovar, one of the most powerful of all the drug dealers in South America, was going to go after Mike Houston in earnest once Mike was back in Peru, Morgan wanted a backup. He didn't want to tell Houston of his concerns for his life, but if Mike got into trouble, Morgan wanted someone with the best medical skills on the planet nearby. And even though Ann was only in her early thirties, she was a top professional in the field.

Ann didn't know why he was sending her to Peru to be near Houston. Morgan didn't want to put that kind of pressure on her. Besides, from everything he and his wife could see, there was a mutual attraction between the by-the-book doctor and the hotheaded, passionate major whose Indian blood kept him running headlong into dangerous scrapes with Escovar. Yes, Ann's cool, calm and collected personality would be a good match for Houston, whose zealous attempts to destroy every drug dealer he could find in Peru could be his undoing.

Morgan admired Houston tremendously, and he'd just gotten information from the highest government sources that Escovar had recently renewed his efforts to take revenge on Houston. In fact, Escovar had just doubled the price on his head. Morgan had no doubt Mike had his own network of spies to warn him of Escovar's movements, but Morgan wanted a safety net for him. And Ann, who was all science and facts, was a good chess piece to put into play down there. She could keep tabs on the footloose major and save his neck, if necessary. No, it was best that Ann go there thinking she would be slaving away in a small clinic. Morgan didn't want her flying in those drug-raid copters and getting shot at. He knew that Houston's network of helicopters could ensure that he was within an hour's ride of Lima should anything terrible happen to him. And Ann would be there waiting, ready with her surgical skills to save his sorry life.

Smiling to himself, Morgan sipped more of his coffee. There was no one better than Houston to go up against Eduardo Escovar. But Morgan wanted insurance for him of a different sort. He felt intuitively that Houston liked Ann—a whole lot. And maybe, just maybe, the hotshot jungle fighter would ease off on the throttles just a little bit, take a few less risks if he knew he had someone to return to in Lima after one of his bloody raids deep in the mountains. *Maybe...* Morgan admitted his plan was risky in itself. It was obvious Ann thought Houston had maneuvered things to get her on this assignment. And in Houston, she had more than met her match. Chuckling to himself, Morgan marveled over the attraction he saw between the cool, level-headed scientist and the passionate jaguar god of Peru. It was the molten steel being thrust into a bucket of icy water. What a combination! Morgan knew the sparks would fly. Secretly, his money was on Houston to endure her scalpel-like reactions and slowly but surely wear her down. Beneath Ann's genius mind, beneath that cold, scientific rationale that fed her intellect, was a hot-blooded woman who was afraid to step out of her ivory tower and experience being wild and free in a man's arms. And these weren't just any man's arms Morgan was pushing her toward.... He was betting that Houston could handle her. Time would tell, though.

"The flight to Peru will be a good shakedown cruise for both of you," he told Ann in his rumbling voice. "A nice chance to talk over how you want to run the clinic for Houston."

Ann glared at Morgan. "I'm not happy about this assignment. At all."

He lifted his hand. "Just be patient," he urged gently. "Mike isn't the monster you make him out to be. He's all-heart if you give him a chance."

That was exactly what Ann was afraid of—Mike Houston's passionate, wild heart. He frightened her. More so than any other man. And in less than three hours, she'd be forced to sit beside him on that airplane. How was she going to deal with her fearful emotions?

* * *

Ann tried to contain her feelings as she sat in the first-class section of the Veracruz flight. Mike Houston, dressed in a pair of dark brown slacks, a short-sleeved, white silk shirt and camel hair sport coat, sat across the aisle. She studied his rugged profile. It reminded her of the harsh granite of the Andes beneath them. They'd been in the air for hours since picking up fuel in Mexico City for the long flight to Lima.

Her conscience prickled. She knew she was being grumpy about this assignment and she didn't like herself for it. Generally, she was unflappable in every situation. Nothing ever caused her to swerve from her focus on saving lives, not even bullets flying around her. This man, this army major, had really unsettled her in ways she'd never thought possible. How could she be so drawn to Mike? *How?* It scared her to even think of him in that way. Ann thought herself incapable of ever falling in love again since— She slammed the lid shut on her memories before she felt the pain of them. Somehow being around Mike made her feel vulnerable once more. He was mysterious; there was something about him she couldn't put her finger on and it bothered her immensely. He was unlike any man she'd ever met—or had been attracted to. Her gut told her that dealing with him would be like handling nitroglycerine—one false move and the attraction between them would explode into something more.

She was a coward, she admitted to herself. A certifiable coward. Mike had been honest and aboveboard in his genuine interest in her. He hadn't manipulated her in this regard. After all, she'd enjoyed his kisses, his incredibly tender explorations, as much as he obviously had. There was no fault in this, really. She was an adult. She had willingly kissed him and wanted his continued caresses. Even now, she felt her lower body tighten with such need of him that she wanted to cry. The past was too strong for her to overcome, though. If she knew Mike for a longer time, those walls might dissolve. And that's what Ann was really afraid of. Six weeks in Lima with him around on a daily basis would surely unlatch a door in her heart that she'd thought would remain closed forever.

Anxiety raced through Ann. She felt bad and wanted to apologize to Mike for accusing him, though she wasn't so sure he was completely innocent of getting her assigned to Lima. She watched out of the corner of her eye as he sipped some amber-colored whiskey. He'd barely spoken a word to her for hours now and he only communicated when she asked him a question. He was still angry with her, despite the fact that he seemed to have cooled down considerably after his outburst in front of Morgan. He'd even apologized to her later as they were packing to leave the ranch. She'd stiffly accepted his apology, but she'd seen the sadness in his eyes, and had fought the tears in her own.

Ann didn't want to hurt Mike, but she knew she had. She could barely stand herself as a result. He was a man of incredible courage, an officer and a gentleman. The kind of man she could fall in love with, if she allowed herself. That's why going to a foreign country and being under Houston's protection was unnerving. She would *have* to rely on him because she was unfamiliar with Peruvian culture. Her rational mind didn't like being out of control like that. Ann had always relied upon herself, all her life. If she got into a scrape, she managed to get herself out—alone, without help.

Yes, she'd dreamed of Mike, of their kisses, of being with him completely. Her emotions unraveled when she was around him, and she felt needy, hungry in a way that she'd never felt before. The thought of six more weeks in his powerful and persuasive presence scared her more than bullets or bombs exploding around her.

Manipulation was something Ann despised. It brought out every conceivable dark emotion within her. But then, she'd been manipulated once, by a master similar to Houston, so why shouldn't she be wary of him? She'd fallen for an Air Force pilot after the one love of her life had died in a plane crash. Robert Crane had said every word, given her every look and done everything she'd ever dreamed that a man might do for the woman he was falling in love with—and she'd fallen hopelessly for him. Now she knew that what she felt for Robert had not grown out of love, but out of the grief and loss of her one true love. At the time, Ann hadn't realized that, of course.

The realization came soon after Crane had lured her into bed.

Once he'd "caught" her, he'd up and left. When Ann confronted him about it a week later, he'd laughed at her and told her the awful truth: he was a hunter, she was the hunted. His quarry. She'd been prey to be taken, used and then thrown away. The humiliation and shame of that disastrous time in her life had branded her forever. Never did Ann want to be manipulated like that again. Yet somehow Houston had gotten beneath her considerable armor. It must be his South American blood, his passion for life, that had breathed hot, molten desire into her heart. Daily, she fought her feelings for him. Daily, she tried to shrug off his heated looks, his gentle teasing, and yes, those wonderful kisses that opened her up inside and made her bare her vulnerability.

Ann closed her eyes and sighed raggedly. What was Houston's real intent? At thirty-two years old, she wasn't stupid or naive. She'd seen the looks he'd given her. She wasn't a young thing who didn't recognize in his dark blue, assessing eyes the smoldering hunger of a man who wanted a woman. He *wanted* her. She felt his longing for her, his unqualified interest. The raw, painful truth was Ann wanted Mike as much as he wanted her. And she was too much of a coward to even try to disentangle herself from the past and reach out to him. She was simply too scarred and too scared. What little emotion she had left was deeply hidden and protected within her. She just didn't have what it took to freely love Houston.

Sighing, Ann wrapped her arms across her chest, closed her eyes and tried to sleep. It was gloomy in the plane now, the lights very low. Most of the people around them in the first-class cabin were already asleep—except for her and Houston. Part of her just couldn't believe that he hadn't dropped several hints to Laura about his struggling clinic to get Ann down here in Lima with him. She knew enough about his dangerous job as an army liaison between the U.S. and Peruvian military resources to realize he had learned how to be very adroit in touchy political situations. She knew Houston had hobnobbed with the rich and powerful at fashionable dinners and society events in Lima. He was a smooth talker. Too smooth, she decided with a frown. Like Robert Crane, a little voice warned her stridently.

As an adviser and the commanding officer representing the U.S.

Army, Houston had to have a lot of skills in place. He had to have the ability to employ U.S. policy and get it to jibe with Peru's political philosophy at the same time. While working out in the field, which was obviously what he loved the most, he coordinated well-planned attacks against the cocaine lords in the jungle highlands. After a successful battle or raid, he'd work his way through the chain of command all the way up to the president of Peru, letting the government know what went down and how many millions of dollars of cocaine wouldn't flow north as a result. Houston handled a big budget and was responsible for keeping ten helicopters flying around the clock, chopping away at the cocaine warlords' domain.

Exhaling forcefully, Ann wondered why a man with such skills would have to manipulate her into coming down to his clinic. The thought made her open her eyes and sit up. She moved across the aisle to the empty seat next to him. Houston lifted his massive head, his dark blue gaze settling warily on hers.

"I just want to know one thing," Ann whispered fiercely. "Why the hell didn't you ask me, face-to-face, for my help? If you wanted me to come down here and help out, why didn't you come to me instead of pulling strings with Laura and Morgan to maneuver me into this corner?"

She saw the hand lying on the armrest slowly flex. She studied the many scars across it and knew every one was a story in itself. The scars were like mini badges of courage in her mind. Then she saw a flinty, cold look come in to his eyes. She felt iciness around him, aimed directly at her.

"Don't you think," Houston growled, leaning forward and nailing her with a glare, "that I would have if I thought you might do it? Sure, the thought crossed my mind, but that was *after* I'd told Laura a little about the clinic."

Ann gripped the seat, her fingers digging into the fabric. "You're saying you're innocent?" She tried to contain the hysteria she was feeling. Mike was so close, so very, very male, and her heart cried out for him, for his embrace. She hated herself for attacking him. He looked completely stunned by the force of her verbal assault. Once again she was hurting him. But she had to protect herself from Mike somehow, keep him from melting her down, little by little. Especially now that they would be working together at the clinic. He'd broken her resistance at the ranch. He would do so again down there, and Ann felt trapped and desperate. She just couldn't give in to her heart. If she did... No, it was too scary to even contemplate.

"For once," Houston rasped, "I am innocent." Reeling from her unexpected attack, he felt his anger explode. "Don't you think I know you don't trust me? You've made that pretty damn obvious, Ann." He set his empty glass down on the table in front of him and leaned slowly toward her, his eyes becoming slits. "Have you ever asked yourself why in the hell I would want to drag someone unwilling down to Lima and spend six weeks with her? That's kinda like throwing two male jaguars into the same pen. You sure as hell know they're territorial—that a male jaguar won't put up with another being in his territory. And they're sure as hell gonna fight each other to the death because each one can't stand the fact that the other is invading his turf."

He exhaled and growled, "One thing I'm not, Ann, is a victim. If you think for one second that I'm looking forward to your sulking, pouting demeanor while I'm working with those two little nuns, whom I love like grandmothers, you're very mistaken. As far as I'm concerned, you can get off this plane at the airport, execute an aboutface and climb right back on for a return flight to the States."

Stung, Ann glared at him, her heart beating hard in her breast. She saw the raw hurt in Mike's eyes, heard it in the rasp of his voice. Oh, why was she doing this? It was as if all the desperation she felt was being fueled by her underlying fear and turning her into this woman she'd never met before. Helpless to stop her response to him, she whispered harshly, "You're very good at twisting words, Major. But then, that's your job, isn't it? Get the dishonest politicians to play ball with you, fund you and your men, your activities. Cross lines in the sand and get both bullies to play the same game together?"

His lips curled away from his teeth. "Dammit, Ann, you're stepping way out of line now. I don't mind if you attack me personally or question my ethics, which you seem to think are very badly flawed, but when you go after my men, who put their lives on the line every day, that's where I draw *my* line in the sand.'' His gaze drilled into her shadowed, frightened eyes. ''Those men have wives and kids and extended families, yet they get paid a pittance to leap out of those choppers and face well-armed cocaine soldiers in the highlands. It's not fair and it's not right. But I'll be damned if some Harvard-graduate medical doctor is going to look down at them. My men are some of the bravest soldiers in the world. Their families are in jeopardy because of what they do, so they're risking more than their lives, they're risking the lives of their loved ones, too.''

Gasping, Ann straightened. The air was tense and she felt his low growl move through her like a tremor from an earthquake. His demeanor had changed to one of controlled violence—aimed at her. She saw the spark in his eyes, like the gleam of a predator stalking her. Fumbling internally, Ann knew she had started this attack. She deserved his reaction. The wounded and vulnerable part of her would rather deal with a man's anger than a man's love. And right now, her heart was hurting so much in her breast she wanted to cry out, throw her arms around Mike and just hold him as she knew he would hold her. If only she wasn't so frightened. Smoothing her gray, light wool slacks against her thighs, she took several breaths before speaking. The danger emanating from Houston shook her. He'd pulled out all his guns, probably hoping she'd back down.

''Okay,'' she whispered, holding his glare, ''I'll apologize for the remarks I just made about your men. They grew out of my anger. I own it and I'll admit it.''

Houston slowly straightened, his gaze never leaving hers. ''You still think I engineered this whole thing to get you down to Lima, don't you?'' He'd give anything to make her realize he was innocent of this. But the look in her eyes told him differently.

''There's no question in my mind about that,'' Ann growled back.

''For what possible purpose?'' he asked, his voice cracking.

Surprised, Ann placed her hands on her knees. ''Why, the obvious one, Major.''

''What? That I like you? That I admire your brains, your gutsiness? I made no bones about that when we worked together up north." He'd have said more, but people were looking in their direction. Even now he would protect Ann from prying eyes and ears.

"And I'm sure those aren't the only things about me you admired," Ann sputtered, feeling heat move up her neck and into her face. She felt uneasy talking about the attraction between them, but dammit, there was no denying it! Oh, she was blushing! Of all the times to blush!

Houston forced himself to lean back in his seat, a mirthless smile slashing across the hard planes of his face. The pain and raw need he felt for her were mixed with anger and frustration. He'd never expected Ann to assault him like this. "And here I thought you were without imagination, Ann. I was wrong, I guess, wasn't I?"

The innuendo struck her full force. Ann saw and felt his derisive laughter as he tilted his head back and allowed the low, growling sound to escape from his throat. She had that coming and she knew it.

"You know what, Doctor?"

She met his ruthless gaze. "What?"

"I have a really tough time thinking you're not a machine. I've seen a lot of medicos in my lifetime, but none of them came across as icy and brittle as you. I heard Morgan say you were one of the best. Well, you're going to have to prove that to me. I won't allow you to step a foot in that clinic with your kind of by-the-book bedside manner. I've seen it for eight weeks now, and I'm certainly not going to subject two nuns who work tirelessly for the poor to your iceberg tactics. As a matter of fact, I don't think you've allowed yourself to be human for a helluva long time. You're happy in your little ivory tower. That's fine. Down there at the clinic, we're all touchers and huggers, and you'll probably misread that, too. Some of the children coming in are orphans off the street, abandoned because their parents were unable to feed one more mouth. Those kids get a lot of hugs, embraces and love showered on them by the three of us."

With a shake of his head, Houston rasped, "And if Miss Anglo with her highfalutin Harvard medical degree thinks she's stepping into our humble abode like the proverbial Ice Queen to order us poor half-breeds and stupid Indians around like we're brainless, she has another think coming. No, I don't want you down in Lima with me, if the truth be known, Ann. Not like this. I'm used to working with people who have heart, who have a passion for living life and who aren't afraid to show their vulnerability. Do me a favor? When you get off this flight, stay at the airport. I'll make sure you get the very next flight back to the States.''

Chapter 3

By the time their jet touched down at Lima's International airport, it was 0600. Pink touched the rim of the horizon, and ordinarily, Mike would have enjoyed the spectacle of color set against the darkness of the Andes mountains, where Lima sat loftily overlooking the Pacific Ocean. Disgruntled, unable to sleep and generally grouchy because of his head-on clash with Ann, he strode off the plane. His heart ached with grief over the loss of the trust he'd forged with her on the ranch. How could he have fallen so helplessly and hopelessly in need of her in two short months? Maybe he was more lonely that he realized. But it was more than loneliness, he realized. He knew now that he wasn't the kind of man who could go through life without a good woman at his side. The tragedy and loss he had endured in his past had told him he had no right to ever try and reach out and love again. Mike never expected to find love again—nor did he want to. He'd always thought of himself as a doomed man. Because of his dangerous life-style, he'd always known it was just a matter of time until his body became meat for buzzards. And then Ann Parsons had walked into his life and he'd begun to dream once more of happiness. What a fool he was.

The dark smudges under Ann's glorious eyes told him she didn't feel much better than he did. Dammit, he wanted to apologize for some of the things he'd said to her in anger earlier. Somehow, she got to him, and he lost his normal ability to hold on to his temper. *Great. Just great.* More than anything, Mike didn't want to leave her with hurtful feelings between them. Ann deserved better than that. He owed it to her to make amends and try to heal the bad blood between them.

Slowing his gait, he waited for her to catch up. One nice thing about first class was that they were off the plane first. He slung the black canvas knapsack he always carried with him over his left shoulder. As Ann approached, he saw that her dark hair was in mild disarray, and he had the maddening urge to reach over and comb his fingers through the thick, gleaming strands, which shimmered with highlights of gold and red. *Better not,* he warned himself. *She'll take my hand off at the elbow.* And then he grinned carelessly. He knew it would be worth it, because she'd once allowed him the privilege of sliding his fingers through her silky hair in one of their stolen moments—in the heat of a hungry, searching kiss.

Once Ann was beside him, he continued toward the terminal. Even at this time of morning, Lima airport was busy. Mike wasn't surprised. Peru's capital was a twenty-four-hours-a-day city. It was cosmopolitan, upscale and surging ahead because of the influence of Japanese investors and the huge population of Japanese people who had left their island home to settle here. They brought money into the economy, and over the years Lima had become the third largest enclave of Japanese in the world. Only Sao Paulo, Brazil, had a larger population outside Japan.

As he stepped into the terminal, he saw a huge crowd of people waiting for folks to disembark from their flight. Too bad he didn't have a special somebody waiting for him. Someone like Ann. Hell, he had too much of the romantic left in him. Or maybe being with a woman he was so drawn to had stirred up that vat of loneliness he'd stuffed deep down inside of him. No, the army was his only wife, and this was one time he was regretting that dictate. Well, it didn't matter anyway, because Ann didn't want him. And if she hadn't before, she sure as hell didn't now after his stupid, stupid remarks to her in the heat of their argument on board the aircraft.

At customs Mike dropped easily into Spanish, Lima's main language. Japanese was a close second and one that he'd mastered with a lot of difficulty over the years because of his position with the Peruvian government. He remained on guard, always looking around. Now that he was back on Peruvian soil, he had to be alert or he could be killed. The young lady behind the desk, obviously Castilian Spanish with her golden skin, thin proud features, black eyes and shining black hair, smiled at him. Mike felt a little better just seeing a pleasant expression on someone's face for a change.

At the check-in desk, he launched into conversation with the ticketing agent about a van that was due to bring the medical supplies, to be carried in on the next flight. In the meantime, he saw Ann halt a few feet away and observe the busy, crowded terminal. She didn't look like a doctor in that moment. No, just a very thin, tired woman. His conscience ate at him big-time. Thanking the agent, Mike turned and sauntered over to where she stood just outside of the streams of people coming and going in the terminal.

"I've never been to Lima," Ann confessed without looking up at him. "This airport reminds me of the Chicago terminal—huge, bustling and busy twenty-four hours a day. I just never imagined it." Mike's presence, especially in the fog of her exhaustion, was overwhelming to her. Ann felt herself seesawing between going with him to the clinic and remaining at the terminal to catch the next flight back to the States. She saw the anguish in his dark eyes, the fatigue clearly marked on his own hard features, and felt a wonderful blanket of protection and care settle around her. She knew that feeling came from being with him. She tried to tell herself that his care didn't mean anything. However, she was too tired to fight the truth of what she felt emanating from him. And she knew the rawness she felt in her chest was her own longing for him.

She'd had a long time on their flight to feel her way through her jangled feelings, her confusion, her fear and her needs. Although she lay in her chair, her eyes closed, Ann hadn't slept because she'd been too upset. How had she come to feel so much for Mike while at the ranch? *How?* No matter what she did, the answer didn't seem forthcoming. Ann had sworn never to fall for a man again...not with her bad track record. How had Mike eased himself into her life? Was it that boyish smile he flashed at her in unexpected moments, always catching her off guard? Was it his obvious passion for living life fully and for the moment? That dancing glint in his eyes that broadcast such warmth and tenderness toward her every time he looked at her? His hot, searching kisses? The way he touched her, fanning coals of passion into wildly flaring flames? It was more than sexual, Ann admitted darkly. She *liked* Mike. His integrity. His continued efforts to help the poor and defend them. She approved of his morals and values. There was nothing, really, *not* to like about Mike Houston, she sourly admitted. Absolutely nothing. Except for the mystery she felt around him—that mystical quality she couldn't pinpoint with her razor-honed intellect. Not all the academic degrees in the world could outfit her to deal with someone like Houston.

"Maybe," Mike growled, despite his attempt to take the sting out of his tone, "if you give Peru half a chance, she'll seduce you like she did me when I came here more than a decade ago." He heaved an inner sigh of relief. At least Ann was talking civilly to him once again. But then, she hadn't slept, either, so he knew she was probably feeling more like a walking zombie right now and the blame game was low on her list of priorities.

Pointing toward where they had to walk to get to the baggage claim area, he added, "They call Lima the Jewel of the Pacific. The city sits up on the slopes of the lower Andes and looks out over the dark blue Pacific Ocean. The first time I came here, I didn't know what to expect. My mother had told me many, many stories of Lima, and how beautiful it was—the apartments that had flower boxes on their balconies and the trees that made the city look more like a park than a maze of steel-and-glass sentinels. She loved this city." Mike risked a glance down at Ann. Even though she was a good five feet nine inches tall, she was still short in comparison to him.

She refused to look up at him. The way her full lips were pursed told him that he'd hurt her earlier with his nasty, spiteful comments. Ruthlessly, Houston absorbed her aristocratic profile. She had high cheekbones, like his Indian ancestors did. With another sigh, he dropped his gaze to her pursed lips once more. *To hell with it.* Somehow, he had to change things so that they parted on good terms at least. He took a deep breath, reached out and gripped her arm gently, forcing her to look at him.

"Listen," he muttered darkly as her expression changed to one of shock as he touched her, "I'm sorry for what I said to you on the plane. It wasn't right and—"

A cry for help halfway down the terminal ripped through the early morning air. People began to slow down or hurry a little faster.

Scowling, Mike dropped his hand from Ann's arm, instantly alert. "Now what?" he growled.

Ann looked in direction of the sound. She could hear a woman sobbing and screaming for help. She saw Mike Houston peering above the heads of the crowd. "You're taller than I am," she exclaimed. "What do you see? What's going on?"

Grimacing, he glanced down at her. "Someone's in trouble. Medical trouble. Come on...." He took off in long, loping strides.

"Mike! Wait!" Ann hurried to catch up. He was a tall, broad-shouldered man and he cut a swathe through the crowds in the airport terminal. She wasn't so lucky and was stopped repeatedly. As she hurried along in his wake, she found herself admiring the way he ran, with a boneless, swift grace that reminded her of a large cat. Perhaps a cougar loping along silently, yet with remarkable power. Other people seemed to sense it, too, for Houston was never elbowed, stopped, nor did he have to change direction. No, the masses parted for him like the Red Sea had for Moses. Ann realized she was witnessing that impenetrable mystery about him in action now. No wonder they called him the jaguar god.

Mike's eyes widened as he made his way through the large circle of people that had formed. In the middle was a woman crying hysterically. A young woman, very pretty, well-heeled and dressed in a purple business suit. He knew her well. It was Elena Valdez, wife of Antonio Valdez, one of the most prominent and powerful businessmen in Lima. What the hell was happening?

"Step aside," Mike growled, opening a path to where Elena stood sobbing, her fists against her mouth. She was from one of the old aristocratic families of Peru, of pure Castilian blood. Normally aloof and serene, her mascaraed eyes were running dark streaks like war paint down her cheeks, her red lips contorted as she stared down at the floor. Mike followed her wild, shocked gaze.

"Antonio!" he rasped. Houston suddenly spun on his heel and roared at the crowd, "Give us room!"

Miraculously, everyone took a number of steps back widening the circle. There on the floor, ashen and unmoving, was Antonio Valdez. The thousand-dollar, dark blue pinstripe suit he wore went with the short, sleek black hair combed back on his narrow skull. His red silk tie looked garish next to his pasty flesh as Mike sank to his knees.

"Antonio—Tony!" He gripped the businessman's shoulder. The man did not respond. Sensing Ann's presence, Mike snapped his head up as he placed two fingers against the man's neck.

"Cardiac arrest," he stated shortly. "No pulse..." He leaned down, his ear close to the man's nose. "No breath." He jabbed at his backpack, which he'd dropped nearby. "There's a bag-valve mask in there. Get it. An OPA, too." He ripped at the man's tie, the silk of his shirt giving way under the power of Mike's efforts. Then he tipped the man's head back to create an airway. He heard Elena sobbing wildly.

"Oh, Mike! Mike! Antonio was just walking with me. Everything was fine. Fine! And suddenly...suddenly he grew very pale and groaned. He collapsed, *mi amigo*. Oh, Mike! Help him! Help him!"

Jerking the tie from Tony's neck, Houston shot a glance at Ann, who was on her knees, digging furiously in his backpack. All the tiredness, the cloudy look in her eyes, had dissolved. When she looked up, protective green latex gloves in hand, he reached out and took them. With expert swiftness, he donned them. "Get the goggles, too. If he vomits, I don't want it in our eyes."

"Right!" Ann handed him a pair of plastic goggles. Her hands trembled slightly as she placed the white OPA, a plastic device known as an oropharyngeal airway, into the patient's mouth. This device would keep his tongue from falling back and blocking his breathing passage once they started pumping air into his lungs.

Ann grabbed the bag-valve mask and moved once more to the man's head. She knelt and settled the translucent, soft plastic mask over his face. The mask was attached to the blue, oval-shaped rubber bag that would start pumping air into him.

Mike watched her get into position. She leaned over the man, ready.

"Have you got paramedics posted here at the terminal?" she demanded, squeezing the appliance.

"Hell, no." Mike looked up and barked at a younger man dressed in business clothes. "You! Get to a white phone! Call security for help. Tell them we've got a cardiac case in terminal three. Tell them to call an ambulance, pronto!"

"Sí, sí!" the man shouted, and he turned and worked his way through the crowd.

"Okay, let's get on it," Ann whispered.

Mike appreciated her cool efficiency as he knelt on the other side of Antonio and placed his hands just below the man's sternum. He laid his large palm flat against his chest, then nodded in her direction. "Give 'em air. Two breaths."

"I know CPR."

He heard the warning clip of her voice. Scowling, he concentrated on his part of the two-person procedure. After two breaths, he leaned over Tony and delivered a powerful downward push over the sternum. The heart lay under that long, flat bone that held the rib cage together.

In moments, they were working like a well-oiled team. Houston forgot the pandemonium around them, forgot Elena's sobbing. He counted to himself, his mouth thinned, his nostrils flaring.

Two minutes into the process, he rasped, "Stop CPR." Anxiously, he placed his fingers against Antonio's neck.

"No pulse." He leaned down, praying for the man to at least be breathing. "No breath."

"Do you know him?"

Houston gave a jerky nod as he repositioned his hands. "Yes. Start CPR."

Ann squeezed the bag-valve mask, delivering a long, slow dose of oxygen into the man's chest cavity. She saw the patient's wife kneel down at his feet, sobbing and praying. She was so young and pretty—she couldn't be more than in her late twenties.

"How old is he?"

"Forty-five."

"Perfect age for a CA."

"Yeah, isn't it, though?" Mike continued to push down on the man's chest again and again. He kept looking at Tony's color. "Damn, this isn't working."

"How long before an ambulance arrives with a defibrillator machine?"

"Too long," he muttered. "Too damn long. Stop CPR. We're going to do something different."

Ann watched as Houston jerked the shirt completely away from the man's chest. She saw him ball up his fist. She knew what he was going to do. In the absence of a defibrillator, which with an electrical shock could jolt the heart into starting again, a medic could strike the sternum with a fist. Sometimes, though rarely, the hard, shocking blow would get the heart restarted. It was risky. She noted the strain on Mike's face, the glistening sweat on his wrinkled brow. His eyes had turned a dark, stormy blue, and she knew all his focus was on his abilities as a paramedic, despite the many other emotions he had to be feeling.

"Is he a friend of yours?" she asked, holding the man's head steady as Mike prepared to strike his chest.

"Yes. A damn good friend. God, I hope this works," he said.

Mike measured where his fist would strike the man's sternum. He gripped Tony's shoulder to hold him in place. Raising his arm, he smashed his fist downward in a hard arc. Flesh met flesh. He heard his friend's sternum crack loudly beneath his assault.

"Come on! Come on!" Houston snarled as he gripped the man's lifeless shoulders and shook him hard. "Damn you, Tony!" he breathed into the man's graying face, "don't you *dare* die on me!" He put his fingers against his neck.

"Nothing," he growled.

"Do it again," Ann ordered in a hushed tone. She saw the fear in Houston's eyes.

"He's dumping on us...."

"I don't care. It's all we got! Hit him again!"

For a split second, Ann met his distraught eyes. And then he balled his fist again. Once the sternum was broken there was a danger that any further strikes to jolt the heart could create lacerations in the liver and possibly the heart itself, from fragments of bone that had been broken by the first blow. Antonio could bleed to death as a result.

"You mean son of a bitch," Houston growled at Tony as he raised his fist. "You live! You hear me?" Then he brought his fist down just as hard as the first time.

The man's whole body jarred and jerked beneath the second blow. Ann held the man's head and neck in alignment and continued to pump oxygen into him. She watched as Mike leaned over to check for pulse and breathing. Whether it was because she was already numb with tiredness and drained emotionally, she didn't know, but for a split second as he leaned down, snarling in Spanish at his friend, she thought she was seeing things.

Houston's growling voice wasn't human any longer. It sounded to her like a huge jungle cat. It shocked her, the primal, sound reverberating through every pore in her body as he leaned over and shook Antonio. She sensed an energy in the air, pummeling her repeatedly like wildly racing ocean waves. She realized it was emanating from Houston as he leaned over Antonio, almost willing him to breathe again.

"You're not dying on me," he rasped, striking him even harder than before, in the center of the chest. "Live! Live, you hear me?"

Ann blinked belatedly. As Houston struck the man a third time, she knew she was seeing things. His head disappeared, and in its place she saw the golden face of a jaguar or leopard, black crescent spots against gold fur. She was hallucinating! Shaking her head, she closed her eyes and opened them again. Mike was leaning over his friend, his fingers pressed insistently against his neck. My God, what was happening? What was she seeing? For the first time, Ann clearly realized that she was on a mission with an incredibly attractive man whose power was beyond her own rational mind.

"Tony!" he pleaded hoarsely. "Don't die on me! Don't!"

Houston's plea shook her. Gone was the hard soldier's mask. She trembled at the raw emotion of his voice. Tears stung her eyes. What a horrible thing to come home to—seeing a good friend go into cardiac arrest and then watching him die. Ann was ready to tell Mike that it was too late. Only seven percent of people suffering from a heart attack ever revived with the help of CPR.

Again she gazed up through her veil of tears. She no longer heard the onlookers or felt them closing in on them, inch by inch. She watched as Houston hunkered over the older man, gripping him by the shoulders and giving him a good, hard shake. Yet again Houston struck him in the chest.

"Mike—" she begged.

"Wait! A pulse! I've got a pulse!" He gave a cry of triumph and watched intensely as the man's face began to lose some of its grayness. "Bag 'em hard," he snapped. "Pump all the oxygen you can into him." He grinned tightly and put a coat beneath the man's legs to elevate them slightly. Leaning over him again, he called, "Tony? Tony, you hear me? Open those ugly eyes of yours and look up at me. It's Mike. Mike Houston. Come on, buddy, you can do it. Open your eyes!" And he shook him again, all the time keeping a firm grip on his friend's arms.

Houston watched the dark lashes tremble against the man's pasty features. "That's it, open your eyes. I'm here. You're gonna be okay. Come on, come on back. You're too mean to die yet...." Then he grinned as Tony opened his dark brown eyes and stared groggily up at him.

Almost immediately, the patient started gagging. Ann removed the bag valve mask from his face, took out the breathing appliance and threw it aside. She quickly replaced the mask, holding it there until she and Mike were both sure he was getting enough oxygen and was breathing well on his own.

Houston heard Elena cry out her husband's name as she bent over him.

"Calm down, Elena," he coaxed, reaching across and soothingly moving his hand against her thin shoulder as she gripped her husband's hand. "He's okay...." Mike wasn't sure how okay Antonio really was. He knew the man had suffered a massive heart attack. How bad, they'd only know after a series of tests at the hospital.

Risking a look up at Ann, who was still kneeling at Tony's

head, delivering the life-giving oxygen, he saw tears sparkling in her eyes. They caught him completely off guard. Returning his attention to his friend, he reached down, got his stethoscope from the bag and listened intently to his heart. It was a good, strong beat. Then Mike took his blood pressure.

"Eighty over sixty," he announced with satisfaction.

"It could be better," Ann said.

Grimly, Mike deflated the blood pressure cuff. "Give him five minutes. He's not dumping on us. Color's flooding his face. His capillary refill is better," he murmured as he pinched the index fingernail of Tony's right hand. Normally, the capillary refill took two seconds or less to flow back into the pinched area. It was a good indicator that the heart was pumping strongly and normally, supplying the life-giving substance to even the farthest extremities of the body.

"Three seconds?" Ann asked.

Houston nodded. He waited to recheck the blood pressure, but five minutes seemed to take forever. Glancing at his watch, he wished the second hand would move faster.

Elena was speaking in hushed tones to her husband. When Tony tried to reach up and touch his wife's wet, pale face, Mike grinned. "You're gonna be fine, Tony. But right now, keep your hands off Elena, you hear me? Just lie there and let your strength come back." He glanced at Ann. "Stop bagging him."

She nodded and watched as he took another blood pressure reading. Houston's expression was intense and hard now. She was seeing his professional side as a paramedic once more. He was very good at what he did. He had an incredible confidence that radiated from him like the sun sending energy earthward. She watched as his thinned lips relaxed. A cocky, one-cornered smile tugged at his mouth as he removed the stethoscope from his ears and settled it around his thick, well-muscled neck. When he looked in her direction, she felt incredible tenderness coming from him. It wasn't for her, but she basked in that invisible glow just the same. In that moment, he looked like a little boy, his blue eyes sparkling with unabashed joy.

"One-ten over eighty. He's stabilizing. He's through the worst of it."

"Yes," Ann quavered, giving him a trembling smile of triumph. "He's going to live...."

Houston stood with Ann at his side as the ambulance paramedics took Antonio Valdez away on a gurney. Most of the crowd had disappeared now that the life-and-death drama was over. Without thinking, Mike put his hand on her shoulder. "Hell of a welcome to Lima."

Ann felt the warm strength of his hand. She recognized his gesture for what it was. People in the medical field had to be devoid of emotion, keep ahead of the curve in any emergency, think rationally and stay calm when everything around them was shaking apart. She lifted her chin and met Mike's blue gaze, absorbing his touch, the energy that seemed to tingle from his hand into her shoulder. It made her feel safe and cared for. His touch felt like life itself throbbing through her. It wasn't the first time she had felt this unusual sensation. Now it was far more palpable and comforting. A soft smile flitted across her face. "Yes, it was...but you were good. Very good. You knew what to do." Her heart expanded wildly. How could she stand the thought of not being near Mike? Suddenly, Ann realized how much her life had changed since he had walked into it.

Digesting the feelings that overrode her normal fears, she understood for the first time how much Houston had become a part of her, and vice versa, it seemed. They had been a good team. They'd worked as one. Perhaps it was due to sleep deprivation, but there in the Lima terminal Ann listened to her heart more closely than she had in a long time.

Houston absorbed that hesitant, fleeting smile Ann gave him. How beautiful she was, even though her hair was in mild disarray and her white blouse rumpled from the long flight. "So were you. We're a good team, you and I." And then he grinned. "Even if we do fight like dogs and cats." He didn't want to remove his hand, but he knew it was best. Allowing it to fall back to his side, Mike thought he saw a fleeting darkness in Ann's wide, intelligent eyes. Unable to interpret what it meant, he cocked his head.

"Let me at least buy you a good cup of espresso before I leave for the clinic. It's the least I can do to thank you for helping save Tony's life. I owe you one...."

Ann frowned. "I'll take the offer, but what makes you think you're leaving this terminal without me?" For better or worse, she had made a decision to stay—because of her feelings toward Mike. She was scared to death, but she had to take the risk. Her mind screamed at her that she was a fool, but her heart was expanding with such joy over her decision that she felt breathless. Inwardly, she knew she was making the right choice, regardless of her dark, haunting past.

Scowling, Houston halted abruptly and turned to face her. There was surprise written on his features. "You made it very clear you didn't want to be down here with me," he began slowly, his voice low with raw feeling. Tony almost dying had left Mike more vulnerable than usual. He was afraid to believe what he'd just heard. His heart pounded briefly to underscore his need for Ann. His fear. Mike searched her calm features. Her eyes shone with hope. The fear was still there, but it had lessened. What was going on? Stunned by her words, he rasped, "Or was I hearing wrong?"

"You didn't hear wrong, Mike. I changed my mind, that's all. You got a problem with that?" Ann held his flaring look of surprise. She felt an avalanche of that powerful energy deluge her momentarily. She remembered how, when she was bagging Antonio, she'd seen the awe in people's faces as Mike worked over the man. All eyes had been riveted on him as he struggled to save his friend's life.

There was no question in her mind why Houston was not only a leader, but one that few people, including herself, could resist. Even if it was dangerous to her wounded heart. She was too afraid, still, to admit for sure why she agreed to stay on. Only time would tell, and another six weeks would hopefully yield the answer she was searching for.

Her mouth twisted wryly. "This is probably the sorriest decision I'll ever make, Houston, but I'm sticking it out down here for six weeks. With or without you. I honor Morgan's commitments. I go where he sends me." She saw hope burning fiercely in Mike's eyes, and more...much more....

Mike just stared at her for a moment. Here was the confident,

gutsy woman he knew lived inside her, but who he'd rarely seen.
The question *why are you staying?* was almost torn from him, but
he forced the words back down. Whether Ann knew it or not, he
had a powerful, ongoing connection with her. He sensed a lot more
about her than she realized. He knew she was scared, but he also
sensed her feelings for him—feelings that had existed all along
but that she'd refused to share with him. Now, for whatever reason, she was doing that. Euphoria robbed Mike momentarily of
words. Was it possible that she was going to allow their relationship to grow? The thought was heady. Wild. Full of promise. At
the same time, he felt full of fear for an uncertain future. Those
he cared for died. She would die, too. No, he had to keep his
distance. He had to protect her from himself at all costs. His whole
life was committed to killing Eduardo Escovar. Mike was in a
death spiral dance with the drug lord and he had no room for a
woman in his life. Especially a woman like Ann Parsons. Another
part of him, one that surprised the hell out of him, reveled in her
decision to remain with him in Peru, regardless.

Ann watched a slow grin crawl across his face. Houston had
such a strong, chiseled mouth. A beautiful mouth, she admitted.
One that she wanted to feel against her lips again and again. For
whatever reason, she felt bolder than she had in a long time.
Maybe seeing Antonio almost die had ripped away something inside her, made her realize life was precious and should be lived
in the moment, not hidden in some dark closet of fear.... Cha-
grined, Ann cut off the thoughts and feelings that seem to grow
like grass whenever she was around the charismatic army officer.

"Well," she challenged, her voice husky, "are you going to
stand there gawking or are you going to buy me that espresso you
promised?"

Snapping into action, Houston slid his hand around her upper
arm and guided her forward. "No, ma'am, I'll buy you that well-
deserved cup of espresso." He felt edgy with fear. He was raw
with wanting. Wanting her. Breath-stealing elation raced through
him as Ann strode at his side. This time she didn't seem to mind
his hand on her arm. Indeed, it was as if she liked it there. But
Houston didn't fool himself. They'd just been through a very intense life-and-death situation. He found it normal that medicos

automatically drew close to one another for emotional support after a crisis was over. It was only human, he warned himself. Still, his fingers tingled wildly as he felt the slip and slide of Ann's light wool blazer against the white silk of her blouse, the firmness of her flesh beneath it. He reveled in the pleasurable sensation, feeling once again like a greedy beggar taking whatever crumbs she'd unknowingly thrown out to him.

Had Antonio's heart attack triggered her own need to live life more fully? To possibly reach out to him? Grinning recklessly, laughter rumbling up from his chest, he said, "This has been one wild ride so far, Dr. Parsons, and the day is young yet...."

She raised one brow and glanced up at him as they walked. "I give you that," she replied, her pulse speeding up. The undisguised happiness in Mike's eyes affected her, left her aching to kiss him, to feel his hands slide around her torso as he pulled her uncompromisingly against his body. She longed to experience his sweet assault upon her senses once again, and it almost overwhelmed her.

When Mike glanced down at her, he realized in that split second that Ann had dropped her guard, because she was grinning, too. There was bright color in her cheeks, and she looked damn beautiful when she blushed. Instantly, she turned away to avoid his eyes. But not even that could mar Houston's happiness at her decision to stay in Peru.

To hell with it. Mike threw all caution aside. "Come here...." he murmured huskily as he drew Ann out of the traffic of the busy terminal. Backing her against the wall, he leaned close to her. In her eyes he read the need she felt for him, and registered in every fiber of his being. The connection between them was as palpable as the feel of his fingers as he grazed the slope of her flushed cheek.

"I need you," he rasped, placing his hand against her cheek and guiding her face upward. The driving need to kiss her and the need he saw in her eyes made him let down his own guard for this one, exquisite moment. He saw her eyes widen momentarily, heard her breath hitch. He sensed her emotional response, and it felt damn good washing through him. Smiling tenderly down at her as he lightly brushed her parting lips with his, he saw the fear in her eyes dissolve. Yes, she wanted this as much as he did.

For one heated moment out of time, all the terminal sounds, the people's voices, faded from Ann's awareness. All she'd longed for moments ago was happening. Somehow, Mike had known she needed him. It was all so crazy. So mixed up. Yet as she lifted her chin and felt his strong mouth settle upon her lips, nothing had ever felt so right. So pure. So devastatingly beautiful. His strong arm moved around her back and she felt him pull her against him. There was no mistaking his gesture; it was clearly that of a man claiming his woman.

Her lashes swept downward and the ache inside her intensified as his mouth skimmed hers. How good he tasted! She inhaled his very male scent into her quivering nostrils, slid her hands upward against his barrel chest, her fingers digging convulsively against the fabric of his shirt, marveling in the strength of his muscles tightening beneath her exploration. His mouth slid surely against her lips, rocking them open even farther, his tongue thrusting boldly into her mouth. She gave a moan of sweet surrender as she lost herself in the fiery, hungry mating. All that existed in that moment was Mike, his maleness, his tender domination of her as a woman yielding to him in almost every way possible. Oh, how stupid she had been not to give herself to him sooner!

His mouth moved possessively and she responded just as hungrily and boldly to his dizzying assault. With him, she felt a primal wildness she'd never felt with any man. He brought out her earthiness, her need to be her untamed, untrammeled self. His hand slid behind her head, holding her, trapping her so he could taste her even more deeply. The sweet hotness and longing built between her thighs as she felt him grind his hips demandingly against hers. There was no mistaking his need of her. Ann felt urgency and frustration. Her fingers opened and closed spasmodically against his thickly corded neck. She couldn't get enough of him and drowned in the splendor of his tender assault upon her.

Ann wanted the hot, branding kiss, the sweet, unspoken promise between them to last forever. As Houston began to ease his mouth from hers, she cried out internally, not wanting to cease contact with him in any way. Yet she knew they must. She was sure they were making a spectacle of themselves in the corridor. People were staring at them but for once, Ann didn't care. Mike had somehow dissolved all her fears, her need to be proper and prudish out in public. He tore away her doctor's facade and stripped her naked, revealing her hot, womanly core of primitive needs and desires. As she looked dazedly up into his narrowed, gleaming eyes, she had never felt so protected or desired.

His face was alive with feelings—for her. Ann saw it in his burning look, his mouth only inches from her own as he stood over her, his arm continuing to press her tightly against him. She tasted him on her lips. She felt the masculine hardness of him against her abdomen and her own heated response to his hunger. Never had Ann felt more alive than now. Never. Her breath was shallow and gasping. She tried to speak.

"No..." Houston rasped thickly, "don't think for once, Ann. Just feel. Feel!" he ordered, and captured her glistening lips one more time.

Sinking against him, her knees like jelly due to his renewed assault on her senses, Ann felt the world skid to a dizzying halt. Only Mike and she existed. She no longer cared what anyone thought as she held him tightly against her, her breasts hard against his chest. Their hearts were pounding; she could feel his as if it were inside her. The sensation was shockingly beautiful and one she'd never experienced before. The sandpaper quality of his beard against her cheek, his hot, moist breath, the taste and power of him as he grazed her lips repeatedly, almost teasingly, left her aching painfully. She wanted to feel him inside her, filling her, taking her, making her his in every conceivable way. Whatever fear had held her was gone now, and in its place, a fierce desire for Mike welled up, surging through her like a tidal wave.

Gradually, ever so gradually, Houston forced himself to ease back from Ann's lips. Lips made of the wild honey he'd found only in the jungles of Peru. Honey that was so sweet it made him dissolve beneath her searching, innocent mouth. There was no question he needed her. None. And as he opened his eyes and stared down into her dazed blue-gray ones, he knew she needed him, too. She was trembling with need of him. But so was he. He regretted kissing her here in the terminal. Anywhere else would

have been better than here. The painful knot in his lower body
attested to the poor choice of location. He wanted to love her
thoroughly, to indelibly print his essence within her. Wanted so
badly to claim her and make her his woman it was nearly his
undoing. The fierceness of his desire for Ann was far more than
just sexual, because he was in touch with every subtle essence
within her—from her emotions to her spirit. Ann didn't know that,
but he knew she could feel his bond with her as much as he did.
That much was clear in the awe he saw reflected in her eyes, the
questions about what she was feeling.

"Shh," he whispered, grazing his thumb across her wet lips,
"just feel, Ann. Just feel.... It's real...all of this is real, I promise
you. You aren't imagining anything." He closed his eyes and
rested his brow against hers, letting himself sink back into that
invisible connection that he'd allowed to fully form between them.
Once Ann could talk to him about her feelings and openly confide
in him, he vowed to tell her all that had happened to him in the
jungle. Another part of him told him he was crazy for allowing
her to get close to him. Did he want to put her in that kind of
danger? How could he? But Ann would have to know the truth
very soon. She had to make her own decision about whether he
was worth desiring or not.

Easing away, Houston cupped her shoulders and gently moved
her away from him. Ann's face was flushed, her eyes soft and
filled with desire—for him. Never had he felt stronger...or more
protective. His mouth curved ruefully.

"Would you like to go freshen up in the ladies' room?"

Swaying uncertainly in his embrace, Ann nodded. Looking
around, she felt embarrassment flooding her. Many people had
stopped to watch them. "Oh dear...yes, yes I would...."

Mike nodded and placed his arm around her. "Don't worry,
folks around here understand lovers. They aren't staring at us because we kissed, you know. Down here, everyone loves lovers."
He guided Ann toward the women's rest room up ahead.

Grateful for his humor, his protective demeanor against the
many prying eyes, Ann tried to contain her escaping feelings. She
pushed strands of hair away from her face and forced herself to
breathe more evenly. *Lovers.* The word flowed through her. Yes,

she wanted to be Mike's lover. Every cell in her body was aching with need of him, more than ever now. Just being close to him was feeding that brightly burning fire that had roared to life in her during his searching, hungry kisses.

Reaching the ladies' room, Ann forced herself to walk into it. She felt drunk. Drunk with pleasure and desire. Somehow, she had to pull herself back together again. At the washbasin, she sloshed cold water repeatedly into her face until she felt some semblance of order returning to her. She spent a great deal more time in there than was necessary; it took a good ten minutes to gather herself. Blotting her face, she quickly ran a brush through her mussed hair and put lipstick back on her soft, well-kissed mouth.

All of her carefully orchestrated life had just exploded. Completely. Ann was no longer thinking with her head, only her heart. The switch was shocking to her. All her life, she'd allowed her head to rule her, not her emotions. In Mike's presence, all she wanted to do was feel—and then feel some more. What was going to happen? Could she control herself where he was concerned? She felt like a teenager with her hormones running away from her, like she had no control over anything. All she had to do was think of Mike, allow his hard features to gel before her, and she grew hot and shaky all over again. Ann thought it was because she'd denied her real feelings for him throughout the last two months. This time his kiss had ripped the lid off Pandora's box.

Groaning, she took a deep breath, talked sternly to herself and left the rest room. She found Houston standing across the corridor, his back to the wall, his arms crossed over his chest. How calm and centered he seemed! Ann stood there for a moment, envying his obvious control. He looked fine. He looked like nothing had happened. But it had. Something life-shattering had occurred within her when he'd held her minutes ago. Something so profound, so deep had occurred that Ann needed time to try and understand what had taken place.

As if sensing she was there, he turned his gaze to her. In that instant, her heart responded violently, and again that sense of warmth and protection he gave her overwhelmed her. Suddenly dizzy, Ann leaned against the wall, unsure of what was happening. Instantly, she saw Mike straighten and walk directly to her.

Before he could say anything, she held out her hand. "I'm okay. I really am."

He smiled a little and placed his hand on her left arm, just in case. "You look beautiful," he whispered huskily. And she did. Her lips were soft from his kisses, her eyes velvet with desire. The flush across her cheeks was still there, and as he drew her back into the traffic, he thought she looked like a teenage girl who had just experienced her very first kiss from the boy she had a crush on.

Ann leaned against him as he placed his arm around her shoulders and led her along. Grateful for his understanding, she managed to murmur, "I've *never* felt like this, Mike. *Ever.*"

Chuckling indulgently, he pressed a kiss to her hair. "I told you Peru would cast her spell on you. Down here, magic happens all the time."

"Magic? Humph. More like a sledgehammer to my head, if you ask me." Ann heard him laugh deeply over her remark. She felt his steadying care and she acquiesced to his superior strength.

"Well," he drawled, giving her a teasing look, "maybe our kiss had a little something to do with that?"

Refusing to be baited, Ann tried to give him a dour look. "You don't have to look like a satisfied cat about it, Houston."

Preening a little, Mike broadened his grin into one of boyish delight. "That kiss has been a long time in coming. And there's no way I'm apologizing for it. Ah, here we are." He halted. "This is just what you need—espresso to settle your nerves."

Ann laughed a little as they stood in front of the restaurant. "Oh, sure, coffee to soothe my jangled nerves. Right." They stood looking at the small café with its red-and-green-striped awning.

"I always stop here, at Federico's Place, to get my espresso when I'm coming in off a long flight." Mike gestured to the brass-and-glass doors. "Come on. He's got the best espresso in Lima. I swear it."

Once they were seated at a small round table covered in expensive white linen and decorated with colorful flowers in a cut-glass vase, Ann smiled gratefully at the waiter. When he delivered their coffee a moment later, she cautiously sipped the tiny, fragile cup of espresso, and studied the man before her. Mike Houston was simply too large for the white wrought-iron chair, the table or even this small café. But it was there that he frequented because the owner, Federico, had recognized him instantly. There had been a lot of backslapping, smiles and greetings. And it seemed the two young waiters knew him, too. She was beginning to wonder who Houston didn't know, but then, he'd been down here more than ten years, and in his line of business, it was good to know a lot of people.

"Well?" Mike demanded. "What do you think?" He'd already drunk half of his espresso, while Ann had only hesitantly tasted hers. He supposed she was like that with everything in her life: cautious and slow. Why? She had that shadowed look back in her eyes as she lifted the English china cup to her lips and looked at him over the rim.

"It's sweet...and tastes surprisingly mild." Ann set the cup down. "I thought it would taste bitter because it's so concentrated."

Chuckling, Mike finished off his first cup. A second magically showed up seconds later, Federico himself brought it over with a flourish. Mike nodded and thanked the restaurant owner. "What you poor folks up in *Norteamérica* get for coffee beans, is a sin," he said to Ann with a laugh. "*Sudamericanos* aren't stupid." He raised the cup in toast to her. "We keep the *best* beans down here, and that's what you're drinking—Andean coffee raised on slopes so high that the condors fly over them daily. Coffee growing in some of the finest, richest lava soil in the world. It *has* to taste good."

Ann couldn't help but smile. "You are so passionate about everything. I've never met anyone like you before." It was Mike's passion that was somehow encouraging her to tap into her own desires on such a primal, wonderful level of herself as a woman.

His reckless grin broadened. "My mother often told me when I was a young kid growing up that if I didn't *love* whatever I was doing, I'd eventually curl up and die. She told me to do things that made my heart sing, that made my heart soar like the condors that hang above the Andes." He sobered a little and sighed. "She was a woman of immense intelligence, I realized as I got old enough and experienced enough to really understand what she was telling me.''

"To live life with passion," Ann murmured. "That's not one I've heard of late.''

"So," Mike said, "do you live your life with passion? Do you love what you do as a medical doctor?''

"I like what I do. It feels good to be able to stop a person's pain, to stop death from cheating a life...but passion? I don't know about that.'' She frowned and picked up her cup once again. "I certainly don't live with the gusto you do.''

"A little while ago," Mike murmured in a low intimate tone, as he turned the tiny cup around and around between his massive, scarred hands, "I saw a different Ann Parsons out there. Not the one I knew for eight weeks in Arizona. This woman, the one I kissed today, was—different. Provocative...passionate...committed...''

"Translated, that means what?''

"Just that I felt a much different woman," Mike said in a whisper, so that no one could eavesdrop.

Avoiding his heated look, Ann tinkered nervously with the cup in her hands. "Mike...give me time. I—I'm just not prepared to say much right now.''

Holding up his palm in a gesture of peace, he added huskily, "You're a woman of immense feelings. I understand. You're like a deep, deep well of water. Not many are privy to the real feelings you hide so well.''

Ann couldn't deny any of it. Stealing a glance at him, she whispered, "I don't know what happened to me today, Mike. Maybe something changed in me when I saw Antonio almost die. I usually protect myself from personal feelings in these situations....'' Her words trailed away as she became pensive. Mike deserved her honesty here. Setting the cup down, she forced herself to add, "I guess your passion for living life with emotion has rubbed off onto me a lot more than I realized. Watching your friend almost die probably shook that loose in me. It was time, I guess....''

Mike nodded, feeling the gravity of her statement. She was being honest on a level he'd never experienced with her before— due to that magical connection forged between them earlier, in that beautiful moment when he'd kissed her. He decided to return some of her honesty. "When I was trying to save Tony, I was afraid," he admitted. "I was afraid he was dead. I wanted him to live so damn bad I could taste it. I could feel myself willing my heartbeat, my energy or whatever it was, into his body. And when I looked up at you in that moment, I felt hope. It spurred me on." With a shrug, he added a little shamefacedly, "I can't tell you what went on between us in that split second, I only know that something did. And somehow, it gave me hope when I didn't really have any left."

"All that in one look," Ann murmured as she sipped the espresso. "I'm amazed, frankly." Still, she felt good at Mike's sincere praise, at the admiration in his eyes. She liked the feeling.

"You have a very healing effect on people, whether you know it or not," Houston said sincerely.

"Something else happened back there, Mike," Ann began hesitantly. "I think what I saw may have been a result of sleep deprivation." She saw him frown. With a wave of her thin hand, she said, "Not that it was bad. It was just...shocking."

"What happened?"

"Promise you won't tell me I had a brief, acute psychotic episode?"

"No problem. You're sane and well grounded." Interested in hearing her experience, Houston asked, "This happened while we were bagging Tony?"

"Yes. At one point," Ann continued, setting the espresso aside and folding her hands on the table, "something changed. You got far more intense than before. You'd hit him twice in the chest and he hadn't started breathing again. I know you were desperate. You wanted your friend to live. That was normal behavior, but..." She folded her hands "...then something happened, and I can't explain it or even begin to get a handle on it."

"What?" Mike's scowl deepened. He saw a flush stain Ann's cheeks. "Something that upset you?"

"It didn't upset me exactly, Mike. I just felt these incredible waves of energy striking me, like waves from the ocean, only...they were coming from you. I actually felt buffeted by them as you leaned over Tony, working so intently with him, willing him to live. And then, the silliest thing of all, I saw this shadow or something.... It descended over you. Well, part of you. And it was only for a split second. I'm sure it was a sleep-deprivation hallucination...."

"*What* did you see?" he demanded darkly.

Taking a deep breath, Ann dived into her experience. "I saw this dark shadow appear above your head. It just seemed to form out of nowhere. I'm not sure anyone else saw it." Moistening her lips and avoiding his sharp, glittering gaze, she added, "I saw it come over you like a transparency of some sort, fitting over your head and shoulders." Embarrassed, she gave an awkward laugh, and said, "For a moment, it looked like a jaguar or leopard over your head. I no longer saw your face, your profile. Instead I saw this huge cat's head and massive shoulders. Well," Ann murmured wryly, risking a look up at him, "I'm sure by now you think I experienced a psychotic episode."

Mike shrugged. "Down here," he muttered uncomfortably, "I carry a name."

"Excuse me?"

His brows knitted and he stared down at his espresso cup. "I have a nickname...." He heaved a sigh. Lifting his head, he met her frank blue-gray gaze. "I'm sure you'll hear it sooner rather than later, so I might as well tell you myself. I'm called the jaguar god. It's a reputation I've garnered over the years. The cocaine lords started calling me that a long time ago. The name stuck." He grimaced.

"It's not a bad name," Ann murmured. "Why are you so uncomfortable with it?"

Mike sat up and flexed his shoulders. "Someday, Ann, I'll tell you more about it. More than likely my friends at the clinic will fill your ears about me, about the legend surrounding me, until you're sick and tired of hearing that name."

Ann frowned. "You mean there's more to this? I wasn't seeing things?"

Mike rose and pulled some sols from his pocket. "You're a trained therapist. You know how sleep deprivation and emotional stress can make you hallucinate during intense moments of crisis," he said, deciding that the truth would have to wait. He couldn't risk her rejection of him. Not after that nourishing kiss. ''Come on, that van should be ready by now and those medical supplies loaded in it.''

Chapter 4

Despite her extreme fatigue, Ann was wide awake as Mike drove the heavily loaded van from the airport to one of the poorest sections of Lima. She tried to minimize in her mind the power and influence of his hot, melting caresses, but it was impossible. It was almost as if her lips were still tingling from his branding, unexpected kiss. She tried concentrating on the road ahead of them, noticing that Mike avoided most of the major freeways and took smaller streets. He probably knew this city like the back of his hand. Even more, Ann was aware of his heightened state of alertness. He was behaving like a soldier out in the bush rather than a man driving in the relative safety of a city. It didn't make sense and she wondered what dangers lay ahead of them.

One thing for sure, Mike was right about Lima. The city was set like a crown jewel on verdant green slopes and surrounded by the raw beauty of the Andes, which towered like a backdrop in the distance. The day was sunny, the sky a soft blue, and Ann found herself enjoying her first views of the city.

"Lima reminds me of Buenos Aires," she said to Mike, as he turned down a dirt road that led into a poor section, what he called a barrio.

Nodding, Mike divided his attention between driving and watching for enemies. He was on his own turf now, and the drug lords had hundreds of spies throughout the city looking for him, trying to pin him down so that a hit squad could corner and murder him.

"Lima and Buenos Aires are a lot alike," he said, distracted. "Plenty of trees, bushes and flowers all over the place."

"Nothing like New York City?"

He grinned tightly. "That place..."

"For once we agree on something," she teased. Moments later, the scenery changed as they crept down the dirt road, which was rutted with deep furrows where tires had chewed into the soil. The winter rains had left the area in a quagmire as usual, and the city certainly wasn't going to waste money on asphalt paving in a barrio. Houston's gaze was restless, his awareness acute. His eyes were scanning their surroundings like radar. Ann felt uncomfortable. Or more to the point, endangered. By what? Whom?

When Mike saw her brows dip, he tried to lighten the feeling of tension in the truck. "Hang around and you might decide I'm not the bad hombre you think I am." He winked at her and delivered a boyish smile in her direction to ease the concern he saw in her eyes. "I've got six weeks to change your mind." He scowled inwardly. What was he saying? He was loco, he decided. There was no way to have a relationship with Ann. Though he'd always known that, the truth of it hit home as he drove through the city. He couldn't place her in that kind of danger. He simply couldn't. The price was too high for her—and for himself.

Ann slanted a lingering glance in his direction. Houston had taken off his sport coat and rolled up the sleeves of the white cotton shirt he wore revealing his strong, massive forearms which were covered with dark hair. The window was open, allowing the spring air to circulate in the van, mixed with the scents of fires and food cooking in pots in the nearby village. "Where are we now?" she asked, sitting up and rearranging the seat belt across her shoulder.

"This is the barrio our clinic serves," Houston said with a scowl. "My home away from home."

"Where do you live the rest of the time?"

"Anywhere in Peru where I can find the drug lords first before they find me and my men,'' he answered grimly. ''Usually I stay at the BOQ—barracks officers' quarters—up near the capital when I come in off a mission.'' He took a beeper from his belt and looked at it. ''Matter of fact, they know I'm here. I've already got five phone calls to make as soon as we get this stuff to the clinic.'' He snapped the beeper back onto his belt.

Ann shook her head as she surveyed the neighborhood. Most of the ramshackle houses were little more than corrugated tin held up with bits of wood, with cardboard as siding. Huge families crowded the doorways as Ann and Mike slowly drove by. ''No one should live in these conditions,'' she murmured. ''The city at least ought to put sanitary sewage systems into a place like this. So many children will die of infections from drinking water from open cesspools.''

''You've got the general idea.''

She heard the tightness in Houston's voice and studied the hard set of his mouth. As they drove deeper into the barrio, living conditions deteriorated accordingly. People were thin and hungry looking, their dark brown faces pinched. They were wrapped in rags and threadbare clothing to try and keep warm. As Mike drove, more and more people greeted him, calling out and lifting their hands in welcome. He called back, often by name, and waved in return.

''It seems like everyone here knows you.''

''Just about.''

''Because of the clinic?''

''Yeah, mostly. Sister Dominique goes around once a week and makes house calls. She carries her homeopathic kit from house to house, family to family, doing what she can.'' He shook his head. ''Oftentimes it's not enough.''

''Hopeless?''

''No,'' Mike said, making a slow turn to the left, down another very narrow street lined with cardboard shacks and crowded with people. ''Never hopeless.'' He grinned suddenly. ''I hold out hope for the hopeless, Ann, or I wouldn't be down here doing this stuff. No, the clinic makes a difference.''

Ann admired his commitment to improving the sad conditions. ''Can't governmental agencies help you?''

"They won't," he said, gesturing toward a redbrick church ahead, its gleaming white spire thrusting above the mire of human habitations. "Peruvians in Lima don't view Indians as human. We're animals to them. Big, dumb brutes to be used as pack animals, is all."

Frowning, Ann said, "You said you were Yaqui?"

"My mother's part Yaqui, from Central America, and part Quechua Indian. She was born in Peru, but her family moved north to Mexico when she was six years old."

"How did your mother meet your father?"

"When you get me good and drunk sometime, I'll tell you," Mike told her with a grin.

He braked the van and turned at the redbrick church, which was surrounded by a white picket fence. Despite the mud, filth and poverty of the neighborhood, the Catholic church was spotlessly clean, with no trash littering the well-kept green lawn. The church stood out like a sore thumb in the dirty barrio, but Ann supposed it was a symbol of hope. A beacon of sorts. When he drove the van to the rear of the church, she saw a one-story brick addition to the building.

"That's the clinic," Mike told her proudly, slowing down. Putting the van into Reverse, he backed up to the open gate of the picket fence. "Sisters Dominique and Gabriella live here. They're the ones who are in the trenches every day, keeping the clinic doors open for the people."

Ann saw at least fifteen mothers with children standing patiently in line outside the doors. Her heart broke as she noticed their lined, worried faces. Some carried babies in thin blankets, pressed tightly to them; others had crying children who clung to their colorful skirts. They were all Indians, Ann observed.

Houston turned off the van and set the brake. He glanced over at Ann. The devastation in her exhausted eyes spoke eloquently of how deeply moved she was by the horrible conditions the Indians lived in. She was easily touched, he was discovering, and it said something about her he'd already known intuitively. Still, he wondered how she would fit in with the nuns here, and he worried that the cool demeanor Ann had displayed toward him when they'd worked together on the ranch might put the nuns off. "The two little old nuns are French. They're from Marseilles, and they're saints, as far as I'm concerned. They've been ministering to the poor since they came here in their twenties. They're in their seventies now and should've retired a long time ago, but they're like horses in a harness—it's all they know and they have hearts as big as Lima. They speak French and Spanish and some English.''

He wrapped his hands around the steering wheel and gave Ann a measuring look. ''I know how you reacted to me off and on for eight weeks up in Arizona. They don't need a *norteamericana* coming in here and telling them what to do. They're homeopaths, not medical doctors. If you don't know anything about homeopathy, try to suspend your disbelief about it, watch them work and watch what happens to the patients they serve before you make any judgment about it, okay?''

Ann met and held his searching gaze. Because she'd kept him at a distance until now, he probably thought she would carry on that way here. ''You're remembering my attitude toward you in Arizona and predicting that I'll treat everyone at this clinic the same way?''

Mike castigated himself. ''There are times when I wish I had more diplomacy, but lack of sleep is making me a little more blunt than usual.'' He opened his hands over the wheel in a helpless gesture. ''I owe you an apology.''

Ann accepted his apology—the second one to come from him since they'd traded parries on the plane. ''Look,'' she said, sighing wearily, ''I understand your being wary. I know I haven't been easy to get along with. But let's just forget our personal feelings about one another, shall we? I have a commitment to honor in Morgan's name for the next six weeks. In a clinic situation or a hospital environment, I'm not the ice queen you think I am. So don't be concerned that I'll ride roughshod over two old nuns. I've got better things to do with my time than pick at them or complain about what type of medicine they practice. No, I don't know a lot about homeopathy. But it obviously works or they wouldn't have been using it here for fifty years, would they?'' But despite her assurances to Mike, Ann knew she would have to make an effort to suspend some of her rational approaches and training. Her medical background was different from a homeopathic practitioner's. This was another situation in which she would have to yield her scientific bent to a more mysterious, even mystical kind of medicine. If she was going to survive these six weeks, she understood that she had to adjust to Mike's world, and that included the nuns' medical procedures.

Mike saw Ann struggling to not be hurt by his request. That said a lot about her. She was confident and didn't let her ego get in the way of better judgment. "I didn't mean to accuse you of being close-minded. It's just that I know a lot of conventional medicine types in the medical field who look down their nose at homeopathy. Hell, the clinic was so poor financially that we couldn't afford to buy the prescription drugs we needed, so homeopathic meds took up the slack instead."

"I'll stand back and let them run the show," Ann promised. "I'm here to assist. All right?"

Satisfied, Mike nodded. "I just don't want any misunderstandings, Ann. God knows, I'm going to be busier than a one-armed paper hanger this next week. I don't have time to come down here and put out brushfires between you and my grannies, that's all." And then he smiled and held her warming gaze. "Otherwise, I think they'll fall in love with you."

She smiled tiredly in return. "Thank you for your brutal honesty, Major. I generally don't cause 'brushfires.' I'm in the habit of putting them out."

"Touché," he murmured with a sour smile. "Okay, let's go inside...."

"Mon petit chou!"

Mike halted just inside the door. Sister Gabby, who was holding her stethoscope on the chest of a baby being held by a young mother, called out in welcome. She raised her soft, frizzy white head, her brown eyes sparkling.

"Mon petit chou, you are home!" she cried. "Oh! How long it has been! We missed you!" Patting the baby with her paper-thin hand, she bustled forward putting the stethoscope around her neck. Then, she threw open her arms and hugged Mike with a fierceness that always surprised him. Sister Gabby was four feet

eleven inches tall—a dwarf in comparison to him. Yet she was strong. Very strong for her age. And she was a giant in his eyes, towering over everyone with her warm heart, her grace.

He gently embraced the nun, dropping into French. "Grandma Gabby, I have great news. Look who I brought with me. This is Dr. Ann Parsons from the States. She's a trained emergency-room physician and she's going to assist you and Granny Dominique for the next six weeks." Mike eased the nun around, praying that Ann would smile.

To his relief, as he brought the two together for introductions, Mike saw Ann's exhaustion melt away before him, leaving a warm, radiant woman whose blue-gray eyes shone with incredible happiness as she reached out and gently enclosed the old nun's hand between her own, and greeted her in flawless, beautiful French.

"Sister Gabriella, I've heard so many wonderful things about you from Major Houston, here. It's a great honor to meet you."

"Ah, call me Sister Gabby, please." The nun directed a beaming smile up at Mike, who had draped a protective arm around her thin, hunched shoulders. "This young one, the one we call 'my little cabbage,' is the true saint around here. And we are so glad to have your help, Dr. Parsons! The Lord knows that we can use a medical doctor of your experience around here, eh?"

Ann smiled pleasantly and released the nun's hand, noticing her dark blue habit which did not cover her silver hair, and the gold crucifix that lay against her thin chest. Although the nun was in her seventies, Ann saw that her aging face was strong and beautiful. And Gabby's adoring gaze never left Houston's. There was no denying the love and admiration the old nun had for the army officer.

"*'Mon petit chou'?*" Ann inquired sweetly, looking directly at Houston, who promptly avoided her inquiring gaze. "Is that the major's name?" Her smile grew as she watched Mike become highly uncomfortable. She knew it was an often-used endearment in France for someone who was precious and beloved. She just found it a little hard to picture big Mike Houston being called a "little cabbage." There was nothing little about this man.

Tittering, Sister Gabby said, "Oh, yes. You know—" she

wagged her finger up at Mike ''—when this young army officer
came to us a decade ago with the offer to build us a small clinic
to help the poor, we knew a miracle had walked into our lives.
Michael is named after the archangel, the destroyer. But he was
an answer to our prayers, believe me! Do you know that he built
this clinic by hand, brick by brick, over a year's time? Instead of
destroying, he built.''

''Granny...'' Mike protested, ''I really don't think Dr. Parsons
wants to hear the history—''

''Sure I do,'' Ann answered, smiling softly as she devoted her
full attention back to the tiny nun. ''So, he built this clinic for
you?'' She was enjoying Houston's obvious embarrassment as he
shifted from one foot to another, his hands behind his back. Let
him squirm. It was good for his soul.

''Ah, yes! He had only the help of the poor who live around
our church. Every day he would come here from his dangerous
duties and roll up his sleeves—'' she pinched his massive biceps
with pride ''—and he would lay brick! He talked the Lima government out of the old brick and he raised money for the concrete.
He was a one-man army! That is when Sister Dominique and I
decided to give him a nickname. Now, you know his *other* name,''
Gabby said in a conspiratorial tone, ''but that doesn't really tell
of what lies in his heart. So we decided to call him 'my little
cabbage' because that's what he was to us, to our people and to
the poor we serve—so very precious and beloved by all of us.''
She reached up, her parchment-colored hand patting Mike's barrel
chest. ''Beneath this shirt beats a heart of gold, Dr. Parsons. His
generosity, his care of the poor is so great! But his heart is even
more large and giving!''

''Granny!'' Mike protested. ''I really don't think we have time
to talk pleasantries right now, do you? Dr. Parsons will get bored
hearing about me. While I get some help unloading supplies from
the van, why don't you introduce her to Sister Dominique?''

Ann chuckled to herself. She liked watching the old woman
ruffle Mike's feathers, she decided, as Sister Gabby caught her
hand and led her down the narrow hall to another room in the
clinic.

''Ah, yes, of course, *mon petit chou.* Time is short! I know you cannot stay long. It is dangerous for you to be too long in one place, eh? Yes, come, come, Dr. Parsons...."

Ann glanced over her shoulder at Houston. He had relief written all over his features. As she proceeded down the narrow hall she saw four different examination rooms. They were pitifully equipped, she realized. The tiny nun moved quickly, switching from French to Spanish as she stuck her head in each of the rooms to tell the awaiting patients that she'd be back in just a moment.

The last room in the clinic was actually an office of sorts. It was the smallest space, and there was a badly dented metal desk in the center of it with another nun in a blue habit seated behind it. Her white hair was cut very short and her wire-rimmed glasses were perched on her very fine, thin nose as she dug through a huge, teetering pile of papers.

"I swear, Gabriella," she muttered without looking up, "we *must* get these homeopathic cases into the files! I am looking for Juan's records. I do not remember what homeopathic remedy we gave him six weeks ago! I must find it!"

"Tut, tut, Dominique," Gabby said, tapping her smartly on the shoulder. "We have a visitor, a medical doctor who is going to help us for six weeks! Dr. Ann Parsons is from the United States. Meet Sister Dominique."

"Eh?" Dominique looked up, her pinched face very wrinkled. Her gray eyes narrowed as she looked Ann up and down. Placing her hands on her hips, she said, "Well, a *real* medical doctor? How did this happen?" Then she suddenly grinned, and Ann saw that all her front upper teeth were missing.

Sister Dominique's handshake was surprisingly strong. Ann smiled. "Major Houston was partly responsible for getting me to volunteer." She released Dominique's hand. "It looks like you could use a file clerk in here?" she added, eyeing the cabinets, which were partially open with all kinds of files sticking out of them.

Sister Dominique looked sadly around at the chipped and dented office furnishings. "I need a clerk. I need five new file drawers." She waved her arms around the stuffy little room. "I need more space!"

"Now, now, Dominique," Gabby chided, waving a finger at

her, "be patient. *Mon petit chou* is home and said he's got two *new* file cabinets for us! He's getting the men to help bring them back here. Isn't that wonderful? He said a *norteamericano,* Señor Trayhern, gave a huge donation to us! Our prayers have been answered—again!" She clapped her hands delightedly.

Dourly, Sister Dominique griped, "Why does God always answer our prayers at the last minute? I swear, Gabby, we must be saying them wrong. There must be something to the process we have obviously overlooked, eh? We pray and pray and pray for *years,* and finally, just when we think the clinic will close, or we just can't go on, He decides to drop us a few crumbs to keep going. No," she muttered, scratching her silvery head, "we must be going about this wrong. Perhaps we need to get up at four a.m. to pray instead of six a.m.?"

Ann smiled gently. Sister Dominique had a vinegar personality, but the tall, lean woman's burning gray eyes sparkled with hints of wry amusement, too.

"I think that God heard you plenty, this time," Ann answered warmly. "Wait until you see what all Mike is bringing out of that van for your clinic. And that donation was for a nice sum—a hundred and thirty thousand dollars to put into the bank for equipment to help you at the clinic."

Both nuns said, "Ahh..." as they looked at each other. Gabby broke into a high-pitched cackle and moved around the desk to hug Dominique. And as they embraced, both nuns began to cry.

Ann found herself with damp eyes as the nuns sobbed on each other's shoulders, their French and Spanish strewn between their joyous bouts of weeping. Digging into her leather shoulder purse, Ann found some tissues and handed them out to each of them.

"Thank you," Gabby sniffed, blotting her eyes. "Oh, this is such a wonderful miracle!"

"*Mon petit chou* made this happen, I'll bet," Dominique told the other nun briskly. "He can squeeze blood out of a turnip, that one!"

"And how many times has he had to do it for us? For our clinic?" Gabby sighed, blowing her nose loudly.

"We must get back to our patients," Dominique reminded her starchly, throwing her tissue into a nearby garbage container. "Dr.

Parsons, why don't you come with me? You can sit and watch and listen. For the next few days, I want you to just get acquainted with what we do, with our patients. They are quite wary of Anglos, you know. Word must get out in the barrio about you. And then—'' she raised her eyebrows, which were so thin they were almost nonexistent, ''we will have a hundred people or more lined up and waiting when we open the clinic doors at seven a.m. No medical doctors ever come down here. No, you will be a curiosity. And they have heard so much about modern medicine that they will think you are heaven-sent to help them with their ills.''

''Ah,'' Gabby said with a sigh, ''they will bring their crippled, those that need surgery, thinking that she can do all those things they cannot afford.''

Dominique grunted and walked quickly around the desk, her long, thin arms flying. ''We'll deal with that when it happens, Gabby. Come, we all have much work to do!''

When he returned to the clinic later that day, Houston poked his head into the largest room, a five-bed area he added on to the original structure two years ago. He found Ann and Sister Dominique standing on either side of the bed of a little girl whose head and right eye were bandaged. The girl's mother, a Quechua Indian, held the child protectively in her arms. As he approached, Mike softened his footsteps across the spotlessly clean hardwood floor, studying Ann.

She sat on the bed, facing the little five-year-old and unwrapping the dressing. He noticed she had changed into a white jacket, her stethoscope hanging around her neck, a blood pressure cuff hanging out of her left pocket. Sister Dominique stood behind her, explaining in detail the child's condition.

The low, honeyed tone of Ann's voice drifted toward him. He halted and watched, unnoticed by all of them except Sister Dominique, who raised her head imperiously, met his gaze and gave him a tight smile of acknowledgment before brusquely returning her attention to the other women. Mike smiled to himself. Sister Dominique never missed a beat.

Curious about Ann's bedside manner, he decided not to make his presence known to her. He knew he should get going. It was dangerous to be at the clinic too long. After unloading the supplies, he'd left for a while to return phone calls and check on some of the operations he had set up, figuring he'd give Ann time to get to know the nuns and see how the clinic worked. But now that he'd returned, he knew it was foolish to stick around. Ann's and the nun's safety had to come first over the selfish yearnings of his heart to stay just a minute or two longer. And his presence at the clinic put them at risk.

But just the way Ann tenderly unwrapped the dressing and gauze from around the child's head made his skin prickle pleasantly with desire for her. He saw the gentle strength in her face, her eyes warm with compassion, her voice low and soothing. And the child seemed to react positively to her ministrations.

For the next five minutes, Houston simply absorbed Ann's presence as she went about her duties, in a manner that indicated her work came as naturally as breathing to her. The child had tripped while carrying a stick and stabbed herself in the right eye. The wound was messy but Ann, with Sister Dominique's help, washed it out and examined it closely. To Mike's relief, Ann was willing to allow Sister Dominique to dispense a homeopathic remedy, Symphytum, in order to reduce the swelling of the tissue and help the injured eyeball heal. He liked the way she worked—with swift, efficient motions—and he realized that came from a lot of field experience under extreme and dangerous conditions. A smile tugged at his mouth as he allowed his hands to drop from his hips.

Mike waited until Ann was getting up before he made his presence known. "Half of healing is the love you put into it," he murmured as he finally approached.

Ann turned in surprise. How long had Mike been in the room? "I didn't hear you come in," she said.

"I didn't want to be heard."

Sister Dominique chuckled. "He's the jaguar god, Dr. Parsons. That is the mysterious part of him and his *other* name. Anyone who lives in Peru has heard of him. He walks like the silent jaguar he is named for. His enemies know his deadly abilities. They fear him. Just as his archangel namesake did, he destroys his enemies, but he does it for the common good and protection of the people. You need not fear him, though. He is like a shadow, you know?"

She came over and patted Mike's shoulder. "He is a good shadow, not a bad one. His enemies want to see him hanged by his feet and stripped of his flesh, one inch at a time. With us—" she smiled benignly up at him "—he's a silent, watchful guardian who protects us and helps us to heal others. No, do not be upset that you did not hear him coming. You are safe with him. Always."

Mike watched Sister Dominique leave the room as the woman tucked her daughter, who was probably staying overnight for observation, into the bed. The other four beds held what looked like worse cases, mostly older men and women. He watched Ann gather up the extra bandages and place them in her pocket.

"How are you getting along?"

Ann walked up to him, her exhaustion dissolving beneath his caring gaze. "Fine." For a moment she thought she saw Houston's eyes change, but it could have just been the fatigue lapping at her that made her think there was something stirring in the depths of those dark blue eyes of his—something so warm and good that it seemed to come out and wrap around her briefly in an invisible embrace. It had to be the jet lag, she told herself, or her imagination was just overactive from being around Mike. Ever since that breathless kiss at the airport, her mind had been creating flights of fantasy.

"You're looking beat, Ann. You've got dark circles under your eyes the size of the Lima airport." Mike said wrapping his fingers under her left arm and leading her toward the door. "I've got to get to my office. How about if I drop you off at your apartment? I think you need about twenty hours of sleep and then you'll feel a hell of a lot better." And he would feel a lot better knowing she'd been safely delivered to her apartment.

Ann walked at his side down the hall. "A hell of a lot better than I look?" she baited, a sour smile edging her lips.

Houston grinned. "Now, *querida,* I would *never* say that." He shook his head. "Nope, in my own male, Neanderthal way, I'd say you can't make a looker look ugly." He'd become painfully aware of how his endearment had struck her when he saw Ann's features grow soft. The word *querida* meant "darling" in Spanish and he'd allowed it to slip out by mistake. He must be tired. Or maybe, in his heart, she was already his woman. Inwardly, Houston fought against himself. He simply could *not* see Ann in that way. He had to protect her, not leave her open to a dangerous life by his side.

Heat suffused Ann's cheeks. Self-consciously, she stuffed the stethoscope into her pocket. Anything to halt the frisson of need that burned through her as Mike's endearment touched her. The intimacy he automatically established with her was shattering. In that moment when he'd looked down at her and spoken that one word, Ann had wanted to step into his arms, drown herself in the rough splendor of his mouth and be loved senseless by him. The raw desire in Mike's eyes made her tremble inwardly. Rubbing the back of her neck, she said, "You *are* terribly old-fashioned." Did he know how *much* he affected her? Ann would just die if he did. She tried to cover her reaction by remaining busy, focusing on little details around the clinic.

"Yeah," he said with a chuckle, "I'm a throwback to the caveman type, I know. As you get used to me, I'll rub off on you and you'll see my bite's not as bad as my bark." The high flush in her cheeks, her nervous gestures told Mike how much his intimacy with her had affected her. He felt her emotional response rock through him like the powerful gust of wind that struck before a storm poured its life-giving rains upon the jungle.

"Somehow," Ann murmured, picking up her purse, which Sister Gabby had stuffed into a drawer of the old metal desk, "I doubt that. Sister Dominique was telling me earlier that there's a reward offered for your head. Never mind the rest of your body." Ann shifted uneasily and searched his suddenly hard, expressionless features as he walked easily down the hall and out the clinic doors with her. "Is that true? The nuns told me a lot of what you do down here." Worry ate at her more than she liked to admit. Mike was so passionate about living, about life. How could anyone want to snuff out this magnificent warrior's life? How? Reeling from the shock that anyone would have a price on his head, she made an effort to look at Mike in the new light. In Arizona, he had been vague about his work in Peru. Now the truth was ugly and frightening to her.

"Nuns don't lie," he said abruptly, opening the door to the

sedan for her. Houston warily looked around the church grounds. It always paid to be alert, no matter how tired he was.

Inside, Ann put on her seat belt and waited until Mike climbed in. She wanted to stop asking questions, but they just kept tumbling out of her mouth. As he drove the car slowly away from the church, she asked, "Well? Is it true? There's a huge price on your head?"

Grimly, Mike nodded. "Let's talk about more pleasant things, shall we?" He saw the shadowed look she gave him. She really *cared* about him. He could not protect himself against the waves of her roller-coaster emotions. The worry, anguish and fear she felt for him affected him powerfully. But if she knew how deeply he sensed her every emotion, she'd be mortified.

Ann rested her head against the seat. "Okay." She sighed and closed her eyes. "I need a hot bath, lots of hot water, I feel so dirty...."

It was on the tip of his tongue to tell her that no one in the barrio had ever experienced a hot bath, but he swallowed his comment. He could tell she was tired by the pastiness of her skin, and he noticed how tight and stressed she had become. "A hot bath can do wonders," he agreed.

Ann whispered, "Yes, it will, but you know what? Nothing will take away the pain of caring for that last little girl we saw at the clinic," she murmured. "It just breaks my heart. She's going to go blind, Mike, and there's nothing we can do for her—no surgery available.... I wanted to cry for her."

Mike glanced at Ann before turning his attention back to the foot traffic along the dirt road. "You might as well get used to it, *querida*," he said, the endearment rolling off his tongue once again. "You're going to see heartbreaking cases every day you step into that clinic to work. It's not a pretty sight."

Mike's endearment took the edge off the sorrow she felt for the child, and his deep voice was soothing to her tension and tiredness. But she also heard the anguish in his tone. There was no question of his commitment to the clinic, to the poor. "Those nuns think you walk on water," she said softly. "They adore you."

"Humph, if I step into water I'll sure as hell go down just as fast as the next poor bastard. My grannies are a little biased toward me, so you have to take some of what they say with a grain of salt."

Through her barely opened eyes, Ann realized he was blushing, his cheeks a decided ruddy color. Lips parting, Ann whispered, "Maybe I drew too quick a conclusion about you, Mike. You are a person of unnerving mystery. I have more questions than answers about you."

He cut her a wry look. "Now, don't go believing the nuns. Every once in a while they stretch the truth a little."

Her lips pulled into a careless smile and she met and held his gaze. "You mean you don't want to suffer from a good reputation?"

Chuckling, Mike flexed his fingers against the steering wheel. "You're hearing only one side of the story."

"I ask you and you don't answer me. So what choice do I have but to believe what others say about you?"

He winced. "Touché."

"So, there really is a reward for your head on a silver platter?"

He saw the genuine worry in Ann's eyes once more and he tried to minimize the danger of his situation. "Thirty pieces of silver or something like that..." he muttered.

"Don't get defensive, Mike. It isn't every day I hear of such a thing. You seem to blow the whole thing off. If I had a bounty on my head, I'd never come back to Peru."

Mike glanced briefly into her drowsy eyes. "Trust me, I'm on guard twenty-five hours a day, eight days a week. Yeah, some drug lords would love to have my head served to them on a silver platter. But that reward has been offered for seven years now and no one has collected it yet. I don't intend to give my enemies the pleasure, either. I'm going to keep hitting them, disrupting their trade and fighting to take back the Indian villages they enslave for their nefarious ends." His mouth reflected the grimness in his voice. "No matter how long it takes."

Ann felt a sweeping surge of power gather around him; it wasn't visible, but she could sense it. In some ways, the sensation reminded her of what she'd felt around Mike at the airport earlier, when he'd saved his friend's life. The pupils of his eyes dilated, making them look huge and black, with only a thin ring of blue around them. His features hardened to emphasize his words.

"I know plenty about the drug lords because Morgan's mercs have been working in the Caribbean, Brazil and Peru on assignment against them," Ann said, watching as they drove out of the barrio and onto the asphalt streets of a more upscale area. "When Morgan and three or four of his mercs were kidnapped by two drug lords down here, I found out a lot more than I ever wanted to know."

"Drug lords are the living scum on the face of Mother Earth," Mike growled. "I'll spend every breath I breathe taking those bastards down and apart. No, I'm their nightmare, believe me. That's why there's a ten-million-sol reward for my head." He saw Ann blanch as he mistakenly revealed the true price his enemies offered for his death.

She stirred and sat up, rubbing her face. Heart beating wildly in her breast, she said quietly, "That's more than thirty pieces of silver. Has anyone tried to kill you?"

Mike wished they could talk about something else, but he knew he owed her the truth—before it was too late. "Sure, many times." He frowned. "That's why you have to be careful, too, Ann. You stay alert everywhere you go. The clinic has never been a target— yet. So far, Eduardo Escovar, one of the drug lords who's after me, has respected the sacredness of church ground. But they've hit the barrio three times in the last seven years. People have been killed by the raids they've made, thinking I was in the area when I wasn't. Thank God, none of the bombs they planted around the barrio went off. The people there know about the druggies and their soldiers. They watch the clinic grounds and they protect those two sisters. I try and vary when I go to the clinic to help out. I never have the same schedule twice, to keep them from setting up an ambush for me. And the nuns are never told beforehand when I'll be coming in. I just show up unannounced."

Shivering, Ann felt suddenly cold. She shouldn't be; the late spring afternoon was warm and pleasant. Rubbing her arms, she wrestled with the harsh truth that Mike's life was on the line every day. "How can you live like this? The stress would kill me."

His mouth curved tightly. "I guess what it boils down to is that my passion to see my people free of oppression is stronger than my need to worry about my own neck." He tasted the fear and the care warring within her. Helpless, Mike could only try to buffer her tumultuous emotional state. Would Ann withdraw from him now? He knew the stakes were too high for her to even consider a relationship with him, and he could see in her eyes that she was realizing that truth now. It was best if she did. Maybe hard reality would make her care less for him than before. He hoped so. It was the only way he could be sure she remained safe.

"And you've evaded capture by them for seven years?"

"So far, so good." He turned onto a main avenue lined with trees. Traffic was heavy, but it was always that way in this section of the city, where the rich and powerful lived in tall, spacious apartment buildings. Morgan Trayhern had not been stingy in getting Ann posh quarters, that was for sure.

"And," Ann wondered in a low tone, "is that because of this jaguar they talk about?" She touched lightly on the topic because every time she mentioned it, Mike closed up and retreated from her. She admitted she was more than just a little curious about this new and surprising facet to him. According to the nuns, the man was a living legend among the Indians in Peru. They idolized him. Because he was also a part of the people due to his Indian blood, they saw him as a spokesman, leader and protector. Mike had such broad, capable-looking shoulders beneath the white cotton shirt he wore. Just how many responsibilities did he really carry? Ann was getting an inkling of his role in Peru and it filled her with a mixture of awe and terror.

She shouldn't be in awe of any man, she thought, berating herself sharply. Awe had gotten her into the worst nightmare of her life. No, no man should be put on a pedestal and worshipped. Bitterly, Ann hoped she'd learned that lesson. It was so easy to want to put Mike on just such a pedestal, though.

When Houston didn't reply to her question about the jaguar, she added, "The sisters said that among the Indian population, people refer to you as the jaguar god."

Shrugging, Mike muttered, "I get called a lot of things. Believe me, you'll want to put cotton in your ears when you hear some of the not-so-nice descriptions that I'm sure you'll be privy to in the next six weeks.''

''I feel you evading me on this, Mike. Why?''

As he pulled into an underground parking facility beneath a relatively new apartment building made of steel and glass, he shot her a quizzical look and then devoted his attention to finding a parking spot. ''There's a lot I need to tell you, to fill you in on,'' he admitted slowly. ''But we're both a little beat right now and I'd like to save it for another time.''

Ann nodded, though her exhaustion seemed to have melted away from her as her curiosity was aroused. ''Yes...that would be fine....''

Mike pulled into a parking slot near the elevators. He frowned and shut off the car engine, all the while looking around the gloomy depths of the garage. No place was safe, as far as he was concerned. ''I'm being more than a little selfish about all this,'' he admitted in a low tone as he held Ann's gaze. ''I was glad I didn't have to leave you in Arizona. But I also knew the risks of your being here and you didn't.'' He shrugged as if trying to rid himself of some invisible load he carried. ''It's not too late to get back on that plane, you know.'' He hated suggesting it, but it was the only right thing to do. Ann shouldn't stay if she was afraid of becoming too involved with him, or putting herself in danger because of him. No, she had to make an informed decision on this. Unconsciously, Mike held his breath and waited for her answer. The smart thing to do was get her on a plane going north as soon as possible. But his heart cried, ''no!''

Pain ripped through Ann's chest; it was as if she were physically connected to Mike for a moment. Something was going on inside her and she didn't understand it. Briefly touching her heart region, she closed her eyes and avoided his searching gaze. Taking a deep breath, she opened them again and looked directly at him. ''I think it's time for a little honesty here.'' She barreled on. ''I'm scared, Mike. Of you. Of myself. And now this...this situation where you could get killed at any second.'' Swallowing hard, she felt tears burning her eyes and forced them back. ''I'd be a liar to say it doesn't bother me, because it does. Horribly, if you want the truth.

But..." She gave him a helpless look and drowned in the burning blueness of his gaze.

"But?" Houston croaked, tension radiating through him as he felt and saw her wrestling with so many unspoken emotions.

"How could I have let myself feel so much?" Ann whispered brokenly. "How?"

He sat very still. Tears trickled down her face, down the taut flesh of her pale cheeks. "Maybe we cared for one another in Arizona and we were just too mule-headed to admit it to each other."

His words were spoken so softly that they felt like a whisper through the tumultuous halls of her mind. She closed her eyes, the pain nearly unbearable. Risking everything, she opened them once more. "Yes...I care for you. God knows, I tried to deny it. I tried to bury it. Dammit, Mike!" Tears splattered down her face. "Damn you...damn myself. Oh, hell, I don't know how it happened...or why...it just did."

Her cry cut through his heart. Acting on blind instinct, he leaned forward and slid his arms around her, pulling her against him. At first she tensed, but within moments, she surrendered to him, her head coming to rest against his jaw. She felt soft and good in his arms, wherever their bodies touched. Mike closed his eyes and pressed a kiss into her hair. He could smell the spicy, faint scent of the perfume she wore. It did nothing but accentuate his need for her. All of her.

"I've never seen someone fight so hard not to care for another person as you have," he whispered hoarsely. "And I know you have your reasons, *querida*." He tightened his embrace around her momentarily. Her hand moved languidly up his arm and he relished the sensation her touch caused. "I should be sorry as hell that this has happened, because my being with you puts you in danger. A danger I'm not willing to expose you to..."

Ann buried her face against his neck. "Hold me," she quavered. "Just hold me?" Right now, she felt like a frightened little girl rather than a woman. Her past haunted her. On top of that, the realization that Mike's life was in constant danger added a new pain to her awakening heart, just when she was trying to reach out and allow herself to love once again—despite her fears.

He pressed small, soft kisses to her hair, her temple and wan cheek. He tasted the saltiness of her tears, the dampness of her flesh beneath his mouth. "I should have told you earlier about the danger that surrounds me," he apologized thickly.

Ann shook her head and buried her face more deeply against him. "No..." she murmured, "how could you? I wouldn't let you. I was still running scared. I was in denial about you...about how I really felt toward you...." Unhappily, she muttered, "And I'm a therapist—I should know better."

Houston brushed several thick strands of hair from her cheek. "Welcome to the real word of people, Doc. You're really one of us, after all...."

The rumbling sound in his chest was comforting to Ann and she managed a slight laugh. "I guess you're right, Mike."

"I know I am." His hand stilled against her cheek. "Do you want me to take you to the airport? You can walk away. If you stay...I can't make any promises about us. Not ever...."

Slowly Ann eased out of his arms. She met his grave, shadowed gaze. "No...I want to stay, Mike. I want...need to explore what we have or don't have—danger or no danger."

Chapter 5

Tension thrummed through Mike as he watched Ann look around her newly rented apartment. It was posh, filled with expensive antique furniture from the Queen Anne period. He checked the dead bolt and the other lock on the door. Below, in an unmarked car, he had Pablo, one of his best soldiers, waiting and watching outside the apartment complex. Escovar's spies in the city were in the hundreds. They all knew Mike's face. They all knew what to do if they saw him: call one of the roving hit squads in Lima—whichever was closest. Then a van filled with the best mercenary soldiers the drug lords could buy would come screeching up, determined to murder Houston and anyone with him.

Rubbing his neck ruefully as Ann looked around the large apartment with obvious delight, Mike knew he had to get going. To stay longer was putting her at risk, whether she knew it or not. As she emerged from the bedroom, he met her halfway down the carpeted hall. Reaching out, he drew her into his arms. She came willingly.

"I've got to get going," he said gruffly against her thick, silky hair as she rested against him.

"You can't stay?"

He groaned. Mike understood the invitation: Ann wanted him to make love to her. But as he ran his hand across her slumped shoulders, he remembered the depth of her exhaustion. "Now, *querida,*" he teased, "if we even thought of trying to love one another, we'd fall asleep halfway through. I don't know about you, but when I take you all the way, I want to be wide awake." Why had he said that? Houston was angry with himself. He had no right to lead her on like this. But his heart was overflowing with need of her. Ordinarily, he resisted such temptations, but Ann was unraveling his emotional control in every possible way and he was helpless to stop her. Somehow, he knew he had to try.

Ann smiled softly and languished in the strength and protection of his embrace. "You're right," she murmured. "I'm so tired I can barely walk...or think."

"See?" Mike said with a slight smile as he eased her from his arms. Her eyes were dark with exhaustion, but he ached to take her even now. "Will a stolen kiss do?" His heart beat fiercely as she lifted her chin and gave him that tender smile filled with undisguised desire. His hands automatically tightened on her arms.

Wordlessly, he leaned down, swept her deeply into his embrace and took her offered lips. How soft and sweet they were! He found himself starving for her. His hands moving of their own accord, he eased them down her back as her own arms came up and encircled his neck. The soft firmness of her rounded breasts made fire burn through him. He heard her moan as he lightly caressed the curve of her breasts. Shamelessly, she pressed her hips against his.

The warning in the back of his mind took over. He had stayed alive this long because he never disregarded it. Reluctantly, he tore his mouth from hers. Fire burned in Ann's eyes as he stared hungrily down at her, cupping her shoulders to steady her, as she swayed in the aftermath of their searching kiss.

"You're one hell of a kisser," he rasped. "Take that hot bath you mentioned. Go to bed, *querida.* I'll drop by and see you sometime tomorrow." He frowned. "And keep your dead bolt on that door, do you hear? I've got a key for it and the other lock."

Vaguely, Ann heard his instructions, heard the concern in his voice. Her mouth tingled. She stared dazedly up at him and her body responded hotly to his narrowed eyes, the primal animal sense she felt emanating from him. For a moment—just a split second—she thought she saw the yellow-and-black eyes of a jaguar instead his blue ones. She had to be hallucinating again from sleep deprivation.

"Okay..." she whispered. "I'll see you soon?"

Caressing her hair, he murmured, "Count on it...."

The apartment seemed so void and lonely after Mike left. Ann dutifully slipped the dead bolt in place and locked the door. She moved to the bathroom, fatigue robbing her of all thought. Her first day in Lima had been by far the most aching, hungry and mysterious she had ever spent in her life. Mike was more of an enigma than ever. Yet she knew unequivocally that she needed him—and wanted to explore how she felt about him. Somehow, she had to put the brakes on her out-of-control feelings where he was concerned, she thought as she readied herself for bed, then climbed wearily between the sheets. As sleep claimed her completely, she had a vivid, colorful dream.

Ann found herself standing by the clearest, most inviting looking water she'd ever seen. The oval-shaped pool was a collecting spot, a depression in the soft earth of the Amazon basin. The humidity that forever blotted out the sun and made the sky look like translucent mist moved above her like a living, breathing thing. As she stood naked and barefoot beside the magical-looking pool, she watched like an awed child as that mist gently twisted, turned, took shape and then dissolved, only to writhe into another form or momentary pattern once again. The swirling humidity made the sun look more like a lightbulb hidden behind heavy fabric.

I should be cold, she thought. But she wasn't. The delicious warmth and humidity of the jungle enveloped her like an invisible blanket. It felt wonderful to be free of her bra and panties and all her clothes! Stretching her arms over her head, she laughed fully, her voice muted by the surrounding trees and lush green foliage beneath the rain forest canopy.

Returning her attention to the glistening, smooth surface of the pool, Ann swore she could feel Mother Earth breathing, in and out...in and out.... As she threaded her fingers through her loose, straight hair, Ann could feel the humidity making the strands curl slightly. What did this place remind her of?

As she gazed about the area, she saw broad-leafed plants, no more than a foot high, growing here and there. Grass did not survive beneath the triple canopy; there wasn't enough sunlight to encourage it. The banks of the pool were scattered with decomposing leaves that had fallen from above and small branches that had been knocked off the trees, perhaps by a colorful parrot or a monkey. The decay that surrounded her wasn't repugnant to her as she knelt down on her hands and knees. No, the ground was soft and yielding, almost like a resilient skin to Ann as she pressed her palms against it, testing it gently in slow, delicious exploration. The odor was sweet—surprisingly sweet and clean smelling.

The faint scent of a flower caught her flaring nostrils and she turned to find a huge silk cotton tree next to the pool, its roots large, thin flat gray wings arching out from the main trunk like flying buttresses. There were at least eight "wings" holding the massive, tall tree in place. On one of them, she noticed a clump of darker leaves and an array of bright, colorful flowers springing from it, hanging over the pool like a series of Christmas ornaments. The flowers smelled like vanilla, and she leaned back on her heels, closed her eyes and drew the fragrance deep into her body.

This place in her dream felt like a birthing chamber to Ann. Slowly opening her eyes, she absorbed that realization within her. Yes, that was it. This very special jungle in the Amazon basin was a living incubator of Mother Earth. By some grace, she'd been allowed into the birthing chamber where expressions of love became life itself. An incredible sense of awe flowed through her as she continued to slowly gaze around her perfect Eden. Ann had had no idea the jungle was this beautiful. It truly was a primal region, as it had given birth to so many beautiful plants, animals and flowers.

Leaning down, she trailed her fingers across the glasslike surface of the quiet pool. The water was invitingly warm. She watched the tiny wavelets become ripples and then disappear halfway across the pool's expanse. Laughing, Ann leaned out over the edge of the bank and looked at herself in the mirrored surface.

How young and happy she appeared! Much younger than her thirty-two years. Smiling delightedly, she admired her reflection. There were faint freckles scattered across her nose and cheeks, which she usually hid with makeup. She saw the bump on her nose—but this time, for some reason, she felt no shaft of pain when she focused on it. That was a miracle in itself, Ann decided. But then, this place she was in was truly magical.

Her gaze moved to her eyes—her best feature, she felt. They were wide and shining. She looked like a child who had just stumbled into a storybook place. Her eyes were no longer ringed or dark looking. Instead, they were sparkling with gold in their depths and shining with joy. Ann felt so happy here and wondered if it was sinful to feel this euphoric. She couldn't recall the last time she'd felt like this, if ever. Her gaze fell to her softly parted, full lips. She had a nice mouth, she decided. It was often pursed, but as a physician, she had to maintain a certain demeanor.

Something whispered to her to slip into the pool's inviting depths, where Ann could see the dark brown of decomposing organic matter scattered on the sandy bottom. A sudden urge overwhelmed her and for once she became utterly spontaneous. Easing her feet into the pool, she was surprised at how warm, how soothing it felt. The water seemed to tug gently at her feet and ankles, calling her to slip farther into its depths. Ann realized the oval shape of the pool reminded her of a woman's womb. That made her feel comfortable and she moved effortlessly into the warm, clear water.

As the liquid enveloped her, dampened her hair, she sighed softly. This wasn't just water, this was energy-ladened, living water. As her feet touched the soft, mushy bottom, she found herself standing with the water just above her breasts. Moving her arms slowly through the clear liquid, she marveled at the energy that stirred provocatively around her. The water wasn't moving, but she felt some force slowly swirling upward from her feet, ankles, knees and thighs. The sensation was lulling and she moaned softly, closed her eyes and floated, her arms and legs outstretched. It felt as if a thousand tiny hands were massaging every inch of her body, and she never wanted the sensation to cease.

As she rolled over on her back and floated, she felt the rest of her hair absorb the living, charged water. Closing her eyes, Ann heard the soft rush of air being drawn into the forested area and felt everything around her begin to slowly expand in order to take in that necessary breath of air. There was no doubt that Mother Earth had given her entrance to her own womb. Ann, a woman, was being blessed by being allowed into the center of the living planet, the womb of Mother Earth, and partaking in the creation of life.

Tears stung Ann's eyes as she realized the enormous gift she was being given. Slowly opening her eyes, she rolled over and found herself at the opposite bank. Her gaze moved to the red-and-yellow flowers that hung over the pool. They called to her. She could hear them, their tiny voices high and filled with such love. They begged her to take the spike of flowers and lace it among strands of her hair. Again spontaneity overwhelmed her, and Ann stood up and gently snapped the end of the spike. The fragrance of vanilla surrounded her as she carefully wound the orchids through her hair.

As she climbed out of the pool and looked down, she could see the red-and-yellow flowers like a brilliant, living crown of fire and sunlight surrounding her head. Even more surprising was that Ann could feel the throbbing, pulsing warmth of those flowers sending wave after wave of sensation from her head downward. Each tiny wavelet moved farther and farther through her as she stood there, appreciating the feeling within her body. As the energy reached her breasts, she felt herself respond sexually, and for a moment that caught her off guard. But as the lulling, stroking movement of the wavelets continued to undulate through her, she sank to the bank of the pool, lay down and closed her eyes.

The golden light and fire made her breasts grow firm and she felt herself suddenly wishing Mike, whom she needed so desperately, was here to touch her, to cup her breast and then place his mouth across the rigid nipple and suckle her gently, provocatively. The moment she wished for that, the energy flowed like the power of a flooding river on the rampage to the center of her body and began to throb wildly between her thighs. Caught within her wish to share this with Mike, she moaned with longing. The throbbing ache continued and she moved her hips in a rhythmic motion, wanting Mike, wanting him to hold her, move his fingers in a rocking motion and slowly open her thighs. Oh, to be touched, to be softly stroked now! The ache built and so did the fire. The energy of the flowers continued unabated, and then she felt a blossoming between her thighs, an incredible shower of golden light bursting forth, as if there was another kind of birth, another creation occurring within her.

A hot, lava-like warmth spilled through her and she sighed with pleasure, holding her arms against herself as the heat and light exploded not only upward in a dizzying spiral of pleasure, but down out of her.

The energy spiraled around her legs and plunged deep into Mother Earth. In that moment, Ann felt a part of the sky and a part of the earth as never before. She felt more alive, more connected to every living, breathing thing than she could ever recall. Slowly, ever so slowly, that sensation began to dissolve. Ann cried out in protest and sat up. No! No, she didn't want to lose this feeling! This incredible sensation of being attached to Mother Earth and feeling her breath, her heart beating and the throb of life pulsing through every cell in her body.

Somewhere in the background, she heard a doorbell ringing— once, twice, three times. Doorbells didn't belong in jungle dreams. With a groan, Ann turned over on her side, her hair swirling across her face and tickling her nose. The tickle took her out of her heated dream state. *Damn.* Forcing her eyes open, she blinked several times. Where was she? It took her a long, groggy moment to remember.

The doorbell rang again. Insistently.

"All right!" Ann grumbled as she sat up and threw off the light cover. The soft lavender curtains over the window of the pale pink bedroom kept light from flooding in, and she was grateful, because it appeared that the sun was shining brightly outside. Rubbing her face, she felt irritated. How badly she wanted to remain in that torrid, luscious dream. Even now, as she forced herself to stand up, Ann felt the last remnants of the warm pulsation between her thighs. It was a wonderful feeling, one that she hadn't experienced in a long, long time. How many years had she tried to deny her own sexual needs? To suppress her sexual appetite and tell her body no? Too many. Far too many. Until now...until Mike had crashed unexpectedly into her life.

Stumbling to the end of the bed, Ann groped for her pale tangerine silk robe. She pulled it over her knee-length, white silk nightgown.

The doorbell rang again.

"All right!" she muttered defiantly as she hurried down the carpeted hall. "Just hold your horses, dammit!"

Pushing her hair away from her face, Ann tried to reorient herself. Yes, she was in Lima, Peru, not her home in the suburbs of Washington. No, it wasn't winter outside, it was spring. She hurried through the living room toward the door. Fumbling with the locks, she managed to dislodge the dead bolt. Twisting the knob, she jerked the door open and glared out at the trespasser who had awakened her out of that very provocative dream.

"Mike!"

Houston's brows flew upward as he stood in the hall with groceries and a bouquet of flowers in hand. Ann stared drowsily at him. Her hair was in disarray, her blue eyes were clouded with sleep and her delicious mouth was parted and looking so damn kissable. Her tone, however, had little civility. She was upset, that was for sure. He gave her a faint shrug and tried a one-cornered smile of greeting to ease her irritation.

"I woke you up, didn't I?"

Ruffled, Ann blinked again. Was she dreaming? "This is a nightmare...I want to go back to bed and keep on dreaming," she muttered thickly as she turned on her heel and moved back into the living room.

Nonplussed, Mike stepped into the apartment. "Well, okay...go ahead," he murmured.

"No...I'm sorry, Mike. I'm just...not here...." Ann had to try and wake up. She felt drugged, groggy. As she stood near the beautifully carved coffee table of dark red mahogany, she rubbed her face.

Mike shifted the groceries and shut the door behind him. "It's afternoon," he told her apologetically as he moved past her toward the kitchen. "Two p.m. I thought you'd be up by now. There wasn't any food in the place, so I thought I'd bring some over so you wouldn't starve to death when you woke up.'' He'd miscalculated her need for sleep, and felt badly. Under the circumstances, he had to see Ann sooner rather than later because the longer he stayed in Lima, the greater the danger. It was only a matter of time until one of the drug lords' spies identified him.

Ann sighed loudly. ''I can't wake up, Mike. Don't talk to me right now. I've got to take a hot shower. Maybe then I can shake this off—this dream, the jet lag....'' She turned and disappeared down the hall toward the master bathroom.

Chuckling indulgently, Mike watched her leave. Did Ann realize just how pretty she looked? How she made that silk robe move in such a provocative, teasing way? Sighing, he shook his head and continued on to the kitchen. He wondered if Ann realized the power she had over him as a woman. Normally, she wore the facade of doctor and therapist in his presence. Even the clothes she chose were mannish looking and understated, usually dull gray or brown. Mike understood why. She was a professional and needed to appear that way at all times. But there was so much to like about her feminine side—the side she seemed so unaware of. He wanted to help her discover the hot, unbridled woman within her. How selfish he was becoming when it came to her. Not even his past, which loomed like a nightmarish warning in front of him, could stop his desire for her.

After setting the groceries on the spotless, white-tiled kitchen counter, he decided to make Ann a cup of espresso. Yes, that would wake her up, he thought, pleased with the idea. He'd surprise her with a cup. She could drink it while she prepared for her shower. That was something he'd like someone to be thoughtful enough to do for him. No one had, of course, but he wanted to do it for her. She looked so pretty and vulnerable when she was sleepy. Her ''I'm in charge'' look was no longer placed like a mask over her soft, flushed features.

Ann had just shed her clothes, the shower creating clouds of steam as she adjusted it to just the right temperature, when there was a circumspect knock at the antique white-and-gold bathroom door.

What now? Ann's mind just wasn't functioning. Jet lag combined with stress and staying up too long had her in an unrelenting grip. Usually she could wake up very quickly and be cheerful. Today she desperately needed a shower in order to raise herself.

The circumspect knock came again.

Jerking at the knob, Ann only belatedly realized she was naked. Quickly stepping behind the door, she glared out from behind it. Mike was smiling lamely and holding out a cup and saucer in her direction.

"Espresso. I thought you might like some before your shower. You look like you need a good jolt to wake up from all that jet lag." He offered her the cup.

Looking down at it, Ann realized there was cream in the espresso. Houston must have observed that she took cream and sugar in her coffee in Arizona.

"Is there sugar in there, too?" she croaked, to make sure.

His mouth curved. "Yeah, just the way you like it, *querida*. Here, take it." For a moment, he wondered if she would. There was such sleepiness still present in Ann's eyes as she looked up at him. He wanted to reach out, take her into his arms, lead her down the hall and love her awake. He brutally squashed the thought. *Distance*...he had to keep his distance from Ann. He couldn't keep being intimate like this woman. Calling her darling didn't help, either. Frustrated, Houston felt torn up inside.

"Come on," he urged, trying to lighten the mood. "There are no strings attached to this. I just took pity on you, that's all...."

Touched by his boyish smile, Ann reached out and took the proffered gift. "Thanks...this is going above and beyond the call of duty, Mike. I'll be out in a little while, okay?"

"Sure. No hurry." He glowed at her tender look of thanks.

Ann started to close the door.

"How do you like your eggs?"

The door halted. "What?"

"Your eggs. How do you like them?"

She scowled. "I don't eat breakfast. You know that."

His brows moved upward again. "No, I didn't know that. At the ranch, I was always done with breakfast and was just coming back after my morning tour when I'd see you in the kitchen. You always had coffee in your hands.... You don't eat breakfast?"

She heard the incredulousness note in his deep voice. "No," she answered lamely, "I don't. I...I...oh, never mind."

Mike saw Ann become flustered. He realized she was naked and hiding behind the door. Soft clouds of mist were leaking out into the hall. "No problem. I'll fix you something you'll *want* to eat. Get your shower, Ann."

She eased the door shut. The fragrance of the espresso drew her. She took a sip and groaned over the luxury of his thoughtful gift. She was being a real grouch and he was being understanding about it, taking her in his stride. The jet lag was turning her into a harpy eagle, she decided unhappily. Taking two more quick sips of the thick, sweet coffee, she smiled. This was just what she needed. How did Mike know? Her heart whispered that he cared enough to want to make her happy.

As she climbed into the welcoming stream of the shower and slid the glass door closed, Ann sighed and thrust her head beneath the water. Yes, this was perfect! How long she stood beneath that soothing, massaging spray reliving that torrid, delicious dream, Ann had no idea. She finally emerged from the eye-opening shower and toweled herself off. Then enjoyed the luxury, finishing the rest of her espresso.

Wrapping a thick yellow towel around herself, Ann padded quietly from the bathroom to her bedroom. A wonderful, spicy odor filled the air and she found herself automatically inhaling the delicious smell. Whatever Houston was fixing in the kitchen sure made her hungry!

That was odd, too, that she should feel this hungry. Like a starved wolf, in fact. Ann laughed softly at herself. Mike seemed to be giving her an appetite for a lot of things.

After pulling on a pale pink tank top, Ann chose a pair of well-worn, dark gray wool slacks. Most of the clothes she'd packed were still in her suitcases. She'd been so tired last night that she'd done little more than take a quick bath and drop, literally, into the beautifully carved mahogany, queen-size bed. She'd slept deeply. Wonderfully. The only thing missing had been Mike—being in his arms and sharing the lovemaking that had occurred in her torrid dream.

As Ann riffled through her second suitcase, she tried to find a

long-sleeved blouse to put over her tank top. She always felt less
a target if she wore big, oversize blouses to hide her body, her
breasts. Men didn't stare at her that much if she was cloaked in a
blouse and then the standard white smock she wore as an MD.

"Damn..." she muttered, and gave up. Luckily, she found her
comb and brush and went back to the bathroom. Even more luckily, she found her toothbrush and toothpaste.

When Ann had finished her toilet, she glanced up into the gold-
framed mirror. Steam still clung to the edges of it and gave her
reflection a very soft, beautiful look. Far prettier than she felt, that
was for sure. Her sable-colored hair gleamed with reddish gold
highlights even though it was still damp and hung unceremoni-
ously around her shoulders. Still, the dark frame of her hair emphasized her blue-gray eyes and the flush across her cheeks.
Touching her light dusting of freckles, Ann muttered, "Oh
well..." She refused to be embarrassed by them for once. Usually,
she wore just enough makeup to hide them from the world. Today
she didn't care. Mike had always said she probably looked beautiful au naturel. Well, today he was going to see her that way.

Her stomach growled. Rubbing the grumbling area with her
hand, she hurried down the hall toward the kitchen, where all those
wonderful smells were originating. Ann felt unparalleled joy at
seeing Mike again so soon. Maybe today they would have
time...time to explore one another at a delicious, leisurely pace.
She found herself eager just to sit and share the afternoon with
him. She'd never allowed herself such intimacy with Mike when
they were at the Donovan Ranch together. What a fool she'd been,
she realized, wanting to explore what might be.

She halted at the entrance to the sunny, pale yellow kitchen,
which contained every conceivable modern appliance. For the first
time, Ann really looked at Houston as he worked busily over the
stove. He wasn't in uniform, but casually dressed in a pair of dark
brown slacks and a cream-colored polo shirt that outlined his magnificent chest to perfection.

Ann noticed once again just now, how terribly good-looking
Mike really was. Although he was tall, he was medium boned and
not heavy. There was an incredible grace to his movements as if
he didn't have joints at all. He reminded her of a sensuous cougar

on the prowl—dangerous and mystical. At the ranch, he'd always worn pressed, starched army fatigues. She liked the way those dark brown slacks emphasized his narrow hips and showed the curve of his butt and his thick, powerful thighs. Yes, he was definitely in good physical shape, there was no doubt.

Disgruntled by her heated thoughts, Ann began to realize the depth of her need for Mike. Normally, she never looked at men in this way. Before Mike, men were to be distrusted, not appreciated as she was appreciating him right now. Hell, it had to be that dream she'd had earlier, spilling into reality, Ann decided. How she would love to feel that alive, that sensual, and have her five senses that lushly awake and receptive! Oh, what a change from how she normally allowed herself to feel! Her heart told her that Mike could make her feel that way. Eagerly, Ann looked forward to some quiet time spent with him today—and tonight. Yes, tonight...

Her gaze moved from Mike's body to his face. He wasn't handsome, at least, not in the conventional sense. But Ann found herself appreciating his square-jawed face, that nose that had been broken too many times to count, the white scars that told how much a warrior he was. Most of all, she found herself wanting to be kissed, to be seduced by this man of mystery who was cloaked in legend and myth.

His mouth was perfect, Ann decided—the most perfect part about him. His upper lip was slightly thinner than his full, flat lower lip. It was a mouth used to giving orders and having them carried out in an instant. She looked forward to those times, she hesitantly admitted, when his mouth would change from that thinned expression of hardness and military authority, and soften, one corner lifting in an amused, teasing smile.

Yes, there was much to enjoy about Mike Houston, Ann admitted. She could feel her breasts start to tingle as she studied the shape of his mouth. As her gaze moved down to absorb his strong, lean body once again, she could feel a slight throbbing ache begin between her thighs. Frustrated with herself for not being able to quench the longing, one she'd never experienced with any man in her life to date, Ann cleared her throat. Despite her head's shrill warning to not allow herself to get involved with Houston, she couldn't help admiring him.

Houston lifted his head and saw Ann leaning in the doorway, her arms wrapped defensively across her breasts, looking at him with that soft, provocative smile of hers. He was more than a little aware of the heat in her eyes—for him.

"Hey, look who just rose from the dead!" he crowed.

"Very funny, Houston." Ann grinned unwillingly as she moved to the kitchen counter.

He noticed she looked damn pretty in that sweet little pink tank top, which outlined her upper body very nicely. She had beautiful breasts. What would it be like to touch them, to feel the soft curve of them flowing into his large hands? The thought was incendiary. Torturous. Instantly, Mike shoved it away. He instinctively knew that if he complimented her on her outfit, she'd never wear it again. Ann always wore bulky clothes, clothes that hid her slender, beautiful body. It didn't make sense. Most women would kill to have a body like hers. That, or diet their life away to achieve it.

"Go sit down in the breakfast nook," he urged her. "I just made a second cup of espresso for you. You'll see it there. I'll have my welcome-to-Lima lunch ready for you in a jiffy."

Ann laughed a little. She couldn't help it. This was a side of Houston she'd never seen before. He was like an eager little boy, not the hard-bitten soldier she knew him to be. There was warmth and teasing in his deep voice, and she melted beneath that burning blue gaze that had sunlight in its depth. Even though he'd shaved this morning, the shadow of his beard gave his face a dangerous look. It made him all that much more mysterious looking—and a danger to her wildly fluctuating emotions.

"You've been so thoughtful, Mike. Thanks...." Sitting down, Ann gratefully sipped her espresso. There were two place settings laid out next to one another at the round table covered with a bright orange, red and yellow cloth. Just as she put the cup to her lips, her gaze settled on some flowers in a crystal vase next to the grocery bags still sitting on the drain board. She choked on the coffee.

As Mike brought over the skillet and put half the contents on her plate and the other half on his, Ann coughed violently. "What are those?'' she demanded in a strained voice, pointing to the flowers on the counter. Her coughing fit subsided.

"Hmm? Oh, orchids. Why?" He grinned as he placed the empty skillet in the sink and ran water to fill it. Grabbing the vase, he triumphantly brought the flowers over and set them on the table so they could be fully appreciated.

Ann coughed again and pressed her hand to her chest. The orchids were red and yellow. They had a distinctive light vanilla fragrance that wafted toward her.

Frowning, Mike took his seat. "You don't like orchids?"

"Well..." Ann murmured with a shake of her head, "this is weird. Just too synchronistic." Taking her gold linen napkin, she spread it across her thighs. The spicy odor of the food before her was making her salivate.

"What's weird?" Mike lifted a forkful of the food into his mouth. He saw a very puzzled expression on Ann's face as she continued to stare at the orchids. "Are you allergic to orchids? Is that it?"

She waved her hand nervously. "Uh, no...no."

Chewing his food thoughtfully, he planted both elbows on the table and tapped her plate with his fork. "You act like you've seen a ghost or something. Come on, eat before you get any skinnier and I lose you to a stiff breeze."

Ann fumbled around and found the fork. "I just dreamed about these very same orchids," she muttered as she looked, for the first time, down at the colorful meal on her plate.

"Yeah?" Mike smiled, suddenly feeling very pleased over that. "A good dream, I hope?"

Ann moved the food around on her plate and refused to look at him. "Maybe it's jet lag," she groused, "or maybe it's this mystical place. Or you. I don't know...."

"You're muttering again, Doctor," he teased, eating voraciously. "Come on, dig in. I'm a pretty good cook, as you well know." He had usually made lunch and dinner for them at the ranch in Arizona.

Ann set the fork down and reached out for the spray of orchids. The petals felt firm and waxy beneath her fingertips. They were a bright yellow, the inner lip red. Very red. The entire shape of the

orchid reminded Ann of a woman with her thighs open and beck-
oning. Flushing heatedly over the unexpected thought, she quickly
pulled her fingers from the flower and forced herself to pick up
the fork again.

"Why did you bring orchids?" she demanded.

"Well, uh, just on a whim, that's all." Mike watched her scowl
deepen. "You don't like flowers?"

"Yes," Ann said, "I like flowers." She forced the food into
her mouth. It was surprisingly delicious. "What is this?"

"The meal?" He saw the surprise in her expression. Relieved
that she'd momentarily forgotten her obvious upset over his bringing flowers, he was glad to talk about the food instead. "*Huevos
rancheros,* Peruvian style." He grinned a little and pointed out the
green peppers, onions and fresh tomatoes among the egg mixture.
"What really makes them special is adding ginger."

"They're good," she exclaimed, suddenly famished.

He preened. "Thanks."

For whatever reason, her five senses were more fully engaged
than she'd ever been aware of before. It was a wonderful discov-
ery. Odors were sharper, more distinctive. The taste buds on her
tongue delectably felt each ingredient and texture. It had to be
because she was with Mike, she thought. That was the only explanation for it.

A silence fell over them. It wasn't stilted and Mike was glad of
that. Every once in a while, Ann would look at those orchids with
a wary, unsettled and confused look. Maybe later she'd share why.
Right now, all he wanted her to do was eat.

When the main course was finished, Mike went to the counter
and made them more espresso. He brought out a coffee cake
smothered in chopped brazil nuts and slathered with thick, sweet
caramel, and sat down once more.

"Here in Peru people serve seven courses at every meal. I took
pity on you and decided eggs and dessert would be enough to
introduce you to our way of living down here."

She smiled a little and took a bite of her cake, which melted in
her mouth. "I'm glad someone has some mercy. That was very
kind of you to do all of this, Mike. I feel so pampered." She
looked up to see his blue gaze growing sad. Why? And just as

quickly, that look disappeared from his countenance. "No one has ever done this for me. Espresso before a shower..." She sighed and rewarded him with a soft, warm smile of gratitude.

Houston reached over and gripped her fingers momentarily. "You deserve to be pampered. Spoiled, in fact." Something in him sensed that Ann had had a very hard life. Now was not the time to speak of that, either. Mike felt frustration curdling deep within him. Time was their enemy right now. He couldn't stay much longer. He couldn't risk Ann being killed because of him. "I'm going to do it every chance I get," he promised her huskily.

Heat swept up her cheeks and Ann laughed a little shyly. She touched her face. "I feel like a teenager, not a thirty-two-year-old woman. I keep thinking it's this place—the mystery, the magic.... Like you said earlier at the airport, the way Peru seduces its visitors...."

He nodded and released her fingers, even though he didn't want to. "There is mystery and magic here," he conceded quietly, "and Indians believe in the mysticism and spirituality of this country, too."

She sobered a little. "I feel out of place here and yet, irrationally, I feel as if I belong, too." She managed a grimace. "Bane of a psychiatrist, you know? The head and eyes see something and look for matter-of-fact explanations about life, but this heart of mine is responding to you, to this country, and it is *not* rational at all...."

He regarded her gently. "Maybe the good doctor is climbing out of her head and into her heart? Peru is about passion, emotions, and yes, the magic and mystery of life and all its incredible and sometimes unexplainable facets." He saw Ann's eyes widen beautifully. Tears glimmered in their depths momentarily and then she forced them away. "I..." He searched for words. "What you're discovering, Ann, is something so special and rare that it scares the hell out of you. The mystery of life isn't so easily explained by weighing, measuring or seeing it with your eyes. Peru is probably more mystical and spiritual than any place you've been before. Right now, you're doing some major adjusting to her...but if you surrender to her seduction, you'll find out so much more about yourself, your own heart and what really makes you pas-

sionate, what makes you want to live your life to the fullest—''
He stopped abruptly.

Touched, Ann nodded. ''I'm beginning to understand a lot of
things about myself of late....''

''Yeah?'' He smiled slightly. ''Really?''

''Oh, yes.'' Ann sighed. She set her plate aside. ''I was just too
scared to admit it to myself, Mike—or to you—until...well, just
lately. I guess I'm still getting used to it all. I'm glad we have the
time down here, because I need it.''

Houston rankled at the word *we*. He felt as if he was on the
edge of a razor-sharp sword and no matter what he did, or how
finely he tried to walk the lines with Ann, he was going to wound
her. It was the last thing he wanted.

Hesitating, Ann whispered, ''I know what I feel for you is special, Mike. I've *never* felt this way with anyone.''

Hope and fear sheared violently through him. He felt the depth
of her admission all the way to his soul. ''Keep your distance from
me,'' he muttered a little self-consciously. ''I'm not worth it, Ann.
Anyone who gets near me is in danger. I don't want to put you
in that spot.'' Yet he admitted with anguish that he was inevitably
heading somewhere with her he'd never been before. All Houston
could do was shake his head in awe of the power of his need for
Ann. Something so deep, so healing was occurring within him that
he couldn't yet put a handle on it, give it a name or even begin
to understand the implications of falling hopelessly, helplessly for
her. He felt like a child in that moment, innocent and full of hope.
And that was the last thing he should be feeling in his circumstances.

Ann nodded and reached out and covered his hand with her
own. ''Danger to my heart?'' she offered softly. ''I feel like a
green teenager again, dumb, inexperienced....'' She laughed awkwardly. She was powerfully attracted to a man of complete mystery.

Mike sensed her discomfort. He raised her hand and kissed the
back of it, holding her uncertain gaze. ''Never dumb,'' he told
her. ''Just because we're feeling things we've never felt with another human being before doesn't make us dumb. Just...'' he
smiled a little ''...inexperienced. Most of the time I feel like I'm

walking on clouds, not Mother Earth, when I think of you. When I picture your face, *querida,* my heart opens up like one of those orchids and I feel this warmth wash through me like the Amazon flooding in springtime. It steals my breath and all I can do is feel. And feel some more..." Mike reluctantly released her hand. Perhaps it was the powerful spirit of love he was feeling toward Ann. That realization scared him deeply. In light of his past, there was no way he could surrender to it—or to her.

Ann stared at the orchids for a moment and then studied him in the tender silence stretching between them. "I'm scared, Mike, but I'm not going to run this time. I'm committed to going wherever this crazy relationship of ours is heading." She touched the orchid tentatively.

Sadness moved through him. Ann had more courage than he did. She truly didn't realize how dangerous caring for him could be. He hated himself in that moment—his life and his commitment to the people of Peru. The price he paid was high. Right now, he felt as if it was too high, but there was no way he could turn back, and he sure as hell wasn't going to allow Ann into his world. He had to protect her and her heart at all costs. Trying to change the subject, he said, "It's the flowers, isn't it?"

With a slight smile, Ann whispered, "Maybe...perhaps they are part of the magic and mystery of Peru? These orchids are special, aren't they?" She fingered the waxy petals thoughtfully.

Sighing, Houston shrugged his broad shoulders. "I couldn't help myself," he admitted. "Well, I guess I could have. There's a story to them. Right outside the grocery store this little old Quechua Indian woman has her orchid stand. She's probably in her eighties, all bent over, shivering in the morning air. I know how hard it is to get orchids, although they grow everywhere here in Peru. This is how she makes her living, to get enough food daily. I stopped and asked her what her most expensive orchid was. She studied me and asked me who was I buying them for. I told her it was for a beautiful *norteamericana* doctor. She cackled and then reached up to the top shelf of her little stand and brought down this spray of orchids. She said that you needed this particular flower."

Ann tilted her head, lulled by his wonderful storytelling abilities.

Mike's face was open for her to examine and she began to realize how completely vulnerable he was with her. There was no hint of the pretense she'd seen in his face during those eight weeks in Arizona. None. It was as if she was meeting the same man all over again, only he was different—and far more provocative to her as a woman. It made her feel a fierce need of him.

"She said I *needed* this orchid?" Ann asked.

Chuckling, Mike finished off his coffee cake and pushed the white saucer to one side. "Yeah, she did. Now, this old lady wasn't just some bag lady on the streets, you know. She wore a leather thong around her neck, with a tuft of black-and-gold hair hanging from it."

"What does that mean?"

"Quechua Indians have a Jaguar Clan, made up of priests and priestesses. These are people who, from childhood on, are recognized as being one with the spirit of the jaguar. They're trained by the medicine man or woman of their village to carry on the sacred and secret ceremonies associated with the jaguar. Those who pass all the tests—and most don't—get to wear jaguar fur as their badge of honor and courage. "

"But what does this all mean? And what does it have to do with these orchids?"

"Patience," he soothed. "Every story that's worth telling shouldn't be chopped up or hurried along." Mike leaned back and tipped the front legs of his chair off the tile floor. His voice was filled with satisfaction. "The jaguar is considered the most powerful of all animal spirits in South America. If a person is able to survive the physical experience of meeting a jaguar in the wild, there's an exchange that takes place between them. The jaguar trades his or her spirit with the student in training. If all goes right, their spirits are forever linked after that. The student passes the last and final test, and then he or she becomes a healer, the most powerful of all healers in South America."

"Because," Ann suggested, "the jaguar somehow bestows on them this power? Is that right?" She noticed the amusement in Mike's eyes. Ann wasn't sure whether he was spinning another tale or telling the truth. She had to admit she loved listening to his unfolding story.

He held up his hand. "There's a lot more to it than I'm telling you, but basically, the power of the jaguar's spirit can be used for ultimate good or ultimate evil. If a person manages to survive their experience with a live, wild jaguar and gets the 'trade,' then they are known as a healer. If they don't, and use it for personal power, selfishness or manipulation of others, they are known as a sorcerer.

"The old woman with the orchids was a healer from the Jaguar Clan. Such people are well known for their psychic ability. It's said that they know what we are thinking and feeling. They walk into our dreams and send us messages, good or bad, sometimes as a warning of some kind. That's the power of the jaguar. He's most powerful at night. That's his kingdom and he is the lord of the jungle when the sun goes down. He's feared by four-leggeds and two-leggeds alike. So..." Mike gave Ann a brief smile "...I think she intuited something when she gave me the orchids, because they weren't the most expensive ones she had. I knew that, and I paid her twice what they were worth because something good, something healing, had gone down between us in that exchange and healers deserve to be paid for their services."

With a shake of her head, Ann whispered, "This is so weird.... I had a dream just before you came and these orchids, the very same ones, with the same fragrance, were in it...."

"Want to tell me about it?"

Flushing furiously, Ann jerked her hand away from the orchid and muttered, "No."

Mike tried to hide his disappointment. "You'll probably get a lot of stories, legends and myths from my granny nuns while you're down here. Everything is steeped in a tale, you know—the truth, B.S. and everything in between. Discernment is the operative word here."

"Still," Ann said, relieved that Mike wasn't going to press her about her very torrid dream, "stories are connections with archetypes, truth and symbols. They shouldn't be lightly dismissed."

Mike nodded sagely and smiled a little. Ann was flushing to the roots of her hair and she wouldn't meet his eyes. She was like a little girl, extremely shy and embarrassed—totally unlike her. Hmm, that old jaguar priestess knew what she was doing, all right. He laughed delightedly to himself. It was obvious Ann was struggling to use her cold, hard, left-brain logic, but in Peru, in South America, one should leave that part of the brain at home.

No, down here the mysterious right brain was what grasped all the unexplained and inexplicable happenings every day. Ann was a psychiatrist and she was going to have a tough time dealing with that, Mike could see. She kept looking at those orchids and then retreating deep within herself. He could feel her wanting to run and hide from something. But what?

Chapter 6

Houston felt his heart squeeze in his chest as he glanced at his watch. It was well past time for him to leave. He was putting Ann in danger by staying so long. Easing the chair back down to four legs, he removed the plates from in front of them. Somberly, he held her gaze and said, "There are some things I need to tell you, Ann...before, well...so you understand why I'm not worth your time or trouble." Shrugging almost painfully, he said, "I wanted to tell you before we left Arizona, but it wasn't the right time. Then, when we got here, I wanted you to get a good night's sleep under your belt before I talked to you."

Ann saw Mike's expression suddenly become serious, the darkness in his eyes and the slashes on either side of his mouth underscoring what he was going to say. "All right," she said tentatively, "I'm listening."

"You probably thought I worked here in Lima most of the time and that I'd be over to the clinic on a pretty regular basis. Right?"

She nodded. "So...you're not going to be at the clinic that often?" Ann felt disappointment in her heart when he nodded. As she watched Mike take his seat again, folding his hands in front of him, she felt a cloak of sadness and fear blanketing her. She realized those feelings were coming from Mike. Shaken that she could sense his emotions so strongly, she found her heart thudding.

"I won't be there very often. I keep in touch with my granny nuns via one of my soldiers, mostly. The last thing I want is to have Escovar's men come crashing into the clinic, murdering everyone in cold blood because they think they're going to find me there." His mouth became a thin line. "Ann, I've got the blood of enough people I loved on my conscience already." He looked at her squarely. "I don't want any more."

She felt his pain and heard it in the rawness of his voice. He looked lost in his memories for the moment and she guessed he was reliving flashbacks of friends who had died while fighting the drug lords. "Losing your men in battle is a terrible thing," she agreed quietly. "They're our extended family. People we care about and want to keep safe even if we know it's an impossibility."

Houston looked down at his heavily scarred hands. "I lost my parents, the woman I loved and my unborn son to Eduardo Escovar."

Ann gasped and felt a ripping sensation in her heart. Houston looked at her, his eyes shadowed.

"H-how terrible...." she managed to whisper, automatically placing her hand against the column of her throat, where a lump of grief was forming for him, for his awful loss.

His mouth twisted savagely. "When it happened, I was half-crazed and in shock over it. Loco with grief, they said at the barracks. I took my best squad out with me and we hit Escovar's men hard. So hard that we stood up to our ankles in blood when it was all over. Originally, I'd wanted to land at his compound. No one had ever done that because it's so heavily fortified—part ammo dump, part heavy-duty artillery and aircraft rockets. Luckily, my sergeant talked me out of that plan, in favor of a second, less dangerous one."

Houston scraped his chair back and stood up, resting his hips against the counter and wrapping his arms against his chest, caught up in that bloody nightmare from the past. "I had intended to capture Escovar's wife and children. To hold them hostage to force him to move out of Peru once and for all. And then I was going to return them to him, unharmed.'' Grimly, Mike lowered his gaze to Ann's pale face. "We caught the family fleeing in a car about ten miles from Escovar's fortress. Everything went wrong. Instead of capturing them alive, we saw them all killed in a terrible accident.

"The driver went around a mountain curve too fast and he rolled the car carrying Escovar's family over a five-hundred-foot drop-off. They all died instantly. There was nothing we could do to save them...and God knows, we tried.'' His mouth hardened with the memory. "Escovar saw their deaths as me getting even with him for killing my own family. That's when he leveled the ten-million-sol reward on my head. Ever since then, we've been in this death spiral dance with one another. He wants me.'' Houston's voice lowered to a growl. "I'm going to get him first.''

A chill worked its way up Ann's spine as she saw the harshness return to Houston's face. Helplessly she opened her hands and whispered, "What an awful tragedy.''

"I understand from Morgan you haven't had it easy, either,'' Mike said.

Ann winced. "He told you about my family?''

"No...he didn't. He only mentioned you'd suffered a great deal.'' Mike saw the devastation in Ann's eyes and the tears she tried to hold back. He hated hurting her like this, but they had to get their cards laid out on the table. Ann had to know the truth about him and why she could not continue to care for him. She had to know that loving him would be her death warrant.

"I was an only child, Mike. My parents lived in Washington, D.C. I was working with Perseus and Morgan for two years going on missions around the Caribbean. Ramirez, a drug lord from Colombia, infiltrated our organization and quietly targeted many of Perseus members' families, including mine.'' She saw Houston's eyes narrow. Her voice became strained as she forced the words out. "Ramirez had hit men kill my parents in cold blood. They were absolutely innocent. The police found them in their home in Fairfax, Virginia, when a phone call was made to the precinct an hour after they were executed. I was out on a mission halfway around the world when it happened. At the same time, Morgan, his wife and son were all kidnapped. One of the other mercs broke the news to me in a phone call.''

''Damn,'' Mike rasped. ''I'm sorry, Ann.'' He wanted to go over and comfort her. Simply hold her because the grief in her large blue-gray eyes tore at him.

''Some days I'm still not over it, Mike. It suddenly feels like yesterday and all the grief comes rolling back over me. And the anger...'' Ann raised her head, his obvious pain for her blanketing her. ''So you see, we share a common background with our families being murdered by drug lords. How long ago did you lose your family?''

''Five years,'' he answered flatly. ''And like you, there are days when it feels like yesterday, and other times it seems like a bad dream with no pain or grief attached to it at all. Everyone told me that over time, the pain would lessen, and it has. But not the memory of what happened.''

''Morgan, Laura and their son, Jason, were kidnapped,'' Ann murmured. ''But, as you know, with the help of the Peruvian government, you and your men, and one of our mercs, Ramirez and his gang were put out of action—permanently.''

''Yeah, I remember that. I worked with that merc, Culver Lachlan. He's up in a village in the highlands, married to that Peruvian ex-government agent, Pilar Martinez, who helped him get to Ramirez. They're friends of mine, and I keep in touch with them because Escovar is trying to regain Ramirez's old territory from the villagers in that area. He's killing people up there right now, to make 'examples' of them.''

''And it's your job to stop him.''

Houston nodded and allowed his tense arms to fall to his sides. Seeing the compassion on Ann's face made him feel raw. This time, she wasn't trying to hide anything from him, and he was glad.

''Want another cup?'' he asked huskily, pointing to the espresso machine.

''No...no, thanks, Mike.''

Somehow, he felt better talking to Ann about his past. It took the edge off his rage, which was never too far beneath the surface when it came to discussing Eduardo Escovar and what he'd done to utterly destroy Mike's life.

"I have to leave soon," he said, glancing at his watch again. "I don't want to, but I have to, Ann."

Terror ate at her as she studied the expressionless mask that had descended over his features now. She was beginning to understand that Mike had been shielding a lot from her. "Are you afraid that because I'm at the clinic, Escovar might attack, since he knows I'm with Perseus?"

"I'm afraid," Mike rasped, "that if Escovar thinks there's something going on between us, he'd gladly make a raid on the clinic to kidnap you. Then he'd kill you to get even with me. Or if he found me hanging around the clinic because of you once too often, he might decide that church property wasn't sacred any longer, and might come in and kill everyone there." Frowning, Mike muttered, "I don't want to take that risk."

Coloring, Ann fumbled with the cup in front of her. "I understand."

Heaving a sigh, Mike stared down at his large, scarred hands. "There's more to tell, Ann. About a year ago, I fell in love with a *norteamericana* woman, an official at the U.S. Embassy. Her name was Tracy. I was very careful about protecting her—us— what we had developing between us. We never went out in public to eat or anything like that. We kept a very low profile. Escovar found out about it, anyway. The Peruvian government is riddled with moles and word leaked out." Mike held Ann's startled gaze. "Tracy was killed in a car bomb explosion right outside her apartment one morning when she was going to work."

"God...." Ann croaked.

"You aren't going to see much of me at all for that reason, Ann. The people I love get killed because of me. I don't want to put you, my friends or my granny nuns into that position, ever." His mouth turned into a suffering line of barely withheld emotions. "The war between Escovar and me has escalated, and anyone who is dear to me will be destroyed. It's a real black-and-white situation."

Suddenly cold, Ann got up and moved slowly around the kitchen. She felt chaos inside herself. Grief mixed with yearning.

Sadness entwined with an ache deep within her. She understood her feelings—she needed Mike and wanted to pursue their relationship. But she could love him, only to lose him. Or die herself, in the line of fire. The look on Mike's face said it all; his suffering was plainly, hauntingly visible on his craggy features. For a moment, she thought she saw moisture in his eyes, but in the next second it was gone. She was probably seeing things again.

Taking a deep breath, she whispered, "So, this is goodbye, isn't it? I won't see you while I'm working over at the clinic?"

Mike watched her halt midway from the table, her arms wrapped around herself, looking terribly abandoned—and it was his fault. Turning around, he murmured, "It has to be this way." His heart was crying out for her, but his head wished she would take the next flight out of Lima and go home to safety. He wasn't sure he could stand losing another woman he cared about to Escovar. Somehow, Mike understood that Ann was his life even though he was pushing her away. If she died... Pain gutted him just thinking about it.

Ann saw gold flecks in Houston's stormy-looking eyes. She felt awful. And angry. And sad. She didn't want Mike to walk out of her life forever, but fear kept her from saying it. That same old knot was forming in her gut, the one that always started whenever she was becoming emotionally attached to someone...especially a man. Oh, it hadn't happened often, but when it did, that fear stood inside her like the Berlin Wall, causing her to retreat.

"It's just that..." Ann hesitated, searching for the right words "...I'm in a strange country with strange customs. I thought you'd be around. Someone I could talk to if I had questions, or whatever.... Oh, hell, Mike." Ann glared at him. "You're asking a lot. A whole hell of a lot."

Nodding, he rasped, "I know I am. That's why it's up to you to decide now, rather than later. I can have one of my men take you to the airport. You can walk away."

Ann slowly stood up and moved the chair away from her. Inwardly, she roiled with anger, fear and need for him as she tried to sort out what she wanted. Pacing the kitchen slowly, her arms folded tightly against herself, she tried to quiet her mind and feel her way to the truth of the situation. He remained silent as she pondered what she wanted to do.

Then she halted a few feet in front of him. She didn't know who looked or felt grimmer at the moment. Her voice was husky with strain. "Because of my past, I shut myself off, Mike. I was pretty successful at it for a long time until you crashed into my life." She saw him smile a little—a smile edged with deep sadness. She saw hope burning in his eyes and a fierce, unspoken need for her. "I'm tired of hiding, of burying myself." She sighed. "No. I want to stay. And if possible, I want to explore what we have on your terms and conditions. I don't like the danger—" she allowed her arms to drop to her sides as she added wearily "—but I don't like the other choice, either. I want a chance to see what we have, where it will lead...don't you?"

Easing to his full height, Mike nodded. Euphoria swept through him at her words. Not only did she want to stay, but she wanted to be with him, despite the danger. He approached Ann, who stood looking like a lost, orphaned child rather than the strong woman he knew her to be. A bitter sweetness flowed through him. Aching to reach out and caress her flaming cheek, Mike lifted his hand. "What I want and what I can have are not the same thing," he rasped, looking down at her, at the turmoil in her eyes. But he knew now that she had chosen to stay, he would *need* to see her. And he would have to be more careful than he'd ever been in his life. He just *couldn't* lose her. "I'll do what I can to come to you, if safety permits."

Ann bowed her head. "This is so hard for me, Mike...because of my past..." She looked up at him, tears stinging her eyes. "You're so strong and brave compared to me. I don't know if I have the guts to go the distance. I want to, but..." She watched that very male mouth curve tenderly. When Mike smiled, Ann felt as if sunlight was blanketing her and making her feel warm and safe once more. Her head warned her that being around Houston would be her death warrant. People who loved him died. Shaken by the thought, she absorbed his healing touch.

"Listen to me," he said, cupping her shoulders and giving her a small shake. "You're one of the bravest women I've ever known. What you do at Perseus is just as dangerous as what I do out in the field. So don't cut yourself down, *querida.* You've got a heart as courageous as mine."

Ann gave him a wry look. "Why do I have the feeling I'm going to find that out?"

His fingers tightened on her shoulders. "I didn't mean to lead you on, Ann...I honestly didn't. But now that you are here with me, the thought of losing you—" He broke off, his voice quavery.

She felt his powerful emotions avalanche through her. "I know," she answered helplessly.

"You know," Mike rasped, "I wanted to tell you before I left tonight that I like your freckles. I've never seen them before. You must have always covered them up."

"Oh, them..." Ann self-consciously allowed her fingertips to brush across her cheek.

"I like them," he told her, his smile deepening as he caressed her thick, damp hair. "It brings out the little girl that hides inside you. She's special, you know. Pretty spontaneous, too."

His words brought back her dream, Ann realized, as she reveled in his undivided attention. It was as if she were standing in front of an incredibly brilliant, shining sun, rather than just an ordinary human being. But he was a flesh-and-blood man and that made her scared and lured her simultaneously.

"I'm not a spontaneous person by nature," she muttered defiantly. "And you know that—freckles or no freckles." Although, for once, Ann found herself realizing that her decision to stay— to see Mike when and if she could—would teach her to be spontaneous. Her heart entertained a notion of what it would be like to meet Mike at that magical pool she'd dreamed about. Oh! Blushing furiously over those lascivious thoughts, Ann hoped that he wasn't able to read her mind.

"If things were different, I'd have the time to find out just what is making you blush like that," Houston murmured as he rested his hands languidly on his narrow hips, studying her purely feminine reaction to him. But he had to go. Time was more than up for his stay at her apartment. Brushing her cheek, he whispered, "I don't care what you say. You look beautiful when you wear your hair down and let those freckles shine through. They're the real you, you know?"

Ann blushed like a proverbial schoolgirl, and that tipped him off. Mike wanted to ask who had made her feel so embarrassed about her natural beauty, but time wasn't going to let him do that. The sight of her set his heart pounding briefly and caused a warm feeling to flow through him. He'd never felt quite like this before. Yes, he'd loved two other women in his life, but the feelings Ann stirred in him were new. She was like a wild, watchful animal around men, he was discovering.

"I've got to go," Houston murmured huskily, allowing his hands to drop from her arms. "I'll be in touch as soon as I can. Through one of my men. He'll use the password *orchid,* to let you know he's my emissary and not one of Escovar's spies."

Ann followed him to the door of her apartment. "All right. Is...where you're going...dangerous?" She knew better than to ask, but her silly heart was in control of her at the moment.

Mike looked out the door through the peephole before unlocking the dead bolt. "Now you're going to worry about me?" he teased, trying to gently parry her concerns so that she wouldn't lose sleep over him or his duties.

"Just a little," Ann admitted with a broken smile.

The crestfallen look on her face confirmed his suspicion that she would worry—a lot. Taking her into his arms one last time, Houston pressed her against him. She came willingly into his embrace. Groaning, he rasped against her hair, "If you *ever* need me, Ann, all you have to do is call out my name. Okay?" He moved her away just enough to hold her startled gaze. "If you are in danger of any kind, just call out my name in your head."

"In my head?" Confused, she frowned.

"Mental telepathy," he explained gently. Trying to ease her confusion, he touched her head with his hand. "From your head to my head. Just call me. I'll get back here to Lima—to you—just as soon as humanly possible."

Stunned, she blinked. "Mental telepathy?"

Unwilling to get into a long discussion on it, Mike nodded patiently. "Yes."

"You—can do that? Read minds?"

"I'm a better receiver than sender," he said teasingly as he saw the wariness come back to her face.

"And how long have you had this ability?"

He ran his hands down her long, slender back, memorizing the feel of her. "About nine years. It happened after I almost died."

"Oh," Ann said, "a gift from a near-death experience? I've heard some people develop psychic gifts after encounters with death."

Mike raised his brows. "Well...something like that. The next time I see you, I'll share some other things about myself with you. Right now, time is gone. I have to leave...."

"You're serious about that, aren't you? This calling you mentally if I'm in trouble?"

"Very," Houston assured her in a growl. "Come here, *querida*. I need to feel you one last time...." He leaned down and captured her lips with his.

Lightning bolted through Ann as she was crushed against his hard, uncompromising body. Tears squeezed beneath her lids as she responded fiercely to his mouth moving against hers. This was their goodbye with one another. Maybe the last time she would ever kiss him. Perhaps the last time she would ever see him. Hot tears rolled down her cheeks, meeting and melding with their hungry mouths as they devoured one another. The saltiness combined with the utter male taste of him. Her world spun only around Mike, around his strong arms holding her, the beating of the powerful, loving heart in his chest against the firmness of her breasts. Oh, how badly she wanted to go to bed with him! To love him fully! She felt the same raw desire emanating from him.

As he tore his mouth from hers, he whispered, "Just stay safe, *querida*. Safe..." Then he turned, opened the door and left.

Ann stood there, swaying unsteadily. She wrapped her arms around herself as the door closed quietly behind him. She felt as if Mike was still embracing her in their final goodbye kiss. Tears flowed unchecked from her eyes. She *felt* his love. It was as real, palpable and surprising as her taking a sudden breath of air into her lungs.

In the next moment, he was gone like a silent jungle cat, leaving her heart pounding wildly in her breast. What had just happened? Unsure, Ann pressed her hand against her chest and went to the door to look out the peephole.

Houston was gone. There was no trace of him. Blinking, she moved away and slid the dead bolt back into place. That warm, loving feeling lingered around her, like a soft caress moving up and down her entire trembling form. Ann turned on her heel and walked slowly down the hall toward her bedroom. She was imagining things! She had to be!

Then why were there tears in her eyes? In that split second, she'd felt his fierce love for her, his raw, unbridled grief at having to leave her and his fear that he might never see her again alive. Picking up her black leather physician's bag from the closet, Ann shook her head.

"It's this damn country, Parsons. You're acting like you've had a temporary psychotic break from reality. It's Peru. Mike said it was a place where magic met reality. More to the point," she growled, grabbing her white smocks to wash them, "where delusions meet hard-core reality. Get a grip, will you?"

She picked up her smocks and headed out of the bedroom with purposeful strides. Houston was gone. Maybe forever. She had been crazy to think there was hope of a relationship with him. And yet, she'd been vulnerable with him. Something she'd never allowed with any other man except Morgan, who knew about her sorrowful past and understood how to deal with her. Yet Ann didn't regret her decision. As scared as she was, she felt exhilarated on another level. She knew then that she *did* have hope. Hope for a future with Mike. Could her feelings, which she'd never even spoken about to him, survive? And would Mike continue to evade Escovar? Her hands tightened around the smocks as she opened the door to the small laundry room.

Later, as she emerged from the laundry room, there was a knock on the apartment door. She looked through the peephole and saw a man in civilian clothes standing there. Who was he? Should she open the door? Ann removed the dead bolt, but left the chain in place and peeked through it.

"Yes?

"Dr. Parsons?"

"Yes?"

He was a young, dark-skinned man in civilian clothes, wearing a black leather jacket, standing relaxed in front of her. Giving her an apologetic look, he said, "Orchid."

She swallowed convulsively. This was one of Mike's men. Mike must have sent him up to her apartment for a reason. Quickly she opened the door and invited him to come in. He thanked her and moved just inside the foyer.

"Major Houston told me you needed a driver and escort while you are here in Lima. I'm Pablo Manuel. He asked me to be your bodyguard for the next six weeks while you are here with us. I am one of Major Houston's best soldiers. I got wounded two months ago and am not yet ready for duty with him, so he asked me, as a favor, to guard and take care of you." He held out the keys to her car. "You are ready to work at the clinic, tomorrow morning?"

"*Sí,*" Ann whispered, leaning against the wall, her heart pounding unrelentingly. "He never said anything about you."

Pablo smiled shyly. He opened his coat and produced the very same type of red-and-yellow orchid that Houston had given her. Only this one was in a small, plastic vial filled with water to keep it alive. "Major Houston said this would convince you. Here, he said for you to wear this on your white coat, that it would bring out the color in your cheeks and make your freckles stand out."

Ann was deeply touched by the parting gift. Taking the orchid, she held it gently.

Pablo nodded in satisfaction. "That's a very special orchid, *señorita,*" he said.

"Oh?" Ann replied. Even now she could smell the wonderful vanilla fragrance beginning to encircle her head. It was as if Mike was embracing her all over again.

Although Pablo seemed very young, maybe in his early twenties, he had a professional soldier's bearing. Ann felt safer, but not as safe as when Houston was with her. But then, she told herself, Mike was head and shoulders above any man she'd ever met in her whole life.

Only Morgan Trayhern was anywhere near to Mike's stature. The two men were different, though, and as Ann stood there, she tried to categorize *how* they were different.

"Did Major Houston tell you the story of that orchid?" Pablo inquired in a friendly fashion.

"No," Ann said.

"Ahh..."

She saw Pablo smile brightly, his strong white teeth a contrast against his dark, copper-colored skin. His black hair was cut military short, and everything about him spoke of his military background, from the way he carried himself proudly to the way he stood with his feet slightly apart for better balance. She decided she liked him. "I guess he didn't have time to share it with me, Pablo," she added.

"*Sí*, Major Houston can never remain in one place too long," he agreed somberly.

Every time Pablo mentioned Houston's name, Ann saw a shining awe come to Pablo's face, as if Mike were some kind of god come to earth to be worshipped. "What does 'ahh' mean in regard to this orchid?" she inquired.

Pablo laughed a little and gave her another apologetic look. "Dr. Parsons, it is not for me to discuss it with you. That orchid and her story should only be shared between you and the man who gave it to you."

"I see," she said. "Does everything in this country have a story attached to it?"

Pablo grinned. "*Sí, señorita*. What does an orchid mean otherwise? A tree? A bush? Without the story, you cannot appreciate it fully, no?"

"I guess not," Ann said lamely. Maybe the nuns would know. Or at least be more forthcoming about it. She could hardly wait to get to the clinic because she desperately wanted to work in order to soothe the loneliness that was cutting into her since Mike's departure. Work always kept her focus off whatever she was feeling. It would be impossible to put Mike and his parting kiss out of her mind—and heart—without it. Hard work always cured all her ills. And the clinic was certainly a place where she could spend twelve to sixteen hours a day doing just that.

"Eh, Ann, you must go home!" Sister Dominique came into the office where Ann sat going over the files of the patients she'd seen in the last twelve hours.

Ann smiled tiredly up at the old nun. Checking her watch, she realized it was midnight. "I lost track of time, Sister." She felt suddenly dizzy and reached out to steady herself on the nearby desk. Earlier in the day, she'd gotten a sudden nosebleed—out of nowhere. She attributed it to the altitude difference, though it was unlike her to get a nosebleed at all.

"Humph," Sister Gabby said, coming up alongside Dominique. "We are tired. We must say our prayers and then sleep. I've asked Pablo to take you home." She waved a finger at Ann. "You work too hard, Doctor."

"I'm used to it," she answered with a weary smile. She closed the file and stood up. Yes, work kept her heart from meandering and wondering about Houston...or the orchid she wore on her smock. When the two nuns first saw the orchid and heard that Houston had gifted her with it, they had cackled like a couple of broody old hens. Neither would tell her about the orchid, however, making Ann even more frustrated.

"The clinic opens at seven," Sister Gabby told her as they walked down the hall together. The gloom of the few lights along the corridor cast deep shadows on the hardwood floor as they walked.

"Okay, I'll be here at seven," Ann promised. She saw Pablo drive the car up to the front door and emerge. Again dizziness swept over her. She felt slightly feverish. Touching her brow, she placed her feet apart a little more so she wouldn't fall over from her sudden bout of weakness. She touched her brow and discovered her skin felt hotter than usual. It was just stress, she decided. Stress and a horrible, gutting fear that she'd never see Mike again. Tears burned in her eyes, and valiantly Ann pushed them back down—as she had all emotional wounds before this.

"Sleep in," Gabby advised gruffly. "Tomorrow we start renovations. *Mon petit chou* has employed bricklayers to build a new wing onto our clinic. Work begins tomorrow."

"And," Sister Dominique interjected with a wistful sigh, "we get a brand-new, much larger office with modern computers. Not that we know how to use them. But we'll learn!"

"Around here," Gabby said, "old dogs have to learn new tricks all the time."

Ann laughed softly. She found the two nuns inspiring and fun to work with. They flew around the clinic in their dark blue and white habits like angels without wings. Today, the first full day at the clinic for Ann, they'd processed over sixty people through the clinic's doors. "I know a lot about computers, so when they arrive, we'll set some time aside and I'll teach you how to use them. Fair enough?"

They nodded sagely and then both clasped their hands in front of them as she hesitated at the glass door.

"They are bringing water trucks tomorrow, too," Sister Gabby added excitedly. "Fresh water for the barrio! This is so exciting! The children will have fresh water to drink, not the stuff found in trenches or mud puddles. It will make our job much easier. There will be less infection. Twice a week, two huge water trucks will drive from section to section, giving away water to the people. Isn't that wonderful?"

Touched, Ann nodded. "This is all from the donations Major Houston got?" A chill swept through her. Looking down, Ann saw goose bumps forming on her lower arm. She was suddenly, inexplicably, icy cold. Was she catching something? It felt like flu symptoms to her. Great. All she needed was to get some acute illness on top of everything else.

"Yes," Dominique said. "He is a man of pure heart and action. We get a new wing on the clinic, which will give us a ten-bed ward in addition to the five-bed one. He has hired a part-time paramedic to help us, as well. His name is Renaldo Juarez, and he will be here tomorrow, too."

"It's shaping up to be an exciting day," Ann said, lifting her hand in farewell as Pablo opened the door for her. "Good night."

"Sleep well, child," Sister Dominique whispered, making the sign of the cross over her. "We will pray for you tonight."

Turning, Ann smiled gently. "I think Major Houston can use our prayers more than me."

Sister Gabby smiled. "He's *always* in every prayer session we undertake. Do not fear, he will not be bumped off our list. We're simply adding you to it."

Laughing, Ann said, ''Believe me, I can use all the help I can get. Prayers are good. Any kind. Thank you....''

Her apartment was dark and quiet. Pablo insisted upon going in first and checking it out thoroughly. He was brisk and efficient as he looked for possible perpetrators, bombs or bugging devices. When he was satisfied her apartment was ''clean,'' he said goodnight and left.

Sighing, Ann wearily dropped her black bag on the sofa. In the kitchen, she gently removed the orchid, from her smock replaced the water it had used and then set it next to the sink. It looked bright and beautiful against the white tile background. And, as always, it reminded her of Mike. Turning, she saw the spray of orchids he'd given her himself sitting in the center of the table.

Why should I feel like this? So lost. Alone. As she moved unthinkingly to the breakfast nook and cupped the spray with her hand, she inhaled its fragrance deeply into her lungs. How was Mike? Was he in danger? Ann couldn't shake those questions even though she wanted to.

Frowning, she straightened and moved down the hall to her bedroom. She was almost dizzy from tiredness, not yet completely over the jet lag, she suspected. Removing the smock and pulling her pink T-shirt over her head, she sighed. Why was her heart feeling like this? There was an ache in it. She knew why but she wasn't willing to admit it to herself. Somehow, she had to climb back into that ivory tower of her mind and be free of her burning, painful emotions. Every time she closed her eyes and pictured Mike's craggy, scarred face, her heart opened like that orchid did. Stymied, she removed her gray woolen slacks and set them aside. It had to do with that invisible connection that somehow existed between them. Perhaps she was still able to feel his emotions toward her? That seemed impossible, yet Ann had no easy answers when it came to Mike. She wanted to find out about the rest of his mysterious past, which he'd hinted about, but feared she'd never see him again to ask such questions.

As Ann took a hot shower, scrubbed her hair and allowed the spray to gently massage her tense, tired body, her heart once again turned to Houston. Frustrated because she had no explanation as to why he was so much on her mind, stirring up her feelings like this, she wondered if she wasn't going a little crazy. As she toweled herself afterward, she swore she could almost feel a direct connection from him to her so that her every feeling was flowing to him and vice versa. It had to be a combination of sleep deprivation, stress and heartbreak.

"You're nuts," Ann growled, slipping into an apricot silk nightgown. And then she laughed at herself. A psychiatrist calling herself nuts. Now, that was the kind of humor Mike would appreciate immensely. He had a wry sense of amusement and would laugh with her about it. Then, as she walked from the steamy bathroom to her bed, Ann had the strangest feeling. Halting in the hall, she automatically touched her heart region with her fingers. If she closed her eyes, she could swear she heard Houston's deep chuckle.

"I take that back, Parsons, you *are* having a psychotic break. Now get your rear into bed and sleep. You're hallucinating." Or was it that mental telepathy Mike had said he could receive from her? Could he pick up on her errant thoughts? The whole idea was a little shocking to Ann. If he could read her mind, then he'd been able to read it since he'd met her. Oh! The embarrassment of that if it was true! That just couldn't be possible, her scientific mind told her.

As she jerked back the pale lavender quilt and sheet, Ann felt that laughter of his once again. The sensation was so warm and easy to surrender to. As she slid her feet beneath the covers and pulled them up, Ann released a weary sigh. Closing her eyes, she found herself wanting to be with Mike, wanting to know more— much more—about this enigmatic man. Today she heard the poor who came to the clinic call him the jaguar god over and over again. The people of the barrio worshipped Houston like a god, there was no doubt. He had produced so much for them, bettering the quality of their lives. Ann was sure that to the poor, his work seemed like a miracle only a god could pull off. He fed them, cared for them medically and often made the difference between life and death for them.

As the wings of sleep enfolded her, she felt as if she were drifting into the warmth of Mike's embrace instead. It was a comforting sensation and she surrendered to it, no longer afraid. Within that invisible warmth, she felt safe—and loved. Very much loved.

Chapter 7

In the days that followed Mike's disappearance, Ann discovered what hell was. The agony of losing him, not having him in her life, gutted her and bled her a little each minute of every hour of every day. Nothing had prepared her for this intense reaction, and she worked tirelessly at the clinic, sixteen hours a day, if possible—anything to stop the pain of her loss. She'd had several more nosebleeds, and though it was unusual for her to get them, she attributed it again to the altitude. The dizziness would come and go, too. And periodically, she'd run a fever for an hour, experience a bone-chilling sweat and then be fine. Her symptoms seemed to worsen, however, as the week wore on. Once, Sister Gabby tried to talk her into getting some blood tests, but Ann just waved off the idea, telling the nun it was nothing but stress, time changes and such. Ann didn't tell her that she was grieving for Mike—for what might never be between them.

For the next seven days, the nuns allowed her to open up the clinic in the morning and close it down at night. They were simply too old to keep pace with her youth. Little did they know her energy was a result of her restless attempts to hide from her aching need for a man she cared for deeply—though she had never told him how much.

I miss him. Oh, God, I miss him and I worry for him.... Ann wearily pushed some strands of hair off her brow as she finished stitching up a jagged laceration on the arm of a teenage Quechua boy, who sat very still on the examination table. Mike Houston had slipped inside the array of defenses she had worked so hard for so long to erect against males in general. In the last week, she'd heard more stories about the jaguar god from people who came through the clinic's doors. They were all eager to tell her of his power, his magic, his superheroic abilities. Of course, to herself Ann scoffed at them, but outwardly she just nodded her head, smiled a little and listened to their fervent stories about *him.*

She arrived back at her apartment at 1:00 a.m. that night. Pablo escorted her home and as always, checked out her premises and then left. She absently tossed the newspaper on the couch, remembering Pablo's words to her ten nights ago. He'd said the apartment was a fortress to keep her safe. Then he'd made a slip and called her "the jaguar's chosen mate" and when she'd stared at him, Pablo had quickly retracted his statement, apologizing profusely over and over again.

Though she'd been rankled by Pablo's faux pas, Ann continued to avoid the raw, twisting feelings of fear she felt for Mike's safety. Was he well? Hurt? How would she ever know? His whereabouts, she discovered, were one of the best-kept secrets in Peru.

Tonight, her head swam with exhaustion and she almost staggered down the hall to the bathroom to take her much needed hot shower. During it, she experienced another spontaneous nosebleed, to her mounting consternation. And then, almost as rapidly, she felt feverish, after which an icy chill worked its way through her bones.

While lying in bed, Ann opened the newspaper, as was becoming her routine, and quickly scanned the headlines. Her gaze was suddenly riveted on a large black-and-white picture with headlines that shouted *Escovar's Army Fights Back.* Sitting up, Ann felt her heart begin pounding as she rapidly read the text:

Escovar's hated enemy, Major Michael Sanchez Houston, has met him in a deadly confrontation in the highlands of north-

*ern Peru, near the village of San Juan. According to reports,
Escovar was attempting to reclaim the territories of the cocaine lord Ramirez, who was killed earlier in the year by
Houston's death squad. In a bloody battle, Houston, who is
a U.S. Army special advisor, took his squads of Peruvian
army soldiers into a trap laid by Escovar. Fighting is heavy
and there are reports of many wounded and killed on both
sides. Because the jungle is dense in that remote northern
region, no further information is available.*

Ann stared at the photo of several dead bodies. Was Mike
among them? Suddenly, she felt nauseous. Her hands tightened
convulsively on the pages of the paper as she studied the photos
more closely. She saw two Quechua Indians, dressed in their cus-
tomary dark cotton pants and white shirts, lying dead. To the left
of them were three soldiers in camouflage uniforms. Her mouth
went dry. A machete had hacked the arms off the Indians, and
two of the soldiers had their throats slit open.

"Dear God..." She allowed the newspaper to fall off the bed
onto the floor. Ann pressed her hands against her face. She felt so
terribly cold as another chill swept through her. None of the men
in the photos looked like Mike, but how could she really be sure?

Anguished, she raised her chin and took a gulp of air. Tears
burned in her eyes and she angrily wiped them away. She jerked
off the covers and climbed out of bed. Reeling with shock, she
walked out to the darkened living room. There was a purple-and-
white afghan on the back of the couch and she took it, pulled it
around her shoulders and curled up on the sofa.

She tried to think rationally, logically, but it was impossible.
Her heart was pounding in her chest. She wanted to cry. She rarely
cried, not since— Ann savagely slammed the door shut on the
incident that had changed her life, changed how she reacted to
men. All men except Mike. He had captured her heart.

Ann sat there, rocking slowly back and forth, as she always did
when she was distressed and feeling out of control. The stories
she'd heard all week about Mike, about his mysterious "jaguar
medicine," as the Indians referred to it... They swore he'd stopped

people from bleeding to death with just his touch! *Baloney*. He was a paramedic. Direct pressure on a wound with his hand *would* stop most hemorrhaging. Ann gazed around the empty, silent apartment. She alone knew that he was just a man.

A sob rose in her throat. Her eyes burned. Bowing her head, Ann rested her brow against her drawn-up knees. The scratchy wool of the afghan felt somehow soothing. She ached for Mike's loving, intimate touch once again. From the beginning, he'd sensed her distrust of him, and he'd approached her slowly, allowing her to get used to him being in her life. He hadn't tried to get her into bed. Rather, his touch, his exploratory kisses, had laid a groundwork of trust between them. Now she was ready to seal her love with Mike completely and it was an impossibility.

Suddenly Ann felt Mike's brief touch on her skin—or at least she thought she did. Her flesh tingled in the wake of his grazing, invisible contact. As she allowed his craggy face to appear in her mind's eye, she felt comforted, the edge taken off her fear that he was dead. The sensation was not new to her; every time in the past week when she thought of him there would be almost an instantaneous returning warmth that soothed her, and she would feel undeniable love sweeping around her, as she did now.

Eventually, Ann fell asleep, curled up in the fetal position on the couch. In her dreams, she was back at the magical pool, wearing that vanilla-scented crown of red-and-yellow orchids in her loose hair. Here, she felt safe. Here, she felt protected from the harsh, brutal reality of the world that she had stepped unknowingly into.

"You are worried?" Sister Gabby inquired sweetly.

Ann had just finished examining a baby with a high fever from the flu that had hit Lima hard in the last week. The mother anxiously looked on. Slipping off the latex gloves which had been bloodied due to the severe nosebleed the baby had suffered during the high fever, Ann deposited them in the new waste container that had arrived only yesterday. "Just tired, Sister," she replied finally.

"Hmm, it is more than that, *mi pequeña*," the nun said, calling her by the nickname she and Dominique had given Ann on her first full day at the clinic. It meant "my little one" and they called her that because she was so thin. Even though Ann towered over them heightwise, the nuns saw her as small and vulnerable, like a child who needed to be protected. Ann had protested, of course, but when Sister Gabby explained that agewise, Ann *was* like a child to them, she relented. Now the words were said with such love that Ann surrendered without resistance.

Thinning her lips, she busied herself around the room, tearing off the soiled paper on the examination table and replacing it with clean paper after the mother and baby left. "Really, Sister. I'm just tired."

"Hmm," Sister Gabby said again, helping her to pick up the bloody gauze she dropped on the floor. "You must have seen the newspaper last night, eh?"

Ann froze. She slowly turned and regarded Sister Gabby.

The nun's brown eyes sparkled fiercely. "You must be going through a very special hell," she whispered.

Ann straightened. The pain in her heart almost exploded. She stood there, wanting to cry. Wanting to sob out her fear for Mike.

"Listen to me, child," Sister Gabby said, coming over and gripping her arms and giving her a small shake, "the newspaper often carries horrid photos. But those pictures may not have anything to do with *mon petit chou,* did you know that?"

Ann blinked. "What are you saying?"

"Oh, the account may be true, but this newspaper likes drama and tries to sell more copies by printing terrible pictures of death. Many are from years ago! I can tell you took that photo to heart last night. Your face is pasty today and your eyes show me grief and longing. But you shouldn't have let it bother you."

Trembling, Ann whispered, "It was horrid, Sister Gabby. I—I was afraid—for Mike...."

"Of course you were, *mi pequeña.*" She smiled tenderly up at her. "The heart has no brain, no eyes, eh? It only knows how to love. That is enough, *oui?*"

Love. Ann stared down at Gabby's kindly features. She instantly tried to reject the word, the feeling. It was impossible, because she felt so helpless and weak emotionally right now. "I worry for him, Sister Gabby."

The nun's mouth drew into a gentle smile of understanding. "Our Michael is a very special man, but I sense you already know that. At least your heart knows that." Patting her arm, she added, "You worry too much for him. He knows how to care for his men and himself. Do not put such great stock in the newspaper accounts of him, eh? You are working too hard. You need more rest."

Still, Ann continued to work endlessly to keep her mind and her aching heart off Mike Houston. What had he *done* to her? she wondered. It was as if an invisible umbilical cord was strung between them. Every hour, Ann could feel him. Actually *feel* his invisible, loving presence. It frustrated her. She couldn't get rid of the sensation or ignore it. Nor could her rational mind find any logical reason for the feeling. At night, in her dreams, when she was by that magical pool, was the only time she found a moment's peace and rest from her anxiety. Maybe she worried so much because she'd been in the military too long herself. She knew what kind of guerrilla tactics Mike was using out there. She knew in the jungle it was simple weapons like knives and machetes that took a man's life rather than bullets, because the foliage was so thick that bullets would easily ricochet off the trees. No, the kind of fighting Mike was waging was hand-to-hand combat in many cases. The worst kind.

On the fourteenth day, Ann closed the clinic early—before midnight—because she wasn't feeling well at all. Both nuns had left for the evening and were more than likely tucked in bed already. Every step up to her apartment was an effort and Ann tried to hide how she felt from the alert and discreet glances of Pablo, who was very concerned about her.

"Eh, Dr. Parsons, should you not take a day or two off? You have lost weight and you work your fingers to the bone. You must rest more, *sí?*"

It took too much effort to shrug. "Pick me up at 5:00 a.m. tomorrow, Pablo."

After he'd checked out her apartment, he nodded. "*Sí,* Doctor."

When she finally shut the door behind him, she sank against it, feeling terribly weak. A chill like she'd never encountered before worked its way up her spine. God, she was cold. Icy cold. Pushing away from the door, Ann picked up the newspaper and went to the kitchen. Despite Sister Gabby's warnings, she couldn't help herself from being driven by an almost obsessive need to check out the evening edition for information on Mike and his men.

There had been a blaring headline in every edition for the last seven days. Houston had launched a major counteroffensive operation against Escovar's attempts to invade and reclaim Ramirez's old territory in the highlands. Every night Ann read with eyes blurry from tears how the body count was rising on both sides. And horrific pictures always accompanied the text. Ann felt herself tense as she opened the paper.

Gasping, she felt her eyes widened enormously. The headlines blared Jaguar God Killed By Escovar!

"No!" Ann cried. Her startled shout sank into the silence of the apartment. She flattened the paper out on the table in desperation. She had to be reading it wrong! She just had to be! There was a photo of Mike in his U.S. Army uniform, the beret at an angle, his face hard, his eyes narrowed. It was an official military photo.

"Oh, God, no... No..." Ann rapidly skimmed the article.

During fierce fighting in and around the village of San Juan, Escovar personally led his men against Major Mike Houston's contingent, which was protecting the village from Escovar's attack. One helicopter was destroyed as troops disembarked from it and it was reported that the legendary Houston, known as the jaguar god to the people of the highlands, was on board. The helicopter had landed with Houston's squad, in an effort to reinforce embattled soldiers who fought bravely side-by-side with the villagers to stave off Escovar's well-planned attack.

A second black-and-white photo showed the twisted wreckage of what remained of a helicopter. White wisps of smoke floated upward from the gutted aircraft. Ann couldn't tear her gaze from the macabre photo. With a horrible, sinking feeling, she felt the pit of her stomach drop away. Uttering a small cry, she sat down before she fell down. Mike was dead! *Oh, God, no! No! It couldn't be! The paper had to be lying! Wasn't it lying?* Her mind reeled. Her emotions and heart exploded with wild, animal grief so raw that she cried out.

Hot, unchecked tears flowed down her taut features as she walked unsteadily to the living room. She had to get hold of Sister Gabby. ''She would know....'' Her hands shook badly as she dialed the phone. There was crackling and hissing on the line.

Groaning in frustration, Ann hung up and dialed again. There were very few telephone lines into the barrio. The one that led to the Catholic church was over thirty years old, and when it rained, as it had earlier today, the water seeped into the cable and calls would not connect until the line dried out. Every time Ann tried to call, the line hissed and went dead.

Ann sat there, wondering who else to call to verify the story. Pressing her hand against her head, she felt another violent chill pass through her. The icy coldness she felt was not to be ignored. It was then, only vaguely, that she realized she was burning up with a fever. She stood up, in a quandary. The earliest she could reach Sister Gabby, *if* the phone started working again, would be tomorrow morning. No one at the U.S. Embassy would tell her anything about Mike. He worked for the Peruvian government, and she knew they weren't about to talk to her, a stranger, to confirm his death.

''God...'' She sobbed as she reeled down the hall toward the bedroom. As she stripped out of her clothes to take a shower and warm up, she knew she'd caught the viral flu going around the city. How many cases had they handled at the clinic in the last week? It must have been over a hundred. It was an upper-respiratory flu with a high, sudden fever, and though Ann knew there was no prescription drug to fight a virus, the sisters had homeopathic potions that seemed to arrest the deadly flu in its tracks.

Yes, she must have contracted the flu. She was run-down. Overworked. Getting too little sleep. Stress had lowered her immune resistance to the nasty virus. Moving in a daze to the shower, Ann turned on the faucets with shaking hands. Shivering, she avoided looking at herself in the mirror. Tears kept streaming down her face. She stood there naked, her arms wrapped tightly around herself as if to hold herself together so she wouldn't explode in a million, out-of-control pieces. She wanted to shriek and scream like a madwoman and give her grief voice.

She had never told Mike she loved him. She hadn't even been able to admit it to herself. Until now. When it was too late. That fact pounded throbbingly through her aching head. It hurt to move, the pain was suddenly so intense. Climbing into the shower, Ann thrust her head beneath the hot, massaging stream of water. She stood under the spray, trembling and shivering uncontrollably. The water was so hot that clouds of humidity filled the bathroom and her skin turned pink.

By the time she staggered from the bathroom dressed in her apricot silk nightgown and robe, Ann was feeling vertigo. She knew her temperature was high, maybe 104 degrees. She could feel her pulse pounding like a freight train through her body; her heart was pumping hard in her chest. Her hand against the wall, she managed to make it to the living room. The door was locked but the dead bolt was not in place. She should secure the door, but she suddenly didn't care any longer. Mike was dead. She felt as if she was dying.

As she crumpled to the couch and weakly drew the afghan over her shivering form, Ann could feel all hope draining out of her, as if someone had sliced open her wrists and was bleeding her dry. As she nestled her head on one of the pillows, she drew her legs up against her body, absorbing the warm comfort of the afghan. She was sick. Very sick. Mike was dead. Was he? Or was it a lie designed to sell more newspapers?

More tears leaked out of her tightly closed eyes. The fever was climbing. Her skin felt hot and dry. The chills racked her body every ten or fifteen minutes. Her mind turned to jelly beneath the violent assault of the burning fever. Tiredness, a spirit-weary kind of exhaustion, swept through her. Never in her life had Ann felt so weak, so alone...so horribly grief stricken. She lay on the couch, the sobs coming softly at first as her fever dissolved the massive control she usually kept over her emotions. Little by little by little, tears flooded her face and her sobs became louder and violently wrenching.

At some point, as the fever skyrocketed through her, Ann's sobs turned to weakened whimpers. The ache in her pounding heart was so painful that she no longer cared if she lived or died. Everything good in her life was now gone. Why hadn't she told Mike she loved him? Ann knew even in her delusional state that her feelings for him were real. *The past.* It was her past. Her fear had not allowed her to reach out, to admit even on some deep, intuitive level that she'd fallen helplessly, hopelessly in love with Mike during those eight weeks she'd spent with him at the ranch in Arizona. What a fool she'd been! A horribly frightened fool. As she lay weakly on the couch, in the grasp of the fever and hallucinations, Ann grieved.

At some point, she fell into a disturbed sleep filled with chaotic visions of the past, when she'd worked with Morgan's mercenaries in dangerous situations. Near dawn, with the apartment swathed in gray light, Ann jerked awake. She was burning up. She could not move, she was in such a weakened condition. Trying to think, she realized belatedly that what she had contracted wasn't the flu. It couldn't be; not like this... This was septic. Deadly. Trying to move her hand from beneath her chin, where it was tucked, Ann felt warm liquid flowing out of her nose. The warmth continued across her dry, parched lips. It tasted salty and metallic. What was it?

Barely able to move her hand, Ann laid her fingertips against her lips. The flow increased from her nose. Fighting to open her eyes, which felt like weights, she lifted her fingers just enough so that she could see them. In the gray light, she saw the darkness that stained her fingers.

Blood. It was blood. Her blood. What was going on?

This was no ordinary nosebleed, Ann thought blearily. No, the blood flowing from her nose was heavy, almost as if an artery had burst, but that was impossible. *I've got to get help. Now.* Ann used every ounce of her reserves and slowly sat up. She sank against the couch, a soft gasp coming from her. Blood flowed down across her lips, her chin, and began to drip down the front of her nightgown. Her panic escalated.

The fever had not broken. She was still burning up. The chills were racking her like birthing contractions every few minutes. *Septic. Somehow, I've gone septic.* Her mind fragmented; her vision blurred and became unreliable. Ann knew for sure now she hadn't contracted the flu. This was something far more deadly. A lethal jungle virus of some kind? Where—how had she picked it up? She'd had all her shots before coming down here. But there were many new viruses that had no vaccination protection available.

And then she recalled that yesterday, a little boy had come in with a broken arm that she had set and placed in a cast. He'd been a brave little six-year-old. His mother had been so grateful for her help and care. One of the last things that little boy did was pull a piece of half-eaten candy from his pocket and give it to Ann. She had ruffled his hair, taken the candy and thanked him. Without thinking, she'd popped it into her mouth and made big, smacking sounds of enjoyment for the child's benefit. The little boy had smiled bravely through his tears, and Ann knew that his priceless gift of candy, which few in the barrio ever got, had been a loving gesture toward her.

Reaching forward now, her breathing shallow and erratic, she knew she was going into septic shock. It was one of the most deadly kinds. She *had* to get help or she'd die! Something in her rallied. As grief stricken and delusional with fever as she was, there was a core in her that refused to give up and just lie down and die. Her fingers closed over the phone. The keypad blurred. Ann tried three times to recall the number at the clinic. *Oh, God, what was it?* Her fingers were shaking so badly that she kept missing the number pads on the phone as she tried to dial.

Everything in front of her began to go gray. She could feel a coldness stealing upward from her feet, flowing like a dark river into her ankles. No fool, she knew this was the shock...killing her. She was dumping.

The phone fell out of her nerveless hand.

Help. She had to get help.

Something drove her to try and stand. Caught in the grip of the fever, not thinking clearly, Ann leaned forward. Her knees buckled. The next thing she knew she was landing on the carpet. A groan rippled through her. She felt the carpet's springy texture against her cheek as she collapsed onto it. All her strength ebbed away. The blood was flowing heavily from her nostrils, unabated. *Dying. I'm going to die.*

It was one of the last thoughts she had. Her final thought was a weak cry for Mike Houston, for his help. That was all Ann remembered as she sank into a dark oblivion.

Ann heard Mike Houston's voice. It was deep and panicked sounding. She felt someone pick her up, the feeling wonderful. Floating...she was floating. Strong arms hoisted her upward. She heard Pablo in the background, the panic clearly audible in his voice as well. She was dying and dreaming. That was it. The hallucinations of fever. Oh, how she wished Mike was here! But he was dead. Dead.... How much she loved him...and he'd never know it...not ever.... Darkness overcame her again.

"What should I do?" Pablo asked, his eyes huge as he stood at the door to the apartment. "Call for an ambulance?"

Houston glared toward him as he held Ann in his arms, her limp form pressed tightly against him. "No, it's too late for that. She's dumping on us."

"I didn't know, Major! She looked very tired last night...but..."

Breathing hard, Houston shook his head. "Get the bedroom door open, Pablo. I'm taking her in there." He looked down. Ann's head lolled against his shoulder, her skin marbleized, cold with sweat. There was a faint bluish color around her parted, badly chapped and cracked lips. Blood was everywhere.

"*Sí!*" Pablo replied, and raced down the hall ahead of Mike.

"Hang on, Ann, hang on," Houston whispered urgently, holding her so tightly against him he thought he might crush her. She was like a limp child in his arms, there was so little life left in her. And whatever life there was was now only a dim flame. His mind raced with questions and possible answers. Somehow, she'd contracted a deadly hemorrhagic fever. Due to the filth, squalor and poor sanitary conditions she worked in, it was easy for her to contract one. He could barely feel her pulse.

Pablo jerked open the bedroom door, his breath coming in gulps. "What now, Major?"

"I'm going to work on her in here. Drive down to the clinic

and get whatever homeopathic remedy the sisters think Ann should have. Make it fast, Pablo. Bring IVs. She's not going to make it if we can't get them into her pronto...."

Pablo nodded brusquely and ran back down the hall.

Houston heard the apartment door slam shut as he looked around the small and feminine bedroom. He saw that the bedcovers had been twisted and thrown aside. The pain in his heart almost overwhelmed him. Ann was dying. It was that simple. That pulverizingly simple.

"You *aren't* going to die on me, dammit," he growled. He knew what had to be done. He'd done it before. Not often, but he knew the procedure, the effects—and the cost to himself. He sat down on the bed with Ann in his arms. Resting his back against the headboard, he spread his legs apart. Quickly, he positioned Ann's limp body between them with her back resting against his chest. He guided her head against the hollow of his right shoulder. He felt the cold dampness of her brow against his unshaved jaw and he pressed his trembling fingers against her carotid artery. There was a faint pulse, that was all. She was dying. Her blood pressure was falling through the floor. No amount of medical help would bring her back now. No, there was nothing known in the high-tech medical world, no drug powerful enough, to pull Ann out of this.

If he'd taken her to the emergency room of the nearest hospital, she'd have died on a gurney in front of him.

Houston breathed savagely, his eyes glittering like shards of icy blue glass. "No," he whispered fiercely, "I won't let you die, Ann. I won't...." He wrapped his arms around her slack form, which fit so heartbreakingly beautifully against his tall, lean form.

Get ahold of yourself, Houston. Get ahold...breathe...breathe in and out for her. Pick up the beat of her heart. Make it one with yours. Breathe with her. And he did. He closed his eyes, his arms firm against her. He could feel the faint, weakening beat of her heart against his stronger, pounding one. They were one now, united. United in a death spiral. Houston knew what must be attempted. He knew the risks to himself. It didn't matter. He wanted her to live. He needed her, dammit, and that's all that mattered in his ugly, dark little world. Ann was his light. His hope, whether he deserved it or not.

His mouth thinned and he felt the power nearby. *Come on, come over me. I need you. I need to save her.... Help me! Help me....* He felt the power gather above him and then, like the sheath of a glove, he felt it move over him. As it did, he felt stronger than ten men. His heartbeat deepened and became five times the power of one human heart. The pulsing life that now embraced him was complete. Visualizing the golden energy now throbbing around and through him, Houston saw it move down his arms, through his hands and into Ann's limp, cold fingers.

He continued to breathe with her, slow, shallow breaths. He steadied her heartbeat and nurtured it. Now there was synchronicity; they were living, pulsing as one. Frightened by how far she was gone, he concentrated savagely on the life-giving energy flowing back into her. He wanted to rob death this time. And without apology. Little by little, he felt her heartbeat begin to pick up, and he felt her breath ease a little, deepen a little. Willing his life energy into her like a transfusion of a different kind, Houston let out a ragged, emotional sigh. He felt tears stinging the backs of his eyes. Ann couldn't die on him! She had to live! She had to! He needed her like he'd never needed anyone before. He'd found that out in the last two weeks while he'd been in that hell of a rotting jungle, fighting Escovar's men. He'd wanted to live—survive—to see her again.

His altered state deepened and he no longer thought, he simply felt. His heart entwined with her weak one. His breath filled her collapsing lungs with not only his oxygen, but his life force. Time ceased. He was no longer aware of the hard wood stabbing into his back or the firmness of the mattress beneath him. All he felt was his heart, filled with fierce emotions and love, as Ann lay in his arms, dying.

Minutes congealed and his world shortened to moments between the beats of her heart, to the time between each soft inhalation and exhalation of breath from her parted lips. He willed his life more surely into her. As he did, he felt the power surrounding him begin to vibrate in a familiar pattern. *Yes!* Yes, he could feel Ann's flesh beginning to warm beneath his hands. It was working!

The energy was flowing into her, giving her life, supporting her weakened heart and moving like a golden river through her, cleansing her, stealing her like a thief from death's grip. Behind his closed eyes, he could see it happening, that golden light flowing down through her thin body, reigniting her form with life instead of giving it over to death, which had hovered patiently, waiting.

Life and death. That was what this was all about and Houston knew it. A deep, throbbing pulse began to move from him directly into Ann's body. With each beat of energy, he began to feel a lessening of his own. He knew he could potentially die in the process, but he didn't care. If he couldn't save Ann, he didn't want to live, either. All his life, people he'd loved had died. He'd thought that by leaving her safe in Lima, it wouldn't happen to her. What a naive fool he'd been. He'd thought that by walking out on her life, he could protect her. But his plan hadn't worked. In that moment, he hated his life, hated what he was, what he had become, hated even the power within him—his taskmaster. It was both his burden and his gift that his presence could give life, or cause it to be destroyed. There was no in between. No trade-offs and never any compromise.

As the golden energy surged through Ann, he felt her body growing warmer by the second. Her breathing was deepening now as she absorbed the life-giving oxygen back into her lungs and fed the starving cells of her body. Her heart was beating strongly now, even as he felt his own solid heartbeat begin to diminish. The exchange was occuring. His mouth twitched. He tipped his head back and smiled faintly. Yes, she was going to live. *Oh, Great Goddess, she's going to live.* His spirit guardian was going to give her life, and not take her this time. Hot tears ran down his stubbled cheeks. He could smell the faint sweetness of Ann's silky hair against his jaw as the flowing, throbbing pulsations continued between them. He was giving her a transfusion of life. The only problem was that it was coming from him. Could he hold on? Could he give her enough to get her stabilized and still have enough left to cling to life himself?

Houston wasn't sure. He felt his guardian's presence even more now than ever before. A low growl of warning vibrated through him, but he felt no fear about death. He'd faced it so many times that it had lost any control over him. All that was important was the woman in his arms. The woman he needed as fiercely as his heart would allow him to need and want. Houston felt his consciousness slipping away. He knew he was at a precarious point in the exchange. He hadn't been this close to looking at death in a long time...

It didn't matter. He found himself sliding downward until he lay on his side on the bed, with Ann tucked tightly against him. Keeping his arm around her protectively, he sighed. Whatever had to happen would happen. He wasn't afraid of dying, but he wanted her to live. As the darkness closed around him, he knew that either he would wake up with Ann breathing easily by his side, or he wouldn't wake up at all.

Chapter 8

Ann felt a butterfly grazing her cheek. Or so she thought. The accompanying sensation was tender. Warm. Filled with love that made her heart pulse more strongly within her breast. She stood surrounded by shining gold-and-white light, absorbing a feeling of unconditional love that flowed not only around her, but through her. As bright as the light was, Ann was not blinded by it. Instead, the swirling, glittering, loving energy that embraced her made her feel carefree and joyous.

The light seemed to twist and become more opaque, taking on an identifiable shape. As it came closer, she felt no fear, only curiosity. Suddenly she recognized it—it was a jaguar with a dazzling gold-and-black coat. Ann could see the animal's huge, slightly slanted eyes, thin crescents of gold against the large black pupils holding her hypnotized. When the jaguar had moved halfway toward her, she watched the beast transform into the shape of a man. Her heart expanded like an orchid opening into full bloom when she realized it was Mike who stood before her. He was clothed in a dirty, bloody camouflage uniform. His face had two weeks' growth of beard on it. His eyes were shadowed and filled with a burning tenderness meant only for her.

A soft smile pulled at her mouth as she held his warming, life-giving gaze.

You came....

There was never a question that I wouldn't be here with you.

Ann stood there, torn between remaining in the embrace of the loving light and staying with Mike. There was no need for words in this realm, she discovered with a thrill. All she had to do was think and her thoughts were sent to Mike. And vice versa.

You have a choice, mi querida.

I know.... She felt his raw anguish, his need of her. Most of all, she felt his powerful love for her. It drew her like a beacon, called to her.

If you come back, there are terrible trials ahead.

Ann sensed that without knowing what those trials would be, exactly. But as she gazed into Mike's weary, battle-scarred face, she could feel the powerful beat of his heart in sync with her own. Every time his chest rose and fell, she inhaled and exhaled. The sense of oneness with him made her step forward. In a graceful movement, she extended her hand to him.

I'm not afraid, beloved. I have you. Ann knew she had expressed the truth, fully and without fear for the first time. It was a liberating moment for her. An empowering one. With Mike, she felt safe. He was someone she could trust. *I've searched for you for so long. It's been so hard, so lonely without you....*

You've held my heart for a long time. Longer than you know, he answered, lifting his hands. *Our search is over. Come back with me, Ann. Let's walk this last path together.*

Their fingers were inches apart. White-and-gold light surrounded them, pulsing with life. The urge to live, to remain with him, was suddenly overwhelming. The love emanating from him toward her was greater than the light that embraced her, such was his undying passion for her body, mind and spirit. It was an easy choice for Ann to make. As she reached across those last few inches toward him, and their fingers met, she felt a surge of energy tunnel through her. She felt his strong, caring fingers wrap more surely around hers, as if to steady her.

Come, Mike urged silently, *let's go home—together....*

Tears burned in her eyes. His face blurred momentarily as the tears formed and fell. Though he was a tired, weary warrior, his head was still held high, his shoulders thrown back with pride. Ann could only admire him. And love him.

I'm not afraid anymore....

As he cupped her hands, Houston smiled tenderly down at her. Squeezing her fingers gently, he leaned forward.

You don't have to be afraid. I'm here. I love you...and our love will keep you safe. He gently framed Ann's face with his hands and looked deep into her guileless eyes, which glimmered with tears. *I'm going to kiss you. As my mouth meets yours, drink my breath into you,* mi querida. *Take my breath into your body and you will live....*

As his strong mouth settled over her parting lips, the kiss felt so right to Ann, so warm and life-giving. Closing her eyes, she slid her arms around his broad shoulders and felt him move more surely against her. It was so wonderful to be drawn up against him, to feel her heart beat as one with his, to inhale his breath as her lips clung to his. Every sensation, from the rough, callused quality of his fingertips against her flesh, to the tender coaxing of his mouth sliding against her lips as he opened her to him even more, was exquisitely beautiful to her, causing fresh tears to stream down her cheeks and wash over their joined mouths.

How long she had waited for this welcoming kiss! Oh, the years, the decades she'd been searching without knowing that this man who held her now, was her one true love for life—her mate. Ann had never realized that until this moment out of time. The lonely, painful years, the darkness she'd carried by herself, began to dissolve beneath the tender ministrations of his mouth. She never wanted this kiss of shared love and incredible beauty to end.

Slowly, she began to feel herself growing heavy as she moved downward in a slow, spiraling motion. The light was dimming and they were moving into the darkness now. Somehow, she wasn't frightened by the dark, though as a child, she would have been paralyzed by fear if someone hadn't left a light on in her room when she went to bed. No, with this man, her mate, she could enter complete darkness and not be afraid.

As her body grew weighted, and different sounds and odors entered her peripheral awareness, Ann understood the true power of love. Love was the light that could cut through the blackness of hell itself. It could pierce the darkest of hearts. It could rescue someone from death and bring her back to life again. These thoughts remained with her as she relished the feel of Mike's arms around her, his strong, capable body against hers, steadying her descent. He was with her—inside her, around her, embracing her, their lips never parting, their hearts still beating as one.

Home, mi querida, *you're home now...open your eyes. Come on, my wild orchid, my woman, open your eyes. I'm here with you now. You're safe and everything is going to be all right....*

Mike's deep voice reverberated inside her like wonderful, ever-widening ripples of water moving down through her body. Her lids felt incredibly heavy and Ann struggled to hold on to Houston's voice as his hands framed her face. The moisture and warmth of his breath covered her as he spoke to her again, calling her back, calling her to his side.

Oh! How she always wanted to be with him! Ann struggled. She felt the terrible weakness of her body, but her heart pulsed strongly as his breath mingled with hers. He was giving her life, feeding her, nourishing her and rescuing her from the grip of death. Homing in on his low, trembling voice, on his hands as they gently held her face captive, she forced her lashes to move. But just barely. The lack of strength in her body scared her badly.

Don't struggle so hard, mi querida, he soothed. *Take your time. You're back with me. Just focus on my touch, my voice, and you'll be fine. Breathe more deeply now. That's it—nice deep, easy breaths. In and out...in and out...*

Ann felt his hands shift on her face, his thumbs removing the tears that continued to bathe her skin. Whatever she was lying on shifted. She felt his arm go around her shoulders and cradle her neck and head briefly. In a moment, she was propped up in a sitting position. Breathing became easier at that point. His roughened hand moved gently down her arm and he stroked her fingers.

Did you know that I dreamed of you when I thought Escovar was going to kill me and my men up in the highlands? I dreamed of you during that walk I took through the dark night of the soul. You were there, beloved. I struggled. I knew I could die if I wanted to, but you kept calling to me, teasing me and laughing with me.

You would dance like a butterfly around me as I stood in the light, unsure if I wanted to come back here or not.

Your laughter was like the beautiful music of the waterfall. Your eyes shone like the bluest of skies above the Andes. The shining love in your gaze was for me alone. You loved me. Fiercely. Protectively. You never gave up on me. You refused to let me die. You begged me, you broke down and wept for me, and I stopped, turned around and came back to you. Your tears were for me, not for yourself, and somehow, I knew that. You cried for me, for all I'd suffered, all that I had lost and would lose in the future if we could not meet again. You held me as I knelt down to take you into my arms to somehow try and comfort you.

I had never had someone cry for me before. As you sat there holding me, rocking me gently against your breast, you told me through your tears that you would willingly give your life for mine—that I had so much to do in the world yet. You told me that my path was hard and that if I had the heart, the courage of spirit to persevere, so many people's lives would be saved.

You cradled my face in your hands, and you looked at me through tear-filled eyes and said you would go in my stead. You would give your life for me, so that I might continue on. It was in that moment, my beloved, that you taught me something I hadn't learned yet about sacrificing for another, surrendering your life to a greater cause, a greater thing...far greater than either of us as individuals. You taught me humility, beloved, and the fierce love you held for me made me decide to live.

So you see, the scales are balanced now. You rescued me when I was ready, more than ready, to leave my life, my mission, behind. Only your undying love, your unselfish heart, taught me the difference, taught me what was really important. Now I've done the same for you. I was more than willing to give my life for yours. You are no less important than me. Your power, your commitment to doing good in this world, equals mine in every way. That is why we are together now. We have earned this gift from the universe, from the great Mother Goddess, to finally be with one another. Jaguar people have only one mate for life, beloved. You are my mate. I pray that when you awake and come back fully into your body, that you are able to walk beyond your fear and reach *out to me. Let my love dissolve those fears you will have to face. Let me help you now, as you helped me....*

Where did reality begin and hallucinations end? Ann wasn't sure as she managed, finally, to force her eyes open to bare slits. At first there was only darkness, but gradually, over heartbeats of time, she began to make out light from shadow. She knew on some deep level of herself that she had one foot in each world. Only the stroking motion against her cheeks, the wet hotness of tears trailing down her flesh, told her that she was still very much alive.

Ever so gradually the light and dark began to take different shapes and forms. Ann fought to keep her eyes open, but it was such a tremendous battle. Struggling, she felt a shift against her hip and thigh. What...? The movement was slight, but enough to snag her wandering attention. Lifting her lids a bit more, she saw huge black pupils ringed in deep blue staring back at her. Her heart opened and joy cascaded through her. She knew these tender, burning eyes; the love reflected in them matched her own.

With agonizing slowness her vision cleared and, the face that held those eyes came into focus. It was Mike Houston. He was here with her. Her sluggish mind whispered that it was impossible—that he was dead. That she must be hallucinating with fever. But as Ann stared up at him in those warm, silent moments that strung achingly between them, she saw tears trickling unchecked from his eyes, rolling down his darkly shadowed, unshaved face, and she knew that he was real.

Mike's tears grazed her soul as nothing else ever would. She'd never seen a man cry before—not like this. In those pregnant moments of clarity, her mind ebbing and flowing between consciousness and semiconsciousness, she knew in her heart his tears were for her. Tears of love. Tears of relief. Of greeting. And though her thoughts were coming so quickly that she couldn't process them all, somehow she could feel Mike's every emotion as he continued to gaze down at her.

She forced her badly chapped lips apart to form a word. One word.

"Mike..."

She had to know if he was really here with her or if she was imagining all of this. Her heart beat harder, full of anguish at the thought that this was nothing more than a mirage, a last-ditch wish from her heart because she'd truly lost him forever.

Houston caressed her wrinkling brow. "Shh, *mi querida,* don't struggle so hard." He broke into a half smile filled with welcome. "I'm real. And no, you aren't dead. And neither am I." He picked up her right hand and brought it to his lips. Her flesh was no longer cool and clammy, but warm and full of life once again. Pressing his mouth to her soft skin, he could smell the faint fragrance of lilac soap she'd last washed with. He watched her eyes widen as he brushed his lips against her fingers.

"See? That was real." He laid her hand across her stomach, which was covered with warm blankets. Placing his hands on either side of her head, her sable hair a dark frame around her frighteningly pale features, he lowered his head until their noses almost touched. He watched her pupils dilate. She was watching him, holding her focus on him. Good, it would help keep her here. Keep her with him. Forever.

"No," he repeated, trying to smile, the corners of his mouth lifting, "you're not dead, Ann. You're here, with me, in your apartment in Lima, Peru."

He saw confusion cloud her eyes as she continued to watch him. She clung to each word he slowly spoke to her. When huge, new tears formed in her eyes, he understood that she was afraid he was nothing more than a fevered figment of her mind, of her broken heart. Lifting his hand, he brushed her tears away with his thumb.

"Reports of my death have been greatly exaggerated," he teased, his voice breaking.

A sob tore from Ann.

He felt his heart being ripped open. He had promised to take it easy and not rush her, but her eyes reflected such anguish that he couldn't stop himself. He couldn't help but reach for her as her sob knifed through him like the unsheathed claws of a jaguar striking out in defense.

"Come here," he rasped brokenly, leaning forward and gathering her limp form against him. She was alarmingly weak, and Mike gently guided her head against his shoulder so that her brow

rested against his stubbled jaw. "There," he rasped, "does that
feel real enough for you now, Ann? Feel me. Here." Lifting her
hand because she was too weak to lift it on her own, he placed
her soft palm against his roughened face. "Feel me. Feel my
beard." He gave a short laugh, but it came out as a choking sound.
"Can't you smell me? Cripes, I smell like the rotting jungle, like
fear, sweat, blood and mud. That should tell you this is real. That
I'm real."

He moved her hand in circular motions against his face. And
then he placed her arm around his waist and he embraced her, so
very much in touch with her chaotic jumble of feelings. There was
a fine trembling in her as he gently rocked her back and forth in
his arms. He felt so responsible for her safety that it nearly overwhelmed him. She shouldn't believe that he could always protect
her. God knew, he wanted to, but he was only human. So terribly,
vulnerably human. Turning his head, he pressed a kiss against her
tangled hair.

"There. Did you feel that? I kissed your hair. How about another one?" Her hair was silky and he liked the feeling of the
strands beneath his lips as he pressed a second kiss against his
temple. Her arm lay limply against him, and for a moment, as he
pressed a third, lingering kiss on her cheek, there was a slight
response.

"Good," he praised huskily. "I see you're beginning to believe
I'm real and not a figment of your fevered state." Sliding his
fingers through her hair, he held her more tightly against him for
a moment. "You came so close to dying...so close.... I heard you
cry out for me. I heard you, *mi querida*. Everything's gonna be
okay. Believe me," he rasped against her hair, "it is. You're very
weak and you need to sleep. I'm going to lay you back down and
I want you to stop struggling, okay? I can feel you. I want you to
take my energy and let it heal you. Don't fight to stay awake or
try to figure all this out. There will be plenty of time for that later,
I promise you."

Mike eased Ann back onto the bed, keeping extra pillows beneath her because that helped her breathe easier. This time, as he
straightened up after tucking her in, he saw that her eyes looked
less cloudy. Her gaze clung to his until her lashes drooped shut.

"Sleep," he whispered, sliding his fingers through her hair in a caressing motion. "I'll be right here. I won't leave you ever again...."

The next time Ann awoke, sunlight was pouring through the curtains of her bedroom, making everything around her glow. As she lay there, she thought at first she was back in that gold-and-white light again. Then a broken snore snagged her drowsy attention. Barely turning her head to the right, she saw Mike Houston sitting, legs splayed, in a chair next to her bed. His head was tipped back, exposing his well-corded throat and Adam's apple, and his arms hung over the chair, which was too small for his large form.

She wasn't dreaming this time, she realized, though it took long, exquisite moments of simply absorbing his form into her wide-open heart before she could think straight. Thinking, Ann realized belatedly, took too much energy. Right now, on an intuitive level, she knew she had to be a miser with that energy in order to get well.

As he slept, Ann saw a depth of vulnerability in Houston as she'd never seen before. His dark hair was tousled and the exhaustion on his face wrung her heart. Dark, deep shadows lay beneath his eyes. His flesh, usually golden colored, was now pasty, as if drained of life. That frightened her. Was he wounded?

She had to examine him closer. As she struggled to try and sit up, the bed creaked in protest.

Instantly, Houston snapped awake, his eyes wide, his entire body tensing defensively. *What? Who?* He jerked a look toward Ann. She was awake. And she was looking directly at him, her eyes clear, her pupils huge and black and surrounded by the most incredible blue-gray he'd ever seen. The seconds strung palpably between them. When he realized there was no danger to guard against, he sat up straight. Then, raking her from head to toe with a searching gaze, he stumbled to his feet.

"Ann?" His voice was thick with sleep and undisguised concern.

She fell back, unable to remain up on her elbows for very long. As she closed her eyes, she felt his hands moving across her face, checking her temperature. And then he sat down next to her, his hip against hers as he picked up her wrist and felt for a pulse. It felt so *good* to be touched by Mike! How she wanted to tell him. She tried to form the words, but they stuck in the back of her dry throat.

"Good," Mike murmured, reaching for the blood pressure cuff on the nearby bed stand, "your pulse is finally strong and stable." Placing the stethoscope to his ears and wrapping the cuff around her arm, he pumped it up. As he released the air slowly from the device, he critically watched the needle. His heart soared.

"One hundred over eighty. Not bad," he said. "Not bad at all." He removed the stethoscope from his ears and the cuff from around her upper arm and watched as Ann slowly opened her eyes again. Smiling down at her, he rasped, "Welcome back to the real world, stranger." Getting up, he moved to the other side of the bed, where plastic IV bags filled with life-giving nutrients flowed into her left arm. Adjusting the drip, he felt relieved when she turned her head and continued to watch him. His heart pulsed with elation. Ann was out of the woods. For the first time in a twelve-hour period, her pulse and blood pressure were remaining stable. As he walked back around the bed, roughly wiping the sleep from his face, he felt exhaustion begin to avalanche upon him. Fighting it off, he carefully sat down on the bed and faced Ann. Should he take her hand as he had before? This time she was fully conscious, not floating in and out of this world.

To hell with it. Sliding his hand around hers, he squeezed her fingers. "Thirsty?"

Ann closed her eyes and drank in Houston's strong, firm touch. How did he know she desperately needed him to touch her? It felt like forever since she'd used her voice, and when she tried to force out a "yes" to answer his question, only a croak issued forth.

Nodding, Mike released her hand and quickly poured her a glass of water. "Hang on, I'll maneuver around here and help you sit up to take a sip."

His arm slid around her shoulders. How good it felt to lean against Mike as he positioned himself next to her. Raising her hand to hold the glass, she found, wasn't possible.

"Let me...." he whispered as he cradled her head against his shoulder, her soft hair against his jaw. "All you have to do is drink. Take all you want...."

Tears formed as she became privy to his incredible gentleness in the following moments. He pressed the glass against her lower lip and tipped it up just enough for her to drink without being drenched in the cool liquid. How good the water tasted! Ann slurped thirstily, some of the water spilling down both sides of her mouth. Houston couldn't tip it up fast enough for her to drink. Her throat was raw and so dry. And one glass was not enough. She saw the surprise in his eyes and then the grin forming on that wonderful mouth of his. She absorbed his warmth as she leaned against him. Just being held by him made her heart soar with joy. Just the strength of his arms around her, his body pressed to hers, fed her own strength.

"More?" Houston chuckled. "I don't have a beautiful woman in my arms, I've got a two-humped camel needing a refill at the oasis."

Ann laughed—or at least tried to. The sounds coming from her throat were raspy, but somehow Houston knew she was laughing. His grin widened enormously as he held her steady, his left arm wrapped around her while he reached for the pitcher on the bed stand. She watched him carefully balance the glass in his left hand while he poured more water into it. The errant thought that he could have laid her back down on the pillow and gotten the water more easily crossed her mind. Somehow, he understood that she didn't want to be physically separated from him just now.

After several glasses of water, Ann was sated. Houston replaced the glass on the bed stand. He should extricate himself and let her lie back down, but he was loath to release her. As he continued to hold her, he felt her tremble slightly and sigh.

"Okay?" he asked near her ear as he clasped his hands across her belly, above the thick blankets that covered her. She was warm and felt so good against him. Worried that he was taking advantage of the situation, he started to ease her up into a sitting position so he could move away from her.

He heard a mewing noise come from her, clearly a sound of protest. Looking down, he saw her raise her lashes. Her gaze clung to his. "No? You don't want me to leave?"

It took every bit of strength Ann had to lift her right hand and allow it to fall across his much larger, darker one. Words refused to come. Body language would have to do. As she tried to send out the impression she didn't want him to move, his mouth curved ruefully and his blue eyes danced with sunlight.

"Okay, I got the message. Just relax, you hear me? I'll sit here holding you for as long as you want, Ann. I'm in no hurry to go anywhere, believe me." And he wasn't. Mike watched as her lashes drifted shut and her lips parted. He heard a ragged sigh issue from her badly chapped lips. She sagged against him, and Houston realized just how much she'd struggled to keep him from leaving her bedside.

"Just lie here," he soothed, capturing her cooler hand between his own. "I'll be your blanket, okay? I'll keep you warm and safe so you can go back to sleep. That's what you need right now, you know. Lots of sleep. That and liquids." He pressed a kiss to Ann's hair and smiled with relief. She moved her fingers slightly within his hand.

Releasing a ragged sigh, Mike closed his eyes, too. He maneuvered himself fully onto the bed, his back against the headboard, his head tipped against the wall behind it. Exhaustion stalked him. He'd barely slept, snatching catnaps between taking her pulse, monitoring her blood pressure and watching over her during the endless hours, days and nights. But as he felt her shallow, slow breaths move moistly against the column of his neck, the hard line of his mouth relaxed. This was all he wanted for the rest of his life: Ann in his arms. Alive. Wanting him to hold her. Wanting him...

Chapter 9

"How long have I been out of it?" Ann heard how rusty her voice was, her words sounding more like croaks than the English language.

Houston stretched his long legs out in front of him. He'd managed to sleep with Ann in his arms, undisturbed, for nearly eight hours. She'd awakened first, and he'd quickly come awake seconds afterward. He'd eased her into a sitting position, given her several glasses of water and watched her orient herself completely to the real world once again. As he sat down, he knew the questions would come like a barrage. A part of him was afraid she'd reject him because of the answers he would have to give her.

Rubbing his face tiredly, Mike looked down at the watch on his left wrist. "Four days, ten hours and thirty-five minutes."

Her brows moved up. "Four days..." she managed in a whisper. She saw a lazy but exhausted smile tug at the corners of Mike's mouth as he regarded her in the dim light of the room, which was almost completely dark save for a small lamp on the Queen Anne dresser.

"Yeah..."

"What hit me? I..." Ann touched her hair with her trembling

hand. Weakness stalked her. "I remember having a fever. It was high. Sudden."

Houston lost his smile. Sitting up, he folded his hands between his opened thighs. "You got nailed with a hemorrhagic fever, Ann."

"What?" Her voice cracked in disbelief. She stared over at him. "But how..."

He shrugged wearily. "I don't know. You tell me. Do you remember anything out of the ordinary at the clinic? The granny nuns couldn't. God knows, we were looking for cause and effect. You had something that I've seen villagers get from living in lousy sanitation conditions. We had your blood analyzed at the hospital. It's actually a parasite. You pick it up from animal fecal matter."

"Yuck," Ann muttered. She pressed her hands to her face and tried to remember. Her mind wasn't functioning fully yet, not by a long shot. Emotionally, she felt completely raw and vulnerable. Having Mike here with her made her feel more stable, despite her weakness. "Wait..." She allowed her hands to drop away from her face. She told Houston about the little boy who had given her the piece of candy in return for setting his broken arm.

Mike's face darkened instantly. He straightened up and scowled. "You didn't eat it, did you?"

"Well, yes, I did eat it.... I mean, I didn't really, but you see, I wanted to make him happy. I know these kids don't get candy that often. I realized when he gave his only piece to me how much it meant to him. I popped it into my mouth and made lots of noises to show him how good it tasted."

Groaning, Mike raised his eyes toward the ceiling. "Ann...!"

"I spit it out into the waste basket as soon as he left," she muttered, defiance in her voice.

Houston got up. He couldn't sit still. "This is my fault, dammit," He began pacing the length of the room. "All my fault..." He ran his fingers savagely through his hair.

"How could it be?" Ann protested. "Mike, stop pacing. Sit here." She patted the side of the bed next to where she lay.

He halted and came and sat beside her once again. There was just a hint of a flush in her cheeks. How good it was to see her blush again!

"How did you know I was sick, Mike?"

He heard the fear in her husky voice. Holding her level gaze, which was filled with questions, he said, "You called me. Remember?"

Closing her eyes, Ann concentrated. Then she remembered something. Mike was here. Alive, not dead. "But," she said hoarsely, opening her eyes and fighting back tears, "they—the newspaper—said you were dead...."

Mouth pursed, he put his hand over hers. "Listen to me, Ann, these damn newspapers exaggerate a lot. Drama is their way of selling more copies."

"Then it was all a trumped-up lie?" Her voice was off-key.

"Not entirely," Mike muttered darkly. "I *was* slated to go on that chopper up to the village of San Juan with my squad. But something warned me against it. I settled for a convoy run up the mountain, instead. Another captain and his men were only too glad to get a lift to the top instead of marching through ten miles of jungle."

"And...they died instead?"

"Yeah...all of them, the poor bastards. Escovar's men have rockets they can launch from their shoulder. The chopper was just about to land when they began firing at it. I was halfway up the mountain with our convoy and saw it happen. We got pinned down, anyway...I lost most of my men...." His brows drew down and his voice faded. He didn't want to tell her how close to death he'd come himself. A bullet had ripped past his head, scoring his skull, and he'd fallen unconscious. Most of his men had thought he was dead because he was bleeding so badly. That was when he'd moved into the light—when Ann had come to him. The choice to live or die was his to make in that moment and he'd known it. Because of her, he'd come back, and thanks to his decision, his spirit guardian had healed the badly bleeding wound and he'd survived. Ann didn't need to know any of this. At least, not right now. She was too torn up already from the lousy newspaper report.

She gripped his hand as hard as she could, and he knew it was because she felt his pain and grief over the loss of his men. The moments strung between them, palpable and heart wrenching.

Never had Houston allowed her to see him like this. There were tears glittering in his eyes, but he refused to look up at her.

"I never realized just how dangerous your work really is...." she said thickly.

Twisting his shoulders to get rid of the tension and grief knotting them, Mike finally forced himself to face her. Her eyes were filled with such compassion. Suddenly Houston was tired of the life he lived. And though he'd found the woman he wanted to be with forever, his path would not—could not—change. The love he felt could never be expressed to her. "It's life and death every damn day, Ann. That's all I've ever known."

The flat finality, the grief behind his words, shook her. "This has been the worst two weeks of our lives. I'm so sorry, Mike— for your men...their families...."

Mike grimaced and admitted hoarsely, "I wanted to protect you from Escovar, from getting killed. Escovar has a sixth sense about people I—I care for. He's like a dog on a scent, and when he finds out who is important to me, he has them murdered."

"Escovar didn't get me," Ann stated wryly, "a damn parasite did."

"This time," he stated soberly. Mike knew he was scaring her, so he changed the subject. "Anyway, I heard you call me. Remember? The mental telepathy? And I felt you were in danger. I thought one of Escovar's killer squads had gotten to you." Releasing her hands, he stood up, frustrated. "It never crossed my mind that you'd contract a hemorrhagic fever and damn near die from it. I thought you were safe. I thought, for once, I'd outsmarted Escovar. He's a dark shadow in my life, always staining it, murdering those I care about. And when I heard—felt—you were in danger, there was no way I wasn't going to come back to Lima." He looked down at her, his voice heavy with weariness.

Ann swallowed hard at seeing the pain in his eyes. "I thought for sure I was going to die."

Rubbing his jaw, he muttered, "When we got here, about three in the morning, we busted down the door to gain entry. You were lying on the carpet, on your belly. You were bleeding from your nose, ears and mouth."

"Oh, God..." Ann connected back to the memory of that night.

"Then I wasn't imagining it? I was burning up with fever. It was at least 105 degrees."

"You had a temp of 106.5," he corrected grimly. "You were dumping. Your blood pressure was through the floor and your pulse was almost nonexistent. Pablo figured you lost two pints of blood on that carpet."

Her eyes widened. Ann heard herself gasp. "Then...I shouldn't be alive...."

With a shake of his head, Mike avoided her look. "No...you shouldn't be...but you are." His voice shook with raw emotion.

"But," Ann said weakly, "how? How did I come back? Medically, I should have died." She saw Houston's face grow closed, that hard mask returning. When he refused to answer her, fragments of memories began to trickle back—chaotic scenes and emotions. Groping, her voice cracking, Ann ventured, "Something happened...I remember being lifted up. I felt like I was in the clouds. I felt so light, so very light.... And I heard your voice. I told myself that was impossible. You were dead. It was then that I knew I was dying."

"Yeah," Mike said roughly, "you were dumping fast at that point. I was scared to death. I—" He stopped himself abruptly. He was afraid Ann would not believe the truth of what had happened. She was fragile right now, and he didn't want her upset. And if she knew the real truth, it would stress her out completely. That was the last thing he wanted.

Instead, he said, "I brought you here, to the bedroom. Pablo went and got Sister Gabby, who gave you a homeopathic remedy. I set up the IVs. When we realized how much blood you'd lost...well..." Damn, he didn't want to admit the rest of this, but he knew Ann was hanging on every word he spoke. He *had* to think of some kind of explanation. And he did—one that she, in her world, could accept.

"Sister Gabby said you were Type O blood. Of the three of us, her, Pablo and myself, I was the only Type O available. Sister set up a transfusion between us. It took one and a half pints from me to get your blood pressure stabilized...."

Pressing her hand against her heart, Ann whispered, "I see...."

The loss of that much blood was critical, she knew. "That's why you look so bad."

He grinned a little sheepishly. "Yeah, it kinda took me for a trip for the next forty-eight hours. I was a little weak after transfusing that much of my blood into you."

"Did Sister Gabby stay here?"

"No, she couldn't," Mike answered. He came back to the chair, and positioning it near the bed, he sat down. Ann was obviously accepting his version of the story of how her life was saved. Breathing a sigh of relief, Mike added, "I couldn't afford to have one of Escovar's spies zero in on this apartment. I know they follow the nuns around. I don't know if they followed Sister Gabby that night or not when Pablo drove her over. I wanted her out of here as soon as possible. I sent Pablo away, too."

"So, it was just you and me? You've been taking care of me through this whole ordeal?"

Houston nodded. Mouth thinning, he rasped, "I wanted to be here. I don't regret it, Ann."

"But," she murmured, "you said that it wasn't safe for you to stay very long in any one place—that Escovar's spies always tailed you...." And he'd been here, with her, going on five days now. Ann suddenly grew afraid—for Mike.

"That newspaper article probably covered my entrance into Lima," he said. "Escovar *probably* thinks I'm dead, too, but that won't last long. He'll send his spies in to see who was on that flight manifest."

"Five days is long enough for someone like him to find out the truth," Ann said. She suddenly felt very weak and very old. Worry for Mike's safety mushroomed within her. "And you look like hell warmed over. You haven't gotten enough sleep after losing nearly two pints of blood."

He lifted his head. "You must be feeling better. You're griping at me again."

Ann laughed spontaneously—a croak, really—but Mike's deep, answering laughter was music to her ears, a balm for her frightened heart. What had changed so much between them that she felt this close to him? Felt this desire to remain in his presence? She secretly hungered for his touch and wondered if she'd ever feel his arms around her again. It had felt so wonderful when he'd held her before.

"I guess," Ann uttered tiredly, "I had that coming."

He rose. "Yeah, you did, wild orchid." The name slipped out before he could stop it. Halting, Mike studied Ann for a reaction. There was a dull flush in her cheeks and she shyly looked down at her hands, clasped in her lap. In that moment, she was such a fragile, innocent young woman. It was torture not to kiss her, hold her close and feel her heart beating in unison with his. Torture not to think that someday.... Oh, Goddess...someday he could love her wildly, passionately, until they were joined on every level of themselves, from the physical to the most sublime. His heart ached for her. But it was a dream never to become a reality.

When Ann saw his wary look at his use of the endearment, her mouth softened. "Wild orchid. That's beautiful...."

"You like it?"

"Who wouldn't?" She laughed, a little embarrassed by the smoldering look in his narrowed blue eyes. Whenever he looked at her like that, she felt so incredibly feminine and wanton—two things she'd never felt before, really, except with Mike. And now, for whatever reason, his look stirred her even more deeply, ripening her yearnings as a woman who not only needed her man, but who wanted to make love with him as she'd loved no other man in her thirty-two years of life.

"I know I'm not beautiful, but I like the idea of being compared to such an exquisite flower."

Angry, but shielding her from it, Mike walked over to the dresser, toward the vase of red-and-yellow orchids that Pablo had brought before he left the apartment. Mike had wanted fresh orchids—Ann's orchids—by her side. They'd been sitting on the dresser through the long, dark nights of her illness, reminding him as he worked to save her that life was stronger than death. That love could delay death. And his love had.

"Here," he rasped as he placed the vase next to her bed, "you just look at these and know they're a reflection of you, okay? I'm going to take a shower, shave and probably keel over afterward."

Touched, Ann reached out and caressed one of the fragrant

vanilla-scented blossoms. "They're lovely," she admitted softly, meeting his exhausted gaze.

"So are you." His tiredness was making him say too much. "I'll check on you before I hit the sack, *querida.*"

Ann nodded. "I'll be fine, Mike. You just get some rest. You look awful."

At the door, he hesitated. Placing his hand on the gold-painted frame, he looked over his shoulder at her. Already he could see that the old Ann was back. Her wry wit. Her sparkling blue-gray eyes filled with warmth—toward him. Heaven help him, but he absorbed it all like a greedy beggar stealing what wasn't rightfully his. "I'll take that as a compliment," he said, and giving her a sad grin, he left.

The phone was ringing. And ringing. And then it stopped abruptly after the second ring. Then it began again. Groaning, Houston rolled over on the couch and damn near fell off of it as he fumbled for the noisy device. Throwing out his hand, he forced his heavy lids open.

What the hell time was it? Sunlight was cascading through the western curtains of the apartment. The watch on his wrist read 3:00 p.m. Groping for the phone, he hesitated, even in his drowsy state. How many rings had it rung? If it was Pablo calling, they'd agreed upon two rings and then hanging up. Then the phone would ring again until the other party picked up. Mike had told his trusted sergeant to phone if, from his watch post in the apartment complex next door, he spotted one of Escovar's men hanging around the apartment. How many times had it rung the first time? Mike wasn't certain, as he knew the caller could be one of Escovar's spies trying to find out if he was here. Answering the phone could mean the difference between life and death. Or it could simply be Sister Gabby, worried about him and Ann. But the granny nun wouldn't be calling, he realized, because she knew it might put him in jeopardy.

Damn. To answer or not? How many times had it rung before he'd awakened? Something told him to do it.

"Yes?" he growled into the receiver.

"Major," Pablo said in a low voice, "Escovar has four armed

men in a car parked outside your apartment building. They've been here five minutes.''

All the sleepiness was instantly torn away. Standing up, Houston snarled, ''Pablo, get the car. Meet us around back, near the exit by the basement door, next to the trash cans. Make sure you aren't seen.''

''*Sí, sí!*''

Son of a bitch! Savagely cursing, Mike pulled on his shoulder holster. He always slept with the nine-millimeter pistol under his pillow no matter where he was. Grabbing his civilian black leather coat, and already dressed in a pair of jeans and a red Polo shirt, he hurried down the hall to Ann's room. They had to get out of here now! Escovar's men would be up at any minute. The yellow-bellied bastards were probably waiting for more backup, more men. More guns.

His heart was pounding as he opened the door to the bedroom. Ann was sleeping. As he hurried to her side, she looked like an innocent in a world gone mad. Shaking her shoulder, he growled, ''Ann, wake up!'' He didn't want to scare her, but time was of the essence. Moving swiftly, he unhooked the IVs and brought them carefully around the bed.

Groggily, Ann raised her head, disoriented. Mike leaned down beside her.

''Listen to me,'' he rasped, ''we've got to get out of here. Now.'' He quickly untaped the IV and pulled it out of the back of her left hand. Blood quickly pooled and he replaced the tape over it. ''We can't take anything. I've got to get you out of here.'' He took the blankets and pulled them around her.

Fear jagged through Ann. ''What—''

''No time to talk,'' he growled, and he slid his arms beneath her. Ann felt light. How much weight had she lost? He shrugged off the thought as his mind spun with tactics. With how to keep her safe.

''Hold on to me,'' Houston ordered as he brought her fully against him. ''Keep this blanket over your head. If I drop you to the floor, don't you dare move. You hear me?''

''Y-yes....'' Ann clung to his neck as he hurried out of the room, the blankets wrapped tightly around her. Terror seized her as she felt the sledgehammer pounding of his heart against hers. She smelled fear around him. She tasted it as she pressed her cheek weakly against Mike's neck. She knew she was a liability to him and the thought pained her.

Outside the door, Houston made a quick, cursory sweep of the hall. Nothing. Breathing harshly, he hurried toward the elevators. *No,* something inside him warned, *take the stairs.* Yes, a better, safer way. Turning on his heel, he jogged to the end of the carpeted hall. Leaning over, he jerked open the fire door. Gray concrete stairs with black pipe railing met his gaze. *Hurry! Hurry, there's no time left!*

The warning shrilled through him. Easing through the door, he rasped, "This is gonna be a rough ride. Hang on...." He gripped Ann hard as he began his rapid descent down the twelve flights of stairs.

Breathing hard by the time he'd gotten them to the basement, Houston ran for the rear exit. The dark, gloomy cellar was empty save for huge conduits, a lot of paper in receptacles and a massive furnace. At the rear door, he halted.

"Don't move," he rasped, and he stood Ann on the ground. He felt her legs begin to buckle. In one swift movement, he anchored her solidly against him, blankets and all. With his other hand, he pulled the pistol from his shoulder holster. He felt her arm weakly move around his torso as he eased the door open just a crack. There! He saw the black Mercedes-Benz. Pablo was only four feet from the door. *Good!* With a swift look in both directions, Houston jammed the pistol back into the holster and picked Ann up.

"Last step," he said huskily, kicking the door open with his booted foot.

Once they were inside the car, Pablo stepped on the accelerator. Houston forced Ann to lie down on the back seat.

"Stay down. Whatever you do, don't get up until I tell you it's safe."

"O-okay," Ann whispered as she felt the car begin to move. Houston's clipped, harsh tone scared her. If she'd been well, she might have handled this situation differently, but being ill made her vulnerable. Once again, she heard Mike's voice from the front seat, low and angry sounding.

"Let's get out of the city. Use all the back streets, Pablo."

"*Sí*, Major, *sí.*"

Houston slid down so he couldn't be seen. This was the lousy life he led. But he couldn't take the risk of anyone spotting him—especially Escovar's hundreds of spies, who salivated after that ten-million-sol reward on his head. Anyone on the street—vendor, beggar or businessman—could be a potential Escovar spy. And all the spy had to do was make a couple of quick phone calls and Mike would be history. Worse, Ann would be killed and so would Pablo.

"Major, where do we go? If Escovar knows you are here, he will have the airport cut off. He will have his spies at the army barracks...so where...?"

"*Aldea para los Nublado,*" Mike ordered. "The Village of the Clouds."

Pablo's eyes blinked, then widened. "*Qué?* Why?"

"Because," Mike snarled in frustration, "I don't have any other choice, so you'd better damn well make sure we don't get tailed."

"*Sí, sí,* Major..."

Ann lost track of time. She grew nauseous as the car twisted and turned down seemingly endless roads. All she could do was try to brace herself so she wouldn't fall off the seat. The blankets were heavy and she was hot in the stuffy vehicle. Perspiration soaked through the white silk gown she wore, making it cling to her. Trying to pull the blanket off her head so she could at least breathe, she felt Mike's hand upon her shoulder.

"We're out of the city now," he told her huskily as he removed all but one blanket from around her. He was leaning over the seat, his eyes narrowed and glittering as he rapidly checked her condition. She was very pale, her eyes huge and dark with fear. "Damn, I'm sorry for this, Ann. This wasn't in the plans...."

She rolled over and lay across the seat as best she could. Mike folded up one of the blankets and, lifting her head and shoulders, placed it beneath her as a pillow.

"Thanks.... What's going on?"

Houston never stopped looking around as he spoke to her. "Escovar got wind of my whereabouts. Pablo was keeping watch in the apartment complex across the way and he spotted a hit squad in a car out front of your place. They were probably waiting for backup before coming in after me.'' He saw Ann's face drain of color. How badly he wanted to protect her from all of this. Reaching down, he smoothed an errant curl off her wrinkled brow. ''It's okay. We're safe. We managed to get out of Lima without a tail, thanks to Pablo here.'' Mike gratefully patted his sergeant on the shoulder in thanks. Pablo glowed at the sincere compliment.

''Where are we going, then?''

Mike heaved a sigh and rested his arms across the seat as he regarded her. ''Home,'' he rasped. ''We're going home, Ann.''

Chapter 10

"Where are we?" Ann asked as she awoke and sat up on a pallet in a roomy hut, the morning light cascading through the window openings. Mike Houston was standing in the doorway, his massive frame silhouetted against the bright sunlight.

Mike turned toward her, smiling a little as he eased away from the door. They had driven for two days, with few stops in between. For Mike, outwitting Escovar was like trying to get his shadow to disappear on a sunny day. However, with more than a little help from the men and women elders here at the village, they'd successfully evaded him. And he was very relieved, he thought, studying Ann sitting before him, her legs crossed beneath the light pink cotton blanket. Her hair was beautifully mussed, her lips softly parted, her eyes still puffy with sleep.

Crouching down, he slid his fingers through her hair and eased errant strands away from her face.

"We're home," he told her huskily, catching her tender look as he caressed her cheek. "And we're safe here. No more running, ducking or dodging."

It was so easy to surrender to Mike. Ann was still healing from her illness and feeling excruciatingly vulnerable. Craving his continued closeness, his touch, she pressed her cheek against his open palm and closed her eyes.

"Home?" she whispered. Mike had been vague about where they were going. She only knew she was someplace safe from Escovar's murdering thugs and spies. She had slept most of the time during their escape because she was still recovering from the fever. Last night, in Tarapoto, they had left civilization behind, and Ann had heard Pablo say, as they slowly moved down a rutted dirt road in the darkness, that he saw a bank of clouds ahead. She vaguely remembered Mike carrying her from the car. She had seen stars overhead between the clouds. She had heard cries and greetings—some in English, others in Spanish and yet others in a language she was too tired to try and identify. Exhausted, all she could do was cling to him as he carried her to a hut and a soft, awaiting pallet. The last thing she remembered was Mike tucking her in with a warm blanket and pressing a kiss to her temple as she drifted back into the arms of sleep.

Now as he placed a feathery kiss on her wan cheek, a tremble raced through Ann and she lifted her chin, looking into his face, which was only inches from hers. "Hold me?" It took all her courage to ask. This was one of the few times in her life that she felt so nakedly vulnerable, so overwhelmingly in need of his protection. It must be the fear of Escovar finding them, coupled with the remnants of the fever, that made her feel this way. Ann searched his shadowed eyes. She had made it a point never to ask a man for anything because of her past. With Mike, it felt normal to ask for his help, his protection. "For just a minute?" she continued.

Houston saw the fear and worry in her drowsy blue-gray eyes. *Forever, if you want,* querida, he thought, though he dared not utter those words. Nodding, he sat down and positioned her between his massive thighs. It was so easy now, Mike mused, as Ann leaned against him trustingly. Her trust had been hard-won, he realized. And it could be shattered all too easily. One mistake on his part would destroy the tenuous connection between them. Especially now, when she was fragile and still mending. Her old walls hadn't been resurrected yet, but he was expecting them to be. Sliding his arm around her shoulders, he laughed softly against her hair. "I held you all night. Didn't you get enough of me then?" he teased.

Ann pressed her face against his neck. She felt the pounding pulse near his throat. He had recently shaved and she could smell the clean odor of soap still lingering on his flesh. She moved her head from side to side, content to be held within his strong, cherishing embrace. "I can't get enough of you...." she quavered. And she couldn't. Being in the back seat of a car for days that melted together like one nightmare had made coping with the ordinary things of life difficult. Mike had done his best to care for her under the harrowing circumstances, but they'd been on the run, barely ahead of Escovar's men, who had tracked them like bloodhounds. Ann had begun to truly understand just how hunted Mike was—and just how many of Escovar's spies were on his trail. Even when they'd stopped to get petrol, she'd had to hide beneath the blanket on the back seat, unmoving where Pablo, the least identifiable of the group, got the gas.

Mike heard the emotion in her voice and felt the stormy chaos within her. Sliding his fingers through her hair and taming it into place, he whispered, "Just tell me what you want, wild orchid, and I'll do my damnedest to give it to you." He bit back so much more he wanted to say to her. Every day they'd been on the run, he'd watched as reality struck Ann, reminding her about the price on his head and the raw danger he constantly dealt with. If anything, their experience on the road demonstrated why they could never have a life together. That made every moment he spent with Ann now even more precious, and like a greedy thief he absorbed her presence into his heart and soul.

The singing of many tropical birds added to the tender stillness ebbing around them as Mike held her. His heart sang, too. How often had he dreamed of Ann coming to him like this? Snuggling into his arms, seeking refuge? Seeking his reassurance? His love? Pain tightened his chest. Love? Yes, he loved her, but that was one thing he couldn't tell Ann. Pressing small kisses against her hair, Mike watched the sunlight strike the silken strands of sable, the red and gold highlights gleaming as the rays crept over the frame of the window and stole into the room.

Ann slowly lifted her hand and pressed her palm against the

center of Mike's chest. She saw that he was wearing civilian clothes still—a short-sleeved, white shirt and dark blue cotton trousers. He pressed his hand against hers.

"I remember...." Ann began in a husky voice as she closed her eyes. "While I was sick, I was dreaming, but I don't think it was a dream, Mike. When I was dying from the fever, I heard you break into my apartment. I remember you were holding me, willing me back to life. I saw the tears in your eyes. I heard your voice break. I saw this shadow near the bed. I—I don't know what it was, but then I saw it move above us. And then..." She opened her eyes and stared at the dried palm leaves that made up the wall of the hut. Ann pushed on, because she knew if she didn't, she'd never again find the courage to address it. "I'm a psychiatrist. This last week has been...bizarre for me. If I told any of my colleagues what I thought I saw, what I think really happened, they'd tell me I'd had a genuine, acute psychotic split from reality."

Mike eased away just enough to look down into her eyes in the warm silence between them. "What's reality, anyway?" he began. "Do any of us really know? I sure don't." His mouth curved ruefully as he studied Ann's shadowed, questioning gaze. He gestured to the door of the hut. "When I came here, to the Village of the Clouds, I was taught to lead with my heart first, *querida,* and my head second. I know I see things here—" Mike pressed her hand more firmly against his heart "—that my eyes don't see. So what's more important? A head's reality check? Or the heart's check of how you or I really feel on a visceral level?"

She managed a slight, strained smile. "I'm confused, Mike. And I'm scared. I feel lost in one way and so terribly vulnerable in another."

His smile dissolved. "I know you're scared. So am I," he confided in a low tone as he held her hands. "Not for the same reasons, though." He lifted his head and gestured toward the door. "We're safe here in the Village of the Clouds. Escovar will never find us here. It's one of the few places on Mother Earth where we're really safe. It's a haven where you can heal, Ann. That's why I brought you here."

She gazed through the doorway. The view outside looked like

any other village in the Andes. Chickens clucked contentedly; dogs yapped and ran among the huts, playfully chasing one another; women cooked over small fires with tripods and black kettles. Yet it felt different here and Ann couldn't figure out why.

"It's a beautiful name for a village," she whispered, returning her attention to Mike. In the light and shadow of the hut, his face looked harsh. She could still see remnants of exhaustion beneath his eyes, and in the way his mouth was set. She realized that Mike was trying to buoy her spirits, to help her feel more at ease here.

"I was brought here many years ago, Ann, when I was dying. My chopper had been shot out of the sky by Escovar and his men. I leaped out of it before it hit the ground and exploded. The blast knocked me into the jungle, but saved my life. Escovar's men were hot on my trail. I took a ricocheted bullet in this thigh," he continued, pointing to his leg. "The damn thing nicked my femoral artery and I lay bleeding to death in a shallow depression as they got closer and closer."

She felt anguish in her heart and she watched a somber darkness cover his face. "What happened?"

"Several things. This old shaman by the name of Grandfather Adaire appeared, almost as if by magic, out of the bush with two of his students, another man and a woman. He saved my life. He brought me here with the permission of Grandmother Alaria..." Mike's voice softened "...to mend. Only my week-long stay with them turned into a year-long stay."

"A year? Did the army think you were dead?"

He chuckled a little. "It was real convenient to disappear. I stayed here, fell in love with the village, with the people, found out a lot about myself that I'd been wondering about for years, and went into training with Adaire and Alaria, the elders here at the village. When I returned to Lima a year later, everyone believed I had died and been resurrected. They thought I was a ghost. I told them I'd survived the crash, but sustained a head injury and had amnesia until only recently. Once I realized who I was, I came back to the real world."

"And people believed you?" Ann demanded incredulously. She saw the mischievous smile creep across his face. There was such a little boy inside this man's body and she found herself starved for a little of his laughter and gentle teasing.

"Why wouldn't they believe me? I was a trained paramedic." Mike touched the left side of his head. "Look at this scar. I got it in that crash. That would have been enough to convince them."

"What were their options? Reality versus...what?"

"Not everything," Mike cautioned, "is a delusional episode, Ann."

"No? I can't tell if I'm dreaming or imagining things anymore."

"Well," he murmured, "there's another choice among the mystical people of Peru."

"This had better be good, Houston."

A fierce tide of emotion swept through him as he saw her rallying for the first time since almost dying. There was a fire in her eyes, her cheeks were slightly flushed and that luscious, orchid-shaped mouth was turned up in a hint of a smile, just pleading to be kissed again. He smiled at her returning spark of defiance.

"Adaire and Alaria would ask you to consider that shamans, such as they are, cross continually between the worlds. They stand with one foot firmly planted in the reality of the here and now that you are familiar with. And—" Mike raised his hand and made a circular motion around the hut—"they keep one foot in the other dimensions, or what they call worlds which intersect this very same space. Most people can't see them, shamans are trained to be aware of them."

"Worlds? I have trouble with just one reality. I'm sure I'd go over the edge if there was more than one continuously overlapping it. Anyone would."

"Patience," Mike chided. "Don't be so quick to judge just yet. Shamans have a special ability to move into what I call an altered state. They can tune in, sort of like a radio set, to one or more frequencies simultaneously. They can be here, with us, or out there, in the other worlds. And they switch back and forth by choice."

"Lately," Ann admitted, "that's how I feel—like I'm being flipped through a hundred television channels. I see so many different, shifting scenes. I hear things, smell and taste things.... I've never had this happen before, Mike.''

"If I told you that what you're experiencing is normal, would it make those worry lines on your brow go away?'' he asked, caressing her wrinkled brow with his index finger. Ann sighed and closed her eyes as he stroked her forehead. Mike understood the power of touch. Lately, Ann was wanting more and more of it.

"Sometimes,'' he began slowly, holding her gaze once she opened her eyes again, "things happen in our life that throw us into chaos. We don't know which end is up. Or what is right or wrong. The only gyroscope I know that will hold the true course is here, in my chest.''

"The heart,'' Ann said, studying his softened expression. She was seeing another side to Mike now. Usually, he was always on guard, wary and alert. Here in this hut, this village, he was not shifting his attention from her to his surroundings continuously. Part of her truly began to relax and believe that they were safe.

"Yep. You're bang on, Doc.''

She grinned a little. "I think I'm getting better.'' She patted her stomach. "I'm starving to death, Mike.''

His brows rose. "Really? You're hungry?''

"I feel like a starving jungle cat.''

"I see....'' Slowly extricating himself, he rose and said, "I'll go get Moyra, then. She'll help you out of that nightgown and into some decent clothes. While she's taking care of you, I'll scare up some fresh hen's eggs and be just outside the hut here, cooking them over the fire.''

Who was Moyra? Ann was about to ask, but Mike disappeared out the door before she could say anything. To her total surprise, a young woman in her early thirties, her hair long, black and shiny, her eyes a lively forest green, skipped into the hut.

"Ah, there you are!'' she exclaimed. "I'm Moyra. Of late, from Canada. I'm a student in training here at the village. You must be Ann.'' She knelt down, setting a colorful skirt and white blouse on the pallet. Holding out her slender hand to Ann, she said happily, "It's so *nice* to meet you at last!''

At last? Ann slowly took her hand. "Th-thank you.'' She regarded her. "You're from Canada?''

Chuckling indulgently, Moyra nodded. "Originally I'm an Irish colleen. I emigrated to Peru. When I was older, I moved to Canada for two years to help a good friend of mine, Jessica Donovan, run her orchid greenhouse. I arrived here a year ago for further training with Grandmother Alaria. And you are from the States, we understand?"

"Yes...I am."

"Well," Moyra murmured, "while you're here with us, I've volunteered to be your maid-in-waiting. Michael isn't too well himself, yet. He did too much. I told the elders I'd step in and be of help when and where I could. Well, what do you think? Will this chemise fit you?"

Her upbeat, joyful mood and quick wit made Ann reticent. She saw the lively sparkle in Moyra's large, slightly tilted green eyes. Her face was oval, and when Ann looked at her, she felt as if she were looking at a cat's face.

"It—looks okay...."

"I'm so sorry," Moyra purred in her husky voice. "I'm rushing on like a wild creek in spring flood and here you are, feeling abandoned to a stranger. Michael isn't far away. He's just outside, as a matter of fact. He felt you might feel a little more comfortable with a woman helping you bathe and dress than him trying to do it."

Moyra was literally reading her mind. Ann stared at her as a red flush crept into Moyra's face.

"Dear me, there I go again. I owe you a second apology, Ann. Don't mind me, the blithering colleen from the Emerald Isle and all. I was just so charged up, getting to meet you. Michael has told us so *much* about you! About your bravery under fire. How you saved the lives of men and women who risked their lives helping others. How valiant and courageous you are." She moved her hands in a nervous, fluttering gesture. "First things first. You must bathe. We have hot springs located just a few steps behind this hut. Do you think you can stand? I'll help you walk to them." She grabbed at a woven bag. "Grandmother Alaria asked me to wash you with this very special soap she made. She said it would make you feel stronger. And heal quicker. It is from a very special orchid with healing powers. Well? Are you up to it?'' She tilted her head, her smile warm and engaging.

Ann managed a soft laugh. ''A bath sounds like a dream come true.'' The feverish sweat had left her feeling very dirty, and she yearned for a warm bath to scrub away the memory of her deathly illness. ''And is Alaria your grandmother?''

Moyra smiled gently. ''We use the terms grandmother and grandfather to honor the elders who keep this village safe for all of us. They're also a term of endearment. In a greater sense, we are all connected by the invisible flow of life around and through us. Therefore, all elders are like grandparents to all of us.''

Ann nodded. ''What a beautiful concept.'' And it was. The warmth and sincerity in Moyra's eyes made Ann smile a little in response.

''Around here,'' Moyra said pertly, rising in one lithe, graceful motion, ''where the clouds meet the other worlds, whatever you need will manifest. It's that simple and wonderful.'' She extended her hand. ''Want to try to walk a bit, luv?''

Gripping Moyra's long, expressive fingers, Ann slowly stood up. Dizziness assailed her momentarily, but Moyra quickly wrapped her long, thin arm around her. ''I've got towels and a robe waiting at the spring,'' she assured her. ''Just look down and concentrate on putting one foot in front of the other.''

''I'm stuffed, Mike,'' Ann protested as he tried to scrape some of his scrambled eggs onto her plate. They sat at a rough-hewn table on handmade chairs cut from mahogany and held together with thin, tough jungle vines.

''One last chance...'' he teased.

With a quick laugh, Ann held up her hands. ''*Finito,* Major Houston. I've eaten enough for three men.''

Darkly, he spooned the last of the tasty eggs into his mouth. ''You must have lost ten pounds. Maybe more.'' Ann was excessively thin and that wasn't good. Still, the bath at the hot springs, getting her hair washed and putting fresh clothes on, under Moyra's warm care, had perked Ann up considerably. But Houston wasn't fooled. He knew she was trying to rally, and that took a lot of energy she really didn't have.

"If I keep eating like this, I'll gain it back in a real hurry," Ann retorted good-naturedly. From the table she could look out the open window over the rest of the village. It was a beautiful place, with white, churning clouds hanging just to the north of them like billowing, constantly moving curtains. It was near noon, she supposed. The sun was directly overhead and shining brightly on the village, which sat in a flower-strewn meadow ringed on one side by jungle and on the other by grassy slopes that led up to the craggy, snow-clad Andes towering above.

Mike took the plates and set them aside. "I think you need to rest now, *querida*. You're looking pale." In fact, he could see the fine blue veins beneath her eyes, a telltale sign of impending exhaustion.

"I'm just a little tired," Ann protested.

Mike got up and pulled her chair back for her. The simple white peasant's blouse with short sleeves and a lace collar that revealed her collarbones made her look excruciatingly beautiful. The red-and-purple cotton skirt hung to her ankles, and Moyra had located a pair of open-toed sandals to protect her feet.

"Come on, I want to take you to one of the hammocks strung just outside our hut. You can let the soft breeze rock you to sleep."

The invitation sounded wonderful. Ann felt his hand settle around her elbow and steady her as she rose slowly to her feet.

"I wish I didn't feel like such a weakling," she complained as he placed his arm around her waist and drew her next to him.

"There's a time to be weak and a time to be strong, wild orchid." He studied her from beneath his dark brows as they left the hut. "I'll be strong for you now. It's your turn to lean on me, okay?"

She gave him a slight smile. "You know I'm not used to asking for help."

"I know." He sighed, squeezing her gently as they slowly moved around the hut. "Especially asking a man." He saw her frown. "I understand more than you realize."

Ann felt sadness and hurt move through her heart. Mike deserved her trust and love—she shouldn't be holding him up as a scapegoat for what another man had done to her many years before. "We need time to talk, Mike."

"And we'll get that—here," he assured her gently. "But not now."

"Okay..." The warm spring breeze wafted several strands of hair against her cheek. Ann noted more men in the village now, gathered around the tripods, eating and talking. Every once in a while she heard laughter. It was good, healthy laughter and she found herself smiling. There were two Pau d'arco trees no more than six feet apart near their hut. Strung between them was a woven hammock.

"Climb in," Mike urged, and he helped her sit down and then stretch out along the length of it. He took a white cotton blanket that Moyra had thoughtfully left behind, and shaking it open, he laid it across Ann. Her lashes were already closing.

"Thanks, Mike," she murmured. "I guess I'm more tired than I thought...."

He gently rocked the hammock, and within moments, Ann had spiraled into sleep. Moyra had made her a cup of herbal tea earlier. It had contained a natural sleeping aid. Right now, Ann needed rest in order to heal.

Mike wanted to remain there, standing over her and watching her sleep, but he felt Grandfather Adaire telepathically call to him. Reluctantly, Mike released his hold on the end of the hammock, giving it one more gentle tug. The breeze and birds would keep Ann company for a little while until he could return.

Moving around the hut, Mike wasn't surprised to see the elder waiting patiently for him. In the years Mike had known him, the old man hadn't aged one bit. Adaire's face was long, and lined like a road map, his shining gray eyes droopy looking, his white hair still peppered with strands of red to remind everyone of his Scottish heritage. His reddish white beard gave him the look of a sage, well deserved.

"She sleeps well," Adaire noted, shifting his wooden staff, topped with bright red, yellow and blue parrot feathers, into his left hand.

Mike sighed with relief. "Yes." He searched the elder's eyes. "Thank Grandmother Alaria for giving us permission to come here. I know you didn't have to allow us entrance. I didn't know what else to do. Everything blew up in our faces. Ann almost died.... I didn't ever expect to have to put all of you in danger like this.''

"It has been five years since your last visit, my son. Alaria said you were long overdue for a visit, and you are always welcome, no matter the reason for your appearance. And you did not put us in danger. We can only place ourselves in danger." He laid his bony hand on Houston's shoulder. "Ann is not unlike us," he murmured as he led him back into the hut. "Her heart is pure. What else can one ask for?" They sat down at the table. Adaire moved very slowly but with ageless grace.

Mike folded his hands and waited as Adaire eased carefully into a creaking chair. To anyone else, he would appear to be a native of Peru, dressed as he was in a pair of threadbare pants made of dark brown cotton and a long-sleeved peasant's shirt too large for his tall, regal frame. Of course, Adaire's skin was white, as he was from Scotland. He had come from a long line of druid priests, Mike knew. Adaire's ancestors had taken care of the sacred oak grove on the Island of Mona, which had been overrun and destroyed by Caesar's army so long ago. Mike really didn't know how old the elder was. Not that it mattered, because Mike honored his wisdom and gentle form of leadership. Alaria, his wife, shared the leadership duties of the village with him. She was the primary emissary in physical form from the Great Goddess and was technically the leader of the village. All queries were taken to the main lodge, but in the end, it was Alaria who made the final decision. Both she and her husband were powerful shamans who led with their hearts.

Adaire's bushy white brows knitted as he placed his hands on his thighs. "We must talk."

Mike grimaced. "I know what you're going to tell me."

"You came very close to giving your life away for hers."

Houston nodded and held the elder's gray, probing gaze. "I did it willingly."

"No doubt."

Becoming grim, Mike flexed his hand and remained very still. "I couldn't lose her, Grandfather."

"Because?"

"I..." He hesitated, his mouth growing dry. "I care...for her."

"You have loved twice before."

Mike held the elder's measuring stare. The word *love* grated on him. Adaire could be very intimidating when he wanted to be, and Mike could feel the man's mind probing his own. Houston offered no resistance to the gentle intrusion. He had nothing to hide from Adaire or Alaria. He knew Adaire was here to get the facts from him and share them with Alaria.

"You have loved two other women and they have been torn from you," Adaire said. "What makes you think Ann's fate will be any different?"

Mike's heart thudded with sudden fear. Pursing his lips, he rasped, "I don't think it would be different—that's why I'm trying to keep my distance from her...not letting her know my real feelings...." Hell, he'd barely admitted them to himself, much less Adaire. Mike knew he could never speak of them to Ann.

Adaire lifted his grizzled head and stroked his beard, the silence thickening. "Does she know?"

"About me? Us? No."

"She must know so she can make her own choice in all of this. You cannot lead her on."

A ragged sigh escaped from Mike's lips. "I know that, Grandfather." And he felt fear eating at him. What *would* Ann do once she knew the truth about him—his "kind"? Would she run in terror from him? Think that she'd gone insane in an insane world? Or would her care for him override the truth about him? And what if she *could* accept him? What did he think he was going to do—put her at risk of Escovar? *No.*

Scowling, Mike looked past Adaire and out the window toward the flower-strewn meadow. "I try not to care what she will think when she finally asks those questions, Grandfather. But I'd be lying if I said I didn't care."

"She's uncertain. And scared. You have little time among us before you must return to your duties in the other world."

Mike studied the old man. "I intend to take her out of here when she's recuperated and get her on the next plane for the States. And then I'm going after Escovar again. At least," he muttered, opening his hands, "that's my plan right now. How long can

Grandmother Alaria and the elders hold the power for us to remain here?''

''Two weeks.''

Two weeks. Mike knew that an outside energy such as Ann's could cause turmoil to the energy grid that made this village completely safe from any enemy encounters. It took the minds and hearts of many villagers meditating all day long to hold the protective shield in place and keep everyone who came here for physical training safe. Could he get Ann to accept him, his way of living, in that time? It was too short a period. Mike rubbed his jaw, and his voice hardened. ''She's been through hell already, Adaire.''

''I can see that. You know of her past?''

Scowling, Houston muttered, ''I've got an inkling. I haven't actively searched her mind. I wanted to let Ann trust me enough over time to tell me herself...to share it with me when she was comfortable.''

With a sigh, Adaire opened his long, bony fingers. The calluses on both his palms were thick and yellow. ''She is braver than you believe, my son. Don't treat her like a weakling, because she is not one. When you love, you protect. That is your nature. You cannot help it.''

Smarting beneath the accusation that he loved Ann, Mike pushed his chair away and stood. ''Yeah, well, it sure as hell didn't stop Escovar from killing the other two women I loved, did it?'' He lowered his voice and tried to control his runaway feelings. Adaire sat there, serene and seemingly unaffected by his stormy response.

''The path of jaguar medicine is not an easy one, my son.''

''No damn kidding.'' Mike raked his fingers through his hair and moved restlessly around the room. ''Don't you think I'm afraid it will happen all over again? Hell, it almost did. I heard Ann cry out for me and I felt her bleeding to death.... I got there almost too late to save her.'' He turned, studying Adaire. ''Yes, I'm protective. And I'd damn well go to the threshold of death again for her. I'm not sorry about my choices, Adaire. I can tell from the feelings I'm sensing around you that you aren't happy with me or what I did to save her life.''

"Please," the elder murmured gently, "be at peace with your-self, Michael. Come, sit down. Sit...."

The lulling baritone of Adaire's voice was like balm blanketing Mike's raging, unchecked emotions. He came and sat down, then he rubbed his face with his hand. "I'm sorry, Grandfather. I'm out of sorts."

Just then Alaria entered the hut. Mike smiled wearily up at her. She, too, was ageless in his eyes, the energy surrounding her like the pulsing of sunlight. Her unconditional love embraced him, and as he met her sparkling, dark green eyes, he felt her smile even though her full lips did not move. She stood nearly six feet tall, and her thin form reminded him of the most graceful of ballerinas. Her face was full and oval, her cheeks high and her nose thin, shouting of her aristocratic roots. Once, Adaire had told him, she had been high priestess of the sacred oak grove in England, though she was originally from Wales. How long ago she had come to Peru, Mike had no idea, but she, too, was descended from a long line of druids, and the stamp of leadership on her bearing was obvious.

"You are weakened by the considerable gift you gave to her, because of the bravery of your heart," Alaria said. "You will need these two weeks to recuperate yourself. Does Ann realize you need to heal, also?"

"No, Grandmother." Mike rose and pulled out the other chair for her. "And I don't want her to know. She's been through enough." He sat back down and stared at the rough, wooden ta-bletop. "Ann worries at the drop of a hat. If she even thinks I look ill, she gets upset."

"Must be love, eh?" Alaria teased gently as she laid her long thin hands upon the table.

He slowly raised his chin and looked into Alaria's large eyes, which were filled with warmth. As leader of the village, she wore around her neck a golden torque with a huge rectangular emerald of absolute clarity. Mike had been told by another student a long time ago that the torque was passed down to each successive leader of the Village of the Clouds. No one could remember how long Alaria had been leader. It was whispered that she was nearly a thousand years old and that because her heart was so pure, she aged very slowly. Right now, Mike thought she looked like she was near eighty, her gray-and-red hair plaited into two thick braids. "I...don't know when it happened. I swear, I don't," Mike rasped. Finally, beneath her gentle gaze, he admitted in a choked voice, "I wasn't expecting to fall in love ever again. Not with my track record." Grimacing, he muttered, "Ann walked into my life like a lightning bolt. I felt like someone jerked the rug out from under my feet."

"I can see that," Alaria said, smiling kindly. "Ann is your true mate, you know. You have shared your blood with her. She is a part of you—of us—because of that, whether she wants to be or not. I hope she will discover that being a part of the Jaguar Clan is not always harsh and challenging. We are glad to hold this energy for you—and her."

Mike reached over and gripped the elder's hand in silent thanks for her graciousness. He felt the parchmentlike skin, the bones of her work-worn fingers and the incredible strength they still possessed. More than anything, Mike felt life pulsing like a thousand suns through her fingers into him.

"Let us help you for a little while, eh?" Alaria suggested. "You need some care, too. You fight what lies in your heart. You are afraid to love again, with good reason. You are so torn now, my son."

Wasn't that the truth? In the past, Mike had had no one to turn to. His family in the Village of the Clouds was never far away, but to run to them and beg for help in every crisis wasn't his way. No, Mike respected what this village was and why it existed. He felt the warm energy begin to flow up into his arm. Within moments, he was very drowsy.

"Lay your arm on the table as a pillow," Alaria suggested, "and close your eyes and allow me to send you the healing energy you need."

Houston nodded and, without another word, did as the elder instructed. As he closed his eyes, head resting on his arm, his hand beneath Alaria's, a sense of utter peace flowed through him and erased all the anguish, pain and anger he'd felt earlier. Still, his last thought was: *How am I going to tell Ann about me? What will she do when she sees I'm not what she thinks I am? How will she react to being a member of the Jaguar Clan?*

Chapter 11

"This place," Ann began, "reminds me of the United Nations, Mike. It's not a simple agricultural village of Quechua Indians as I first thought." She sat with her back against a stout tree at the edge of a flower-strewn meadow, the shade of the tree shielding her from the sunlight. Above, churning white cumulus clouds drifted through the sky like a long roll of white cotton against the high slopes where the meadow met the magnificent snow-covered Andes. She picked at the ripe papaya that he'd peeled and carefully sliced to share with her.

"No one eats meat around here, I've discovered. Just fruits, vegetables and grains. And there are no babies here. Just adults." She met Houston's gaze as he sat less than a foot away from her, legs crossed, his arms resting on his thighs. "In the past five days, I've discovered a lot of what I'd call inconsistencies." She pointed to the fruit in his hand. "This is spring, not summer. This fruit shouldn't be available here yet. What did they do, ship it from somewhere? There are no automobiles, no trucks that I've seen to bring it here."

Ann looked around the meadow. "Yet it's a beautiful place. I love it here and feel so at peace." Her gaze traveled back to Mike.

"And I've never seen you as relaxed as you are here." Or as playful, she thought, realizing once more how precious his little-boy side, his frequent, teasing grins or the laughter reflected in his dark blue eyes, were to her. Frowning, she bit off a piece of the sweet, dark orange fruit.

"And now that I'm well and my brain's functioning again, I've got a lot of questions. Like, how did you hear me call you? I didn't pick up a phone and yell for help. And the nuns didn't know what was going on." She held his shadowed gaze. "So how did you know? I mean, I know what you told me about your telepathic skills, but still, it seems so unusual. And looking back and remembering more and more of what took place, Mike, I *know* without a doubt that I should be dead." Her voice lowered. "And I'm not. Something extraordinary—maybe an inexplicable miracle—happened, involving you...and...a large cat of some kind. This time, I don't want you to be evasive. We need to sit and talk about this. Every time I try to broach this topic with you, you start teasing me and we get to laughing, or you...well, you hold me, kiss me, and I lose track of where I wanted to go with the conversation...."

Houston watched the puzzlement and confusion in Ann's expression. It was time and he knew it. He'd been trying to delay this day, but he knew it would come. Ann was simply too intelligent, too curious, to let her near-death experience go without explanation. Before, he'd been able to distract her—with himself, with the attention he showered on her, the love he shared with her. At night, they slept in one another's arms. He would hold her and she would sleep like an innocent child in his embrace. It was sweet agony, because Mike would not take advantage of Ann or the situation. He wanted to, but he didn't dare. Things had to be that way between them or the solid trust that was being built would be seriously fractured. Mike knew this day of truth was coming and he hadn't wanted to let his raging hormones get out of control. Too many more important things were at stake.

Lifting his head, he gave her a strained smile. Today Ann wore a lilac-colored cotton blouse. It was very simple, the scoop neck accentuating her collarbones and slender neck. He watched as she nervously smoothed the folds of the dark blue cotton skirt again and again around her legs.

Setting the knife and the papaya aside on a small red cloth where they had placed the rest of their lunch, he moved to her side. Settling behind her, he drew Ann between his outstretched legs and allowed her to lean back against him. He savored these intimate moments with her. They were natural. And they both needed it—and each other. Her dark hair tickled his chin as she lifted her face to gaze up at him. Their mouths were a bare inch from one another. The urge to lean down, to take that wild-orchid mouth of hers was nearly his undoing.

"I have a story to tell you," he began in a low tone. "And it may sound like I'm making it up, but I'm not. You're going to have to trust me like never before. Don't ask questions until I'm done, and then I'll try my best to answer them as fully as I can. Fair enough?" His heart was beating hard and his fear sent a rush of adrenaline through him. In telling her the truth, he knew there was every chance she would leave him—today, forever. Yet Grandmother Alaria was right: Ann had a right to know. He would not live a lie with her. If she loved him enough, and he wasn't sure that she did, then her love would sustain her through this coming hour of bare-bones truth telling, and she would remain at his side. But even that thought tore him apart. Did he want Ann to love him? Mike was more scared now than at any time in his life.

"Fair enough," she whispered. Ann took his arms and guided them around her waist, placing his hands in her lap and covering them with hers. How she loved these special times with him, alone in this beautiful meadow. She was grateful Mike did not take advantage of her need to be held. On some level, he understood exactly what she needed.

"Okay," Houston murmured, easing her head back against her shoulder, "close your eyes and listen." He felt terror seizing him. Mike had known fear in his lifetime, but never this bad. The lump in his throat seemed to grow. To hell with it. He *had* to reveal who he really was.

"My mother was part Yaqui, part Quechua Indian, born in northern Peru. She was one of ten children, a middle child. When she was six, her parents moved the entire family to Mexico City. She got a job and worked hard. She literally pulled herself up from poverty, eventually making a middle-class living as a typist at the U.S. Embassy. It was there she met my father, a marine corps officer attached to the embassy.'' Mike nudged several reddish gold strands of hair away from Ann's cheek, where the breeze wafted them. How peaceful she looked. His heart ached with the loss he knew was coming.

''They fell in love with one another. It took a year for my father to get orders stateside, but once he did, they got married and she became an American citizen. I came along four years later, their only kid. When I was old enough, I realized I was different. For one thing, the color of my skin in a school of white kids set me apart, but it was more than that. It went a lot deeper. When I was nine, my mother sat me down and told me of her people's—her family's—unique history.''

Ann opened her eyes and looked up at him through her lashes. Mike was gazing away from her now. His profile was marked with tension. Why? Feeling his turmoil, she automatically smoothed her hand down his darkly haired arm. ''How were you different?'' she asked gently. Instantly, she saw his brows dip. His mouth tightened. Truly concerned, Ann eased from him enough to turn and place her arm around his broad shoulders. ''Mike?''

A ragged sigh tore from his lips. ''I—my mother said she was a priestess from the Jaguar Clan. I didn't know what that meant— at least, not at that time. She told me that one member of each generation could choose to become a member of that clan. It is the oldest continuing medicine line in the Americas. Jaguars used to roam the U.S., particularly the Southwest, until they were all killed off by white men who wanted their skins for their women to wear.'' He ran his hand through his hair in an aggravated motion and refused to look at Ann, although he could feel the probing heat of her gaze on him. Desperately, Mike searched for the right words, the right way to tell her.

''Among the Indian nations, there's always a family heritage of healers and doctors, just like there's a line of people with other finely honed skills, such as artisans, weavers, hunters or leaders. My mother was a healer and a member of the Jaguar Clan. From the time I was nine until I was eighteen, she gave me special training exercises to do every day. She told me that at the right time, I would meet a teacher who would help open these gifts within me, the ancient wisdom I carried, genetically, and I would begin to use this knowledge.

"I didn't know what that meant." Mike looked down at the grass beside him. "I do now..." His stomach tightened into a very painful knot. Unconsciously, he rubbed that area with his hand. Ann's fingers lightly stroking the back of his neck eased the tension there. But then, her touch was always healing to him. "My mother said that I would have to go to Peru to meet this teacher. Well, as fate would have it, I joined the army and was sent to Peru over ten years ago because I spoke fluent Spanish and I was good at what I did as a training advisor. I'd long ago forgotten about my destiny, the event that my mother had said would happen at the 'right' time."

Lifting his chin, Mike gestured toward the distant village shimmering in the sunlight. "When I came to Peru, I heard all kinds of myths and legends about jaguars down here. How they would track a man in the jungle for days, look directly into his eyes, freeze him so he couldn't run and then pounce on and eat him. I'd heard about the mysterious Jaguar Clan that lived up in the highlands, near the foot of the Andes. Things like that."

"When Escovar shot that chopper out from under me, and I was bleeding to death, it was Grandfather Adaire who rescued me. I was dying and I knew it. I was a paramedic—I knew the score. And I knew that a grizzled old man draped in a jaguar skin with two younger students in tow wasn't going to save my hide, either."

"Well," Mike rasped, "I was wrong. I've never told anyone about this, Ann. You're the first to know...." He met and held her somber gaze.

"Whatever you tell me, Mike, is safe with me. You know that." She reached out and laced her fingers with his.

He nodded, lifting her hand and kissing the back of it gently. "My life has always been in your hands," he whispered, meeting her widening gaze. "My trust of you is not the question."

Her flesh tingled and a slight ache began deep within her. Ann knew that feeling, for it often occurred when Mike touched her, or even kissed her fleetingly. "Unless Adaire had a surgical unit hidden somewhere in this village, there's no way he could have repaired your torn femoral artery," she agreed softly.

"Exactly," Mike said, turning and looking across the meadow. His voice lowered. "I passed out shortly after that, from blood loss. I had this wild, incredible dream that really wasn't a dream." He pointed toward the center of the large meadow.

"When I came to, I was in one of these huts like you found yourself in. Grandmother Alaria was with me, sitting serenely on a pallet next to me, just regarding me in a very kind, motherly way. She told me she was the leader of this village and that I was welcome to stay with them. As I got oriented, I realized there was someone else in the small hut with us, in the shadows. I was very weak, and it took everything I had to turn my head in that direction.

"I damn near had a cardiac arrest, for I saw this huge, stocky female jaguar suddenly appear and come toward me, where I lay. I thought I was a goner. She had a huge, flat head with the biggest, most incredible gold-and-black eyes I'd ever seen. I feared her. I started to look around for something—anything with which to protect myself from her charge. I knew I was fooling myself, because the jaguar is a massive animal. Before I could do anything, she was there at my side, licking at the wound on my thigh. I could feel her rough, pink tongue as she licked that area again and again. I felt this strange, hot wave of burning energy enter my leg. I remember moaning in pain, and then I lost consciousness again."

With a slight, strained chuckle, Houston shook his head. "Brother, was I naive back then. Grandmother Alaria laughed at my reaction. After I regained consciousness, that big cat lay down next to me, purring loudly and just watched me. I was so scared I didn't know what to do. The cat just lay there, switching her tail every now and then and watching me like a mother might her child. Gradually, my fear was replaced with...something else. It was then that Alaria told me it was about time I met my guardian, this beautiful female jaguar who had saved my worthless neck many times over. It was the first time I ever met her in this reality."

Puzzled, Ann stared at his profile. Houston's features were hard and uncompromising now, like those of the soldier she'd seen earlier in Arizona. "This guardian...does it have to do with your mother's medicine? Her predictions for you?"

Mike knew Ann would piece it together. "Yes...."

"But," Ann murmured, opening her hands, "how did this jaguar heal your torn femoral artery? That's impossible, Mike."

He slowly turned his head. "I was demanding the same answers from Grandmother Alaria. I told her I was dead, that this was heaven or something. I didn't understand. I couldn't have survived my wound. I should have bled out in four minutes or less, game over."

"Exactly." Ann saw a sheen of perspiration covering his dark gold skin. The suffering line of his mouth made her reach out. The act was intimate. As she brushed the tight line of his mouth, she saw the startled look in his eyes and the instant, burning desire for her. "I feel your fear," she whispered, again caressing his mouth. It was a strong, good mouth. One she wanted to kiss, to cling to and learn from forever. The day was coming soon, Ann felt, when she would walk beyond her last fear barrier and do just that: fully love him. If only he would stop pushing her away...if only he would admit what was so obvious in his touch, his eyes and his voice.

Ann's touch was unexpected. Searing. Hope suddenly threaded through Mike. He captured her hand and pressed a long kiss against her palm. And then he pressed it to his cheek. "Ann, I'm going to tell you something now, and I pray...I hope you'll believe me...."

The words came out filled with such anguish that she didn't know how to respond. "I know I'm pragmatic," she said softly, "and I can't explain how your guardian saved your life, but Mike, there's a lot in our world that can't always be explained in rational ways." She shrugged. "I believe in miracles. I always have, whether science can explain them or not. Things like this, what you've shared with me, make me curious. They don't scare me."

Taking the last of his fleeing courage, Houston met and held her warm blue-gray gaze. There was such compassion and love in her eyes for him. He felt it through every cell in his tense, frightened body. Still, he had yet to discover how much of his spiritual heritage she would truly be able to accept. "I want you to look out there, in the center of the meadow," he ordered her darkly. "And no matter what happens, know you're safe with me, Ann."

Puzzled, Ann watched him stand. He leaned down, grasped her hand and pulled her to her feet. She felt his arm go around her in an almost protective motion and a warm feeling spread through her. "Okay," she said "what am I suppose to see?"

As she stood beside Mike, their bodies lightly touching, Ann watched the meadow. Though she couldn't see it, she felt a strange shift of energy around Mike. And then she saw a dark, nebulous shadow begin to form no more than a hundred yards from where they stood. Frowning, she blinked. Was she seeing things? The darkness began to take a more identifiable form. In the next minute, there was a powerful female jaguar standing before them. Her gold-and-black coat gleamed in the sunlight.

Gasping, Ann took a step back. Instantly, she felt Mike's arm tighten around her.

"You're safe," he rasped. Would she run in terror? Risking a look down at her, he saw Ann's gaze riveted on the jaguar standing serenely in the meadow. His guardian looked at them, her tail twitching lazily from side to side. The terror, the shock on Ann's features, made his heart sink. His gut tightened painfully.

"Ann, listen to me," he pleaded, "that's my spirit guardian. That's the jaguar that saved my life years ago."

"But," Ann argued hoarsely, "she wasn't there a minute ago. She gave him a wild look and then stared back at the gold-and-black cat. "Or was she? Was she there, lying in the tall grass all along, and just stood up? The grass is four feet deep there..."

Turning, Houston gripped her shoulders. "No," he admitted, "she wasn't lying in the grass, Ann. I called her mentally. She came on my command from the other worlds. That's what really happened."

Ann gave him a strange, guarded look. Houston's eyes were narrowed and intense, and she felt the desperation in his voice. Peering around him, she stared at the jaguar in the distance. "What do you mean, you called her? I didn't hear your voice."

He smoothed some strands away from her cheek. Her face had gone pale. She was truly frightened. And so was he. He soothed her tight shoulders in a stroking motion. "You felt me call her, didn't you?"

Torn between the magical appearance of the jaguar and Mike's intensity, she muttered, "Well—yes, I felt *something*...but—"

"You felt me mentally call my guardian," he said slowly and firmly, "that was all. Mental telepathy, Ann. It's not something foreign to your understanding. I know it isn't."

She swallowed hard. "Oh, God, Mike, that's the *same* jaguar I saw when I was...dying, I'd swear to it." She gave him a confused look. "She came first. She was standing in the light with me. And then she changed—into you.... Now I remember. Yes, you were the jaguar—and vice versa. Oh, God..."

The way she looked at him made him want to cry out. He was losing Ann. He felt her slipping away from him as the fear, the realization sank into her. Grimly, he pulled her into his embrace. He felt her resistance and then it dissolved. "Just let me hold you, okay?" he rasped. When her arms went around his torso, he breathed a small sigh of relief. At least she hadn't run from his arms—yet. She still sought safety there, instead of running away from him.

"For a year in this village, Grandfather Adaire and Grandmother Alaria trained me to do what I can do now. They said I had the necessary skills and talents to become a member of the Jaguar Clan, if that's what I wanted. At first," Houston breathed harshly against her hair, "I was like you. I was scared. I thought I was going crazy or that I'd died and was trapped somewhere between heaven and hell in this insane place where the impossible happened every minute of every day. If you wanted a papaya to eat, all you had to do was think it, and it appeared physically in front of you. If you were hot, you could visualize a cooling shower from overhead, and it would happen within minutes." He caressed Ann's hair and felt her heart beating like a caged bird fluttering in her breast. Anguished, he wanted to somehow protect her from the truth, but it was impossible.

"This place," he began awkwardly, "is so very, very special. In North America, there is a similar place, a sister to this, on the East Coast, in North Carolina. It's called Spirit Lake. The Cherokee people are the guardians of it. Places like this—if you aren't

supposed to see them, you won't. You can't gain access to them
without...meeting certain requirements. That's why we're safe
here. The Brotherhood of Darkness, our opposite energy, can't get
to us here. This place is off-limits, in a sense, to them. That's why,
when you awoke that first morning, you felt different. You mentioned it a number of times to me."

Ann eased away just enough to look up at him. "Y-yes."

"It's the energy here, the people who live here or visit here,"
he said simply. "That's the reason it's special. They are heart
centered, very spiritually advanced, and they can hold or create an
energy or reality. This village exists because of them."

"That jaguar just appeared out of *nowhere,* Mike. How can you
explain *that?*"

The trembling in Ann's voice tore at him. He gently turned her
around so that they could watch the jaguar, which stood patiently
out in the meadow. "I can't...at least, not in a scientific way—a
way you'd accept. Maybe later, when you understand more about
us..."

"Is she always with you?" Ann found herself wanting to know
if the jaguar was a mirage or if she was physically real. Her fear
was giving way to curiosity.

"Always." His mouth twisted in an effort to smile. "Usually,
she's invisible. I asked her to come and to appear so you could
see her."

"Would I see her if I wasn't here with you?"

"You saw her when you were dying of that fever, *querida,*
didn't you?"

Ann nodded, so many more memories of that terrible night
flooding her being. Throughout the last few days, more and more
of that night had been coming back to her. Now she vividly recalled it in its entirety. "She was there with me..." Ann breathed
raggedly.

"Yes," Mike admitted, "I sent her ahead to help you, to stabilize you the best she could energetically, until I could reach you
myself."

"Then I wasn't dreaming it! I saw her next to the bed while
you were holding me in your arms. I was lying between your legs

and you were holding me against you. I felt your heart, your breath in me..."

"And at that point, my guardian came over me and supplied the extra energy, the gift of life to you through me," Mike said humbly. "That is the gift of the jaguar, Ann—life or death."

She gripped his arms and closed her eyes, caught up in the entire sequence. Mike held her steady. "My God...then it really did happen. I didn't dream it. I thought I was having hallucinations due to my high fever...."

"Nice medical explanation for the magic of possibility," he told her wryly. Ann opened her eyes and he watched as her lips parted.

"That's why they call you the jaguar god? It isn't just a myth?"

Gently, Mike turned her and, placing his arm around her shoulders again, drew her against him. "Some of the stories being told are true, Ann. Some of them are gossip. The myth builds, changes and becomes ridiculous."

"I heard Pablo say that you brought people back from the dead."

Mike laughed, but the sound was strained. With a shake of his head, he said, "No, that's something I can't do. Only the Great Goddess could do that, and I'm afraid I'm only a terribly flawed human being. No...I can ask for intervention for someone who's dying...and if it's allowed, my guardian will help me pour my own energy and hers into that person to help save them."

"And that's how you saved me? You not only gave me your physical blood, but you gave me part of...you?" Ann searched his harsh face, his shadowed eyes. "A transfer of—what? Your life energy along with a blood transfusion?"

His hand tightened briefly on her shoulder. "Yes, exactly. I couldn't do it if I didn't...care for you, Ann," he told her in a low tone. "There are two types of Jaguar Clan members—those belonging to the Sisterhood of Light and those belonging to the Brotherhood of Darkness. I chose the path of light, Ann. And in order to help someone who's hurt or dying, I have to be in good stead with my heart and my emotions toward them."

"And your friend Antonio? I saw the jaguar come over you that time in the airport."

"Yes," Mike admitted, "you did."

"And he lived."

"My jaguar spirit and I interceded on his behalf, Ann. And it wasn't his time to go. The Goddess allowed him to survive. My guardian and I were only tools, if you will, for that life-giving energy to flow back into Antonio and save him. It's not an unlimited source. If I give too much of my energy, I could die. It's a delicate balance."

She was very quiet, digesting his explanation. "And the same thing took place to save me?"

Mike held her steady, demanding gaze. "Yes." He saw her wrestling with his explanations. She was honestly trying to accept them—and him. He felt it. There was one more test to go, and he felt the fear eat away at him.

"There's one more thing I need to show you, Ann," he told her. "You don't know everything about me, and it wouldn't be fair to you if I didn't tell you the rest."

She stood back as he began to unbutton his white, short-sleeved cotton shirt. Her mind reeled with possibilities, with confusion. "What are you talking about, Mike?"

He stripped out of the shirt, let it drop to the grass between them, then faced her. "When I finished my training, when I took my guardian as part of myself, something happened... My body became marked for life, to identify me as a member of the Jaguar Clan. It happened during the initiation when the exchange of spirits—of hers—" he pointed to the jaguar in the meadow "—and mine occurred."

Ann tried not to stare at Mike as he stood barechested before her. This was the first time she'd seen him partially unclad. He always wore cotton pajamas when they slept together. His chest was magnificent, the dark hair spread across the broad, well-muscled expanse. There wasn't an ounce of fat on him, and when he moved, each set of muscles bunched with clear definition telling her how physically powerful he was.

She scowled at her wandering thoughts. "Are you saying you and the jaguar experienced a transfusion of some kind?"

"Exactly. I hope—pray—that what I show you won't scare you, Ann. It could—and..." He took a deep, ragged breath. "I'm going to turn around and I want you to look at my left shoulder blade...."

This was it. The final truth. Houston felt as if the guillotine was coming down on his exposed neck as he slowly turned around so that Ann could look at his back.

"Oh, my God!"

He froze. And he waited. His heart contracted in anguish over her terror-filled cry. Twisting to look over his shoulder, he saw Ann standing, her eyes huge, her hands pressed against her mouth to stop a scream as she stared wildly at him—at his shoulder.

"It's real," he soothed. "Just try and get ahold on yourself, Ann. There's nothing to be afraid of. Believe me, there isn't. How long have you known me? Have I ever done anything to make you think I'm not—Mike Houston? Not a man?"

As his words fragmented in her mind, Ann felt dizzy and she had to force herself to remain standing. She had to be hallucinating! She had to be! This was impossible! But Mike's words were filled with urgency, with fear. She fought her own fear. Fear of what was real and what was not.

"My God, is that—this—real?" she asked, finally looking up into his blue eyes, which glittered with pain.

"As real as you and me, Ann. Touch it—me...and find out. Whatever you do, don't run, okay? I'm not some kind of—of monster, I'm a man. The same man you knew before you saw this—this mark of initiation into the Jaguar Clan."

Heart pounding, Ann tried to allow his pleading tone to soothe her fear. The mark on his body seemed impossible, and yet it was there. And it didn't go away when she blinked her eyes. No, it wasn't a hallucination. There was a moon-shaped patch the size of her palm that was covered with sleek dark gold fur with black crescents—the same fur as that of the jaguar that stood out in the meadow watching them. Ann wanted to reach out, to touch it to see if it was real.

"Touch me," Houston demanded. "Touch *me,* not 'it,' Ann. Don't separate the jaguar fur from me as a man, because you can't. That fur is a part of my flesh. It's not pasted on, like you're thinking. The first time I saw fur on my body was during my near-death experience. On my arm. But that disappeared when my guardian's energy left me. Then, when I took the initiation into the clan, this—happened. That's why I never let you see my upper body naked before this. I was afraid that if you saw it, you'd run away from me. You'd—'' his brows dipped ''—you'd be scared of me....''

Ann allowed her hands to drop from her mouth. She took a step back. "This is a lot to handle, Mike. You have to admit."

He turned to her. Grimly, he whispered, "Believe me, no one's more aware of that than me. I don't want to lose you...what we have, Ann. But I also know that I won't keep secrets from you, either. If you care for me...then you have to know. I can't live a lie. I never could." He avoided her searching gaze.

"And your wife? Did she know—about this?"

"I met Maria here at the village," he said wearily. "She was from Spain."

"And she was...part of this Jaguar Clan, too?"

He slowly bent over and retrieved his shirt. "Yes. We met and fell in love with one another while I was here that year, in training. Grandmother Alaria married us. We took our vows and we left the village and went back to the 'real world,' Lima."

"And she had that same...mark on her body?"

Grimly, he nodded. "Same mark, same place. Those who go through the initiation receive this mark."

Ann watched him knot the white shirt in his fist as he stood there before her. The suffering in his eyes tore at her and she felt his fear of losing her. "And why didn't it save her and the baby when Escovar murdered her?"

Houston looked up at the brilliant blue of the sky above them. "We have limits on our ability. We're not all equal in skills. Some of it is genetic ancestry, the rest has to do with where we are as a human being on our own spiritual path. We can be killed just like any other human being. When Maria was murdered, I went insane with rage. Escovar..." Mike shook his head. "He's pure evil. I don't know why I'm caught up in this death spiral dance with him, but I am. I didn't mean for his wife and children to die in that accident, but he believes I did it on purpose. I didn't. He even killed the man I sent to persuade him that it was an accident."

"And then," Ann whispered, "you met Tracy?"

"Yes. We fell in love. She worked as an intel officer at the American embassy in Lima."

"And she was a member of your...clan?"

"No," Mike said, studying Ann's face. Did he dare approach her? Or would she back away from him, the fear he saw in her eyes multiplying. He ached to know if she cared for him enough to deal with this revelation, with him being more than a man in some ways, and in others, so terribly flawed and human.

"Did Tracy know about that?" She pointed toward his left shoulder.

He nodded. "About six months into our relationship, I showed it to her, and I told her the truth, like I'm telling you now."

Ann nodded and rested her hand against her beating heart. "H-how did she react to it?"

"She was scared at first," he admitted. "Like you are now. But she loved...trusted me enough to transcend her fear of the unknown, of something...different and unexplainable in her rational view of the world."

With a shake of her head, Ann muttered, "Houston, you sure as hell know how to throw a woman a real curve."

He didn't know whether to laugh or cry. "Translated, what does that mean?"

Ann dropped her hands. "I need time to think through this, Mike. All of it—my nearly dying, what I saw and felt. This is all just too incredible, and yet it happened. And it's real or I wouldn't be standing here today, alive, and I know it." Moistening her lips, she gave him a beseeching look. "I want to be alone for a while."

"You've got it." Mike tried to control his fear. He knew Ann's proclivity for cold, hard logic. She couldn't be a psychotherapist without that left-brain ability. But would she try and explain all of this away with that powerful and intelligent mind of hers? "I just have one thing to say." Opening his hand toward her, Mike rasped, "This one time, don't let your head do all the talking and deciding for you. Let your heart have a say in this, too. That's all I ask, Ann...just that..."

She wrapped her arms around herself and stood feeling very alone in that moment. Mike was suffering cruelly from her decision to separate from him in order to think all of this over, but it was the only thing she could do. "My heart is always involved in every decision I make," she said gently.

He nodded. "I know it is. It's just that..." Fear consumed him. He'd nearly said *I love you....* The words froze in his mouth. His jaw ached because he so badly wanted to say them to her. "I know that it's your decision and in your hands—and heart." Mike tried to smile but didn't succeed as he pulled the shirt back over his upper body. "I'll move out of the hut for now. Whatever you decide, I'll abide by it, Ann. If this is too much for you to accept, I'll call Pablo and have him drive you back to Lima. You can catch the first flight going north, to the States, no questions asked. If you want to stay, on the other hand, I can't guarantee it's going to be a picnic. You know what's happened to the other two women I loved." Sadly, he whispered, "And I couldn't protect them...."

"But you did me," Ann said brokenly, tears welling into her eyes unexpectedly. Houston was terribly vulnerable right now. She'd never seen a man drop his guard with her as he had. He looked so lonely, so beaten down by life and its harshness, that in her heart, she knew he was a man of tremendous good. After all, she'd been privy to that side of him. He'd almost died giving her back her life.

Flattening his mouth, he rasped, "Yes, for once..."

"Maybe," Ann said, hope in her tone, "that means something has changed—for the better? I don't know, Mike. I have to think all this through."

Taking in a deep breath, he nodded. "I'd give you anything you want, Ann. Come on, let's go back. I'll move my stuff out of the hut."

Ann stepped aside as he walked over to her. Shamed by her reaction, she couldn't meet his eyes. She felt the hurt radiating from Mike by her actions. She couldn't help herself, but wanted to. Helplessly, she looked out at the meadow. The jaguar was gone! Quickly, Ann looked up at Houston. The agony she saw reflected in his eyes tore at her heart.

"I asked her to leave," he told her apologetically. "You've had enough shocks for one day."

Ann walked back with him, down the well-trodden path. They had walked out here arm in arm, laughing and talking animatedly about so many things. Now, as they walked back, each was well aware of the space between them. She saw Mike fighting himself not to reach out and hold her hand. God knew, she wanted to hold his. She wanted to be held by him right now, but that wouldn't make what she'd just seen or realized go away.

She stole a look up at his strong profile as they walked. Was he man or monster? A genetic freak? Something from Dr. Moreau's Island? A scientific project gone insane? And yet, as her mind clipped along, going over a hundred different events that had involved Mike during the last three months she'd known him, she realized he'd always treated her with respect, and that she had blossomed like an unwilling orchid beneath the sunlight of his personality...and his very large, giving heart. No, it wasn't fair to him to call him a monster. He'd be terribly wounded by that. He'd not acted like a monster toward her or anyone else she'd seen him interact with. If she didn't know he carried the mark of the Jaguar Clan, she would have said he was a normal human being just like anyone else.

Why couldn't she let herself see him for what he was? Maybe because he'd brought her in touch with a reality she'd never seen before—and understood very little about. Here at the village, everyone carried the mark, he said. And, the races and nations represented were as diverse and fascinating as any melting pot of human beings anywhere else she'd been on earth. She understood that hereditary Jaguar Clan blood had been shared around the world over the past millenium. It started in the Americas long ago and over time, due to inter-marriage, the genetic gift was passed on around the world, which explained the diversity of people who came to the village to receive their training. The people here were so uplifting, Ann had discovered. Everyone treated everyone else with such courtesy and genuine warmth and sincerity. There were never harsh words here. No, just the opposite, ever since she'd been here, harmony, beauty and an incredible peace had permeated her like a healing balm.

At the hut, she waited outside while Mike gathered up his few belongings. As he exited, she called, "Wait...."

Houston turned, his bag in his hands. Ann's face was shadowed and thoughtful. He could feel her thoughts, her heart as he could his own, though he'd try to shield himself from most of what was going on inside her. And it took everything to hide his reaction to her wondering even whether he was some kind of monster. Some genetic freak.

"You saved my life," Ann said.

"Yes," he answered, not understanding where she was going with this.

"What do I owe you for that?"

His heart shattered. He tried to keep the disappointment out of his voice. "Not a thing, Ann. Why?"

"I don't know," she began with an effort. "How do you pay someone back for saving your life? I wouldn't be standing here now if you hadn't done what you did."

He cocked his head, trying hard to understand her. There was such a quandary within her presently. "Listen very carefully to me, Ann," he growled. "What I did for you was a gift from my heart to your heart. There are no strings attached to it. Do you understand? Don't factor anything I did to save your life into whatever decision you might come to. That's separate. It has to be. You owe *me* nothing."

She regarded his narrowed eyes. "I owe you the truth."

He raised his head and took in a deep, ragged breath. "Yes, that's all. That's enough...." And it was. His life hung in a real balance now. He could not share with her that she was his one true mate for this lifetime. Even though he possessed paranormal powers beyond most human beings, his life was led and dictated by the Sisterhood of Light code. That meant that he would never willingly force anyone into doing something he or she might not want to do. As fiercely as he loved Ann, he would never allow her to know she was his true mate until—and if—she decided to accept him—all of him—for the way he was.

Mike could taste his love for her. They had so much to explore, to share with one another—and yet he shielded Ann from all of that. It wouldn't be fair to try and influence her like that. He knew he could probably persuade her, but at what cost? No, it wasn't his way. Ann had to decide on her own, based on the experiences she'd already shared with him and the information he'd placed in her hands about himself. His hand tightened around the paramedic pack he held at his side.

"If you need anything, Moyra will be around. She'll help you, okay?"

Ann almost took a step toward Mike. She wanted to reach out, touch him and tell him everything would be all right, but she didn't know that. At least, not yet. The harsh mask was in place on his face. He was hiding a lot from her now.

"Okay...."

He turned and left.

Ann stood there for the longest time. Her need for him was so real that she felt tears form in her eyes. Turning, she sobbed and moved into the hut. Sitting down at the table, she buried her face in her hands and began to cry in earnest.

Chapter 12

"Grandmother Alaria..." Ann called out as she entered the elder's hut.

"Ah, my child, how are you this morning?" She turned slowly, a bowl of bread dough in her floured hands, her eyes crinkled with pleasure beneath her thin, arched gray brows.

Ann clasped her hands nervously. "I've made my decision." She glanced out the window at the clouds beginning to withdraw across the meadow, the sunlight revealing the brilliant colors of the flowers among the knee-high grass.

"I can see that you have." She set the bowl aside. "You are looking for Michael?"

In the last four days, Ann had grown accustomed to Grandmother Alaria's ability to read her mind. At first it had scared her, but during their frequent long talks, Ann had realized the elder would never take advantage of such knowledge. Now the old woman's ability simply reminded Ann that this world was foreign to her and that she needed to suspend her own beliefs. And, because everyone here was like Alaria, it was Ann who felt this great cosmic joke was on her.

"I—yes. Have you seen him?" Ann had seen Houston only

twice, and then only fleetingly. Since he'd left her alone at the hut, which stood on the eastern edge of the village, he seemed to have almost disappeared. Around here, that wouldn't surprise her.

Alaria gently patted her shoulder. "Why, I saw him just a few minutes ago." She pointed a bony finger toward a well-used trail that led down into the jungle near the village. "I think he was taking Sasha, his guardian, to the waterfalls to bathe her. She dearly loves her playtime with him. It's rare she gets it, so Michael is taking advantage of that time here with her."

"Sasha...that's a Russian name, isn't it?"

Alaria smiled kindly, her eyes twinkling. "Wasn't it you who said this was a village of the United Nations?"

Nodding, Ann slid her hand into Alaria's. The woman felt so old and fragile, yet so timeless. She was beloved by everyone here. And now Ann knew why. Something—a small voice within her heart—had urged her to see Alaria and Adaire after Mike left the hut, to ask them the questions that burned through her. She had needed answers. A lot of them. They'd willingly complied. Ann had lost count of the hours she'd spent in their warm, generous company over the last four days.

Releasing Alaria's hand, Ann stepped away. This morning she had awakened early after a deep, healing night's sleep, and had bathed in the hot springs behind the hut. Moyra had brought her a pale pink cotton blouse with short sleeves. Ann loved the tiny bits of lace around the throat and the pearl buttons down the front of the blouse. Nervously, she wiped her damp hands against the white cotton skirt that fell to her ankles.

"Grandmother, I have just one more question."

"Hmm? Yes?"

"I'm sure you already know what it is." She laughed a little out of nervousness. Here in the village, she'd observed, few people spoke because they were in constant telepathic communication with one another. Grandmother Alaria had hushed her worries that everyone could read her thoughts by explaining that in the Sisterhood of Light, it was part of the Jaguar Clan code never to enter another's space on any level without his or her conscious permission. Alaria had revealed to Ann the sensation of someone connecting with her thoughts. Once Ann recognized it, she was able to identify the brief, feathery touch. Because Ann always granted both Alaria and Adaire permission to enter her mind, neither elder spoke to her verbally very often. They usually answered her mentally. She, on the other hand, had no capacity for such a skill and had to use her voice to communicate with them.

"You carry Michael's blood in your veins now," Alaria confirmed. "And you wonder what that means. Are you one of us? One of the outsiders? Or neither? Or both?"

Ann moistened her lips and held Alaria's forest green gaze. "Yes...I wondered."

Picking up the dough, Alaria said, "Until recently, there was no way to share our blood with another. Michael is one of the first of our clan to have made the decision to do this. It is not against our code to do so, but heavy responsibility falls on the shoulders of the clan member who initiates such a process."

"Ever since that transfusion took place, I feel different, Grandmother. It's a little scary. Maybe it's this place...my imagination.... I don't know."

"What is different?" Alaria inquired kindly, plumping the dough on the table.

"I feel things more...more easily, I guess. And I can feel people's emotions and thoughts from time to time."

"And does that bother you?"

"Yes and no. Is that how it is with all of you?"

She chuckled. "Oh, yes, my daughter. It is not something we can turn off or on like a faucet. Like the jaguar, we sense and receive impressions that are so subtle that most humans would never be aware of them. But we are, at times, excruciatingly aware of them. *All* of them."

Ann shook her head. "It must be very painful to live among us."

"If your heart is in the right place—if you stand in balance with yourself—that is all the protection you need, my child. When you have compassion, it does affect how you respond to others, but it does not hurt you. Only if you are out of harmony will it tear you apart internally."

Ann hesitated for an instant. "I *am* different now? Changed?" she finally asked, waiting anxiously for Alaria's response.

"You are, let us say, in the midst of a great change." Chuckling, she pointed upward as a monarch butterfly with huge orange-and-black wings fluttered past the window of the hut. "Like the butterfly which waits within the cocoon until its time is ripe, your gifts will, over time, be revealed to you. But how you will utilize them remains unknown at the present. Michael's blood has mixed with your own. It is a gift of love, my child. Nothing bad will come of it. Later, you may want to return to the village for further training in the arts of the clan. That choice is up to you, though. There will never be pressure on you to develop your abilities or to come here to train. There is no coercion in the Sisterhood of Light. Not ever. Everything is always free choice."

Ann nodded. "Thank you, Grandmother." Now she understood that because of Mike's blood being transfused into her veins, she was considered a member of the clan as well. And she was the first person ever, according to Grandmother Alaria, to be permitted here without genetic ancestry. Ann had found out earlier from Alaria that clan members choosing to violate the laws of the Sisterhood of Light were no longer welcomed back into the village; and if they came without invitation, their rebel-like energy could destroy everything the clan had painstakingly built here over the centuries. Now Ann began to understand that her being here was a special privilege, granted because of Mike's actions. Otherwise, he would not have been able to bring her to the Village of the Clouds at all. That was the code. No one without Jaguar Clan ancestry could come and seek safety here.

"Go see him," Alaria coaxed softly as she kneaded the dough.

"Yes," Ann whispered. "Thank you, Grandmother." She saw the old woman nod, her eyes sparkling as she embraced Ann with feelings of love. Ann left the hut and headed down a well-worn dirt path through the village. Moyra had been showing her the many paths, the stream, and just yesterday she had shown her the rainbow waterfall, which had made Ann gasp with delight and awe. It, too, was otherworldly, more like an artist's rendering of some far-off place. And it, too, was real, for she had dipped her fingers into the warm, healing waters to see if it was. Her left brain, her mental faculties, were always questioning, testing and asking why. Of course, here that question was never asked. The

Jaguar Clan members had no such need; they simply accepted. She could not do that, however—at least not yet—and perhaps she never would.

Her heart pounded with fear and she forced herself to walk briskly even though she wanted to drag her feet. Mike had suffered long enough, and she knew these past four days had been hell on him as much as they had been on her.

The jungle enveloped her, and as she hurried down the sloped path, bushes and vines swatting gently at her legs, Ann prayed for the right words. She prayed for courage. She was so scared.

The path opened up. In front of her was the hundred-foot waterfall. In the morning sunlight the mist rising from around the tumbling water created a vibrant, colorful rainbow across the large, dark pool at the bottom. She searched for Mike and his jaguar guardian. There! Trying to compose herself, Ann forced herself to rehearse what she was going to say to him. Would he understand?

Mike was standing in ankle-deep water. In front of him, lying down in the water, was the huge female jaguar that Alaria had called Sasha. The cat was powerful, with thick, stocky legs and a broad, massive head. Her coat glowed gold, with black crescents over it. Ann swallowed hard as she realized Mike was stripped to the waist, and that the loose cotton pants he wore clung to his lower body emphasizing his powerful thighs. He and his guardian had obviously just been swimming in the deeper part moments before her arrival. His hair gleamed with rivulets of water. When her gaze fell upon his left shoulder, on the mark of the jaguar, Ann felt fear knotting her stomach once again. She was frightened as never before in her life.

Houston sensed Ann's approach. He forced himself to continue to sluice handfuls of water across Sasha's broad, strong back, though his heart was focused on Ann's presence. What had she decided? Mike had not allowed himself to invade her emotional field or her mind while they'd been apart. To have done so was against the highest code of personal ethics in the Sisterhood of Light. He respected Ann too much to breach that code even if the woman he ached for might tell him goodbye.

Slowly straightening, he turned around and met her shadowed, wary gaze. She stood near the bank, her hands clasped nervously in front of her. The soft breeze caressed her loose hair and the sunlight made strands of it come alive with red and gold highlights. He met her gaze and managed a tender smile of welcome. Sasha slowly rose and stood at his left side, her body touching his leg.

"She's so beautiful," Ann murmured, gesturing to the jaguar, which stood gazing up at her.

"What I'm looking at is beautiful to me," he said huskily. There was no more than six feet between them, but there might as well be a chasm. He saw a flush creep into her cheeks, but she avoided his eyes looking around the clearing instead.

"I need to talk to you, Mike. Can we sit down here?"

He nodded, feeling like a man before a jury as the judge was about to read the verdict. To him, it was either going to be a death sentence or a new life. And if it was a new life, what kind of life would it be? Did he really want to put Ann in danger by sharing his life with her? How selfish was he, really? Selfish enough to condemn her to death at Escovar's hands, sooner or later? A bitter taste coated his mouth. He reached down and slid his hand across Sasha's broad, sleek skull. Mentally, he asked her to leave them for a while. The jaguar moved sensuously out of the water and trotted up the trail that led back to the village.

Ann sat down, tucking her legs beneath her and smoothing the cotton skirt over them nervously. Mike sat down no more than two feet away from her, his legs crossed. The sunlight bathed him and he looked so strong and powerful compared to how weak and frightened she felt. Ann saw the ravages, the toll that waiting had taken on him. There were dark rings beneath his eyes and the slashes on either side of his mouth were deeper than usual, as if he were trying to protect himself from bad news. She realized he probably hadn't slept much at all.

Opening her hands, she forced herself to say, "I'm scared, Mike. More scared than I've ever been in my life." She closed her eyes because she couldn't stand the gentleness that came to his expression as she spoke. "You are so heroic, in my opinion. And I'm such a coward. You knew the risks you were taking when you brought me here. You could have left me in that apartment. You could have left me anywhere between Lima and this village." Ann opened her eyes and clung to what little courage she had.

"You didn't have to risk your life to come into Lima, either, when I got ill." Her hands fluttered in the air. "And most of all, you didn't have to risk your life to save mine. On top of it all, you gave me blood. Your blood."

Hot tears stung her lids. Ann looked up and willed them back. "I must have cried buckets in the last four days. More than I've ever cried in my life. And then I realized why. Something happened to me a long time ago. It was something I tried to forget. Something I wanted to forget. But now, more than ever, I realized that pushing it away, trying not to feel the pain it created in me, was staining my life in every possible way."

The tears wouldn't stop and Ann sniffed. She saw the anguish in Mike's features as she rattled on, speaking in hoarse undertones. It was so hard to look him in the eye. So hard. Ann knew she'd been a coward all her life and now was the time to meet Mike with the level of courage he'd shown her. "I know this sounds disjointed. I've done a lot of thinking about it. I cried so much my head ached, but the deeper I got into my emotions, the more I realized what was really going on inside me."

Mike forced himself to remain very still, his hands resting on his knees. How badly he wanted to reach out and touch Ann, to soothe away some of the fear he heard in her voice and felt around her. "What did you discover?" he asked her quietly.

Ann shut her eyes tightly and gripped her hands in her lap. "When I was in the Air Force, working as a flight surgeon, I was both a psychiatrist and medical doctor, helping pilots work through their fears after a crash so they could fly once again. But the military is a hard place for women. I loved flying and I liked the pilots, but I began to feel very vulnerable because of the way the men often harassed the women. It got so I feared men—the looks, the catcalls, the innuendos, the subtle and not-so-subtle ways they wanted to control me or any other woman who was in the military.

"I became so wary of men, of what they could do to me, that I put up strong walls to protect myself from them. I know behind my back they called me the Ice Queen but I didn't—couldn't—care. I lived inside my head. My world as a doctor was safe because I could weigh, measure, prove and see the different aspects of it with my own eyes. Science became my wall of protection.

By remaining there all the time, I could survive." She sighed raggedly. "And I did survive very well within that reality, Mike."

Opening her hands, she said, "Then I met Casey Cameron and I found myself beginning to love him little by little.... He worked hard to gain my trust." Some of the anguish began to leave the region of her heart and Ann knew it was due to Mike's warm, quieting presence. She ran her hand across his strong, firm arm. "Just as I was ready to trust, Casey died in a jet crash. He was torn from me. I stood there thinking that no matter what I touched or tried to love, it died. And then I had a disastrous affair a year after Casey died. Captain Robert Crane..."

Ann squeezed her eyes shut. "I was so horribly lonely after Casey died.... I had grown used to having him in my safe little life. Casey had accepted my world of logic and science. He didn't try to change it or me." Opening her eyes, her voice hoarse, she met and held Mike's compassionate gaze. "Crane was a manipulative bastard. He had seen me and Casey together. He knew the score, and like a predatory animal, he waited until I was at my most vulnerable and stepped into my life. He had all the right moves, the right words, the right everything. He took my reality and twisted it, used it against me. I'm ashamed to say I fell for it and him—completely."

Houston took a deep, raw breath. "He got you on the rebound, Ann."

Quirking her lips, she nodded, too ashamed to meet his gaze. His voice, though, was like a healing balm to her pain. "You could say that."

"The son of a bitch..."

With a helpless shrug, she whispered, "At the time, Morgan Trayhern contacted me and asked if I'd like a challenging position as part of his rescue operation. I leaped at the offer, because to stay in the Air Force would have reminded me too much of Casey—of what might have been with him—and I could no longer cope with the memories. Morgan's offer got me out of the mess with Crane, too. I just didn't have the guts to face him down and tell him what I really felt. That's one thing I've left undone. Morgan provided me an escape, an opportunity to move back into the safe little world of the mind. I could still do the job I loved and feel safe from my heart and feelings." She forced herself to look up at him. "Until you crashed into my life, that is..."

He managed a sour smile in return. "There's nothing safe about me, is there?" And he realized more than ever how many changes and demands she'd encountered since being with him. And yet, miraculously, she was still here, with him. Houston felt the powerful connection between them. Would Ann be able to reach out and trust him based upon that? Was she willing to leave her safe little world forever for him? For a life that promised her only danger in the long run?

"Last night, Mike, I finally got it. I got the answer I needed about us." Ann eased away from him and, twisting around, she held his somber gaze. "Your life has been just as rough as mine. People you loved were torn from you, too. The difference between us is that you didn't let your fear of losing me stop you from reaching out...."

Risking everything, he rasped, "It hasn't been easy, Ann. My heart wanted to reach out to you. But my head, my experiences, told me I had no right to even try. All I could offer you besides my...love...was the threat of Escovar killing you."

Her heart bounded with joy and dread. Mike had finally used the word *love*. She understood clearly why he had hesitated in using it with her and she knew now that he loved her enough to want to protect her from himself, from his dangerous way of living. She, too, had been afraid to use the word—but for different reasons.

Ann closed her eyes as he caressed her cheek. It hurt to breathe. It hurt to continue to feel on this so very raw, vulnerable level, but Ann pushed on. She met and held his tender, burning gaze as he continued to cradle her cheek. "I wanted so desperately to reach out from behind my walls and love you in return, but I was afraid, Mike. So very, very scared. You made me happier than I ever thought possible. You've made me laugh more deeply than I ever have before. You've given me so much by having the guts to not let your past, those awful events, crush you, like they did me. I've been running scared all my life. I realized that, too, last night." She slid her hand over his and whispered brokenly, "You were the one with the courage to confront me with the truth of who you are. And I was still hiding and running.''

She leaned forward and slipped her hand, palm down, across his shoulder. Instantly, she felt his flesh tense beneath her touch. ''You wear a badge of honor on your back. I wear scars of my past around my heart.'' Her palm reached the jaguar fur on his shoulder blade. She felt him tense again, as if to try and shield himself from her reaction. Throwing her fear to the wind, Ann moved against him, pressing her breasts to his chest as she slid her hand slowly, purposefully across the patch on his back again and again.

''The crosses you bear are many. The path you've chosen to walk is paved with risks and death. How can I, someone with so many emotional wounds, judge you?'' She moved her hand in a delicate, circular motion, allowing the sensation of his skin against her palm to course through her. His flesh was sun warm and firm. The jaguar fur was soft and thick in comparison, a seamless part of him. Ann eased back on her heels and allowed her hands to come to rest on her thighs as she looked at him. ''You never judged me, Mike. I have no right to judge you or this strange world you live within. Four days ago, you told me I had to make a decision about us. That's not true. We both had a decision to make—for ourselves, about ourselves. If you can love me, faults and all, then I can give myself permission to love you even if you are a part of a greater family known as the Jaguar Clan.''

Her words echoed through him like mission bells being rung on a cool, clear morning, like the music of the heavens and earth combined. Without a word, he slid his dark fingers around the whiteness of her wrists. Gently, he drew Ann's arms downward. ''The love and pain you held for Casey is not something to be ashamed of, *querida*. And what Crane did to you wounded you even more, made another scar on your heart. In a sense, those scars are medals of courage, purple hearts, if you will, that speak of the battles you were in, the wounds you sustained.''

Just his warming, firm touch eased her anguish. There was no mistaking his feelings for her as she drowned in his blue gaze. Tears glimmered in his eyes. Tears for her...

"They were battles I lost, Mike. I'm not proud of what I did, what happened...."

"You didn't lose any battles, Ann. Listen to me," he rasped fiercely, "you were frightened and alone. So very, very alone. I just thank the Great Goddess you didn't stop trying to reach out— especially to someone like me. But then, you're walking a unique path, too. And that path is the same as mine."

Hanging her head, Ann listened to the fierceness behind his words, which sounded like a growl. It wasn't a growl that frightened her, but rather moved through her, sustaining her, nurturing her.

His hands tightened briefly around hers. Ann's fingers were so cold and Mike knew it was because she had been so scared of coming face-to-face with her ugly past and sharing it openly, with trust and vulnerability, with him. "Your courage," Houston rasped, "is magnificent, Ann, in my heart, my eyes. There's not a damn thing you need to be ashamed of. You were young and you were impressionable with Casey. When he died, Crane took advantage of you and you believed in the bastard."

She pulled her hand from his and slid her fingers along his recently shaved cheek. "Walking wounded, aren't we?"

He took her hand and pressed a kiss into the palm. "But we aren't dead, Ann. And we sure as hell have hearts that belong to one another."

"I'm afraid," she quavered. "Afraid for you...afraid of a possible future between us. I'm afraid of the strangeness of your world compared to mine. In the last four days, I've come to accept it on some level, but it's very hard, Mike...so very hard...."

With a groan, Houston nodded. Her palm was so soft and yet so strong. He could smell the faint scent of the spicy orchid soap that she'd used. "I know...and it's your choice, Ann. I love you. For me, right or wrong, selfish as it is, there's no other answer except that I want you. All of you. For the rest of the time I have on our mother, the earth." He smiled tenderly at her. "I know it's not so simple for you, though.... By telling you I love you, I'm placing you in harm's way. Because of that, I can't and won't ask you to stay with me. This has to be up to you. Entirely."

Ann moved into his arms, curled up between his legs, wrapped her arms around his torso and laid her head against his chest. It was such a beautiful sensation—the strength of his sun-warmed flesh beneath her cheek, the powerful thud of his heart against her ear. Mike pulsed with such life, such hope, that it gave *her* hope.

"My whole life has been based upon my fears, Mike. I constructed my safe little world up in my head to avoid feeling. Well, I've found out the real world, reality, doesn't work like that. Every time I think I've got everything in place, life comes along in one form or another and destroys my order." She moistened her lips. "I think I finally got the message that there's no safety in living the life of the mind. I have to step outside of it once and for all. I'm willing to do that, to try that with you. Yes, Escovar is a threat to us. I've lived too much of my life with what-ifs, and with you, I have to surrender all of that. I can't have life on my terms, I've discovered. I have to learn to flow with it, not against it."

"My wild-orchid woman," he whispered huskily against her hair, sliding his fingers around the curve of her shoulder to the juncture of her slender neck. "We can live our lives in fear or we can walk free. That's the choice before you."

"I can be a coward like I've been all my life, or I can choose freedom, can't I?"

"Yes," he murmured, "and freedom always has a price. And in this case, the price could be very high. It could mean your life," he said soberly, his fingers stroking her head.

His touch was silken. Her breasts tightened in need of him, of the love he could shower upon her. Every time Mike stroked her hair, she felt joy replacing her fear.

"The other day, when I was out in the meadow trying to think my way through all of this," Ann told him in a low voice, "I watched a monarch butterfly land on some gold flowers at my feet. It stayed there, close enough for me to touch. I began to look at it in a different light. In a way, I feel like a butterfly. Almost a third of my life has been spent in a cocoon, Mike. And then—" she laughed a little breathlessly "—I met you. My chrysalis cracked open. My world changed. It was opening up and I grew afraid, because the only home I'd ever known was the prison of my orderly, rational cocoon. I'd equated that hard shell around me with protecting me, when really it was imprisoning me and stopping me from growing and being fully human...from being myself.''

Mike's hand stilled on Ann's slender neck. He could feel her pulse beneath his fingers. Smiling against her slightly curled hair, he said, ''So are you going to crawl back inside that prison or be a butterfly, *mi querida?*''

She twisted her head to look up at his wry, smiling features. His eyes burned with such tenderness and love that they melted the last of her fear and replaced it with a growing euphoria that made her feel as if she could do anything—anything in the world—and succeed at it. Even love Houston fiercely, fully when she'd never allowed herself to love at all.

''Butterflies are very delicate.''

''Yes,'' he murmured, leaning down and kissing her nose lightly, ''but they will fly two thousand miles on their migration journey to come back to their home. They might be delicate, but they're tough.''

Ann sat up and spontaneously threw her arms around his neck. ''Oh, Mike, I love you so much it hurts. Please, love me. That's all I need, that's all I ever want from you. Please...''

Chapter 13

The anticipation, the longing, was exquisite as Ann watched the tenderness burning in Mike's eyes turn to undisguised hunger and need of her. He eased up on his knees so that only inches separated them. As he towered over her, his shadow falling across her, her gaze was riveted on his eyes, on his mouth, which had become so terribly vulnerable looking in those seconds after she'd asked him to love her. Ann understood what their lovemaking meant, where it would lead. But today was the first day of forever for her. She was now a butterfly, free to fly, no longer imprisoned in a cocoon that hid her from life, from the man she loved. They had been in a sense like aliens from two very different cultures and times, but the language of the heart had been their mutual connection, the one language they both spoke and understood. It was enough.

His fingers, rough and callused, slid against the planes of her face, eliciting tiny tingles of pleasure. A ragged sound escaped her parting lips as he framed her face and gently angled her chin upward. He was going to kiss her. Ann allowed her hands to come to rest on his powerful chest, the dark mat of hair wiry beneath her fingertips. He had kissed her senseless before, and her body quivered with the memory of those stolen moments, heat flowing

and pooling languidly in her lower body. But this was different.
She was going to love Mike in return. She was going to breathe
her breath of life back into him. This time, it would be an equal
exchange as they shared with one another as never before.

Ann felt Houston lean over to claim her parted, waiting lips.
Her fingertips dug into his chest as she anticipated—needed—him.
She felt his large fingers curve against the base of her skull, strands
of her hair tangled within his grasp. His body swayed slightly
forward. His moist breath caressed her face. And then she strained
upward to meet his descending mouth.

The first skimming brush of his lips against hers brought tears
to her closed eyes. His touch was like that of a butterfly, so light
and tentative. She could feel him restraining himself, and feel the
leashed power vibrating within him as he took her mouth a second
time. Hungrily, she opened her mouth as he rocked her lips open.
He tasted of sunlight, of the sweet water of the rainbow waterfall,
of the lush scent of orchids that grew in nearly every tree that
surrounded the Village of the Clouds.

His breath mingled with hers. She took his breath deep within
her, and she felt him tremble. As their mouths clung wetly, sliding
greedily against one another, she allowed her own breath to flow
into him. There was such a connection forged in those meltingly
hot moments. She was no longer thinking, guided only by her
heart, which asked her to give herself on all levels to Mike. Never
in her life, had she done that—she'd always been too afraid. With
Mike, with his tender mouth touching, cajoling and teaching hers,
she gave as much of herself as she could, knowing that it would
take time to surrender herself completely. Only time would help
her to truly accept who and what he was.

Everything about him was primal—the pressure of his mouth
against her own, the hunger building in his powerful embrace. She
heard him groan, the reverberation moving through her like a drum
being beaten as her hands slid upward across his bunched, tense
shoulders following the curve of his thick neck. An explosion of
heat begged to be released within her. As she brushed against him
with her breasts, an incredible wave of pleasure shimmered
through her. She felt her nipples tightening, clamoring to be
touched, cherished and suckled.

Lost in the splendor and heat of his mouth, his breath warm and ragged against her, she buried her fingers in his dark, thick hair. She couldn't get enough of him, she discovered. Her body throbbed and cried out for him. With each movement of his mouth, his tongue sliding provocatively across her lower lip, she whimpered. He was trembling in earnest now, and it wasn't her fevered imagination. Slowly, very slowly, Houston eased away from her mouth.

Barely opening her eyes, her breath shallow and fast, Ann met and clung to his burning gaze. The raw power of him as a man, as someone who desired her, poured through her like cooling rain on a very hot day, it was so welcome. Ann tried to speak, but her heart was skittering wildly in her breast. She kept touching him, unable to stop from exploring his neck, shoulders and magnificent chest. It was as if she'd never realized how love could make her feel. But then, she understood that because of her past, she had never before trusted herself to open up to any man, never allowed herself to feel the divine pleasure that now exploded simultaneously through her body and heart.

"I want you to love me," she said unsteadily. "I want to love you…"

Houston nodded, unable to speak for a moment. Caressing her flushed cheek, he drowned in Ann's upturned gaze, which glowed with such life that he wanted to cry. Here was the woman he knew had lain dormant beneath that mask, that armor she'd worn so long to protect herself. Suddenly she seemed like an innocent in his eyes, not a mature woman with experience and life behind her. And he knew that emotionally she *was* terribly naive. Getting to his feet, Houston drew her upward. Not wanting to lose contact with her, he slid his arm around her and drew her against him.

"Come on, I know where we should go," he rasped.

Ann felt as if she were walking on air rather than the ground. The sunlight felt different, too. The breeze seemed to caress her like invisible hands, making her vibrantly aware of her body as never before. Each time she moved, she felt the action within her body. The sensation was so surprising that she lost herself in the fluidity, the gracefulness, of her own motion. Talk was unimportant.

At the same time, Ann felt Mike's every emotion. Alaria had made her understand that those of the Jaguar Clan had the very same senses as a jaguar; they were incredibly attuned to all living things and could absorb every impression, every emotion and thought without effort. This morning, Ann was glad to be in such intimate attunement with Mike. And even more surprising, she could feel his returning joy, his raw hunger for her, not only in her mind, but in her heart as well, and it left her reeling with euphoria.

They walked for perhaps half a mile down a winding, twisting mountain path in the jungle. At the bottom of the slope, a barrier of thick bushes and trees had grown like a dark green wall where the path ended. Mike halted and turned to her. He smiled knowingly.

"I think you'll remember this place," he said as he moved some branches aside to allow her entrance.

Puzzled, Ann slipped past him. Beyond the barrier of foliage, she saw an oval-shaped pool. Gasping, she halted, her eyes growing large.

Mike stopped beside her. Ann had pressed both hands against her lips, the surprise more than evident on her face. He chuckled softly and drew her against him as they viewed the pool together.

"This is the place in my dreams!" Ann whispered in awe, and she looked up at him. "I dreamed this, didn't I?"

Mike broke into laughter and pulled her fully against him, embracing her hard and swiftly. "Dreams are a part of our reality, *mi querida*. They are the stuff that helps us bring things into this physical manifestation, into the here and now." He kissed her hotly for a long, long time and felt her begin to melt bonelessly into his arms. Reluctantly, he broke away. How easy it was to love Ann. Even more joyful, more wonderful, was her ability to love him equally in return. Mike thought he might die of happiness. The threat of Escovar faded. At least, for a small space of time.

Ann sighed and looked at the pool, shaking her head. "So many times, Mike, I dreamed of this place! It was the only place I could come to—to...help myself. If I undressed and slid into the water,

I felt hope. I felt strength, as if I could keep on going, and I could survive...."

He heard the trembling in her lowered voice. Caressing her hair, he sighed heavily and simply held her. "This is known as the pool of life," he told her. "It's shaped like a womb to remind us that all creatures, two-legged and four-legged, come from the body of a woman, that we are all part of the tapestry of the Great Goddess, that we are all from her." He gestured to the clear water, which looked like glass, the sunlight reflecting off of it like dancing diamonds. "There are many legends about this pool among the Indians of Peru. It is said that anyone who can find it and bathe in it will become healed. Many people, dying of disease, try to find this place."

Ann studied his face and realized how happy he was; there was no longer any strain in his features. "And...do they ever find it?"

Houston smiled tenderly down at her. "The Village of the Clouds is accessible to anyone, two-legged or four-legged, whose heart is in the right place. The Great Goddess judges that, we don't. Many have found this beautiful place and some, with their last breath of life, have fallen into this water, only to be revived, healed and reborn."

She moved her hand against his lower back and felt the deep indentation of his strong spine, the tight muscles on either side of it. "This pool saved my life in my dreams. I knew that—every time I woke up and remembered being here, swimming in it."

"Your heart, *mi querida,*" he said huskily, framing her face and making her look up at him, "is so pure that I have no question as to why She allows you to come here any time you want."

Drowning in his tender smile, in the burning desire in his eyes, Ann took a deep, tremulous breath. It was so easy to lean against his strong, steadying body. "I love you so much," she quavered. "I'm so happy I think I'll burst, Mike."

Houston rocked her in his arms. "I love you, Ann. I always have. I always will." The deep timbre of his voice resounded around the intimate place, ringed by the wall of high, thick foliage. "I never knew I could feel this way, my wild-orchid woman. And it's because of you. You and that very brave, courageous heart in this tiny body of yours."

She eased away and studied him. "I'm not tiny, Mike Houston—I'm five foot nine and one hundred and forty-five pounds. *That* is not tiny and you know it!"

His grin widened and he threaded his fingers through her hair. She leaned forward like a cat, desiring even more of his touch, and he felt her purr against him in sheer pleasure. "Tiny compared to me," he whispered teasingly, capturing her mouth, feeling her respond like an opening orchid to his cajoling. His hand slid to the back of her head, which he angled so that their mouths fit deeply against one another. She tasted like the sweet honey that formed in translucent globules on the stems of blooming orchids. It was a heavenly sweetness that engulfed him, set him on fire with need of her.

In one smooth motion, he leaned down, and without breaking contact with her luscious, wet mouth, picked her up and carried her forward. The forest ground was soft and warm beneath his bare feet as he laid her on her back against the brown leaves and bark, naturally decaying to make more rich earth for seeds to take life within. He was again reminded of the circle of life—that even in dying, the body surrendered to the power of the Great Goddess, became part of her once again and nurtured and supported new life as a result.

Mike lay next to Ann, bathed by the warmth of the sunlight that fell over them like a loving blanket. In the distance, he could hear the roar of the waterfall. He saw colorful birds flitting among the branches of the tropical trees that surrounded this miraculous place, their songs swelling with joy, a musical tapestry proclaiming life and the sheer beauty of living.

The smile he saw lingering in Ann's eyes made him smile in return. She took his hand and pressed it against her pale pink blouse. The longing, the need for her, embraced him. Mike eased the first shell button from its buttonhole. And then a second, third and fourth. He knew he could not lose control over himself. No, he had to keep a close rein on those basic, almost violent needs. Over the years, with the blood of the jaguar coursing through his veins, he had learned to balance his primal urges and needs with the more refined ones of a human being. And now he understood that the test before him was a daunting one. In his heart, he was afraid that he'd wound his mate instead of drawing her out of that chrysalis and inviting her to be loved fully and without fear. Could he do it? Could he control the animal instincts surging and growing within him, straining to be released and expressed toward her? As the last button slipped free, he looked up and met her half-closed eyes. The softness of her parted lips, the longing in her gaze transformed and tempered his raging hunger for her.

It was all so simple, Mike realized in that moment as he slipped his fingers beneath the edge of the garment and moved it slowly away from her breasts. If he loved her from his heart, and did not allow his primal needs to drive him, he would know what to do. Within seconds, he felt that shift occur within him and his fear dissolved.

Ann wore no camisole beneath the blouse, and her skin shone white and almost translucent in the sunlight. As the fabric fell away, he absorbed the beauty of her breasts, and following his heart, he slid his fingers up around them, feeling her tighten deliciously in response to his caress. He heard her whimper, and she rolled to her side, against him, wanting more...much more.

Leaning over, he suckled her in slow, teasing sips. The honeyed taste of her body was an unexpected gift. Closing his eyes, he felt her arch against him each time he suckled her. The moan of pleasure coming from her only increased the throbbing of blood through his lower, hardening body. In a matter of moments, he had removed her blouse and devoted equal attention to her other breast. She trembled violently as he laid his hand against her bare midriff and eased his fingers beneath the waistband of her skirt, slipping it downward across her hips and legs.

He smiled to himself. Ann wore nothing beneath her clothes. Why would she? The veneer of modern civilization was gone and he was glad. He grazed the gentle swell of her abdomen to her flaring hips and down her firm thighs. He lifted his head and met her smoky eyes, which begged him to continue his exploration of her.

"You are so beautiful...." he rasped unsteadily, and he shed his cotton pants and pushed them aside. Now they were both naked, as it should be. This time, when he slid his arm beneath her neck and eased closer so that she could touch him at will, he saw the languor in her eyes, the heat in them. Leaning down, he felt her lift her head to meet his mouth, to kiss him. As her breasts grazed his chest, he groaned. Her lips were soft, hungry and searching against his mouth. He felt her shyly move her fingers against his chest, beginning to explore him. Understanding her shyness, the hunger driving her as a woman wanting to mate with her partner for life, he placed massive control over himself. Allowing his hand to fall upon her hip, he waited. It was exquisite torture for Houston; every fleeting touch of her fingers, every warm stroke across his hard, tightening flesh, made him feel as if he was caught between heaven and hell.

Nothing could prepare him for her butterfly touch as her exploring fingers ranged downward across his flat, hard belly to his hip. He clenched his teeth and groaned as she innocently caressed him. Perspiration beaded his brow and he trembled savagely as the warmth of her fingers surrounded him, lingered upon him. He drew in a deep, ragged breath. Blood pulsed and throbbed through him. How badly he wanted to open her thighs and thrust hard and deep into her!

Yet he knew that her exploration was motivated by more than just desire. In some part of her, she was still afraid. The errant thought that he was too large for her slipped through his dissolving mind as he sank rapidly into the bubbling cauldron of primal need of her. He knotted his fist in her hair and tried to concentrate on breathing, on controlling himself.

When her hand left him and she slid it around his waist and pressed herself wantonly against him, he had his answer. An explosive breath came out of him as he felt the warm satin of her skin against his taut, throbbing flesh. Capturing her mouth in one swift, hot motion, he eased her onto her back. This time, he would touch her in the most sacred of places that a woman could be caressed, a place of beautiful creation, of life, birth and love.

Lost in the exploding heat and strength of his mouth as he plundered her lips, Ann barely felt his fingers come to rest on her hip. But as he slid his roughened hand across her abdomen, she welcomed it. The ache between her legs intensified to such a degree that she began to moan, her body moving spontaneously at this point. She felt the strength of his hand as he caressed her left thigh, her skin feeling as if on fire beneath his stroking, exploratory touches. As he eased his hand between her damp thighs, she opened to him and gave him access to herself. It was so easy, so beautifully natural as she drowned in the searching splendor of his mouth.

She felt his fingers move in a caressing motion against her, and she moaned and tore her mouth from his. Lights and explosions went off behind her tightly shut eyes. She pressed her face against him and gasped for breath. With each wet, silken stroke, another jagged bolt of heat rippled up through her. It was sweet, unfulfilled agony and she writhed and twisted in his arms, wanting...wanting....

The moment his mouth settled over the peak of her left breast and he slid his fingers into her wet, moist depths, she cried out in startled reaction, but it was from the intense pleasure that gripped her in that moment. She opened completely to him, wanting more, much more of him, more of his stroking, fiery touch. The ache built so rapidly within her that she moaned. Each caress, each stroke made her cry out. Her fingers dug deeply into his shoulders and she arched against him like a bow too tightly drawn. As he suckled her strongly, she suddenly felt a white-hot explosion deep within her body. A little cry of surprise, of relief, tore from her lips.

Yes, yes, my beautiful orchid, open up for me...give yourself to me. Spill your honey over my fingers...spill your sweet, beautiful life over me....

Sobbing for breath, she clung to him in those moments afterward, not understanding what had occurred. She heard his low, growling laugh of raw pleasure as he moved over her, his body like a huge, heavy blanket across her. She felt him slide his hand beneath her hips and guide her fully under him. How natural it was to ease her thighs apart and welcome him to her throbbing, fiery entrance. As he placed his hands on either side of her head, she opened her eyes and looked up, up into his narrowed stormy eyes, burning with a savage fire that consumed her. His heart thundered against hers. Her nipples were tight and taut against the dark, springy mass of hair on his chest. He was smiling down at her, a smile so tender and yet so wild and untrammeled.

She felt his power for the first time. Every inch of his body was taut under his brutal control. Every time she touched him, he quivered. As she settled her hands on his hips and guided him against her entrance, he growled. It was a low growl of such utter pleasure that the sound traveled straight through her, to the heated cauldron boiling and throbbing with life in her lower body. She felt him press against her, and she moved her hips to invite him into her. He lifted his head, his teeth clenched, the perspiration standing out on the taut planes of his face. His fists knotted against her hair. She felt his massive control and began to dissolve it by following her heart, allowing the love she had always felt for him to flow out of her toward him in those golden moments.

Just as water gives nourishment to the dry, thirsty land, she understood that she was the water, the nourishment he sought, that he needed as a man. How easy it was to lift her hips and capture him, invite him into her most sacred place. Her lashes fluttered downward as she felt him surge forward, deep and swift, taking her, being consumed by her wet, warm depths. A cry tore from her—a cry of triumph, of elation as she rocked with him in a rhythm that matched the beat of their hearts.

His arms came around her, molding her against him. Crushing his mouth to hers, he clasped her to him, burying himself deeply in her welcoming, responsive body. The gliding, throbbing heat, the pressure and rhythm combined, and she felt the world slipping away as, locked in a tight embrace, their breaths ragged, their cries mingling, their slick bodies moving with the ancient, throbbing rhythm of the earth herself, they fused into oneness.

Sunlight danced and shimmered within her. She could not get enough of the taste of him, the smell of him, the texture of his roughened face against her own, softer one. He held her hard against him, thrusting into her, taking her, loving her and making her one with him. Why had she waited so long for this? For him? Those thoughts dissolved beneath the shattering, splintering explosion that occurred within her. His arms tightened. Breath rushed out of her. She arched against him, her head thrown back, her fingers digging deeply into his massively bunched shoulders. His responding growl of absolute pleasure, of absolute authority, resonated through her. A rainbow of colors continued to explode and expand through both of them as they gave each other the gift of themselves. Nothing else mattered in those raw, primal heartbeats out of time. Their love, so long denied, was finally satisfied, fulfilled. For Ann, it was like dying and being reborn all over again, the pleasure was so intense. So heartbreakingly beautiful.

The living warmth of the water being sluiced across her breasts and shoulders made Ann smile languidly. She lay in Mike's arms, floating bonelessly in the pool, the water like millions of hands touching her, healing her and making her feel every emotion within like a million blazing suns. He was lounging in the shallows, cradling her between his massive thighs. Each droplet of water that fell from him onto her made her sigh with pleasure as she nuzzled her face against the column of his massive neck.

"You have the most beautiful, giving body," Houston rasped against her ear. "You're just like an orchid—mysterious, closed until just the right amount of heat, sunlight and water are provided, allowing one lucky man to watch you grow, blossom and share the honey of yourself with him." He cupped his hand in the water and moved it down across her left breast. The nipple tightened automatically as he followed her luscious curves. She moaned and pressed a kiss to his neck as he held her tenderly.

"I like being an orchid," Ann whispered, resting her head on his shoulder and looking up at him. Mike gazed down at her. The undisguised happiness in his eyes embraced her as nothing else could. Did he know how young he looked now? So many of those stress lines had disappeared from his face that she marveled at what love, expressed and fulfilled, could do to a person. She wondered if she looked any younger, and then laughter bubbled up through her. She watched his mouth curve in response to her mouth.

"Do I look younger, too?" she asked playfully.

Chuckling, he smoothed her damp hair from her flushed cheek. "Love always makes you feel like living, *mi querida.*"

With a contented sigh, Ann took his hands and moved them across her belly. His dark fingers splayed out against the stark whiteness of her flesh. Light against dark. And hadn't they both suffered cruelly in their own personal darkness for so many years?

Alone? Hurting, yet trying to go on? Ann closed her eyes and rested completely against him. The solid beat of his heart was so steadying, so reassuring to her.

"I'm afraid to feel this happy, Mike," she admitted softly. "I've never felt like this before, ever...."

He caressed her face with his wet hand. Leaning down, he licked the droplets of water off her cheek. "Me either. But," he said with a laugh, "I'm not going to let my stupid head get in the way and ruin a perfectly beautiful day with my mate, either."

His laughter vibrated through her and she smiled winsomely. "You're right—I think too much."

Gently moving his hand across her belly, he whispered, "Think about this, then. Think about the child of love that will come from our being together today...."

Instantly, Ann's eyes flew open. With a gasp, she twisted around in his arms. "What?"

Mike regarded her through hooded eyes. "Didn't you know the other legend about this pool?" he asked as he drew her back into his arms.

She melted against him, her arms curving around his neck. "No, what?" Her abdomen tingled where he'd gently rubbed her with circular motions of his large, dark hand. She brushed several damp curls off his brow.

"That lovers come here, wanting a child to express their love for one another, and conceive?"

She lay very still in his arms for a moment. "I—I didn't know that..."

Mike eased her over him, positioning her so that he could look into her shadowed features. "Does it bother you?"

Ann shook her head and stroked his face. "No...it's just that...I felt something, too, when we...when we were loving one another. I thought that because I was finally able to love you so openly, so freely, that a baby would be created by us."

"Well," Houston murmured, satisfaction in his voice, "in about nine months, my wild orchid, I'm going to be here to help you deliver that gift into my hands."

She saw the tears glitter in his eyes as his hand splayed against her abdomen and he looked down at her belly. There was such raw hope and emotion in his voice.

"Oh, darling..." she whispered, and she pressed his face against her breast and just held him. Mike had lost his wife and his unborn baby. How could Ann have ever forgotten that? As happy as he was, Ann saw flecks of fear deep in his eyes and knew that Mike was afraid for her—for them.

Some of her euphoria dissolved as she held and rocked him in her arms. He trembled violently, once, and then she felt him release his fear. Sliding her fingers through his damp black hair, the sun warm and bright above them, she whispered, "I love you with my life, Mike Houston. And if I'm lucky enough to be carrying your baby in my body, then I'm the happiest woman on the face of this earth. Do you hear me?" She framed his face with her hands and forced him to look up at her. The fear was still there, maybe a little stronger than before. He was human, after all, she realized. Being of the Jaguar Clan didn't guarantee that life would be any easier. In fact, just the opposite was true. Smiling tenderly at him, she kissed his closed eyes, his nose and the corners of his suffering mouth.

"It won't happen again, Mike. I know it won't. Like you said before—we've paid all the tolls along the road. We got to meet...to love one another because we've *earned* this privilege. I don't believe for one moment that I'll be torn from you like Maria or Tracy were." Ann sniffed and blinked back tears as his lashes lifted and he studied her. Looking around at the beauty and peace of the pool, Ann quavered, "I may not know much about metaphysics like you do, but I know in my heart of hearts that we'll be here, nine months from now. I want to have our baby in this pool. I want her to be born into all the love she can possibly experience. Do you hear me?" She pinned him with a fierce gaze, her voice low and trembling.

Instinctively, in a protective gesture, Mike slid his hand across her belly once more. "I hear you, *mi querida*. I hear you..."

Another thought occurred to Ann in that moment. She decided to give voice to her fear. "Will this baby be like you?"

Tenderly, he smoothed the hair from her cheeks. "You mean, will the baby be 'different'?" He saw concern banked in her beautiful eyes and understood the nature of her question. It was one thing for Ann to try and adjust to his alien world. It was another to raise a child with special attributes.

"Does a baby who has the possibility of becoming a great artist or writer differ any more than the child we will have? No," he rasped, "our baby will be a blend of both of us. Whether or not he or she ever chooses to use the skills inherited from the Jaguar Clan is not up to us. Right now, I want to think of marriage, *mi querida.* I want our baby to have my name. I want it to have you as its mother and me as its father. Whatever talents or gifts it is born with remain to be seen. Let's take this one step at a time. It's all we can do."

Closing her eyes, Ann felt the safety of Mike's arms, heard the low growl of his voice, and they soothed her fears, her questions and uncertainties about their future. She was seeing his male side now, his need to fulfill his obligations to her. Mike would never be satisfied with just living with her; he wanted to marry her, to give her his name and what little protection he could offer her and the baby she now carried deep within her body. His possessive instincts were overpowering and she didn't try to combat them. There was something so primal about him, about those of the Jaguar Clan, that it would be useless to fight their sense about some things. *Marriage.* The word held such sweet promise and yet such fear for her.

"Marriage..." she whispered uncertainly.

Concerned, Mike gazed deeply into her blue-gray eyes. "You're worried that we can't make it as man and wife? That our worlds are so different that we won't be able to find any middle ground?"

Ann realized he was reading her heart and mind again. Gently, she slid her fingers across his roughened cheek. "Yes..."

"Life has to be lived one day at a time, wild orchid. One moment at a time. Outside the walls of this place, it's a crapshoot. There are no guarantees. Nothing. The moment we step back across that bridge, our lives are at risk." Leaning down, he caressed her mouth tenderly. As he eased away, his eyes burning with the passion of life that ran through him as surely as sunlight stroked the heated earth, he whispered, "The cosmic joke is that everyone's life is at risk every day. We don't know when our time will be up. We don't know how we are going to die. Billions of people on the face of Mother Earth live this way. Life is risky, Ann. I have an added danger in mine—Escovar. And yes, that does put you in greater jeopardy. All we can do is be careful, watchful, and stay ahead of him and his men. I promise you," he said in a deep, resonating tone, "that I will do *everything* in my power to keep you and our baby safe and shielded. With my life, I promise that to you...."

Tears stung her eyes as she closed them and pressed her brow against his thickly corded neck. His arms drew her tightly to him. All her senses were wide-open and she felt his fear, his suffering and anguish for her and the baby she carried. Mike was right— life was tenuous at best. She could step on a venomous snake and die. Or she could contract a hemorrhagic fever and bleed to death. Yes, he was right—life was a risk twenty-four hours a day. Again, she had to adjust her attitude toward living, toward marriage and becoming a mother and a wife.

A quivering smile touched her lips as she caressed his strong, naked shoulder. Mike felt so invincible to her, strong and pulsing with the power of life. She wished that same strength could live within her. Perhaps that was the gift of the jaguar. At least her baby would have that same powerful vital force, that sheer determination and will to not only survive, but to live life on the edge and with passion—a passion she was only now beginning to understand and appreciate by loving Mike.

"One day at a time," she promised him. "One hour at a time."

Caressing her hair, he pressed a kiss to the sunlit strands. "We can do this together. I know we can." His fingers curved about her skull and he closed his eyes as he rested his cheek against hers. "Love is the most powerful, the most healing emotion we have. It's ours, Ann. If we have the courage to embrace it fully, without reserve...if we can surrender to it entirely, then we've got more than most people will ever have...."

Raggedly, she whispered, "Yes, I understand that...and I'll try, Mike. I swear I'll try with every breath I take into this body of mine. I'm not there yet, but I'm going to try...."

Houston's fingers tightened on her silken hair. It was all he could ask of Ann. He knew she had not yet surrendered all the way to him—nor had she completely accepted the possibility of being his wife and the mother of his child. Only time...and the will of the Great Goddess...would allow her to cross that threshold between them. Only then would their love be strong enough to carry them forward into their new life together. The commitment needed to be at a soul-deep level, like a foundation being laid. For their lives to entwine fully, that foundation had to be there; otherwise, their relationship would deteriorate over time. He knew she didn't want that, and he didn't, either, so he would give her the time and space necessary to adjust, accept and then surrender to him, in all ways. He wanted this to happen naturally. Beautifully.

Chapter 14

Ann's heart was heavy. They were going to leave the Village of the Clouds within the hour. It was her understanding that because she was an outsider to the energy forces that kept all those within the village safe, she and Mike had to leave in order to ensure the protection of the villagers. Further, Mike had received disturbing news from his government sources that Escovar was mounting a campaign to take another village. No, real life was intruding upon them, whether they liked it or not.

Grandmother Alaria sat at the table in their hut as they packed their meager belongings. A number of new friends Ann had made over the last two weeks had dropped by individually and embraced her, blessed her and wished her a safe journey on her newly chosen path.

She was kneeling on the mat in the bedroom of the hut, folding clothes that she'd recently washed and sun dried. Mike was nearby, looking through the black paramedic pack he always carried with him no matter where he went, checking the contents and organizing items in case he had to use them.

Ann's body glowed from recent lovemaking they'd shared. She lifted her head to look at the man she loved. As if sensing her attention, Mike glanced in turn. Their gazes met. Her lips parted and she drowned in his tender look. His love for her was so strong and palpable that wave after wave of warmth embraced her. She sighed softly. Yesterday, they had been married by Grandmother Alaria, with the entire village in attendance. It had been a beautifully moving ceremony, the thought of which still made tears come to her eyes. Ann was beginning to understand on a much deeper level about the people of the Jaguar Clan. She knew now that the incredible loving power they held was centered in life and family.

Because she was now considered one of them due to her blood transfusion and becoming Mike's mate, she had to learn to accept the unsettling feeling of being in touch with the villagers' subtle emotions. And her own startling ability to share her thoughts and emotions with Mike was remarkable.

Mike didn't have to say "I love you" aloud. All he had to do was think about the love he held in his heart for her and a warm euphoria flowed through Ann just like a physical embrace. It was, as Grandmother Alaria put it wryly, a gift and a curse. There would be times, the old woman had explained the night before, as they shared their last meal with her and Adaire when they would fight and disagree, and Ann might want to ask Mike to shield himself from her. After all, that was the only fair thing to do, since she didn't possess his more advanced abilities.

Or did she? Ann wasn't sure. She eased back on her heels and continued to fold the clothes across her lap. Nestling her hand against her abdomen, Ann could sense the baby she and Mike had created down by the pool of life. She knew as a doctor that it was impossible to know this soon that she was pregnant, yet there was a warm flame of feeling, a thrilling joy that resonated throughout her belly and up to her heart ever since that day. Grandmother Alaria had confirmed that she was carrying a baby—a very special little girl soul, she had told them with a twinkle in her eyes.

Suddenly a voice startled her out of her reverie. "Have any names come to you yet, Ann?" Grandfather Adaire asked softly as he leaned on his staff at the door, watching her through kindly eyes. He then exchanged a tender smile with his wife.

Ann looked and laughed, a little embarrassed. She'd given

Adaire and Alaria permission to monitor her thoughts and feelings while at the village. They and Mike were the only ones, however, and everyone else remained shielded, as was the policy.

Mike smiled and placed his paramedic pack aside to welcome Adaire. He took the folded clothes off Ann's lap. "I know she's thinking about it, Grandfather."

"Aye...."

As Mike's hand settled over hers, Ann leaned against his strong, steady body. Today he was dressed once again in his combat uniform. That frightened her. It was a reminder that once they left the safety of the village, Mike would be a hunted man again—but so was she, now.

"How do you name a baby you haven't seen yet?" Ann teased them. "This is not fair. You know so much more than I do...." She leaned over and pressed a kiss to Mike's recently shaved cheek. Each minute here with him was precious, moments she wanted to brand into her heart and memory.

A rumbling chuckle rolled out of Adaire. "She is a child of the Jaguar Clan. She will come into your dreams very shortly, my dear. Believe me, she will become a pest to you each night you close your eyes. You think you will sleep?" He slapped his thigh and chuckled again. "This little girl is precocious. She will tell you exactly what she wants to be called when she arrives."

"That is true," Alaria said as she rose slowly to her feet. "I am being called," she told them. "I will meet you down at the bridge?"

Mike nodded. "Of course, Grandmother."

Ann saw the love between Adaire and Alaria as the old woman reached out and touched her husband's hand briefly and then was gone. With a sigh, Ann said, "I don't care what our baby wants to be called so long as she's born healthy." She cast a glance up at Mike, who had sobered slightly. "That's all I want. And a safe place to have her..."

Houston's arm tightened around her shoulders briefly. "I'm going to do everything I can to keep you—and her—safe." Frowning, he glanced at Adaire, then continued, "The best thing, we believe, is to have you go back to the States. Wait for me there.

Escovar won't follow you. I could fly up every few months and
see you and—"

"Absolutely not!" Ann muttered defiantly. "I'm not leaving
your side. I need you, too, you know."

"Ann," Houston soothed, keeping his voice purposely low and
shielding her from his chaotic feelings, "we've discussed this before."

"Yes," Ann said firmly, "and we've agreed that I'll work in
the villages as a doctor. My name will change because we know
Escovar has linked me to you, as well as to Morgan, whom he
hates almost as much as he does you. Yes, I know—" Ann held
up her hand as Mike started to interrupt, "—that he'll try to find
me and kill me because of that link. What is in my favor is that
he doesn't realize we love one another, or that we're married. I
can pose as a doctor from the Peruvian Red Cross, on assignment
to this region. You said yourself that Escovar usually leaves the
medical people in the villages alone. He won't kill priests or nuns,
either."

"It's the only place of light in his dark heart," Houston
growled. "I don't know what stops him. He kills everyone else—
babies, children, women and men. His murdering soldiers don't
give a damn about life, not at all...."

Ann felt his raw, cutting anguish even though she knew he was
trying desperately to shield her from his worries about her safety.
Moving her hand from beneath his, she pressed it against her abdomen. "Mike, don't do this to yourself. Please. I'm a doctor. I
can help the people—your people. God knows, they need someone
like me in every village, but that's not going to happen, either. I
promised you that I'd stay in areas that you considered safe, far
away from wherever you're going to engage Escovar as he tries
to take over Ramirez's territory. I won't like not seeing you for
weeks at a time, but I know you have a job to do. I'm not asking
you to stop doing what you need to do, and you can't ask it of
me, either."

Mike tried to protest.

Ann held up her hands. "I'm a doctor," she repeated. "I save
lives in my own way, just as you do. Besides, I've grown to love
the people of the villages—they are born and bred in the same

mystical land that is our child's heritage. We're both committed. Neither of us is going to leave the field of battle we've chosen to take a stand on.''

''But,'' Houston said huskily, glancing over at Adaire for help, ''you're pregnant, Ann.'' He slid his hand across her belly in a tender motion. ''I lost one family—'' He stopped abruptly.

Ann reeled internally as his feelings deluged her. His terror over losing her and the baby were haunting him even more than she'd realized.

''Children,'' Adaire counseled soothingly, ''be at peace with yourselves. Each of you must trust and surrender to the other. Each of you must respect the needs of the other to pursue the goals you've chosen to work toward. It is that simple. You must make your individual decisions work for, not against one another.''

Bitterly, Ann admitted, ''I wish you could leave Peru, Mike. That would solve everything. If you could come back to the States, lead a normal life there—''

''My child,'' Adaire said in a low tone, ''Michael is in a death spiral dance with Escovar. No matter where in this world he tried to go, Escovar would seek him out, find him and try to kill him. It is better that this dance be played out here, in Peru, on the turf of the jaguar. It is to Michael's advantage that it be done here. I know that the constant threat to his life is very hard on you. But it would be a threat wherever you tried to live. You cannot outrun fate.''

Frustrated, Ann fought back tears. ''I keep hearing of this death spiral dance.'' She glared at Mike and then at Adaire. ''What is it?''

Houston sighed raggedly. ''It's something that was chosen by both of us—Escovar and I—before we ever came into physical bodies in this lifetime. There is some old karmic debt still unresolved between us. Only someone like Grandmother Alaria would know what that debt is. She is the only one allowed to see the Akashic Records, a place where all our deeds, actions and words in our hundreds, maybe thousands of lifetimes, are accurately recorded.'' Shrugging, Mike gave Ann a gentle squeeze. ''I don't know why Escovar is after me like this. I can't explain why his family died in that accident, or why he chose to murder my family in revenge...."

"It's like a stain on the soul," Adaire interjected gently, his gaze on Ann. "A stain can be caused by some terrible decision made by one soul against another in a particular lifetime. In order to remove the stain, the same event must be turned around, opposite of what it was before, and played out again. In that way, the scales of karma are once again in balance."

Struggling to understand, Ann whispered brokenly, "Lifetimes? Reincarnation? My God, I've never even considered them as possibilities. But then, to tell me that Mike murdered Escovar's family in one of these so-called lifetimes—"

Adaire held up his hand. "Wait, child," he murmured, "you cannot know all the possibilities that occurred between Michael and Escovar. I'm not at liberty to speak of it, either. To do so would be to interfere in the karma between them, and the clan can never interfere on that level. To do so is to break the code. Michael understands this, and I know it's very daunting for you to try and comprehend it all. A death spiral dance is a simple way of saying that Michael is locked in a life-and-death struggle with another person. In this case, Eduardo Escovar. And like actors, they must play out their parts. They must walk through the scenes, make decisions and work through their karma with one another."

Sniffing, Ann gave Mike a dark look. "And no one knows what the outcome will be, right?"

Unhappily, Mike gently rubbed her tension-filled shoulders. He wished that this topic hadn't come up. "That's right, *mi querida.* Look, don't worry about it. I've been evading that bastard for over ten years now. I'm slowly but surely getting the upper hand on him. We stopped him at the village of San Juan. I'll stop him at the next village he's preparing to attack in a couple of weeks. The people here are *worth* protecting, Ann, regardless of the death spiral he and I are locked in."

"Call it what it really is, my blood brother—a major death spiral confrontation between the Sisterhood of Light and the Brotherhood of Darkness," a woman's voice interjected. "It is the first of several clashes between the light and dark before the darkness descends upon all of us and we are hurled collectively into the pit of hell.''

Ann snapped her head toward the entrance to the hut. A woman, very tall, built like a lithe, well-muscled jaguar and dressed in camouflage combat fatigues just like Mike, stood there looking commandingly at them. The power emanating from her made Ann gasp. The woman had a rifle slung over her left shoulder. Her hair, backlit by the morning sun, was a shining blue-black waterfall, like a glistening raven's wing. It was her proud, almost arrogant carriage that made Ann tense. This was no ordinary woman. No, she was special...and dangerous.

Quickly, Ann perused her golden face, which glistened with a sheen of perspiration. Her willow green eyes were large, intelligent and slightly tilted. Her black hair framed her oval features, emphasizing her high cheekbones and full, grimly set lips. On the web belt around her slender waist were weapons of war. Ann saw: grenades, a deadly knife and a canteen. Across her shoulders were bandoleers of bullets for the rifle she carried.

Ann had seen female combat soldiers before, stateside, but never anything like this woman. She saw the glittering laughter in her eyes, the supreme, unshakable confidence in her proudly thrown back shoulders, and the way she lifted her chin at a cocky angle. There was no doubt in Ann's mind that this woman was, indeed, a member of the Jaguar Clan—she *looked* half human, half jaguar. One second Ann thought she saw a jaguar covering the woman soldier, the next, that stunning human visage reappeared. Power emanated from her in battering waves of such magnitude that Ann found herself recoiling.

''Shield yourself!'' Adaire growled. ''This woman is with child, Inca. You know better than that.''

Ann watched the woman give Grandfather Adaire a smile of annoyance, a one-cornered lift of the right side of her mouth. ''Old One, as usual, you are here to chide me.'' In the next instant, Ann felt the battering waves of energy cease, and she breathed an inward sigh of relief. Mike leaped to his feet, calling out Inca's name. Ann looked up at him in surprise as Adaire moved aside, scowling heavily in displeasure.

"You came!" Mike said, opening his arms to the newcomer as he walked toward her.

With a husky laugh, she stepped into the hut, opened her arms and gripped Houston hard, slapping him heartily on the back.

"Of course I did, my blood brother!" She buried her face against his shoulder and hugged him fiercely.

Ann blinked. Who was this woman? Even when shielding herself, she was like a thousand suns radiating in the small space of the hut. Her raw animal energy, her power was palpable. She was a leader, there was no doubt. And, Ann noticed, she was only a few inches shorter than Mike. The woman's willow green eyes grew huge and black as she held Mike in her tight grip of obvious warmth and welcome. There were tears in them, Ann realized. Slowly standing up, she felt very weak and terribly human in comparison to this woman Adaire had called Inca. She was of Indian origin, no question. Her dark golden skin, thick black hair and classically beautiful face indicated that she was from somewhere in South America.

"It is so good to see you," Inca whispered huskily as she finally released Houston.

He laughed a little and gently cupped her shoulders. "I don't believe it! I never thought I'd see you again, Inca.... Hell it's *good* to see you!"

Ann heard raw, undisguised emotion in Mike's voice. Confused, she looked from her husband to Grandfather Adaire. She'd never seen the elder angry before, but he was angry now. It was nothing that overt, but clear in the way his brows were drawn down and the line of his wide, usually gently smiling mouth spoke of displeasure.

"You are not welcome here, Inca. You broke our code a long time ago and you know our laws. You were never to step foot back into the village."

Grandfather Adaire's voice felt like thunder to Ann. And she reeled internally. Inca glared momentarily in the elder's direction. "I am not welcomed anywhere, Elder," she snarled back. "Do not get tied in knots over this. I am leaving very shortly, I promise." Then she wiped the tears from her eyes. "I had to come, Michael. Your guardian told me you were here, that you'd taken a new mate...." Inca turned, suddenly devoting her considerable attention to Ann, who stood uncertainly before her. Without hesitation, Inca strode over to Ann, her hand extended in friendship.

"I am Mike's blood sister, Inca. I am sure no one has told you of me. I am the black sheep of the Jaguar Clan—not quite pure enough of heart to be accepted and yet not dark enough of heart to be embraced by the Brotherhood of Darkness, either." She laughed heartily.

Stunned by her warm regard, Ann stared down at the woman's extended hand. How beautiful she was, in every way—full of such grace, such sinuous movement that it took Ann's breath away. There was an unearthly glow around her and Ann wasn't sure what that meant. Forcing a nervous smile, she lifted her hand and slipped it into Inca's.

"I'm Ann Houston. It's nice to meet you." Ann felt the strength in Inca's callused hand, realized the woman soldier had monitored the amount of pressure she used in her grip. Yet, as Ann met that willow green gaze, she felt an incredible joy embrace her. It was real. This woman was real. Her emotions were sharper, more ragged, less steady than Mike's or Grandfather Adaire's, but Ann felt only goodness radiating from her.

"It is good that my blood brother found the mate he has been searching a lifetime for," Inca told her in a low, purring tone. "I have prayed to the Great Goddess to ease his pain, his suffering and loneliness." She looked at Ann, her eyes narrowing as she studied her from head to toe. "Yes...you are the one." Inca turned and grinned at Mike. "This is truly a day to celebrate, my brother!"

Mike moved to Ann's side. He slid his arm around her shoulders and drew her gently against him as he met and held Inca's glistening gaze. "Yes, it is. I'm glad you could meet Ann."

"I am sorry I could not be here for the joining ceremony yesterday." Inca looked to the left and glared defiantly at Adaire, who stood tensely. "The Old One would probably have hemorrhaged on the spot if I had shown up, unannounced, on one of the five most sacred days a Jaguar Clan member can have." She laughed harshly. "Do not worry, I'm leaving, Old One. I can feel your anger stalking me."

Ann saw Grandfather Adaire's face grow shadowed. "You threaten all of us by coming here without permission, Inca, and you well know it. As usual, your own selfish needs and whims take precedence over the safety and consideration of others. You have not changed at all."

Scowling, Inca returned her attention to Mike. "There is trouble out there," she whispered tautly. "I ran into a couple of jeeps with Escovar's men not more than ten miles from here. They are like jackals hunting and sniffing around—for you." She placed her hand on his shoulder. "I must leave. I must journey back to Brazil, to my own death spiral dance, my brother. I wanted to be here, in person, to be a part of your happiness and to meet Ann—your life mate."

Ann felt the powerful love that Inca held for Mike. It was a stunning, fierce kind of love yet one that was very different from her own love for Mike. So many questions pummeled her, but she remained silent as the drama played out between the three members of the Jaguar Clan.

Gripping her hand, Mike rasped, "I had hoped to see you—but I knew the decision of the village elders about you, so I never thought you'd come back...."

Inca grinned wickedly. "Elder Adaire knows that I make and break rules as I need to, my brother. That is another reason why I'm not welcome here. Black sheep never are." She chuckled and released his hand. In one motion, she took a leather thong from around her neck.

"I have a gift for you, Ann," Inca said, her voice becoming a silken purr. "Here, this is for you—you are now my sister-in-law because you are my blood brother's mate."

Ann watched as Inca lifted the leather loop with a white claw hanging from one end of it and settle it over Ann's head, arranging it against her neck.

"I do not have much money." She grimaced. "I'm just a green warrior in the name of Mother Earth and the Amazon Basin which is being destroyed acre by acre. I do not have a job in São Paulo or Rio de Janeiro to make coins for anything fancy but—" she pressed her hand against Ann's upper chest, where the necklace now lay "—this is a gift from my heart to yours. This is a jaguar's claw. In time, you will understand what it is, what it means to you. Wear it—'' her eyes narrowed upon Ann's ''—*always*. Don't ever be without my gift, my sister.''

The heat of her hand was like a burning brand into Ann's flesh. Though Inca was not pressing hard, it felt like the thick, heavy claw was being pushed through Ann's flesh, into her bones and body. As she stood, riveted by Inca's closeness, she saw the woman's face change into that of the jaguar guardian who protected her. It was the face of a huge male with glittering green-and-gold eyes. Closing her eyes, Ann could barely contain the power and fierce sense of protection that Inca covered her with in wave after wave of heat and light.

As Inca slowly removed her hand, Ann swayed. She felt Mike's grip become more firm. Dizzy, she opened her eyes, stunned at the feelings in her chest. Without words, Ann lifted her hand. Yes, the claw was still resting there. No, it was not inside her, as it felt right now. She looked up at Inca. The hardness, the arrogance was gone in that fleeting moment. Instead, Ann saw a very beautiful woman, childlike in her terrible vulnerability and with eyes filled with such loneliness that it caught Ann completely off guard. She realized Inca was allowing her to see the *real* her, rather than the mask she wore. And suddenly Ann connected to her on a very familiar level. Inca was a lot like she herself had been all her life—a butterfly trapped in a cocoon. Yet as she met and held Inca's glittering gaze, Ann felt a depth of pain in her that was so overwhelming, she wondered how the woman was surviving it at all.

"I must go," Inca whispered hoarsely, self-consciously wiping her eyes and then stealing a look at Adaire, who stood near them threateningly. "I have overstayed my welcome." Swiftly, she leaned forward and kissed Mike on the cheek. Then she carefully embraced Ann.

"Be strong, my new sister-in-law. Love him. He has gone too long without it. Having you strengthens all of us, believe me...." She released Ann and shared a gentle smile with her. Then she extended her hand toward Ann's belly. "May I? May I bless you and the baby you carry?"

Touched to the point of tears because she saw and felt Inca with such compassion, Ann nodded. "Of course..."

Kneeling down on one knee, Inca gently pressed her cheek against Ann's abdomen. "Little one," she crooned, "know that you are loved, so loved.... If I had parents like yours, I would be eager to come into this world, too. Even in the darkness to come, I am here. I am your aunt. I promise you, I will protect you with all my heart...my spirit...with the last breath I take. May the Great Goddess bless you, your mother and your father." Inca closed her eyes and pressed her hand more surely against Ann's belly. "I swear this...."

As Inca rose in one fluid motion, Ann felt an incredible sensation of love, of commitment, tingle up through her entire body. Even though Grandfather Adaire disdained Inca, Ann found herself admiring her. She was a woman of immense power, there was no question. Perhaps a woman who was not afraid to embrace her power fully, and thus threatened men. Yes, Inca would threaten most men—but not Mike. No, Mike loved her; that was obvious by the tears glimmering in his eyes as Inca raised her hand in farewell to them.

"I will see you in your dreams, my blood brother." She turned her gaze on Ann. "If you call me by name, I will come." She pointed to the jaguar claw around her neck. "Or call him." Giving Ann a mysterious smile, she turned around and with a deferential nod of respect in Adaire's direction, left as abruptly as she had come.

Suddenly dizzy, Ann whispered, "I need to sit down for just a moment, Mike...."

He eased her to the mat and knelt beside her. "You okay?"

With a slight, embarrassed laugh, Ann said, "I'm fine...fine. She's just a bit overwhelming, that's all. I'll be okay in a minute..."

Adaire hobbled slowly to the door. "There is less than an hour left, my children. Time is of the essence now.... I will meet you at the bridge over the stream."

"We'll be there," Mike promised.

Ann rubbed her brow as the dizziness slowly disappeared. When she looked up, Adaire was gone. Sometimes she wondered if these people just materialized from the surrounding air. She'd never seen it happen, but Adaire could not move that fast, for he had a bad limp.

"Wow," she murmured, giving Mike a wry look, "what a morning, huh?"

He grinned a little and knelt in front of her. "Inca doesn't exactly make quiet entrances," he agreed with a chuckle. Removing her hands from her brow, he said, "Hold still, I'll help steady you. Just close your eyes, take in a nice, slow breath while I hold you...."

It was so easy to surrender to Mike in this way, as he cradled one hand against the back of her head and pressed the other gently to her brow. Almost instantly, she felt the dizziness dissolve. In its place was a sense of stability again, of complete harmony with herself and with him. In less than a minute, it seemed, he withdrew his hands. When Ann opened her eyes, he was smiling tenderly down at her. Reaching up, she slid her hands up around his hard jaw and settled her palms against his cheeks.

"Thank you, Major. I think I like this form of medicine. Much quicker, less invasive than the kind I practice." She leaned upward to meet his descending mouth.

The moments slowed to a molten halt as his lips met hers. The joy of his mouth sliding, rocking her lips apart, was all that mattered. It was so easy to center her entire universe on Mike, on his touch, on the fierce love she felt in his heart for her alone. She drank from him, shared his breath within her and drowned in the splendor of his tender, searching kiss.

Gradually, he eased back from her lips. Ann's lashes lifted. "Now I'm dizzy all over again." She laughed softly as he caressed the crown of her head with his hand. She loved being stroked by him, touched and held. Feeling his unshielded love for her left her breathless and euphoric and filled her with so much hope.

Chuckling, Mike released her and sat back on the heels of his black leather boots. "I'm a little dizzy myself. But then, you're one hell of a kisser, *mi querida....*"

She flushed at his compliment and fleetingly touched her cheeks. She was not used to that burning look he shared so brazenly with her, that look of a man wanting his woman in every possible way.

Her entire body responded to his heated, smoldering gaze. An ache began to build deep within her, a yearning to be one with him again and again and again. Ann thought she'd never get enough of Mike, of what they'd shared every time they'd loved on these mats here in this hut.

Reaching out, he caressed her hot cheek. "There will be other mats, other huts," he promised her huskily.

"You're reading my mind," Ann said. And then she laughed, even more embarrassed than before. "Mike, I'm going to have to get used to this...."

He grinned broadly. "I can shield, if you want me to. It's not a problem, you know."

Slowly getting to her feet with his help, she said, "No...it's just different, that's all. I *like* our connections. In fact, when you shield yourself from me, I feel like we're only half-connected. It's an awful feeling...."

He moved the paramedic bag to the table and zipped all the compartments shut. "Now you know how a jaguar feels without his mate. The jaguar has that same kind of open mind and heart connection running between him and his mate twenty-four hours a day."

She picked up the folded clothes and brought them to the table where he was working. "It's a beautiful thing," she admitted, "like being fully alive, Mike, instead of half-alive. Do you know what I mean?"

He saw the quizzical look in her expression. A love so fierce and pure welled up in him that he couldn't speak for a moment. Ann might not be a genetic member of the Jaguar Clan, but her heart was so pure that it rocked him as nothing else ever had. Raising his hand, he eased several strands of reddish brown hair from her wrinkled brow. "Yes, I know exactly what you're talking about because we share it."

With a sigh, Ann looked around. "Will it still be there when we leave here, Mike?"

Hands stilling over his black canvas bag, he held her gaze. "What we have will be with us until the day we die and even beyond mere physical death, *mi querida*. It will only grow stronger, more sure and more beautiful with each passing day, week and month. Love, once it takes seed and you surrender completely to it, does nothing but grow.''

She nodded and sat down on the chair, her hands resting on the pile of colorful clothes Moyra had loaned her. ''In some ways, that's scary. In others, it makes me feel so hopeful about the future for us.'' Ann knew she had not yet given over, surrendered completely, to Mike yet. Time...they had to have time....

''Yeah, I feel scared and hopeful, too,'' Mike agreed wryly. ''The future is iffy. But then, it's always been that way with me.'' His expression sobered. ''It's you who's going to go through some tremendous adjustments because of it.'' His brow wrinkled. ''And that's what worries me.''

Ann saw and felt his agony over having to subject her to his life on the run from Escovar. She knew he worried that the drug lord might put two and two together and realize their connection— and then murder her to get even with Mike for the death of his family. It was all part of the death spiral dance.

Anxious to distract him, Ann said, ''Tell me about Inca. What an incredibly powerful woman she is! What did she mean when she called you her blood brother? Is that another custom here in the Village of the Clouds?''

She saw him release his worry and focus on her questions. Folding his hands on the table, he said, ''Over time, you'll get to understand a lot about the Jaguar Clan and its customs. When I came here to this village after being wounded and nearly bleeding to death, it was Inca who cared for me. She was in training with Adaire and Alaria at the time. She'd been Adaire's prize pupil for two years, and she was one hell of a powerful woman even then.

''At the time, I didn't know I was one of the Jaguar Clan. I lay on a pallet in a hut like this, and I fought against the energy, the healing, that Adaire was trying to send to me, to pump into me, to save my worthless neck. I fought it—and him—every step of the way because I was scared and I didn't understand.'' He gave Ann a humored look. ''Like you, my left brain, the paramedic in me, said I should be dead, and I wasn't. When you believe something like that to that degree, you can stop healing energy from coming in to help save you.

''I was semiconscious from losing so much blood. I kept fading in and out, and yet Inca devoted herself to caring for me. She *refused* to let me go. Adaire released me. She did not. He ordered her to let me die. Inca defied his direct order and said no, which helped create more problems for her. At that moment, she broke a basic clan law—you cannot save someone who is supposed to die. That is what brought her banishment from the Village of the Clouds. Adaire wanted her not only banished, but her jaguar guardian stripped from her for disobeying. Alaria said no—that banishment was enough.

"Adaire has yet to forgive Inca for this, I think. They were so close before that. Inca had never had a father figure until she came here, at age sixteen, and Adaire loved her like the daughter he'd lost many years earlier. Inca more or less replaced that lost daughter in Adaire's heart. When she defied him, it cut him to his soul. He'd never entertained the possibility that she could do that to him. He thought her love and respect for him was more powerful—but he was wrong.... She took things into her own hands and fought for me on every level to get me to accept the healing energy. I don't know how many nights she bathed me with a cool cloth, or talked to me or...sang to me. She has a beautiful, angelic voice...." Houston smiled at Ann. "Back then, Inca was...different, and she usually obeyed the laws of the clan. But one night, as I was slipping away, dying, Inca broke clan law."

Mike frowned heavily. "She shouldn't have done it, but she did anyway. Inca was only eighteen at the time, young, impetuous and rebellious. I don't know whether it was out of spite for Grandfather Adaire, who had released me to make my choice to die, or if it was just that damned stubborn streak of hers to save a life.... Anyway, Inca joined with me...as I joined with you to save your life in Lima. My spirit was too weak to fight her, and so she was able to stop me from going over the threshold, into the light, and dying.

"The next morning, I awoke and I was coherent. I remember weakly sitting up, and I saw her lying curled up in a fetal position, next to me. I saw blood all over the damn place around her. She'd bled out. I was terrified. About that time, Grandmother Alaria appeared and quickly went to her side. I saw her do something that just blew me away. She knelt over Inca, gently cradled her in her arms like a child and held her face very close to hers. Inca was a gray-blue color. I knew she was dead. I saw Alaria breathe into her slack, parted lips. I watched—and saw—this golden, living energy flow back into Inca. I was transfixed. I knew that what I was seeing was a miracle. There was no question of it.'' His voice shook with emotion. ''Alaria brought Inca back to life.''

''My God, Inca died giving you life? Is that what you're saying?''

Mike nodded. ''I'm going to skip the technical stuff with you and just say that Inca struggled to stop me from choosing death *and* tried to heal me, and she didn't have the necessary power to do both. She'd had two years of training with Adaire and Alaria, and she knew a lot of different healing methods. With her energy, she managed to stop me from crossing over the threshold. She had very little left with which to heal me, though. Instead, what Inca did was transfer my wound, my condition into herself. She gave me her own life-force energy so that I could live. That's what killed her.''

Ann's eyes widened. ''Then...she acquired your wound?''

''Yes.'' Houston sighed. ''Inca knew if she could bring me back, that I'd still die. I'd bleed to death on the floor of that hut. Grandfather Adaire had released me, so that meant I'd be the way I'd been before he found me in the jungle.''

''And Inca willingly sacrificed her life for yours?'' Ann quavered.

''Exactly.'' Houston raised his eyes to the roof of the hut. ''She was a wild, impetuous young woman then. I think she thought that she could pull it off and heal herself of the wound she took on from me. She bit off more than she could chew. Usually she is very good at taking care of her own needs first, above anyone else's. She still is.''

''Even if that's true,'' Ann said, feeling the truth of Inca's goodness in some deep intuitive level of herself, ''Inca gave her life for you.''

''No question,'' Mike murmured.

''And Grandmother Alaria really did bring her back to life?''

He nodded, then frowned. ''Grandmother Alaria is very, very ancient....'' Awkwardly, he continued, ''Alaria and Adaire are role models here at the village of what we can become, if we follow our heart's path. But we're all terribly human, too, and each of us has our own flaws, problems and weaknesses to overcome, first.''

''Yet,'' Ann said, ''it's obvious Adaire didn't want Inca here.''

''That is his karma, something he must work through with her,'' Mike explained. ''He has yet to do it, or she with him. It's still an open, bleeding wound between them. Alaria has forgiven Inca, which is why I suspect she allowed her back here to see us just now.'' He smiled a little. ''Grandfather Adaire isn't happy about it, but there's not much he can do. I pray that he and Inca make peace between themselves. The sooner, the better.'' He opened his left hand and showed Ann an inch-long white scar in the palm of his hand. ''Once I understood what Inca did for me, when I'd mended and finally accepted that I was one of the Jaguar Clan, I sought her out. I asked her what I could do to balance the scales of karma between us. To thank her for fighting for my life and saving me even when I'd given up and was ready to leave this body. She said she wanted me to be her blood brother. She had no family of her own and she wanted to be part of my family.''

''So, you shared one another's blood?'' Ann asked.

''It's more than that, but yes, it's one of five powerful ceremonies we have: life, death, birth, joining and adoption. The adoption ceremony is like a linking between our spirits, but not like the marriage that took place between you and me. It's different, but in some ways similar. She loves me and I love her—sister to brother and vice versa.''

''And Inca came here when she wasn't supposed to? To see you?''

Houston smiled thinly. ''Inca comes and goes where she damn well pleases. She treads where angels and spirit guardians fear to go, believe me. She's a hellion, a rabble-rouser, a zealot, an extremist, but I love her and admire the hell out of her for what she's been able to do...for what she is doing to save the rain forests of Brazil.'' He opened his hands. ''Because she's so driven, so focused, she's out of balance. But she doesn't care. She has the power of the Jaguar Clan in her veins, she has her guardian and she knows how to use—and abuse—the power she has. As she said earlier, she walks a fine line between darkness and light. To her enemies, she's the devil incarnate. To the people of Brazil, who love her, worship the ground she walks on, she's known as the jaguar goddess.''

"Like you're known as the jaguar god here in Peru," Ann ventured.

"Similar, though I play by the rules set out by the Sisterhood of Light. Inca plays by her own rules. But then, if I'd gone through the living hell she did when she was a child, and later as a young adult, I don't think I'd be half as good as she is about it. I'm afraid I'd have been very tempted to side with the Brotherhood of Darkness and go after my enemies, one by one, to even the score....''

Sliding her hands over his, Ann said, "I like her, Mike. I don't care what Inca's done. When she leaned down and pressed her face to my body, I felt and saw the real her.''

Mike entwined his fingers with hers. "Yes," he rasped, "you did. That's only the second time I've seen Inca unshield herself completely. I was stunned that she'd do it here, with Adaire present. But..." he gazed at her "...she can see how pure your heart is, how pure you are, and she knew she could entrust herself entirely to you without fear of reprisal. And Inca runs on fear.

"She gave you two gifts. The first was her friendship, her heart, and the second is something that I know you don't understand— that jaguar claw. It's half of her protection, something she always carries with her. She gave it to you...to our baby...." He blinked a couple of times, his voice suddenly emotional. "I don't know about her. She's so damn unreliable, and yet she turns around and does something like this. I saw and felt her just like you did. We were seeing her good side, the side of her that's whole and not shattered by what life's done to her.''

"It was a real privilege, then?"

Mike slowly rose, wanting to continue the conversation but knowing it was time to go. "It was a gift, *mi querida*. A gift of such unselfish proportions that I would never in a million years have expected it from Inca. I know she put herself on the line for me once, but she has been very protective of herself ever since.'' Mystified, Mike held his hand out to Ann and helped her stand. "Inca knows something we don't. But then, she's farseeing, like Grandfather Adaire, whether he admits it or not. She's got tremendous skills and abilities in place—far more than most of the Jaguar Clan members. More than I do, that's for sure. I know she saw something...and that's why she gave you that gift, that protection...."

Ann slid her arm around Mike's waist and leaned on him. She hated to leave, yet it was time. "Then, darling, she's given the gift not only to me, but to our baby and you."

Mike caressed her hair. "I know," he murmured worriedly. "I know...."

Chapter 15

"Ann, you must rest," Pilar Lachlan pleaded, guiding her over to a rough-hewn chair in the hut where Ann had been seeing patients all day. "Eight months along and you work like you're not pregnant at all!"

"I can pretend, can't I?" Smiling wearily, Ann allowed Pilar, who was married to one of Morgan Trayhern's ex-employees, Culver Lachlan, to sit her down. It was late afternoon and Ann was tired and thirsty.

As if reading her mind, Pilar, a petite woman, of Quechua and Spanish heritage, poured her a glass of water from a clay pitcher on the table. "You can try, my friend, but I see dark circles under your eyes. I can tell your tiredness goes to your bones." She frowned and handed Ann the glass. "I know it has been a month without a visit from Mike. I'm sure it's been hard on both of you. But he'll be here tomorrow morning." Reaching out, Pilar patted Ann's hand.

Ann moved her other hand gently across her very swollen belly beneath the pale pink cotton smock she wore. "I think we're both excited about seeing Mike. She's kicking up a storm in here."

Grinning knowingly, Pilar murmured, "I remember the feeling well. My daughter Rane, who is ten now, was our first child."

She cast a glance toward the straw cradle in the other room of the hut. "Maria is only four months old. She is our second heart child."

Smiling softly, Ann studied the tiny little baby with reddish hair sleeping soundly in the cradle. "She's so pretty, Pilar."

Squeezing her hand, Pilar laughed and said, "Yes. All children born of love are beautiful. Yours will be, too, though you won't think that when she gets you up every two hours to be breast-fed!"

Ann smiled. She didn't know what she would have done without Pilar's help during her pregnancy. Ann had traveled on a monthly circuit to five different villages in the highlands, all within a hundred miles of the nearest fighting that Mike waged against Escovar's men. During that time, Morgan had put Ann in touch with Culver, who lived in the village of San Cristobal. It was Culver's wife, Pilar, the daughter of a jaguar priestess, who had not only helped Ann establish a circuit and routine, but had been her right hand all these months, even while she'd been carrying her own baby! Ann had helped Pilar deliver the strapping eight-pound Maria four months earlier, with Culver there to catch his second daughter as she crowned and slid into his large hands. It was in Culver's hands that Maria drew her first breath. It had been a beautiful birth.

Ann sighed and blotted the perspiration from her brow with a pink linen handkerchief. It was September, and it was hot and humid. She felt the heat more than usual because of her pregnancy. "You need to get home," she murmured, looking out the door at the angle of the sun on the horizon. Pilar drove ten miles over heavily rutted roads to be with her each day, her daughter in tow on some days. The rest of the time, Rane and Culver took care of Maria, providing Pilar had stored up enough breast milk to make that possible.

To look at Pilar, who wore a blue cotton skirt and white blouse, her black hair long and flowing, one would think she was like any other Indian villager. Yet she was a college graduate and once had worked for the Peruvian government as an undercover spy, as well as for Morgan Trayhern. She and her *norteamericano* husband had met and fallen in love ten years ago. But it wasn't until they had rescued Morgan Trayhern from Ramirez's fortress in the highlands that they finally admitted their love and married. Everyone had said Morgan's rescue couldn't be done, but this brave woman had teamed up with a giant of a man—a hardened mercenary—and accomplished the impossible.

Mike had played a role in Morgan's rescue, too. And he knew Culver and Pilar very well. Ann was glad to have such friends, because Mike was gone more than he was at her side. It had been a terrible period of adjustment for her in many ways. Yet every few nights Mike entered her dreams, and she made love with him at the pool of life, or they walked hand in hand in the Village of the Clouds. Sometimes they sat by the rainbow waterfall and talked over what their day had been like. She loved this added form of communication, another hidden plus to his being a member of the Jaguar Clan. His visits in her dreams didn't take place every night, because often, he was attacking Escovar's holdings in dangerous night raids.

"Tonight," Pilar said, standing and smoothing her skirt, "is the first night of the jaguar moon."

Ann tilted her head. "That's a term I've never heard before."

Pilar went over and gently eased her baby daughter from the straw cradle and nestled her against her breast. "The jaguar moon is the seven days before a new moon, when the moon sheds no light on Mother Earth." She walked back and stood near the table. "It is said that this is the time when the Brotherhood of Darkness is at its greatest strength because the Great Goddess and her symbol, the moon, cannot shed her light of protection across our mother, the earth, and all her relations. It is the time when evil spirits have power over the force of light. The Goddess cannot protect us as this evil stalks our land."

Ann raised her brows. "I don't feel anything different," she said.

Pilar caressed her sleeping daughter's chubby little face. "Soon I will know more of these things. I am going into training, my grandmother Aurelia told me. I'll become a member of the Jaguar Clan."

"What do you do for seven days in the dark of the moon?" Ann teased. "Hide?"

With a chuckle, Pilar shook her head. "My grandmother, who is in her nineties, is a very wise woman. She told me to tell you that when the sun goes down, you must remain inside this hut and meditate or pray. Do things that allow you to go inward. These seven days are a time of introspection, of moving deep within ourselves, to see our truth and to feel our way through this time of darkness. It's not a time for many external events, or to start new projects. This is, she has told me, a time when a seed is planted in the ground. It's very dark for that seed in the soil, no?''

''Yes,'' Ann said, pouring herself more water, ''it certainly is as dark as a night with no moon for that little seed buried in fertile earth.''

''So,'' Pilar said, ''use this time to plant new seeds of awareness within yourself.'' She smiled and raised her hand in farewell. ''I will see you tomorrow morning? Mike said he will be here no later than noon?''

Ann nodded. She held up her crossed fingers. ''If everything goes according to plan, he'll helicopter in.''

''And I will do what I can here tomorrow, at your clinic, to help out until he arrives.''

Ann waved goodbye, thankful for Pilar's care and love. Without her friendship, she knew that she wouldn't have fared half as well. Sitting at the table, she gazed down at the white-and-purple orchids that Pilar had brought that morning. Though they were beautiful, they had no scent, not like those gorgeous red-and-yellow ones Mike had given to her in Lima. With a sigh, Ann rested her head on her arms on the rough-hewn table. Exhaustion ate at her. How she missed her husband! She never knew when he would visit until a day or two beforehand, because he feared Escovar finding out.

This time, however, was going to be different. Mike was coming to take her to the Village of the Clouds for the last month of her pregnancy. He wanted her to have a month of serenity, with him at her side. Grandmother Alaria, bless her, had given Mike permission to bring her ''home.'' Ann understood enough to know that the village was indeed a very special place. It was available only to those of the Jaguar Clan, or to a person whose heart was in the right place and who sought healing at the pool of life. Otherwise, one could look at the slopes of the Andes and never even see the village. Ann couldn't explain how that could be and had given up trying. All she knew was that the village was real, and she was eager to be a part of incredible peacefulness and joy that always resided among the heart-centered people who lived there.

In the distance, Ann heard a car entering the village. Frowning, she wondered if Pilar had forgotten something. Or perhaps it was Mike? Her heart lifted a little at that thought. Sometimes he came by car, with Pablo as his driver.

Ann heard the chickens clucking and squawking in protest as the car slowly came to a halt just outside her hut. She didn't sense it was Mike and swallowed her disappointment. She would know if it was him; he always sent his jaguar guardian ahead to tell her of his approach. At those times, Ann had felt the guardian's warmth and strength like an embrace. Hearing two car doors open and then shut, she straightened up in the chair and waited.

Sometimes people in the surrounding villages brought their sick to her. Some of the farmers who made a better living could afford some old clunker of a car to get around in, instead of traveling by foot or donkey, which was the usual means of transportation up here in the highlands.

A man, very lean and around six feet tall, dressed in a short-sleeved white shirt and tan slacks, stepped into the doorway.

Instantly, Ann went on guard. She met his dark, narrowed eyes as they settled on her.

"Yes?" she asked firmly. "May I help you?"

He suddenly smiled. His thin face lost its hardness.

"Ah, are you...Dr. Barbara Forest?"

Ann nodded. Her "other" name was what she went by. No one knew her real name, except for Pilar and Culver. "Yes, I am. Are you ill?"

"Well." He laughed apologetically. "I was driving to my land holdings, up east of here, and I suddenly got very dizzy. Very dizzy." He touched his brow. "They said there was a Red Cross doctor here in the village. So I said, 'Why not stop?'" He walked into the hut and stood in front of her table. "What could cause my dizziness, Doctor?" His gaze moved to her left hand, where there was a plain gold wedding ring on her fourth finger.

Ann slowly rose. "If you'll have a seat, *señor,* I'll take your blood pressure and pulse. We'll see if maybe it's due to high blood pressure. Are you on any medications right now?" She reached for her black physician's bag, put the stethoscope around her neck and drew out the blood pressure cuff.

"No...no medications, Doctor. Ahh, I see you are with child. Soon, eh?"

Ann smiled her perfunctory doctor smile as he pulled out the chair and sat down. Something bothered her about this man. He was, for this area, very richly attired. His shirt was not made of cotton, but of silk, and it clung to his rounded chest. As she approached him, she judged him to be in his middle forties. His skin was a pale gold color, and she guessed that he might be of Spain's Castilian aristocracy. From a very rich family, no doubt. His features were sharp, almost gaunt looking, and his dark brown gaze ferreted around the silent hut.

"Well," she murmured, affixing the blood pressure cuff to his right arm, "let's see what we've got...." She pumped it up, let off the pressure and watched the dial as she listened for the first beat of his heart. He was watching her with great interest, and that bothered her. She had pinned her hair up to keep it off the back of her neck because it had been exceedingly hot of late, and suddenly she felt very self-conscious.

"*Señor,* your blood pressure is normal," Ann informed him, removing the cuff. She saw him nod and appear relieved.

"That is good." He looked around some more as she put the cuff and stethoscope back into her bag. "I had heard of a doctor up here. They said she was very beautiful. A *norteamericana.* I said, 'No, how could that be?' And the gossip was that you'd appeared one day, like an angel from heaven, in February of this year." He snapped his fingers and grinned, showing a row of clean, white teeth. "It's quite unusual for a doctor to be up here. A blessing, yes, but very, very rare."

Ann didn't like him—at all—but she hid her irritation. Moving around to the other side of the table, she said, "I work with the poor, *señor....*"

"Eduardo," he said genially, "you may call me Eduardo. After all, your husband, Major Mike Houston, knows me very well."

The icy grating of his words shattered her. Ann froze. She stared at him. He was relaxed, sprawled out in the chair, his arms across his chest. He smiled up at her, but it wasn't a pleasant smile. It reminded her of a predator's smile right before it killed its frozen prey. That was how Ann felt right then—absolutely unable to move. Her heart thudded harshly in her chest. She felt as if she couldn't breathe.

"Eduardo Escovar at your service, Dr. Ann Houston." He rose and made a sweeping gesture as he bowed in her direction. As he straightened up, he snarled an order in Spanish. Instantly, two armed guards entered the hut, their gazes locked on her.

With a gasp, Ann tried to move. Escape was impossible. Eight months along, she was about as fast as a lumbering elephant. Besides, Ann knew that any violent exercise could induce premature labor. She rested her fingertips on the edge of the table, feeling the blood flowing out of her face.

"*Señor,* I don't know what you are talking about. My name is—"

"Silence, bitch!" he snarled, his lips lifting away from his teeth. "I have tracked you for eight months. Ever since that bastard, Houston, stole you from your apartment in Lima, I have had my loyal spies out, searching." He made a stabbing motion toward her. "My spies have discovered you are Ann Parsons. You work for Perseus. For that slimy Morgan Trayhern." He smiled a little, picking at some imaginary lint on the front of his shirt. His voice softened and became cajoling. "You are Houston's wife. That, I have no doubt." His dark, angry gaze settled on her swollen belly.

Instinctively, Ann shielded her baby with her hand. Terror ate at her. She tried to think, tried to find a way to escape, but it was impossible. Her only help would have been Pilar, but she was gone until tomorrow morning. A coldness flowed up through Ann, more chilling and haunting than she'd ever experienced. Escovar was going to kill her—and her baby.

"Listen," she pleaded hoarsely, "don't hurt my baby! I'm eight months along...can't you—"

In one lightning motion, Escovar lunged forward and with his open hand, slapped her as hard as he could across the face.

Her head exploded with light and pain. Ann cried out and staggered backward. She felt herself falling from the unexpected blow. Somehow, she threw out her arm as she was knocked sideways, and her hand struck the wall of the hut, breaking her fall. She crumpled heavily to the mat beside the table. Liquid flowed hotly out of her nostrils and across her parted lips. She tasted the salty, metallic taste of her blood. Automatically, she pressed her fingers against her throbbing nose and cheek.

"Get her up!" Escovar rasped.

Instantly, his two guards, heavily armed with modern rifles, moved forward.

Their hands bit savagely into Ann's arms as they jerked her to
her feet. She cried out as pain serrated her belly. *No! God, no!*

"In the car!"

Semiconscious, Ann was literally dragged between the two
guards. She saw several villagers hiding behind their huts, their
eyes huge with terror. The door was opened and the men shoved
her into the back seat. Sobbing, Ann was sandwiched in the rear
seat of the white luxury sedan by the two large, muscular guards.
The air in the car was hot and humid. She watched through narrowed eyes as Escovar's driver quickly opened the front passenger
door for him. Escovar looked down before getting in.

"Comfortable, Señora Houston? I hope so. We are going for a
little ride to a place not far from here that's very, very famous."
He grinned savagely and slid into the leather seat.

Ann tried to compose herself. The guards were tense beside her,
and when she tried to wipe the blood from her nose, they glared
at her. Emotionally, she was in such terror that her mind was
frozen, and she could taste death in her mouth. She had to try and
think! *Think!* Mike wouldn't be here until tomorrow, at noon. Did
Escovar know he was coming? Oh, God, she had to keep his
arrival time a secret at all costs! A sob caught in her throat as she
protectively covered her unborn daughter with her hands. The glittering hate that Escovar had for her—for Mike—was palpable.

"W-where are you taking me?" she demanded in a wobbling
voice.

Escovar turned his head and smiled generously. "Ah, Señora
Houston, this is a place you must visit." He turned in his seat and
devoted all his attention to her. "Tell me, when does your very
famous husband come home, eh?"

Ann avoided his piercing gaze. "I—I don't know. I never
know...."

Chuckling, Escovar nodded. "Yes, well, that's very wise of
him. He always operates on a need-to-know basis. I thought," he
said with a sigh, "that since you are the one he loves most, he'd
certainly let you know when he was coming for a visit. My guards
persuaded several of the villagers where you have your clinic to
talk. Pity. None of them seemed to know when the jaguar god
was going to appear."

Coldness crept over Ann. She knew Escovar was prone to use
torture to get the information he wanted. Yet she'd not heard of

his arrival in the village. That was a clue to her of how lethal he was at what he did. He was almost like a jaguar in some ways, a shadow until he wanted to be seen.

As they bumped along the rutted road, the bouncing and jerking was hard on her. Ann could feel telltale pains around her belly. As much as she could, she held her abdomen, held her daughter from the jolting motions on the rutted road. Soon they were on another dirt road, one lined by a thousand-foot dropoff into the jungle below on one side and in a thousand-foot cliff of yellow-and-red soil on the other.

Escovar hummed a tune and seemed to be enjoying the scenery. Ann shook in fear. She couldn't help it. Without a doubt, Escovar would kill her—and her baby. It was only a matter of time. Her mouth was cottony and dry. She tried to call Mike, but the terror broke her concentration. Again and again, Ann tried to call him. She knew he would hear her, but it had to be an intense, concentrated thought before he could pick it up. Oh, dear God, what was she going to do? Closing her eyes, she felt hot and nauseous. Ann knew there was no talking Escovar out of anything. She felt the full extent of his rage and hatred and it battered her senses.

As the sun was setting on the western horizon, the sky becoming gray with gathering clouds, Escovar snapped at the driver to stop. Ann looked around. They were parked in the middle of the dirt road, its green, grassy edge littered with bushes and big gray rocks before it fell away into space.

"Get her out!" Escovar ordered as he left the car.

Her legs wouldn't work and Ann was dragged between the guards to the edge of the cliff. Her eyes bulged as she struggled to push away from the precipice. Dirt and stones tumbled down with her movements. The first hundred feet was nothing but rock, littered with branches from trees and bushes that had tumbled, over time, from the cliff above them.

Escovar sauntered over. He lit a cigarette and took a long, deep drag of smoke into his lungs. His eyes glittered as he studied her.

"You know this place, Señora Houston?"

Her skin crawled. Wildly, Ann looked around. "N-no, I don't."

He smiled a little and took another drag on his cigarette. "I'm surprised, frankly, because your husband has made this a very famous place." He stabbed with his cigarette down the slope. "Look," he snarled. "You see those four white crosses down there, about five hundred feet below? Just before the edge of the jungle?''

Ann tried to gather her composure. Sweat was dripping into her eyes and they burned with pain. Tears of terror ran down her cheeks. Blinking rapidly, she tried to concentrate on where he was pointing. Halfway down the slope, she saw four white crosses with huge bunches of fresh flowers around each one.

''Y-yes, I see them,'' she whispered hoarsely. The guards' hands bit deeply into her arms, the pain constant.

Escovar took another drag on his cigarette. He looked at her, his face raw with grief. ''Those four crosses are my wife, my two sons and my daughter, *señora*,'' he rasped. ''Your husband murdered them in cold blood! Look at them, damn you! Look at them because it is the last thing you are going to see!''

With a cry, Ann jerked her head toward him. ''Señor Escovar, please, don't do this! Mike didn't murder your family! I swear it! It was an accident! He was following them in a helicopter and trying to land in front of them. The driver of your family's car panicked. He was going too fast for this road. The car flipped!'' Ann sobbed as she felt the guards move her within inches of the cliff edge. ''Oh, God, you've *got* to believe me! Mike never meant to harm your family. I swear it....'' She sobbed as she clung to his angry features with tear-flooded eyes. His gaze was black and glittering as he stepped toward her.

''Do you know how *much* I loved my wife?'' he screamed into her face. Reaching out, he wrapped his hand through her hair and jerked her head forward.

Ann felt his breath against her face, hot and nauseating. She was held captive, her neck and head twisted at a painful angle as Escovar glared down at her. Her scalp radiated in pain. She tried not to cry out as tears slipped from her eyes.

''My children. The babies my beautiful Juanita carried in her belly, which I tenderly caressed every day she carried them....'' His voice cracked. ''I *loved* her. I loved them! Your murdering husband took them from me. The coward didn't come to me. No,'' he rasped, his spittle splaying across her face, ''he picked on innocents who could not protect themselves.''

Suddenly, he released Ann's hair.

With a cry, she was jerked upright by the guards once again. Escovar was smiling, but there was no life in his eyes. Only death. "Let me see..." he murmured, composing himself. "I have killed his first wife and I understand she was pregnant. Too bad. I counted that as one death. To make up for the death of my sweet little daughter, Elizabeth." He shrugged. "And then the second woman he loved, that *norteamericana* who worked in the embassy. Poof!" He threw up his hands and laughed.

Ann winced. She thought he was going to strike her.

"Her death paid for Ernesto's death, my youngest son...."

Escovar reached out, gripping her belly hard.

Ann screamed and kicked out, trying to protect her baby from his clawlike hands.

Escovar dodged her attempt, his hand loosening on her belly. He grinned savagely.

"I should have both your legs broken for that," he snarled, staying just out of range of her flailing feet. "Ordinarily, I would," he told her archly. "But I am not a man without honor, not like your bastard husband...." Again, he inhaled deeply on the cigarette, regarding her from hooded eyes.

Ann sobbed for breath. She hated his touch on her belly; she felt his hatred and revenge and tasted it in her mouth.

"So, you will pay for my Juanita, my heart, who I grieve for daily." He turned and pointed to the largest of the four crosses at the bottom of the cliff, the one with the most flowers around it. "Every day, did you know? I have one of my men come here and place fresh flowers near these crosses. Oh, they are not buried here. No, they are at the compound, in proper graves where I can go and talk to them daily. It is a custom, you know, *señora?* To place a cross to remind everyone that they died a needless death at the hands of a murderer."

She saw Escovar's eyes glitter with tears. His voice became laced with grief and grew harsh with emotion as he turned back to face her.

"Well, now, Houston can place a white cross of his own down there." Escovar smiled, showing his white teeth. "You and your unborn baby will be an even trade for my wife and my other son's death. Yes, that feels right to me. When he finds you—if he can find you—he will understand it all...my plan. I knew someday he would fall in love again. And I waited.... I have the patience of a jaguar, also." He dropped the cigarette to the yellow dirt and crushed it out with the sole of his expensive loafer.

"I will not torture you, *señora*. Ordinarily, I would. But you are a woman, I can see, of great courage. Most people who are dragged in front of me lose their bowels and scream for mercy. You did not. You begged only for your baby's life. I find that— commendable. Houston, when he finds you, will find your body eaten by buzzards. There won't be much of you left to grieve over." He smiled. "Say your prayers, *señora*. For you are going to die...."

"Nooo!" Ann shrieked, her voice cracking. She tried to yank free of the guards, but they were simply too strong, and she too far along to do anything more than struggle in their grip. She saw Escovar's face grow cold and expressionless. His eyes went dead. She dug her heels in as the guards propelled her forward, toward the edge of the cliff.

And then everything slowed down. Ann closed her eyes. She drew a deep, quavering breath into her body. Opening her heart fully for the first time, she pictured Mike's hard, scarred face in front of her. She sent out a cry for help that reverberated through her, through everything surrounding her in that moment. For the first time, Ann surrendered fully to her love for Mike. She felt all her emotions build, felt the thunderous power of feeling grow within her, and as she pictured him, she sent everything she felt to him. Within those long, drawn-out seconds, she surrendered fully to the magic of possibility, to his world, his belief in the mystical, the unseen. This was one time when she must reach out, embrace him fully and believe—for her baby's sake...for any chance of survival....

Seconds later, she was hurled out into space. Her last view was that of the sharp, gray rocks racing up to meet her. Her scream was for Mike...and then darkness was upon her and she remembered no more.

Chapter 16

The dawn was a thin, bloody ribbon along the horizon. Houston tried to keep his focus, his concentration, but the pain in his lower body, on the left side of his rib cage and head kept shredding what little composure he could muster. The shaking of the helicopter around him, the humid wind whipping into the open craft where his squad of hardened soldiers sat as they flew toward their destination, didn't help.

Hours earlier, he'd heard Ann scream for help. Far south of her in the Andes, in the middle of a firefight with some of the heaviest opposition Escovar had thrown against his men to date, Mike knew she was dying. He could feel it throughout his body. He'd known it the instant he'd felt her scream rip through him. And he knew...oh, hell, he knew.... Sweat trickled down the hard planes of his features, across his stubbled beard as he anxiously sought out the grayish black ground a thousand feet below him.

His jaguar guardian was with Ann and he could feel everything that Ann was experiencing. She was unconscious and bleeding to death. The massive pain he was feeling in his abdomen were savage birthing contractions. Trying to keep his anguish at bay, his need to sob, Houston sat in the copilot's seat, gripping his fists in his lap. He'd tried to withdraw from the firefight when Ann's cry shattered him, but it was impossible. Escovar's men had launched such a massive counterattack that Mike had finally had to call in army reserves from Lima itself to come and help extricate him and his squads.

Now, as the bloodred color on the horizon thickened to announce the coming morning light, Houston had managed to get two chopper loads of men—his handpicked, well-trained soldiers—out of that hellhole and into the air to fly to Ann's side. He knew where she was and it sickened him until he wanted to vomit. Escovar had planned this so well, so very well.... Mike couldn't believe Escovar had found out his connection to Ann, they'd tried so carefully to hide her status. The spies in the Peruvian government on Escovar's payroll had won again.

Over and over, Mike sent Ann energy. But he had to be there in person, he had to be there at her side for it to make a real and lasting difference. Judging from all the pain in his body he was picking up from her own, he knew she had broken ribs and a wound on the side of her head. The cutting pains in his abdomen told him his daughter was in the process of being born—alone to die if he could not reach them in time. Closing his eyes, Houston tried to steady his reeling emotions, his love for Ann, his terror in knowing that he was feeling her life slowly leaking away from her.

His mind spun wildly with plans and tactics. It wouldn't be unlike Escovar to set up a trap, as Mike came to rescue the woman he loved more than life. Escovar could be waiting for him on the cliffside his own family had accidentally driven over, rolling end over end and dying five hundred feet below as the car smashed into the jungle.

Rubbing his face savagely, Houston took deep, gulping breaths. Never had he expected Escovar to make a stand against him over the graves of his lost family. That was sacred ground to him—and to Mike. But he'd broken that taboo. Escovar's hatred of him was so complete that he'd captured Ann, taken her to the spot where his family's car had run off the road, and he'd either shot her, tortured her or pushed her off that cliff. Mike didn't want to consider that he might have done all of those unthinkable things to her and then hurled her down the slope, thinking she was dead or dying. Then he had left her for the black buzzards to find as the sun rose this morning.

Choking on bile, hatred consuming him, Houston struggled to clear away his emotions and remain focused on Ann and her rapidly deteriorating condition. The plan he'd formulated swam in his head. He would leap out of the helicopter just above the ground when they located Ann. And then he'd deploy the two chopper loads of men above him—just in case Escovar was laying a trap for him. Once his men had secured the area, both choppers would land.

Mike had his paramedic pack; he had his other skills.... If he could stabilize Ann and the baby, they could possibly fly them to Tarapoto, the nearest city with a hospital, a hundred miles west.

So much could go wrong. Mike knew Ann had been injured at dusk yesterday. For six hours, she'd not received any stabilizing medical help. He wondered how, with the severity of her injuries, she'd held on this long. Alone, abandoned by him in her greatest hour of need... He felt her life ebbing away rapidly now. Mike felt her fighting, but she didn't have the necessary strength to do it much longer. His eyes narrowed as the helicopter rose over the last jungle-clad hill to that road where Escovar had lost his family.

The bloodred ribbon was turning a deep pink color as the sun's rays neared the horizon. Houston ordered Captain Sanchez, the pilot, to bank away from the road they paralleled and head toward the jungle below. There was an abandoned car on the dirt road, the doors open and no sign of life around the vehicle. As the helicopter turned steeply the spinning of the thick blades sending out heavy, drumming sounds in the humid morning, Mike anxiously searched the slope below for Ann.

In the meantime, the other helicopter, armed with a door machine gun, began to prowl the territorial limits of the area Houston had laid out for them earlier. They would be the guard dogs—in case Escovar was waiting...waiting to spring his trap. Mike's mind raced with questions. Why was there a car abandoned up on the road?

Houston would not endanger his men for his own personal needs any more than necessary. He would try to locate Ann, leap off the chopper and send them high enough, far enough away, to stay out of the range of rifles and rocket fire as he worked to save her life.

"There!" Pablo cried from the rear of the aircraft. He made

stabbing motions out the door of the helicopter. "Major Houston! *¡Commandante! ¡Commandante!* See?"

Mike got out of the copilot's seat and made his way through the tightly packed squadron of heavily armed men. Kneeling down at the door, where the wind whipped into the cabin, he gripped Pablo's shoulder. The young soldier was jabbing his finger repeatedly toward the edge of the jungle. Squinting, Mike could make out nothing at first as the helicopter bobbled and shook in the early morning air currents rising off the humid land.

Yes! His heart slammed in his chest. Mike saw it—he saw— Wiping his mouth, he leaned farther out the door. In the grayish light, he could barely make out Ann's still form. She was on her back, seemingly unconscious. And alone. So alone...

No...wait! As the helicopter skidded closer, descending rapidly in altitude, Houston blinked away the sweat stinging his eyes. Heart pounding, he saw a soldier in green-and-black fatigues jogging down the road toward the abandoned car.

Inca! It was Inca! But—how?

Stunned, Houston froze momentarily, his eyes widening. Inca halted and lifted her face toward them, her expression one of rage mixed with terror.

"Get closer!" Houston roared to Sanchez. "She's one of us." He leaned down and grabbed his paramedic pack. The helicopter dropped rapidly, within fifty feet of the grassy slope. His mind spun with questions. If Inca was here...how the hell had she gotten here? She didn't have the ability to physically transport herself from one place to another. Or did she? *No, impossible.*

The battering air slammed against Mike as he made a five-foot leap off the lip of the helicopter to the earth below him. Houston had thrown out his paramedic bag first. It landed and rolled twenty feet away from where Ann was located. The instant Mike leaped, he bent his knees to absorb the shock of contact. The slope was too steep and he'd have to roll. As he hit the wet, slippery grass, he heard the helicopter's engine rev to full power and pull up high and fast.

"Michael! Michael!"

He threw his arms and legs out to halt his roll. The wet grass soaked his clothing. He sprang to his feet. Inca's call was hoarse. Desperate. Turning, Houston grabbed his black paramedic bag and dug the toes of his boots into the soft, wet earth, heading for Ann.

He whipped a look to his left as he ran. Inca had leaped off the road, rifle in hand, and was scrambling down the rocky slope toward him.

With each running stride, he wondered if Escovar was nearby and waiting. But his gaze was riveted on Ann, who lay unconscious on her back, looking like a splayed-out, broken doll in the dreary gray light of dawn. He heard Inca approaching. Her green eyes shone with tears and utter desperation.

"I got here just as fast as I could," Inca sobbed. She dropped her rifle as she hurried toward Ann. "Get the baby! The baby's coming..." she cried over the noise of the helicopter's departure.

Pushing for breath, Houston dropped to his knees beside Ann. He tore open the paramedic pack. Inca fell to her own knees, breathing heavily. She immediately placed her hands on the sides of Ann's bloodied head.

"How long have you been here?" he rasped, jerking out the labor supplies. His gaze shot to Ann's pale, unmoving face. How pasty she looked! Her lips were parted. He saw dried blood from her nose, the bruise around her left eye. Inca was holding her with all her strength, all her energy, he realized.

"A few minutes after Escovar threw her off that damn cliff. She must have hit the trees, which broke her fall. I've been trying to help her hang on. At one point, I think she regained consciousness." Inca rasped. "I'm tired, Michael...I'm almost out of energy. The baby is being born...Ann's bleeding to death from the inside...."

"The placenta has been torn away from her uterus," he whispered raggedly, quickly examining Ann. He saw the bloody mass on the right side of her head. He feared the worst: a deadly head injury.

"Can you keep stabilizing her?" he asked anxiously. If she'd become conscious earlier, that meant that even though the head wound looked bad, it wasn't a subdural hematoma, which could cause brain damage.

Inca laughed hoarsely. "Even I run out of energy eventually. It took nearly everything I had to get her to this point."

Mike spread the silver-lined blanket beneath Ann's hips. He moved her as gently as possible. He saw the baby's head crowning. It was a matter of moments before his daughter would be born. He had to hurry. Snapping on latex gloves, he grabbed the scissors and clamps that would be necessary. Positioning himself between Ann's legs, he placed his hand on his daughter's head. Life and death. It was so horribly entwined. He knelt there, sobbing for breath.

As his daughter entered the world, her tiny head resting in his large hands, joy filtered through Mike's terror. Her tiny face was flushed pink with health. In the next contraction, he allowed his daughter to turn on her shoulder, and then the rest of her perfectly formed body appeared and slipped into his awaiting hands.

"I've got her!"

Inca nodded. She rested her brow against Ann's hair and closed her eyes. "Thank the Great Goddess..." she whispered unsteadily. Tears choked her voice.

Rapidly, Mike placed a small blanket around his daughter, keeping her cradled in his arm, against his body. The last of the blood pulsated through the cord. He placed the clamps on the umbilical cord. His gaze went to Ann. Tears blurred his vision.

"She's slipping," Inca cried. "Oh, damn, I can't hold her anymore.... Michael!" She collapsed beside Ann, her features pale.

There! Houston quickly cut the umbilical cord. Just as he did, the rest of the placenta delivered. That was good. Quickly tying off the cord, he wrapped his daughter tightly in the blanket. Rising up on unsteady legs, he moved forward. In one motion, he gripped Inca's shoulder as she lay there, sending Ann the last of whatever energy she had left in her.

"Here," he rasped, pulling Inca away. "Lie down on your side. Hold the baby next to you. Just hold her against your chest and keep her warm. That's all you have to do...." He looked into Inca's watering eyes. He saw the devastation, the hopelessness in them. She did as he instructed and rolled over. As he tucked the baby into her arms, against her bandoleer-laden chest, he gave her an unsteady smile of thanks.

"Save her...." Inca sobbed. "Save Ann—you have more energy than I do...."

Houston wasn't sure Ann could be saved this time. As the light grew from the coming dawn, he saw the dark stain of blood around her lower body. How much blood had she lost? With the birth of the baby, the bleeding should stop. Gently, he gathered his wife, the woman he loved so fiercely, into his arms. He was careful, because he knew she had broken ribs, and any movement might puncture her left lung.

He heard the helicopters droning above him. He sensed that Escovar was nowhere around. For whatever reason, the man was not going to engage him in a firefight on his family's graves. As he moved his hand across Ann's limp hair and closed his eyes to make contact with her spirit, Mike knew that Escovar wanted him to feel the same anguish that he had when he'd discovered his family dead at the bottom of this slope. No more than fifty feet away from where Ann clung to life in Mike's arms were the four crosses ringed in fresh flowers, a poignant reminder of that terrible event of so many years ago....

Tears stung his eyes as he worked to forge the fragile connection with Ann. There was so little life left in her. He heard a baby crying piteously and realized belatedly that it was their baby—their daughter—crying out for Ann, for her nourishing milk, her loving arms. A sob ripped through Houston, shuddering through his entire body. Ann couldn't die! She just couldn't! Yet compared to the time she'd nearly died from that hemorrhagic fever in Lima, she was much weaker.

The baby's cries became stronger. More insistent. Houston concentrated. He focused on holding on to Ann, on to her spirit, which stood at the threshold of death. Did he have the power to pull her back? He felt his composure shredding. He felt his anguish over the possibility of losing her. Ann couldn't die! He needed her! He loved her! Their daughter had to have a mother, dammit! Ann had to come back! The sobs ripped out of his contorted mouth as he leaned over her, cradling her helplessly in his arms. She was so cold, her body limp, without life. No! He'd just found her! He didn't care what laws of the code he had to break. He wanted her back! He loved her too much to let her go!

The cry of a baby made Ann fight for consciousness. She struggled against the weighted feeling of her eyelids as the baby's cries became more plaintive. It was her daughter—she knew it. As she barely lifted her lashes, Ann saw someone leaning over her, staring down at her. The effort to try and see who it was was almost too much for her. She felt a hand, strong and firm, on her arm.

Mike...it had to be Mike! Her lips parted and she tried to smile. He'd come...he'd come for her....

"Ann?"

Yes, that was Mike's voice. Off-key, ragged sounding, but his voice. Ann rallied and tried to open her eyes once again. This time, she was more aware of her surroundings. The white walls behind Mike as he stood leaning over her, anxiety written in every plane of his dirty, perspiration-streaked features, told her she was in a building of some kind.

Again, she heard the cry of a baby. Her baby...their daughter.

Her mind wasn't functioning well. She saw Mike's grim mouth part. He reached over, and with a trembling hand, kept stroking her head.

"*Mi querida?* You're safe. You're in a hospital...."

Safe. The word rang through her like a breath of life-giving air. Mike was here, with her. He was dirty. He was in uniform. His face was deeply lined with exhaustion. His eyes were red rimmed and she knew he'd been crying. Why? And then the entire series of events with Escovar came flowing back through her. It was too much. Ann tried to take a deep breath, but it hurt too much, the left side of her rib cage reminding her that she'd broken some of those bones in the fall after Escovar had pushed her over the cliff.

Closing her eyes, Ann focused on Mike's hand, which gripped hers so tightly. She remembered Inca. Opening her eyes, she looked up at him. Inca was not there with him. Had it been her imagination? Ann did not know where reality began or ended anymore. It didn't matter. Not at all.

The cry of her daughter made Ann rally. Her gaze moved left, toward the sound of her baby.

"You hear her?" Mike asked hoarsely, praying that Ann could. She'd sustained a nasty concussion from the blow to her head, near her ear. The doctor had given her twenty stitches to close up the wound.

Ann opened her chapped, dry lips.

Mike smiled a little. "Hold on. I'll get her," he whispered unsteadily.

Closing her eyes, Ann wished for more strength, and had none. Incredibly weak, she could feel the IVs in both her arms, sending life-giving fluids to sustain and stabilize her. She became aware of throbbing pain every now and again in her lower abdomen. Her baby, at some point, had been born. She watched through half-closed eyes as Mike moved away. He returned moments later with a tender look on his face. In his arms, in a soft, pink blanket held gently against him, was their daughter.

Anxiously, Ann looked. She tried to lift her head.

"Don't struggle," Mike whispered unsteadily. He sat on the edge of the bed, facing his wife. Very carefully, he laid their daughter across her abdomen.

"You've got broken ribs on the left side," he warned as he held their daughter so Ann could look at her for the first time. The joy in Ann's eyes, the tears that sprang to them, made him smile tiredly. "She's healthy and doing just fine, *mi querida*." His voice broke. "And you're going to be fine, too..." Houston allowed his tears to flow freely down his stubbled, dirty face. They had arrived here at the Tarapoto Hospital three hours earlier. With the help of the emergency room doctor, Ann had been stabilized and whole blood given to her by himself and Inca. He had been right; as soon as their daughter was born, Ann's internal bleeding ceased. The birth had been the biggest threat to her life. She had been bleeding to death with each wave of contractions.

Ann sobbed. It hurt to move, but she weakly lifted her hand and placed it on her tiny daughter's dark-haired head. She saw Mike's mouth curve tenderly upward. He gazed down at her.

"I love you," he rasped, and he leaned forward and placed a very gentle kiss upon her mouth, welcoming her back, welcoming her into his heart once again.

Ann drowned in the splendor of his mouth. Mike was so strong and cherishing as he moved his lips against hers. His breath gave her life, and more energy. In her hands, on her belly, she held their baby daughter, who had stopped crying the moment she was with her mother. Ann was alive. Mike was here, with her. And most important, their baby was with them—alive and well. As he eased his mouth from hers, hot tears spilled from her eyes.

"I...love you..." Ann whispered brokenly, clinging to his stormy gaze. In that moment before she'd been hurled off the cliff by Escovar, she had surrendered fully to his love, to him. Ann understood now, as never before, what Grandfather Adaire had talked about, and what Alaria had hinted at. The complete surrender of herself on all levels to the love she felt for Mike had occurred. She was stunned and warmed by the strength and nurturance of his love for her as she lay there. She felt Mike grip her shoulder momentarily as he looked down at their baby.

"She's beautiful," he said hoarsely, his voice cracking, "just like her mother...."

Outside the private room, Houston sank against the white-washed wall of the small hospital. His knees were weak. He could barely think. The hospital personnel moved around him in a ceaseless flow of traffic up and down the hall. A bone-deep weariness struck him so hard that for a full minute he didn't think he could move, much less walk. Down the hall, in another private room, Inca was sleeping. Right now, Ann was breast-feeding their daughter for the first time. The baby would sleep, and then so would she. They would be together. And now he had to get some sleep or he was going to keel over right here.

Shoving himself away from the wall, Houston blinked back the last of the tears burning in his eyes. As he headed toward the room where Inca slept, his heart felt bruised with all the emotional upheavals he'd experienced in the last twenty-four hours. Opening the door, he entered the room and saw Inca sitting up on the edge of the bed. She was still in uniform, like him. The bandoleers of ammunition she always carried across her shoulders were hung over a chair nearby, with her rifle. Her black hair was mussed, an ebony waterfall spilling over her slumped shoulders as she sat there, head bowed.

Forcing himself over to her bedside, Mike drew up the chair with the bandoleers hanging across it. Searching Inca's pale features as she lifted her head, he realized for the first time what it had cost her to try and save Ann and his baby. Being able to transport herself physically, from one country to another was known as bilocation. The power it took to do it was beyond his comprehension, but she had that ability and had used it to try to help Ann. He drew the chair under him and sat down, his arms resting across the top. "How are you doing?" he asked huskily. He was slurring his words.

Inca shrugged weakly. "Like hell itself ran over me," she joked tiredly.

"Makes two of us," Houston teased huskily, and shared a one-cornered smile with her. "I don't know how you did it, but I owe you more than I can ever repay you, Inca." And he meant that. Mike watched her shadowed, willow green eyes narrow briefly as she sat there, her hands gripping the edge of the bed.

"You owe me nothing."

"How did you know?" He searched her pale, exhausted features.

Lifting her head, Inca took a deep, shuddering breath. "When I touched Ann's belly, when I laid my head against her to bless your baby, I saw it...." Her voice deepened with despair. "I saw all of it...."

Houston scowled. It was on the tip of his tongue to ask why she hadn't told him, but he knew why. As many laws as Inca might break regarding the Sisterhood of Light, some she would never break because it would mean permanent excommunication from the village, and from the Jaguar Clan. She would be stripped forever of her guardian and become a rogue clan member, only to be hunted down by the Brotherhood of Darkness. Even she did not want to lose her status, though at times she fought against the elders of the village like a rebellious, headstrong child.

"I—I wanted to, my brother." Her voice broke with fervency. "Believe me, I wanted to."

Mike nodded and rested his chin against his hands as he held her glistening gaze. "So you did the next best thing—you teleported from Brazil and then came in and picked up the pieces?"

Her mouth stretched a little. "I did what I could within our laws, my brother." She slowly sat up and pushed her thick, black hair away from her face.

Houston cocked his head, regarding her quizzically.

Inca laughed. The sound, faint in comparison to her normal husky laughter. But she seemed close to her old self. "Less than thirty seconds after Escovar threw Ann off that cliff, I took him down." Her eyes glittered. Her voice lowered to a growl as she met Houston's widening eyes. "He is dead, my brother. And so are the two thugs who were with him. I appeared there, ten feet away from them, right after they threw Ann off the cliff. They picked up their guns and shot at me."

Stunned, Houston stared at her. The silence was like a sharp knife ready to fall between them. His mind whirled.

"Then that's why the car was up there...but no bodies."

Her mouth twitched. "I called in the jaguars. They disposed of the bodies. Fitting end, don't you think, to this death spiral dance you've been in with him?''

Mike shut his eyes tightly. "Inca...."

Reaching out, she gripped his arm. "By the time Ann had stopped rolling, I was being fired upon. Escovar ran. His two henchmen hid and there was a firefight on the road. It took more than ten minutes before I could kill the two of them. I called the local jaguars, a male and female who own the territory, and told them to carry off their bodies. I didn't care what happened to them." Her eyes flashed dangerously. "Then I went after Escovar. I knew you were on your way to Ann. I saw your guardian with her and knew that what could be done was being done for her. So I set off after Escovar, to track him down and make sure he would not be there when you arrived. To take care of him once and for all.

"I tracked him down with my guardian." Her green eyes glittered with satisfaction. "Escovar shot at me, missed, but I did not. He died with a bullet in his head." She lifted her chin imperiously. "A fitting end to a brother of the darkness, do you not think?"

Mike was stunned. He could only nod.

She chuckled. "The local jaguar had her fill of Escovar, I'm sure. The rest of his carcass is buzzard bait out there right now. His men will never find him. That I am sure of. A good end for a murdering bastard like that, is it not?" She slowly flexed her hand, pleased with herself, and stared at Mike.

Houston lifted his head. He saw the glittering hate in Inca's green eyes, and the satisfaction in them, too. "He's dead?" Stunned, he saw Inca nod and then give him a lethal smile. It was the smile of a jaguar that had won a heated battle.

"If you think for one moment that I was going to let that murdering son of the darkness take Ann and your baby's life, you are mistaken, Mike. The Great Goddess did not give me that vision of Ann's future for nothing and you know it."

"I didn't know you had that kind of power," he murmured, still shaken by the fact that Escovar was dead.

"Ahh, brother, you are so dense sometimes!" Inca slowly unwound, like a sinuous jaguar, from the side of the bed. Ruffling his dirty hair, she stepped over to him and slid her arm around his heavy, slumped shoulders. "If it had not been for the fact I gave Ann that jaguar claw, my guardian's symbol, I would never have been able to do what I did.'' She patted Mike's shoulder gently. ''You see, the last thing Ann did before she hit the ground was grab for that necklace she wore. She called you...and then she called my guardian.'' Grinning tiredly, Inca held his gaze. ''I did not break code for once, my brother. By giving Ann my second guardian, I made sure she had every right to ask for divine intervention and help from me—and them. I could come once she called me. Before that, I was helpless to intervene—even though I wanted to.''

''So she had two guardians working to save her?''

''Yes,'' Inca said, satisfaction purring in her husky voice. ''That is what saved her, my brother. Elder Adaire will not be appearing before me to chew me out over this mission.'' Inca chuckled indulgently and raked her fingers through her thick, dirty hair. ''I am filthy. I am going to take a shower and then I am going to eat. I'm starving! You, on the other hand, look like hell warmed over.'' She slapped his shoulder and pointed to the other narrow hospital bed. ''Go lie down. I'll keep guard over your wife and daughter. After all, I am the little one's aunt. And this is the first time I get to practice being one. You sleep. I will guard and take care of your family for you....''

Ten hours later, Houston awoke. He felt groggy, but he had much of his strength back. The smell of the jungle, the mud and dried blood, was too much even for him, so he stripped out of his fatigues, took a quick, hot shower, shaved, put on a fresh set of clothes and quickly headed back to Ann's room. The watch on his wrist read 0300. The hospital hall was deserted except for one nurse at the desk. At both ends of the hall, Houston had stationed guards—his own men—in case Escovar's thugs tried to make an attempt on their lives.

He had business to attend to and that had to come first, even though he wanted to peek in on Ann and their daughter. Using the telephone at the nurses' station, he reported in to a top official in Lima that Escovar was dead. The satisfaction Mike felt was small in comparison to the relief. With Escovar out of the picture, that meant an end to the death spiral dance for him—and more important, for Ann and his baby daughter.

Finishing his call to the official, Houston ordered his two squads to fly back to Lima for a well-deserved rest. He himself had been given a month's leave, on the spot, by the official. As he walked back down the hall, toward his wife's room, his heart felt lighter and lighter. For the first time since everything that had happened, Mike felt joy replacing dread. Hope replacing fear. As soon as Ann was well enough to travel, he would take her and his daughter to the Village of the Clouds. Grandmother Alaria had promised them a month there, and he was going to take her up on it, without question and with gratitude.

Houston quietly opened the door to Ann's room and slipped in. The harsh light from the hall flooded in around him. He saw that Ann was sleeping soundly, their baby daughter nestled in her arms. A soft smile tipped the corners of his mouth. Inca lay on the floor, next to Ann's bed, only a blanket for a mattress beneath her. She, too, was sleeping deeply. Her rifle, which was never more than a few inches from her, lay at her side, her fingers draped across it. That was the way of Inca's life: she was a green warrior in Brazil, a hit-and-run specialist against those who would destroy her rain forest home, which was really the womb of Mother Earth.

His gaze moved back to Ann's shadowed face. Already she appeared to be stronger and have more color. He felt her growing strength as he unshielded to allow himself to feel her and their baby fully. Yes, life was pulsing through them once again. The ache to be with them overwhelmed Mike. Quietly crossing the room, he was careful to move slowly. If Inca sensed any danger, she'd snap awake and grab that rifle so fast that he knew it would make even the head of a seasoned military man like him swim.

But he had jaguar blood and could pad so softly as to never be heard—not even by Inca. Easing himself onto the bed, Houston settled his bulk gently against his wife's form. Sliding one arm beneath Ann's neck, he lay on his side and placed his other arm across her until his hand closed over his baby daughter, wrapped in the fleecy pink blanket. Tiredness flowed over Mike once more as he pressed his brow gently against Ann's hair. How good it was to feel her soft, shallow breath against him. An exhausted smile tipped the corners of his mouth as he closed his eyes and allowed the peace, the joy, to thread through him. In moments, Houston was asleep, with the woman he loved so fiercely in his arms and their baby daughter beside them.

Chapter 17

Ann shared a secret smile with Mike, who sat on the edge of her bed, his arm draped casually around her shoulders. Next to him was Grandfather Adaire, who had materialized before them little less than fifteen minutes earlier. Mike had warned her he was coming and *how* he would come. Teleportation was something that only a few of the Jaguar Clan could accomplish.

Grandmother Alaria had other duties to fulfill, so she'd asked her husband to come in her stead. Ann was disappointed, but knew that when they reached the village, Grandmother Alaria's love and support would be there for their daughter. One of the many things Ann was getting used to was the ebb and flow of situations and not to assume or expect. As Mike always told her, "Expect nothing, receive everything." And judging from Grandfather Adaire's expression and tender regard for their new baby daughter, he was the perfect person to perform the ancient ceremony they had gathered together for.

Grandfather Adaire stood beside Ann's bed, leaning heavily on his staff, which had colorful parrot feathers attached to it. Everyone's attention went to the door as it slowly opened.

Ann held out her hand. "Inca...come join us." She saw the

woman warrior's hesitation as her gaze settled darkly on Adaire. "Please," Ann murmured.

"You are invited to the naming ceremony," Adaire rumbled. "Enter!"

"I thought Grandmother Alaria would be here," she said stiffly. But the flash of rebellion in Inca's eyes softened immediately as she closed the door and centered her focus on Ann.

"It should not matter who is here," Adaire said to her sharply. "We are gathered because of this child. *That* is what you should be focused upon."

For whatever reason, Ann knew that Inca trusted her with the very core of her wounded being. And she could literally feel Inca's distrust and dislike of Adaire. As Ann held out her hand, the woman warrior walked around the bed and grasped her fingers.

"I'm so glad they found you," Ann told her.

"I was in the hospital cafeteria, eating."

Houston grinned. "Is there any food left?"

Chuckling, Inca released Ann's fingers, leaned over and very delicately touched the baby's soft black hair. "I left you a little, my brother. Ahh, look at her. She is so beautiful!" Inca smiled up into Ann's eyes. "She has your beauty and this ugly guy's stubborn personality. What a combination!" She laughed fully in that husky, purring tone as she straightened up.

Ann cradled her daughter in her right arm. She gazed from Inca to Adaire. "Now we can begin, Grandfather."

He nodded his aging head. Placing his staff against the wall, he drew out a small glass vial with a cork in the top of it. "Let us bow our heads in prayer, in grateful thanks for this child's entrance into our lives, that she is alive and healthy."

Ann closed her eyes. She felt Mike's arm move comfortingly around her shoulders. This was all she wanted, all she would ever need: him and her daughter. Three days after the horrendous event, Mike had suggested the naming ceremony. She was still too injured to be moved, to make the trip to the Village of the Clouds. Another week here, in Tarapoto, was what the doctors recommended. Ann didn't like the idea of staring at four white walls for another seven days when she could be "home" in the village, but she didn't fight Mike on the decision.

Adaire's low, rumbling tone filled the room. "Allow the light of the Great Goddess and her heavens to come through you, Cath-

erine Inca Houston.'' He reached over and gently touched the
baby's hair with the fragrant orchid oil. Moving it in a clockwise
circle, he pronounced, ''Your connection to this life, in this body,
is now complete.''

Ann watched through glistening eyes as Grandfather Adaire
rubbed a tiny bit of oil on Catherine's brow, her throat, over her
heart, stomach and abdomen. Adaire's hands were so gnarled and
aged looking against Catherine's new, pink skin. The little girl
slept as he touched her, as if she knew he would never hurt her.
And throughout the moving ceremony, Ann saw tears in the elder's gray eyes.

More surprising to Ann, as Grandfather Adaire called out the
baby's name, was that Inca's head jerked up, her eyes widening
in total surprise that her own name was part of it. Just as quickly,
she hid her reaction by placing her hand across her eyes, bowing
her head so no one could see how she really felt about it.

Adaire then raised his hand and placed a drop of the oil on
Ann's heart region. ''From daughter to mother, the Great Goddess
bless this union between you.''

He then moved around the bed in slow, limping strides. Mike
eased off the bed and unbuttoned his white cotton shirt to expose
his chest. Adaire placed a drop of oil above his heart and rumbled,
''From daughter to father, the Great Goddess bless this union between you.''

Ann felt Inca stiffen. She hoped her friend would not rebel,
would not refuse the gift that they had given her. Mike had told
Ann earlier that those who accepted the drop of oil at a naming
ceremony accepted an unbreakable bond with those who shared
the oil; becoming, in essence, an extended family even if they had
no blood or family lineage in common. For Inca, who was an
orphan, and almost an outcast of the Jaguar Clan, this would mean
that someone wanted her enough to invite her into their family
unit. Honored and loved no matter how bad her reputation was,
or what she had done in the past. Mike had warned Ann that Inca
might balk and refuse to be part of the ceremony because Grandfather Adaire would be overseeing it, instead of Alaria. Inca had
always gotten along with Alaria. Her quarrel was with Adaire.

Although it hurt to move her left arm because of her broken
ribs, Ann reached out, entangling her fingers in Inca's strong ones.

Inca snapped her head to the right, looking down at her.

Ann tried to smile through her tears, silently asking her to be a part of their family. She saw Inca valiantly try to shield emotions, but for whatever reason, she could not. Maybe it was the baby that had exposed Inca's deeply hidden vulnerability. Ann wasn't sure.

As Adaire approached her, Inca stiffened, but turned her attention upon him.

Ann squeezed her fingers in a pleading gesture. She saw Mike nod gently at Inca, as if encouraging her to allow the ceremony to take place. She also saw Adaire wrestling with his own judgment of his former apprentice. There was such bad blood between them.

Inca wore a sleeveless, dark green T-shirt. With her left hand, she yanked it down enough to expose her heart region between her small breasts. Her lips were set as Adaire moved forward to place the oil on her skin.

"From daughter to aunt, the Great Goddess bless this union," he rumbled.

Ann closed her eyes as Adaire placed the oil upon Inca's chest. She thanked her friend mentally. Little Catherine stirred and opened her eyes. They were so large and blue-green in color. Ann knew without a doubt that her daughter would have her husband's deep blue eyes as she grew older. Smiling, she placed a soft kiss on her tiny brow. Catherine's bowlike mouth curved in a smile.

Adaire moved around to the other side of the bed. He leaned down and carefully bundled Catherine into his arms. Ann watched as he cradled her daughter against his thin chest, his gray eyes glittering with tears as he placed his trembling hand upon her small chest beneath the blankets.

"This is a child of our hearts. She has her family here with her now. She also has her extended family of the Jaguar Clan. May she be blessed by the Great Goddess to walk a path of light in harmony with her heart. May she always see through the eyes of her heart. Blessings upon her, her family and the Jaguar Clan, into which she is welcomed."

Ann sniffed. She glanced over at Mike as he went and stood beside Inca. There wasn't a dry eye in the room, though Inca tried to hide her tears. It was impossible. Adaire was beaming as he held Catherine, rocking her gently in his arms.

"Thank you, Grandfather," Mike whispered, extending his

hand across the bed. "Ann and I are grateful you could do this for us...all of us...."

Adaire carefully cosseted Catherine as he reached out and shook Mike's hand. "My son, I would go wherever Alaria asked me to. This is a blessed moment." He released Mike's hand and turned his attention to Ann.

"It is a custom of our people for the elder who blesses the newborn to tell you something of her future. I know Alaria wanted to be here, but circumstances prevented her from doing so. She sends her love to all of you."

Ann nodded and leaned back against Mike as he sat down on the bed and placed his arm around her shoulders again. "I hope Catherine has a good future, Grandfather," she quavered, sniffing and blotting her eyes with a tissue.

Inca came and carefully sat down on the same side of the bed, near Ann's blanketed feet, facing her. She placed her hand across Ann's ankle and looked at her through tears that she refused to allow to fall.

Adaire sighed. "For once, I can tell you with great assuredness that Catherine Houston will be a catalyst in our world as she blossoms into an adult."

"Don't you mean Catherine *Inca* Houston, Old One?"

Adaire scowled and refused to look down at Inca, who had prodded him unmercifully, with blatant sarcasm in her voice.

"Of course—Catherine Inca Houston."

Mike reached out and gripped Inca's hand as if to tell her to let the slight go, that he and Ann loved her and that was all that mattered. Adaire, as spiritually advanced as he was, was not perfect. Inca was still his open wound, one that he had not been able to heal within himself. Mike fervently prayed that someday these two would make their peace with one another.

"Catherine Inca Houston," Adaire intoned gravely as he held her, "you will become a light among lights. A woman of great and balanced power who will help our mother, the earth, and bring two-leggeds in harmony with all our relations."

Leaning down, Adaire kissed her brow. "The Great Goddess blesses you, little one. Go in peace, in step with her heart, for you are made in divine image of her."

Gently, Adaire handed Catherine toward Ann.

"Please, allow Inca to hold her," Ann murmured.

Instantly, Inca gasped and recoiled. She released Mike's hand. "But—"

"Hold her," Mike ordered quietly. "You're her godmother now. More than an aunt, you know." He saw Adaire's scowl, but the elder controlled his reaction and managed to tame whatever feelings he had toward Inca as he limped around the bed to stand before the woman warrior.

Ann smiled through her tears. Mike gripped her hand gently and they watched Adaire set Catherine into Inca's arms. Maybe, just maybe, this little innocent baby could help begin to heal the rift, the chasm between them. Ann knew Inca never wanted to be touched by Adaire. But now, as they carefully passed the baby between them, they had direct contact. She hoped the baby would become a bridge and connection between them.

Inca's face changed instantly as she cradled Catherine very carefully in her arms. All the anger, the distrust, melted away. As she held Catherine, she bowed her head, her black hair falling across her shoulders and acting as a shining curtain, hiding her face.

Adaire moved away, but there was a kinder expression on his face as he watched Inca's unexpected reaction. It was as if he was surprised but pleased by her acceptance of the baby.

Ann felt a tremendous unleashing of emotions from Inca. There was no need to see her features; Ann felt her tears. Catherine started to move very actively in Inca's arms, her tiny hands flexing, as if to reach up and touch her face.

"Kiss her," Ann urged brokenly. "She wants you to kiss her...."

Inca slowly raised her chin. Tears were streaming down her taut face. "N-no...I cannot.... I do not deserve such a gift—"

"Nonsense," Ann whispered. She gestured firmly toward her child. "She wants you to kiss her. You're her aunt. Her godmother. If anyone should be holding her and kissing her and loving her, it's you."

Inca's shoulders sank. She struggled hard not to sob as Ann reached out to her, heart-to-heart. "You do not realize all I have done—how bad I really am—"

Mike sighed raggedly. "Listen to us, Inca," he said in a low, emotional tone. "Ann and I don't care what you've done. We don't stand in judgment of you or what's happened in your past. Our daughter wouldn't be alive today—" he looked tenderly down at Ann "—nor would my wife, if you hadn't been there...if you hadn't helped to save their lives by protecting them against Escovar and his men. This isn't about karmic payback or balancing things out among the four of us. Two people are alive here today because of your courage and bravery. Catherine belongs to you as much as she does to us. You're her family now, you know. You're not an orphan anymore, Inca."

Inca winced, shutting her eyes tightly for a moment, then carefully lifted Catherine so that she could look at the baby's face and waving, active arms. "She is so precious. So clean and innocent...without sin...."

"We were all like her once," Mike reminded Inca gently. "Life changes us, but somewhere in your heart there's light, Inca, or our baby daughter wouldn't be happy to be in your arms, and you know that. Babies sense who's good or bad. If Catherine didn't want to be with you, she'd be screaming her head off." He grinned a little down at Ann.

Ann agreed. "We love you, Inca, sins and all. We aren't perfect, either."

Inca cast her a tear-filled look. "You are not anything like me. You know nothing of the blood that stains my hands or what I have done.... I am not a good person like you. I have acted in revenge, which is against clan code, and I have not yet learned my lesson—"

"Tell that to the baby in your hands," Adaire rumbled warningly, scowling at Inca. "Can you not allow the purity of a baby, newly born, to wash away some of that eternal darkness that stalks your soul?"

Shaken, Inca refused to look up at Adaire. Lowering her head, she pressed a hesitant kiss against her soft, ruddy cheek.

Ann watched as something magical occurred when Inca allowed herself to kiss Catherine. She felt a shift, a dramatic one, in the room. Whatever demons, guilt or darkness Inca was fighting dissolved within that moment. Ann was mesmerized as Inca's drawn, pain-filled expression disappeared. And for a second time that day, Ann felt the shield completely fall away from her friend. Ann wasn't sure what had happened, but she understood that something very powerful and healing had taken place between Inca and Catherine. Her daughter cooed and waved her arms, as if excited by the touch of Inca's lips upon her cheek.

Inca smiled brokenly as she brought the baby to rest against her breast. In a tender motion, she wrapped her arms around little Catherine, closed her eyes and rocked her gently.

Mike shared another tender look with Ann. Then he turned to Inca and saw huge tears squeezing from beneath her thick, black lashes, her lower lip trembling with a sob that desperately wanted to be released. He watched Inca fight against being human and vulnerable. He knew it was because Grandfather Adaire was in the room that she wouldn't cry, wouldn't allow her feelings to be displayed. Mike looked up to see the expression on the elder's face. No longer was Adaire scowling. No, the old one was staring at Inca with such compassion and love that it shook Mike. Wave after wave of emotion emanated from Inca. It was as if she could no longer control them, and on some level, Mike understood that this was good because Inca rarely released her feelings freely. But this innocent little baby did. Babies were pure love, as far as Mike was concerned. Pure, radiating love, so clean and innocent in this insane world they lived in. And only something as pure as Catherine would be able in some unfathomable way to reach effortlessly into Inca's dark, wounded heart, and help release her past.

Mike felt Ann press her cheek against his chest. Leaning down, he threaded his fingers through her clean hair and gently held her against him. Yes, whatever they were sharing in this miraculous moment, it was a powerful healing for Inca, made possible by the daughter whom she had saved. Kissing his wife's hair, Mike lifted her chin a little and met her widening blue-gray eyes. There was such love burning in them for him...for her new, extended family. Mike smiled brokenly as he caressed Ann's pale cheek. He couldn't wait until he was within the sanctuary, the serenity of the village with his family.

"Look at her," Mike said with a chuckle, "she's a hungry little jaguar today." He sat with his back against the huge silk cotton tree, the long, thin gray roots surrounding them like protective arms. Ann was curled up between his legs, resting contentedly against him. Catherine lay suckling noisily from her left breast. Mike's arm was positioned below Ann's to help hold their daughter in place as she fed.

Dappled sunlight filtered down through the leaves, dancing

around them like gold, glittering coins. Mike listened to his daughter's noisy, happy sounds. He grinned down at Ann. Her face mirrored her happiness, her absolute contentment. Watching Catherine suckle, Ann softly caressed her daughter's curling black hair. "She is hungry," she said with a laugh. "Every day since we've been here Catherine gets stronger, hungrier and more active."

Mike agreed. He moved his hand in a caressing motion across Ann's sable hair, the reddish gold highlights gleaming in the sun. "One more week," he said with a sigh, "and then we have to leave."

"I know..." Ann tried to keep the disappointment out of her voice. She looked out across the wildflower-strewn meadow. There were red, purple and white flowers mixed with the verdant green of the grass. This was their favorite place to come, besides the pool of life. Mike had surprised her earlier by making a picnic lunch over at Grandfather Adaire's hut before picking her and Catherine up and bringing them here to the ancient tree they enjoyed so much.

"I think Grandmother Alaria is sad that we're going to have to leave," Ann whispered. "She is so taken with Catherine." Without fail, the elder would walk over to their hut midmorning shortly after Catherine's feeding, to sit with Catherine in the hand-hewn rocker outside the hut and rock her in her arms for an hour. Inevitably, all six elders would come over, touch, hold and love Catherine. It seemed the child had several doting grandparents.

"Alaria might be the leader," Mike said, "but she's lonely, too. I think, with us, she can be more herself—just another human being."

"Yes," Ann said softly, gazing out across the meadow. It was near eighty degrees, the sky a deep, cloudless blue. To the north, she saw that white roll of clouds hanging against the grayish blue snow-covered Andes. The day was perfect. Everything was perfect. "Members of the Jaguar Clan come and go from here constantly. She is their leader," Ann noted, "and she has that role to fulfill for them."

"Not with us, though," Mike whispered, and leaned over and kissed Ann's brow.

Closing her eyes, she nestled her face against the curve of his neck and hard jaw. "I don't care where we go when we leave here, Mike. I just want to be with you."

The trembling in her voice touched him deeply. Easing his arm around her, Mike held Ann tightly against him. Catherine continued to suckle noisily, her small arms waving every now and again, as if cheering for that rich, nutritious milk she was gobbling down.

"Yesterday, I left the village and met Pablo down below the bridge," he confessed in a low voice.

Ann opened her eyes. "So that's where you went. I wondered...."

Chuckling, Mike slid his fingers along the smooth curve of her cheek. He ached to make love with Ann, but the time wasn't right yet. She was recovering from the birth and her ribs were mending nicely, but she needed to recuperate fully, first.

"So what were you conspiring with Pablo about?" she demanded wryly. Gently she moved Catherine to her other breast to continue feeding. Mike drew the edge of Ann's blouse away to expose her other breast and helped position the baby against her. Just having his strength, his support and assistance meant the world to Ann. He'd helped deliver so many babies over the years in the villages of the highlands that he knew a lot more about them than she did. However, the women of the village, many of them mothers many times over, had also helped her pick up the necessary mothering skills, and Ann was more than grateful for their knowledge and guidance.

"I know you're worried that when we leave here, we'll be in the same danger as before," Mike began quietly. He watched Catherine's little mouth suckle strongly. Smiling, he felt his daughter's strength, her determination to latch on to that nipple and feed. A drop of milk formed at the corner of her mouth, and with his finger, he rescued the bubble. In one motion, he placed the milk onto his tongue. He heard Ann chuckle.

"Two hungry jaguars here," she teased, smiling up at him.

He grinned. "I'm hungry, all right, but it's not the same hunger little Cat here has," he growled darkly.

Blushing fiercely, Ann held his burning blue gaze and knew exactly what Mike meant. She felt her lower body respond to his look. How badly she wanted to love him! Waiting was necessary, but it was a special, unfulfilled agony. With a frustrated sigh, Ann muttered, "Let's talk about the future, shall we?"

Laughing deeply, Mike cradled his wife and child more securely against him. "Okay, okay...." Then he sobered. "I've been talking to Morgan off and on. He's made us an offer we can't refuse."

Ann felt her heart squeeze a bit in terror. "What do you mean, Mike?"

"I told Morgan I'd talk to you about his proposal first. And then, when we decided, I'd get back with him with a firm answer one way or another."

"This had better be good, Mike," she warned.

He grinned a little sheepishly and caressed her flaming cheek. "Oh," he whispered conspiratorially, "I think you'll like his offer...."

Ann relaxed in Mike's arms. Happiness continued to flow through her. What else was there besides lying against the man who loved her with a fierceness that defied description, while holding the child created out of that love in her arms? "Okay, what did he offer you?"

"Us," Mike corrected. "Morgan knows the score down here. He's had mercenaries working with all the governments in South America for some time now. He has a plan—a big one—to go after all the drug kingpins at once in one massive concerted effort. To do so he needs people like myself, who have been in the field for a long time and know the score, to help develop tactics and strategies that will break the grip of the drug lords once and for all."

"That means he want you to help him come up with a battle plan."

"Yes," Houston murmured, "but not like you think." He smiled a little. "Morgan has got the guarantee of the U.S. government to form a top-secret department under the code name Jaguar."

Ann gave him a significant look. "Now, I wonder who came up with that name?"

"Hey, I'm innocent—for once," he said. "Morgan came up with this all on his own."

"Does he know about you...the Jaguar Clan?"

"No. He might have an inkling about us, but as an outsider, no, he doesn't have much information."

"I see...."

"He wants to move us to Montana, where he lives, near Philipsburg, a small town deep in the Rocky Mountains. He has key government officials from ten countries coming there, with their families. This is so damn secret that only the president and two members of his cabinet know about this plan, Ann. And it's going to be kept that way. We'll work at an office in Philipsburg during the day, forming plans, and we'll be staying in contact with each of these governments at the highest of levels. This minimizes possible leaks to spies who are moles for the drug lords."

Ann considered his plan. "Montana?" She looked around. "A far cry from the humid jungle, isn't it?"

He nodded. "Yes, it is."

"Will you miss it? This?"

Shaking his head, Mike placed a kiss on her wrinkled brow. "No. I have exactly what I want in my arms right now," he whispered huskily. "As long as I'm with you, I don't care where I live, *mi querida*. Do you?"

Ann closed her eyes and rested against him. "No," she whispered softly, "I don't care either, Mike. I just want our baby— and you and I—safe, that's all."

Sighing, Mike nodded and held her gently. "I know," he said heavily. "Going north will be safer for us. If word ever gets out about the organization we're planning, it won't matter where we live, we'll be in maximum danger. Escovar is dead, but someone will take his place. It's only a matter of time. The difference is my death spiral dance is over. If we continued to live in Lima, you and Cat would be exposed to the same dangers. Drug lords go after family members of people like myself. I want you *out* of that danger as much as possible. By moving to Montana, we'll have a modicum of safety and a chance at a peaceful life."

"I know...." Ann raised her head. "But we have an advantage, Mike, and you know it."

His mouth drew into a slight smile. "It might be hell sometimes, being a member of the Jaguar Clan, but in some ways it's a blessing, too."

"Your guardian will tell us if trouble is coming. That can be an early warning system for all of us—even for Morgan and his family."

"Yes, but they'll never know that we're operating on a different, invisible plane."

Ann shrugged. "It doesn't matter. We'll be able to tell them if our cover is blown. Then we can still get out in time and keep our families safe.''

Mike nuzzled her cheek. ''Well? Want to move to Montana, Mrs. Houston?''

''Yes,'' Ann whispered, her voice emotional. She gazed down at Catherine, who had stopped suckling and was now asleep in her arms. ''I want as normal a life as we can have for her, Mike. And for ourselves...''

''Well...'' He sighed, smiling against her cheek. ''Being a member of the Jaguar Clan isn't going to guarantee total normality, but for the most part, we can have it.''

Lifting her head, she met and drowned in his deep blue gaze. A fierce sense of love overwhelmed her. ''Kiss me?''

''Any chance I get....''

As she met his descending mouth, felt the power of his lips upon hers, she gave herself completely to Mike in every way. When they gently drew apart, he began rummaging in the loosely woven sack that he'd brought the lunch along in.

''I have something for you,'' he murmured, and he withdrew a red-and-yellow orchid from the sack.

Gasping, Ann eyed the blossom. ''Mike, that's the same kind of orchid you gave me in Lima!''

He grinned and pinned it in her hair. ''Yep, the same one you saw in your dreams a long time ago. Remember that?'' He carefully affixed the flower so that it rested against her left ear. The vanilla scent enveloped them.

''Yes, the same one you gave me when you first came to my apartment in Lima.''

Chuckling indulgently, he said, ''You were mine then and you didn't even realize you'd been caught.''

''What's that supposed to mean?''

Very pleased with himself, Mike said, ''You don't know the story of this particular orchid yet, do you?''

''No, but you're going to tell me, aren't you?'' Ann flashed him a smile. His eyes danced with a mischievous glint in their depths.

''It's called the marriage orchid,'' he told her, his smile widening. ''A man who wants a woman to marry him will bring her this orchid. It's a proposal. If she accepts the orchid, well, it's a done deal—she has, in effect, agreed to marry the poor slob.''

Ann gave him a dirty look. ''No fair, Mike. I didn't know what

I was taking from you when you handed me that spike of orchids in Lima!''

''Oh, yes, you did, *mi querida*. On some level of yourself, your spirit knew. That's why you grabbed them.''

''I did not grab them, Michael Houston, and you know it! You always embellish things so much!''

Laughing deeply, Mike rocked her in his arms and gave her a swift, hot kiss on her parted, smiling lips. ''You can never outwit a jaguar. He will *always* trap you.''

''Pooh!'' Ann muttered. ''You were being just plain sneaky, Major Houston, and you know it!'' She fingered the orchid in her hair. ''But it's a beautiful gift and a beautiful way to say that you love someone.''

''Sneaky?'' Mike muttered, pretending to be wounded. ''I'm not sneaky.''

''Okay, how about another adjective, like underhanded?''

His laughter rolled across the meadow, absorbed by the inconstant breeze and warming sunlight. As he held his wife and baby, he realized he had never been happier. The life that stretched out before them wouldn't be easy, but Mike knew they had the strength and courage to weather whatever was thrown at them. And more important, they had love. Forever.

*   *   *   *   *